CU00683976

The
MX Book
of
New
Sherlock
Holmes
Stories

Part XIII – 2019 Annual
(1881-1890)

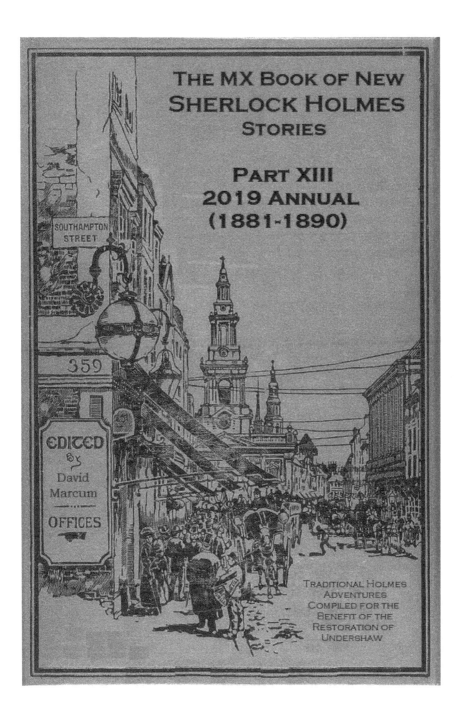

THE MX BOOK OF NEW
SHERLOCK HOLMES
STORIES

PART XIII
2019 ANNUAL
(1881-1890)

SOUTHAMPTON
STREET

359

EDITED
by
David
Marcum

OFFICES

TRADITIONAL HOLMES
ADVENTURES
COMPILED FOR THE
BENEFIT OF THE
RESTORATION OF
UNDERSHAW

First edition published in 2019
© Copyright 2019

The right of the individuals listed on the Copyright Information page to be identified as the authors of this work has been asserted by them in accordance with the Copyright, Designs, and Patents Act 1998.

All rights reserved. No reproduction, copy, or transmission of this publication may be made without express prior written permission. No paragraph of this publication may be reproduced, copied, or transmitted except with express prior written permission or in accordance with the provisions of the Copyright Act 1956 (as amended). Any person who commits any unauthorised act in relation to this publication may be liable to criminal prosecution and civil claims for damage.

All characters appearing in this work are fictitious or used fictitiously. Except for certain historical personages, any resemblance to real persons, living or dead, is purely coincidental. The opinions expressed herein are those of the authors and not of MX Publishing.

ISBN Hardcover   978-1-78705-442-4
ISBN Paperback   978-1-78705-443-1
ISBN AUK ePub   978-1-78705-444-8
ISBN AUK PDF   978-1-78705-445-5

Published by
MX Publishing
335 Princess Park Manor, Royal Drive,
London, N11 3GX
www.mxpublishing.co.uk

David Marcum can be reached at:
thepapersofsherlockholmes@gmail.com

Cover design by Brian Belanger
www.belangerbooks.com and *www.redbubble.com/people/zhahadun*

CONTENTS

Forewords

Adventures

(Continued on the next page . . . .)

(Continued on the next page . . . .)

The following can be found in the companion volumes
The MX Book of New Sherlock Holmes Stories
Part XIV – 2019 Annual (1891-1897)
and
Part XV – 2019 Annual (1898-1917)

(Continued on the next page . . . .)

**These additional Sherlock Holmes adventures
can be found in the previous volumes of**
The MX Book of New Sherlock Holmes Stories

(Continued on the next page . . . .)

PART III: 1896-1929

PART IV – 2016 Annual

(Continued on the next page . . . .)

(Continued on the next page . . . .)

PART VI – 2017 Annual

(Continued on the next page . . . .)

(Continued on the next page . . . .)

Part IX – 2018 Annual (1879-1895)

(Continued on the next page . . . .)

(Continued on the next page . . . .)

Part XII: Some Untold Cases (1894-1902)

The following contributions appear in this volume:
The MX Book of New Sherlock Holmes Stories
Part XIII – 2019 Annual (1881-1890)

"Bootless in Chippenham" ©2018 by Marino C. Alvarez. All Rights Reserved. First publication, original to this collection. Printed by permission of the author.

"The Grosvenor Square Furniture Van" ©2018 by Hugh Ashton and j-views Publishing. All Rights Reserved. Hugh Ashton appears by kind permission of j-views Publishing. First publication, original to this collection. Printed by permission of the author.

"The Folly of Age" ©2018 by Derrick Belanger. All Rights Reserved. First publication, original to this collection. Printed by permission of the author.

"The Case of the Enthusiastic Amateur" ©2018 by S.F. Bennett. All Rights Reserved. First publication, original to this collection. Printed by permission of the author.

"The Shackled Man" ©2018 by Andrew Bryant. All Rights Reserved. First publication, original to this collection. Printed by permission of the author.

"An Ongoing Legacy for Sherlock Holmes" ©2019 by Steve Emecz. All Rights Reserved. First publication, original to this collection. Printed by permission of the author.

"The Adventure of the Missing Cousin" ©2018 by Edwin A. Enstrom. All Rights Reserved. First publication, original to this collection. Printed by permission of the author.

"The Mystery of the Patient Fisherman" ©2002, 2018 by The Estate of Jim French. All Rights Reserved. First publication, original to this collection. Printed by permission of the author's estate.

"Sherlock Holmes in Bedlam" ©2018 by David Friend. All Rights Reserved. First publication, original to this collection. Printed by permission of the author.

"The Yellow Star of Cairo" ©2019 by Tim Gambrell. All Rights Reserved. First publication, original to this collection. Printed by permission of the author.

"A Word From the Head Teacher of Stepping Stones" ©2019 by Melissa Grigsby. All Rights Reserved. First publication, original to this collection. Printed by permission of the author.

"The Adventure of the Worried Banker" ©2018 by Arthur Hall. All Rights Reserved. First publication, original to this collection. Printed by permission of the author.

"The Clerkenwell Shadow" ©2018 by Paul Hiscock. All Rights Reserved. First publication, original to this collection. Printed by permission of the author.

"When I Glance Over My Notes and Records . . . ." ©2019 by Roger Johnson. All Rights Reserved. First publication, original to this collection. Printed by permission of the author.

"Editor's Introduction: The Great Holmes Tapestry" ©2019 and "The Coffee House Girl" ©2018 by David Marcum. All Rights Reserved. First publication, original to this collection. Printed by permission of the author.

"Inscrutable" ©2019 by Jacquelynn Morris. All Rights Reserved. First publication, original to this collection. Printed by permission of the author.

"The Fashionably-Dressed Girl" ©2018 by Mark Mower. All Rights Reserved. First publication, original to this collection. Printed by permission of the author.

"The Adventure of the Winterhall Monster" ©2018 by Tracy J. Revels. All Rights Reserved. First publication, original to this collection. Printed by permission of the author.

"The Odour of Neroli" ©2018 by Brenda Seabrooke. All Rights Reserved. First publication, original to this collection. Printed by permission of the author.

"The Golden Star of India" ©2018 by Stephen Seitz. All Rights Reserved. First publication, original to this collection. Printed by permission of the author.

"The Roses of Highclough House" ©2018 by Matthew Simmonds. All Rights Reserved. First publication, original to this collection. Printed by permission of the author.

"The Adventure of the Ambulatory Cadaver" ©2018 by Shane Simmons. All Rights Reserved. First publication, original to this collection. Printed by permission of the author.

"The Mystery of the Green Room" ©2018 by Robert Stapleton. All Rights Reserved. First publication, original to this collection. Printed by permission of the author.

"Take Up and Read!" ©2019 by Will Thomas. All Rights Reserved. First publication, original to this collection. Printed by permission of the author.

"The Recovery of the Ashes" ©2018 by Kevin P. Thornton. All Rights Reserved. First publication, original to this collection. Printed by permission of the author.

"The Dutch Impostors" ©2018 by Peter Coe Verbica. All Rights Reserved. First publication, original to this collection. Printed by permission of the author.

"The Adventure of the Missing Adam Tiler" ©2019 by Mark Wardecker. All Rights Reserved. First publication, original to this collection. Printed by permission of the author.

"The Voyage of Albion's Thistle" ©2008, 2019 by Sean M. Wright. All Rights Reserved. First publication, original to this collection. Printed by permission of the author.

The following contributions appear in
Part XIV – 2019 Annual (1891-1897)

"The Lancelot Connection" ©2019 by Matthew Booth. All Rights Reserved. First publication, original to this collection. Printed by permission of the author.

"The Horror in King Street" ©2018 by Thomas A. Burns, Jr. All Rights Reserved. First publication, original to this collection. Printed by permission of the author.

"It's Time" ©2018 by Harry DeMaio. All Rights Reserved. First publication, original to this collection. Printed by permission of the author.

"Child's Play" ©2013, 2018 by C.H. Dye. All Rights Reserved. This story originally appeared on-line in a slightly different form. All Rights Reserved. Printed by permission of the authors.

"The Adventure of the Crossbow" ©2018 by Edwin A. Enstrom. All Rights Reserved. First publication, original to this collection. Printed by permission of the author.

"The Adventure of the Delusional Wife" ©2019 by Jayantika Ganguly. All Rights Reserved. First publication, original to this collection. Printed by permission of the author.

"The Second Whitechapel Murderer" ©2019 by Arthur Hall. All Rights Reserved. First publication, original to this collection. Printed by permission of the author.

"The Adventure of the Scarlet Rosebud" ©2018 by Liz Hedgecock. All Rights Reserved. First publication, original to this collection. Printed by permission of the author.

"The Poisoned Regiment" ©2018 by Carl Heifetz. All Rights Reserved. First publication, original to this collection. Printed by permission of the author.

"The Adventure of the Modern Guy Fawkes" ©2018 by Stephen Herczeg. All Rights Reserved. First publication, original to this collection. Printed by permission of the author.

"The Carroun Documen" ©2018 by David Marcum. All Rights Reserved. First publication, original to this collection. Printed by permission of the author.

"Skein of Tales" ©2019 by Jacquelynn Morris. All Rights Reserved. First publication, original to this collection. Printed by permission of the author.

"The Case of the Persecuted Poacher" ©2019 by Gayle Lange Puhl. All Rights Reserved. First publication, original to this collection. Printed by permission of the author.

"The Adventure of the Silent Witness" ©2018 by Tracy J. Revels. All Rights Reserved. First publication, original to this collection. Printed by permission of the author.

"The Collegiate Leprechaun" ©2018 by Roger Riccard. All Rights Reserved. First publication, original to this collection. Printed by permission of the author.

"The Adventure of the Jeweled Falcon" ©2018 by GC Rosenquist. All Rights Reserved. First publication, original to this collection. Printed by permission of the author.

"Mr. Clever, Baker Street" ©2018 by Geri Schear. All Rights Reserved. First publication, original to this collection. Printed by permission of the author.

"The Tower of Fear" ©2018 by Mark Sohn. All Rights Reserved. First publication, original to this collection. Printed by permission of the author.

"The Threadneedle Street Murder" ©2018 by S.Subramanian. All Rights Reserved. First publication, original to this collection. Printed by permission of the author.

"The Adventure of the Royal Albert Hall" ©2018 by Charles Veley and Anna Elliott. All Rights Reserved. First publication, original to this collection. Printed by permission of the author.

"The Case of the Fourpenny Coffin" ©2018 by I.A. Watson. All Rights Reserved. First publication, original to this collection. Printed by permission of the author.

"A Malversation of Mummies" ©2009, 2018 by Marcia Wilson. This story originally appeared on-line in a slightly different form. All Rights Reserved. Printed by permission of the authors.

The following contributions appear in
Part XV – 2019 Annual (1898-1917)

"The Mysterious Mr. Rim" ©2018 by Maurice Barkley. All Rights Reserved. First publication, original to this collection. Printed by permission of the author.

"The Adventure of the Weeping Stone" ©2018 by Nick Cardillo. All Rights Reserved. First publication, original to this collection. Printed by permission of the author.

"The Case of the Haunted Chateau" ©1944, 2017 by Leslie Charteris and Denis Green. First publication of text script in this collection. Originally broadcast on radio on October 30, 1944 as part of the *Sherlock Holmes* radio show, starring Basil Rathbone and Nigel Bruce. Printed by permission of the Leslie Charteris Estate. Introduction ©2018 by Ian Dickerson. First text publication of this revised version, original to this collection. Printed by permission of the author's estate.

"Introduction – The Case of the Haunted Chateau" ©2018 by Ian Dickerson. All Rights Reserved. First publication, original to this collection. Printed by permission of the author.

"The Adventure of the Fatal Jewel-Box" ©2018 by Edwin A. Enstrom. All Rights Reserved. First publication, original to this collection. Printed by permission of the author.

"The Incomparable Miss Incognita" ©2019 by Thomas Fortenberry. All Rights Reserved. First publication, original to this collection. Printed by permission of the author.

"The Silver Bullet" ©2018 and "The Boy Who Would be King" ©2019 by Dick Gillman. All Rights Reserved. First publication, original to this collection. Printed by permission of the author.

"A Skeleton's Sorry Story" ©2018 by Jack Grochot. All Rights Reserved. First publication, original to this collection. Printed by permission of the author.

"The Adventure of the Silent Sister" ©2018 by Arthur Hall. All Rights Reserved. First publication, original to this collection. Printed by permission of the author.

"Alas, Poor Will" ©2018 by Mike Hogan. All Rights Reserved. First publication, original to this collection. Printed by permission of the author.

"The First Floor Ghost" and "Sherlock of Aleppo" ©2019 by Christopher James. All Rights Reserved. First publication, original to this collection. Printed by permission of the author.

"The Devil's Painting" ©2018 by Kelvin I. Jones. All Rights Reserved. A substantially different version of this story originally appeared in *Carter's Occult Casebook* ©2011. Printed by permission of the author.

"An Actor and a Rare One" ©2018 by David Marcum. All Rights Reserved. First publication, original to this collection. Printed by permission of the author.

"The Whitechapel Butcher" ©2018 by Mark Mower. All Rights Reserved. First publication, original to this collection. Printed by permission of the author.

"The Adventure of the Throne of Gilt" ©2018 by Will Murray. All Rights Reserved. First publication, original to this collection. Printed by permission of the author.

"The Adventure of the Twofold Purpose" ©2018 by Robert Perret. All Rights Reserved. First publication, original to this collection. Printed by permission of the author.

"The Adventure of the Green Gifts" ©2018 by Tracy J. Revels. All Rights Reserved. First publication, original to this collection. Printed by permission of the author.

"The Notable Musician" ©2018 by Roger Riccard. All Rights Reserved. First publication, original to this collection. Printed by permission of the author.

"The Turk's Head" ©2018 by Robert Stapleton. All Rights Reserved. First publication, original to this collection. Printed by permission of the author.

"The Seventeenth Monk" ©2018 by Tim Symonds and Lesley Abdela. All Rights Reserved. First publication, original to this collection. Printed by permission of the author.

"Mass Murder" ©2018 by William Todd. All Rights Reserved. First publication, original to this collection. Printed by permission of the author.

"A Ghost in the Mirror" ©2019 by Peter Coe Verbica. All Rights Reserved. First publication, original to this collection. Printed by permission of the author.

"The Adventure of the Three Telegrams" ©2019 by Darryl Webber. All Rights Reserved. First publication, original to this collection. Printed by permission of the author.

The 2019 Annual, Parts XIII, XIV, and XV of
The MX Book of New Sherlock Holmes Stories,
are dedicated to

Joel Senter

Joel passed away in July 2018.
He was a wonderful and very supportive
Sherlockian, and he will be missed.

Editor's Introduction:
The Great Holmes Tapestry
by David Marcum

W ay back in early 2015, when the world was a much simpler place, I woke up early one morning from a very vivid dream where I had edited a Sherlock Holmes anthology. Instead of going back to sleep, I arose and started thinking about it. What a wild hansom cab ride it's been since then!

Who would have then suspected the future of *The MX Book of New Sherlock Holmes Stories*? Since that time, we've had over 330 new Sherlock Holmes adventures, plus poems and forewords, from over 150 contributors, and along the way, through the very generous efforts of the participants, we've raised over $40,000 for the Stepping Stones School for special needs students at Undershaw, one of Sir Arthur Conan Doyle's former homes. Additionally, the books have raised awareness of the school around the world.

Back in 2015, when the initial hope for a single book of possibly a dozen new Holmes tales had grown and grown to three massive simultaneous volumes of 63 new stories, I sat down to write a foreword. In it, I referred to a phenomenon that I had observed during my previous four decades of collecting, reading, and chronologicizing literally thousands of traditional Holmes stories: All of these different narratives – the pitifully few original sixty of The Canon and all the rest from so many other later literary agents – fit together remarkably well as one wonderful whole. To describe it, I coined the term *The Great Holmes Tapestry*, and I've been proud since then to see it mentioned that way in other places when describing *The Big Picture* of all these stories, and not just Watson's initial sixty tales that crossed the *First* Literary Agent's desk.

As I've explained in other locations, this Tapestry consists of the overall and complete lives of Holmes and Watson from birth to death, filling in all those pieces of the picture that the original Canon does not. The Canon indisputably makes up the main fibers of the illustration, but there are so many other pieces to examine. Another way to look at this is to think of all the days in a life. I'm sure that someone somewhere has calculated the amount of time in Holmes and Watson's lives that are actually represented in The Canon. (There are always people who are carrying out these various scholarly tasks – counting the exact number of times a gasogene is used, for instance, or the total number of words uttered by Inspector Lestrade during all of his combined appearances. This information is undoubtedly out there – *somewhere* – if one just knows where to look.)

The actual amount of on-stage time chronicled in The Canon adds up to just a limited number of days. In Holmes and Watson's full lifetimes – and as a deadly serious player of The Game, I emphatically declare that Holmes and Watson *had very full lifetimes!* – there were far more moments that have not been "officially" described than the little bit that is related within The Canon. Some would be satisfied with only ever knowing what's related in The Official Sixty Adventures, endlessly examining and re-examining these cases and preferring to think of Holmes spending the rest of his time between cases moping about the Baker Street sitting room in a brown study limbo for weeks on end. And that isn't correct at all. There is more to the complete lives of Holmes and Watson than the little time recorded in The Canon.

Even during those years when the First Literary Agent was still alive, before he had a chance to examine and evaluate first-hand his spiritualistic assertions, new stories from other directions were appearing to start filling in the missing pieces of these complete lives. Consider Vincent Starrett's "The Adventure of the Unique Hamlet", which was published in 1920. There are people who know much more about Starrett than I do, and they can probably relate what the First Literary Agent's reaction was to someone bringing forth one of Watson's manuscripts from a different source. What interests me is that someone so revered in the legendary Sherlockian Halls of Fame as Mr. Starrett chose to make public an extra-Canonical adventure – and such a well-regarded one to boot! – more than a decade before he produced his scholarly work, *The Private Life of Sherlock Holmes* (1933). In this regard, I like Starrett's priorities, and commend them to those who favor the more scholarly side of Holmesian Studies.

Some people – too many, actually – are satisfied only with The Canon, and go no further – either through ignorance or stubbornness. I'll admit that there is a certain completeness to the solid and wonderful Canon. I well remember the first time that I finished my reading of all sixty of the "official" adventures. I can only imagine how sad it must be for someone to reach that final story and mistakenly believe that there are no more. I was quite fortunate that I knew better from nearly my first encounter with Mr. Holmes. I discovered him in 1975, when I was ten years old, reading the abridged Whitman edition of *The Adventures* that only had eight of the twelve stories. I next found a tattered paperback copy of *The Return* – and I still have both of those very books on the shelves holding my collection. After obtaining *The Return*, I plunged into "The

Empty House" – thus learning how Holmes survived his encounter with Professor Moriarty at the Reichenbach Falls before I even knew that he was believed to have died – an incredibly valuable lesson in reading things in chronological order! And very soon after that, I discovered pastiches, and it became apparent that there was no need to feel sad when finishing The Canon, because it was simply a gateway to a much larger world, and not simply a closed and finite sixty-sided dead-end room.

Not long after my first introduction to Holmes, I received a copy of Nicholas Meyer's *The Seven-Per-Cent Solution* (1974). I recognized, even then, that some parts just didn't fit with the True Canon, and I was much more thrilled from beginning-to-end with Meyer's next book, *The West End Horror* (1976). In those early days, still before I'd even read all of The Canon, I was electrified by William S. Baring-Gould's biography *Sherlock Holmes of Baker Street* (1962 – and it's hard now to get my head around the fact that when I read Baring-Gould's incredibly influential masterpiece in the mid-1970's, it was only thirteen years old to my ten years.) And over the next few years, I occasionally found other Holmes books that thrilled me as well, including *Enter the Lion* by Sean M. Wright and Michael P. Hodel (1979) – which showed that a Holmes adventure doesn't have to come by way of Watson's pen to give a true account – and various books by the prolific and fun (and sadly deceased) Frank Thomas, such as *Sherlock Holmes and the Golden Bird* (1979) and *Sherlock Holmes and the Sacred Sword* (1980).

Through the years, I've been very fortunate to have the opportunity to track down and acquire literally thousands of traditional pastiches – as well as to read and study and chronologicize them. In the mid-1990's, I began to make notes as I re-read my favorites and also caught up on all those stories that I had acquired at that point but hadn't yet explored. In the years since, I've been constantly expanding and revising those original notes while acquiring many more pastiches, and now I have a massive Sherlockian Chronology of both Canon and pastiche, well over 800 dense pages, stretching from 1844 – with a story relating the meeting, courtship, and marriage of Holmes's parents – to January 1957, and Holmes's death, as shared by Baring-Gould. (I'm a staunch Baring-Gouldist, although I'll admit he didn't get everything right.) Through this entire Chronology, I've broken down traditional adventures in my collection – novels, short stories, radio and television episodes, movies and scripts, comics, fan-fiction, and unpublished manuscripts – by book, story, chapter, or paragraph into year, month, day, and even hour. And it never ceases to amaze me how well it all fits together.

As I've related elsewhere, all of the traditional Canonically-based Sherlock Holmes stories are linked together to that spark of imagination that sets these narratives in motion, *The Great Watsonian Oversoul*. Although there are contradictions and incorrect statements at times – and usually the blame can be placed upon modern editors who foist their own agendas or unverified assumptions onto Watson's original notes – the overall consistency of this myriad of adventures is astonishing. For example, an obscure story brought forth by one later literary agent in the 1940's will fit perfectly – chronology-wise – with another written in the last year or so, and I'm almost certain that the more recent literary agent didn't have any clue about the earlier one when tapping into *The Oversoul* to bring forth the narrative. Somehow, as each of these little sparks from *The Oversoul* are revealed, their connection to the whole becomes apparent. And while editing these current three simultaneous volumes, *Parts XIII*, *XIV*, and *XV*, I saw this same thing happening yet again.

When I solicit and receive stories for these books, I only set out a very few requirements: The stories must be absolutely traditional. They have to be set in the correct time period, of equivalent Canonical length, and with no aspects of parody, anachronisms, or actual supernatural encounters. Sometimes participants will want to float an idea by me before beginning, or even send a draft of a story to get my input along the way, but I refuse to read it. I want the first version of a submission that I read to be the final version. But by doing it this way, I cannot say ahead of time if someone is going to submit something that has a relationship or connection to another entry. I'll leave it to perceptive readers to have fun spotting the overlaps in this new collection.

A few times through this amazing journey of over 330 stories (so far), there have some overlaps. In one volume, two of the contributors submitted stories that were both set within days of each other, and in one Holmes fools Watson with a false investigation, while in the next Watson fools Holmes (or tries to) in the same way. Rather than tell one of the contributors, "No," I happily used both of their stories, side-by-side, as to my mind they strengthened rather than diminished each other. On another occasion, one author was worried to discover that his story about a jewel theft had been placed chronologically in that particular book next to another story that was also about a jewel theft. However, the two narratives were so different, and diverged immediately into such varying directions, that I don't believe that anyone noticed or was bothered by it.

That's one of the thrills of reading a Holmes story – one never knows which way it will go. It may be a straight-forward narrative or convoluted, with international consequences, or of huge importance only to one person. It might be comedy or tragedy, or a procedural investigation, or gothic horror. It might have a London setting or take us to the countryside, or to the Continent or North America, Asia or Africa. It could cover just hours, or be spaced to relate connected incidents that occur years apart. We might find ourselves early or late in Holmes career. Holmes or Watson – or neither! – might not even appear at all. There may be a comfortable trope, such as Holmes and Watson hiding in a supposedly empty location waiting to trap the criminal, or something brand new.

Mysteries may range all the way from murder down to nothing more than a simple misunderstanding with a crime-free solution. The tale may involve great historical events or the tiniest of mysteries that only affect the lives of a few people. It might be Victorian or Edwardian, or possibly a little bit later. The story could be narrated by Watson or Holmes, or someone else. There may be a treasure hunt or a series of mysterious warnings, brought to Holmes from high-born clients or low. The majority of the story might consist of the client's strange tale, narrated while sitting in front of the fire in the Baker Street sitting room, or we may find Our Heroes in the foreground from start to finish.

To paraphrase Bilbo Baggins, who warned his nephew about the dangers of stepping onto the road: "*It's a [fascinating] business, [Watson]. You [start a new adventure], and . . . there's no knowing where you might be swept off to.*"

It never gets old, and there are never enough.

I mentioned my requirements for a story to be included in these books, but I neglected to list perhaps the most important one of all: Holmes and Watson have to be *heroes*.

When I first dreamed of editing a Holmes back – specifically on January 22nd, 2015, as evidenced by the email that I still have proposing it to publisher Steve Emecz – the reason that I wanted to do so was simple: People were forgetting that Sherlock Holmes is a hero. More than just forgetting, actually – they were desperately going out of their way to actively destroy him. It has become fashionable to use the names of Holmes and his associates in ever-more lurid and demeaning and insulting representations – as if each iteration has to outdo the one before it in terms of just how outrageous and broken Holmes can be. He has to be absolutely hopeless and irredeemable, or a sociopath, or a murderer. He can only function if Watson serves as a caretaker at best, and Watson is given his own set of defects as well. A push-back was needed.

I'm so fortunate to have been able to find like-minded individuals who also want to support Holmes the Hero, and who write stories about the True Sherlock Holmes. In the four years since the idea first occurred to me, these 330-plus adventures have served as an alternative against those who would erase and replace the heroic Holmes of the Victorian and Edwardian years, instead trying to make him some sort of damaged goods, or Van Helsing, where "Ghosts can apply after all", or a Dr. Who-like character who regenerates in a multitude of decades or formats, or worst of all, as a morally defective creep. Playing The Game means that Holmes is not a Magic Man who lives forever, or someone whose spirit dances into different realities or even completely different personalities with the same name. There are still bulwarks that stand to defend the True Holmes – these books and others like them – and I cannot thank those enough who contribute to and support them for all that they have done and continue to do.

Luckily, the True Holmes has continued to burn like a beacon through all of the greasy fog that still threatens to obscure him. There are still legitimate adventures appearing – *almost daily, it sometimes seems, and thank God for that!* – that tell us more – *but never enough!* – about Mr. Sherlock Holmes of Baker Street.

As these anthologies continue – and there's no end in sight, as at this writing, as I'm already receiving stories for the next two collections! – what will *not* change is that Holmes and Watson will continue to be represented as *heroes*. You won't find a story where Holmes or Watson turn out to be murderers, or Holmes deduces that he's been created by a writer. (I regularly turn these down, along with many other stories with objectionable premises.) One thing that has changed, however, is an informal rule that I had for a long time with the earlier books – only one story per author per collection.

This seemed to make sense for a long time, as I didn't want to be appearing to favor someone over another, and also because initially space was limited. After all, the first collection had humble ambitions, although it grew over time. At first, Steve Emecz and I had many discussions about what to do as more stories arrived and the initial single book grew fatter. Keep making the font size smaller as more stories arrived? The contributors kept contributing, and I didn't want to keep any new Holmes adventures away from the public. Just when I thought that things were about to get locked into place in that spring of 2015, I had a sudden surge of new submissions. What to do? Why, expand to two volumes. And as that year progressed, what was two books then became three, containing 63 new Holmes adventures.

When we decided to continue beyond the initial record-breaking three-volume set as an ongoing series, the plan was to have modest one-volume editions. That worked for *Parts IV* and *V*, when we we had ended up having enough contributions to issue new collections in both the spring and the fall. Then came *Part VI: 2017 Annual*, which was huge and really should have been split into two books. After that, when the number of contributions pushed the boundaries, we decided to expand into multiple simultaneous volumes, as needed. (We were happy to discover that these multiple volumes were more popular anyway.) So the next sets have appeared in twos: *Parts VII* and *VIII*, *IX* and *X*, *XI* and *XII*. And now, with this new collection, I've again received so many stories that they can only be contained in three large books, and this time with more stories than the initial record-breaking 63 from *Parts I*, *II*, and *III* in 2015.

And part of this is due to allowing multiple contributions from authors. In *Parts XI* and *XII: Some Untold Cases*, I had two different stories from the great Mike Hogan that fit the collection's parameters, and I couldn't pick one or the other. Then I saw that one would go in the *Part XI* and the other *Part XII*. Problem solved. It wasn't my intention to make this a new accepted policy – it just worked out that way. Then, when I first began assembling and editing another anthology, *The New Adventures of Solar Pons* (2018), I was worried that I wouldn't have enough stories, so I also said that authors could contribute more than one. We ended up with a really great collection of 20 stories with some from multiple participants, so I needn't have worried. By then, my mind was open to additional contributions.

I was in the early days of preparing this set in mid-2018 when I received an email from reader Ed Enstrom. I'd never heard from him before, but he reached out through the email address shown at the end of this foreword to discuss errors that had slipped through and into the previous book. (I'm always mortified when this happens, but I have to point out – as I did to Ed – that sadly I can't devote a professional amount of effort to these books, as professionally I'm a licensed civil engineer, and my editorship is as an unpaid amateur who does this in his spare time. I look upon this work as that of a missionary of The Church of Holmes. I don't have any true publishing software, just the common version of Microsoft Word in which to assemble the book files.) I replied to Ed's email and, as a diligent amateur editor, I concluded – as I often do – by asking if he'd like to write a story.

He'd never considered such a thing, but he went away and, eight days later, he sent me his first-ever pastiche. I read it and saw that it was exactly what I'm always looking for, and promptly confirmed that I could use it. And then, soon after, Ed sent me a second story. And then a third. He had the fever.

Of course, just like in the case of Mike Hogan's two stories in the previous set, I hated to pick one over another when I could bring *all* of them to the public's attention. I was happy when this ended up being three volumes, because that way I could put one of Ed's stories in each book.

By then, some of the other much-treasured regular participants – Tracy Revels, Mark Mower, Roger Riccard, Arthur Hall, Dick Gillman, and Peter Coe Verbica – had sent more than one story as well, and I was very pleased to include all of them. And then, having written my own initial contribution, I decided to have a go at another, and then another – thus making me a multiple contributor to the books too. And that's how we reached *66* stories this time, beating the record of *63* set with *Parts I, II*, and *III* in 2015, way back at the beginning . . . .

> *"Of course, I could only stammer out my thanks."*
> *– The unhappy John Hector McFarlane,* "The Norwood Builder"

These last few years have been an amazing. I've been able to meet some incredible people, both in person and in the modern electronic way, and also I've been able to read several hundred new Holmes adventures, all to the benefit of the Stepping Stones School at Undershaw, one of Sir Arthur Conan Doyle's homes. The contributors to these MX anthologies donate their royalties to the school, and so far we've raised over $40,000 – maybe $50,000 by the time you read this! More importantly, thousands of people have been made aware of the Stepping Stones School, and this has been a wonderful and unexpected added benefit.

There are many people to thank. First and foremost, as with every one of these projects that I attempt, my amazing and incredibly wonderful wife (of thirty-one years by the time you read this!) Rebecca, and our truly awesome son and my friend, Dan. I love you both, and you are everything to me!

I have all the gratitude in the world for the contributors who have used their time, energy, and creativity to be part of this project. I'm so glad to have gotten to know all of you through the process. It's an undeniable fact that Sherlock Holmes authors are the *best* people!

I also must thank the people who buy these books and support them in so many ways. And don't forget – if you like reading them, considering joining the party and *writing* a story too! One of the things that makes me most proud of these books are the first-time authors who sent a story, and sometimes another for the next book, and so on, and now some of them have had enough for their own books to be published, and along the way they've learned about writing and publishing.

Next, I'd like to thank those who offer support, encouragement, and friendship, sometimes patiently waiting on me to reply as my time is pulled in so many other directions. We often go great amounts of time between communications, but I always enjoy our discussions. Many many thanks to (in alphabetical order): Bob Byrne, Mark Mower, Denis Smith, Tom Turley, Dan Victor, and Marcia Wilson.

Additionally, I'd also like to especially thank:

- Steve Emecz – From idea to book, and then repeating the process, I've had a wonderful time ever since I first emailed Steve back in December 2012. Everything that has happened since then is amazing for me personally, and I owe so much of it to Steve, a great guy in every respect. Thank you for each opportunity!

- Will Thomas: I first heard of Will when I bought and read his first Barker and Llewelyn book, *Some Danger Involved* (2004) when it was initially published. I was thrilled. There are several authors who have taken Canonical characters and made them their own, filling in the details beyond the cursory Canonical descriptions – Marcia Wilson and the Scotland Yarders (especially Lestrade) for instance, Michael Kurland's Professor Moriarty, Carole Nelson Douglas and Irene Adler, Sean Wright and Michael Hodel's Mycroft Holmes, and Gerard Williams's Dr. Mortimer – and now we know the truth about Barker, Holmes's *"hated rival upon the Surrey shore"*. Others have written about Barker – he's been in one of my stories, and he appears in another by someone else in this very volume – but Will told us his first name ("Cyrus") and provided his background and a circle of friends and has given us so many amazing adventures.

   I've been able to make three Holmes Pilgrimages to London (so far), and while nearly everywhere that I went related to Holmes, I did work in a few other stops, such as the former homes of Solar Pons, Hercule Poirot, and James Bond. And several times I've stopped into Craig's Court in Whitehall – both because it was one of the locations of Watson's old bank, Cox and Company, and also because it was where Cyrus Barker's office was located. (As is the case with Mr. Holmes and several others, I also play *The Game* in regard to Barker and Llewelyn.) I'm only on one certain social media succubus to connect with other Sherlockians, and it was amazing fun to photograph myself and my ever-present

9

deerstalker in front of Barker's office on several occasions and post the photo, letting Will know in real time that I was right there right then, and then to see him immediately respond.

I'm very thankful that he both wrote a Holmes story for the first three-volume MX collection back in 2015 ("The Adventure of Urquhart Manse") and now that he's a part of this set too. Long may he continue to chronicle the adventures of Barker and Llewelyn!

- Roger Johnson – To one of the most knowledgeable Sherlockians and one of the most gracious and supportive people that I know! I'm incredibly grateful that Roger reviewed my first book, and then others after that. He and his wife Jean Upton have done so much to help promote these books, and they wonderfully hosted me for a few days during my Holmes Pilgrimage No. 2 in 2015, when the first MX anthologies were published. Since then, there have been many other projects – these books, and others – where Roger has stepped up and written scholarly forewords, no questions asked. I can't imagine these books without him.

- Derrick Belanger – Derrick and I started emailing in late 2014, and haven't stopped since. Soon after, I had the idea for the MX anthologies, and he was one of the initial group that I asked to join the party. (He recently reminded me that my invitation led him to write his first traditional pastiche.) Since then, he and his brother Brian have gone on to create Belanger Books, home of many successful projects – several of which I've been fortunate enough to edit – and Derrick has also written a great deal more new Holmesian material. Derrick: Thanks very much for your friendship, and for all of the additional Sherlockian opportunities.

- Brian Belanger – Although we've yet to meet in person, I've really enjoyed getting to know Brian over the last few years, both in connection to these projects, as well as those with Belanger Books. He's an incredibly talented graphic artist who continues to amaze me even more with each new project – and all of the people who have book covers designed by him will certainly agree. Brian: Thank you so much for all that you do – it's appreciated by many people besides me!

- Sean M. Wright – Finding pastiches in my hometown was difficult when I was a kid, just starting out as a Sherlockian. As mentioned above, one of the first pastiches that I ever encountered was the Mycroft Holmes-narrated *Enter the Lion* (1979) by Sean M. Wright and Michael P. Hodel. It's still an amazing book forty years later, and it showed me that others besides Watson could provide narratives within The World of Sherlock Holmes. Others have written about Mycroft since then – Glen Petrie, Kareem Abdul-Jabbar and Anna Waterhouse – but for me the best and most definitive will always be *Enter the Lion* by Wright and Hodel. I was thrilled a few months ago to be put in touch with Mr. Wright and, as your diligent amateur author, be able to ask him for a new Mycroft Holmes story. Amazingly, he has several which he hopes to publish in the future, and more amazingly, he allowed me to use one of them here first. The boy Sherlockian in me, who back then had a Holmes collection on his shelf only about one-foot wide – including *Enter the Lion* – is thrilled, and so is the adult Sherlockian, and I cannot thank Mr. Wright enough!

- Ian Dickerson – In a couple of contributions to previous MX anthology volumes – "The Strange Adventure of the Doomed Sextette" in *Part IX (1879-1895)* and "The Giant Rat of Sumatra" in *Part XI: Some Untold Cases (1880-1891)*, Ian explained how he came to be responsible for a number of long-lost scripts from the 1944 season of the Holmes radio show, starring Basil Rathbone and Nigel Bruce, and written by Denis Green and Leslie Charteris (under the name Bruce Taylor).

  Since then, he's published two sets of the scripts – *Sherlock Holmes: The Lost Radio Scripts* (2017) and *Sherlock Holmes: More Lost Radio Scripts* (2018). There are still a few more of them that remain unpublished, and I'm very grateful to Ian for allowing "The Haunted Chateau" to appear here. When I first discovered Holmes as a boy, I quickly found a number of Rathbone and

Bruce broadcasts on records at the public library, and that was where I first "heard" Holmes. I can't express the thrill of getting to read these rediscovered lost treasures, having been tantalized by their titles for so long. Many thanks to Ian for making these available.

- *The Nashville Scholars of the Three Pipe Problem* – The area where I live in eastern Tennessee is not noted for Sherlockian activity, or even awareness of the great man. I've worn a deerstalker as my only hat year-round since I was nineteen in 1984, and no one ever seems to recognize who I'm honouring. The closest Sherlockian Scion is in Nashville, a nearly-four-hour drive each way. Understandably, I don't get there as often as I'd like, but I'm very grateful to be a member of The Nashville Scholars, now in its fortieth year, and to visit when I can. In particular, I'd like to thank four of the Scholars:

  o *Jim Hawkins*, who works tirelessly to promote the group, and with whom I was very glad to spend some time at the 2018 *From Gillette to Brett V* Conference in Bloomington, IN;
  o *Shannon Carlisle, BSI*: I met Shannon, an award-winning teacher, at my first Scholars meeting. She is noted for using Holmes as the basis for much in her classroom, and her students were particularly interested in Stepping Stones and Undershaw. I was able to provide some information, including descriptions of my visit there in 2016. I'm grateful for her friendship;
  o *Bill Mason, BSI*: I met Bill at *From Gillette to Brett III* in 2011, when someone mentioned that we were both from Tennessee. We exchanged copies of our first books and have stayed in touch ever since. He's very supportive, and I've enjoyed hearing much of his insight since then;
  o *Marino Alvarez, BSI*: I became aware of Marino when he published A Professor Reflects on Sherlock Holmes (2012 MX Publishing.) I met him at *A Gathering of Southern Sherlockians* in 2012, but I doubt if he remembers it. I next met him at my first Nashville Scholars meeting. And

then, to my great surprise and enjoyment, he unexpectedly submitted a Holmes story for this collection. I'm very happy and thankful that he's a part of this!

- Ray Betzner, noted Sherlockian and especially noted Vincent Starrett Scholar: Thanks for taking time to answer a Starrett question!

- Melissa Grigsby – Thank you for the incredible work that you do at the Stepping Stones School at Undershaw in Hindhead. I was both amazed and thrilled to visit the school on opening day in 2016, and I hope to get back there again some time. You are doing amazing things, and it's my honor, as well that of all the contributors to this project, to be able to help.

- Joel Senter and his wife Carolyn have been legends in the Sherlockian community I personally got to know Joel through telephone conversations, starting in the late 1980's, when I would order items from their amazing *Classic Specialties*. Later, I would call Joel with product ideas or questions. When my first book was published by a publisher who didn't actually intend to sell it, Joel gave me great advice, and furthermore, he sold the book for me through *Classic Specialties.* I only met him and Carolyn once in person, at *A Gathering of Southern Sherlockians* in 2012, and they arranged for me to sell books at a vendor's table (shared with Tracy Revels, whom I also met there for the first time,) and at that same event, Joel made a point of presenting me with a check in front of everyone for the profits my books that had sold through their business. When I first thought of the MX anthology, Joel was an incredible supporter, and he and Carolyn wrote an amazing story, "The Adventure of the Avaricious Bookkeeper", which closed out the final of the first three volumes with a case set just before Watson's death. It was an amazing way to conclude those books. Joel and I continued to communicate by email until shortly before his death in July 2018, and I – like so many Sherlockians – was devastated to learn that he had passed. He helped so many people with his enthusiasm and support, and this set of MX volumes is dedicated to him.

In addition those mentioned above, I'd also like to especially thank (in alphabetical order): Larry Albert, Hugh Ashton, Deanna Baran, Jayantika Ganguly, Paul Gilbert, Dick Gillman, Arthur Hall, Mike Hogan, Craig Janacek, Tracy Revels, Roger Riccard, Geri Schear, and Tim Symonds. From the very beginning, these special contributors have stepped up and supported this and other projects over and over again with their contributions. They are the best and I can't explain how valued they are.

Finally, last but certainly *not* least, **Sir Arthur Conan Doyle**: Author, doctor, adventurer, and the Founder of the Sherlockian Feast. Present in spirit, and honored by all of us here.

As always, this collection, like those before it, has been a labor of love by both the participants and myself. As I've explained before, once again everyone did their sincerest best to produce an anthology that truly represents why Holmes and Watson have been so popular for so long. These are just more tiny threads woven into the ongoing Great Holmes Tapestry, continuing to grow and grow, for there can *never* be enough stories about the man whom Watson described as *"the best and wisest . . . whom I have ever known."*

David Marcum
March 20th, 2019
The 122nd Anniversary of the
Radix pedis diabolic *experiment*

Questions, comments, and story submissions
may be addressed to David Marcum at
thepapersofsherlockholmes@gmail.com

"Take Up and Read!"
by Will Thomas

I cut my teeth on Sherlock Holmes. I still recall being enthralled by Basil Rathbone at ten, and reading *The Boy's Sherlock Holmes* a year later. When I was seventeen I joined a Holmes scion, The Afghanistan Perceivers, in which the average age was fifty. What does one do with a rambunctious seventeen-year-old? One makes him the book reviewer for the club journal, something that doesn't require attending actual meetings. I didn't mind – I was studying The Canon, the history of Victorian London, and the other great fiction of that golden age. I was giving myself an education of sorts. Then Nicholas Meyer came along with his *The Seven Per-Cent Solution* and rocked my world.

There is an itch many writers have to pen a Sherlock Holmes story. Twain had it. What is *Pygmalion* but an homage by George Bernard Shaw? It is an itch that begs to be scratched. Picture a bear upright against an old oak tree. I've never thought to myself, "You need to write a Hemingway story," or "A sequel to *The Catcher in the Rye*! Brilliant!" Yet countless times I have put pen to paper and scribbled "It was in the year 1894 that I first . . . ."

What is the fascination? I cannot explain it, but I feel it keenly. Many Sherlockians do as well. We want to create our own tale, or to read others' in the hope that for twenty minutes or so we can be transported back to when we read our very first Sherlock Holmes story.

Some cannot visualize a time when The Canon was so sacred one wrote a pastiche with trepidation. It would be like walking on Doyle's grave. Luckily, we live in more enlightened times now. The book in front of you, featuring stories from a slew of modern masters, is proof of that. The world of Holmes has become less stodgy, and a lot more fun, if such a thing is even possible.

I never wrote that Sherlockian novel I was planning. Another pair of fictional detectives . . . sorry, make that private enquiry agents . . . came along and demanded my time and attention. Yet I admire the attempts others have made to try on Doyle's slippers, if only for a brief while. Holmes fans are the better for it.

Rather than quote from Doyle, let me turn to St. Augustine, who said:

"Take up and read!"

The book lays in front of you, open and insistent. Shall you heed its siren call? Oh come, what are you waiting for? The game's afoot!

Oh, look. I quoted Doyle after all.

Will Thomas
February 2019

"When I Glance Over
My Notes and Records . . . ." *
by Roger Johnson

. . . I realise, with a certain surprise, that this remarkable series of books began only four years ago. And here we are in 2019, celebrating the 160th anniversary of the birth of Arthur Conan Doyle in an entirely appropriate manner by helping to maintain the house that he helped create for himself and his family.

But there are other anniversaries this year. On the 30th August 1889, for instance, J.M. Stoddart, who had come from Philadelphia to commission material from British authors for *Lippincott's Monthly Magazine*, gave a small dinner party at the Langham Hotel. His guests were Thomas Patrick Gill, Oscar Wilde (whose 165th birthday falls on the 16th October) and Arthur Conan Doyle. Gill may have been invited on the strength of his own editorial experience. If so, he can share the credit for the magazine's publication the following year of *The Picture of Dorian Gray* and *The Sign of the Four*.

Conan Doyle published no new Holmes stories in 1919. The masterly "His Last Bow" had appeared two years before in both *The Strand Magazine* and *Collier's*. "The Mazarin Stone", rather less inspiring, was published in 1921, adapted from Conan Doyle's one-act play *The Crown Diamond*, which had enjoyed a brief and unsuccessful run earlier in the year.

But if we look two decades further back, we see that *Sherlock Holmes: A Drama in Four Acts*, credited to Arthur Conan Doyle and William Gillette, had its copyright performance at The Duke of York's Theatre in London on the 12th June 1899, with Herbert Waring as Holmes. Gillette himself was the star, of course, when the play opened on the 23rd October in Buffalo, transferring to the Garrick Theatre in New York the following month. Its success, which owed much to Gillette's performance, certainly helped stimulate public demand for more adventures of the great detective – a demand that was shortly to be satisfied in part by the publication of *The Hound of the Baskervilles*. (Gillette's play was triumphantly revived by the Royal Shakespeare Company forty-five years ago, with John Wood magnificent as Holmes.)

1929 saw both the last silent Holmes film, *Der Hund von Baskerville* (now restored and made available *this year* for home viewing) and the first talkie, *The Return of Sherlock Holmes*, with Clive Brook in the lead. A print of the latter is held at the Library of Congress, but is apparently inaccessible to the public.

In 1939, however, there was a true cinematic landmark. Fox's lavish production of *The Hound of the Baskervilles* paired Basil Rathbone and Nigel Bruce for the first time as the detective and the doctor. Moreover, it was the first Holmes film to be set in the correct period. Late Victorian London was superbly re-created in Hollywood – and the sets were used again that same year for a similarly excellent production, *The Adventures of Sherlock Holmes*.

Twenty years later, Hammer's flawed but entertaining version of *The Hound of the Baskervilles* presented Sherlock Holmes in colour for the first time, and showed that a British studio could match Hollywood for action and suspense. In its sixtieth anniversary year, critical appreciation of this good-looking film, with its fine performances from a cast headed by Peter Cushing and Andre Morell, has grown. (I remember when the *Radio Times* critics gave it a rather harsh two-star ranking. Now it merits the full five stars. *Tempora mutantur . . . .*)

In 1954, while Carleton Hobbs and Norman Shelley were playing Holmes and Watson in a series for children on the BBC Home Service, the Light Programme transmitted twelve new dramatisations from the Canon, starring John Gielgud and Ralph Richardson. Unusually, these were produced by an independent company, and for some reason the BBC declined to broadcast the remaining four plays, though the whole series was eagerly taken up by stations in America and elsewhere. (Hobbs and Shelley remained British radio's definitive pairing for another fifteen years. 2019 marks the fiftieth anniversary of their final series as Holmes and Watson, which concluded, most appropriately, with *His Last Bow*.)

That same year, American audiences could see the great detective on television, in a light but very enjoyable series of short films with Ronald Howard and Howard Marion Crawford in the leading rôles. On this side of the Atlantic, we had to wait until video recordings were released some fifty years later, but meanwhile we had something rather better to look at. Fifty-five years ago, in an anthology series called *Detective*, BBC TV presented a superb, authentic Holmes and Watson. The actors were Douglas Wilmer and Nigel Stock, and the story was *The Speckled Band*. Its success led to a fondly remembered series the following year.

2019 also marks the thirty-fifth anniversary of Jeremy Brett's first appearance as Holmes, with David Burke as his Watson, in Michael Cox's series for Granada TV, *The Adventures of Sherlock Holmes*. It was the start of an extraordinary decade-long world-wide phenomenon, which at its best was unbeatable. In Burke we saw the true Watson, brave, intelligent, loyal and down-to-earth. Brett, for many, remains the ideal Holmes.

What else? Well, eighty-five years ago, The Baker Street Irregulars, which, in terms of its combined age and influence ranks as the world's senior Holmesian fellowship, was founded. Moreover, The Sherlock Holmes Society held its inaugural meeting in London at the same time as the BSI's first meeting in New York. Indeed, the two groups exchanged congratulatory telegrams! But while the Irregulars' sodality persisted through the hard times of the thirties and forties, the very differently constituted British society survived only until 1938, lying dormant until its revival as The Sherlock Holmes Society of London in 1951.

I can't conclude without mentioning the twentieth anniversary of two remarkable achievements. In 1999, thanks to the imagination and hard work of certain members of the SHSL – notably, of course, the sculptor John Doubleday – and the financial support of Abbey National plc, an imposing statue of the Great Detective was at last erected in London. Its unveiling on the 23rd September was the focal point of a week-long festival, which included an evening at the Cockpit Theatre to see *Sherlock Holmes: The Last Act!* written by David Stuart Davies for Roger Llewellyn, who had first staged it earlier in the year at the Salisbury Playhouse.

I doubt that even the author seriously believed that it would become an international success, but that's exactly what has happened. The play itself is first-rate, and even then Roger Llewellyn's interpretation was revelatory. Roger died last year, but his performance in *The Last Act* and its successor *Sherlock Holmes: The Death and Life* can still be enjoyed, as he recorded the two plays for Big Finish in 2010. (And as I write, we're less than a month away from the premiere of David's new play, *Sherlock Holmes: The Final Reckoning*, in which Michael Daviot and Mark Kydd play the detective and the doctor.)

I remember the explosion of interest in 1987, stimulated by the centenary of the first Holmes story, *A Study in Scarlet*. 2019 is another year peculiarly rich in significant anniversaries – *and opportunities*. David Marcum, MX Publishing, and the many contributors to this volume have created one of those opportunities. Let's make the most of it!

Roger Johnson, BSI, ASH
31st January, 2019

* "The Five Orange Pips"

An Ongoing Legacy
for Sherlock Holmes
by Steve Emecz

Undershaw
Circa 1900

As we enter the fourth year of *The MX Book of New Sherlock Holmes Stories*, we reach a staggering fifteen volumes – by far the largest collection of new Sherlock Holmes stories in the world. Through authors donating royalties and licensing, the series has raised over $40,000 for Stepping Stones School. With this money, the school has been able to fund projects that would be very difficult to organise otherwise – especially those to preserve the legacy of Sir Arthur Conan Doyle at Undershaw.

There are now over three-hundred-thirty stories and well over a hundred-fifty authors taking part – many MX authors, but many others including bestselling authors like Lee Child, Jonathan Kellerman, Lyndsay Faye, and Bonnie MacBird.

Volumes XI and XII continued the tradition of getting starred reviews from *Publishers Weekly*:

"Each of 17 Sherlock Holmes pastiches in Marcum's stellar 11th anthology (after Part X) is based on one of the teasing references that Conan Doyle made to cases that were never published. The end result is another triumph of ingenuity and faithfulness to the spirit of the canon . . . .This is an essential volume for Sherlock Holmes fans."

"Marcum continues to amaze with the number of high-quality pastiches that he has selected."

MX Publishing is a social enterprise – all the staff, including me, are volunteers with day jobs. The collection would not be possible without the creator and editor, David Marcum, who is rightly cited multiple times by *Publishers Weekly* and others as probably the most accomplished Sherlockian editor thus far. In addition to Stepping Stones School, our main program that we support is the Happy Life Children's Home in Kenya. My wife Sharon and I have recently returned from our 6th Christmas in a row at Happy Life and can report back that huge progress has been made and the lives of over 600 babies saved. You can read all about the project in the 2nd edition of the book *The Happy Life Story.*

Our support of both of these projects is possible through the publishing of Sherlock Holmes books, which we have now been doing for a decade.

You can find out more information about the Stepping Stones School at: *www.steppingstones.org.uk*

and Happy Life at: *www.happylifechildrenshomes.com.*

You can obtain more books from MX, both fiction and non-fiction, at: *www.sherlockholmesbooks.com.*

If you would like to become involved with these projects or help out in any way, please reach out to me via *LinkedIn.*

Steve Emecz
February 2019
Twitter: *@steveemecz*
LinkedIn: *https://www.linkedin.com/in/emecz/*

21

The Doyle Room at Stepping Stones, Undershaw
Partially funded through royalties from
The MX Book of New Sherlock Holmes Stories

A Word From the
Head Teacher of Stepping Stones
by Melissa Grigsby

Undershaw
September 9, 2016
Grand Opening of the Stepping Stones School
(Photograph courtesy of Roger Johnson)

"The world is full of obvious things
which nobody by any chance ever observes."
– Arthur Conan Doyle, *The Hound of the Baskervilles*

As we travel into the next journey of Stepping Stones School, the words of Arthur Conan Doyle ring so very true. Our developing outreach and employment support programs based at Undershaw focus on social mobility for young people with Special Educational Needs. Our work sits with Business and Companies that so often miss the obvious things and get caught up in practical barriers, rather than seeing the potential of the young people on our watch.

The funds gifted to us have allowed us to start developing a more sophisticated communication systems, which in turn will open doors to allow the world to observe the obvious things and look deeper at the skills and opportunities the young people of Undershaw bring to the community.

23

Dr. Mortimer looked strangely at us for an instant, and his voice sank almost to a whisper as he answered:

"Mr. Holmes, they were the footprints of a gigantic hound!"

The royalties we receive are the footprints in a gigantic story for Undershaw and the young people that learn under its roof.

Melissa Grigsby
Executive Head Teacher,
Stepping Stones, Undershaw
January 2019

Sherlock Holmes (1854-1957) was born in Yorkshire, England, on 6 January, 1854. In the mid-1870's, he moved to 24 Montague Street, London, where he established himself as the world's first Consulting Detective. After meeting Dr. John H. Watson in early 1881, he and Watson moved to rooms at 221b Baker Street, where his reputation as the world's greatest detective grew for several decades. He was presumed to have died battling noted criminal Professor James Moriarty on 4 May, 1891, but he returned to London on 5 April, 1894, resuming his consulting practice in Baker Street. Retiring to the Sussex coast near Beachy Head in October 1903, he continued to be associated in various private and government investigations while giving the impression of being a reclusive apiarist. He was very involved in the events encompassing World War I, and to a lesser degree those of World War II. He passed away peacefully upon the cliffs above his Sussex home on his 103rd birthday, 6 January, 1957.

Dr. John Hamish Watson (1852-1929) was born in Stranraer, Scotland on 7 August, 1852. In 1878, he took his Doctor of Medicine Degree from the University of London, and later joined the army as a surgeon. Wounded at the Battle of Maiwand in Afghanistan (27 July, 1880), he returned to London late that same year. On New Year's Day, 1881, he was introduced to Sherlock Holmes in the chemical laboratory at Barts. Agreeing to share rooms with Holmes in Baker Street, Watson became invaluable to Holmes's consulting detective practice. Watson was married and widowed three times, and from the late 1880's onward, in addition to his participation in Holmes's investigations and his medical practice, he chronicled Holmes's adventures, with the assistance of his literary agent, Sir Arthur Conan Doyle, in a series of popular narratives, most of which were first published in *The Strand* magazine. Watson's later years were spent preparing a vast number of his notes of Holmes's cases for future publication. Following a final important investigation with Holmes, Watson contracted pneumonia and passed away on 24 July, 1929.

Photos of Sherlock Holmes and Dr. John H. Watson courtesy of Roger Johnson

The MX Book
of
New Sherlock Holmes Stories
Part XIII:
2019 Annual
(1881-1890)

Inscrutable
by Jacquelynn Morris

Bellamy was remarkable
Her instinct was invaluable
Her strength was in her character
Women are inscrutable.

Winter's motive indisputable—
The Baron was despicable—
Revenge is quite delectable
Women are inscrutable.

Hunter worked for Rucastle
Her appearance substitutional
The plan was convolutional
Women are inscrutable.

A solitary cycler
The swindle matrimonial
Woodley was detestable
Women are inscrutable.

They are puzzles most insoluble
To Holmes, incomprehensible.
But none of them forgettable
Women are inscrutable.

The Folly of Age
by Derrick Belanger

It was on the morning of September 21st, the first day of autumn in the first year of my friendship with Sherlock Holmes. We were sitting at our dining table, enjoying a cup of Darjeeling and sharing sections of *The Times*. From the ground floor below arose a lively conversation between Mrs. Hudson, our landlady, and a man I did not recognize. The volume of the man's voice was booming and ebbed and flowed like the movements of a symphony, occasionally crashing with a loud crescendo.

Though our door was closed, so loud was the man that when his voice hit a high mark, I could make out snippets of his conversation. "A woman like you can do so much better! Stocks and bonds, my dear! Stocks and bonds! Invest! Invest! Invest!"

Hearing the conversation, which was more like a monologue, from below, I lowered my newspaper and asked Holmes if he knew the identity of Mrs. Hudson's caller.

Holmes folded up the agony column and handed it over to me. "The gentleman is here not for Mrs. Hudson, but to see me."

"Are you sure?" I asked with a raised eyebrow. "He is certainly having a serious conversation with her."

"I have a feeling, Watson, that he has a similar conversation with all he meets. Ah, there he is now, coming up the stairs. Let's see if this man, clearly an investor with ideas to share, shall pause long enough in his salesmanship to tell us of his case."

The young man practically stormed into our abode, his eyes darting wildly around our room, noting every crack in the china we had upon our table, every notch in our walls. He was a squat man with a rounded face, his black hair slicked back, and his thin mustache waxed and curled at the ends. His suit was black and his bow tie red. He carried a top hat in his right hand and I thought if he put it upon his head, he'd look like the ringmaster of a circus.

"Tut-tut, Mr. Holmes," the man scolded. "I have just had a chat with your landlady and I explained to her the importance of investing in stocks and bonds. A renowned detective like yourself should be living high above the rank depicted in this setting. Perhaps I could schedule an appointment with one of our market investors for early next week. Here is my card sir."

It almost seemed to appear like magic as he removed it from a pocket within the sleeve of his suit coat.

35

Holmes and I remembered our manners, put down our papers, and stood from our seats. My detective friend made a slight bow to the gentleman and accepted his card. "'*Mr. Arthur Ludlow, Manager at Bloomfields*'" he read. "And how did you come to seek out my services?"

"A constable provided your name. Delightful fellow. Said if I need something found, just ask Mr. Holmes and Dr. Watson. Described you, sir, the fellow did – gaunt with a beak of a nose. It was easy to tell who was detective and who was doctor. Now, as you've noted," Ludlow said with a conductor-like wave of his arms, switching topics as a symphony changes movements. "I work for Bloomfields. We are a small but growing company, my friend, small but growing," Ludlow clapped his hands together then pulled them as far apart as he could to show how quickly they were growing. "Mark my word! With just thirty minutes of your time, we will have you on your way to a state of luxury. You as well." The man barked, now turning his attention to me. "Both of you think on it. Detective and Doctor, living in a fine London house!"

Holmes and I turned to look at one another, a slight smirk on both of our faces. Holmes shifted his gaze to the manager, "A fine offer, Mr. Ludlow, and perhaps Watson and I shall take you up on it. However, I believe your purpose here today is not to seek out new clients."

"Ah, but one can always have two purposes Mr. Holmes," the man chuckled. "I am always at the service of one who wants to invest and invest wisely."

"Please have a seat, Mr. Ludlow, and let us turn to the original purpose for your visit."

We took our cushioned chairs, while Mr. Ludlow sat across from us on our sofa. After several more attempts of keeping the conversation on stocks and bonds, Holmes steered the man towards telling us of the primary reason for his visit.

"It's the folly of age, my dear Mr. Holmes, the folly of age!" Ludlow said with a theatrical wave of his hands. "I warned my mother several times about keeping such a large sum of money in her house. Just sitting in a safe, not earning any interest, not working for her. What good is that, I ask you? But she wouldn't listen. Father had come around before his passing, but Mother was a strict one – very religious, kind-hearted, wanted to help the poor – and I told her that the best way to help them is to invest and share the wealth. A church-going woman, my mother."

"My good man," I said interrupting Ludlow, trying to make sense of all he was saying, "was your mother robbed?"

"Indeed, she was, Dr. Watson, indeed she was. Window was left unlocked. The safe door was open. The combination was written on a scrap of paper glued to the inside of her top desk drawer. What kind of security is that, I ask you?"

"Mr. Ludlow, if you will kindly start at the beginning of your story, Dr. Watson and I shall have a much easier time assisting your mother in finding her stolen money."

"Of course, Mr. Holmes, I do apologize. The affair happened two days ago, but I must go back in time a bit further to explain my mother's situation. My father was a merchant. He started as a captain, and then over time he was able to invest in his own vessel. By the end of his life, he'd fully owned his own ship, *The Mercurier*. He passed two years ago this October, bless his soul.

"Father wasn't skilled at investing. He allowed for far too much of his money to sit in bank vaults and not be invested in other lucrative ventures. At least he did invest in shipping, and my parents were able to afford a fine house, two servants, and a cook.

"When my mother became a widow, she allowed things to continue as they were. Despite my arguments for investing in stocks and bonds, Mother continued to allow her money to sit in the bank until six months ago. At that point in time, gentlemen, my mother removed all her savings from the bank and stored it in her home in the family wall safe.

"I argued extensively with her about the folly of such a move, but she wouldn't hear of investing her money elsewhere. She said the money was safely locked away at home, and that the Bible is clear about making money off interest."

"Your mother is particularly religious?" inquired Holmes.

"Oh yes!" boomed Ludlow, a look of disgust crossing his animated features. "She always attends services with her sister every Sunday. Since my father's death, she's attended several times a week. She's always been a good Anglican and gives generously – in my opinion a bit *too* generously."

"How generous?" Holmes sat back his fingers now steepled before him.

"Oh, nothing outrageous. Ten pounds a week, at times. She is most concerned for the less fortunate. But I told her she'd be better off investing that ten pounds a week, taking the interest and sharing it with the church. She'd have none of it, though."

Holmes nodded, then said, "Tell us about the robbery."

"Yes, yes, as I was saying it occurred two days ago. Mother was out visiting her sister, my Aunt Christina. Those two had been inseparable after my father's death, going to church together, hosting luncheons, attending the theatre and symphony. They were both widowed and provided each other companionship.

"That morning, my mother was running late to her appointment with Aunt Christina. She says that she went to the family safe which is hidden behind a portrait of my father in the office, opened it, removed two pounds sterling, and closed it up. She does remember opening the window to get some air in the room as it was stuffy, and she believes she closed it, but cannot say whether or not she remembered to lock the safe.

"That afternoon, she returned from her engagement. In her haste, she had forgotten to record the removal of the sterling in her record book. She entered the office and found the window open and the door to the safe ajar. When she looked inside, all of her money was gone!"

"My word!" I ejaculated. "The poor woman! Did the servants hear anything?"

"Jameson, the butler of the house, swears that he heard nothing. He arranged the silverware in the dining room next to the office for dinner, but he did that at around two that afternoon. It is assumed that the thief had absconded by then. The maid and the cook were out gathering food for the evening meal. My mother often allows them to shop when she is away with my aunt for the day. It gives them time to socialize. She does the same for Jameson occasionally, allowing him time to go to the races."

"So this Jameson is a gambling man?" I asked gruffly, thinking of my own vices. While I've always been able to keep my debts from becoming overly burdensome, I've seen many men ruined by placing their fortunes on losing horses.

"He is indeed, Doctor, and he was the prime suspect of the police. However, Jameson, though holding the title of butler, does multiple jobs for my mother as must occur in a household with few servants. He does repairs around the house and tends to the garden. Several neighbors witnessed Jameson mending one of the front steps that day. While it is possible he could have taken the money quickly anytime mother was gone, his behavior of repairing the house and polishing the china seemed unusual for a man stealing more than three-thousand pounds."

"Perhaps not so unusual for one wanting to appear innocent," said Holmes. "Was Jameson arrested?"

"He was not, Mr. Holmes. As a matter of fact, when Mother reported the money missing, it was he who ran off and fetched a constable. The police certainly had enough circumstantial evidence to hold him, but Mother vouched for his character and refused to have any of her household arrested. She refused to make a statement to the officer if it meant ruin for any of her servants. And so, if she would not officially report the crime, the police could not investigate. The puzzled officer was sent away."

Holmes pursed his lips and squinted his eyes for a moment, taking in the information. "And what has happened since the crime took place?"

"Much, Mr. Holmes, much indeed!" Jameson removed a handkerchief from his front pocket and mopped his brow. He had become flushed in the excitement of telling the story, his face red as if he had sprinted down the street. "That evening, according to Jameson, he was awakened by harsh whispers coming from Mother's bedchamber. He swears that he heard two distinct female voices arguing about the money and what to do about the servants. The next morning, my mother called all three of the servants to the parlor and sacked the lot of them. She gave them their wages and said that she just didn't know who to trust anymore. After dismissing the staff, she then had all the locks changed on the doors and windows. She's refusing to see anyone, including my aunt and even me. Believe me, I've tried Mr. Holmes, but she won't open the door. She just yells at me to leave her alone.

"The folly of age, Mr. Holmes! If only she had taken me seriously, none of this would have happened. You can't steal bonds locked away in a bank!"

Holmes sat up suddenly, lowering his hands to his palms. "Your mother's situation is intriguing, Mr. Ludlow, and in the absence of the police's aid, I am happy to take your case. A few questions, if you please."

"Of course," said Ludlow deflating a little, his excitement tempered with relief.

"I assume you have your own suspicions about who took the money?"

"I do."

"Tell them to me, please."

Here Ludlow became a bit uncomfortable and squirmed in his seat. "Well, with the ground floor window open, really anybody could have come and taken the money. Someone from the street."

"Come now, Mr. Ludlow. Jameson was outside or next to the office most of the time in question. From your own inquiries, you know the neighbors saw Jameson in the yard and had a good view of the house. Yes, Mr. Ludlow, don't look so surprised. If your mother dismissed the police, then it must have been *you* who made those inquiries. I know that you have also been in touch with Jameson. It is the only way you could have known that he heard your mother's conversation with the other woman on the night of the robbery."

"Yes, you are correct Mr. Holmes. Jameson does have his vices, but he's a good man. Still, I can't completely rule him out as a suspect, though it breaks my heart to say so."

"Whom else do you suspect?"

Ludlow let out a long sigh. He fidgeted with his handkerchief and shifted in his seat. "I hate to speak ill of family, but I suspect my Aunt. I've heard she gives much more generously to the poor box than even my mother, and she lives alone in a small flat such as your own. She can't afford to spare the money she gives away."

"But you've said that your mother was with your aunt the entire time she was gone," I reminded him. "This seemed like an impossible feat for the woman."

"I know it doesn't make sense Dr. Watson, but she's the only one that I can identify who would be arguing with Mother in the dead of night. It could be that Christina sent someone to get the money. I know it isn't much to go on, Mr. Holmes, more like a hunch, but it might explain why my mother sent everyone away and refuses to see visitors. She may have realized the truth and was too heartbroken to admit it."

Holmes nodded, taking in the man's reasoning. Then he rose. Ludlow and I did so as well. "You may call on me at this time tomorrow, Mr. Ludlow. I do believe I shall have answers for you by then. Please give me the address of your mother, your aunt, and Mr. Jameson. Watson and I shall need to ask them some questions."

I provided Ludlow with pen and paper. He leaned over to use the side table, wrote the addresses for us, and handed me the paper. He then turned to Holmes, grabbed his hand, and shook it vigorously. "Thank you, Mr. Holmes! Thank you so much!" He finally released the hand and put on his hat. "I do look forward to seeing you tomorrow."

Ludlow turned to leave and then Holmes added, "Just one more thing, Mr. Ludlow."

"Yes, anything," the man said excitedly, his boisterousness returning.

"Is your mother in any fear of becoming destitute?"

"Oh, no sir," the investor said, his eyes wide in shock. "The missus and I would never allow any of our relatives to be out on the streets. Mark my words, Mr. Holmes, whatever the solution to this matter, my mother has no fear of becoming destitute."

"Very good, sir. I shall see you tomorrow."

"What do you think?" I asked Holmes after Ludlow left. Holmes had returned to the newspaper as if he had heard nothing interesting from his client.

"In my opinion, investing in stocks and bonds can be as risky as betting on a roll of the dice. If one does not take the time to study the financial world carefully, one could lose everything. Though Mr. Ludlow makes some very strong arguments, I would have to say that I would rather spend my mental energies on different tasks than following market trends."

"I mean about the case," I explained crossly. I could tell Holmes was having a bit of fun with me.

"Ah, that," said Holmes. He folded up the paper and now gave me his undivided attention. "I believe the knot in this case is but a single loop, and with the gentle pull of one thread, the knot shall come undone. There are several paths we can take to start our investigation." Holmes paused for a moment. He eyed me in the way that a kitten eyes a ball of string. "You've now assisted me on several occasions, my friend. What say you? Where should we start our inquiries?"

"I believe it is always best to start at the scene of the crime," I answered.

"Very well, Watson, then that is what we shall do."

About an hour later we were standing before an elegant multi-story Georgian home. There were spots along the front of the house where chips in the white paint were flaking, and signs of mending along the exterior beams were apparent. Though one could see that Jameson did his best to keep up the house, the repairs were too much for one man to handle, and if care wasn't taken, the house would begin to fall away to the ravages of time.

Holmes and I walked up the front steps and I saw the repair work completed by Jameson. The poor man must work non-stop, I thought to myself, then realized that alone was motivation enough for the servant to run off with his master's money.

"Do not draw conclusions without facts," Holmes scolded me. He realized where my thoughts were leading. The detective rapped loudly on the door. We waited, and he did so again. Still, no answer. Holmes called loudly, "Mrs. Ludlow, I am Sherlock Holmes, and this is my associate, Dr. Watson. We have been hired by your son to find your missing money! We believe we can discover the thief who robbed you if we could only look around!"

"I don't need any help," shouted a deep, raspy voice from a window above us.

"Please, Mrs. Ludlow! I implore you to open this door!" Holmes shouted back in return.

"I don't need help from you or anyone else! You tell my son and the others! Now go away!" She yelled with finality and slammed the window shut.

I cringed at her behavior. "I suppose we should have expected this," I grumbled. I looked to Holmes, and he looked as though he were enjoying himself.

"Come now, Watson. You know as well as I that we can enter the house whenever we please. Now is not the time, though. Where to next, my guide?"

41

I mulled it over for a second and then said, "I believe that Mr. Jameson isn't staying too far from here. Just a couple of stops away. Let's interview him next."

"Very well," Holmes concurred. "It is a lovely day for a stroll Watson. Perhaps we can walk the mile."

I agreed, and we were off. Along the way, Holmes stopped at a small grove of trees on some undeveloped property. He admired the leaves and noticed the maples were already changing to their red hues. I enjoyed seeing the leaves as well and said as much, though I couldn't fathom why Holmes was in such high spirits. He was having such a good time with a case that he admitted had a fairly simple solution once we uncovered it. I had seen Holmes dismiss clients with more tangled knots than this because he found the case intellectually unstimulating.

We took our time on our walk, continuing to admire the leaves, stopping at times to examine lilac bushes in well maintained gardens, and enjoying the heat of the sun as the rays flowed through the partially clouded sky, brightening up the day. Eventually we meandered to the inn which currently housed Mr. Jameson.

We found him sitting in the inn's tavern, enjoying a glass of ale. He was a stout man with thinning hair, wiry limbs, and a puffy brown beard. He was in good shape for his age. I estimated he was my senior by a decade. His eyes crinkled as he heard that we were hired by Ludlow to find his mother's missing money.

"I'm right glad someone's going to get to the bottom of the matter. It pains me to see Mrs. Ludlow so grief-stricken. I'd love to continue on working for her, but alas, I've already found employment elsewhere. Start tomorrow. I'm not sure she'd ever take me back anyway. Not sure she could afford her help much longer. One ship's income can only go so far." He paused and took a swig of his ale and then wiped some froth from his beard with his sleeve. "I am loyal to her, though. She could have had that constable arrest me. I blame myself for that money going away, for not hearing nothing."

"Yet, you did hear something the night of the robbery," Holmes corrected the man. We had joined the man at his table and also were enjoying glasses of ale while we talked.

"That's true. Odd it was, as well. In all my years working for Mrs. Ludlow, I never heard a caller at night – certainly not another woman."

"Was the visitor's voice recognizable?" asked Holmes.

"Uh-uh," Jameson wagged his finger at Holmes. "I know what Master Ludlow is up to, trying to pin this on his aunt, Mrs. Thurston. She's a fine, upstanding woman, that Mrs. Thurston. She couldn't take a sterling left on the pavement without going and confessing at church. To be honest, I could just make out that there were two voices in the room. I could tell they were women. That's about it. I tell you, though, the other one wasn't Mrs. Thurston."

"Did you hear any of their discussion?"

"Can't reckon that I did, except for one point where I heard Mrs. Ludlow say, 'What shall I do?', and then something about the money. They weren't being loud and I'm not one to eavesdrop. Sorry, gentlemen. I wish I could be more help."

"Actually, you've been most helpful."

Jameson was surprised by Holmes's remark. The detective then asked the man a few more questions about himself and the other servants. I was taken aback by the questions that Holmes didn't ask, such as more about his whereabouts during the robbery, if he saw anyone suspicious, or any questions about his debt. Holmes merely inquired about the cook and the maid, finding that both had also secured employment elsewhere. He then asked some questions about the character of the late Mr. Ludlow. Jameson assured Holmes that the Ludlows were upstanding and treated their servants kindly. He again bemoaned the fact that the robbery occurred while he was nearby and didn't stop it.

We finished up our drinks and bid Jameson goodbye. We then left the inn and Holmes hailed a cab. "Why didn't you ask for the new addresses of the maid and cook?" I questioned as a hansom stopped at the curb before us.

"Because I have no reason as of yet to suspect them in this matter. Come along, now. Our next stop is the residence of Mrs. Thurston."

Mrs. Thurston's flat was a small, tidy two-room abode a few blocks from the Thames. "I like being near the water and hearing the sounds of the shipyard. It makes me feel close to my dearly departed husband, Walter," the elderly woman explained as we heard the ringing of shipyard bells echoing in the background.

The white-haired woman was gracious and spry. She invited Holmes and me into her flat, made us feel comfortable, and insisted on serving us tea and cakes. She ran about the flat, despite her bow-leggedness, preparing our meal. Her table was set with a checkered doily, and she quickly added plates, utensils, jams, and teacakes. While the tea was steeping, she insisted that we join her in prayer. She thanked the Heavenly Father for our meal and asked for His blessing. Her prayers were soft and her Amen almost inaudible.

"Has your sister always been a loyal member of the church?" asked Holmes after we had been served our tea.

"Oh yes. She and I both," Mrs. Thurston said as she carefully spread a thin layer of raspberry jam on a biscuit. "We have been since we were children. Both raised Anglican in the strict sense. All of our schooling was through the church. Why, if we hadn't fallen in love with our husbands, we might have joined a convent."

"So your sister is just as pious as you?"

"Oh, yes," Mrs. Thurston answered solemnly.

"Not a sinner?"

"Dear me, sir!" Mrs. Thurston was taken aback at such a question, and was quite stern in her answer. "We are all sinners in the eyes of the Lord."

Holmes gave one of his silent chuckles at his unintended impropriety. "I apologize, Mrs. Thurston. Of course, we are. What I meant to say is that your sister follows the path of the righteous, that she is her brother's keeper."

"Yes, why bless your heart," Mrs. Thurston had a grin from ear to ear, impressed by Holmes's biblical knowledge. "She most certainly is. My dear sister Bethany has always followed The Good Book. She says her prayers and follows the commandments. She helps those in need by tithing and giving generously to the poor box."

"Do you know if that is why your sister took her money out of the bank and kept it locked in a safe at her home? She told her son that she did so because she didn't want to collect interest."

"I don't know. We didn't discuss money, but with Bethany she may indeed have felt it was too sinful to collect interest off of her money. The Bible is clear on that," Mrs. Thurston explained, as though we were Sunday School children.

"Did she ever borrow money from you?" Holmes inquired.

Mrs. Thurston leaned back in shock as though an invisible force had shoved her. She was stricken by Holmes's question and clearly felt he had once again crossed into impropriety. "Mr. Holmes," she started bluntly. "My sister has always had more money than me, as you can see." She motioned to her bare walls and the simple dishes on her table. "My husband was an honest man. I've never been poor, always had a roof over my head, and I am grateful for what I have, but Bethany has so much more than me. There is no reason for her to ever ask to borrow from me. Of course, if she ever was in need, I'd give her all that I could."

"Thank you, Mrs. Thurston. It is good to know that Mrs. Ludlow has a sister like you who doesn't have the inequities of the selfish. Do you have any idea who might have stolen your sister's money?"

"Oh, Mr. Holmes, it was probably some poor unfortunate soul who knew not the gravity of what they did. I have prayed for my sister and prayed for the unfortunate soul who stole from her. I do so hope they return the money to Bethany. It is far better to pay for one's sins now than in the afterlife." Mrs. Ludlow put her palms together as if in prayer. "As you know, sir, those who hurt their brother's keeper shall be struck down with great vengeance and furious rage."

Holmes looked solemn and nodded, understanding the gravity of the thief's situation.

"Are you concerned that your sister has locked herself away and dismissed her staff?" I asked Mrs. Thurston.

"I am," she admitted. "A great wrong has been suffered by my sister. I feel that she just needs time to pray and try to understand how this could happen to her – how there is a lesson in all of this. The Lord works in mysterious ways. Rest assured, though, that Sunday is just a few from now. I'm sure she will emerge from her home on the Lord's Day and accompany me to church. Under the eyes of God, she will be able to begin her healing."

After our questioning, we joined Mrs. Thurston in praying for both her sister and the robber. We then thanked her for the delicious meal and for being such a wonderful hostess, said our goodbyes, and departed her flat.

"I think that's the most praying I've done since I was a schoolboy," I admitted to Holmes when we had stepped out to the pavement.

He gave a silent chuckle. "For men like us, Watson, I'm sure that it didn't hurt."

Holmes had me hail a cab while he took out his clay pipe and stuffed it with shag. I gave the driver our Baker Street address, but Holmes corrected me and gave the address of Mrs. Ludlow.

We jumped in the hansom and as it moved out into the traffic of the day, I asked sarcastically if we would be needing his lock picking tools.

"She will see us this time, Watson."

"And why is that?" I inquired.

"Because she is a pious woman," Holmes responded firmly. I was going to ask more questions, but I had already learned that my friend would tell me more when he was ready to say more.

On the way to Mrs. Ludlow's house, Holmes had the driver stop at the residence of a botanist he knew who specialized in the Japanese bonsai style.

"Do we have time for this?" I asked. It was now late in the afternoon.

"Come now. Mrs. Ludlow shall be locked away in her home whether we arrive in a few moments or an hour later. Let us enjoy this fine day a little longer by spending time in the splendor of Mr. Takahashi's garden."

We spent a good thirty minutes in the man's back garden, admiring his tiny elms, pines, and junipers. Mr. Takahashi, a gaunt, bald oriental, explained how the trees were created through wrapping wiring around the limbs and branches to shape the trees and then trimming them back to ensure they maintained their size and shape.

"Aren't they extraordinary, Watson?" Holmes said admiringly while eyeing a tiny pine. "The Master molds these trees to perfection much like Prometheus molded man from clay." Holmes gently stroked one of the thin pine tree branches, letting the course bristles flow through his fingertips. "We never have to worry about such beauty falling from grace."

It wasn't long after thanking Mr. Takahashi for his time that we returned to the doorstep of Mrs. Ludlow's residence. Once again Holmes gave a harsh rapping on the door. Once again, the window above our heads opened, and Mrs. Ludlow called out harshly, "Go away!"

"I will not!" Holmes yelled up to the window, his fists clenched in the air. "You listen well! I am here to speak with you about your breaking of the Ninth Commandment. If you don't open this door at once, I will shout, so all of your neighbors can hear!"

My mind reeled as I tried to remember which Commandment was the Ninth. I thought it might be to honor your mother and father but wasn't certain. Could it be about stealing? No, that was the eighth one.

My mind grappled for a few brief seconds and then I heard a clicking of the front door. The lock was undone, and slowly with a loud creek, the wooden door pulled inward ever so slightly. A wrinkled face topped with thin gray hair and dull hazel eyes peered through at us.

"How much do you know?" the woman asked, her raspy voice spoke softly.

"I know everything, and I would prefer to discuss it inside rather than on your front steps," Holmes answered firmly.

The woman stepped away from the door, and Holmes and I pushed it open. We entered a well-kept luxurious home. Mrs. Ludlow's form was like her sister's, short and bow legged. She almost waddled forward through her house and we followed behind. We strolled through several rooms, and I was surprised at the contrast between this house and the flat of Mrs. Thurston. Here were fancy oriental rugs which adorned hardwood floors and exquisite artwork which hung upon fine papered walls. We finally arrived at the parlor where we sat down in soft leather chairs.

"You should see the office," said Mrs. Ludlow in a soft monotone. She sat with her hands limp resting on her inner thighs, spread as though invisible irons held her in place.

Holmes's lips pursed and then he said gruffly, "There is no need for that."

Mrs. Ludlow gave a slow nod. Tears welled up in her eyes and she dabbed at them with a handkerchief she removed from a pouch on the side of her chair. There was an overwhelming sense of melancholia about the woman. She was rounder than her sister, almost cherub-like, but cast down by a heavy burden, as though she were carrying melancholia itself upon her back.

I was about to say some words of comfort to the woman, but Holmes's eyes glared at me and told me to hold my tongue. I was about to have all of my questions answered.

"There was no money stolen," Holmes said still sternly but his tone was now tempered with a sense of compassion.

"No, that's not true," Mrs. Ludlow countered, the raspiness returned to her voice. "There *was* money stolen – stolen in international laws, in trade disputes, in sailors making simple mistakes."

"Your husband's ship is *The Mercurier*, is it not?"

Mrs. Ludlow gave another slight nod.

"I have read about the ship's trouble," Holmes explained, his tone now soft and gentle. "How it mistakenly landed in the wrong port outside Osaka, how there was a dispute between the captain and the port master, how all of their goods were confiscated."

"Yes. The poor crew has been stranded for months while my lawyers argue with the Oriental lawyers. All this time locked up in court, and the insurance won't pay out because nothing has been lost or damaged – just locked away. The expenses have risen at a staggering rate, with no end in sight. So, I took all my money out of the bank. I couldn't have Arthur know of my troubles and, being in investments, someone could have told him. He has friends at the bank. It is how he knew I'd emptied my savings. So, I put it all here. All in my house, and I paid out my bills until all that was left was fifty pounds."

"Fifty-two pounds," corrected Holmes.

"No, it was just fifty. I made up the whole bit about the two pounds, another violation of the Ninth Commandment. You can add that to my sins. When I saw that the safe was finally empty, I panicked. A deep sense of fear invaded my soul. I knew I'd have to admit to my son and to my servants that I'd done them all wrong. I just couldn't bring myself to do it, to admit I'd lost all my savings, my poor husband's money."

"So, you made up the story about being robbed."

"Yes, and once I said it, I thought this might be a solution to my problem, a way for no one to get hurt. After all, anyone could climb through an open window, see the safe combination in my desk drawer, open the safe, steal the money, and be gone.

"But I should have known better. Should have known that the Lord was watching my every move, that breaking commandments never results in good. Once Jameson got that constable, I quickly realized from his line of questioning that Jameson was suspected and would be arrested. That's when I sent the police officer away. My son got word of the theft, and he was most upset at my sending away the constable. He started interviewing the neighbors, and I knew eventually he'd find out the truth. That night I didn't sleep well. I argued with myself aloud, like a mad woman, grappling with what to do."

"Did you argue with anyone else?" I inquired.

"Why what do you mean?" the woman looked truly puzzled by my question.

"Watson only asks because Mr. Jameson had told us he thought he overheard you speaking with someone on the night in question. Clearly with the changes in your tone as you talked aloud, he mistakenly thought there was another woman in the room when you were just speaking to yourself," Holmes explained.

"Yes . . . yes, I could see that," admitted Mrs. Ludlow.

"Pray continue with your story. What happened on the day after the supposed robbery?"

"That morning, I decided I needed more time, so I sent away all the servants. I didn't have money to pay them. With what little I had left, I had all the locks changed. I locked myself away from the world. A woman of shame. I was tested, gentlemen, tested like Job, and I failed." Mrs. Ludlow broke down in a harsh fit of sobs.

"There, there, my dear woman," Holmes said softly and reassuringly, like a mother speaking to a babe. "You are wrong. Your test is not over. You have done the hard work of realizing your mistakes. You have nothing to fear."

Mrs. Ludlow looked up at Holmes. A spark of hope entered her dull eyes. "I don't, sir?"

"No, you have found yourself a victim of no more than chance. But rest assured, all shall be resolved."

Mrs. Ludlow reached out her quivering hand and placed it on Holmes's head. "Are you real? Are you a messenger from God?"

Holmes smiled at this. "No, my dear. I'm no more than a detective who has a solution to your trouble. I can tell you that all has been resolved with your legal troubles. The crew has been released from custody, all charges dropped. *The Mercurier* has delivered its shipment and is now heading back to port in London."

"Oh, bless you, kind sir," Mrs. Ludlow choked the words through her sobs. "Bless you. 'Tis a miracle."

"A miracle it may seem," a sternness returned to Holmes's voice, "but there is more you must do. You still need to atone for your sins."

Mrs. Ludlow's sobs ceased at Holmes's proclamation. She looked to Holmes with abject terror crossing her face. "Wha-wha-wha" she stammered.

"What must you do?" Holmes asked for her. "You must write to your discharged servants, your sister, your son. You must confess your sins and ask for their forgiveness. Have faith, Mrs. Ludlow," Holmes snapped as she shook her head in fear at what she must do for absolution. "You will find that when you do this, you shall once again feel His grace upon you."

After Holmes finished, Mrs. Ludlow slowly lowered her head back down and raised her hands. I thought she was going to start sobbing again, but instead, she put her palms together and began to pray, to thank the Lord for sending us to her door, to give her the strength to confess her sins to those she had wronged.

She was still in prayer when Holmes and I rose from our seats, and quietly left the room.

"Our services, my dear Watson, were never really needed in this case," Holmes explained while riding in a cab on our way home. The sun was now setting, and the sky displayed purples and reds, a living vibrant painting. "When Mr. Ludlow first told us his story, I suspected Mrs. Ludlow of taking her own money or of having no money within the safe. Often when one changes all the locks to one's home, it may be to keep someone out, but it also can be to lock oneself in. Why would she take such harsh actions unless she herself had something to hide?

"When Mr. Ludlow left, I remembered seeing an article on *The Mercurier* in today's *Times*. An agreement had been reached and the ship's crew was free to go. Their shipment was delivered, and they were on their way back to port. When we first visited Mrs. Ludlow, she said that she told us to go away just as she had told the others. I surmised that the others were messengers from the law firm representing her to tell her of the good news. She didn't answer, so she didn't know that her legal troubles were over."

"While Mrs. Ludlow's savings have dwindled, I'm sure her coffers will be full as soon as her ship returns to business. In the meantime, I am certain that her family will take good care of her once she confesses to them. Her son will cover her expenses, and her sister will help with the spiritual healing."

"A pity about her losing her servants," I said. "Mr. Jameson in particular was most loyal to her."

"Ah, Watson, but Mr. Jameson admitted that she could not afford her servants much longer. This was as good a time as any for them to leave her employment, and all of them have found new jobs. Perhaps instead of servants, she can have her sister."

"Her sister?"

"Yes, the two widows would make wonderful companions, don't you think? It is time for Mrs. Ludlow to sell her home, a home that was beginning to fall into disarray, and buy a smaller dwelling. Her sister could move in with her, and I'm sure they could find a nice cottage in close enough proximity to the Thames as to satisfy Mrs. Thurston. Why, I believe I shall make such a recommendation to Mr. Ludlow when we see him in the morning."

"You have it all wrapped up neatly. Just one more thing," I said. "I still don't know why you took the case. It sounds as though you solved it before Mr. Ludlow left our flat this morning. There was no reason to even leave our rooms today."

"Really, Watson," Holmes said taken aback, "and miss such a beautiful day outside! Look to the sky, my friend, and enjoy what little sun is left on this fine and glorious day."

The Fashionably-Dressed Girl
by Mark Mower

Those of you that have a mind for these things might well remember that in *A Study in Scarlet*, I recorded some of the early visitors to our Baker Street apartment in the days before I appreciated fully the nature of my friend's singular occupation. As a throwaway line, I wrote that, *"One morning a young girl called, fashionably-dressed, and stayed for half-an-hour or more."* It was Holmes himself who pointed out, sometime afterwards – when he had first read what he referred to as my "amusingly anecdotal" account of our earliest adventure together – that the young woman I had seen that day was later to feature in another of his cases. To that point, I had been wholly unaware that when Miss Madelaine Fremont called at 221b one afternoon in the November of 1881, it was not the first time she had entered the upstairs consulting room.

Holmes later explained that her first visit had been a trifling affair about a family inheritance which he had been able to sort out with very little effort. The case I now set before you was an entirely different matter.

With her cape and hat removed, I could see that the young woman was a little over five feet in height, slim, graceful, and pretty. Her small oval-shaped face was framed with a high crown of auburn hair in the style of a French twist, with a loose fringe across her delicate forehead. In her early-twenties, she was quite the society lady – her blue crinoline fan skirt was narrow-fitting with a long bodice extending down to her tiny waist. I had rarely seen a more engaging and fashionable girl.

Holmes seemed oblivious to her charms and, with a thin smile, terse greeting, and single wave of his hand, directed her towards the seat nearest the fire. She seemed unperturbed, sitting most elegantly and taking time to remove her long blue gloves which she placed deftly on the arm of the chair. My colleague took it upon himself to lead the introductions. "My dear Miss Fremont, this gentleman is my colleague, Dr. Watson, with whom I share this apartment. Watson has recently been assisting with a number of my cases, so you may trust his discretion on any matter you wish to bring to my attention."

She nodded and responded in a clear, confident voice, with just the hint of a foreign accent. "Thank you, Mr. Holmes. That is understood. And I am very pleased to make your acquaintance, Dr. Watson. My name is Madelaine Fremont." I thanked her quickly, allowing her to carry on. "I am a woman of independent means and make a comfortable living

51

assisting a number of wealthy ladies in matters of style and taste. In short, I help them to choose the most appropriate items for their wardrobe."

My surprise at the nature of her vocation must have been evident, for she felt it necessary to explain further. "While my father was English and I grew up in Oxford, my late mother, Genevieve, came from the province of Lorraine in the north-eastern corner of France. She was an accomplished dressmaker, and when I was fourteen, encouraged me to train as a seamstress. I was fortunate in securing a position working for the couturier Charles Frederick Worth in his prestigious Parisian fashion house on the Rue de la Paix. My mother was so proud, but sadly died before I could complete my apprenticeship . . . ."

She paused at this point and I could see that the mention of her mother had clearly moved her. Regaining her composure, she then added, "Two years ago, my father also passed away and – after some family shenanigans – I was left with a modest inheritance . . ." She cast a quick glance towards Holmes, although my colleague displayed no reaction. "Monsieur Worth was very understanding when I announced that I would be leaving his employment. Since that time, I have used my knowledge of fashion to guide my wealthy patrons and have introduced many British and American women to the delights of Parisian *haute couture*."

I was slightly bewildered as to where this was all heading but felt it polite to respond. "I see. Well, I cannot claim to know much about dress making, but your name intrigues me. You said your father was English, but the name 'Fremont' has a distinct Gallic ring to it."

She nodded. "Yes, it was my mother's maiden name – deriving, I believe, from the village of Framont in Lorraine, close to where my forebears lived. My given surname was 'Strathclyde', but when I began working in Paris, I thought the name 'Madelaine Fremont' would be more acceptable to my Continental colleagues. I have been known by that name ever since."

Holmes then interjected, somewhat brusquely, "Miss Fremont, your earlier telegram mentioned something about a strange visit that you had couple of days ago and some fears you have about your safety. Perhaps you can enlighten us as to the basic facts and sequence of events?"

Our client seemed to take no offence at my colleague's directness. She sat forward in the chair and addressed him. "Certainly, Mr. Holmes. I appreciate that you are not one for blather. As you know, since moving to London, I have rented a very pleasant house on Upper Brook Street. It has proved to be an ideal location for my work – close to the fashionable heart of Mayfair and providing me with sufficient space to store my extensive collection of dresses and fabric samples. I arrange appointments with my ladies and they visit my home to choose outfits which suit them. Two days ago, on the Tuesday, a couple called on me at the address. They introduced themselves as 'Mr. and Mrs. Reynolds'."

"And had they made a prior appointment?" asked Holmes quickly.

"No. It struck me as being unusual at the time. So far so, that my first question to the woman was how she knew of me, for I have nothing on the front of the building to advertise my business, which is all conducted by word of mouth. She said that 'a friend of a friend' had once used my services and I therefore came 'highly recommended'. I was at once flattered and invited them inside.

"In order to properly display all of my dresses and other items, I have given over the sizeable front parlour and a further adjoining room to the business. The parlour is used for the initial consultation with my clients, who are then invited through to the back room to browse my collection. While seated in the parlour with the Reynolds, I asked my young assistant, Abigail, to bring us a pot of fresh tea, and then began to ask Mrs. Reynolds how I could assist her. But then a strange thing happened . . . ."

"Which was?"

"Mrs. Reynolds had to this point been carrying a most remarkable cat in a small wicker basket. It was a chocolate-brown colour, with a delicate triangular face, pointed ears, and light-blue almond-shaped eyes. She explained that it was a rare female Siamese cat. With no warning whatsoever, the animal started to make the most hideous wailing sound and began to scramble to get out of the basket. At one point it scratched Mrs. Reynolds on the hand, drawing blood and, having exited the basket, proceeded to run around the parlour in a desperate attempt to evade capture. As it did so, two small silver bells on its collar rang melodically, making the whole scene rather comical. This carried on for some minutes until Abigail entered the room carrying the tea tray and provided the cat with an escape route. Mrs. Reynolds screamed uncontrollably and said the pet must not be allowed to get away as it was 'an extremely valuable housecat'."

I had imagined that Holmes might be disinterested in this feline caper, but he was listening intently to every word.

"We chased the cat as it made its way through the downstairs rooms and through to the kitchen at the back of the house. With the kitchen door ajar, the Siamese ran at speed out into the back garden. Mrs. Reynolds screamed once more and directed her husband to go after it. I tried to explain to her that my high-walled garden would easily contain the cat. And so it was that, five minutes later, I was able to coax the petrified animal from beneath a box hedge.

"We made our way back to the parlour and resumed our discussions, but the cat would not be parted from me and hissed every time the

Reynolds approached her. I have always had an affinity with cats and the animal warmed to me. The pair seemed content just to have the Siamese back and Mrs. Reynolds began to explain what it was she wanted. In short, she had a very specific green dress in mind – one that had been launched in Paris that very summer. She had even brought with her an advertisement for the dress that had appeared in *The Queen* magazine. She asked whether it would be possible to obtain a dress similar to that advertised, for much less than the cost of the original and in a short space of time. I explained that it was indeed possible, as most *couture* is immediately copied by less prestigious dressmakers and sold at more affordable prices. I needed only to take her measurements and could have a dress ready within a couple of days. Mrs. Reynolds was delighted and said that she would return for the dress on Friday. I then took her measurements and wrote out a receipt for the deposit she paid on the dress, before seeing the couple to the door."

"And what did Mr. Reynolds do while all of this was taking place?" I asked, imagining the poor fellow to have been like a fish out of water.

I received a coquettish grin from our guest. "Like most men, he had little to say about his wife's choice of dress. For the most part he sat quietly, nodding occasionally and agreeing with everything she said. I took Mrs. Reynold's measurements in the back room, leaving him in the parlour. When we returned, he had somehow managed to get the cat back into the basket, although it did not look happy with the arrangement at all. The couple then left, hailing the first hansom that passed by."

Holmes reached for his churchman and began to fill the bowl with a pinch of tobacco. "What were your immediate thoughts when the couple first left, Miss Fremont?"

"I had the distinct impression that the cat did not belong to the couple, Mr. Holmes."

"I see. Anything else?"

"Yes. While they were reasonably well-dressed, their attire did not suggest that they were particularly wealthy. Mrs. Reynolds' outfit was drab and inexpensive, a distinct contrast to the dress she wished to purchase. When the Siamese was sat on my lap, I could not help but notice the leather collar around its neck. In addition to the two silver bells, there was a small gold locket beneath the cat's throat and the collar was studded with diamonds."

Holmes looked up sharply. "Diamonds, you say? *Real* diamonds?"

"Without a doubt. Working with the many fashionable ladies that I do, I know a real diamond when I see one. And these were diamonds of the very best quality. It also seemed odd, if the pet was 'an extremely valuable housecat', that the couple should carry it around in such a cheap wicker basket. Altogether, I was left with the uneasy feeling that something was not quite right. And yet, Mrs. Reynolds happily paid the one-third deposit for the dress and seemed eager to return for it later in the week."

"Yes indeed. But why is it that you now fear for your safety? Has something else happened?"

Miss Fremont's demeanour changed and she began to look more solemn. "Yes, Mr. Holmes. Again, it was all very odd. Abigail works with me until about five o'clock each day. Beyond that, I live alone. I suppose it must have been about nine o'clock that evening when I retired. I had something of a headache and decided to have an early night. My bedroom is at the front of the house. It was quiet at that time, and as I lay in bed I thought I could hear the jingle of bells out in the street. Instantly, I was reminded of the Siamese. And as I listened, thought I heard a cat meow. I got out of bed and walked to the window. I could not see below the porch of the door, but again heard a cat. Intrigued, I wrapped my dressing gown around me and went down to the front door. When I opened it, a cat ran in and began to rub against my ankles. From the lights in the street I could see that it was indeed the Siamese cat with the ornate collar."

I was intrigued by her account and, like Holmes, keen to hear what had happened after that. Miss Fremont continued in her confident tone.

"The poor cat seemed hungry and eagerly consumed some chicken I had in the pantry. She was content to follow me upstairs as I returned to my room and slept soundly on the bed at my feet for the rest of the night. So when I awoke yesterday morning, I had to decide what to do. Somewhat against my better judgement, I determined that I ought to try and find where Mr. and Mrs. Reynolds lived, so as to return the cat to them. In the event, I thought the task would be easy, for on the underside of the cat's collar was stamped an address in Piccadilly."

Holmes was relishing the narrative. "No doubt the address of the cat's real owner. So what happened next?"

"I took a cab and travelled the short distance from Upper Brook Street to Sutherland Place, a grand property close to Devonshire House. I knew before I arrived at the front entrance that this was unlikely to be the home of the Reynolds. A smartly-tailored butler answered the door and was delighted to see me holding the Siamese. I explained how I had found the cat and had taken it in for the night, but deliberately did not mention the Reynolds. The butler said that his mistress would be delighted and invited me to step in off the street. The lady of the house was a Mrs. Sarah Van Allen. She was overjoyed at seeing the cat and could not thank me enough for finding and returning her beloved pet. While she was expressing her gratitude, I noticed that she paid particular attention to the locket around the cat's neck. I had not thought to check it myself, but watched as she opened it quickly and glanced inside. In that brief moment, I saw that it contained a small key and noted also that Mrs. Van Allen appeared to be very visibly relieved having checked this."

"Capital! Your observational skills do you credit. I believe we are beginning to get to the bottom of this mystery."

"Yes. But I haven't yet told you the most remarkable feature of my encounter with Mrs. Van Allen."

Holmes beamed. "I really do not wish to steal your thunder, Miss Fremont, but was she wearing a distinctive and fashionable green dress, just like the one that Mrs. Reynolds wished to procure?"

Our client looked astonished. "How could you possibly know that?"

"It was really the only solution which would fit the facts as we know them. There is a criminal endeavour at the centre of this, I am convinced of that. And I take it that your security fears are based around the fact that you now know the Reynolds to be charlatans of some kind."

She nodded reluctantly. "That is exactly my fear. I am terrified that they will arrive tomorrow for the dress and have some ulterior motive for wanting to gain entry to my house for a second time. I implore you to help me, Mr. Holmes."

I knew already that my colleague had no intention of letting the matter rest there. And I was equally clear that I would do everything I could to protect this remarkable young woman. Holmes gave her an assurance that he would look into the case further and promised that both of us would be at Upper Brook Street when the Reynolds arrived the following morning at ten o'clock.

Miss Fremont left us a short while later. I escorted her to the door and hailed a cab for her outside 221b. When I had climbed back up the steps to our apartment, I saw that Holmes had donned a thick overcoat and deerstalker hat and had a walking cane to hand. At my polite enquiry, he announced that he had a couple of errands to attend to, but would be back for supper. In the short time that I had known him, I already recognised that Holmes sometimes preferred to work on his own and at his own pace.

It was close to eight o'clock that evening when I heard him return. Mrs. Hudson had prepared a large Shepherd's Pie for our supper and was placing it on the table of the sitting room. She seemed relieved that my colleague had arrived back at just the right time.

"Mrs. Hudson! Your timing is impeccable. I am ravenous! And I think Dr. Watson and I will enjoy a bottle of *Beaujolais Nouveau* with our meal. I have just received twelve bottles from a grateful French client, so we ought to sample its delights!"

We both tucked in to the hearty faire and Holmes explained the nature of his earlier enquiries. "I paid a short visit to Mrs. Sarah Van Allen. An extremely genial lady who was most concerned to hear that a scheme had been hatched to dispossess her of the Siamese cat. When I explained that the thieves had sought only to obtain the key secreted within the gold locket, she was astounded. With what she had to tell me, I now have a clear outline of the crime being planned by the Reynolds."

"Which is?"

"Grand larceny. Mrs. Van Allen's husband spends most of the year working in the Dutch East Indies. He trades in tea and silk mainly, but is also something of a gem collector. Each month he sends his wife a parcel containing one or two precious stones. Fearful of leaving these in Sutherland House, Mrs. Van Allen makes a monthly trip to Coutts and Company in The Strand. Here she has a large safe deposit box into which she deposits the gemstones – "

" – and the key that opens the box is kept in the gold locket around the cat's neck!"

"Exactly! Our would-be thieves took the cat on Tuesday and had a fresh key cut to match the original. They then hoped to return the animal to Sutherland House before its absence had been noted."

"A task that they cleared botched. But how did you know they had a duplicate key made?"

"Before visiting Mrs. Van Allen, I called in at the cab depot closest to Upper Brook Street. I took a punt, but figured that the driver who had picked up the Reynolds outside Miss Fremont's may have been locally-based. It was a gamble that paid off. I tracked down the very helpful Mr. Trimble, who clearly remembered the couple, *and the cat*. He explained that they set off, having asked to be dropped off at an address in Pimlico. The hansom had not travelled more than a couple of hundred yards when the cabbie heard a frantic knocking from inside. He pulled over, only to see a brown cat leap from the cab and sprint off down the street. With no hope of catching the animal, his exasperated passengers had asked him to carry on towards their destination."

I laughed at the humour of it all. "So that explains how the cat was still in Upper Brook Street when Miss Fremont took it in."

"Yes. Now the couple alighted from the cab at the Marquis of Westminster public house. I went there myself and discovered that there is a locksmith close-by. Having knocked at the door of his premises for some minutes, the proprietor answered, and – with the inducement of a few shillings – recollected that a couple had called earlier in that day, requesting that a duplicate key be cut from the one they presented. He said the woman had been carrying a wicker basket in which was a sleeping cat.

In fact, the Siamese looked to be sleeping so soundly that the locksmith wondered if the cat was actually dead!"

"Very suggestive, Holmes. Do you think it had been drugged?"

"Most likely. It would explain how they were able to take the cat in the first place without raising any alarm in the house."

We finished what remained of the pie and downed another glass of the excellent *Beaujolais*. I was still unclear on a number of points and continued to ask questions. "Surely the Reynolds cannot hope to carry on with their plan? Having lost the cat, does that not give the game away?"

"Not necessarily," replied Holmes. "They still have the duplicate key. And until I alerted Mrs. Van Allen, she had no inkling that anyone might plot to steal the original key. You see she was under the impression that only she knew of its hiding place."

"A-ha! Then if the Siamese is a house cat that can only mean one thing . . ."

". . . that one of the household staff is implicated – my thoughts exactly, Watson. Mrs. Van Allen has a butler, an under-butler, a housekeeper, two maids, and a carriage driver. In the short time I was at Sutherland House, I was unable to speak to any of the staff, but have my suspicions. I hope to put my theory to the test tomorrow, when hopefully we will get the chance to meet the Reynolds."

Before turning in for the night, I had one final query. "I understand that they have a key for the safe deposit box, but how do they expect to walk into a reputable bank like Coutts and Company and be given access to the vault? Mrs. Van Allen is likely to be a recognisable figure given her frequent trips and the bank prides itself on its very personal service."

Holmes nodded and grinned widely. "I believe that is where the newly-commissioned green dress comes in to its own. Coats, hats, scarves, and gloves are relatively easy to obtain, but an expensive piece of Parisian fashion is a different matter. A discerning manager will have an eye for such things in a bank like Coutts and Company!"

I slept fitfully that night, turning over all of the facts of the case and trying to imagine what would happen the following morning. I woke a little after six o'clock and was shaved, washed, dressed, and breakfasted before Holmes stirred.

We set off in good time. It was another cold yet sunny day and Holmes insisted on walking the mile and a half to Upper Brook Street. Miss Freemont was overjoyed to see us and looked every bit as radiant as she had the previous day. We were introduced to her assistant, Abigail, and Holmes then explained what would happen. Abigail would greet the couple at the door and show them into the front parlour. Miss Freemont would then enter and explain that she had been unable to obtain the dress and would return the Reynolds' deposit to them. This would be the signal for Holmes and me to enter the room and confront the pair. Until that point, we would be hidden away in the front room opposite the parlour.

Our couple arrived a few minutes before their appointed time. Standing behind the net curtains of the front room, Holmes and I had an opportunity to study them as they stepped down from a cab and walked up to the door. The man was a little over six feet in height, strongly-built and clean-shaven. The woman at his side was also tall, elegant in her features, yet plainly clothed. Both looked to be in their mid-thirties.

The plan worked like clockwork, and it was quite clear that, until Holmes and I barged our way into the parlour, the Reynolds had no idea that their underhand scheme had been exposed. On seeing us, it was the man who immediately turned defensive. "Who are you? What is it you want from us?"

Holmes came straight to the point. "I think it is more a question of what you wanted from Mrs. Van Allen, Mr. Beerton."

The use of his real name had clearly shocked the man. He looked as if he was about to say something further, but could not seem to articulate the words. The woman beside him then spoke. "I think we're done for. These gentlemen must be the police."

"We are not the police, Madam," replied Holmes, "but will be accompanying you to the nearest police station in a short while. We just need some further information from you to complete our investigation into your scheme to rob Mrs. Van Allen's safe deposit box."

Beerton had clearly found his voice again and rose from his seat to confront Holmes. "How do you know who I am? In fact, how do you know any of this?"

Holmes stood face to face with Beerton. "Sit down, sir. My name is Sherlock Holmes and I am a consulting detective. This is my colleague, Dr. Watson. You have nothing to gain by offering violence."

Beerton looked from Holmes towards me and then sat back down. Holmes then continued.

"I have neither the time nor the inclination to provide you with the full details of *how* we uncovered your plot to rob Mrs. Van Allen. But I will tell you *what* I know. Firstly, your name is Andrew Beerton and you work as a groom and carriage driver for the Van Allen family, a post you have held for the past five years. Each month, Mrs. Van Allen takes a trip to Coutts and Company in The Strand. Here she deposits the precious gems that her husband sends her from overseas. It is your job to drive the carriage and to then accompany Mrs. Van Allen into the bank, nominally ensuring her safety as she carries with her a bag containing the valuables.

59

"In this role, you observed a pattern. Mrs. Van Allen enters the lobby, walks to the reception area, and then asks to see one of the bank's managers. She is greeted by one of four managers each time. They exchange a few pleasantries and accompany her to the locked door of the vault in which the safe deposit boxes are held. Here they leave Mrs. Van Allen in the capable hands of a bank employee who asks for the number of her deposit box. Then, for security, he requires her to produce the safe deposit key. When she does this, they unlock the heavy security door and allow her to go into the vault alone where she is able to deposit her valuables. While you are required to wait outside the vault, you know from overhearing this conversation many times that her deposit box number is '4457'.

"The monthly trips to the bank are known about by all of the household staff. In fact, I imagine it is often a source of some gossip. But you found out the one piece of information that none of the others knew – namely, where Mrs. Van Allen hid the key to the safe deposit box . . . ."

At this point, Beerton felt inclined to speak. "It was so simple. I was passing the window of her study one day and looked in to see Mrs. Van Allen stroking the cat. Unaware that I was watching, she reached for the locket and opened it. Inside I could see a small key – the same key I had watched her produce at the bank dozens of times. In that moment, I knew that with the key it would be possible to access the safe deposit box."

"But your challenge was how to get someone to pretend to be Mrs. Van Allen, someone convincing enough to fool the staff and managers at the bank. Is that when you enlisted the help of your sister here?"

It was the turn of "Mrs. Reynolds" to look shocked. Like Beerton, she had clearly realised that there was no point in lying to my colleague. "How did you know, Mr. Holmes?"

"There is no mistaking the likeness. You are clearly siblings. And I'm certain that your name is not 'Mrs. Reynolds'."

In spite of the position that she now found herself in, the woman could only chuckle. "No, my name is Annalisa Beerton. I never married. And you must not judge my brother too harshly. It was me that put him up to it. When he told me about the key, I said it would be easy for me to assume the part of Mrs. Van Allen. She is a similar height and age to me, has the same hair colouring, and an identically shaped face. For some years, I have made a rather precarious living in the theatre, so it is second nature for me to pretend to be someone else."

This time it was Madelaine Freemont who spoke. "But I suppose you realised that you needed to have a convincing costume to pull off the pretence, and that was why you approached me for the dress."

60

Annalisa Beerton smiled at her without any hint of malevolence. "I told Andrew it was essential. Both to convince those snooty managers at the bank that I was the well-heeled Mrs. Van Allen, but also so that I would feel appropriately dressed for the part. I had seen Mrs. Van Allen in the dress once before and knew it to be an expensive outfit. But I also knew that we could find someone to replicate it. I was not lying when I said you came highly recommended, Miss Fremont."

Our client looked somewhat embarrassed at the unexpected compliment. Annalisa Beerton then added, "Our mistake, of course, was taking that damned cat!"

Holmes could only agree with her. "Yes. I imagine that your plan was to take the Siamese for a short time, having drugged it in some way, and while the cat was comatose to arrange for a duplicate key to be cut from the original. I know that you visited a locksmith in Pimlico on your way to Miss Fremont's. Having then come here to procure the green dress, you then planned to return the cat to Sutherland House."

Andrew Beerton answered him directly. "I knew the cat was temperamental. But I was fearful of just taking the key. If Mrs. Van Allen had chanced to look in the locket and had found the key to be missing, I felt certain that she would suspect foul play. But if the cat went astray for only a few hours – and was then returned with the key – I believed that would work in our favour.

"As the groom, I have access to lots of horse treatments. I took a mild sedative and put some in the cat's food, having no real feel for how much would be needed to knock out such a small animal. It was enough to put it to sleep when I first removed the Siamese from the study, and for our trip to the locksmith's, but when we arrived here, the cat came round in a highly agitated state."

"And then you lost her altogether on the cab journey back to Pimlico . . . ."

"Yes. At first I thought it would prove to be a disaster, but hoped that the cat would find its way home. Either way, I thought that no one would be able to guess that we had taken the Siamese and would have no clue as to our real intentions in removing it in the first place. So when I saw that the cat had indeed come back, I told Annalisa that we should continue with our plan."

Miss Freemont then interposed once more. "Did you not know that it was me that returned the cat?"

Beerton looked at her quizzically. "No, not to this point. It is less than a couple of miles from here to Piccadilly. I just assumed that the cat had made its own way back."

Holmes then continued. "Having taken the decision to continue with the robbery, were you planning to pick up the dress and then visit the bank this afternoon?"

The groom answered somewhat sheepishly. "Yes. I told Mrs. Van Allen this morning that the carriage needed some minor repairs and would need to be driven down to the blacksmiths. I expected to pick up the dress, travel back to Sutherland House, and then, with Annalisa suitably attired, drive the carriage to the bank. Having successfully stolen the gemstones, we believed we could return the carriage and make our escape tomorrow. I didn't think that Mrs. Van Allen would realise she had been robbed until she next went to the bank. By then, Annalisa and I would have made the passage across to Holland and be living a new life abroad."

"Then I am sorry to disappoint you," said Holmes. "Watson and I have no option but to hand you over to the police for the attempted robbery. How you will fare at the hands of a judge and jury I do not know."

It was some weeks later when I next saw Madelaine Freemont. Holmes had asked her to call in at Baker Street for he had some news on the attempted robbery.

She was punctual in arriving just a few minutes before eleven o'clock that morning. I decided to meet her at the door and show her up. She was dressed in a deep-red velvet skirt and bustle, with a matching jacket. Her very fetching hat, parasol and slim scarlet shoes completed the overall look. I stood in admiration of her.

"How good to see you, Miss Freemont. I trust you are well?"

"Thank you, Dr. Watson. I am very well and hope the same can be said of you?"

When we entered the study, Holmes was in the process of dismantling a flintlock pistol. Miss Freemont seemed both surprised and bemused by the sight. Holmes was unperturbed. "Ah, Miss Freemont. I thought you might like to know what has happened in the case of Andrew and Annalisa Beerton. They were examined by the magistrates earlier this week on the charge of attempted robbery and have been committed to face trial at the Old Bailey next March. In all likelihood, they can expect heavy prison sentences if found guilty."

"Thank you, Mr. Holmes. I feel some sympathy for them, but I suppose the crime was very audacious."

"Yes, they were foolhardy in their endeavour. But the law cannot be seen to make exceptions. And the crime is viewed all the more seriously because Andrew Beerton broke the time-honoured bond of trust that is supposed to exist between a servant and his employer. Anyway, on a much lighter note, I am pleased to say that Mrs. Van Allen is very much in your debt for what you did in helping to expose the robbery plan. She has invited you to call on her at your convenience, for she would very much welcome your advice on matters of style and taste. And she has lots of very wealthy friends that she is also prepared to introduce you to."

Miss Freemont was clearly overcome to hear this. "Thank you, Mr. Holmes. That is indeed good news!"

"Yes," he replied, "but I think you have some good news of your own? If I am not mistaken, that is an engagement ring on your finger."

She blushed as he said this and went on to say that she had accepted a proposal of marriage from Gaston Lucien, the twenty-eight-year-old son of Charles Worth, her former employer. They were to be married the following summer.

I was stunned to hear the news, made all the more surprising because I had failed to notice the ring myself. I added my congratulations to those of Holmes and wished her all the very best for the future. When she came to leave, I walked her out of the house and once more insisted on hailing her a cab. It was with more than a touch of sadness that I waved her off, little realising it would be the last time I set eyes on that fashionably-dressed young girl from Upper Brook Street.

The Odour of Neroli
by Brenda Seabrooke

During the years that I was associated with the cases of Sherlock Holmes, either while residing in rooms on Baker Street or my own, he seldom revealed how he would solve a case at the outset, preferring instead to explain at the end how he reached his conclusions. However, a few times in our association he told me in the beginning what he would do. One such case occurred early in our association, a case unique in that all involved were professionals in some quarter.

I was late rising after a night listening to the wind announce its presence on loose shutters and rattled windows, shivered tree limbs, and flung debris. Holmes had been up for hours by the time I joined him in the sitting room of our shared flat.

"No time for breakfast, Watson. It's late and you have an invitation. I suspect it's urgent." Holmes spoke from his chair by the fire where he was already dressed for going out. He held up an envelope. I couldn't read the writing across the room, so I moved to the other chair by the fire and reached for it.

"Read it aloud," Holmes said handing it over.

"But it's addressed to me."

"Nevertheless, read it. It was brought by messenger not ten minutes ago. I heard you faintly astir, so I waited for you to emerge."

I opened the envelope and drew out the message.

> *Dear Dr. Watson,*
>
> *Please come to early luncheon at 12 Park Crescent. Bring your medical bag and your friend Dr. House. If anyone enquires, say only Dr. Lister is ill and the two of you are consulting.*
>
> *Yrs most sincerely,*
>
> *Joseph Lister, M.D.*

I looked up, mystified. "The envelope is addressed to *me*, but the letter appears to address *your* talents."

"Precisely."

"Do you know Dr. Lister?"

"No, I have never met him. What do you make of the letter?"

"He must surely know your name is Holmes, not House. I can't imagine why he would make such a mistake."

"A mistake – I doubt that. He is a man of science and such seldom make mistakes. Yet this day he seemingly made one. Therefore it had to be a deliberate mistake."

"Assuredly, but what could have prompted this peculiar invitation?"

"I thought you might have some suggestions."

"He may have noticed me at his lectures at King's College Hospital. He may have enquired and found that I share rooms with you and got your name mixed up."

"Perhaps. Did you meet Dr. Lister in your medical student days?"

"Meet him, no. Not many of the students or doctors caught his lectures, so I may have stood out when I repeatedly attended. Most of the profession thought him a joke."

"A joke. Hmm. A man with sound ideas on improving the profession and he wasn't taken seriously. Is he now?"

"Yes and no. He was at the Royal Infirmary of Glasgow, and later Edinburgh, and now he is at King's College Hospital here in London, so he has to be accorded some respect. However, you know how Londoners regard Edinburghers as impossible people with an impossible language – and that's when speaking English."

"Lister is not a Scot." Holmes steepled his fingers. "I believe he grew up in Newham, which is not far from here."

"Yes, I think you are correct."

"Then why the negative opinion of him?"

"It's his ideas."

"And these are?"

"Washing his hands and instruments before surgery. Using surgical instruments with handles of metal instead of bone or wood, which are porous and catch-alls for bacteria. Wound cleaning. The use of phenol crystals derived from coal tar to make a solution to spray on incisions and lacerations. Using a clean towel pinned to his clothing each time he takes up a scalpel. These are strangely unacceptable to many in the profession, and you know how hidebound doctors can be. You've spent time in medical facilities."

"Not since we moved here. I've been able to conduct my experiments in our rooms."

I refrained from saying anything about the noxious clouds of sulfur and other chemicals that perfumed our rooms until they were aired out. I'm comfortable with the aromas of my profession, but do not care to live with them. "Old habits die hard. Many of the surgeons think the more blood and gore on their surgical gowns, the more experienced it makes them look. They profess to like the reeking effluvia attendant to surgical procedures in their theaters. 'Old Reekie' they call it, and they are averse to washing their hands or even their surgical instruments."

"Did you use his methods in India?"

"My instruments have metal handles, but as to carbolic acid, it wasn't available far from the sea in the mountainous regions where the fighting occurred. I did what I could under the worst of circumstances, airing the wounds in the sun and washing what I could and cauterizing."

"Hmm. Why do you suppose he sent an envelope to you with a luncheon invitation asking you to bring me along?"

"I cannot imagine. Perhaps a secretary's mistake in the address on the envelope? Or Mrs. Lister's?"

"Envelope and letter are in the same hand."

I shook my head. I didn't want to suggest all those noxious fumes had deranged Dr. Lister's mental clarity. I knew some who might think so, but I doubted it. I'd read his papers, and he was as clear-thinking as Holmes.

"He is practicing deception, but for whom, I wonder?" Holmes rose abruptly. "Make yourself presentable, Watson. We need further information to solve this case."

"Presentable?" I was impeccably dressed as always.

"Your hair could use some attention."

He was right. In my haste, I had forgotten to complete my toilette. My hair looked like someone had used an eggbeater on it. I attended to it and picked up my case. My overcoat and hat were hanging by the door with my stick, which I needed now less and less, but I felt more comfortable with it. Holmes had donned his hat, coat, and scarf, and awaited me downstairs.

"I sent a boy 'round for a cab. Ah, there it is now." Holmes rushed out, leaving the door to me.

The wind was braw twixt door and cab and I was glad for the three-and-a-half-sided protection of the hansom driven by a man whose face, snugged into a scarf, was red – whether from drink or weather, I could not tell. Perhaps both since libation might be needed to carry on in the teeth of that wind. I gave the address and with a flourish of his whip we were off. The horse wore a blanket and didn't feel the flick, even if it touched him.

The ride wasn't long – along Baker Street, into Marylebone Road and right into the curve of Park Crescent. The cabbie could have taken a more direct route, but the streets were narrower and promised to be more crowded. This longer route took not fifteen minutes.

Park Crescent started as a palace for the Prince Regent, but when he became king the plans were dropped. The circular building of white stuccoed blocks was girded by a balustraded balcony resting on pairs of Ionic columns. This ran the length of the building and was backed by arched windows on the second floor. The Crescent today was a prime London address facing Regent's Park with its over-sized statue of the Queen's father in the fenced garden staring down Portland Place as it bisected the two arms of the Crescent.

A wrought-iron fence behind the façade columns of the Crescent kept wandering animals out, assuming any were still loose in this area of London. The cab stopped in front of Number 12 and, because the trip had been brisk, I gave the driver an extra tip for his horse. "He gave us a smooth ride."

We stepped under the balcony and I rang the bell. The door opened immediately and I wondered if the man had been standing on the other side waiting for us. Holmes looked as if he thought the same thing. He lifted his eyebrows at me.

"Dr. Watson, Dr. House, please come in. Dr. Lister is waiting for you in the parlor. Please follow me."

He didn't appear to be the usual butler. His dress was more akin to what a doctor would wear on his rounds rather than the formal penguin-like suit worn by the head servant of a smart London address. He announced us and we entered the parlor where the Listers sat on either side of a cheery fire, rather in the same way that Holmes and I did in our sitting room – Mrs. Lister on Holmes's side, the right. I was soon to learn she was an equal partner in the doctor's work. Her father had been Dr. Symes of Edinburgh, whom Dr. Lister replaced before coming to London.

Mrs. Lister rose to greet us, but the doctor remained seated, a lap robe covering his legs. "Thank you for coming so quickly," she said, taking my hand.

They were a handsome couple. Mrs. Lister, whose given name was Agnes, wore a gray dress with a blue cameo pinned in the center of a froth of lace at the neck. She had fine eyes and smooth dark hair, parted in the middle and drawn over her ears. The doctor wore clothing much like that preferred by Holmes and me, with dark morning coats and trousers.

"I came as soon as I received your summons," I said, keeping to the subterfuge of the letter. I opened my case and removed my stethoscope. "What symptoms have you exhibited?"

"Please be seated, Dr. House, and I will relate my symptoms to you." Dr. Lister said in a low quiet voice.

"Crichton," said Mrs. Lister, "you may be excused. I will see the doctors out."

"Very good, Madam."

When the door closed behind him, Mrs. Lister listened for a moment. "We have given the staff the afternoon off. Crichton was the last one left." She went to the hall door, opened it, and stepped out.

"I realize my request was unusual," said Dr. Lister. "I appreciate your responding with alacrity, and I apologize for my subterfuge, but you will understand."

Mrs. Lister returned. "Crichton is off, walking at a fast clip toward the Underground."

Lister threw off the robe and stood up.

"You do not wish to be examined?" The stethoscope dangled from my hand.

"No. Indeed, I am hale and hearty." Lister spread his hands as if inviting us to look at him.

Holmes raised his eyebrows.

"You have been wondering why I asked you here. Why all this secrecy, these pseudonyms, this feigned illness."

"No," Holmes said, "I have not."

At the same time I said, "Yes, we have been wondering."

Mrs. Lister focused on Holmes. "Really, Mr. Holmes, You don't wonder why we told our man to expect Dr. Watson and Dr. House?"

"It is perfectly clear to me that you have a problem and do not wish to be known to consult a detective. Therefore, you suspect some person or persons are working against you, and that he or she may in fact be in your own household."

Mrs. Lister stared at him while her husband nodded.

"Short of assassination, the person or persons may be attacking you through your work, which I believe is paramount in your life," Holmes continued.

"Correct," Dr. Lister said.

Mrs. Lister shook her head. "Your reputation is well-earned, Mr. Holmes."

He inclined his head at the compliment. "You set up this scheme to consult with Dr. Watson as a pretense to examine you for a sudden onset of illness."

"You are quite correct. Something has happened serious enough to warrant this elaborate deception."

"The question is then, besides *who*, is *why*. If we solve the *why*, perhaps it will shed light on the *who*. Do you have any enemies?"

Both Listers laughed, but not with pleasure. "They are legion," Dr. Lister said. "I think it is reasonable to say that roughly two-thirds of the medical profession in this country despise me."

"Surely not that many," I said. "I have attended your lectures at King's College Hospital. I am in complete agreement with your precepts regarding surgical cleanliness."

"The medical profession is slowly coming around. My surgical successes have proved that carbolic acid or phenol sprayed on wounds and cleanliness in the operating theater promote healing and prevent gangrene. Now, as to why I asked to see you: This is confidential. As you may know, earlier this year I was elected president of the Clinical Society of London. Things have happened that may endanger that honor."

"Accidents in the laboratory that may impugn your practices," Holmes said.

"Exactly."

"At first small things," Mrs. Lister said. "A mislaid canister or tool. A broken vial. The cat could have done that. Spilled milk for experiments. Again the cat. But a mislabeling is beyond the smartest cat's abilities."

"Last week a Bunsen burner fell off its stand. The lab and possibly my house could have been destroyed," Dr. Lister said.

"The entire Crescent," Mrs. Lister added.

"All accidents, surely," I said.

The Listers nodded. "Taken separately, these have happened to us at various times in lab work," Lister said.

"But taken together, they add up to something intentional," Holmes said. "And that is serious. The solution to this case lies in three parts: First *what*. Next *how*, and last, *why*."

"What about *who*?" Mrs. Lister asked.

"The perpetrator will follow. I will, of course, need a list of your servants and anyone else who might have access to your lab."

"Oh it couldn't have been anyone in our household," Mrs. Lister protested.

"Was your house broken into?"

"Not that we have been able to ascertain," Dr. Lister said.

Mrs. Lister named the servants. "You have met Crichton, the butler, but he is so much more. He lends a hand in the lab when needed. Mrs. Gladys Mayton, the cook. Polly the kitchen maid. Iris the upstairs maid. Nellie the parlor maid. George the knife boy, who also does much more than sharpen knives. They have all been with us for years and from time to time lent a hand in the lab. We are less formal here than other London households, and I would trust all of them – but in any case, I will provide you with a list." She went to a desk across the room and occupied herself with writing.

She didn't mention a nursery maid or governess. I recalled hearing that the Listers were childless.

"Add the lab assistants to the list," Dr. Lister said. "My nephew Rickman Godlee. Watson Cheyne, Newbold Smith, and John Stewart. I would trust them with my life."

"I would also," Mrs. Lister said handing the list to Holmes. "I don't think you will find them involved in this treachery."

"I hope your trust in them will be proven," Holmes said, placing the sheet in his pocket.

She gave him a warm smile as if she trusted him to do so. Holmes nodded in return. She appeared to be the type of woman that he tolerated – no nonsense, cutting to the heart of the matter, and no subterfuge except perhaps when needed. I admired her and thought the Listers a lucky couple to have found each other in the world of frills and furbelows and idle chatter in which so many women indulged themselves – as well as some men, I had to admit.

"A tour of the house would be helpful," Holmes said.

Mrs. Lister led us down to the kitchen rooms and sub-cellar below stairs, where Holmes inspected every nook and cranny that an intruder might have used to enter, including the passages that led to the mews behind the Crescent where the horses and carriages were kept.

Holmes questioned her about deliveries made before these accidents began. Mrs. Lister insisted they had known the tradesmen and deliverymen for at least a year. The coal chute was one way of entry but after delivery, the chute was always padlocked inside and only opened again when it was time for another delivery. "Otherwise, the coal would be stolen at night by people small enough to go up and down," she explained.

"Anyone entering from the mews would have to pass through the kitchen to the stairs that lead to the floors above," Mrs. Lister continued as if anticipating what Holmes was looking for. "And Mrs. Mayton keeps a strict eye on whomever enters, tradesmen and the like."

"No doubt," Holmes said agreeably. "You and Dr. Lister surely must have suspicions," he continued. "Else why would you have gone to such trouble to consult me, rather than coming to see me or asking me to come here openly? Someone is causing those accidents. The fire could have destroyed your work, your house, perhaps the entire Crescent, and even lives. I need the *what* now, please. What was the incident that prompted you to need to consult me?"

"I was to give a demonstration of carbolic acid's efficacy today to visiting doctors and professors from America and Canada. I always run a pre-test to make sure everything is in order. The test showed something was wrong. If I hadn't taken the precaution of testing, the demonstration would have failed."

"Indeed. That is serious. It could cost lives in the future if the delegation had returned with a negative report."

Lister nodded.

Mrs. Lister led us to the stairs. The upstairs bedrooms and servants' rooms in the attic completed the living area of the household.

"Now we need to see the laboratory where these accidents occurred," Holmes said at the end of the tour.

Dr. Lister joined us in a large room along the back of the house, no doubt used as a family sitting room by previous tenants, but now serving admirably as a laboratory. Long narrow tables held lab paraphernalia, racks of test tubes, canisters, large glass jars of crystals, chemicals, microscopes, and boxes of slides. I recalled that Lister's father was a wine merchant who also had designed the achromatic lenses which led to the perfection of the optical microscope now used by his son.

"You have contributed a great deal to science," Holmes murmured.

"As, I believe, have you, Mr. Holmes," Lister said.

Holmes took a keen interest in the laboratory and I could tell he wished for one such as this in his rooms instead of a table beside the fireplace.

The area around the Bunsen burner bore scorch marks from the accident there, despite recent vigorous application of emery cloth. Mrs. Lister noticed when I ran my hand over the marks.

"Newbold worked on it a long time, and would have worked on it again today, but we told him to visit his family. We don't suspect him or any of our assistants, but we are treating all of the household the same. It's only fair."

"To be sure," I said.

Holmes fiddled with the burner's apparatus. "It seems to be in order. What happened that day?"

"My nephew had gone out to a play or cards, or whatever young men do these days," said Lister. "The others had retired early, as had the staff and Agnes. I wanted to read a monograph I'd left in the sitting room. As I came down the stairs, I smelt smoke and roused the household before opening the door to the laboratory. The blaze had taken hold, and if it had reached the chemicals, then this house and perhaps others would have been lost. I poured water on a towel and smothered the flames as the others joined me. We turned off the burner's gas supply. It hadn't been left on from our day's work. I'm sure of that. We are all careful in the use of our lab equipment. As you know, some of it is costly and volatile."

"And the experiment yesterday that prompted you to write to me today?"

"As I said, I was to give a demonstration of carbolic acid, or phenol. I normally check my equipment the day before to make sure everything is in working order." He showed us the sprayer he had designed to apply the chemicals to the wound. "In this case, I would be using only a small amount on some rotting meat. I planned to use a hand sprayer and didn't need as large a supply of crystals as I would for a surgical situation. I mixed the chemicals using crystals from that container." He pointed to a medium-sized jar like those apothecaries use with a glass lid, but this one had a wire apparatus around it to keep the lid in a tight seal.

"I mixed the solution and used the hand sprayer. The subject did not change. It sat inertly. I watched it all day in case it was slow for some reason, but nothing changed. That's when I realized something was wrong. I sent a telegram postponing the experiment tomorrow and wrote to you."

Holmes looked at the crystals. "How long have these been in the present container?"

"I filled it the day before yesterday," Mrs. Lister said.

"You noticed nothing different about it?"

"No."

"Where were the crystals kept before you put them in the container?"

She showed us the large covered glass vat of crystals in the corner of the lab. "I removed them using the metal scoop, as I always do."

"How many scoops?"

"Six for this small demonstration."

"How many did you use for the solution?" he asked Dr. Lister.

"Two."

"So four should remain. A scoop if you please, and a receptacle."

Mrs. Lister handed him a glass bowl and her husband gave him a scoop. Holmes opened the container and asked me to scoop the crystals into the bowl. I did so carefully without dropping any. I removed three scoops. Only a sprinkling remained in the glass jar.

"It seems we have a missing scoop," Holmes said.

Mrs. Lister frowned at the bowl of crystals. "Maybe I forgot to put in the last one. I believe that I was in a hurry because we were going to that reception for the visiting dignitaries."

"Dignitaries?"

"Yes. The demonstration was to be given today for the American and Canadian doctors, and hospital representatives and professors – a sort of magic show for medicine to demonstrate my findings. Only my 'illness' prevented it. The demonstration is rescheduled for tomorrow, presuming I have recovered."

"That is the most critical phase of this situation. Send a telegram to the college that you have recovered and will be there tomorrow for the demonstration. Where are your assistants?"

"My nephew has gone to visit a colleague in Brighton."

"Send a telegram telling him of the postponement and rescheduling."

"Surely you don't suspect my nephew?" Dr. Lister protested.

"No, certainly not, but if he is questioned by anyone, he needs to give the correct answer without any hint of subterfuge.

"Where are your other assistants?"

"They are visiting their families. I was insistent that they leave in case I might prove to be contagious."

"Send them telegrams as well with the same information. Now you must test the crystals you will be using to see if they will work and I will test this one." He reached for the glass jar where I had returned the crystals to and opened it. He sniffed and held it out to Dr. Lister. "Is this how it's supposed to smell?"

Lister leaned over and sniffed. "Yes, it smells a bit of the tar from which carbolic acid is derived.

"Watson?"

I sniffed. "That's exactly how it smells."

"Mrs. Lister?"

She sniffed and nodded.

He turned the glass lid over to reveal a perforated circle of paper cut to fit inside it and we all sniffed again. It smelt like creosote or tar.

"The Navy used tar or creosote on stumps after a sea battle," I said, "and with good results."

"No doubt the person who also used creosote to contain rot on sewage was also familiar with that practice," Holmes said.

"That was what gave me the idea to use it for surgical wounds," Lister said as Holmes removed the perforated paper.

Underneath we saw the lid was smudged with a tar-like substance. Another circle of paper under the lid hid it from view above.

"Here is the source of that odor that has permeated the jar," Holmes murmured. "The crystals are ineffective."

"Devious," Mrs. Lister said.

"Yes, the person who did this was devious. Tweezers."

Dr. Lister handed him tweezers and Holmes removed the tarred paper circle. In turn, we all sniffed the glass lid. The creosote odor lingered on the glass, fainter now but still recognizable.

Holmes separated the glass lid from the jar of crystals.

"Now, Mrs. Lister what do you smell?"

"Something sweet. That's how phenol smells, sweet and tarry."

We took our turns sniffing.

"Definitely sweet. Perhaps a lady's perfume, or *eau de cologne*." I was certain I had smelled it before – at the opera or a play, perhaps.

"Perhaps a perfume of some sort, or orange blossom oil or neroli derived from the bitter orange flower," Mrs. Lister said. "It would have been easy to add a drop to the crystals and shake them up."

"Taken with the creosote, the crystals in this glass container smell like phenol crystals." Dr. Lister looked at Holmes. "I think we are in agreement this jar smells like phenol."

"Indeed, someone went to a lot of trouble to make you think so."

Dr. Lister examined a crystal from the large canister of phenol crystals and declared them to be genuine.

Holmes raised his eyebrows. "I thought as much. Someone entered your house after Mrs. Lister filled the glass container. That person substituted this container for the other, which he then removed with him. The stage was set for your experiment to fail."

"What did he substitute for the crystals?" I asked.

"Glass."

"Glass?" We all echoed the word.

"How could anyone think we would mistake glass for phenol crystals?" Dr. Lister said.

Holmes smiled. Nothing makes him happier than discovery, whether chemical in nature or human. He scooped out some of the crystals from the large container and put them on a tray. He then tweezed up several from the small container. We stood for a moment regarding them.

"Side-by-side, it is obvious they aren't the same. This person knew you wouldn't check the crystals if they resembled phenol crystals. In looks they are close enough, and the correct scent has been applied. You had no reason to compare the crystals. You would have taken the container and used them in the experiment, and it would have failed. By the time you ferreted out the substitution, the delegation would have returned to America, and you would have missed your chance to spread your findings to the new world."

"And you might possibly have been removed from your position as president of The Clinical Society of London," I said. "Who stands to benefit from your failure?"

"Any number of doctors. The Society has grown since its inception in 1868 with one-hundred-and-ten members. It's nearly three-hundred now."

"Who might be your competition for president?" Holmes said.

"I cannot say. It would be another surgeon. The Society alternates presidency between physicians and surgeons and the president serves for two years."

"I understand your reluctance to name anyone," I said, "but surely it could be someone who disagrees with your surgical sterilization theory."

"Not necessarily, Watson," said Holmes. "Human nature being what it is, it could be someone jealous of Dr. Lister's discovery. Or someone who wants to be president badly enough to try to destroy his competition to the detriment of scientific progress and resulting loss of life. The person or persons unknown may possess abhorrent personalities that are carefully hidden. But we must not get ahead of the events."

As Dr. Lister prepared to send the telegrams, Holmes wrote one of his own to be sent to Scotland Yard. He picked up the jar of false crystals.

I was half-turned toward Holmes and saw him raise the jar and bring it down hard, letting go halfway down. The crash was loud as the container shattered and glass shot all over the laboratory floor and added a myriad of glass bits to those in the jar. "Another accident in the laboratory."

The Listers, although quite surprised, prepared to clean the mess, but Holmes stopped them. "The sooner the telegrams go out, the sooner we can solve this case."

I didn't know how we would do that, but I was sure Holmes had already formulated a plan.

"I must prepare another container of crystals," Dr. Lister said.

"That can wait. First the telegrams."

Mrs. Lister took up the broom and pan and the doctor left the laboratory.

"The broom, please, Mrs. Lister. Unless you don't mind losing another measure of phenol crystals, you will need to prepare a dummy container exactly like the previous one using these bits of glass."

She gave him a perplexed look but did as he asked and using the same scoop, took smaller bits from the pan as he swept. When she had five scoops in the container, she sniffed the crystals.

"It doesn't smell quite like the previous ones. Should we try to replicate the scent?"

"That will not be necessary," Holmes said. He emptied the remainder of the glass into a bin and found some rags to toss in on top of them. "These must go out in case anyone is checking your bins. Now you must measure out the phenol crystals for tomorrow's demonstration."

"I'll do it," I said.

Dr. Lister returned as his wife finished her task. Holmes placed the *faux* crystals on the table where the previous one had been when we entered the laboratory. Holmes was punctilious in his preparations for his cases. He didn't like to leave details to chance. Because he said anything can go awry, he tried to limit the scope of unknowns within the equation of an investigation.

When I'd once accused him of using mathematics to solve cases, he denied doing so. 'Really, Watson, how could one possibly apply such methods to human beings? They are often so unpredictable?'

My reply was that a love triangle often fit the Pythagorean Theorem neatly, which made him laugh for several minutes, possibly a record.

At Holmes's suggestion, the Listers prepared the equipment for tomorrow's demonstration – sprayer, chemicals, phenol crystals, the glass container of putrifying pork – and put all under lock and key in Dr. Lister's study. "I can lock the laboratory," he said.

"That won't be necessary. Your study will suffice. Now I suggest we prepare for tonight's business."

"Tonight?" Mrs. Lister echoed raising her eyebrow. "Business?"

"If I am correct, we can expect a visitor tonight, and it's too early for Father Christmas."

I laughed. Holmes rarely joked. The Listers didn't know what to think.

Holmes sensed their perplexion. "Forgive me, this is serious business, I know. Lives will depend on what we do here tonight. Your discovery of the use of carbolic acid in the surgery came in 1865, too late for the American war which had just ended, but it can help people in the future. I suggest you retire now for naps. Tonight promises to be tiring. What time do the servants return?"

"They should all be in by six o'clock," Mrs. Lister replied.

"When they are back, I suggest eating a light supper. We must be prepared for a long night."

Holmes and I returned to our flat and had our tea early. I decided that a nap would be in order and lay on the sofa before Holmes could claim it. Mrs. Hudson had kept a small fire burning cheerily. Holmes disappeared into his bedroom for what I assumed would also be a nap. I drifted off and thought that I was dreaming when a rough workman emerged from his room.

"Here now, what are you . . . ."

I was interrupted by laughter of the Holmes timbre.

"Where are you going?"

"I am visiting a few pubs in the vicinity of the hospital to drop a few hints."

"Shall I come?"

"Certainly not. You need your sleep and would ruin my disguise."

"Why so?"

"A workman would not make pub rounds with a doctor."

"We could separate. I could be disgruntled about having to return for the demonstration."

Holmes stopped in the act of placing a flat cap on his head. "Watson, that is brilliant. Come along then. We can divide up the pubs."

"Perhaps you should dress as a doctor."

"I think not. My face might be recognized. If yours is, it will not matter. You are what you are – a doctor through and through. As a workman, I will complain about having to return tomorrow to help the doctor transport his equipment."

We made appearances in seven pubs altogether, learning nothing before we returned to our rooms, where Holmes changed back into his regular attire. Then we made our way to Park Crescent, but this time took a cab to another address and then back to Number 12 on foot. Mrs. Lister admitted us.

"Crichton hasn't yet returned, but soon the staff will be straggling in. Our nephew is back and we expect the other assistants soon as well. They know something is amiss from the telegrams. Normally we wouldn't inform them of a rescheduling."

Dr. Lister joined us and we went to the laboratory as the clock in the hall chimed six times. "I hope you all had more sleep than I did. The thought that someone would do this – jeopardize lives for selfish or spurious reasons – is intolerable. I wouldn't expect this from a man of medicine. We swear a sacred oath not to do what this perpetrator is now doing."

I nodded. I had sworn the same oath. "I hope that a doctor isn't involved in this scheme."

"As do I," Holmes said, "but it has to be a person with chemical knowledge. He or she knew how to simulate the precise smell of phenol crystals. I can't see a chemist going to these extremes to discredit Dr. Lister's work."

"It has to be another doctor – most likely a surgeon," Dr. Lister said with sadness. "I've been reviled and ridiculed for my strange discoveries, but for one to be this devious, I suspect a sickness in the brain."

"Many people walk around in their daily lives with jealous, sick minds," Holmes said. "Criminals often look just like us."

Crichton was the first of the staff to return, and the only one to come upstairs to inquire if the Listers needed anything. Our presence was not revealed to him.

We made ourselves comfortable in the laboratory and talked of desultory events. Holmes walked over to the windows on the back wall and looked at them. Outside, night drifted down on London. "Do you draw the curtains in this room?"

"We do," Mrs. Lister said, rising to do so, but Holmes said he would do it. He suggested the Listers retire but they refused. "This may take a while," he told them.

"We want to be involved," Mrs. Lister said.

"This is too important," Dr. Lister said. "I need to know who would jeopardize the lives of others for gain."

Holmes asked Dr. Lister to lock the door from the inside and turn down the gas jets. We settled down in silence in the darkness to wait. The hall clock chimed eight times. The front door opened with a key and closed. One of the assistants returning early. At various times the others straggled in. When the hall clock chimed the eleventh hour, I realized I must have nodded off.

No one spoke. The only sounds in the laboratory had been the sighing of cushions when one of us sought a new position in the confines of our chairs.

If I were the perpetrator, I would give the household another twenty minutes to sink into a deep sleep. Soon something bumped the outside window. Possibly a cat. We waited.

We heard fidgety sounds, metallic in origin. Holmes threw off the knitted throw that Mrs. Lister had provided. I did the same and heard the others as well. We were ready for what was about to happen.

A scraping sound was followed by a *clink*, and then cold air rushed in through the opening window. The curtain was pushed aside. A darkened lantern led the way as someone jumped lightly down through the window. The room brightened as someone opened the lantern's slats.

I drew my revolver from my pocket as Holmes did the same. Mrs. Lister gasped. Perhaps she hadn't anticipated the possibility of gunfire.

The intruder, intent on his errand, didn't hear her. Holmes and I advanced out of the darkened area of the laboratory, our weapons at the ready, Dr. Lister behind us.

"Barston! How could you?" Dr. Lister cried out.

The intruder froze at the sound of his name but only momentarily.

Quick as lightning, he turned to leap for the window ledge, but Holmes was too quick for him. "Cease and I will not be forced to use this," Holmes barked at the man, showing his gun.

Mrs. Lister lit the lamps. The man before us held a glass container of *faux* crystals. He swung it high. "Back off or I'll break this container."

"Oh, don't do that, Dr. Barston," Mrs. Lister said. "The servants have retired and I really don't want to have to sweep up glass in this room, even with the help of Mr. Holmes."

"Mr. Holmes? Sherlock Holmes?" The man's eyes shifted beyond the gun.

"The same," Holmes said.

The man identified to us as Dr. Barston flung the glass container at Holmes while turning toward the window. He swung up on the ledge and was outside and away before we could stop him.

Dr. Lister launched himself but was too late. "He got away!"

"He won't get far in that direction," Holmes said. "I've alerted Scotland Yard. Constables should be on post behind the mews."

We rushed for the front door, with Holmes thinking to pick up the man's lantern on the way. On the street behind the mews, we found one bobby lying in a shadow. His helmet lay on the ground as a thin line of red trickled from his hairline. We carried him into the house through the below-stairs entrance, laying him on the kitchen table. With Dr. Lister's medical kit, we patched him up after the bleeding stopped. He didn't need stitches, but enjoyed a medicinal brandy provided by Mrs. Lister.

He was able to tell us Scotland Yard had sent only one bobby – him – to deal with this potential problem. Holmes, who had assumed that Barston was being pursued by the police, was not pleased. He stepped back outside and used his police whistle to summon any constables in the area. They came on the run and combed the shadows on the Crescent and Portland Place, but found no one of our description. No doubt the man had escaped into the park – but his identify was known.

The staff rushed downstairs when they heard the commotion, and the assistants straggled down as well. Within the half-hour, Number 12 Park Crescent swarmed with minions of the law. Inspector Lestrade himself soon followed.

"I told Metters he should've sent more men and gone himself," said Lestrade. "We know who did this and should have him picked up soon. What was his name again?"

Dr. Lister shook his head. "I thought he was a friend. Dr. Leroy Barston. We met for lunch just last week."

"At your behest, or his?" Holmes asked.

"His. I thought he agreed with the importance of sterile surgery."

"Perhaps he does," Holmes said, "but perhaps he wants to be president of the Clinical Society more than saving lives."

"Twice," Mrs. Lister said. "He got in twice. We need new latches on those windows."

We returned to the laboratory with Lestrade who examined the window latches. "Did Barston ever come here to visit the laboratory?" the inspector asked the Listers.

"No," Dr. Lister said.

"Yes," Mrs. Lister said.

The doctor raised his eyebrows.

"He came one day when you were at the hospital. He said he had left his stethoscope in his coat pocket, and wondered if one of the assistants had picked it up by mistake. It sounded plausible. Doctors are always doing that kind of thing. I let him look at the coats in the laboratory."

"Did you accompany him?" Lestrade asked.

"No."

"Did he find his stethoscope?" I asked.

"Of course he did," Holmes said.

"He showed it to me. It had his name engraved on it," Mrs. Lister said.

"You had no reason to doubt him." Dr. Lister patted her shoulder. She smiled faintly.

"He took the opportunity to examine the latches and no doubt determined the best way to open them. Tonight he prepared another container of false crystals and stashed it in a knapsack," Holmes said.

Lestrade spoke to a constable who exited and soon returned with a ladder the likes of which none of us had ever seen before. Made of thin metal, it had been smeared with a coat of plaster and painted white so it wouldn't show up against the stucco of the Crescent.

Holmes examined it. "If Dr. Barston made this and the curved jimmy, he might be following the wrong profession. He seems to have a knack for creating the right tool."

"He will not be practicing medicine now," Lestrade said. "When he's caught, I'll put the word into the proper ear that he's not to be allowed near any tools."

Holmes and I accompanied Lestrade to Dr. Barston's rooms. We were too late. Cupboard doors hung open. Drawers were pulled out, and in one case had fallen on the floor. Books, clothing, and valuables that would be of no value during an escape were strewn over the rooms. The man was on the run and there was no knowing which direction he would take.

"Where can a discredited doctor go?" Mrs. Lister said.

"We'll catch him," Lestrade said as dawn spread over London.

Holmes wasn't so sure. "This man is clever – perhaps too clever for his own good. If he applied his ability to manufacturing tools, surgical or other, he could've been as revolutionary as Dr. Lister, but he chose to use his gift wrongly. I don't think that he will be caught."

Holmes was right. He hasn't been seen in England to this day. After some enquiries along the docks, Holmes concluded that a man of similar description had signed on as an able seaman on a ship bound for Africa using the name Joseph Park from Crescent Green.

"With the Boer War recently concluded, the need for surgeons is great. He could easily slip himself into place using a different name. At least his talents won't be wasted," Holmes said.

"I do not like to think of a surgeon with his ethics caring for unsuspecting patients," I said.

"Perhaps he learned his lesson and will be grateful to have a second chance," Holmes said.

"I would like to think so, but I've seen too many leopards prowling the streets, pretending to be tartanized or striped, but still committing the same spotted mistakes. The arrogance that propelled Barston to attempt to stop such a life-saving discovery as Dr. Lister's from dissemination, merely to remove him as president of the Clinical Society, will trip him up in any future endeavors."

Holmes raised his eyebrows. "Excellent character prognostication, Watson. I pray this will be so if he should attempt to use his gifts for any but the improvement of the human lot."

Holmes refused remuneration for his services. "This was a case involving professional courtesy amongst professional men and a scientific contribution for the benefit of mankind."

Dr. Lister thanked him, but the following week a basket was delivered to Drs. Watson and House at 221 Baker Street. Upon opening, it proved to be filled with oranges – not the neroli kind, but sweet ones grown in an orangerie on someone's estate – and a bottle of excellent champagne. The card was signed by Agnes and Joseph Lister. Holmes placed it on the mantel, where it remains to this day.

The Coffee House Girl
by David Marcum

In those early days in Baker Street, when my friendship with Sherlock Holmes was still relatively new, tolerating his eccentricities was always balanced by the belief that, once my health was recovered, I would be finding lodgings elsewhere, and those things, both large and small, that had vexed me would be relegated to the past – becoming amusing anecdotes for friends or family, and certainly fodder to my need to write, which had been with me as far back as my earliest memories.

On a particular morning in early 1882, I came downstairs to enter a sitting room that had been ill used, and certainly with no consideration by one lodger for the other. Even before I had opened the door, I had a fair idea of what to expect, as the fumes from my friend's latest chemical experiment had permeated the entire building.

"Holmes!" I coughed as I made my way vaguely in the direction of the windows. My eyes were stinging from the combination of some acrid smell that was bound up in a swirling fog of pipe smoke. Throwing up the sash resulted in a gasp from the icy outside air, reminding me of when my father and I had plunged into the sea when I was a boy. Yet the sudden shock was worth it, as the noxious vapors were soon pulled from the room. The thought crossed my mind that when I did find new lodgings, the memory of these would never be far away, as everything I owned would now be permeated with this smell.

"If the matter is that urgent," I told him while shivering, "I believe that the laboratory at Barts is open at all hours. Perhaps in future . . . ." There was no response.

"There is a reason," I continued, turning towards my friend, who was hunched on a stool, leaning over his deal chemical table and intensely observing the bubbling retort before him, "that real chemistry laboratories have ventilation systems. I'm sure that at some point in the past, after an employee or student was found dead beside an experiment, it was worth the extra effort to provide breathable air."

Holmes didn't move, but at least he spoke, which indicated that he was still among the living. "I suspect that Mrs. Hudson would not be agreeable to constructing the elaborate ductwork system that would be required."

The room now reasonably clear, I lowered the window, thinking that there were simpler ways to circulate air than what he suggested. Moving to build up the fire, and hoping that whatever fumes remained weren't volatile, I noticed by the mantel clock that it was later in the morning than I had thought. "Has Mrs. Hudson been up yet?"

"Hmm? Possibly." He moved then, making a note in the small journal that he kept to carefully record all steps and conclusions from his experiments, no matter how insignificant. Then, having transcribed the results of this particular olfactory offense, he leaned forward to shut off the Bunsen burner. "The bitumen in the samples scraped from Vicar Denis's bedroom floor show conclusive signs of Welsh origin. I believe that I have enough evidence to force a confession from Welwyn – if I don't spook him. We'll have to go carefully, and warn Gregson to do the same."

Only then did he spin to face me. His face looked weary, and I could see that he had been up all night. "I do have some sense that Mrs. Hudson opened the door earlier this morning," he said with a tired grin, "but then she immediately departed. At least," he added, rising and stretching, cat-like, before pivoting and settling in his armchair, "I assumed it to be her. A bit early for an assassin – or late, as they usually prefer to strike around midnight so as to get home to their well-earned rest."

I continued attending to the fire, considering whether to question his own personal knowledge of that assertion. However, before I could comment, he had risen again, his nervous energy preventing him from tarrying for too long. He went into his bedroom and shut the door.

I rang for breakfast, which wasn't long in coming. Mrs. Hudson opened the door rather cautiously, as if fearing that she might be overcome by billowing fumes. After ascertaining her safety, she entered and placed bacon and eggs on the table, wrinkling her nose in distaste.

It was a wonder to me how, in those early days, she didn't turn Holmes out into the street, and me along with him for simply being a passively complicit bystander.

For a number of years, I regularly pondered just why she let us stay. At times Holmes could be charming, but he countered that just as often with an impatience that could border on rudeness. Both of us were timely with our rents, even when we sometimes had to do without food or tobacco when Holmes's cases were few and far between, or when my own expenses exceeded my wound pension. However, Mrs. Hudson could have found countless other people who would also pay the rent on time – there was nothing special about the way that we simply met our required and agreed-upon obligations for shelter and meals.

It was only much later that I learned the truth from the lady herself, during a conversation that occurred during those bleak months of mid-1891, following Holmes's supposed death in Switzerland. I had stopped by to say hello, and talk had turned, as it must, to that most unique of individuals. She smiled, even while wiping away a tear, and explained that there were two reasons why we hadn't been turned out after the destructive incident when Jefferson Hope attempted to throw himself through our sitting room window following his capture in early March of '81. While Holmes often vexed her, Mrs. Hudson had explained, she had known him when he was a teen, some years before that last day of 1880 when a chance encounter between them had led to their reacquaintance and made him aware of her intention to rent the Baker Street rooms, providing an opportunity for him to move from his lodgings in Montague Street, if only he could find someone to go half on the rent. His mention of that fact the next day to our mutual acquaintance, Stamford, had resulted in my introduction to this most unusual fellow.

The other reason was that Mrs. Hudson was worried for *me*. She knew that my resources were limited and my health shattered, and that splitting the rent with Holmes gave me a chance to live in much better accommodations than I might otherwise have been able to obtain. And she also perceived quickly that my interest in Holmes's affairs, and then my participation in them, as rambunctious as they often were, did more to heal me in those months after my return from Afghanistan than anything else that might have come my way.

Not for the first or last time did I bless the good fortune that had led me to 221 Baker Street.

But on that icy morning in January 1882, with none of that knowledge in my head, I wondered again if I should not be seeking a different arrangement.

As the day progressed, I became more and more impatient. There was nothing in the newspapers. None of my books interested me. I didn't feel like writing. I would stand and wander to the window, or pause before my desk and see various sorted stacks of papers which awaited my attention. Then, without doing anything about it, I would return to my chair by the fire, aware that the day was slipping by.

When I was young, my brother and I called these spells "The Deadly Wanderings", wherein our toys and books, or distractions in other forms as we grew older, would suddenly hold no interest at all. Through the passing years, I came to understand that this temporary *ennui* would pass, and that the favorite things that meant nothing to me on a certain bleak day would again hold my interest on the next. Sadly, my brother never quite grasped this fact and, as he aged, he assuaged his boredom with certain destructive habits that darkened the rest of his attenuated life.

As I sat in my armchair, I considered Holmes, who had returned to his chemistry table sometime before noon, resuming his experiments but, thankfully, without generating the noxious fumes. I'd seen signs in him over the previous year of these same "deadly wanderings", but fortunately he seemed to work it out rather quickly for himself, either in the form of working on some new monograph, or research to gain a bit of finely focused knowledge to aid him in his profession, or when a new client would fortuitously seek his services. I was also aware that my own spells of boredom had also now been conditioned to dissipate when presented with one of Holmes's cases.

But there was nothing like that today, and I felt the walls of the sitting room closing in.

It was then that Holmes, without looking my way, said, "Why don't you adjourn to that coffee house you've favored over the last couple of months? You've been pacing like a caged tiger all morning."

My first response was to toss aside that suggestion, as it seemed as pointless and unfulfilling as anything else. But then I vaguely realized that the change of scene might do wonders. And I had come to enjoy visiting the shop upon occasion.

It took me a bit to work myself around to it, but I was eventually well-wrapped in hat, scarf, and coat, making my way down Baker Street, stopping not too far from Marylebone Road at a tidy building on the corner of the lane leading to the Portland Mansions, and so into East Street. In recent months, the building's ground floor had been refurbished into an atmospheric little coffee house, and one could smell the roasting beans for nearly a block in each direction.

I stepped inside and the old wooden floors creaked beneath me in welcome. I passed through a small alcove, as always never certain if the place would reveal itself to be empty or crowded. I always hoped for it to be quiet, but even on a busy day I enjoyed my visits.

Upon entering, I found it to be somewhere in the middle, with a number of tables occupied by my fellow Londoners in quiet conversation, some with coffee, and others with the more traditional tea. I saw that my favorite table was available, so I walked over and placed my hat upon it, as well as several of my journals, containing the records of a few of Holmes's recent cases that I planned to revise over coffee and pastries. I'd found that I was able to accomplish quite a bit while here, in spite of the buzz of conversation and the movement of patrons, as sometimes attempting to do the same thing at home led me to recall too many other necessary distractions that got in the way of completing my tasks.

Now considered something of a regular patron, I followed the prescribed routine and stepped to the counter, where I ordered a small cinnamon-filled cake and received a large empty mug. Following the appropriate exchange of coin, I shifted a few steps to my left, where several urns of coffee stood upon the counter, each roasted and brewed to various degrees of strength. Filling my mug with a moderate blend, I carried my comestible back to my table, arranged items to my satisfaction, and lost myself in my notes.

At some point in my labors, I realized that my unsettled mood had passed, as I knew it would. I was fortunate to understand that this would happen, without falling into a greater malaise. I'd just returned from refilling my mug when I became aware of someone approaching my table, taking a direct and unmistakable path toward me, rather than that of someone simply weaving his way to the urns.

Looking up, I saw that it was Jennie, the manager and daughter of the owner. She was in her mid-twenties, and had always greeted me with a twinkle in her eye. I cannot say that it went unnoticed. Though still recovering from my wounds of nearly eighteen months before, I was in my twenties then too, although I had thought more and more of my approaching thirtieth birthday, now just months away instead of years. Though still unsure as to what my greater future held, I was certain that marriage would be a part of it. And while I had no such intentions toward Miss Jennie Gains, I was a young man that was always open to possibilities.

"Excuse me, Doctor," she interrupted, a slight lilt of a Derbyshire accent in her speech. "I don't mean to bother you, but might I have a word?"

I stood and nodded toward the opposite chair at my small table for two. She smiled and I stepped forward, pulling out the chair for her. She then sat and then placed her own mug of coffee before her, while I returned to my own seat.

"I see that you enjoy your own wares," I said, nodding toward her cup. "I know of certain cooks who can no longer abide those things that they produce."

She shook her head. "I have to be careful," she replied, "or I'll be drinking it all day long. That happened when we first opened the shop. I fairly had the shakes every afternoon, and then I couldn't sleep, until I was able to limit myself." She leaned a bit closer, her voice lowering a tad. "I'm sorry to bother you, especially when I can see that you're busy." She cast her eyes toward my journals.

"Not at all," I said, pushing them aside and closing the ink. "How may I help you?"

She smiled, and a dimple appeared in her left cheek. I noticed for the first time that, with the light behind her just so, her hair – which might tend to curliness if not worn so long and kept wound in a fashionable manner – had most unusual rosy highlights. After just a second or two of hesitation, she continued. "I understand that you're friends with Mr. Sherlock Holmes, the detective-man from up the street."

I nodded. "We share rooms." I cleared my throat and added, "I've been fortunate enough to assist him on several of his cases."

"Oh, that's fine, then," she said. "I wanted to tell you about something that has happened, and see if you thought that he might have any advice."

"Certainly," I replied, a bit disappointed that my own experience wouldn't be sufficient.

She took a sip and related her story. "You probably didn't know, but we've – that is my father and I – have had several businesses here before the coffee house. There was a small used furniture store, with some storage upstairs. That's what it was for most of the years when I was small. Then, in the mid-seventies, my father tried to make a go of it with a shoe repair business. He'd found some of the necessary machinery for sale and purchased the lot of it. I think that he was tired of the furniture. He didn't know what he was doing at first, but he was always clever, and he learned quickly. But then, last year he had his stroke, and I didn't know what we were going to do.

"We've always had some money put aside, I believe that my father inherited it before I was born, and he's always been careful with it. That was how he bought the lease on this building, when I was very small, not long after my mother died. After his stroke, he couldn't work, and I thought about hiring someone to carry on with the shoe business, but I longed for something else – maybe I was as unhappy with shoes as my father had been with furniture. In any case, the father of one of my friends' owns a coffee house in Bloomsbury, and he gave me some advice. He was very gracious and never seemed to worry about me setting myself up in competition, as we're located quite a distance away. I sold the shoe equipment, as well as all of the stock, and with what I made from that, along with using our savings, which were quite a bit more than I had believed, I remodeled the building into the coffee house. Additionally, we import and roast our own coffee beans upstairs. In the months since we opened, we've been doing quite well.

She leaned closer and became even quieter. "I don't tell anyone, Doctor, but I actually run everything." Her lovely face had a glow of pride, mixed with sadness. "I still have to give the impression that father is making the final decisions, because the idea of a woman managing a business would be shocking to many, and there are people with whom I have dealings who wouldn't hesitate to cheat me otherwise. I make a show of consulting with father, but truth be told, he isn't any help. He can't be any longer."

I nodded, and realized that I wasn't particularly surprised. I had often seen her father in the shop – he was there that day, as a matter of fact – carefully placed in a comfortable chair in a back corner near the fireplace. Once I happened to pass nearby when the two of them were there and the old man was coughing. I had offered my services as a doctor, but Jennie had smiled and politely declined, indicating that she had the matter in hand. It had been the start of our very limited acquaintance.

Nearly every time that I'd been there, her father was located in his spot, an elderly and enfeebled wreck of a man, slumped down and collapsed upon himself, and seemingly disconnected with his surroundings. And yet, I recalled any number of instances when Jennie had gone over and whispered to him, seemingly having some sort of conversation. While the man gave no indications of making any responses, she would nod as if receiving an answer before giving him a kiss and then returning to her place behind the counter. Now I understood that it was all theatre.

"I had no idea," I said. "I've seen you speak with him on numerous occasions."

"All mummery," she said, rather matter-of-factly. "I don't know if he's there or not. But when a question arises that seems to require more than my own authority, I make a show of asking him before providing my own decision.

"The business has been doing well," she continued. "We're making a profit. I'm in the process of hiring a new cook, and there will soon be more food on the menu. Father and I lived in some of the upstairs rooms for years, but after his stroke, we've moved down to this floor, through that door over there. Because there is only so much space here on this floor for the public, I'm considering opening up the additional rooms upstairs. Things seem to be going well – and yet, recently things have taken an unusual turn.

"It started late last year, just a month or so ago, really, when one of the walls in the cellar collapsed. It's in one of the rooms at the very front of the building. Like most of them here, it extends a bit under the pavement and out beneath the street. We don't have an areaway in front, so there are no windows down there and the cellar is quite dark. My father always claimed that there had been some structural damage back to when they installed the Underground, and that it still causes problems, but the station and the lines are a block away, so I'm not sure why he believed that. I just know that for as long as I can remember, he would periodically inspect the cellar, looking for problems.

"I'd pretty much ignored this as an eccentricity, but just before Christmas, I happened to be down there for another reason, and decided to take a look around. I was more than a little surprised to see that the brickwork under the street had crumbled, and that a void had opened up. Afraid that the pavement above would collapse and that I'd be somehow liable, I summoned a building contractor that we know. He said that it didn't seem to be a problem, as long as it was repaired quickly. The opening under the street was only a cubic foot or two, or so he told me after measuring it, and he packed it with bricks and cement. Then, he set about repairing the cellar wall. I was down there watching as they were clearing away the old rubble, and I noticed that he tossed something odd into the canvas bag they were using to carry the waste up to the street. It didn't quite look like a brick, and I stepped forward to ask about it. He seemed surprised, but I reached past him into the bag, pulling out a small metal box, not much larger than a brick. It was made of a heavy gray metal, and had a little lock through its hasp.

"This builder, who I've known since I was a child, seemed a bit perturbed, and said that he didn't realize in his hurry to clear the rubble that he'd picked up something other than a brick. I theorized that it must have been buried in the wall, and he agreed. And then he reached out to take it from me! I stepped back, clutching it and looking at him with surprise. For a long moment, we simply stood there, no words spoken, and for the first time in my life I was a little afraid of him. He's long been a friend to my father, and that was why I had called upon him to begin with. Now, I felt as if I'd never seen him before. He was quite terrifying in that moment, his eyes wide and his nostrils flaring as if he were a bull about to charge.

"I'm not sure what might have happened next, but I turned and dashed up the steps. Without stopping in the shop, I went up to the next floor, to the roastery, and looked for a place to hide the box. No one was around just then, so I was able to place it behind a piece of the baseboard along one wall which I knew to be loose. The box just fit between the lower part of the wall and the flooring, and when the baseboard was replaced, no one could tell anything at all. Then I went downstairs to the shop and resumed my duties.

"Later, my father's friend, Mr. Chesham, came upstairs and told me that the work was finished. He acted as if nothing had occurred, but there was still a tension between us. When he asked if I'd like to accompany him downstairs to inspect the repairs, I declined, telling him that I was busy and would check it later. That seemed to irritate him, but what could he do? With a scowl toward my poor father, he turned and left.

"Of course, my curiosity got the better of me, and even though I tried to put it off, it wasn't long before I'd climbed back upstairs, retrieved the box, and gave it a closer look. It was apparently made of iron, quite smooth, and well fashioned. Of course, I had no key, and no skills to open a lock. I retrieved a tool from the roastery and began to pry at it. The old lock gave way before the hasp did, and soon I had it open. Inside, curiously, was a single sheet of paper. It was in my father's handwriting, and signed by him. All that it said was, '*I owe you*' and his name, '*Will Gains*'.

"What was there about this box that had made Mr. Chesham try to sneak it out with the rubble – for I have no doubt that is what he intended to do. Did he think there was something else in there – or at least did he hope for something valuable, as I had? If so, he would have been as disappointed as I was. And why had my father taken the trouble to hide it down there in that odd place? I was greatly saddened that I couldn't ask him what it all meant. It was probably his work in digging out a spot behind the cellar wall that led to the weakness there that resulted in the collapse.

"Convinced that it would forever remain a curiosity, I re-hid the box behind the roastery baseboard and went back downstairs, wondering often about the curious paper and why it was worth that much trouble.

"I should mention that, ever since the shop has been open, we've been fortunate enough to be supported quite well by my father's old friends. There is Mr. Chesham, of course, and Mr. D'Abitot, who sells wine from his shop in Bingham Place, near the cripples' home. Mr. Brent sells knitted goods from Scotland in the Bazaar, and Mr. Stadhampton works as a clerk for one of the banks. They've all been like second fathers to me, and offered more good advice than I could have ever expected when I decided to open the business. They stop in frequently, sitting with my father and keeping him company, in spite of the fact that he likely doesn't know that they're here. One of them – Don't look! – is with him now. Mr. D'Abitot usually comes by in the middle of the day

"After Mr. Chesham found the box, things changed. Each of them still comes by, but their behaviors have changed – or at least it seems that way to me. They seem more guarded, and they talk with me in clipped tones and with narrowed eyes. Mr. Chesham has only been in once, and even though neither of us spoke of the matter in the cellar, it's clearly something that isn't forgotten.

"Then, last week, I came back from an errand, and as I entered from the front door, I looked over and saw Mr. Stadhampton stepping into the shop through the doorway to our apartment in the rear, pulling the door closed behind him. He was acting in a most suspicious manner. He didn't see me, and he returned to a seat near my father, where Mr. Brent was waiting. There were two cups of coffee on the table, one for each. I can assure you that Mr. Stadhampton had no business being in our rooms.

"After that, I became more careful, and I've seen subsequent signs that there have been intruders, as if our things were searched. Although I trust my employees, there are none that I can ask to help keep watch without some sort of explanation – it would simply start too much gossip, and I sense that this affair, whatever it is, should be kept quiet.

"Last night, after the shop was closed and father was in bed, I had put out the light and retired to my own room. However, I couldn't fall asleep – the curse of working in a coffee house where my own product is too tempting! – and I simply lay awake for quite a while. It was then that I heard footsteps – slow and careful – moving across the roastery in the floor above my bedroom!

"I am not a fearful woman, Doctor. My father didn't raise me that way, and starting and running a business has made me bolder than many. But I assure you that the sound of that intruder, passing just a dozen feet above my head, paralyzed me with terror. How had this person entered the shop? What was he looking for? And did it somehow relate to the mysterious iron box that was revealed several weeks ago? Somehow it seems that it must be connected, for only when it was found had my father's friends begun to act so suspiciously.

"After a while the sounds stopped – whoever it was had left. Later, I found the courage to go upstairs and check. The box and the note were still hidden where I had left them. I didn't know what to do, and then," she smiled, "it seemed as if fate has brought you here today.

"I'd thought of making the trek up Baker Street to visit with Mr. Holmes, but perhaps you can intercede for me, and see if my story suggests anything to him. It is said the he sees light where others only perceive darkness. My friend, Alice Cumnor, still recalls a time five years or more back when Mr. Holmes visited their house at the invitation of her father and located a painting hidden in plain sight, as well as pointing the finger of guilt at her own uncle as he attempted to defraud the family of a much-needed heirloom. Would you be willing to repeat for him all that I have told you?"

Of course I was willing, and I earnestly assured her of that fact. She laid a warm hand on the back of my own, and my heart beat a bit faster as she looked into my eyes and thanked me. I looked for the dimple, but it had vanished with the concerns of her tale. Then, removing her hand, she pushed back her chair, lifted her cup, and walked behind the counter.

I looked at my own coffee, now grown cold while I had listened to her strange tale. It was a small series of happenings, and yet, in her world, it was proportioned to fill the horizon. How could I not offer to help in any way possible?

I considered rising right then and asking if I might examine the scene of these matters myself, but then I recalled that one of the men in question, her father's friend Mr. D'Abitot, was currently in the room, and I decided that it wouldn't do to seem too curious. I turned in my seat and leaned down, untying and then retying my shoe, allowing me to see across to the fireplace where Jennie's father slumped in his chair. Beside him was a small, dark man of approximately the same age, sipping coffee and reading a newspaper. At any other time, I would have disregarded him as simply another face in the background of any other day, but now I saw him with a new perspective: One of a suspicious group who had some common secret, the existence of which had led to them causing fear in the heart of this admirable girl. Watching him, sitting there unaware of my interest, made me feel as if I were an agent on a vital mission, or a knight on a quest.

Then I realized that there was nothing that I could accomplish at that moment. I therefore sat upright and pulled my journals back to the center of the table. Opening the first, I began to read through, making notes and corrections as needed, but I found that my interest simply wasn't engaged any longer. Instead, I puzzled over the strange box and its meaningless message, and what could have brought about the sudden change in the behavior of these old family friends. It crossed my mind that Jennie might well be imagining it, but I quickly dismissed that notion. She didn't seem that type of woman at all, and to even those thoughts felt like some sort of betrayal of our new alliance. She had asked me for help – although it was really a request for me to obtain the help of someone better qualified – and as such I had to be her advocate, and not her doubter.

After a few minutes, I found that I could focus on my journals as planned, and I had several more productive hours as I recalled matters that I'd felt merited memorialization. Some had been quite serious, such as the terrorizing of Lucius Kintner at Old Radford, while others had drifted toward being quite ludicrous. Here I refer to the Prancing Minister of Dunchurch, and his unique marriage proposal to the Old Widow Ditton, and the singular misunderstanding that had provided him with a ducking in his rival's pond.

Recalling that affair, and how Holmes had held his tongue for so long before revealing the truth, forcing the minister to blurt out his true feelings, left me in a much better mood than when I had arrived. When I reached that point where I instinctively knew that it was time to go, I gathered my various materials, nodded toward Jennie, and walked toward the door. Along the way, I saw that D'Abitot had departed during the time my memories had been turned towards Dunchurch. Now her father, old Will

Gains, was left sitting alone. Who knew what he could have told his daughter, if only he'd been given one more chance?

Stepping outside was like launching one's self into icy water. With a gasp, I pulled my coat tighter and faced toward home. Within moments, I had briskly covered the distance and entered and closed our front door behind me. Mrs. Hudson heard my arrival and came from her domain in the back, informing me that Holmes had departed an hour or so before without saying when he would return. I thanked her and, in spite of the prodigious amounts of coffee consumed during my time down the street, agreed when she offered to bring up tea. The pure taste of it, I felt, would cleanse my palate from the bitterness that currently washed over me, seeming to smoke from my very pores. Anyone who drinks coffee to their limit will understand.

Upstairs, I returned my journals to their proper place and then made myself more comfortable, with no intention of vacating the premises again that day. Mrs. Hudson soon arrived with the tea, and as I settled in my chair before the fire, I felt that all was right with the world. The Deadly Wanderings of the morning had been vanquished, as they always were. Reaching for and finding my place in the sea novel that was currently holding my attention, I settled back with a sigh and began to read.

I have no memory of emptying my tea cup or setting aside the book and falling asleep. Upon waking, my first thought was surprise that I had been able to do so, especially after consuming so much caffeine. However, it must be recalled that, even in those days, I was still recovering from my injuries, and I tired rather more easily than might be expected.

Not long after, Holmes came in, removing his Inverness and fore-and-aft cap. Hanging them behind the door, he rubbed his hands briskly and informed me that Welwyn had confessed with an almost grateful urgency as he attempted to free himself of the guilt which was consuming him. I was still rather sleepy, and knew that I'd need to question Holmes about the specific details later, should he be in a mood to relay them.

In fact, after dinner I was able to obtain how he had seen his way to a solution – a narrative which I will record elsewhere. It was only when he was finished with that narrative that I remembered to share with him Jennie Gains's tale from earlier in the day. As I spoke, he progressed from casual interest to a much more intense curiosity, leaning forward with his elbows upon his knees, sometimes waving his fingers as if to make me tell it faster. Then, something he heard seemed to please him, because the tension released, and he leaned back with a smile before immediately rocking forward again to stand while I was finishing my thought. He walked around me to the shelf holding his commonplace books, pulled one loose, and returned to his chair. Opening it carefully across his knees, he turned sheets until he found what he sought. Then he sat back and explained.

"You've heard me lecture the Yarders upon the history of crime?"

"Indeed. You've often commented on the fact that you are generally able, by the help of your knowledge of the history of crime, to set them straight."

"It is a valuable tool towards earning my bread and cheese. My researches started early, as I recognized the importance of identifying criminological patterns. During those bleak stretches when I first set myself up in practice, and clients were few and far between, I made good use of my time researching the old cases – both solved and otherwise. And one such was what the newspapers called 'The Duntisbourne Jewel Theft'."

"I've never heard of it."

"I would be surprised if you had. It occurred in 1858, and more accurately it took place in Perrott's Brook, rather than in nearby Duntisbourne proper. You may read the account here – " He tapped the page before him. " – but in short, a box of jewels – an iron box, mind you! – was stolen from a manor house, the hidden accumulated treasure of the manor's owner. Five of the servants were suspected, but nothing was ever proven. The jewels were never recovered, and the five men were sacked, disappearing into the fog of history. Or so I thought, until today. Here, read this."

He passed me the awkward book, with clippings threatening to spill to the floor and pages heavy with pasted news articles pulling loose from the feeble binding. Adjusting it toward the gaslight, I saw that the five listed servants of one Dr. Edward Benton all had very familiar names: Will Gains, of the stables; Arthur Chesham, the handyman; Richard D'Abitot, the butler; Jonathan Brent, the valet; and Clark Stadhampton, Benton's private secretary.

The case was quite simple: The jewels, kept in an iron box poorly secreted in Dr. Benton's bedroom, had been found missing. The eccentric doctor had summoned what passed for the law in those times and had accused his entire staff, including several of the maids, whose names were not listed. When the jewels weren't found, despite searches of the staff's possessions, they were all turned out. A final clipping showed that less than a week later, Dr. Benton had died naturally, succumbing to a wasting illness.

"In my youthful research," said Holmes, "the matter was interesting, but hardly instructive. No solution was ever discovered. I corresponded for a bit with a local vicar, presenting a few sincere questions, and he was quite willing to reply, but he had nothing useful to add. He told me that all of the accused had long since departed from the area, and that old Dr. Benton, who was eccentric in the best light and probably mad in an accurate light, had died without any heirs, and that his small estate had been finagled and quickly absorbed by the locals in a most shocking manner, with the land being taken by a wealthy neighbor through passage of a special ordinance. And so the matter ended . . . until today, when you bring me a tale that effectively shackles all of these men together once again by their presence at another common location, and the reappearance of an iron box that holds their apparent fascination. But for this girl's story to you, as brought to me, it's unlikely that this connection would have ever been noticed."

I closed the book and sat back. "So . . . so Will Gains had the jewels, then, all this time? And the others knew of it, and now their interest has been aroused. That's what is implied by the iron box hidden in his cellar, with a note written in his own fist. But what of the note? '*I owe you.*' What does he owe? And to whom?"

"Why, surely that is clear. He owes the jewels – or at least an equivalent payment. And who to but the other men, his cohorts in the crime, all of whom shared in the original theft, and have since found London jobs and residences and lives near one another, staying in touch through the intervening years. It doesn't sound as if there was any animosity during that time. Your coffee house girl spoke of the men as being 'second fathers' to her, and there is no sign that they weren't her father's close friends throughout."

"She is not my 'coffee house girl'," I informed him. "Is she in danger?"

"I think not. If she considers them to be second fathers, then they certainly see her reciprocally as a daughter. It was only when the box was found that Chesham seems to have shown an unexpected covetous side. He has obviously spoken to the others, and they have since started to display this sudden grimness and suspicion. They don't know that the box is empty, save for the note. They only know that the jewels have been brought to light, and with Will Gains effectively out of the picture, their interest in their share has apparently been awakened."

"What shall we do?" I said. "The jewels must be gone. Will Gains was keeping them, but he's instead left a note of debt in their place." I stood up. "Should we arrange to hide in the coffee house, tonight perhaps, and give these men another chance to break in and be caught red-handed?" I took a step forward. "I can pop down the street and notify Jennie – that is to say, Miss Gains – of our intentions."

Holmes smiled and waved me back to my seat. "No need, Watson. I believe that I shall ask a few questions here and there on the morrow, and perhaps borrow that box from your Miss Gains. Then we shall have a little gathering here and settle this matter."

I nodded and walked to the shelf, returning the book to its place. It was curiously labeled "*L*", which as nearly as I could tell, had nothing whatsoever to do with the names of any of the principals or locations involved with the missing jewels. I doubted that I, or anyone, would ever understand Holmes's curious filing system.

The following morning proved to be possibly colder than before. I had awakened to discover one of those days when an unseasonable plunge in the temperatures had combined with a thick fog, making it quite unpleasant to step outside. The freezing mist had coated every surface – building and tree and pavement – with a thin rime of ice that resembled fairy tracery. As I dressed, I looked from my bedroom window at the bare yard behind our house to where the ice had limned the branches of the plane tree, delicately illuminated by light from the windows of the adjacent buildings. There was no sign of the sun.

Downstairs, I called for breakfast, observing that Holmes was already curled in his chair, seemingly fascinated with some textbook. I spoke a greeting but received no response. When Mrs. Hudson carried in my rashers and eggs, we exchanged glances of understanding.

Within the hour, Holmes had set aside his book, risen abruptly, and vanished into his bedroom. He soon returned, *sans* dressing gown, and fully dressed for the outside world. He confirmed that I would be at home in the early afternoon, and then he departed, wrapped well to face the bitter temperatures.

All morning and well past lunchtime, I fiddled with this or that distraction, but curiosity as to Holmes's actions, as well as what he might be arranging in connection to the matter of the Duntisbourne jewels, kept me from doing anything constructive. Several times I considered walking down to the corner at Portman Mansions in order to report on what Holmes had revealed to me the previous night, but I sensibly remained inside, knowing that I might cause whatever edifice he was constructing to fall apart by some inadvertent action on my part.

It was mid-afternoon when the doorbell rang, and after some murmured conversation downstairs, I heard light footsteps seemingly dancing up the stairs. In seconds the door was thrown open to reveal a rather effete fellow, accompanied by a much burlier youth, carrying a basket and a large flat box. "Mr. Holmes?" asked the first, and then ignoring the shake of my head, he snapped, "Fortnum and Mason." Then he and his assistant quickly and efficiently laid out upon the dining table a pheasant, a couple of brace of cold woodcock, what turned out to be *pâté de foie gras*, and a couple of tidy bottles of a respectable vintage. I became aware that Mrs. Hudson was standing in the door, watching with a mixture of amusement and skepticism, as displayed by a tolerant smile and two vertical lines between her brows. Without further explanation, the two men departed, leaving me to ask the reason for this surprising intrusion.

"I don't have the faintest," said our landlady. Then, with a muttered comment concerning hope and the expense of such victuals when the rent was due soon, she departed, while I tried and failed to find the words to explain that Holmes had recently received a very handsome reward for the recovery of Lady Drake's missing maid and the tiara she had taken with her.

Not long after, Holmes returned, noting with satisfaction the various items upon the table. Then, humming to himself and ignoring my requests for an explanation, he began to drag chairs around, making up something of a semi-circle before the fireplace. Counting the seats, I realized his intention. "You have invited the four old friends of Mr. Gains."

"Excellent, Watson."

I nodded toward the deliveries from Fortnum and Mason's. "This doesn't seem to be planned as an unpleasant afternoon of accusations and denials."

"Indeed. I have a proposal for them, and there is no reason for it to be contentious."

As he stood, seemingly satisfied with the room's arrangement, the doorbell rang again, and soon four men were shown into the sitting room.

D'Abitot, whom I had seen the day before, led the way. His past position as the butler of old Dr. Benton's household apparently still made him the *de facto* leader. He was a smaller man than the figures that followed, but he looked around, almost belligerently, as if he were a terrier seeking something to shake to death.

Behind him was a big individual whom I would learn was Chesham, the building contractor. It was easily deduced by his clothing, which was more worn than that of his compatriots. Next was Brent, a dark and solid fellow whose face, by inadvertent construction, seemed always to be smiling with a secret. His profession as a salesman of Scottish knitted goods was belied by rather colorful wool coat. At the rear was Stadhampton, the bank clerk, a thin faded chap who would disappear into the background if one wasn't careful.

D'Abitot glanced my way but then turned his attention to Holmes. "We're here," he snapped, obviously advancing with the idea that an immediate aggressive stance would place them on a better footing. "You have no leverage, sir. The events to which you referred in your invitation were long ago, and never proven. Still, we felt that it would be better to discuss it with you and nip this business in the bud now, rather than let you start asking questions where you shouldn't."

"Peace, Mr. D'Abitot," replied Holmes with raised hands and a smile. "Please find seats, and I'll tell you what I know for certain and what I've concluded. Then perhaps you'll find that there isn't as much need to worry as you might have believed. "

They looked at one another and then seemed to come to a common agreement, for they moved into the circle of chairs and the settee and arranged themselves. Holmes introduced me, and let me know the names of the four men. D'Abitot glanced my way, Chesham and Stadhampton nodded, and Brent flicked an indifferent glance my way before again focusing on Holmes.

"I had to be somewhat mysterious when issuing my invitation," explained Holmes. "How else to convince you to join us?" He nodded my way. "It was Watson who brought the matter to my attention, following a conversation with Miss Gains yesterday at the coffee house."

D'Abitot nodded. "I saw her speaking with you." He frowned. "We try to keep an eye on Jennie."

"In case she happened to reveal the existence of the iron box to a stranger?" I asked, rather more hotly than I'd intended.

The wine merchant was taken aback. Suddenly he seemed less angry, and more like a rather weary middle-aged man. "Why . . . why no. Simply to make sure that she's safe. Since her father's illness, she's done quite well, and demonstrated an impressive amount of strength and ability. And yet, each of us makes sure to regularly stop in and verify that all is well."

Holmes nodded. "That's what my own little researches have concluded. Miss Gains stated to Watson that the four of you are like second fathers. It's difficult to believe that you would suddenly reverse that position and pose a threat to her. While it is possible that any one of you might harbor greedy thoughts regarding the contents of the iron box, together you serve to check one another. However, Mr. Chesham – " Here he turned his attention to the contractor. " – you caused a bit of a fright the day that you reacted at seeing the iron box revealed in the cellar. As did whomever it was among you that got into the building the other night to search the premises for the box's hiding place."

Brent cast his eyes down. "That was me. Will had given me a key long ago, and I used it to look around, hoping to discover where Jennie had hidden the box when she removed it from the cellar. I thought that I was being quiet, but I suppose something gave me away."

"She was in the room below," I explained, "and heard your footsteps. I gather that she was quite terrified." Perhaps this was putting it on a little thick, but I wanted this man to feel ashamed.

"Be that as it may," said Holmes, again taking control of the conversation, "we are here to put that behind us. I have a general sense of the events at Perrott's Brook nearly a quarter-of-a-century past. Several years ago, in my studies of the history of crime, I became aware of the unsolved jewel theft, and corresponded with Vicar Dill. I was happy to learn that he is still among the living, and a wire to him this morning confirmed my hypothesis – specifically that your employer, Dr. Benton, was a rather cruel and unpleasant individual while he slid through dementia toward death. In fact, he refused to help treat Mr. Gains's wife, who was the housekeeper, during her long and eventual fatal illness – making life rather more difficult for that family than it needed to be. I suspect that this led to a feeling of ill will, at best, toward him during his final days."

They men looked at one another, and then nodded in unison.

"You don't have to confirm anything, of course," said Holmes, "but I suspect that my understanding of events hews close to the truth. Knowing that Dr. Benton was not long for this world, and that he had no heirs, and also likely realizing that the local community in that remote area had already made plans to absorb his estate by whatever means – legal or otherwise – you probably saw no harm in taking his box of jewels, little realizing that he might rally long enough to discover that they were gone and thus summon the authorities. But fortunately, he chose to simply dismiss you *en masse*, allowing you to depart unhindered to new lives. You gravitated to London, where your shares were used to establish yourselves in new professions."

D'Abitot cleared his throat and decided to acknowledge Holmes's assumptions. "True enough, for the most part. But we didn't split the jewels equally and separate as strangers, never to see one another again. We were all good friends, like brothers really, and have remained so. Will convinced us that after the jewels went missing we might be watched, perhaps for a long time, and that it would be best if we kept our true names, lived innocent lives, and made use of the funds realized from the jewels gradually, rather than each suddenly spending an unlikely amount and making a fast leap to a substantially higher station. Thus, only a few jewels at a time were carefully sold and the profits divided. The rest were kept hidden by Will, to be divided gradually as the years passed."

"I helped with the banking side of things," explained Stadhampton.

"And I used my own skills to make improvements and expansions at our homes and businesses, as needed," added Chesham. "By paying me for repairs, I was able to charge what they were really worth, and it helped keep the money in the family, so to speak."

"But then," Holmes said, "Mr. Gains had a stroke, and you all realized that he'd neglected to tell you exactly where he hid the remaining jewels."

They nodded, and D'Abitot said, "It's a measure of the trust that we had with one another that we never needed to know."

"I never meant to frighten Jennie," added Chesham. "I recognized the box as soon as I saw it in the rubble. I tried to slip it out with the broken bricks, so that we wouldn't have to explain to her what it was or where it came from, but she saw it. I'm afraid that my surprised reaction scared her."

"It did," I explained. "She felt that all of you acted differently toward her after that."

They had the good grace to lower their heads. Then Holmes continued.

"I fear that your trust in Will Gains may have been misplaced after all. I stopped to see Miss Gains this morning, and she gave me this." He reached into his waistcoat pocket, pulling out a folded sheet. "It is what she found in the box – not jewels, but rather a simple note in her father's handwriting: '*I owe you.*' I expect that you understand his meaning." He handed it to D'Abitot.

The other's half-rose, leaning over to see before returning to their seats. Brent still had the half-smile on his face, which would likely be there if he were angry rather than pleased. Stadhampton had no expression, a skill likely learned in his position as a bank clerk. Chesham was surprisingly indifferent, while D'Abitot only shook his head. "Poor Will," was his unexpected comment.

"Indeed?" responded Holmes, who was clearly as unprepared for this reaction as I was.

D'Abitot looked over at him with a sad expression on his face. "You may not know that our friend Will had several unlucky occurrences in his life. He was the only one of us to marry, and then she died. When we set up in London, we all found – if not riches, then at least security – in our new lives, but he continued to struggle. Oh, he was able to obtain the lease on the building, but whichever venture he tried there never seemed to find its footing. His most recent – the shoe business – likely did much worse than he let on. I can only imagine how desperate he must have felt to have violated our trust and used the last remaining jewel for himself. And for Jenny."

"The last jewel?" I asked. "They had all been sold over the years?"

Stadhampton nodded. "There were never that many. Dr. Benton had greatly exaggerated the amount when he reported the theft, and how could we disagree with him? We only converted a few at a time every few years to supplement our incomes, and when we last met to make a 'withdrawal' two years ago, there were only three left. We determined that selling two of them would meet our needs, and that the last one – the finest of the lot – should remain in the box. There was some mention of a tontine arrangement, wherein the last survivor would have it, but nothing was formalized – and how could it be? In the end, the box was closed with the final stone – a ruby – still inside. Poor Will," He said, shaking his head. "He must have been feeling quite pressed to have been forced to take from his friends in that way. I wish that he had come to us. It must have shaken him terribly to use the jewel."

The others seemed to share this sentiment, and I was impressed at how this band of men had stayed linked together during the intervening years, willing to think the best of their friend who had been forced to breach their agreement and trust.

"It seems," said Holmes, "that there was still enough left for Miss Gains to renovate the building into a coffee house. Some of these funds must have been paid to you, Mr. Chesham, for your labors."

"It's true," said the contractor. "She said that she realized a profit from selling the shoes and equipment, but I should have realized that paying me, along with buying the coffee roasting equipment, probably took more money than she would have rightfully had. The rest must have come from Will's account, where the proceeds of the last jewel rested."

"And further," said Holmes, "you have all benefitted from the arrangement in other ways. You have had a place to go, keeping your friendship alive in yet another way, and additionally your support has allowed a young woman who thinks of you all as second fathers to find both success and a firm footing."

"You're right," said D'Abitot. "None of us have families, other than each other really, and Jennie is truly like a daughter to all of us."

"Then she should know it and be certain of it," said Holmes, "rather than feeling unsettled, and now even a bit fearful towards all of you. Which is why," he said, glancing at the clock upon the mantel, "I've invited her to join us, so that you can explain the old bond shared between all of you and her father – and I trust let her know that his '*I owe you*' should be considered paid in full."

In a most timely fashion, the doorbell rang.

"That will be Miss Gains," noted Holmes. "Shall I instruct our landlady to let her in?"

D'Abitot said in a rueful tone, belied by his smiling face, "You don't give us much choice, Mr. Holmes."

"It's best that the truth be known," said Holmes, rising from his armchair. "I've researched each of you in the short time since I learned of this affair, and I learned that you are all honest, respected, and honorable.

You have led good and useful lives, and now you can do some good in another way. You and Miss Gains have much to discuss. I'm certain that, with the now open assistance of all four of you, the coffee house will became even more successful than it already is, ensuring that your informal daughter will be quite secure."

And such was the case. Jennie entered the sitting room to find the six of us standing in greeting. She seemed nonplussed, although she explained that Holmes had informed her beforehand that she was invited to discuss his findings related to the iron box in her cellar. As the history behind it was revealed, and then elaborated upon, Jennie went through a variety of emotions before finally succumbing to joyful tears, revealing in a quavering voice how much more difficult the preceding months had been than she had ever dared to let on, with her father's illness and the uneasiness of operating a business that each day might suddenly veer into failure, despite every effort and indication otherwise. Gradually we made our way across the room to the table and its fare, filling plates and glasses, and letting the little family – which is what they were – become known to each other in an entirely new way.

With the enthusiastic support of the four men, the coffee house went from success to success, and in the years since, it has become hard to recall when it wasn't in business at that corner. Jennie's father died not long after that little party in our sitting room, but she confided in me sometime afterwards that she was certain her father somehow knew that she was well cared-for, and that he had turned loose of life without any worries left.

I continued to go there for a few of those early years, finding it a convenient haven when an escape from our quarters for this or that reason became a necessity. I was intrigued by Jennie, still occasionally referred to by Holmes as my "coffee house girl", but nothing ever came of it. Within a year or two, she had been introduced to some fellow that was an acquaintance of Brett – a tall, dark, and rather gangly chap that didn't seem as if he would be her type at all – and they eventually married. I eventually frequented the place less and less as my own interests turned elsewhere, and as I instead spent more time involved with Holmes's investigations, along with visits to my club, and then later at my own hearth with my wife. But I never yet walk down the street in front of Jennie's coffee shop without thinking of that space in the cellar stretching out under the pavement, wherein the iron box of jewels was hidden, and wondering how many other similar treasures are scattered around, unknown and just underneath one's feet.

The Mystery of the
Green Room
by Robert Stapleton

"How is the girl, Watson?" Sherlock Holmes posed the question the moment I stepped through the door of our sitting room in Baker Street and sat down heavily in my customary easy chair.

Our acquaintance was still in its early days, and I had been too preoccupied with my patients to take a great deal of interest in Holmes's latest activities. "The girl is not at all well, Holmes."

"I am sorry to hear you confirm the fact."

"But how do you come to know about my young patient?" Now, in that summer of 1882, I was accustomed to the singular skill of my friend to make deductions based upon even the most sparing of facts, but this turn of events made me look up at him with renewed awe.

From his seat beside the laid but unlit fire, Holmes smiled, and studied me through steepled fingers. "You have been out visiting the sick. That is evident from the fact that your medical bag now lies on the floor beside you."

"I'll admit that appears obvious."

"And the expression on your face suggests that the condition of your patient is a cause for concern."

I nodded. "True enough."

"The bulge in your coat pocket could be made by nothing other than a bag of sweets. That, together with the fact that the bag appears to be full, suggests that the child was in no mood or condition to enjoy them."

"Surely you are now taking your skills of deduction into the realms of speculation?" I retorted.

"Not at all. It is merely a matter of observation and deduction."

"Very well. I have to admit to the truth of it. But how could you tell that the child was a girl?"

"Now there I have to admit to a certain amount of duplicity. You see, I was in the public gardens at the center of Morpeth Square when you approached the front door of Number Eighteen."

I stared back at him in amazement. "You were there? I have to admit, I was complete unaware of your presence anywhere near the place."

"I am glad to hear it. Otherwise my disguise would have been entirely without value."

"The only person I saw was the gardener." Then it occurred to me. "*You* were that gardener."

"Correct."

I remembered the scruffily clad figure employed upon pruning a bed of roses. "I would never have guessed."

"That was my intention."

"But what were you doing there in such a disguise?"

"I was watching the very house you called upon this afternoon. As you will already know, it belongs to a certain Jeremiah Edlingholm, the manager of the branch of the London and South Coast Bank situated in Horsegate Road. I know that Mr. Edlingholm is married and has a young daughter of eight years."

"The girl's name is Amy," I explained, in an attempt to regain a measure of dignity in the face of this surge of revelations.

"I also know that he and his family moved in there no more than three months ago."

"I believe that is true.'

Holmes laughed at the discomfort evident in my expression. "Please do not be offended, Watson. It was not you I was there to observe. And anyway, I left shortly after your arrival. It was a matter of balance. If I had spent too little time there, my time would have been wasted, but if I had spent too long there, I might have risked drawing undue attention to myself. I arrived back here shortly before you did – with just sufficient time to change out of my work clothes."

I nodded. "You are quite right in saying that I am worried about the girl. The parents called me in because nobody else was able to provide them with any hope of recovery. And, quite frankly, at first I was not sure I could either. One physician had pronounced that the constriction in the girl's throat meant she was suffering from diphtheria. Another suggested cholera."

"Dear me!" said Holmes. "That is yet another blow to a man who has faced a great deal of trouble during the last few months."

"How do you mean?"

"Mr. Edlingholm's bank suffered a robbery at the end of May," he elucidated. "Banknotes were taken, to a considerable value. Although the numbers printed on them are known, Scotland Yard has had little success in tracing any of them. The crime has left them completely baffled."

"And for that reason, they called in yourself," I concluded.

"As you will remember, I was otherwise preoccupied at the time. There had been one definite attempt to assassinate Her Majesty, and at least one other had been contemplated. Scotland Yard were busy arresting every suspect they could lay their hands on, whether sane or insane."

"I remember they called you in, but I know nothing of the details."

"It continues to be an extremely delicate matter," said Holmes as he stood up and moved across the room to the window, where he remained looking out upon the busy street below.

"But you decided to assist them with their enquiries into the crime."

"Indeed, and the more I have looked into this matter, the more intriguing I have found it to be. And baffling. I have to admit, I am as perplexed as the police. The matter appears simple enough, but I'm at a loss to find any way forward with the investigation. I can cope with facts, information, and evidence, but in this case there seems to be nothing for me to work with. What we do know is that when the bank's strong-room was locked on the Saturday afternoon, nothing was amiss. Then, when it was opened again on the Monday morning, a large amount of money was discovered to have gone missing. And the strong-room door was found to be still locked."

"Somebody must have used a key to gain entrance."

Holmes turned to face me again. "In the absence of any other indications, that had to be the assumption at which we arrived. The same was true of both the front door of the bank and the door to the staircase leading down into the vaults. The inevitable conclusion was that a complete set of keys had been used. But the only two sets were in the possession of the two most significant men at the bank: The manager himself, Mr. Edlingholm, and the Chief Cashier, Mr. Obadiah Mitchelson."

"I suppose you are going to tell me they both still had their keys in their possession on the Monday morning."

"That is exactly the situation, Watson. When Scotland Yard was brought in to investigate the theft, they took both men in for detailed questioning. It turned out that both sets of keys had remained securely in their possession throughout the whole of the weekend. Both were able to give detailed accounts of their activities since the Saturday afternoon. Mr. Mitchelson and his family had been away from home, staying with his wife's parents at their home in Kent. Mr. Edlingholm was busy preparing to move house, and had been busy packing the family's possessions into tea-chests, under the careful scrutiny of his wife."

"I do remember you being somewhat preoccupied at the time," I told him, "but you felt unable to share any of the details with me."

"Beyond what I have just told you, there were no details."

I nodded. "Are you suggesting, Holmes, that a *third* set of keys had been employed for this robbery?"

"That had to be the only solution. I carefully examined both sets of keys, and discovered that those held by the Chief Cashier had traces of wax adhering to the teeth of some of the keys, with none at all on those belonging to the Manager."

"And yet neither man could account for this."

"Obviously somebody had borrowed Mr. Mitchelson's set of keys and had made wax impressions of them without his knowledge. When it became clear that Mr. Mitchelson could shed no further light on the matter, we realized we had come to the end of our investigation, and could see no way forward. The suspicion still remained that either man could have been responsible for the theft, as no evidence could be found to link the crime to anyone else."

"That was why you were watching the house. On the lookout for anything unusual in the bank manager's behaviour."

"Quite right."

"And then I came along."

"Indeed. I have been watching surgeons and medical men come and go at that house for much of the week, but your appearance proved the most hopeful event to have taken place since the girl was taken ill."

"That is kind of you to say so, Holmes."

"Think nothing of it, Watson. It is merely my personal observation."

"Although it is my professional opinion that the illness is more likely to have been caused by poisoning."

"What makes you say that?"

"Observation and deduction," I replied. "Elementary, Holmes."

"Hmm." He smiled, and inclined his head slightly.

"The symptoms, including headaches, stomach pains, vomiting, and diarrhea, might just as easily have resulted from poisoning by a salt of some heavy metal."

"And you have one particular culprit in mind?"

"Precisely. But I am not prepared to name it at this time. Not until I am sure."

"I have a certain expertise when it comes to the detection of poisons," said Holmes modestly. "I would be more than happy to accompany you on your next visit to that house. My opinion might prove useful to you."

The following morning, I paid another visit to Number Eighteen Morpeth Square. And this time I was accompanied by Sherlock Holmes.

Here was a district of the capital city which displayed affluence and privilege. Simple and secluded, yet with an air of quality and self-confidence. The houses had been built in terraces along three sides of a rectangle, with the entrance at the far end of the square. Separated from the road by a row of iron railings, with a front door approached by a flight of stone steps, each house looked out onto a small public garden occupying the center of the square. A couple of elderly men and were wandering among the shrubs, bushes, and flowerbeds. Others were sitting on the benches set out along the footpaths. I found it difficult to envisage Sherlock Holmes spending several hours here acting – and indeed working – as the gardener in that place.

The maid opened the door to Holmes's knock, and invited us both to step inside. We waited in the morning room until the door opened and Mr. Edlingholm himself stood in the entrance. He was a big man with auburn side-whiskers and the appearance of one who has achieved comfortable success in life. At this moment, however, his face exhibited considerable mental strain.

"Mr. Holmes," said he. "It is good to see you again." The two men shook hands. "Have you made any progress with that terrible business at the bank?"

"Not yet, Mr. Edlingholm," replied Holmes. "But I am sure Scotland Yard is making every effort at this moment to locate your money and to bring the thief to justice. Today, however, I am here to assist my colleague, Dr. Watson."

The bank manager turned to me, and raised his eyebrows as though enquiring as to the purpose of our visit.

"I should like to examine your daughter again, Mr. Edlingholm," I told the man.

"Amy? Yes. She has shown no signs of improvement since your visit yesterday, Dr. Watson. As we told you, the previous physician indicated cholera. You yourself examined her and said nothing to contradict his opinion."

"Having given the matter my full consideration since I was last here, I am prepared to do so now," I replied. "I'm hoping to explore another possible cause of your daughter's illness. May we have your permission to revisit the sick-room?"

"Certainly. My wife is sitting at the bedside."

The air in the little girl's bedroom felt stuffy and oppressive. The heavy drapes covering much of the closed window made the room appear dark and dismal. On one side of the room stood a dark-brown wardrobe. On the other side stood a simple washstand. The ambient color of the room was green. Woodwork throughout the room had been painted green. The walls of the bedroom were covered with an expensive paper, thick in texture, with raised decorations of flowers in bright green. A green coverlet lay across the sickbed, wherein lay the little girl, looking pale and sickly.

"Amy loves that wallpaper," said Mr. Edlingholm as he noticed my interest in it. "She finds the texture comforting, and she strokes it lovingly every night."

Holmes looked at the wallpaper, and then towards me.

I nodded. The very same thought was evidently occupying both our minds.

The child's mother rose from her chair beside the bed, and greeted us. "Dr. Watson. It is good of you to come again so soon."

"I have brought a friend with me this time," I told her. "Mr. Sherlock Holmes."

"The detective?"

"On this occasion, here as a colleague."

She turned to face Holmes. "But what about the theft from my husband's bank? Are you not helping out with that investigation, Mr. Holmes?"

"That is another matter entirely, Mrs. Edlingholm," said Holmes. "Today, I am concerned with Amy's health."

Leaving Holmes to inspect the wallpaper, I took a second the chair and examined the little girl. "Good morning, Amy."

"Good morning, Dr. Watson."

"How do you feel today?"

With her eyes fixed upon Sherlock Holmes, she tried to smile. "Still sick."

I proceeded to give the child a thorough physical examination.

"She still has moments when her mind is disturbed," said Mrs. Edlingholm.

"That is understandable," I told her.

"She keeps imagining somebody coming into the bedroom during the night."

"Her father, perhaps?"

"No. Someone she doesn't recognize."

"The sick mind can play the most amazing tricks upon us," I explained, soothingly.

After several minutes, I stood up, looked down at the child, and announced my diagnosis. "I am convinced that Amy is not suffering from cholera, or any other contagious disease."

Her mother appeared relieved by this news.

"I believe, however, that something else is making her ill," I continued. "I feel that I know what it is, but I'm not prepared to commit myself until I'm certain. Whether I am correct or not, I would like you to remove Amy from this room."

"Remove her from the bedroom?" Her mother sounded shocked. "But she is far too sick to move, Dr. Watson."

"Nevertheless," I returned, "I believe it is essential for the recovery of her health."

The mother nodded. "In that case, I shall arrange the matter when you have gone."

"Arrange the matter now," I told her.

After a moment's pause, Mrs. Edlingholm opened the bedroom door and called out, "Molly."

The housemaid appeared in the doorway almost at once. "Ma'am?"

"Arrange the settee in the lounge. We're going to transfer Amy to sleep down there for a while."

Still examining the wallpaper, but being careful not to touch it, Holmes took out his pocket-knife, scraped away a sample of the green decoration, and proceeded to drop it onto a sheet of paper torn from his pocket-book. He then folded it up and tucked away beneath his coat. He next scraped away some of the paintwork, and added a small sample of this to his inner pocket. Holmes turned to the girl's father. "How long have you had this wallpaper, Mr. Edlingholm?"

"We had it hung just before we moved in here."

"That must be no more than three months ago," Holmes determined.

"That's about right, Mr. Holmes."

"And the paintwork?"

"A similar length of time."

"And Amy has been sleeping in this room all that time?"

"Indeed. And becoming frailer by the day."

"I agree with Dr. Watson," said Holmes. "I believe it is imperative that we remove the girl to a more secure environment as soon as possible."

Whilst I opened the window, allowing the outside air to refresh the heavy atmosphere of the sick-room, Mr. Edlingholm picked up the little girl, together with her bedclothes, and carried her from the bedroom.

"I need to undertake some investigation," I told her girl's parents once I was sure the girl was comfortably settled, "but I'll return later in the day."

On our return to 221b Baker Street, I went immediately in search of my medical books, and returned to the sitting room a few minutes later with an armful of learned tomes.

"Well, Watson," said Holmes. "What says your professional opinion?"

"I am increasingly convinced of my medical diagnosis," I told him. "But I await to hear your opinion first, Holmes."

"Then you shall have it," said he, gathering together some of his scientific equipment and arranging it upon the dining table. "You have no doubt heard of the Marsh Test."

"I have certainly heard of it," I told him. "But, if you intend to carry out such a procedure here, it would undoubtedly be safer to have the fresh air before we start." I opened the window and allowed the warm summer air, together with the raucous noise of the Baker Street traffic, to invade the quiet stillness of our room. It seemed strange to me that the ordinary world should continue to turn whilst we delved into the mysterious chemistry of poison.

Holmes turned his attention to the apparatus now assembled on the table. "As you can see, Watson, I have set up an asymmetrical U-tube, held in place by a wooden clamp."

"Indeed."

"The longer end of the tube remains open, whilst the shorter end is fitted with a narrow glass tube secured by a simple cork bung. This glass tube tapers to a narrow aperture at the end, and is fitted with a tap halfway along its length, allowing gas to flow from the tube toward the end of the opening."

"I'm following you," I told him.

"Before closing the tap, I admit into the bottom of the tube a small amount of diluted hydrochloric acid, together with several small pieces of zinc."

"Producing an immediate chemical reaction," I observed. "Bubbles of hydrogen gas."

"Then, in order to prove that we have no contaminants in the tube, I close the tap, and wait for the hydrogen gas to build up inside the U-tube. When the pressure inside the tube has built up sufficiently to push the acid up the open end, I turn the tap, and allow some of the gas to escape through the narrow aperture. I then apply a lighted match to the resulting gas."

I watched carefully as the experiment proceeded. "Which burns with an almost invisible flame."

Holmes took up a white, glazed saucer, and held it against the flame. "See, Watson, the flame leaves the white surface unmarked. This verifies the purity of the ingredients," he explained. "Now, I extinguish the flame, close the tap, and repeat the experiment, but this time adding to the U-tube the scraping I took from the sickroom wallpaper earlier today."

I watched with keen interest as Holmes opened the folded paper, and poured the green powder into the U-tube. For several few minutes, we both stood watching the chemical reaction.

"Once again," continued Holmes, "the gas in the closed end of the tube has built up sufficiently to cause the liquid in the open end to rise."

I nodded. "Just as on the previous occasion."

"Now, I open the tap, and apply a flame to the resulting gas."

"Which now burns with a very slight mauve-tinged flame."

"This time, when I apply the flame to the white saucer, it leaves a dark, silver-gray deposit. Indicating the presence of a metal."

"Which might turn out to be antimony."

"Then allow us to remove any doubt. I apply a small quantity of sodium hypochlorite solution to the deposit."

He picked up a bottle from the table beside him, and allowed a few drops to mix with the dark deposit. The silver-gray deposit rapidly dissolved.

"Now we must clean the equipment," announced Holmes, "and repeat the experiment using the scraping I took from the paint."

The result turned out to be similar to the previous sample.

"Once again, we take a further sample. This time of the girl's bodily fluids. I notice you have such a sample with you, Watson."

"Indeed. What sort of a doctor would I be without having collected a sample from my patient?"

This time, at the very moment that the silvery deposit dissolved, we looked at each other in triumph.

"Proof positive, Watson," declared Sherlock Holmes.

"The little girl is suffering from arsenic poisoning, absorbed from contact with her bedroom environment," I concluded. "Science confirming my own medical opinion."

On our return to Morpeth Square, we discovered that Mr. Edlingholm had returned to his place of business, and Amy was asleep in the front sitting room.

"It is a little too early to say," said her mother, "but Amy does appear to be calmer now that her bed has been made up downstairs."

I looked down at the sleeping child. "Mrs. Edlingholm, my colleague and I are now of the same opinion, that your daughter's illness has been caused not by any contagious disease, but by arsenic poisoning."

"Oh, dear!" The child's mother held her hand to her mouth, looking deeply disturbed by this news. "We've always tried to be so careful about what we feed to our daughter, Doctor."

"We are also agreed that the poison is coming from various items in her room – particularly the wallpaper. The coloring is heavily contaminated with arsenic."

"The green?"

"Indeed. Scheele's Green. Not only is it present in the wallpaper, but also in the paint work. I suspect also that it might also be present in some of the textiles in the room. The arsenic is being transmitted to Amy by small particles in the air, and through physical contact with the wallpaper and other contaminated items."

Mrs. Edlingholm looked even more shocked. "Poor Amy. What can we do to make her better, Dr. Watson?"

"You have already done the first thing necessary, which is to remove her from the source of the contamination – her bedroom. Down here, she can at least begin the process of recovery. I would suggest that you also open the windows, so that the fresh air can dilute the arsenic-filled air which has undoubtedly contaminated the entire house. After all, this is the middle of summer."

"If you consider it important, then we can certainly do that."

"Then we must cleanse her of all traces of the poison. To begin with, you must wash her down, from head to foot, to make sure none of the poison remains on her skin, threatening to enter her system. And wash all her clothing. Next, you must give her plenty of water to drink. This should help clear her stomach of any poison that she might have ingested. Then we need to cleanse her bloodstream. The inclusion of garlic in her diet would be one good way of helping with that."

"Garlic?"

"Indeed, if you can find a ready supply – even if only for a few days."

"Don't worry, Dr. Watson. If our daughter needs it, we can get hold of it for her. Is there anything else?"

"Oh, certainly. You must try to persuade her to drink plenty of milk." I reached into my bag and drew out a sheet of paper. "Here is a list of the kind of foods that will help. I shall leave it with you."

"I'm still concerned about that bedroom," said Holmes, who had been sitting quietly in the corner of the room. "Has the girl repeated her assertion that a man entered her bedroom?"

"Indeed, she has," replied Mrs. Edlingholm. "She insists that a man used to come into her room during the night."

"How often was that?"

"On a number of occasions during the last few weeks, Mr. Holmes."

"Hmm. Interesting. With your permission, I should like to make another inspection of the sickroom."

"Please, feel free to help yourself."

I stood in the doorway of the now-empty bedroom, whilst Holmes once more examined the wallpaper.

"What are you looking for now?" I enquired. "You have already tested samples of the pigment."

Holmes was holding a magnifying lens in his hand as he now examined the surface of the paper. "Somebody has been making holes in this paper. Extremely carefully. Whoever was here has cut thin vertical slits, as though with a sharp razor."

"How extraordinary! Are you sure?"

"Oh, the matter is beyond doubt. I can only conjecture that whoever it was had been looking for something hidden beneath the surface layer. See how thick and bulky the paper appears."

"It might simply be the high quality of the paper they used."

Holmes opened up his pocket-knife and slid the blade beneath the wallpaper. "Watson, would you please ask the maid to bring me a bowl of warm water and a sponge?"

I watched carefully as, a few minutes later, Holmes applied water to the edges of the wallpaper roll, and eased the edge of the paper away from the wall. "There is definitely a gap under here," said Holmes. "Only the edges of the paper have been properly secured to the wall."

Intrigued, I watched him carefully. "Is anything hidden underneath?"

"I am sure of it. Do you happen to have a pair of forceps with you?"

I opened my medical bag, drew out a pair of forceps, and handed them to Holmes.

"Now we shall see," he said as he pushed the forceps between the paper and the plaster behind.

I watched with growing astonishment as my friend slowly withdrew the forceps, together with a sheet of white paper. "What have you found?" I asked.

He held the paper up to the light, and examined it carefully. "A Bank of England banknote," he declared, handing it to me.

Holmes repeated the operation, and had soon retrieved a further two banknotes from behind the wallpaper, which he handed to me.

I examined the notes now in my hands. One was to the value of twenty pounds, whereas the other two were valued at fifty pounds each. "Could this be Edlingholm's own personal bank deposit?" I submitted.

"I am sorry to say, Watson that we may well have uncovered some of the money stolen from his bank earlier this year. Scotland Yard are bound to come to the conclusion that Edlingholm concealed the money here himself."

That was indeed the conclusion that Inspector Lestrade reached when we visited him at Scotland Yard later that afternoon. This shrewd, rodent-faced policeman had already proved himself to be a good detective, and he was already developing a guarded respect for the skills Sherlock Holmes had exhibited on more than one occasion.

"I have to admit, Mr. Holmes, you have done an exceptionally good job in finding these banknotes," said the inspector. "The numbers tally precisely with some of those missing from the bank. Although, it has to be admitted, these are not the first we have come across."

"Really?" Holmes's ears pricked up. "Have others surfaced?"

"Only the occasional one or two, and all within the last couple of days. They were paid in at large stores across London – and one at the Dorchester Hotel for a meal. Another was furnished in payment for a bank loan. But by the time we were able to respond to both occasions, the person in possession of the banknotes was long-gone, leaving no trace whatsoever of his identity."

"What do you intend to do next, Lestrade?" asked Holmes.

"You need hardly ask a question like that. We have no choice but to arrest Mr. Edlingholm on suspicion of stealing that money from his own bank and concealing it upon his own premises."

"And why do you imagine he would have taken such a risk?"

"That is one of the questions he will need to answer. Both here, and in a court of law."

"If you intend to arrest Mr. Edlingholm, then I would ask you to refrain from passing this information on to the gentlemen of the Press – at least for the next forty-eight hours."

Lestrade rubbed his chin thoughtfully. "I suppose you have been helpful with this case, Mr. Holmes, so I think I can allow you twenty-four hours. But then I shall need to bring my suspect before the magistrate, in open session. The Press will inevitably be there."

"Then we have just one day," said Holmes, turning to me. "Let us make sure we use our time in the best possible manner."

We returned to Baker Street in a dejected frame of mind, myself thoughtful of my patient, my colleague brooding over the unenviable task before him. Holmes filled the bowl of his churchwarden with a plug of shag, and was soon enveloped in a thick cloud of smoke. We both sat silently staring into space.

Holmes eventually broke the silence. "On the surface, Edlingholm's guilt appears to be sealed. But can we really believe that he would steal the money from his own bank and then hide it in his own daughter's bedroom?"

"The idea seems preposterous," I replied. "It's hardly the sort of devious trick in which a doting father would involve his only daughter."

"And yet, Lestrade was right. The questions need to be asked, and answered."

I was distracted from my thoughts by the sound of two pairs of footsteps on the stairs outside our rooms. The door opened to reveal Mrs. Hudson.

"Mr. Holmes. There is a lady here to see you."

"Very well, Mrs. Hudson. Please show her in."

With all the fluster of a whirlwind, in stormed Mrs. Edlingholm. "Mr. Holmes," she roared. "What have you been doing? No doubt you are aware that the police have arrested my husband, on suspicion of stealing the bank's money. They tell me that you discovered it hidden behind the wallpaper in my daughter's bedroom."

Without rising from his seat by the window, Holmes nodded. "That is true."

"And you never thought to tell *me* about this?"

"With so many other problems besetting you, Mrs. Edlingholm, I did not wish to add to your worries."

"Not wish to add to my worries? How dare you! Anything that brings my husband into disrepute and threatens to send his wife and child into the workhouse has everything to do with me!"

"I do not think it will come to that."

"Really? Are you planning to come up with some amazing new piece of evidence to completely reverse the opinion of Scotland Yard?"

"It would not be the first time," replied Holmes.

"Or do you intend to wave a magic wand and set my husband free again?"

Holmes arose abruptly from his seat, clearly agitated, and wishing to calm this difficult state of affairs. "Maybe not a magic wand," said he, "but perhaps some information which you alone can provide."

"Me?" Mrs. Edlingholm scowled. "I don't see what more I can do to help you."

He fixed her with his steely stare. "Tell me about that wallpaper. The paper covering the walls in your daughter's bedroom."

For a moment, she turned her gaze away from him. "Until Dr. Watson informed me, I was totally unaware that it carried poison." Then she once more riveted him with her glare, "I would never knowingly have placed my daughter in any kind of peril."

"So I would imagine. And you have only been living in that house for the last three months."

"That is correct."

"Then I assume you had the place decorated before you moved in."

"That is also true. We were fortunate enough to be able to afford a professional decorator to come in and apply fresh paint and wallpaper to all the rooms."

"Then I need to know the name of the firm you employed to do the work."

"We were recommended a firm with offices in the West End – a firm called Paradise Home Adornment. A man called Wallace Goodwell is the proprietor there. He proved to be extremely helpful, and had the work completed in good time for our removal."

"Who recommended this firm to you?"

"My husband's Chief Cashier. Mr. Obadiah Mitchelson."

An expression of enlightenment lit up Holmes's face. "And did Mr. Mitchelson also employ this firm to decorate his own house?"

"That is what he told us, Mr. Holmes. Indeed, he invited us 'round to his house to see the quality of the work they had carried out for him. We went, and were so satisfied with the results that we decided to book Mr. Goodwell's firm to complete the decorations in our own new home."

"Which he proceeded to do."

"Indeed. I think he valued our business, and considered us priority customers."

"In that case, I think we ought to pay Goodwell a visit. What think you, Watson?"

"Indeed, I heartily concur."

"And I would like you to come along with us, Mrs. Edlingholm."

"You think my presence might be of value on this occasion?"

Holmes gave her a wry smile. "We need to reach the bottom of this business, and our visit to Paradise Home Adornment is where we have to now extend our search."

The moment we stepped outside into the scurry of Baker Street, Holmes hailed a cab which brought us presently to the entrance of a smart, glass-fronted shop bearing the name Paradise Home Adornment.

Holmes inspected the front of the premises. "Is this the place, Mrs. Edlingholm?"

"Yes. It doesn't appear to have changed in any way since I last visited the establishment."

Holmes opened the door, and led the way inside.

A smartly dressed man approached us. "Good afternoon."

"Good afternoon," returned Holmes. "Mr. Goodwell, I presume."

The man gave a slight bow of acknowledgement.

"I am Sherlock Holmes, and this is my colleague, Dr. Watson. And I believe you already know Mrs. Edlingholm."

"Certainly. Good afternoon." Turning back to Holmes, he continued, "How may I be of assistance?"

"I am interested in the work you recently carried out at the home of Mr. and Mrs. Edlingholm."

"I hope all is well."

"Sadly," said Holmes, "it turns out that the wallpaper put up in their little girl's bedroom is impregnated with arsenic, and it has been poisoning the child."

"Are you certain?"

"The matter is beyond doubt," I responded. "Along with some of the paint employed."

"Dear me," said the man. "I had no idea it would put anybody's life in danger. Believe me, we do our best to provide the public with the materials they require, making sure they are of the very highest quality. Those new colors are extremely popular nowadays. So vibrant. So lively. They bring light and brightness to rooms which have always been shaded in darkness."

"An admirable ambition," said Holmes. "But I would urge you to be more circumspect in your choice of the materials you employ."

The man appeared suitably humbled.

"However, that is not the matter which brings us here today."

"Then perhaps you'd better come with me to my office at the back of our store," said Goodwell, looking around him at the other staff and customers. "We can speak there freely and without the danger of being interrupted."

Once seated in the office, Holmes leaned forward, stared at the proprietor, and came to the point of our visit. "I need to know from you, Mr. Goodwell, who it was who carried out the decorating work at the Edlingholm property. You must be able to provide me with that information."

Mr. Goodwell stood up, reached to the shelving above him, and brought down a large, leather-bound ledger. "We employ teams of workers to carry out the decorations, Mr. Holmes. Groups of two or three men, each detailed to a separate district of the city. It is an efficient method of working, and has resulted in nothing but approbation from our clients. Until now."

"Are you able to give me the names of those who worked on this particular project?"

Goodwell searched through his records. "Ah, yes, here we are. Two of our men worked on the property. William Ardley was the foreman. And a man called Harris Greep helped him with the work."

"What do you know of them?"

"Ardley is a responsible and trustworthy employee who has been with our firm for many years. Of the other man, I know very little. He has been carrying out some casual work for us during the last year – learning the trade as he went along, is what he told us. Which was just as well, because, sadly, Bill Ardley's usual assistant was killed in a tragic accident shortly before work began on one particularly important job."

"Where was that piece of work carried out?"

"At the home of Mr. Mitchelson, Mr. Edlingholm's Chief Cashier. We were delighted when Mr. Greep stepped in at extremely short notice to help complete the assignment. A very nice job of work he made of it, as well."

"You say the man who was supposed to help with the work was killed."

"That is correct. A very nasty accident. You might remember it. He was standing among the bustling crowd on the platform of the underground railway at Paddington Station when he slipped and fell beneath the wheels of an approaching train."

"Yes, I remember reading about it," I told him. "A nasty business."

"Are you sure it was an accident?" Holmes asked him.

Mr. Goodwell appeared shocked. "Dear me, Mr. Holmes, are you suggesting he might have been pushed to his death? That really is a thought too terrible to contemplate."

"It is merely one line of enquiry," admitted Holmes.

"The police have always considered his death to be an accident."

Holmes nodded. "Of course."

Sherlock Holmes and I returned with Mrs. Edlingholm to her home in Morpeth Square, and she invited us inside. Little Amy, still lying in the front room, was giving every appearance of recovering slowly but steadily from her illness.

"I should like to pay another visit to the upper part of this house, Mrs. Edlingholm," said Holmes. "I believe there's something more to be discovered there."

"Certainly," she told him, "but I can't imagine what you have in mind."

"First, can you tell me what lies above? Is there an attic of some kind up there?"

"If there is, I have to admit, I've never been there to find out."

"Do you know of any trapdoor which might give access to a space above?"

"No. I can't recall ever having seen anything of the sort."

"And yet, there must be some such access," mused Holmes. "Do you happen to have a pair of kitchen steps?"

"Yes."

"May I borrow them for a few minutes?"

"Certainly, if you think they can be of any help."

118

I followed Holmes up to the landing immediately outside the green bedroom door, while Mrs. Edlingholm waited downstairs. I was keenly interested to discover his intention.

The landing area gave access to the master bedroom, and to other rooms on that upper level of the house. It also gave access to the rear of the house, and to the bedroom set aside for the use of the housemaid.

Holmes now stood on the landing, looking up at the ceiling. In the shadows, it appeared to be as professionally papered as the rest of the house.

"A-ha!" said he, setting the steps close to the rear side of the landing. Then he climbed them and pushed against the ceiling above him. I was amazed to see a section of the papered ceiling push upward on a hinge, and fall over softly onto the ceiling joists somewhere in the darkness.

Holmes heaved himself up to the opening and peered through. "Now, this is very interesting," came his report, as he allowed a coil of rope to drop through the gap. A length of knotted rope now reached from the floor to the opening above.

"Do you need a light?" I called up to him.

"Not at the moment," he replied. "There appears to be plenty of illumination provided by a skylight in the roof above my head – and a number of others along the full length of this terrace. This is undoubtedly the means of ingress and egress for Amy's night-time visitor."

I watched Holmes disappear up into the attic space and decided to follow. I climbed the steps until I could see over the lip of the trapdoor, looking along the entire length of the highest part of the entire row of houses. Weaving its way between buttress walls and chimney stacks, a passageway led as far as I could see. Rough-hewn planks of wood had been laid down along its length, to establish a secure passageway. I could see Holmes in the distance, kneeling down and examining the wooden surface.

"What have you found now?" I called.

"A skylight above each of the houses illuminates a trapdoor leading down into the dwelling. Most show no signs of recent use, but one or two have rope handles attached to them for easy raising."

"Can you see any trace of the intruder?"

Holmes returned and followed me down the steps until we were once more standing on the landing directly outside the girl's bedroom. There Holmes took out his pocketbook and showed me a few scraps of wool. "The intruder had to make his way along that passage at night, and as silently as possible, in order to avoid being detected from below. In order to accomplish that, he had to make his way in stockinged feet. As a result, he has left traces of wool caught on splinters attached to the boards."

"Is that significant?"

"In itself, maybe not. It merely proves that somebody has been up there in the fairly recent past, attempting to move as silently as possible."

Holmes thanked Mrs. Edlingholm for allowing him to investigate and led the way outside. There, we stood in the roadway and looked up at the top of the terrace buildings. "You can see the skylights from here, Watson. But where does that passageway lead?"

I looked along the street. "To the left, it ends at a blank gable-end."

"No, no," said Holmes. "The wool from his stockinged feet lay in the other direction."

We made our way to the far end of the terrace. "Now what do you see, Watson?"

"By George! It's a tobacconist's shop, adjoined to the end of the terrace – a place that might well remain unoccupied during the night. But how would our intruder make his way in there at will?"

We made our way round to the back of the shop. "There you are, Watson," cried Holmes triumphantly. "A side-entrance, leading directly from the access lane and into the back yard."

"Harry Greep?" said Inspector Lestrade, when we informed him of our progress in the case. "Now there's a name that rings a bell, as loud and clear as Big Ben himself."

"I remember the name from our initial investigation into the bank robbery." said Holmes.

"Indeed, you would, Mr. Holmes," said the detective. "He was one of our strongest suspects at first. But when we made our investigations, he came out cleaner than a shirt fresh back from the laundry. He even demanded that we search his house from top to bottom."

"Always a suspicious thing for a criminal to do," I replied.

"Naturally, you found nothing," said Holmes.

"Not only did he have none of those missing banknotes on the premises, but he appeared to be more in debt than in credit with the local commercial traders."

"I seem to remember he had been in trouble before."

"He has quite a record, has our Harry," said Lestrade, "but he told me he was now a reformed character. Said he had turned over a new leaf and was learning a new trade."

"That is certainly true," said Holmes. "He seems to have become an expert in wallpaper-hanging."

"That doesn't sound like Harry Greep. The fellow's as bent as a hairpin – one of a network of villains who make a habit of targeting the vulnerable across London."

Holmes nodded. "And since then, you have made no progress at all with the case."

"And neither have you, Mr. Holmes."

"But now we have a connection between an employee of the London and South Coast Bank, and a member of the criminal fraternity – a connection through the Chief Cashier."

"And not a scrap of evidence to be used against him."

"But enough to cast doubt on your accusation that Mr. Edlingholm was responsible for the theft."

"That remains to be seen."

Holmes returned a knowing smile. "I'm certain the Chief Cashier is not our man. But if we can catch this fellow, Greep, in the act of retrieving some of his stolen banknotes, would that be sufficient to allow you to release the Bank Manager?"

"It would unquestionably cast the case in an entirely new and very different light, Mr. Holmes."

"Capital! Then allow me to place an article in the local evening papers, warning people of the dangers of arsenic poisoning in wallpaper, and suggesting they redecorate their houses immediately. I shall make no mention of the Edlingholm's home, but the thief, whoever it turns out to be, will want to remove the evidence before the walls can be stripped and the money uncovered."

"Very well. When do you anticipate he might come to collect those notes?"

"As soon as ever possible, I should imagine. Perhaps as early as tonight "

"Then we must be ready for him."

We gathered at the Edlingholm home late that evening. The shorter nights of summer meant that our time would be limited, but we still had to be prepared to remain there all night if necessary. Holmes asked to borrow my service revolver, a request to which I readily acceded.

Lestrade had come with five of his most reliable constables. "I'll take my place in the green bedroom," he announced.

"In that case," said Holmes, "I elect to remain at the rear of the tobacconist's shop, ready to apprehend our man if he manages to escape your clutches. However, I would value the use of two of your constables, Lestrade. Perhaps Rand and Murcher, by choice."

"You may have them, although I doubt that you will need them."

"And I shall leave Watson with you."

As the darkness deepened and, as a local church clock chimed off the early hours, I stood with Inspector Lestrade in the darkest corner of the bedroom. The door stood open so we could see the landing. The three remaining constables waited in a room on the other side of the landing, ready to emerge when summoned. Lestrade had a lantern on the floor beside him, closed on all sides, and turned down low.

At what must have been the darkest hour of the night, we were disturbed by a scuffling sound coming from the roof-space above us. The trapdoor, which I had seen opened from below by Sherlock Holmes, now hinged upward, and the knotted rope dropped abruptly but noiselessly down into the landing.

In the light of the moon shining through the window, I observed a dark figure climb down the rope as nimbly as a monkey and step silently into the green bedroom, only feet away from where we stood. The man seemed to know his way around in the darkness, and I half-expected him to see us and make his immediate escape. Instead, he turned his attention to the wallpaper directly opposite the window and ran his hand along the paper. The steel of a cutthroat razor flashed as the man proceeded to make a slit down the paper.

I would have pounced upon the man at once, but Lestrade held me back, and shook his head.

Even with the man's back against the outside light, I could see him extract something from behind the wallpaper. Now we had the man in possession of the stolen money, Lestrade opened the lantern, and held it high. "Hello, Harry."

The intruder turned abruptly to face the policeman, and the constables as they entered from the landing. His face showed both surprise and terror.

In the ensuing confusion, Greep threw himself toward the rope and climbed up it at a remarkable speed.

When two of the constables set off in pursuit, I realized they had little chance of catching up with the little man. Our only hope now lay with Holmes at the tobacconist's shop. Lestrade had come to the same conclusion, and followed me as I hurried down the stairs, and ran out through the front door and down the street.

We arrived at the rear of the shop to find Sherlock Holmes holding my revolver and facing the intruder, now securely in the hands of the two constables assigned to accompany him.

"Harris Greep," said Lestrade, "I am arresting you on suspicion of theft and murder."

Greep glared back. "I went to great lengths to keep my business secret. How did you manage to find out what I was doing?"

"We had a little help from Mr. Sherlock Holmes here."

Greep glared at Holmes. "Life for us criminals is bad enough without amateurs like you getting involved in crime detection. Why couldn't you keep your nose out of my business?"

"Your business has gone on long enough, Greep," returned Holmes. "This has been the result of long-term planning on your part. You decided to concentrate upon the inhabitants of wealthier streets, such as Morpeth Square, and the sort of people who could afford to pay for the professional decoration of their homes. You inveigled your way into working for a decorating firm, and became proficient at wallpaper-hanging. You waited for the right chance to come along, which it surely would.

"When you heard that the Chief Cashier at the London and South Coast Bank wanted his house redecorating, you went along to act as another hand, and you took the opportunity to make wax impressions of his bank keys. Then you waited. But your waiting proved short-term, because you heard that Mr. Edlingholm wanted his house decorating in view of his imminent removal there."

"This is all speculation," cried Greep.

"Not at all," replied Holmes. "It is merely deduction based upon the facts. I might even be able to place you at the scene of the death of the firm's previous wallpaper-hanger. You pushed him to his death beneath the wheels of an underground train, so you could step in and take his place with the decorating firm."

"You have no proof of any of this."

"Perhaps, but then you undertook the robbery and immediately set about hiding the stolen banknotes behind the paper on upper floor bedroom in several of the houses you were working on, both in Morpeth Square and other streets in that part of London."

"Which streets?" Greep challenged him.

"We'll find them easily enough," replied Lestrade bluntly.

"Now," continued Holmes, "with the stolen banknotes hidden, and with no way of linking them to yourself, you were able to enter the rooms from above whenever you needed to draw upon your stolen plunder. However, your luck ran out when you targeted the room of Mr. Edlingholm's daughter and the poisonous nature of the wallpaper was discovered. The Edlingholms will have to arrange for their child's bedroom to be redecorated. But I suspect they might select a different firm to undertake the work next time."

A few days later, as we traveled by cab along the side of Hyde Park on our way to Baker Street, we happened to notice the Edlingholm family standing together in the late summer sunshine, listening to a brass band concert.

"They look intensely happy together, do you not think?" I asked.

"Indeed, considering all they have gone through together in the last few months."

"And yet, about the case, I realize I am not yet in possession of all the facts."

"Are you not? What do you still wish to know?"

"I find it difficult to imagine that this fellow Greep has been working alone."

Holmes nodded sagely.

"Lestrade described him as part of a network of criminals working in the city. Who else was involved with him in this particular project? Was the decorating firm involved? Was Goodwell involved? And what about Ardley? Was he working with Greep in his nefarious scheme?"

"I think none of those," replied Holmes, as he sighed and stretched out his legs as far as they would go in the confined space of the cab. "Consider the tobacconist's shop."

"The tobacconist's? Do you mean the one at the corner of Morpeth Square?"

"Of course. If you wish to find a den of thieves, then I would suggest that shop, Watson. The time I spent watching the square was not confined to simply observing the Edlingholm household. I also paid close attention to those who frequented the tobacconist's shop, and I recognized among them several of the most notorious criminals in the city."

"I can hardly believe such a thing of a small shop in a prosperous and upmarket area of London. The place looks so innocent."

"And yet, it is true. I happened, on one occasion, to enter the shop, purporting to be in search of a particular brand of pipe tobacco. I recognized the man behind the counter as one who is high up on the wanted list of Scotland Yard."

"Did he recognize you?"

"Hardly. You yourself failed to see through my disguise as a common workman."

"Lestrade will want to make a number of arrests now," I ventured.

"When we sprung the trap and caught our thief, I fear the rest of the birds flew to other bushes."

"To be taken another day."

"Let us hope so, Watson."

"This completes another case for my journal," I cried. "The public shall learn the true story of the Green Room."

"And yet, just for the moment, we must allow Scotland Yard to enjoy the limelight of publicity."

"Even though the solving of this entire investigation was down to you, Holmes."

"It was a mere matter of observation and deduction," he said smiling genially. "The entire process was quite elementary, Watson."

The Case of the
Enthusiastic Amateur
by S.F. Bennett

It may come as no surprise to readers of the accounts of those cases which have been committed to posterity that amongst the correspondence received by Sherlock Holmes has invariably been numerous requests for advice on how one may pursue a similar career. I would not deny that, on paper at least, it appears to hold some attraction. There is a difference, however, between perception and reality, and in the gap between, therein lies disappointment. If I have been responsible, as Holmes oft reminds me, for presenting the life of a consulting detective as a thing of airy delight, then it falls to me to set the record straight. To those who would aspire to follow in my colleague's footsteps, I say with no hesitation it is no easy existence. In this, I speak from bitter experience.

So it was on a chill, raw morning in March 1883, when Holmes was away on the Continent on a case of the utmost delicacy, that my path happened to cross with an old acquaintance, Roger Thurston. It had been some time since I had seen him and I was struck by the change in him. The fresh-faced youth of my college days had been replaced by a man who wore his troubles openly, whether in the deeply-engraved creases of his forehead or the spider's web of fine lines etched around his mouth. Bruised beneath the eyes and pinched of cheek, his air was one of deep suffering. I had known tribulations enough in the years that had separated our last meeting to have some sympathy with his plight, and at my urging we found ourselves a table at the nearest public house and shared our troubles over what the landlord claimed to be his finest brew.

"To tell you the truth, Watson," he confided after we had covered the initial pleasantries, "I'm in a devil of a mess."

"Personal?" I enquired.

"Were it that simple!" said he. "It's more serious than that. You remember I used to dabble in stocks and shares?"

I did. I also remembered how he had advised me to invest in a honey farm on one occasion. I saw nothing for my consideration save a few jars of rancid produce that would have put any respectable bee to shame.

"Well, I became rather good at it," he continued. "I made a fortune on coal." He grimaced. "Then lost it on aluminium. It happens," he said ruefully. "One has to take a longer view of these things."

I said nothing. A distant memory came back to me of a younger Thurston saying much the same thing when he told me the honey farm had gone out of business.

"After that, I turned my attention away from metals to agriculture. Well, it seemed like a safer bet. Everyone needs to eat, after all. I did very well for a time too. For a while, I could do no wrong. I had clients – rich, influential clients, Watson, not your average clerk with a few pounds to invest." He drained the last of his ale and stared dismally at the residue gathering at the bottom of the glass. "Then came the years of bad harvest, and we couldn't compete with imported grain prices. People lost a great deal of money and my name has been mud ever since."

"I am sorry to hear that," said I. Indeed, I was. Thurston, for all his faults, had no malice in him, and I imagined he had taken the losses to heart. I had every certainty he had believed at the time his investment choices were correct. If anything was to be questioned, it was his judgement, not his probity.

"Oh, it isn't so bad," he replied, forcing a smile. "Some people still believe in me."

There was something about his tone of voice that put me on my guard. Thurston was possessed of a great deal of charm. I imagined it was how he had persuaded so many to put their faith in him in the first place.

"I am a little short myself," I said. "If it is money you want, I cannot help you."

"No, it's nothing like that. Although money would be useful, I won't deny."

"Then what is the problem?"

"Another of my investments." He shook his head. "It seemed like a good idea at the time."

"It always does. What was it?"

"Shares in a cab business." He must have seen my expression. "Don't look at me like that," said he. "Food and transport are always safe investments."

"Apparently not."

"Do you know how many cab licences were issued in London last year?" said he earnestly. "Nigh on ten-thousand."

I confess the figure took me aback. "As many as that?"

"People will always need transport. There's many folk would like their own carriage, but until the day they can afford them, they have to travel in cabs like the rest of us."

I could not deny the truth of what Thurston said. All the same, I couldn't shake the impression he was trying to sell me something.

"Do I take it you bought a cab?"

He stifled a laugh. "Don't be silly, Watson."

I acknowledged it was an elementary error on my part. The thought of Thurston doing a hard day's work in any capacity was risible.

"Just over two years ago, I came by information that a cab business in Hoxton needed extra capital for vehicles. The proprietor's name was Mandergast, and after a little checking, I found he had a viable business with twenty-nine cabs which he rented out on a regular basis. Now, I ask you, sixteen shillings a day for a growler, a few shillings a day extra for a hansom – well, it all adds up."

"I'm sure it does. Then what is the problem?"

Thurston pulled an unhappy face. "I found an investor willing to provide the funds for a thirty-five-per-cent share of the business."

"You took a commission, naturally."

"Yes." He squirmed in his seat. "Twenty-per-cent. Not unreasonable," he added quickly. "I had to have something for my trouble. Well, things were going well until three months ago. Then the business was beset by one problem after another: Accidents, fines, unexplainable damage to the cabs, horses ill with influenza, and so on. Profits fell, and my client wasn't getting the return he expected."

"Isn't that the nature of speculation?"

"Quite." There was a note of reticence in his voice. I suspected there was more to this story than he was telling. At my urging, he finally relented. "Because of my past record, I had to give this man certain assurances, that I could guarantee the return on his investment for a period of no less than three years."

"That was unwise," I said. "I gather this part of the agreement did not appear in the contract."

"Contract?" He stared at me as though I was being unreasonable. "There was no formal contract. This was a gentleman's agreement, sealed with a handshake. My client has peculiar ideas when it comes to money – especially his own."

"Which makes me question why you became involved with him in the first place."

"What else could I do? I have to live."

"In that case, you have to cut your cloth according to your purse."

Thurston bridled at this. "That might be all very well for some, but why should I accept second best? All I needed was a safe investment. Mr. Llewellyn, my client, had the capital. It seemed ideal. Who could have predicted this would happen?" He sighed heavily. "It could be worse, I suppose," he went on. "At least Mandergast has agreed to return Llewellyn's original investment in full, although the business is worth less now."

"Most generous of him. How much will you still owe your client?"

"Just over £300."

I caught my breath.

"I have it, but the capital is tied up elsewhere and I cannot touch it. Not to mince matters, Llewellyn isn't a man who likes to be kept waiting. He's given me until close of business on Friday to come up with the money."

I could imagine what failure on Thurston's part might entail. "Or else?"

"Well, he has threatened to break both my legs." He ran his hands through his hair. "It's the way my luck goes. If I invested in a graveyard, I'm sure people would stop dying."

He had my sympathy, but there was little else I could suggest, apart from an urgent need to put distance between himself and the egregious Mr. Llewellyn.

"If only the business hadn't failed," said he, shaking his head. "I'll be honest with you, Watson, I find it mightily peculiar. Mandergast's family has been in the carriage business for over a hundred years. There has never been greater demand for vehicles for hire."

"You suspect foul play?"

He shrugged. "I did wonder if a rival might be trying to put him out of business. Mandergast says not, and I dare say he would know. The truth is, all I know about cabs is how to hail one. If I could prove someone was intentionally trying to ruin Mandergast, it might buy me more time with Llewellyn."

I began to see a way in which I might be able to help Thurston. For all his ill-advised dealings, I would not have liked to see him come to harm.

"I have an acquaintance," I said. "He is a consulting detective."

"I couldn't afford to hire him," he cut in.

"I dare say not. In any case, he is out of the country at present."

"Then how—"

"I am not unfamiliar with his methods, Thurston. I could look into this affair for you."

The light of gratitude flared in his desperate eyes. "Would you? I'd be in your debt."

I gave him my assurance that I would do all I could. With that, we parted. As I headed home, I started to have my misgivings. In the cold light of day, what had appeared to be a good idea at the time seemed fraught with difficulties. Today was Wednesday. On Friday, Llewellyn would call on Thurston for his pound of flesh. I had no time to waste on idle doubts.

It seemed to me that the best course of action was to determine how Holmes would approach the case. Mandergast was the first person to interview. I did wonder how receptive he would be to being interrogated by a stranger about the failure of his business. Equally, if someone did have a vendetta against him, then the other cabmen might well be able to shed some light on the identity of such a person. A fanciful notion took shape in my mind about how I could enter their world and gain the information I needed without raising their suspicions.

Accordingly, I delved into Holmes's cache of disguises and found myself a set of ginger whiskers and a threadbare Inverness cape of indeterminate pattern. I completed my appearance with a disreputable hat which had seen better days, a waistcoat which had once been my bullpup's bed of choice, and a gaudy yellow neckerchief. When I inspected my appearance in the mirror, I appeared the very image of every jobbing cabman I had ever seen. Pleased with what I saw, I affirmed my approval in my finest east of Aldgate accent and doffed my hat in farewell to my amiable reflection.

An hour later, I had presented myself at Scotland Yard at the Public Carriage Office. After a brief interview as to my suitability and knowledge of the principal routes and points of interest in London, I emerged clutching my one-day licence. From there, I took a cab to Hoxton and, much to the consternation of my cabman, alighted at the premises of the Mandergast Carriage Company.

The yard itself was set in a side street dominated by red-brick factories and furniture workshops. Away from the main thoroughfare, the looming edifices of industry seemed to block out the very light, casting the rows of stables behind their sturdy gate into permanent gloom. It might have been my fancy, but I couldn't shake the impression that an air of despondency hung over the premises – even the very dogs seemed too lethargic to stir themselves when I entered. Straw drifted across the grassy cobbles from empty stalls and gaps in the sheds where cabs once had been housed told of the business's decline.

A squat building which I took to be the office at the rear of the yard seemed to be my natural destination until I was arrested by the sight of a sturdy, middle-aged man, bristling with greying whiskers emerging from one of the stables leading a limping bay horse with a hollow back. Close on his heels came a tall, loose-limbed younger man, wearing a battered tweed suit and hat set at a jaunty angle. The first man brought the horse to a halt and ran his hands down the hind legs.

"Spavined, as I thought," said he, shaking his head. "He'll never sell looking like that. All right, Jimmy, you'll have to get him over to the knacker's yard. Get what you can for him."

130

He straightened and caught sight of me. There was a momentary pause as he looked me up and down.

"And what can we do for you?" said he.

"Mr. Mandergast?" I asked.

"That's me," he grunted in reply.

"I want to hire one of your cabs."

The younger man came round from the other side of the horse to look at me. I saw a glance pass between him and the cab master.

"And what will you be wanting? A hansom or a four-wheeler?" asked Mandergast.

"A hansom."

"I see." He sniffed loudly. "Ever driven one afore?"

"Many times," I lied. "I have my licence."

"Good. You wouldn't be taking one of my cabs without one. Jimmy, get Hector ready for the gent. Now, Mr. . . . ?"

"Watson," I replied.

"Mr. Watson," Mandergast continued, "what made you come to me?"

"I was recommended."

He gazed at me down the length of his nose. "Now who would do a thing like that?"

"Another cabbie," I said. "He said you had the best horses this side of London."

Mandergast made a noise at the back of his throat. "That might have been true once. Times are hard, Mr. Watson. Take a look at Achilles here." He patted the lame horse on the neck. "You wouldn't think his grandsire was a Derby winner, would you? I always had thoroughbreds for the hansoms. Ex-racehorses, all of them. The customers liked the look of them, made them think they had a bit of speed in them. Now they're only fit for the cat's meat man."

"You're selling off your horses?"

"I have to. The business is on its knees. I blame the middle classes."

I struggled to contain my surprise. "Indeed?"

"Everyone wants their own carriage these days. If the neighbours run their own carriage, then they have to have one. Then there's the independents, wanting to run their own cabs and put us large owners out of business." He was warming to his subject and would not be denied. "You know who else I blame? These doctors keep talking about infection. I ask you, is it the driver's fault if he has to take people to the hospital in his cab? Now, in the olden days, you had your plague and your miasma. You knew where you were. Nowadays, it's 'fever' and 'filth in the water'. My great-grandfather drank water straight from the Thames for years and never did him any harm. He lived till he was eighty-four."

131

I imagined he was the exception rather than the rule. I kept my peace, however, smiled, and said nothing.

"Saying that, if you get anyone asking if the cab is clean, you can tell them from me I have 'em all washed down every night with carbolic."

"Do you?"

The look he gave me suggested that I should have known better than to ask.

"So," he said, appraising my appearance yet again, "you're doing a night shift, are you? Well, you come back here at two o'clock for a fresh horse. You got your oats?"

He must have seen my puzzled expression.

"For the horse. You've got to feed the beast." He grabbed a stained feed bag from the corner of the yard and thrust into my hands. "Don't know much about horses, do you? Tell me, Mr. Watson, what really brought you here?"

"As you said, Mr. Mandergast, times are hard. I need the extra income."

"Well, mind you stay out of trouble. The police have been harassing my drivers lately. Have you got the Authorised Book of Fares with you?"

I pretended I had, and thought myself lucky when Mandergast didn't ask for proof. I had decided it was unnecessary for one night's work. As I would be out of pocket for the hire of the vehicle, I saw no virtue in throwing good money away after bad on books and tables of fares. I had no intention of collecting customers in any case.

Mandergast's attention was drawn away from me by the clatter of hooves. His assistant had led a grey gelding into the yard and was busy backing it up into the shafts of a cab.

"Now this here is Hector," said Mandergast. "He'll take good care of you."

"A fine beast," I said. "Named after the Trojan warrior naturally."

"No, after my wife's dog." He gave me a withering glance. "You bring him back safe and sound. I've got a buyer for him coming tomorrow."

I assured him I would do my best. I fear I was not entirely convincing, for I began my career by struggling to mount the driver's seat. It took a push from Mandergast's assistant to propel me into place, near pitching me straight over the cab in the process. Under the disapproving gazes of both men, I gathered up the reins and urged the horse on with a flick of the whip.

I am not entirely unacquainted with the intricacies of the driving horse, but even my closest friends would say that I did not acquit myself with good grace on that evening. We snaked across the road, encountering

132

the roars of oncoming drivers to keep to the proper side of the street. Hector appeared to have his own mind and took a left when I wanted a right. Several times we circled Hoxton Square until I persuaded the horse to head towards the heart of the City. As we shambled past Spitalfields Market, a thin rain began to fall. My misery was complete.

It had been my intention to visit the many cabmen's shelters that proliferated throughout London. There surely I would able to initiate a conversation with many of the working cabbies to see if Mandergast's complaints about the changing nature of the business were valid. If memory served, the closest was near the Church of St. Clement Danes in the Strand.

With my destination in mind, I wrestled Hector down Ludgate Hill and onwards along Fleet Street. It was not with incident. Four times, another cab darted out in front of us, nearly jolting me from my precarious position at the rear of the vehicle. But as night tightened its grip on the land and the rain gathered in intensity, the glistening streets began to empty of people and traffic. Soaked though I was, there was almost something joyful about rattling through the empty thoroughfares of London, gazing at the hidden life of the city through first storey windows that kept their mysteries from pavement-bound pedestrians.

I should have continued in this vein if not for the appearance of an obstruction in the road ahead where several men were working on the gas pipes. Hector slowed to a halt before I had dragged on the reins, tossing his head furiously at the interruption of our journey. As we waited for a water cart coming in the opposite direction to pass, I heard a call and suddenly saw an elderly man running towards me. I tried to wave him away, but the weather had stiffened his resolve to have a cab at any price. His error was in jumping onto the footplate before I had gathered up the reins. Sensing the weight of a customer, Hector started off at a trot, nearly into the path of an oncoming coster's donkey cart. The would-be passenger gallantly tried to cling on as we swerved across the road to avoid a collision, only to fall into a puddle. His cry of outrage, coupled with the sudden appearance of a mangy dog that ran from a doorway, barking and nipping at our heels, caused the horse to rear. The next thing I knew we were galloping along the Strand out of control.

At what speed we covered the next mile, I dare not say. A few sodden pedestrians scattered before us, a startled policeman blew his whistle, and the oaths of other cabmen followed us all the way to Waterloo Bridge. Only then did I manage to haul on the reins to bring the horse to a shuddering halt. Hearing the whistle still sounding behind us, I decided to press on to a different shelter, lest the forces of law and order catch up with us.

We took a circuitous route, more by luck than judgement, and finally came upon a shelter with bright yellow light streaming from its windows and a plume of smoke curling from the vent in its hipped roof. I gave the horse his feed and headed inside. The warm interior of the small hut was a welcome sight to a wet and tired man. Several cabmen with their hands wrapped around chipped mugs were seated on benches at trestle tables in a *U*-shaped arrangement that allowed a man to pass up the centre aisle. Curious and somewhat wary eyes fixed upon me as I entered. I took a seat nearest the door and waited to be served. A moment later, a mug missing its handle had been placed before me and was rapidly being filled by a man with an apron about his waist holding a tin teapot. I had been hoping for something stronger to fortify my spirits against the cold.

"Do you have anything else?" I asked, throwing myself in the character with what I considered to be a first-rate East End accent.

"You can have milk in it if you want," the man grunted.

"Anything else?"

"Sugar?"

"No, I meant did you have another beverage?"

The man stared at me with the sort of studied patience that comes from years of dealing with the public. "Milk."

I appeared to be drawing unnecessary attention to myself. "The tea will be more than adequate."

In its favour, it was strong and hot, which went some way to ridding the chill that had settled in the pit of my stomach. Having come this far, I was determined to make the most of it.

"This is welcome," I said to my neighbour, a taciturn, dark-eyed man, swaddled in heavy coat, scarf, and gloves, despite the warmth emanating from the stove.

I received a grunt in reply.

"The name's Watson," I said, offering him my hand. "I'm new around here."

He turned his head slowly to look at me. "You don't say."

"Yes, I got my licence this morning."

My companion gave a stifled snort. "More competition," I heard him mutter.

"Hired my cab from Mandergast. Do you know him?"

"He used to run a good yard," said a driver who was sitting opposite. "I heard he was packing it in to run a hop farm in Kent."

"Decent horses, he had," said another. "I've just got my second from him. Part-thoroughbred he is. Got a fair few years left in him, I dare say."

"His cabs weren't in bad shape either," said the first man. "Henry Smith bought one from him for £30. He's setting up in business for himself now the little 'un has come along."

"That's the way they're all going," agreed his fellow driver. "Not much call for cab masters these days."

"That's a pity," I said. "I thought Mandergast was a good egg."

All eyes turned on me. The silence lingered.

"Is he not?"

My sullen neighbour suddenly rose to his feet. "Yes, he's 'a good egg'. S'cuse me, I've to work to do."

He pushed past and opened the door, allowing a blast of cold night air into the shelter. He paused and looked back at me.

"Is your horse the grey?"

"Why, yes, he is. A fine beast."

"I wouldn't know," came the reply. "He's walking off down the street."

I left my money and hurried out of the shelter in pursuit of my wandering horse. So began a pattern that repeated itself throughout the night. I had meant to return to the yard for a fresh horse as Mandergast had instructed, but time seemed to get away from me. The streets took on a different aspect in the dark and the slanting rain made visibility poor. It was nearly dawn when I stumbled into a shelter near Holborn, despairing of learning anything to help poor Thurston's cause.

I had scarce taken my first sip of tea than the serving man let out a warning cry. "Look lively, lads, there's a copper about," said he, peering out of the steamy window.

There was a rush to the door that left me in its wake. I was on the threshold when I was confronted by the forbidding presence of a tall policeman.

"Evening, sir," said he. "Is this your cab outside?"

He read out my plate number.

"Why, yes, Constable, it is."

"Do you mind coming with me?" The nod of his head indicated I should follow him out to where the horse stood, its head drooping and mane black with rainwater. "I've had complaints that a vehicle matching this description was being driven in a reckless manner along the Strand last night."

"Yes, that might have been me. The horse was alarmed."

"Oh, was he now?" The policeman inhaled a deep breath, making his nostrils flare. "Well, there was a good few folk who were 'alarmed' too. May I see your licence, sir?"

I pulled the damp paper from my inside pocket.

"And your *Book of Fares*?"

After a moment of hesitation, I had to admit I did not have it on me.

"Most forgetful of you, sir," said the constable, fixing me with an unfriendly eye as he took out his notebook and pencil. "Not looking good, is it?"

The events of the next few hours are not ones that would ever stand in my credit. I was charged with reckless driving and failure to produce the necessary paperwork, and had to appear before the magistrate that same morning. I left the court with a fine and a deep sense of failure. I didn't have the heart to return Hector to Mandergast in person. A lecture about my shortcomings as a cabman, I fear, would not have improved my temper. Instead, I paid a driver outside the court to deliver the cab and horse back to his owner. It cost me two guineas, and another for the cabman who followed his colleague with a view to returning him to his stand.

Back at Baker Street, it took a hot bath and several plates of our landlady's beef stew before I began to feel anything approaching my old self. As the afternoon dwindled, I fear I must have fallen asleep, for I was roused some time later by a voice calling my name and a hand patting my shoulder. I opened my eyes to find Holmes at my side, a faint smile touching the corners of his mouth.

"Good evening, Watson," said he. "Forgive me for disturbing you."

"When did you return?" said I, wiping the sleep from my eyes.

"Five minutes ago, to find the house in uproar and you insensible on the couch. You appear to have been busy in my absence."

I did not yet feel equal to admitting my part in the events of the day. "On the contrary, it has been rather quiet."

Holmes chuckled and drew out a folded newspaper. "You made the evening press. '*Mr. John Watson appeared before magistrates this morning charged with the reckless driving of a licensed hansom cab and failure to produce the Authorised Book of Fares when asked to do so by a police constabl*e.'"

"That could be anyone," I said defensively. "There must be more than one John Watson in London."

Holmes ignored me and read on. "'*Mr. Watson of Baker Street pleaded guilty to the charges and was fined 40 shillings.*' Do I need to continue?"

"It isn't how it sounds."

"Is it not?" Holmes considered. "It sounds to me as though you have been pursuing an investigation of your own, Watson. If we set aside your reasons for driving a cab through the centre of London in the middle of the night, we are left with your appearance. The remains of spirit gum on your jaw suggests the application of false whiskers. And then there is this." He reached behind him. In his hand he held my yellow neckerchief. "I struggle to believe that this is a part of your usual wardrobe."

"Very well," I admitted. I sat up and felt my head swim with the dizziness of interrupted sleep. "I was making enquiries on behalf of a friend of mine, Roger Thurston."

Holmes tilted his head slightly in an effort of remembrance. "Would this be the Thurston to whom you lent five guineas in the second year of your studies and was never repaid?"

I was amazed he remembered. It had been a passing remark made in the first year of our acquaintance, and at the time I was sure he had not been listening.

"And is this the same Thurston who advised you to invest in a honey farm that boasted a single hive?"

"Well, yes," I admitted.

"Then I must confess I am not in least surprised to hear he has found himself in difficulties. Men like Thurston are born to trouble as surely as the sparks fly upwards." He rose from my side and sought out a cigarette from the mantel. Lighting it, he took his place before the fireplace and regarded me gravely. "Not content with manufacturing their own downfall, they contrive to share the misery to all and sundry. Now, Watson, if you would care to explain the circumstances of this grim farrago, we may see what can be done."

By the time I had recounted every sorry detail of the affair, Mrs. Hudson had bustled in with our supper. In the manner that the plates were being slapped onto the table, I took it that all was not well with our landlady.

"I expected this sort of behaviour from Mr. Holmes, but not from you, Doctor," said she in answer to my question. "I don't know how I'm going to look the vicar in the eye on Sunday, I really don't." She left, still aggrieved, but not before delivering one final parting shot. "This is why Mrs. Davies stopped letting rooms to unmarried men!"

"Dear me, Watson," said Holmes in evident good humour. "If you continue on this path of crime, we may well find ourselves evicted."

"I don't find it amusing in the slightest."

He sobered. "I agree. It is most serious." He took his index book of biographies from the shelf and flicked through the pages. "I am familiar with several men by the name of Llewellyn, but there is one in particular who springs to mind. Ah! Here is the fellow. Hmm! If this is the gentleman in question, then Thurston will not be the first business partner he has maimed." He snapped the book shut and threw in on the desk. "Well, well, what did we learn from your escapade, Watson?"

"Precious little," I said.

"And hardly the better for it."

"I tried to apply your methods, Holmes," I protested. "If you were investigating the case, I thought you would have used one of your disguises to interrogate the other cabmen."

A laugh escaped him. "My dear fellow, you could not be further from the truth! To masquerade as a member of that particular fraternity requires more than whiskers and a neckerchief. Why, your very appearance would have put them on their guard."

This stinging assessment of my endeavours I considered to be excessively harsh. "I thought I was rather convincing. My Cockney accent, I have been told, is authentic."

As I gave him a sample of my skill, I saw Holmes wince. "It has overtones of the East End, I grant you. Which 'East End', however, and where it might be located, I cannot say."

"Then what would you have done?"

"What I should have done – and what I shall do – is to ask Robinson, our usual cabman. He is a fount of untapped knowledge. What I would not have done is hire a cab and gallop about town in a state of confusion."

"The horse was mettlesome," I said in my defence. "You could have done better, I suppose. You'll be telling me next you are used to driving four-in-hand."

Holmes smiled as he threw the last of his cigarette into the grate. "Not recently. I had the pleasure some years ago of borrowing the Earl of Whippington's team of Cleveland Bays for the pursuit of a jewel thief who was attempting to escape on the milk train to Paddington."

"And caught him, I dare say."

"No, the carriage overturned in a ditch – an unpleasant experience and not one I recommend. To your credit, Watson, the cab horse is a different creature entirely. You are to be congratulated for your persistence in the role."

"Most generous of you. But what am I to tell Thurston?"

"Businesses fail," said Holmes succinctly. "That is the risk every investor accepts. However . . . ." He trailed off into silence. His gaze was directed at the ceiling and I thought for a moment something had arrested his attention until he spoke again and I realised he had been lost in grave contemplation. "I tend to agree with your friend, Thurston. What is the most common complaint one hears about town? 'Never a cab to be had when you need one'. I can testify to the veracity of that lament. Transportation would appear to be an industry where demand will always outstrip supply. Indeed, Mr. Mandergast seems to be the only cab owner in the capital to defy the robust nature of the market. If a man cannot make a decent living in a city teeming with the masses in need of a cab, then he is either fortune's fool or prey to a malign influence."

He took a turn about the room and collected a worn map of London. "It has been a while since I was obliged to frequent Hoxton," said he, running his finger across the creased sheet. "I seem to remember pockets of gentility interspersed with the twin evils of poverty and industry."

"It has not changed much," I replied. "That was my impression."

"If memory serves, Mandergast was situated in Birch Street. To the east was the Martin Brothers Furniture Warehouse, whilst Ryman's Cabinet Makers lay to the west."

I thought back to the brief impression I had obtained of the area. "Ryman has gone. I believe a firm of upholsterers had taken over the building."

Holmes nodded. "That does not surprise me. The area was always known for the rapidity with which premises changed hands."

So saying, his mood abruptly altered, from one of severity and censure to conviviality. At such times, I envied him his ability to put the troubles of the world aside so easily.

"Well, there is little we can do tonight," said he, throwing the map onto an ever-growing pile of books and papers. "I suggest supper and a concert. Hmm! Oxtail soup. It appears we are both out of favour with our landlady. Since dining out appears to be the order of the day, there may well be a table for us at Orsini's. The manager said he would be happy to oblige after I cleared up that business for him concerning the curried lentils and the litigious patron."

Company and a good meal went some way easing my disquiet. Holmes elaborated about the case that had taken him abroad, the violin concertos of Torelli and the limitations of postmarks as a means of establishing opportunity in criminal cases. By the end of the evening, my constitution was feeling the strain of the last few days, and I was grateful to return to the comfort of home. By the next morning, I awoke with an aching head and the unmistakeable beginnings of a cold. Holmes had already left, and I wandered down to find a meagre breakfast waiting for me. As I contemplated the offering of stewed tea and congealed eggs, I heard Holmes's key in the door and his cheery call from downstairs.

"Good morning, Watson!" said he as he entered the room, with an enthusiasm I could not muster. "Whilst you have been slumbering in your bed, I have had a most productive morning."

"You spoke to Robinson?"

"Indeed. He is waiting downstairs for us now." He had pulled a drawer from his desk and tipped the contents onto the floor. After a brief rummage, he gathered up a small white card and thrust it into his pocket.

"Robinson confirmed what you were told – that Mandergast was a first-rate cab master until recently. He seems to be of the opinion the fellow has grown tired of the business. That may happen, of course. I can foresee a day when my own sights may turn to pastures new. When I am in my dotage, no doubt," said he when he saw my expression. "For now, however, we have the curious case of Mr. Mandergast to keep us out of mischief."

Holmes gave a sudden, hearty chuckle.

"Speaking of which," he continued merrily, "your foray into the business of detection caused quite a stir at the cab rank. The consensus, according to Robinson, is that you were a journalist sniffing around for a story or, failing that, you were a 'toff' attempting to poke fun at the working man. Phrases like 'a good egg' – which I have yet to hear outside the pages of stories about public school boys – gave you away. In any case, you may consider yourself fortunate: Had you not been arrested, your evening might have had a painful termination. Now, if you can bear to tear yourself away from this poor repast, we have an appointment in Hoxton."

An hour later found us in Birch Street outside Mandergast's premises. Robinson gave me a peculiar look when I paid him his fare, and I only hoped I hadn't been recognised and named by his associates. As the cab rattled away, I joined Holmes, who was staring up at the adjacent five-storey premises that housed the firm of upholsterers. The board above the main door announced the name of the business owner as Bryce.

To my surprise, Holmes strode up to the door and rapped upon the wood. A hatch opened and there appeared a red-faced man wearing round spectacles.

"Is Mr. Bryce in today?" Holmes asked.

"Who wants him?" demanded the man.

"Mr. Faraday of the Faraday Furnishing Emporium." He took the card he had taken from his drawer and held it up to the hatch for inspection. "I am currently based in Birmingham, but I am planning to open a new branch in London. I am looking for suppliers. Your name was recommended to me."

The door promptly opened. There is nothing quite like the lure of a potential customer to transform obstreperousness into obsequience. "Come in, Mr. Faraday. I am Mr. Miller, Mr. Bryce's representative." He wiped his glue-stained hand down his apron before offering it to us. "I am sure we can accommodate you."

Holmes smiled. "I trust you can. If I like what I see, the order will be a generous one. I select only the finest stock. Mr. Fellowes here is my Chief Buyer." I nodded when he gestured to me. "He has an eye for quality that is second to none."

Miller offered to take us on a tour of the factory, which we accepted. After passing rows of craftsmen busy with the wooden skeletons of sofas and chairs, admiring abundant rolls of fabric of luxurious material of every shade and hue, and commenting on the airy and agreeable working conditions, Holmes expressed himself satisfied.

"But tell me, Mr. Miller," said he, "my order will be sizeable. Nor do I tolerate delays. Do you have the capacity to accommodate my requirements?"

Miller nodded enthusiastically. "We have plans for expansion, Mr. Faraday. The business is growing every year. Mr. Bryce has considering moving to larger premises, perhaps outside London."

"That would be a pity, since your location makes you convenient for the City. Could the present site not be altered? I thought I saw a vacant site next door."

Miller rolled his eyes. "The Mandergast Carriage Company? He would never sell."

"You have asked him?"

"Once, years ago. He sent Mr. Bryce away with a flea in his ear about how his ancestors started the business when all there was in Hoxton was green fields and cows."

"A pity." Holmes extended his hand. "Well, thank you, Mr. Miller. You may tell Mr. Bryce I shall be in contact."

"Mr. 'Faraday'?" I asked him when we were outside once more.

"I have always found it useful to have a store of business cards for every occasion. Faraday has opened more than a few doors in the past."

"And the purpose of our tour?"

"To test a theory. Come, Watson, let us beard Mr. Mandergast in his den."

Holmes led the way through the open gate of the cab yard. Mandergast was busy inspecting a hansom with a broken wheel and only looked up when his assistant alerted him. His face flushed red when he saw me.

"Not you again!" he said, taking up a long whip as he strode over to confront us. "Damn near killed my horse keeping him out all night. Get out of here!"

"Calm yourself, Mr. Mandergast," said Holmes. I took a step back in the face of the man's fury, but Holmes remained resolute. "You may want to hear what we have to say."

"I doubt it," said he, scowling as he turned on his heel.

"That is your prerogative. I would be negligent in my duty, however, were I not to warn you of the consequences should Mr. Llewellyn learn of your arrangement with Martin Brothers."

Mandergast stopped in his tracks. "I don't know what you're talking about."

"How much did they offer you?"

His mouth fell open. "How on earth – "

"How I know is not important," said Holmes. "*What* I know is that approximately three months ago, Martin Brothers offered to buy your premises – a handsome sum, I dare say. You had your own reasons for wanting to sell, but needless to say, it could not have come at a worse time. Your business was thriving, and you had recently received investment from a third party, Mr. Llewellyn. Not wishing to share the proceeds of the sale with your investor, you set about sabotaging your own business. Exposure to an infected horse would have caused equine influenza to spread in your yard, and it was easy enough for you to damage your own equipment. The cabmen to whom you once hired your vehicles began to drift away and your yard began to fail. Your mistake, Mr. Mandergast, was in offering to repay the original investment. It is a rare man who would honour his obligations in the face of financial ruin. You did so because you needed to buy out Mr. Llewellyn, and to do so fast. You knew he would settle for nothing less."

Mandergast was glaring at us, his fists balled. "What nonsense is this?"

Holmes smiled, a gesture that did not touch his eyes. "Mr. Bryce is eager to expand. It stands to reason the same might be true of the Martin Brothers factory on the other side of your yard. I imagine they have been eager to keep their offer a secret lest their competitors hear of their plans."

For a long time, Mandergast stood in silence, before sighing and throwing the whip away. "I knew there was something odd about him," he said, pointing at me. "I should have known it was something underhand. Well, out with it, how much do you want?"

"Nothing at all," said Holmes. "My concern is for your continued well-being. Mr. Llewellyn is not a man with whom one should trifle. If he retains his liberty, it is only because he has been careful. When he learns of your deception, as surely one day he must, he will demand his due."

"He can try. There is nothing in writing."

"Llewellyn will not waste his time with the courts. I trust whatever you have been offered is equal to the value you place on your life."

Mandergast stared at him. "Who the devil are you?"

"My name is Sherlock Holmes. I am a consulting detective."

"Working for Llewellyn, no doubt. I suppose you're going to tell him all this."

"No. I have no interest in your arrangements. The matter has been brought to my attention by my associate, who has a passing acquaintance with Mr. Thurston. He tells me Thurston has been threatened with violence."

"What is that to me?" Mandergast retorted. "He was well paid. I have worked my fingers to the bone in this business. Why should I have to share what's mine?"

The defiance in his eyes suddenly died. He raked his hand through his greasy hair and released a long, troubled breath.

"It's true, what you say," he admitted. "Fifty-two years I've worked here, man and boy. To be honest, gentleman, I've had enough. There's a hop farm I've had my eye on down in Kent. Well, it's come up for sale, and I say that would suit me at my time of life. Martin Brothers has offered me a decent price, although it's not half of what the land is really worth. But it's better than ending my days being kicked in the head by one of these old nags, like my father was."

"Then take Mr. Llewellyn into your confidence and argue for better terms. He may prove a valuable ally in the negotiations, and you may well find there is more interest in the land than you anticipate. The ability to sleep soundly in your bed at night without fear of future violence would be worth whatever sum you have to pay him."

Mandergast held his gaze for a long time before slowly nodding. "There may be some truth in what you say, Mr. Holmes. I will give it due consideration."

"If I were you, I would make my decision before close of business tonight. The sooner, the better, it seems to me. Nor should I mention your prior arrangement with Martin Brothers. Mr. Llewellyn may be less amenable to reaching an agreement if you are too candid about recent events. That is my advice – the choice is yours. Good day, Mr. Mandergast."

With that, Holmes turned to go, leaving the cab owner exchanging thoughtful glances with his assistant. I hurried after him and caught up as he strode along Birch Street.

"An interesting fellow, that Mandergast," said Holmes. "A shame about the scurvy."

I stared at him. "Scurvy, Holmes? He was as healthy as any man of his age."

"But the assistant, surely there were clear indications of consumption?"

"Not at all. He appeared to have a very robust constitution."

Holmes stopped abruptly. "Then you would agree, Watson, that when it comes to the field of medicine, our few years of association have not made me an expert?"

I could see where this line of questioning was heading. "I take your point."

He chuckled. "Capital! We can agree then. I will not diagnose your patients, and you will refrain from undertaking investigations. It is the safest course for all concerned. Now, I suggest we return to Baker Street. Spring is in the air and I have observed that Mrs. Hudson is readying her duster and floor polish. Since you have already caused our fall from grace, I dare say we should not tempt fate by leaving our rooms in a state of disarray. My collection of business cards is a handsome one, and I would not care to see them join the rest of our possessions on the pavement should our tenancy be suddenly terminated!"

The Adventure of the
Missing Cousin
by Edwin A. Enstrom

"Watson, I shall go mad if I do not have some stimulation soon."

I looked up from my book to watch Holmes pacing nervously about our sitting room. It was a beautiful spring morning in early May 1883, but neither of us were in the mood to enjoy it. Holmes had not had an interesting case for several weeks, and the lack of focus was affecting his composure. For my part, my medical duties had few patients, and my days were filled with boredom.

"Watson, come look at this. What do you think of the man in the checked suit?" asked Holmes as he looked out the window at the people streaming by below.

I joined him and looked out at the man indicated. He was walking very oddly. He would move quickly for several paces, then slow to a crawl. Then he would walk quickly again and then slow again, over and over. All the while he was turning his head to the left and right, as if he were trying to work out a crick in his neck.

"Why, Holmes, I think the poor man must have some kind of nervous disorder. He doesn't seem to have full control of his muscles."

"I think it's much simpler than that. He is looking for the number of a house. Ah, he has stopped. Yes, he is coming across to our door. Watson, I think we are saved."

Holmes doffed his mouse-colored dressing gown and pulled on his coat while I picked up the newspapers he had thrown willy-nilly about the room. The doorbell rang and we heard voices in the hall, followed by steps on the stairs. Shortly thereafter, there was a knock on our door and Mrs. Hudson appeared with the young man behind her.

"Come in, sir, and make yourself comfortable. Whom do I have the pleasure of addressing, and how may I help you? Mrs. Hudson, some tea if you please," said Holmes, with a twinkle in his eye.

The young man went to Holmes with his arm outstretched and said, "I am Charles Parkhurst and I need your help. My cousin has disappeared. I have been to the police, but they think that he has just taken himself off, and I know that cannot be true. He would never do such a thing."

"Sit down and tell us your story," said Holmes, indicating the basket chair. "By the way, this is Dr. Watson, my friend and associate. Anything you say to us will be held in the strictest confidence." Holmes refilled his pipe, lit it, and sat back in eager anticipation to hear the man's story.

"Well, I don't think anything I say is confidential, but thank you for the assurance," said Parkhurst. "I am a teacher at a grammar school in Sussex. I have two cousins: Reginald Parkhurst, who has a chemist's shop in Islington, and his older brother Giles Parkhurst, who is a lay brother in the India Missionary Alliance. Giles has been in Calcutta for the last eight years, working in the hospital and school run there by the Alliance. Two months ago, Giles and Reggie's father died of heart failure and Giles was notified. He sent this telegram."

Parkhurst reached into his coat pocket and brought out a telegram. He gave it to Holmes, who read it and passed it to me. It read thus:

> *Arriving Southampton May first MS Britannia STOP Will see Reggie first STOP Will send further itinerary later STOP Giles STOP*

"Mr. Holmes, on May second, I received a telegram from Reggie asking whether Giles was with me. Not knowing what to make of this, I came up to London today and spoke to Reggie before I came here. Giles did indeed stop by the chemist's shop on the first. He and Reggie made plans for dinner at Reggie's flat that evening. Giles never appeared."

"Thank you, Mr. Parkhurst. I will take on your case. First, however, I would like some background information about your family. Was their father wealthy, and who inherits the estate?"

"Oh yes. Their grandfather made pots of money in the cotton mills and left it all to their father, who was an only child. He had a large estate in Staffordshire and wanted to keep it intact, so he left the bulk of it Giles, with small annuities to Reggie and myself."

"Is Giles married, and who is his next of kin?" I blurted out. Holmes shot me a glance and I saw that he was unhappy with my intrusion into his questioning.

"He's unmarried, and I suppose that Reggie is his next of kin. There are no other brothers or sisters."

"Well, Mr. Parkhurst, I think that is all we need right now," said Holmes. "Where may we get in touch with you if necessary?"

Parkhurst took out a visiting card and a pencil and wrote something on it, handing it to Holmes.

"I'll be staying for a few days at the Metropole Hotel, and after that I will be returning to my home in Sussex, which address is printed on the card. I have added the address of Reggie's shop if you should wish to speak to him."

146

"Admirable, sir," said Holmes as he rose and escorted our client to the door. "Well, Watson, what do you think?" asked Holmes a moment later with a sly grin.

"Mr. Giles Parkhurst may have taken off entirely for reasons of his own, or there is some villainy going on here," I replied. I had no other ideas to offer.

"Exactly my thoughts, Watson. We shall have to do some initial investigation to see which of the options applies. In any case, we have something to occupy our minds, at least for a while."

Ten minutes later we were in a cab rattling off to Reginald Parkhurst's shop in Islington. Arriving there, I saw that it was worse for wear. The paint was peeling, and the windows looked as if they hadn't been washed in months. Upon entering, I saw a man of medium-height, alone behind the counter. He appeared to be about thirty years of age, with slicked-back black hair and gold-rimmed glasses.

"How may I help you, sirs?" he inquired.

Holmes introduced us and explained that Charles Parkhurst had engaged us to look into his cousin's disappearance. "Will you tell us what you know?"

"Yes, I will. Giles came by on the afternoon of May first. We chatted for a while and then he said he had to go find a hotel. We made arrangements that he should come to my flat for dinner that evening and he left. That's the last I saw of him. He never came."

"Did he seem perturbed, or otherwise out of sorts?" inquired Holmes.

"Not at all, although he looked very thin, almost emaciated, and his skin appeared sallow. He also seemed somewhat shaky in his movements. I asked him about this, and he told me that the Alliance had few funds and its members are on practically a subsistence diet. He added that when he had control of the estate, he would make a sizeable contribution to the Alliance." As he said this, Reggie's face contorted with anger and was suffused with blood.

"I take it you aren't in agreement with this proposal"

"Agreement! Giles has no call to be using our patrimony for the benefaction of some dirty heathens on the other side of the world!" fumed Reggie.

"I see. Do you by any chance have a photograph of Giles? That would be very helpful to us."

"Why yes, I do. I have it at my flat. It was taken shortly before he left for India about eight years ago. He still looks very much the same, although much thinner. I will give you a note to my wife." So saying, he scribbled an address on a pad, tore it off, and handed it to Holmes.

We left the shop and found a cab to take us to the location that Reggie had given us. It was a tower block in a run-down part of the city. Peeling paint, boarded-up windows, and weeds in the courtyard testified to its meanness. Parkhurst's flat was on the second floor and our knock was answered by a youngish woman. Her dress was old and patched, but very clean. Her face was that of one who has been eaten down by the vicissitudes of life.

Holmes explained who we were and gave her the note from her husband. She moved back and invited us inside. The room was neat but with very little furniture, all of which was threadbare. It was easy to see that the Parkhurst couple were barely getting by. Mrs. Parkhurst disappeared into another room and came back with a photograph, which she gave to Holmes.

"Mrs. Parkhurst, can you tell us anything about Giles' disappearance?"

"I'm afraid not. Reggie sent me a message that he would be coming for dinner. I had to scrounge a bit to get enough for a third person. Giles was supposed to come at 7:30, but he never came. We waited until 8:30 and then gave it up and ate our dinner. That is all I know."

Holmes thanked the lady and we descended to the street.

"Well, Watson, what do you think?"

"I think the Parkhursts are living very near the edge."

"My thoughts also, Watson. And Reggie is very angry that his brother would give a lot of money to a missionary alliance and not a farthing to his brother."

"Homes, you don't think . . . ."

"Watson, I don't think. How many times have I said that is a capital mistake to theorize before one has all the facts?"

As we approached the steps to our lodgings, Holmes turned to face the street, put two fingers in his mouth, and let out four shrill whistles.

"Holmes, what in the world are you doing?" I cried.

"Summoning Wiggins. Either he or another of the street urchins will hear it and know that I want him. Now we can only wait."

Wiggins was the self-declared leader of a band of ragtag boys whom Holmes called his "Irregulars". They could go anywhere in London and were virtually invisible to adults. Holmes periodically used them to run errands or to find people. We had barely started tea when there was a clatter on the stairs and the door burst open. Wiggins rushed in and ran up to Holmes.

"Here I am, sir."

"Yes, I see. Wiggins, I want you to find Dawkins and bring him here. He usually hangs around Paddington Station."

"Yes, sir," cried Wiggins and tore off down the stairs.

"Who is Dawkins, may I ask?" I inquired.

"He is a cabman for whom I did a small service some time ago. It was really a very trivial matter, but Dawkins is as grateful as if I had saved him from the gallows. He knows practically every cabman in London and the pubs that they frequent. I am looking for the cabman who drove Giles Parkhurst from his brother's shop to a hotel."

We had barely finished tea when Wiggins appeared again, this time in company of a middle-aged fellow who was obviously a cabman.

"Well done, Wiggins. Here's a shilling."

"Thank you, sir!" said Wiggins and stormed down the stairs.

"Dawkins, I need your help. I am looking for a cabman," said Holmes.

"I am always ready to help you sir," replied Dawkins.

"Good. I want to find the cabman who drove this man from a chemist's shop in Islington to a hotel somewhere," said Holmes, while handing him the photograph.

The expression of surprise and astonishment on Dawkins' face was so comical that I could hardly keep from bursting out laughing.

"Why, Mr. Holmes, are you japing with me? I myself drove this man!"

"Remarkable! The Fates seem to be smiling on us. Tell us what happened."

"Well, sir, I had taken a fare to Islington and was returning to Paddington when this gentleman hailed me. He asked if I could recommend a good hotel that was economical. I said that I could, and he climbed in and I took him to the Columbus Hotel, which as you know has cheap rooms."

"And did the gentleman actually take a room there?" asked Holmes.

"Yes, sir, he did. In fact, he didn't look too healthy, kind of wobbly on his pins, and I took his valise into the hotel for him. Not a very good tipper, though."

"Excellent, Dawkins. Here is a crown for your time and trouble. And wait outside with your cab."

"Thank you, sir," said Dawkins and left the room.

Holmes disappeared into his bedroom and emerged shortly with his valise.

"What are you doing, Holmes?

"Watson, I think that we need to spend some time investigating the amenities available at the Columbus Hotel."

We descended to the street and Dawkins drove us to the hotel, where Holmes dismissed him. The hotel was unprepossessing, just the sort that would be frequented by those with limited means. We pushed through the double doors and entered the lobby.

The desk clerk welcomed us with a smile. "How may I help you?"

"I would like a single room for one night, or possibly two," answered Holmes.

"Very good sir. We have a nice room on the second floor facing the courtyard. If you would kindly sign the register," said the clerk, before moving to the other end of the counter to deal with another hotel guest.

Holmes signed the register and then motioned to me to come and look at it, pointing to the spine between the two open pages. I could clearly see the ragged edge where a page had been torn out. He then ran his finger down the top three signatures on the right-hand page. At first I didn't see what he wanted me to notice. All three entries were for May first, while the next entries were for May second. Then I noticed that the first three seemed all to be in the same handwriting. I looked questioningly at Holmes and he just gave me a sly smile.

"Watson, I shall go to my room and unpack. Can you come back here tomorrow, say about eleven?" said Holmes.

I knew that I was being dismissed and I agreed that I would return on the morrow. I went back to Baker Street and tried to make some sense of all that I had seen. A disappearing missionary, a hard-up chemist, and a provincial schoolteacher. Peculiarities in a hotel register. Despite cudgeling my brain for several hours, I couldn't see anything that tied all these together.

Next morning I went to the hotel and, upon entering Holmes's room, I found him in conversation with one of the hotel's housemaids.

"Ah, Watson, allow me to present Mary Langton, a most perceptive and inquisitive lady. I have shown Giles Parkhurst's photograph to Miss Langton, and she recognized it immediately. Please go on, Miss Langton."

"Well sir, the gentleman had a room right on this floor, just across the hall. The next morning after he came, our manager Mr. Johnson called the doctor, and they both went to the gentleman's room. An hour or so later, the doctor went downstairs with the gentleman, whose head was all wrapped up in bandages. The housekeeper told me that he had fallen and hurt his head."

"And what did you do then?" asked Holmes.

"Some hours afterwards, I went to his room to straighten up and saw that all of the bed linen, as well as the mattress and pillow, had been removed from the bed. There was also a strong smell of carbolic in the room. I asked the housekeeper about this, and she told me that the linens and mattress were stained with blood and had to be disposed of."

"Thank you, miss. Do you know the name of the doctor?"

"Yes, sir. Dr. MacPherson in Canary Street."

"Very good. Here is a little something for your trouble," said Holmes, handing her a guinea, at which she smiled prettily and left us.

"Come, Watson, let us reconnoiter the area a little. I think we may find someone who can give us some more information."

We exited the hotel and Holmes led me down an alley that ran alongside the hotel to a courtyard in the rear. There we found a boy of ten or twelve years old loitering by the rear entrance.

"Hello, young fellow. I would like a word with you," called Holmes.

The boy shambled over and looked up at Holmes expectantly.

"I have seen you several times from my hotel window. Are you in this area frequently?"

"Yes, sir. I live in the next street over and I come here because the cook or housekeeper sometimes asks me to run errands for them. I get a few shillings, which helps my mum."

"Capital. Do you know if the hotel has a carriage or a dray or some such conveyance, and have you seen it recently?" asked Holmes.

"Yes, sir. They have a dray and I saw it just yesterday. The manager and the desk clerk loaded it up with a big laundry hamper. It must have been very full and heavy, because they struggled a bit with it."

"And where did they go with it?"

"I don't know sir, but they drove off in the opposite direction from the laundry."

"I see. Here is a shilling for your mum and another one for you," and the lad scampered off.

Holmes stared at the façade of the hotel but I knew that he wasn't seeing anything. "Watson, I have almost all the threads in my hands. We have one more loose end to tie up. Let us visit Dr. MacPherson."

The doctor was between patient appointments and we were ushered into his office. Holmes introduced us and told the doctor that we were looking into the disappearance of Giles Parkhurst. At this, the doctor gave a start and looked away.

"I understand that you treated Mr. Parkhurst on the morning of May second," said Holmes.

"Er, yes, that is so. He had fallen and cut his head badly. I brought him here and stitched up the wound and he left," replied MacPherson.

"Do you know where he went after he left here?"

"No, I assumed that he went back to the hotel. Now I must terminate this conversation and get back to my patients. Good morning, gentlemen."

Back on the street again, Holmes said "Yes, Watson, it is all clear to me now. The evasiveness of Dr. MacPherson supplies the final piece of the puzzle. I shall go back to the hotel and check out, and then send a couple of telegrams. Will you be free tomorrow at eleven?"

"Yes, I will. Do you mean that you have solved the mystery of the disappearance?"

"Yes, Watson. All will be made clear tomorrow. Have patience."

I still didn't know what was in Holmes mind the next morning as we made our way once again to the Columbus Hotel. Holmes had made an appointment with the manager for eleven o'clock and we were ushered directly in. Holmes wasted no time but asked the manger to call in the desk clerk and the housekeeper.

"What in heaven is this all about?" carped the manager.

"We are going to clear up the mystery of the disappearance of Giles Parkhurst. Perhaps you may suspect this already?" said Holmes.

The manager's face paled, but he rang the bell and told the page to send the clerk and housekeeper to his office. While we were waiting, the door opened and Dr. MacPherson entered.

"What did you want me for, Johnson?" asked the doctor.

"Pardon me, sir, but it was I who invited you here and I took the liberty of using Mr. Johnson's name," interjected Holmes. "It is necessary for you to be here to supply a key piece of information."

Just then, there was a knock at the door. Holmes opened it and ushered in Charles Parkhurst and his cousin Reggie, looking somewhat bemused at what this meeting was all about. There was a short wait while enough chairs were brought in to seat everyone, and then Holmes began. Striding up to the manager, he cried, "What did you do with the body?" Then pivoting to the doctor, "And what was the cause of death?"

Turning to the Parkhurst cousins, Holmes said, "Yes, I am sorry to have to tell you, but your brother and cousin is dead. We will now hear the story of what happened."

The faces of the manager and the doctor were a picture of fear, consternation, and confusion. The manager rose and motioned to the doctor, and they retired to a far corner of the office where they conversed in low tones for a few minutes.

Returning to his desk, the manager said, "I see that you have divined most or all of this sad situation. While we will admit to breaking a few laws, we didn't commit any capital crimes. I shall tell you the full story." He looked around the room and the doctor, housekeeper, and desk clerk all nodded their heads in agreement.

"I think you are wise," said Holmes. "I'm not a policeman and have been known to bend the rules, so long as no one is hurt and there is an overarching reason. I feel that this is the case here."

"Thank you, sir. On the morning of May second, the housekeeper went to Mr. Parkhurst's room and found him dead in bed. I called Dr. MacPherson, who came immediately. Will you continue, Doctor?"

"Yes," said MacPherson. "I examined the body and was horrified to find that he had died from the plague! Fearing that there would be widespread panic in London if this news became public, I called Mr. Johnson, and we discussed what should be done. We decided that we would try to hush it up. I know that, as a doctor, I should have reported it, but I also knew that the office of public health cannot keep secrets. Please continue, Johnson."

"We decided that we needed to show the gentleman leaving the hotel, so we made up the story of Mr. Parkhurst being injured, and my desk clerk played the part of his leaving the hotel wrapped in bandages. We know that plague is spread by fleas and we didn't find any in the room, but we burned the bed linen and the mattress just to be safe. We also scrubbed the whole room with carbolic. We were waiting to see if any other cases of plague appeared. If they did, we were going to tell what we had done."

"I see" said Holmes. "I would probably have done much the same thing in your position. And what did you do with the body, doctor?"

"I'm not proud of that, but I didn't have much choice. The body was still contagious, so I issued a bogus death certificate and had it cremated." He turned to the Parkhurst cousins and said, "I am truly sorry, but there was nothing else that I could do."

"Well, it is a sad story, but I think we can all see the necessity for what was done. I think it best if none of us were to repeat what was said here today," said Holmes. He looked around the room and all of us nodded our heads in agreement.

Back in Baker Street a few days later, Holmes referred again to the Parkhursts. "Dr. MacPherson has issued a valid death certificate for Giles Parkhurst, although he listed the cause of death as heart failure. This was duly filed at Somerset House, and Reggie Parkhurst succeeded to the estate. Since it was quite large, he shared some of it with his cousin, Charles. All in all, a good outcome for a few days stimulation."

The Roses of Highclough House
by M.J.H. Simmonds

Chapter I

The young man was shown in by Mrs. Hudson and we heard him race athletically up the stairs, two at a time. A loud single rap at the door was followed, a second later, by the appearance of a face, youthful but anguished, peering round the half-opened door.

"Excuse me gentlemen, but is this the residence of Mr. Sherlock Holmes?" he asked, his red cheeks and bright blonde hair in stark contrast to eyes deep and dark with obvious distress.

"Please come in, young man. Take a seat, catch your breath, and then tell us everything that vexes you," ordered Holmes, with careful authority. "I am Sherlock Holmes. And you?"

The young man fully entered the room and, after a quick look around, sat down where Holmes had gestured. He was unlikely to have yet reached his twentieth birthday, but he was tall and strong, his face displaying the rosy cheeks and light tan of a youth spent outside in the country air. His face was wide, honest, and open. His eyes, despite their shadows, were a bright blue. He wore a light-coloured suit at least one size too small. Clearly the lad had recently suffered a late growth spurt.

"I am from Highclough House. I mean, sorry," he stumbled. "My name is Matthew Newton and I live up at Highclough House. A terrible thing has occurred, a murder, but no one else can see it for what it is. I know that I am right, but I am ignored and pushed aside. And what is worse, I know that I will be next! They won't stop until they have everything!" Newton's voice had risen to the point of panic, his black-rimmed eyes were open wide with terror.

"Please help me," he begged. "If I go back to Highclough, I know I willn't survive the night!"

"Good heavens!" I declared. "Do you know who is trying to harm you? If you do, tell us their names and I swear that we will keep you safe," I promised, rather prematurely.

"Of course I know them. They are my sisters," replied Newton.

Chapter II

I was dumbstruck, but Holmes simply raised an eyebrow, almost imperceptibly, before responding.

"I see. Now why, pray tell, do you believe that your sisters are trying to kill you?" Holmes asked, in his calm, matter of fact way.

"Because they then stand to inherit the House and everything that we have, of course," Newton spurted out, quickly.

"Very well," Holmes replied, gently. "Why don't you start at the beginning? What has happened up at the House, who has died, and why do you believe it to have been murder?"

"Perhaps the young man would like a glass of water first?" I interjected. I would usually recommend brandy, but I felt that our guest was a little young for hard liquor.

Newton nodded, so I fetched and filled a glass, which he took in his trembling hands. After gulping down half of the contents, Newton seemed to calm down and collect his senses.

"Just over a week ago, my father – " Newton stopped, struggling to overcome his emotions. "My father died," he finished, quickly.

"How did he die?" I asked. "I am a doctor, so please tell us every detail that you can remember and everything that you were told."

Holmes nodded in agreement.

Newton took a deep breath. "He was found hanging in his bedroom. They say he took his own life." Newton now avoided our eyes. As he spoke, he looked down towards the floor. His loss clearly exacerbated by the guilt and shame associated with a suicide.

Carefully, his head now appearing to harbour a great weight, he began to look up. His tired blue eyes were now filled with tears, but these sparkled in defiance. "But he would never do this, not in a million years. He was a strong, religious man. A good man, a great man. *They* did it. Somehow, *they* killed him! They have been poisoned. Possessed. Turned against us by evil forces."

"A week ago, you say?" asked Holmes, seriously.

Newton nodded.

Holmes swore, quite unnecessarily in my view.

"Holmes, remember yourself," I admonished.

"I am sorry, Watson, Master Newton, but a *week*? There will be nothing left for me to examine after such a long time. I assume that servants, doctors, and various members of the police have all spread their contagion throughout the room since the body was discovered?"

Newton looked surprised. "Well, no, Mr. Holmes. My father was discovered when a maid attempted to enter and found the room locked.

She knocked but there was no response. Seeing that the key was still in the lock, but on the other side of the door, she became concerned and called out for me. I knocked and shouted for a minute or so before I decided that something must be seriously amiss. It took several hard shoulder charges to break through the sturdy door, but the frame suddenly gave way and I fell in, flat on my face to be honest. Then I heard her scream when she saw the terrible sight before us. But she never entered the room. I took his body down and removed it to the parlour, where I lay him upon the large table. There I, rather foolishly, tried to administer brandy in a desperate attempt to revive him. I know it sounds ridiculous now, but I had to attempt everything I could to try and bring him back . . . ." Newton tailed off, sadly.

"The doctor arrived about three hours later and examined him," continued Newton, when he had recovered his nerves. "He acted with commendable discretion, but it was clear right from the start that he believed that my father had taken his own life. Once he was satisfied that the cause of death matched my account, he took a brief look upstairs. After no more than a quick glance into the bedroom, and seeing the remains of the rope still hanging down, its end frayed and torn from where I struggled to cut it with my pocket knife, he returned to me and quietly delivered his verdict.

"The authorities had been alerted, and early the following morning, a police sergeant arrived from Stocksbridge. It was clear that he had previously been in contact with the doctor, as the questions he asked appeared to have been designed simply to confirm what he had already learned. He also made little effort to examine the bedroom and left soon afterwards, seemingly content to have confirmed the doctor's verdict."

"The undertaker called later that same day, but by then I had already secured father's room as best I could. I didn't want anyone else to go in there before I could find time to take a good look around myself. The room has remained that way ever since."

Holmes rose and patted Newton on the shoulder, one of the few times I ever saw him make physical contact with anyone of his own accord.

"What you thought of as foolish may just have given us a chance of solving this case and restoring your father's reputation. Time is now very much of the essence. I will return with you to Highclough House, and on the way you must tell me more. I wish to know of your family background and, essentially, about your sisters and what you believe now holds such an influence over them.

"But, most of all," Holmes continued, "I need to know exactly what it was that made you decide to secure your father's bedroom. This was, I believe, the exact moment that you first came to suspect that your father

156

had been murdered, and by someone close to you – someone who had daily access to the house.

"In addition, I am quite sure," Holmes added, "that Doctor Watson would be delighted to join us. His mind may only be above-average, but his heart is hewn from the finest English oak. You could not have a better man at your side. Fear not, Master Newton – we shall uncover the truth of this matter. We need just a moment to pack a bag, write a few messages, and then we will be ready to go."

Seeing a smile slowly break upon Newton's big, honest face for the first time was all the incentive that I needed. However, a thought then struck me.

"Where exactly is Highclough House?" I asked.

Chapter III

Highclough turned out to be six miles west of Stocksbridge in what has become known as the Peak District. We took the twelve o'clock train to Sheffield and then a further hour on a branch line. We left Stocksbridge station in a four-wheeler just after four in the afternoon, making slow progress along the difficult road to Highclough.

Once Newton had answered all of Holmes's exhaustive list of questions, we sat mainly in silence, which gave me an opportunity to enjoy the majestic views framed by the carriage windows and consider what the young master had revealed.

The Newton's modest wealth had come directly from an invention patented by Matthew Newton's grandfather. Born the year the Napoleonic Wars ended, Augustus Newton enjoyed a mostly uneventful life until, in 1855, he created the bi-cyclical valve regulator. Although fiendishly technical, the device increased the efficiency of all steam engines by nearly fifteen percent. He shrewdly licensed his invention to separate companies in Britain, Europe, and the United States, and was soon receiving many thousands-per-year in royalties.

Augustus was a genuine eccentric. He donated large sums of his fortune to the poor of his hometown of Sheffield and spent much of what was left on the construction of Highclough House. As the name suggests, the house overlooks a steep-sided valley, but the difficulty involved in the building of a large mansion in such a remote location meant that costs were huge and progress was slow.

Augustus' son, Hadrian, was a completely different character. Studious, religious, and careful with money, he regularly bemoaned his father's lavish expenditure on the half-finished house. However, it is important to note that he never criticised or opposed any of his father's

157

charitable work or his regular, generous donations. When Augustus died in 1871, Hadrian, to the surprise of everyone, pledged to continue his father's work and spent the next years completing the house. Matthew Newton even commented that, under the control of his more serious and efficient father, the work began to progress at a much increased pace and costs were reduced dramatically.

Master Newton had, therefore, grown up during the final stages of the construction of the house. In 1866, two years after having had Matthew, Hadrian's wife, Lily, gave birth to twin girls, Rosalie and Rosalind. Tragedy hit the family ten years later when Lily was struck down with consumption, from which she later died, after having endured six months of terrible suffering.

Matthew was, by then, already away at boarding school and only returned to the house during the holidays. He soon noticed a change in his father. He became withdrawn and almost entirely ceased his, up until that point, regular correspondence with his son. The letters that his son had, hitherto, so looked forward to receiving, simply stopped arriving.

Things always seemed to improve somewhat during the long summer breaks, but it wasn't until Master Newton finally finished school and moved back into Highclough House permanently that he witnessed his father slowly returning to his old, active self. He had involved himself in local issues once more and had for the first time, at the direct request of his son, rented out some of his large estate to the local sheep farmers, albeit at a much-reduced rate.

Father and son truly bonded and both finally found happiness after many years of individual loneliness. The only thing preventing this from becoming a bucolic idyll was the presence of the two girls. They seemed to have always attracted trouble and, having been expelled from several schools, the only solution appeared to be to send them to separate institutions. This seemed to have curbed their waywardness until, having also completed their studies, they were reunited.

The girls had become close to some of the younger men who had worked on the house during its final year of construction. Hadrian had always made a concerted effort to recruit locally, much to the benefit of the surrounding villages. Work there was scarce and what there was to be found was particularly hard, especially in the harsh, unforgiving winters. However, he had, on more than one occasion, been forced to dismiss a worker who had become over familiar with one, or both, of his young daughters. Predictably, this had led to even greater friction between the girls and their father.

Hadrian Newton was discovered hanging in his bedroom barely a week after the final such incident, the young man in question having been employed to carry out some basic maintenance to the roof.

The answer to Holmes's question, "What had convinced Matthew to lock up his father's bedroom?" had been fascinating, if not quite conclusive. Once Hadrian had sacked the impudent worker, harsh words were spoken by the girls. This seemed to amount to a threat that, once their father was gone, they would take over the house and do as they please. On discovering his father's body, young Matthew hadn't only remembered these chilling words, but had also made a further realization: There was still one obstacle remaining, and only after his own death could the girls ever inherit the estate. Although neither Matthew nor the girls had yet to read it, the contents of Hadrian's will were no secret. The house and all of his possessions were to pass directly to his son, just as expected. The girls would get a small stipend until they were married, and then a moderate dowry would accompany them on their way.

I have to admit as to being rather sceptical about the whole business. Arguments between parents and their children are commonplace and often far more vicious than either side would ever later admit. However, most of this vitriol is hot air, and tempers inevitably cool over time. To me, this supposed threat sounded far more likely to be just that: A simple, childish attempt to cause emotional injury to the father. In that light, Master Newton's fear for his life seemed rather over dramatic, perhaps even obsessive. Whatever Holmes had seen in this case to warrant us racing up north was quite beyond me.

After an hour-and-a-half, we passed through an iron gate and onto the Newton estate. Thankfully, the track was now firmly gravelled and progress increased markedly. We still had nearly a mile to travel and the road began to climb noticeably, clinging to the side of a dark green valley. Low dry stone walls formed large, mostly arbitrary-shaped, fields. The steep hill cast a long shadow far down the valley, hiding much of the detail below. Small groups of sheep grazed, the lambs now grown enough to be almost indistinguishable from their elders.

As we neared the crest of the hill, we had our first glance at Highclough House. Perfectly square, it had four short, round turrets on its corners, each one topped with a cone-shaped tile roof. The house was faced with warm, yellow stone, which helped soften its rather fortress-like appearance. Large, rectangular windows on the ground floor suggested grand, airy rooms for entertaining. However, the bedroom windows above were rather mismatched, being numerous slim openings topped with gothic arches – designed, I would imagine, to resemble ancient loopholes.

However, the most striking thing about the house wasn't its style or construction, but how it could possibly have been built up there at all. It was several miles from the nearest village, and all of these were steeply uphill. Newton had insisted that the house had all of the facilities one would expect: Running water, a heating system and modern plumbing. It may have not have had gas laid on, but in every other aspect it was a modern, comfortable house. It just happened to sit at the top of what many people would consider to be a small mountain.

We were greeted by a butler, Joseph, and a maid, who led us to our rooms, where we freshened up before joining Newton downstairs in the study. The interior of the house was a strange mixture of traditional and modern, but mostly it gave off an air of being unfinished, or at least unfurnished. Corridors were often just painted walls and a wooden floor. Several rooms, including even some of the larger ones, contained little other than a few chairs and tables, all surrounded by plain, unadorned walls.

The study was one of the few exceptions. Sitting on a large Persian rug were several comfortable armchairs and two long settees. A large fireplace dominated one side of the room, and above this were various portraits of the family. The opposite wall held a modest library of leather-bound volumes. The large windows let in the last of the evening light, and the candles that had already been lit completed a friendly, warm atmosphere.

Newton greeted us and then, almost as if he had read my mind, declared, "This had always been my favourite room. The rest of the house is rather too austere for my tastes."

He handed us each a glass of fine single malt. Now that he was more relaxed, and back in his home environment, he appeared rather more mature and thoughtful.

"Where are your sisters this evening?" asked Holmes, sipping his whisky.

"I have no idea, sir, is the honest answer. Joseph, the butler, said he saw them upstairs this afternoon, and they might well be somewhere in the house, but unless they call down to the kitchen for supper, I cannot be certain."

"Very well," Holmes declared. "To examine your father's room properly, I will require better light than that which we now have left to us. I suggest we take a light supper and retire early. Newton, for reasons of safety, you will swap rooms with myself, if you don't object. It is essential that we all lock our bedroom doors, and keep them locked all night."

This rather changed the mood and, after we had eaten, we headed upstairs, where Holmes slipped quietly into Newton's room while our host took the bedroom next to mine. I wasn't yet ready to sleep, so I invited Newton to my room for a few hands of cards and a smoke. He may not have been a smoker, but he was a fine card player, and had the best of me over the next couple of hours. He left around eleven o'clock and I heard him close and lock his door. Now tired from a long day, I lay down and was soon fast asleep.

Chapter IV

I woke to find myself lying in complete darkness. Somewhere, deep in my subconscious, I was certain that I had been roused by a sound coming from just outside the door. I sat upright, straining to hear if the noise had been real or simply imagined.

I waited for several minutes, and was just about to lie back down when I heard the queerest sound. It was a swishing or whooshing, from right outside the closed and locked bedroom door.

My mind raced as I wondered upon the possible causes of this most unusual sound. A gust of wind from an open window? Surely, not possible. An animal, perhaps a pet cat, or a trapped bird, brushing past the door? Not impossible, but would a cat's fur rustle so as it touched the door? Would a bird not call out in distress? No, it was something else, something more familiar.

The realisation suddenly hit me, I knew that sound. It was the sound of moving fabric – or more precisely, several layers of cloth, almost certainly fine silk. Although usually almost silent when moving, the act of rushing by the door at pace had given it a quite otherworldly tone. That I had heard no accompanying foot-falls only added to my growing sense of unease.

I leapt from my bed and unlocked the door. I peered, carefully into the hallway but all was dark and silent. After a few moments, I began to feel rather foolish. I had, of course, concluded that it must have been one or both of Newton's sisters, running along the corridor, but it soon began to dawn on me that I was almost certainly worrying over nothing. This was, after all, their house and they had every right to walk, or indeed run, wherever they wished, no matter the hour, day or night.

I let out a small sigh, and moved to step back into the bedroom, when I heard a sound so aberrant and disconcerting that I halted, frozen upon the spot.

From both ends of the hallway came a small laugh, barely more than loud sighs, but in perfect, unnatural unison. I stared, intently, first one way then the other, but could see nothing in the darkness. Two uncannily synchronised giggles followed, echoing eerily along the long, narrow

161

passage, followed by a swish of silk skirts, as the girls moved, unseen, in opposite directions, away from my position.

Feeling quite unnerved, and not wanting to be a victim of such games, I withdrew back into the bedroom and shut the door. I turned the key swiftly and with great relief. My first encounter with the Newton sisters had left me quite unsettled. In the distance I heard another laugh, both voices again in exact harmony, as if but one.

I turned and leaned back against the closed door. My heart rate was just beginning to return to something approaching normal. I breathed out, deeply.

The sudden, double burst of laughter that erupted at that exact second, just the other side of the door, shook my very nerves and made me leap involuntarily forwards, desperate to be as far away as I could from that awful sound.

I quickly gathered my wits and steeled myself to return to the corridor to confront my tormentors, when I remembered one of Holmes's myriad sayings: "Follow, Watson, but never be led."

I forced myself to return to bed. I refused to be intimidated, or influenced by, such childish tricks. I turned away from the door, covered my exposed ear with a large duck down pillow, and made to fall asleep.

Chapter V

The remainder of the night mercifully passed without incident. I awoke later than I had planned, well after eight o'clock and, sensing that the others had already risen, quickly dressed. As I rinsed my face in the cool water bowl, I recalled the *outré* events of the previous night. I decided that I should make no mention of these until I had time to discuss them with Holmes. Once presentable, I walked along the corridor and, having received no answer when knocking on Holmes's and Newton's doors, descended the dark wooden stairs and headed for the dining room.

I found Newton sitting at the far end of a long mahogany table, and he rose to greet me with his usual wide, infectious smile.

"Doctor Watson, good morning. I trust you slept well. Help yourself to coffee – the pot is hot. Eggs and bacon will be with us in a few minutes."

I poured myself a cup of the steaming brown elixir. The smell was wonderful. Coffee in the morning truly is one of life's great pleasures.

I took a sip. "Ah, exquisite, thank you. Have you seen Holmes? He wasn't in his room when I knocked."

"Oh, Mr. Holmes has been up and about since dawn, at least," replied Newton, slightly surprised that I wasn't already aware of this. "The kitchen staff – well Cook and Jenny, the maid – both swore that they had seen him

162

wandering around outside the house as they came in to work, and both start well before seven."

"That sounds like him," I sighed, feeling the usual guilt that haunted me when I couldn't share Holmes's fierce drive once engaged in a case. "I would be surprised if he fails to find at least something of interest," I volunteered, hopefully.

I was rescued by the arrival of both the hot food and Holmes himself. He sat and, without a word, helped himself to coffee along with an egg and a single rasher.

"Erm, Mr. Holmes, good morning, sir. Might I venture to inquire whether you have discovered anything of interest during your examinations?" Newton asked. His uncertainty had an edge of nervousness that I hadn't previously detected.

"Why, good morning, Master Newton. Doctor." Holmes smiled. His light, airy manner was a complete surprise to me. "And to answer your question," he turned to Newton, "no, not a thing. Nothing at all. Many footsteps – some old, some new – but nothing of relevance to this particular case."

"How can you be so sure?" Newton asked, "Surely any recent activity outside the house must be of interest?"

"There was a possibility that some imprints may have been of use to us, but it has been too long and nothing is distinct or, more importantly, individual. I have matched almost all of the footprints to those resident at the house, and the remainder appear to be those of staff or regular visitors.

"There isn't one singular set of footprints in all of the grounds surrounding the house," Holmes declared. "All of those, which I could identify, appear on at least three separate occasions."

"What does this mean?" I asked. "Does it help or hinder the investigation?"

"It helps us, exponentially, of course," replied Holmes. "It supports our client's belief that the party responsible for the death of his father was someone based at the house, or at least a regular visitor."

"Then you do believe me. Mr. Holmes. I am so relieved." Newton again smiled his big country grin. "I suspect that you would like to examine father's room now," he said.

"We would," answered Holmes, "but alone, if you would allow us. We must remain neutral at all times, and your presence may create undue influence."

"Oh yes, of course. Actually, I have some paperwork to which I really must attend. Please, have the freedom of the building. No door will be barred to you. I will be in the study, at the back of the house, overlooking the valley. It was father's favourite room. The views are sensational. He used to sit there and watch the seasons change, a glass of single malt in his hand," Newton concluded wistfully.

Newton quickly finished his coffee and left with a polite nod to each of us. Once he was beyond earshot, I whispered loudly to Holmes.

"Undue influence? When has anyone held even the slightest sway over you?" I tried not to laugh at Holmes's *faux* earnest expression.

"We must be alone, Watson," he retorted, now genuinely serious. "It seemed as good an excuse as any. Something isn't quite right here. I have yet to interview the twins. In fact, I have hardly laid eyes upon them since we arrived. But that is for later. Now we must take a look upstairs."

"Actually, old man, I have something rather important to convey regarding events which occurred last night," I interjected, quickly. "I also thought it best only to do so once we were alone."

I proceeded to recount, in as much detail as I could remember, what had happened that previous night. Holmes remained silent, but nodded at what he determined to be pertinent points in my account.

"Interesting, Watson. A childish prank or a deliberate attempt to unsettle us? Probably both. However, we have more immediate issues of far greater concern."

Chapter VI

Newton Senior's room was indeed at the rear of the house, directly above his study. This had been by deliberate design. He had posited that if he weren't in one room he would more than likely be in the other. This would ensure that he would never be disturbed by any noise from either above or below. We learned this from the butler, whom we encountered on the way up the stairs. He was most keen to help and followed us to Hadrian's room, with the complete approval of Holmes.

"Can I speak candidly, sir?" asked the butler.

"Of course, Joseph. I would expect no less from a former member of the Royal Artillery," replied Holmes, casually.

Joseph looked surprised, "But how did you know I was in the R.A.?"

"I could point to seven different signs, including burn marks on your right hand, friction scarring on your palms from hauling rope, and a slight deafness in your right ear," Holmes replied.

Joseph's mouth dropped open. Holmes then smiled, an open genuine smile that could put anyone at ease.

"But it was mostly the regimental badge pinned upon your waistcoat. The unmistakable, unique design of the Royal Artillery."

Joseph laughed, "Of course, sir. I forget I even have it on most of the time."

"But please do continue," I quickly added, trying to capitalise on the butler's now more-relaxed manner. "You were about to tell us something."

"Well, yes. I just wanted to ask you to promise to do you level best in this matter. I have known Mr. Newton for nearly twenty years, and I have to agree with his son that he would never take his own life – especially in such a manner, without leaving so much as a note."

"That troubled me also, Holmes," I agreed. "In most cases of suicide, the deceased leaves a letter or note, often explaining the reasons why they took such a course, and sometimes just a simple apology for their actions. I had meant to ask young Newton whether a note was found, but now we know there was nothing.

"In addition, I noticed that there were several guns locked in a cabinet in the dining room. I have yet to hear of a man who owned a gun ever having hanged himself," I finished, grimly.

Holmes seemed to think for a moment before replying. "You have both made very important points, and when these are added to what we already know, suicide does seem to be a rather unlikely cause of death. However, we must still examine all of the evidence with an open mind. I have several theories, but I hope to be able to significantly reduce the number of these in the next hour."

The door to Newton's room was closed but not locked. A wooden bench had been placed across the front in a weak effort to keep others out. Holmes sighed when he saw this and moved it quickly aside with exaggerated ease.

"Secured the scene?" he whispered under his breath.

The butler and I stayed back as Holmes knelt to examine the door and lock. He poked at it with a selection of illegal-looking tools that he produced from a leather roll, kept in some pocket hidden deep within his jacket. After a few minutes and seemingly satisfied with his work, he briefly examined the door frame before entering the room. He gestured that we should wait outside for now.

We watched as he carefully crept in, minutely examining each inch of the floor beneath him before stepping onto any part of it. After he was happy that he had inspected every iota, he knelt, then lay flat and picked at the carpet. He seemed to find several tiny shards of something of interest and placed these in his handkerchief. He then leaned over the bed and somehow, balancing without touching the surface, managed to examine this in intimate detail, this time using tweezers to remove minuscule particles. He then checked the windows thoroughly, searching the glass, frames, and latches.

"You can now enter," he declared. "As I hoped, I have enough data already to discount several of my theories," he admitted with unusual candour, "but not yet enough to come to a firm conclusion."

"I'm still waiting to hear the official account of what happened. I wired the local police yesterday," he added, "but I think I can predict most of what will be in their report."

"So, I believe, can I," I agreed. "It will state that suicide is the most likely cause of death, the man had a known history of depression, and there are no clear signs of foul play. The lack of a note will be put down to mental stress. Not all suicides leave a note, it is true. Case closed."

"Apart from the report lacking your admirable brevity," Holmes agreed. "I fear that you may very well be correct, Doctor."

He then appeared to be in two minds over something. He looked as if he was about to make a statement but stopped himself, just as the words were forming on his lips. He frowned, looked up at the ceiling, and then seemed to slip into a state of deep thought.

"Are you alright?" I asked, with some concern. "You look like you have taken a turn there."

Holmes's head suddenly snapped round to face me. "No, not at all, Watson. I just need to think. Joseph?" he asked. "Would you be a good fellow and find out whether any mail has arrived for us?"

Holmes beamed a sincere smile, which the butler saw straight through, but he politely agreed to Holmes's request and left us alone in the bedroom.

"You could have just asked him to leave, you know," I stated, matter-of-factly. "He is a decent fellow. He would have understood and taken no offence."

"What matters is that we are alone," replied Holmes, waving away my light protest.

He stood, stone-still, deep in thought. His eyes were focused, but not upon anything that one present could see. After almost a minute, he declared, "There are problems with this case, both logical and practical."

"I agree. The most glaring issue is that the whole notion of the girls wanting to kill young Newton to gain control of the estate is absurd," I declared. "I mean, all he has to do is – "

"Draw up a will that leaves nothing to his siblings." Holmes declared, effortlessly completing my sentence. "Yes, and that is just the most obvious flaw."

"Could it be a mere oversight? Has it simply not occurred to him that he can protect himself by rendering his own death unprofitable to his sisters?" I asked.

166

"No. He may have the air of a country bumpkin, but he isn't an uneducated man. I believe him when he says his father was murdered. However, I am, as yet, undecided as to whether anything else he has told us is true. I'm far from certain that we have ascertained the real motive for his father's killing."

"Or maybe, even, the true identity of the perpetrator?" I was beginning to share Holmes's misgivings and a theory of my own was beginning to form.

"Holmes, when I was with the army in India, I came across a clever trick. By childishly simple means, it was often possible to not only gain entry to a locked room, but also to retrieve the key itself from the other side of the door."

"By poking the key backwards with a sharp object until it drops upon a sheet of newspaper slid under the door? Pull the sheet back and *voila*, you have the key! Really, Watson, how is this relevant? The door was locked with the key still *in situ*, in the lock on the other side."

"Actually, that was just my starting point," I continued. "Imagine this scenario. The suicide is faked. Newton is strangled and then hung up. The killer leaves the room and locks the door from the outside. He then works the key hard, left and right, in the lock until the shaft weakens and snaps. He then pockets his part of the key, absconds, and disposes of the evidence later at an undisclosed location."

"Do continue this most fascinating theory," encouraged Holmes, with only the merest hint of sarcasm.

"Don't you see?" I asked, earnestly. Holmes raised an eyebrow but said nothing, so I continued.

"The room is found locked. The observer quickly kneels and looks to see if the key is still in the door. From his point of view, it would appear that, indeed, it is, and that the door has been locked, presumably from the other side. In the confusion and panic that follows, is it not possible that this has been overlooked?"

Holmes walked to the open door and closed it. The key was in one piece and protruding proudly from the lock.

"Very well, but the key might have been replaced later. A pair of needle-nosed pliers and a screwdriver would make the task of removing the broken key a simple one – a minute at most. A spare could then be placed where we see it now and no one would be the wiser."

"Watson, I applaud your imagination and logic. I would only add that your plan is actually aided by the fact that domestic doors almost invariably open inwards. This would hide the lock on the inside of the door from view for valuable seconds at least, and in all probability for far longer. Nobody would take the time to examine the hidden side of a door when a man was hanging right in front of them."

Excitedly, I continued my theory, "There is only one person here who could have manhandled a body in such a way, if we discount the butler. Do you think that maybe – ?"

"No." Holmes cut me dead in my tracks. "Your theory is really rather brilliant, Doctor, but, almost sadly in this case, it isn't correct."

My face fell. I genuinely thought I was on the right path for once.

"Don't be despondent, Watson," consoled Holmes, in a rare show of sympathy. "I formulate multiple theories for each problem I encounter, and ninety percent of them are quickly proven wrong. As long as you learn something from each failure, you will always continue to improve.

"In this case," he added, kindly, "the fault isn't yours. You have been stymied by something that I have yet to disclose. Having examined the locks on both sides of the door, and the key itself, I can state that there are no signs of force having been used. The brass plates on both sides of the door are polished and unmarked. Any violent movement of the key would have left a clear trace."

"Oh, very well, I understand," I replied, meekly, before recovering. "But were you not, yourself, on the verge of making a pronouncement on the case?" I asked.

"I was simply about to state that when it comes to motive, there is only one person who definitely gains from the death of Hadrian Newton."

"Yes. Matthew Newton." I agreed. "Could this whole story of his sisters and their madness just be a blind to throw us off the scent?"

"This has occurred to me, also. But why, then, did he call upon us for help? He has what he wants. Everything is his. Why risk it all by calling in an outside agency? The police are certainly giving him no cause for concern." Holmes walked slowly around the room as he spoke.

Holmes again looked up. "What do you make of the apparatus Newton used to end his life?" he asked, completely changing the subject.

"Well, I haven't seen the rope itself, but I believe you are referring to the chandelier hook in the ceiling, as I have observed you looking up at it on at least three occasions."

Holmes nodded in agreement, but his eyes remained fixed upon the stout hook protruding from a large boss in the centre of the ceiling, decorated with an artistically elaborate carving of a rose.

"Well, what can I say? It is a standard iron hook, strongly fixed in place to support a sizeable chandelier. Perfectly normal up here, I suppose, where there is no chance of having gas laid on. Without asking Matthew, we won't know for sure, but I would bet that his father removed the chandelier once he realised that he would never use the thing. After all, who needs a chandelier in their bedroom?"

"But what of the boss, itself? Does nothing about it strike you as unusual?" Holmes asked, finally taking his eyes away from the sinister-looking hook.

"Perhaps," I stumbled, failing to see what Holmes had observed. "I suppose, well, it is rather large. In diameter I mean, it must be more than twenty inches across."

"Twenty-four," Holmes corrected.

"Yes, maybe it is," I grumbled. "But we haven't seen the chandelier was to hang from it. Perhaps it was unusually heavy and needed additional support. What could be the significance of a slightly unusual ceiling boss?"

"Possibly nothing." Holmes clapped his hands. "Anyway, we are finished here for now," he declared. "Time to return downstairs and put our findings to Master Newton."

Chapter VII

We found Newton in his father's study, where he appeared to be struggling with some legal documents. "Gentlemen, I hope you return with some good news. I, for one, am completely out of my depth here." He held up buff coloured folders in each hand. "I'll have to engage a professional to help me with these, I think."

"That would be very wise, but choose carefully. Find someone that your father knew well and trusted." Holmes advice was as sincere as it was serious.

"Yes, you're quite right. Old Mr. Goldman in Stocksbridge is, or *was*, father's solicitor. I thought I could work through all this on my own – that the challenge might take my mind off my terrible suspicions."

"As a doctor, I would suggest that a combination of the two would be the healthiest course. Keep yourself occupied by learning what you can from your father's papers. Then you can take everything you have to Goldman, who will then explain to you whatever remains."

"Very good, Doctor. But now onto more pressing matters," said Holmes, gently moving the conversation forwards. "Was your father a heavy sleeper?" he asked.

"Why, yes he was. He may have been an early riser, but once his head hit the pillow at night, he was dead to the world." Newton's face reddened as he realised the inappropriateness of his metaphor.

Newton started to apologise, but Holmes simply raised a hand and offered an understanding smile. "As I thought," he replied, quietly. "Well, I can now confirm two things, Mr. Newton," he added, after a pause, in a louder, much more confident tone. "Firstly, your father was indeed murdered and, secondly, I know exactly how the vile deed was done."

There then followed a moment of total silence as we took in what Holmes had declared. Once I had recovered my composure, I began to think about his statement and a thought occurred.

"But who was responsible?" I asked. "Surely, that is the most important issue here."

"All of the issues are equally important, Watson. Without any single one of them, we have no case. I am now confident that I can demonstrate that murder was done here and how it was actioned. The identity of the killer is the one missing piece of the puzzle. We need proof of all three."

"But I've told you who is responsible, Mr. Holmes. It was my sisters," Newton implored.

"Perhaps," Holmes muttered, his mind clearly elsewhere. "However, you've never adequately explained how you came to know of your siblings' plot against their father," he stated, with more than a hint of accusation.

Newton was momentarily shocked, but regained his composure most admirably. "It was exactly as I recounted earlier," he replied, confidently, almost defiantly. "I had overheard the threats that they made to my father, as he dismissed yet another enamoured employee. I was also certain, beyond any doubt, that my father would never end his own life, so when I discovered his body, I knew that there was only one possible cause of death: Murder. In addition, there was no-one else present that night. It could only have been them."

"We shall see," Holmes replied, enigmatically. "But now I need a smoke. Watson, please join me in the living room. Master Newton, could you please ask Joseph to join us there, I require his help in organising what I hope will be the conclusion of this affair."

Chapter VIII

Holmes spent a good twenty minutes conversing with and giving detailed instructions to Joseph the butler. They huddled together, closely, by the large bay window, but I overheard little of Holmes's plan, excepting that it would involve the authorities at some point. Once their little tryst was concluded, Holmes excused himself and left me alone in the empty but comfortable sitting room. I filled my pipe and sat back to ponder the case.

After turning it over in my head for nearly an hour, I realised that I was no closer to solving the mystery. I was still torn between the possible culprits. Newton seemed such an open and honest young man, yet he was

170

the direct beneficiary of his father's death. His story seemed more incredulous with each closer inspection. The sisters were no real risk to him, surely. Moreover, how on earth could two slight young women have hanged a fully-grown man without outside help?

I was just emptying my pipe into the grate and preparing it for a refill when Holmes returned and joined me in front of the fireplace.

"Well, it appears that you have opened the final innings," I said, as I filled my pipe.

Holmes ignored me and pulled out a sorry-looking briar from his jacket pocket. I offered him my tobacco pouch, which he accepted, and proceeded to fill his awful pipe three-quarters to the brim. Before he lit it, he took a sniff of the tobacco pressed into its bowl.

"Mm," he declared, with obvious satisfaction. "A Cavendish from the former colonies. Not too scented. A hint of vanilla – or nougat I think. Nice and dark – should be a cool smoke. Slightly moist. I think the doctor has had a delivery from H. and S. in the last three – no, *two* days." Holmes smiled and lit his pipe with a long match.

"Arrived yesterday morning, direct from Bedford," I confirmed, with a smile.

Holmes nodded, took a deep draught, and exhaled a writhing cloud of steel grey smoke. Looking down, he rubbed at his trousers, releasing a smaller, white puff of dust.

"Wherever have you been to get in such a state?" I asked.

"Oh, just a quick visit to parts of the house less travelled," was his rather cryptic reply, upon which he steadfastly refused to elaborate.

I treasured these precious moments when we could forget everything and simply enjoy a pipe together in shared friendship. We spent a blissful, almost entirely silent, hour smoking and appreciating each other's company. Just as I was beginning to nod off, Joseph rapped lightly and then nudged open and peered around the door.

"Sirs, many apologies for the interruption," he began, and then addressed Holmes, directly. "You asked me to inform you when . . . ." the butler deliberately left the sentence hanging, unfinished.

"Ah, yes, Joseph, thank you," Holmes replied, leaping to his feet. "Come now, Watson, we will have but one chance to interview them on their own, before events overtake us!"

"The sisters? You know where they are?" I asked with renewed enthusiasm, but Holmes had already passed Joseph, sped into the hallway beyond, and was almost out of earshot.

I struggled to keep up as he swept up the wide staircase to the first floor landing, two steps at a time. He turned left and rushed along the plain, unadorned corridor until he reached its terminus. Directly ahead was a solid oak bedroom door, heavily lacquered in brilliant gloss white paint. To our left, but a few feet further back along the hall, was another identical bedroom door. Holmes ignored these and turned right, into a much narrower passageway that dog-legged back left and, having no windows, was shrouded in darkness. I followed, in silence, as the tall detective before me crept along this narrow hall towards the rather more humble pine door that lay at the far end.

We were barely six feet from this barrier when we began to hear voices. It was the sisters, talking in short bursts, followed by simultaneous giggles. I admit that I paused, as the events of the previous night flooded back and the hairs on the back of my neck rustled against my collar.

Holmes reached for the door handle, just as the voices within suddenly stilled. He quickly pulled open the door, and burst inside.

I swiftly followed but, to my utter astonishment, the room was empty.

That Holmes didn't seem at all fashed simply added to my sense of bewilderment. He began, frantically, to search the room, thrusting aside a full length mirror and pulling open the wardrobes, until he stopped for a brief moment, his head buried deep inside one of the closets. I moved forward to see what he had discovered, but he leaned forward, pushed aside the hanging garments, and stepped inside. The dresses swung back behind Holmes, leaving no trace of him ever having entered.

I took a step back, before calling out. After a few seconds, a voice responded, muffled, but just about discernable.

"For heaven's sake, Watson, go back and watch the hallway to the landing."

Holmes's order was exactly what I needed to break free of my stupefaction. I ran back along the dark passage, along the hallway, and onto the landing. I took position at the top of the stairs. Unless there was another hidden flight of steps, anyone wishing to leave that wing would have to pass this way.

Barely ten seconds later, I heard a disconcertingly familiar sound. A rustling of skirts, along with the very lightest of footfalls. Out of the gloom rushed two figures. They skidded on the carpeted floor as they attempted to change direction, but a combination of their light shoes and the forward momentum was too great and they fell upon the floor, a mere eight feet or so from my position. They scrambled to their feet and turned to run, but the imposing figure of Sherlock Holmes loomed into view, just behind them.

"Ladies, please, there is no need for alarm. I only wish to ask of you a few, simple questions," Holmes stated, with open arms.

The girls move closer to each other. They suddenly seemed very small and vulnerable – two pale, white faces barely distinguishable in the dark corridor.

A small, soft voice broke the silence.

"We have . . ." declared one of the sisters –

" – nothing – " they chimed in unison –

" – to say," concluded the other.

Holmes paused to consider the situation, before replying.

"Very well, that is your right."

He stepped aside and the girls, tentatively, crept passed him, presumably to return to their room.

Once they were out of sight, I rounded on Holmes.

"Why did you let them go? Surely, we have learned nothing," I protested.

"Far from it. I believe I now have all of the pieces needed to solve this little puzzle."

Knowing full well that he would refuse to expand any further upon this enigmatic pronouncement, I followed him back down to the living room without comment.

We had barely lit our pipes when Joseph reappeared at the door.

"The ladies of the house have been seated, along with the young fellow. The police will be another hour at least, I am afraid."

"That cannot be helped. We must begin and hope that the authorities gain an extra stride in their step," Holmes announced.

"The dining room is prepared, sir," replied Joseph, beckoning us toward door.

Chapter IX

The table was laid for eight. Newton was already present, sitting in his father's chair at the head of the table. On either side of him were his sisters. They were nearly identical in appearance, a slight difference in the way that they wore their thick red hair being all that separated them. Both had porcelain white skin. They wore indistinguishable lilac satin dresses. They made no effort to acknowledge anyone else present, instead they sat, stock-still, staring straight forwards at one another. Which was Rosalind or Rosalie, I couldn't begin to guess.

Next to the girl on the left was a young man of perhaps twenty years. His clothes were poor and his rough hands attested to a life of hard manual labour. He appeared to be extremely nervous, constantly fidgeting and looked particularly uncomfortable and out of place.

Joseph, along with Jenny, the very attractive and efficient maid, served a fine dinner of chicken soup followed by succulent lamb chops, accompanied by local vegetables. The meal was eaten in complete silence. At any moment, I expected Holmes to rise and deliver a damning speech to settle the matter once and for all, but he remained silent, picking at his food in his usual, bird-like, fashion. I must admit that I was the only one to finish my plate. All of the other dishes, including those of Newton, were barely touched.

I took a large draught of the excellent claret and happily refilled my glass from the decanter. As I had no idea what Holmes had planned, I decided to wait and see what would happen, rather than waste my time in idle and probably fruitless speculation. Newton seemed as puzzled as I was and looked, if anything, even more uncomfortable than the mysterious young stranger who sat before us, struggling with both the cutlery and his table manners.

The identity of the unexpected visitor slowly became clear to me as I observed him throughout the awkward repast. He shot an occasional pleading glance at Holmes and myself, but mostly, when not staring directly at his food, he looked from one flame-haired Newton daughter to the other, his eyes begging for assistance. Not once did he look at Matthew Newton. He must be one of the young men dismissed by Hadrian Newton when he became too close to his daughters. Logic would suggest him to have been the most recent casualty of Newton's strict familial code, the one who had recently worked on the roof.

The meal ended with the reappearance of Joseph and the maid, who quickly cleared the table and replaced the wine decanter with another two-thirds filled with a deep ruby-red port. I couldn't have been the only one who noticed how perfectly it matched the rose-red hair of the two young ladies sitting to either side of it.

I helped myself to a glass and passed the bottle left to Holmes, but he subtly waved it away. He then stood and tapped his glass, rather unnecessarily, to gain the attention of all of those present.

"You have all enjoyed a fine meal, freshly prepared entirely from the finest local fare," Holmes began. "I have allowed this as, I fear, that for one or more of you, it may be the very last time that you taste such finery."

Four pairs of eyes were now fixed upon Holmes, but they all appeared equally troubled. I would have to wait a little longer for the answers to this sad episode.

"The slaying of Hadrian Newton was a cold and terrible act, one made even worse by the identity of those responsible. Even the very fact that it has now been proven to have been murder has, in itself, also become part of the mystery," began Holmes, most enigmatically.

"However, we must first begin with the act itself, and explain how the foul deed was committed," continued Holmes, the shadow of his tall figure now looming large in the candlelight.

"What was required was the death of Hadrian Newton. However, it was imperative that this terrible act should appear to the authorities to be nothing other than a suicide. It was clear from the onset that the best way to achieve this deception was to strike when he was apparently safely ensconced in his bedroom, behind a heavy, locked door. Surely, a body found hanging in such circumstances could only be recorded as death by their own hand.

"But," Holmes exclaimed, plangently pausing as his voice echoed around the sparsely-furnished, wood-panelled dining room. "Was there any way that ingress could have be made without breaking a window or forcing a lock? It so happens that there was one way into that apparently secure room, but one that could only be known of and fashioned by someone who had worked for many years on the construction of the house."

Holmes again paused for a moment, and then suddenly, almost violently, his right arm shot up, index finger stretched towards the chandelier.

"The ceiling?" I asked, with no little surprise. "The killer came down from above? But how?"

"The ceiling boss, Watson!" Holmes exclaimed, dramatically.

He waited for this revelation to sink in before continuing in a far calmer tone.

"The murder itself was clever and sophisticated," explained Holmes. "Our villain had discovered a way by which he could access the upper rooms of the house from the attics above the bedrooms. The killer knew that the large ceiling bosses were now redundant. No chandelier would ever be hung from them. In the attics, directly above the bedrooms, he was able to adapt the boss above Newton's bedroom so that it could be removed and replaced at will. Here, he was free to act in whatever way he wished during the day, knowing that he wouldn't be disturbed by Hadrian, who never returned to his bedroom during daylight hours."

"His scheme was diabolically clever. As I learned from visiting the attic, he cut out the boss from above, but rather than let it fall, he fixed to it a pair of sturdy cross-beams, which allowed it to be removed and replaced with only minimal effort. Everything was now in place."

"Waiting for Newton to fall into his usual deep sleep, the assailant removed the boss from the attic above. He descended through the hole left in the ceiling using the very rope that he then proceeded to wrap around the neck of Hadrian Newton. Violently, he pulled the cord tightly until all life had left his pleading, uncomprehending eyes. After securing the rope in a noose around Newton's neck, the killer climbed back up and completed his work from above. He positioned the boss halfway across the hole in the ceiling and rested it upon the recently fitted cross-beams. He then slipped the rope through the hook of the ceiling boss and heaved up the body with, perhaps, the aid of a pulley, until it dangled listlessly. The rope was then secured to the hook and, finally, the boss, now fully supporting the weight of the body, was carefully pushed back into place.

"To anyone entering the room, it would appear that suicide was the only possible cause of death." Holmes looked round, from one pale face to another.

"How fiendish," I whispered, barely able to comprehend the lengths that someone might go to kill another human being. "Who was this man, this cold, calculating devil?"

"Now I should introduce Mr. Edward Holding." Holmes gestured towards the unfamiliar young man. "Master Holding has worked on the house, on and off, since he was a boy of just fourteen years. He witnessed the final phase of major construction, and all of the subsequent interior work and decoration. He was in a unique position to advise on how to gain access to the bedrooms. Joseph, here, has confirmed to me that, until very recently, he was employed to carry out minor repairs to the roof of the house. He was also the last worker to be sacked for becoming inappropriately close to the Newton sisters.

"This much is all easily proved, for I have seen the doctored ceiling boss myself from above while examining the attic." He then turned to the pale faced newcomer. "When added to the testimony of Joseph, and that of the foreman of works, there can be little doubt that you are responsible for these 'alterations', Holding.

"Whether you were also responsible for the installation of the hidden doors, false walls, and various other hidden passageways that appeared to allow the girls to traverse the length and breadth of the house as if by magic, completely unseen, is of no real importance. It does prove, however, that these young ladies have used their strong powers of persuasion, successfully, on previous occasions."

"Wait a minute," Holding suddenly exclaimed. "Yes, all right, I admit it. I made the changes to the boss, but I didn't kill Mr. Newton. I was supposed to, but I just couldn't do it. He was a good man. It was all wrong. I refused to. Then he sacked me and that was that. I haven't set a foot back inside this house since then, I swear it."

"Oh, I believe you, Holding, don't worry. The charge you will ultimately face may yet be one as lenient as conspiracy to murder, so there is still a possibility that you just might survive to tell of this sorry business in your dotage," Holmes replied, with some venom.

"There is a history here," Holmes continued, "one that has manifested itself several times during the latter stages of the completion of Highclough House. As we already know, several young men, after becoming close to one, or possibly both, of the young ladies present, have been dismissed by their father for inappropriate conduct.

"This seems to have increased the enmity which already existed between father and daughters to a disastrous level. This was when the girls made the fateful decision to take revenge, and began plotting."

This, so far, tallied with what we had already suspected, and with what Matthew Newton had claimed right from the beginning. I was preparing for a sad but predictable end to Holmes's speech.

"It didn't take the sisters long to identify Holding as a most useful and malleable ally. His interest was probably piqued by the overt attention they paid to him, his complicity no doubt guaranteed by the promise of future riches. His face was already well-known, so he was free to wander the house uncontested."

"However, before he could realise his scheme, he was summarily dismissed. The plan was left unfinished, hanging in the air," Holmes stated. "But then, just a week later, someone enacted the remainder of this evil plot." exclaimed Holmes.

The tall detective paused, stared intently deep into the eyes of each of the young suspects sat before us, and continued.

"Now, finally, we come to the real conspiracy here. Who, after Holding had refused to carry out the act of killing, was actually responsible for the death of Hadrian Newton, but a week later?"

"First, we have ascertained for whom Holding was initially acting when he so cleverly adapted the ceiling boss in Newton's bedroom. That part was simple – he worked for Rosalie and Rosalind Newton. I cannot be certain of what they offered him to carry out this egregious plan, but it seems that it wasn't quite enough for him to risk his liberty or even, perhaps, his life."

Holmes then addressed the two girls, directly.

"I have no doubt that you will require to see the proof against you before making any statement, but I have the distinct impression that young Holding is about to confirm my theory."

"He's right. They offered me a share of their inheritance if I helped them," Holding blurted out, right on cue.

Holmes smiled. "Ah yes, of course, and that also explains why you failed to carry out the plan. It was only once you had completed the practical work on the scheme that it finally dawned on you that there was absolutely no certainty that the Newton daughters would ever receive any inheritance at all. This is when you withdrew from the plan altogether."

"It's true, sir. I couldn't take such a risk with nothing in it for me at the end. I didn't even want to kill him. I had nothing against the man. They have a way about them, sir. They poisoned my mind," Holding sobbed, wringing his now-shaking, hands.

"But, nonetheless, Newton was murdered, and in the exact method schemed up by his own daughters. We have a witness here who, I am sure, would be happy to testify against you," Holmes gestured from one sister to the other. "But it matters little, for the law is on its way. They will take things from here and decide who is guilty, although they may not be quite as reasonable as I."

Holmes made to sit back down when we suddenly heard a new voice speak. It was quiet but assured and came from the left side of the table.

"We will not sit here and be accused of murder when we did no such thing," declared one of the, up until now, completely silent sisters.

"So, what, exactly, did you do?" asked Holmes, with great precision.

"Don't," hissed the sister opposite.

"No, we must tell Mr. Holmes everything. It is the only way that we can now save ourselves."

The girl turned back to Holmes. "Yes, we planned a terrible fate for our father, but we didn't enact the scheme."

"We have lived a life of suffering and separation," continued the girl. "Rosalind and I are as close as any two people can be. We have never meant to cause any trouble, but we cannot bear to be apart. It is only then that we transgress, but always, and only, with one goal: That of being reunited."

"It was only when father began to change that they started to separate us," interjected Rosalie from across the table. "After mother died, he could barely even look at us. I think the sight of the two of us, young reminders of his lost wife, drove him slightly mad. Someone decided that we should be sent away and that we must be kept apart. By then, Father had lost his remaining spirit and meekly agreed." She made no attempt to hide the bitterness in her voice.

"One evening, during a summer break, we were exploring the house. It was late, after eleven, and most everyone had gone to sleep. We enjoyed these times, when we could roam the house without fear of chastisement. We found that father had left his study unlocked and ventured inside. We could only assume that he had been drinking, as he had also left the door to his safe unlocked and indeed wide open."

"What else could we do?" Rosalind picked up the story, without a pause. "We looked inside. Of course, most of what we found was meaningless to us – papers, certificates, and accounts. But, eventually, we discovered father's will. We nearly left it alone. After all, he had made no secret of what was contained within. But we were curious, and so we opened it."

"What we found shocked us. But excited us, also." Rosalie continued. Although it brought back uncomfortable memories of the previous night's unpleasantness, I couldn't help but be fascinated by the way they could relate the story in such a fashion, almost as if they were, in fact, a single consciousness.

"What we read wasn't at all what father had always described. He wrote that the will hadn't only been drawn up in accordance with his own wishes, but also those of our late mother. She had convinced him to share the entire estate between all of us. Half for Matthew and half for ourselves."

"Now I do see a motive for murder," I thought grimly.

"Yes. We were angry with father for our suffering and we now saw a way to extract revenge and also secure our futures. We would be free of the torments of both separation and financial insecurity. We would have no need to ever marry and could remain together. Forever."

The girls smiled at one another. That last word, spoken in unison, had chilled my blood. For a second time, I had seen something of what the local men had spoken of, something disturbing, almost unnatural in their behaviour.

"However, your plan came to an abrupt halt when Holding had second thoughts. Without having seen the will for himself, he only had your word that he would receive what you had promised and not just a long drop at the end of a short rope," Holmes declared.

"But then what happened?" I asked. "You must know who did, eventually, carry out your evil scheme?"

"Do you really need us to tell you?" sneered Rosalind. "Who else could have become aware of the contents of the will and who would benefit from our incarceration? Who followed us in the darkness and eavesdropped as we spoke our secrets?"

I shot a look towards Matthew Newton, who now wore an expression of complete disgust and growing malevolence.

"Why, you of course!" I exclaimed.

"You discovered your sisters' plot, just as we have heard," Holmes interjected. "However, rather than feel any concern for your father's safety, you were struck by the sudden realisation that you stood to lose half of his estate to your siblings upon his death.

"This was quite unacceptable to you. You were the heir. You were the one who had stayed with him through all of the dark times. You had endured his slow recovery, all the time holding his genuine affection and friendship in utter contempt. This was all done in the knowledge that, one day, all of this would be yours. You felt betrayed and angry."

"Your true personality is, after all, not the one you have worked so hard to create and exhibit, both in public and in front of Doctor Watson and myself," Holmes continued. "It is here that you made a mistake – a common one, often made by the wealthy and the arrogant. You discounted the intelligence of your own servants."

"I did what?" Newton roared, his face now incandescent with rage. "You have no idea what you are talking about. You know nothing! I had no hand in my father's death. We were close, just as I told you. It was *them*!" He pointed to his sisters on either side of him, his outstretched finger shaking as he tried to control his anger.

"Yes, you told us many things, most of which were a pack of lies. I simply asked those who serve you to verify these claims of yours. Those around you, those whom you rarely acknowledge and barely even notice – but they are always there, waiting to serve. They have been party to many of your confrontations with your father and they told a rather different tale – one of aggression and myriad heated arguments. The subject of these was, almost universally, money.

"You wanted rid of your father, but you lacked both the courage and imagination to act yourself. When you stumbled upon your sisters' plot, you saw the perfect solution to all of your problems. You would complete their terrible scheme and then simply wait for their plot to be discovered and your siblings arrested. They would either hang or spend the rest of their lives in gaol, leaving you to inherit the estate in its entirety. However, the plan, as plotted and finally enacted, proved rather too convincing, the estate appeared destined to be split, just as was intended. Your frustration grew as the local authorities refused to believe your insistence that there had been foul play. You were finally forced to bring in outside help. Sadly for you, you chose to knock upon my door."

"You puffed-up amateur! You have no proof of my involvement – nothing at all!" Newton snarled, his lip curling, menacingly.

"Do I not?" replied Holmes, dismissively. "Other than, of course, the fact that you are the one person present upon that terrible night who could have carried out the deed. All of the house's other occupants were always in the company of at least one other. Additionally, I've determined that the footprints that I found in the attic are a match. No one else in the household wears hand-made boots with such a distinctive fine pattern of nails set into their leather soles.

"However, the most damning evidence was found earlier today by Joseph. I asked him to examine your clothes for signs of damage or scuffs from heavy manual labour. Before you object, Joseph didn't trespass into your private rooms or breach any trusts."

Newton's fists were now white balls, shaking with fury. I casually picked up the largest knife that remained before me, secreted it below the table, and prepared my body to pounce if Newton's temper should get the better of him.

Holmes continued, quite unaffected.

"Here, once again, the arrogance of your class has betrayed you. Joseph had no need to cross a line because you had already, to your mind at least, disposed of the offending garments. To your kind, those who serve you are merely the invisible, unknown drones attending to the every whim of the hive. You give them your problems, your cast-offs, and they deal with them, quickly and quietly. Joseph simply visited the laundry. There he found various articles of clothing, stained and dirtied with the unmistakable plaster flakes and dust acquired from having moved the heavy ceiling boss."

"If we add to this the testimony of Holding and that of your sisters, I believe the police will have ample evidence to charge you with the murder of your father, Hadrian Newton."

Holmes stopped and listened. We could hear carriages arriving, crunching gravel beneath their iron-rimmed wheels.

"Master Newton," Holmes declared. "You aren't the first to try to deceive me, and I am certain that you won't be the last. It may, or may not, be of interest to you to know that each attempt only increases my overall knowledge and experience, making every subsequent effort less likely to succeed. For this, I thank you."

Holmes then addressed the two, now ashen-faced, girls. "I am sorry, but in order to give evidence against your brother, you will have to admit to your part in the affair. A charge of conspiracy to murder, even with extenuating circumstances, will almost certainly mean time in gaol, but I will do all that I can to ensure that you are both tried and incarcerated together."

The door opened and half-a-dozen burly policemen entered the dining room. Holmes rose, bowed slightly to those before him, and left. I followed quickly, having no stomach to witness Newton's struggles as the men in dark blue attempted to arrest him.

Chapter X

After Holmes had briefed them, the police were happy to take us as far as Stocksbridge, from where we just made the last train to Sheffield. Once we reached the steel city, we took a late train home to London and were back in Baker Street at just after one in the morning. Our guardian angel, Mrs. Hudson, had left out some bread and cold meat on the dining room table. I happily indulged, while Holmes leisurely picked at a piece of ham. Shortly after our small repast, we were sitting in our chairs, pipes filled and lit, happily smoking away in quiet contemplation.

"Holmes," I asked, after taking a deep draw upon my pipe, "how on earth did you first know that the killer had come down through the ceiling?"

"I found small pieces of chipped paint and plaster upon the bed and the carpet. An attempt had been made to clean up, but it was rushed and far from thorough. The presence of paint could be explained in a new house, it might have been brought into the bedroom on an item of clothing, or footwear, but the plaster on the bed could only have come from the carved ceiling boss above. Nothing else in the room was made from such a material. That is where I ventured, before we took our memorable dinner. With the aid of the ever-efficient Joseph, I examined the attics above the bedrooms. I soon discovered the machinery with which the plan was enacted, along with the other vital clues. I then recalled your experience of the sister's preternatural night time behaviour and suspected that Newton himself may have witnessed something similar, from which he learned of the foul scheme being constructed above."

"Later confirmed by the girls themselves," I nodded. "At least I will sleep better tonight, now that I know how they moved around the house as if ghosts."

I puffed upon my briar for a few moments, as the events of the past few days swirled around in my head, slowly forming into a cohesive whole.

"The ceiling rose." I whispered, half to myself. "Just one of the roses of Highclough."

Holmes didn't reply. We sat quietly and continued to smoke for a while, a spicy-scented blue-grey fug now gently floating around us. Then he finally broke the silence. "There are only two types of people who are unaffected by money: Those who have always had it, and those who have never had any at all. Those of us caught in between the two ruin our lives in its endless pursuit."

"Is that why you rarely seem to charge a fair rate for your work?" I asked, mischievously.

"But to whom, exactly, in this affair could I send an invoice?" Holmes shrugged, with unexpected humour. "This may be unique among all of my cases. In the end, when I addressed all of the concerned parties, every single one present was, to a greater or lesser extent, guilty."

I looked into Holmes's sincere face, not knowing how to respond. But his lip twitched and then the corners of his mouth raised, slightly. He tried to stop himself, and then laughed, loudly.

I couldn't help but join him.

The Shackled Man
by Andrew Bryant

We sat apart and had not spoken for nearly a quarter-of-an-hour – not because of any animosity between us had we not spoken, but merely because we were both involved in activities that needed no explanation, consultation, and, in fact, no conversation of any kind. The window was slightly open, and the noises from the street drifted up to us, giving us a comfortable background of sounds. I was holding the newspaper that my friend had put into my hand the moment I entered the room. Holmes was cleaning a pistol.

I was reading a story on the murder of one William Jones, actor, formally of Cardiff.

Mr. Jones had been found in late winter, chained to a wall in a guard's room of the ruined Caerphilly Castle, ten miles north of Cardiff. Mr. Jones had been dressed only in shirt and trousers, was bare foot, and had been gagged with a woman's scarf. Mr. Jones had also been soaking wet prior to his death, and was frozen when found. The police were now in the process of investigating the guilt or innocence of the last known person to see him alive, his alleged *paramour*, a Miss Mary Llewellyn.

The pistol was an old British East India Company flintlock, .70-calibre, that I had picked up in Afghanistan and brought back with me, and that I had given to Holmes as a gift. To my knowledge he had never fired the weapon, but seemed to enjoy handling it, cleaning it, and working the action before returning it to its case.

I finished reading the story and folded the paper. Holmes put the pistol away.

"So, Watson. It's unusual, isn't it?"

"Unusual?"

"The death of Mr. Jones."

"It's certainly not usual."

"It's uncommon."

"It's not common."

"I've been following the case, in the newspapers for a few weeks now."

"And?"

"And we have a visitor."

I had heard nothing at the door downstairs. Holmes stared at me, unnervingly, until there was a knock on the outer door.

"Footsteps?" I said.

"What else?"

Shortly I heard the footfalls of Mrs. Hudson and the visitor surmount the stairs. Mrs. Hudson knocked, opened the door, and was followed into the room by a slim young woman, well dressed, and not at all shy at having invaded our privacy unannounced.

"A Miss Llewellyn to see you," Mrs. Hudson said.

I rose to my feet and waited for Holmes to do the same and introduce me. When he did neither, I introduced myself. I attributed my friend's lack of manners this day to a sad mixture of lethargy, *ennui*, and inverse sycophancy.

"Miss . . . ?" Mrs. Hudson began.

"Miss Mary Llewellyn, yes, yes," Holmes said, and waved Mrs. Hudson off.

I offered my seat to Miss Llewellyn, who took one look at the worn armchair and declined. Instead I brought over to her a prim and uncomfortable desk chair. She sat and waited for Holmes to speak, which he did not.

"Would you like some tea?" I said.

"No, thank you, Mr. Watson."

"*Doctor* Watson," Holmes said.

"My apologies, Doctor."

"Not at all," I said.

She spoke with what can only be described as a lovely, lilting voice, with that soft way the Welsh have of letting the last syllable fall away before the uptake of the following word.

Holmes looked at her now, a little interested, perhaps, because of the timbre of her speech.

"Miss Mary Llewellyn," Holmes began. "Cardiff socialite, niece of Lord Glamorgan, and – if the newspapers are to be believed, and it is not too indelicate a phrase to describe your relationship – the *paramour* of the late Mr. William Jones. You are in London yourself to seek assistance because you are about to be charged, in spite of some spurious evidence, with the murder of the poor Mr. Jones.

"The police have no other suspects than you, no other motives except yours, no other evidence than what they have gathered against you. And, your uncle, the good Lord, not wanting the embarrassment of your arrest and trial attached to his good name, has sent you here to me as a last resort."

"Yes, Mr. Holmes. And I prefer to be called friend, not *paramour*."

"And I prefer to be a first resort."

"It was at my uncle's instigation."

185

"Yes, of course. You, as a socialite, cannot be burdened with such things as accountability and responsibility."

"Holmes, I . . . ."

He held up his hand and cut off my attempted protest against his rudeness. He had been reading Dickens again over the winter and had developed a heightened social conscience which had not yet worn off.

"Not to worry, Miss Llewellyn. You did not murder Mr. Jones."

"Why, thank you, Mr. Holmes. You are very kind."

"No. It is not kindness. It is simply evidence. And evidence is never kind nor unkind, it is simply . . . evidence."

"But Holmes," I interjected. "The police, according to the newspapers, have some crucial evidence against Miss Llewellyn. The scarf . . . ."

"I'm not talking about the police's evidence Watson, I'm talking about mine."

"Yours?"

"Mine."

"You haven't been to the crime scene. You haven't spoken with the police. You've only read about the story in the papers, along with everybody else."

"Not quite correct, but, none the less, our visitor is innocent."

"But how can it be proven?" Miss Llewellyn said, her voice rising, and becoming a little harsh with the change in tone.

"First, you need to answer two questions, Miss Llewellyn. And then you will tell me your story, and then I will tell you mine."

"Of course."

"Did Mr. Jones love you?"

"Yes, he did. He spoke often of his undying and unconditional love for me."

"And did you love him?"

"No, I regret to say that I did not."

Her beautiful voice had returned.

"And you told him as much on your late winter jaunt to Caerphilly?"

"Yes."

"In fact, that was the purpose of your expedition, one last outing before the axe fell on him."

"Yes. We had been there before on picnics, in summer, and I thought it would be a suitable place to end it – "

"So to speak."

" – before he became entrenched in his belief that I might love him in return."

186

"Nothing like choosing a place of fond memories to announce the ending of it all." Holmes said this as if he himself had been the victim of the rebuff, and not the poor Mr. Jones. "Tell me your story," he added.

"About a year ago, I was in the front row at the Theatre Royal, and William was holding a spear . . . ."

"Was he on stage or in the audience?" Holmes asked.

"On stage . . . ."

"Drama or comedy?"

"Drama. William was prone to drama."

"What was the play?"

"*Hamlet*."

"A tragedy."

"Yes."

"Carry on."

"We noticed each other, and, after the performance, we found each other in the lobby. We talked, and the short of it is, that we exchanged addresses . . . ."

"And he was in love with you before the crowd let out onto Wood Street?"

"He seemed very interested, yes. You have been to Cardiff, Mr. Holmes?"

"Of course. But you were not as interested in him?"

"No."

"You thought that he was a mildly interesting young man from a world quite different from your own, and you found his ardor rather charming."

"Yes."

"Carry on."

"We met several times for dinner after his performances, and then later on went for walks and picnics . . . ."

"How many times did you picnic at Caerphilly?"

"Three times during the summer."

"And you explored the castle while there?"

"Yes. We would picnic in the inner ward, and then walk the walls and the grounds . . . ."

"So you knew your way around there? You had been into the guards' rooms?"

"Yes."

"What did you find there?"

"Nothing but the old shackles on the walls."

"And Mr. Jones put his hands and feet into the shackles and pretended to struggle, and pretended to be a prisoner in the castle."

"Yes."

"And you found this . . . ?"

"Amusing, if a bit immature."

"Let me describe the shackles to you, Watson, so you can have a complete mental picture of the scene. There are four of them, made of heavy black iron. They are circles, or cuffs, attached to the stone wall with short chains that allow very slight movement. One pair is at ground level, at a distance apart slightly wider than shoulder width. The other pair is at shoulder height, and anchored to the wall just at the limit of the average man's arm span. The cuffs open and close around the wrists and ankles on a hinge, and on each cuff is an opposing pair of tabs with matching holes that hold the cuffs closed by a choice of three methods: A padlock, a loose pin, and, a captured pin that is attached to the cuff with its own piece of chain."

"Yes, school boy stuff," I said.

"Except that the whole case depends upon the method of locking used in that particular guards' room."

"But Holmes – " I began.

"Carry on, Miss Llewellyn."

"After William became increasingly adamant that we would be engaged and then married, I decided that I must cool his enthusiasm, as my feelings were not compatible with his."

"So you invited him for one final picnic."

"Yes. The weather was quite fine when we left Cardiff. Easily pleasant enough to sit outside if you were away from the wind. And the weather was reasonable enough even after we arrived at Caerphilly. But as we walked from the station up to the castle . . ."

"It's a quarter-of-a-mile, Watson," Holmes said.

". . . the clouds began to move in from the mountains, and a light rain began to fall."

"And because of the weather, and the lateness of the season, there were no other visitors."

"We were quite alone. We had planned to picnic in the lee of the leaning tower but abandoned our plans when the rain turned to snow. I had intended to tell William of my decision while we ate, but we turned back from the tower and I stopped with him on the bridge over the moat instead and let him know that this was to be our last meeting, and that my feelings were not equal to his. I said that we would be cordial to one another if ever we met again, but that any thoughts of intimacy must be banished from his head."

"And he pleaded and implored, and, possibly, begged?"

"It was something of an embarrassment."

"And?"

"And I walked away down the hill to the village and the station."

"And you carried the picnic basket with you. None was found at the scene."

"Yes."

"Did you turn to look back?"

"No."

"It would have been a tragic sight, don't you think? The spurned lover standing on the snow-swept bridge over the moat of Gilbert de Clare's abandoned castle. Even more tragic when considering that Gilbert de Clare was one of your ancestors, Miss Llewellyn."

"I suppose it would have been tragic if I had looked. And de Clare *was* a distant and indirect ancestor."

"As an actor, Mr. Jones must have been struck by the theatricality of it all."

"Most likely."

"What next?" Holmes asked.

"I boarded the train and went home."

"Did you not wonder, as the train left the station, where Mr. Jones was?"

"I assumed that he had decided to stay the night in the village and return the following day."

"In truth, you gave no thought to his whereabouts at all, did you? He was just one more young man not up to your or your family's standards."

"It was over between us, and I had no reason to think of him any longer."

"How easy it is for you to be as cold as charity."

"Holmes . . . ." I protested.

"And you did not find out about his death until the police began making inquiries with Mr. Jones' acquaintances, and your name was brought forward by his friends in the theatre."

"Yes."

"Tell me about the scarf. Did you give it to him, as a souvenir, or did he take it from you?"

"When I turned away from him on the bridge, he moved to restrain me and took hold of my scarf, pulling it from my shoulders. I didn't wish to confront him over a scarf, so I kept walking and left it with him."

"I believe your story completely. You are innocent – of any criminal offence, at any rate."

"But Holmes, what about the locking method of the cuffs?" I said.

"The cuffs had to lock with captured pins."

"Why?"

189

"Padlocks are out of the question, as keys would be quickly lost and, even in the most honest of communities, four padlocks would not remain in their place for long. The same with the loose pins, they would quickly be lost or taken, rendering the cuffs useless. The only option then was that the shackles had the pins attached."

"But there has been no mention of that in the newspapers."

"As I said, I have been interested in this case for some weeks. A letter to the local constabulary confirmed the exact configuration of the shackles. And that was all the information that was required."

I knew what his answer was going to be to my next question, but I asked it anyway.

"So if Miss Llewellyn did not commit this crime, then who did?"

"It's obvious, isn't it?"

"I'm afraid not."

"Actually, it is."

"Shall I take an educated guess?"

"An education does not necessarily make you good at guessing, and, besides, guesswork has nothing to do with it. The evidence points the finger, as always."

"Mr. Jones was the victim of robbers who were in the castle awaiting the arrival of incautious visitors," I said. "During the proceedings, the robbery went cruelly awry."

"No. There was no one else involved."

"No one else involved?"

"Small Welsh villages are hardly a hot bed of robbery and murder, especially that late in the season, when very few, if any, visitors would be expected to visit the castle."

"He killed himself?" I shrugged the question.

"Precisely."

"Suicide?"

"No."

"Holmes, you are being more than a little obdurate."

"Killing oneself is not always a suicide, Watson. His was a death by misadventure. Miss Llewellyn was obviously not physically capable of gagging and chaining up Mr. Jones, against his will. And if it was done as a young couples' lark, then she would have unchained him and it would have been nothing more than an amusement for them both. The criminal element was eliminated due to the inclement weather, the lateness of the season, and the general honesty of the locale. And then there was motive."

"Who had the motive?"

"Certainly not Miss Llewellyn. Since Mr. Jones had become an embarrassment to her, and she had already rejected him, she had no reason to harm him physically. The robbery motive? Even if we accept that robbers may have been present, a turning out of pockets by Mr. Jones, and an explanation that he was an actor, would have made our criminals put away their cudgels, as even robbers know that actors have no money. That leaves only Mr. Jones himself. Who, as our Miss Llewellyn. here has pointed out, was *prone to drama.* Prone meaning both, *naturally inclined to,* and, *groveling.*"

"What could his motive be, to do that to himself? And, how could he physically do it? And, what happened to his clothes?" I said.

"That's where my story begins: Exactly where Miss Llewellyn's leaves off. As our visitor walked away from him and disappeared into the falling snow, Mr. Jones had the romantic notion that, like the majority of women, she would kindle her affections towards him by rescuing him from himself. Take note Watson – or better yet take care, of that female motivation to save a man from himself. For, once saved, the man is remade in the woman's image and to her ideal.

"Having previously been in the guards' room on earlier visits, and having noted the shackles, Mr. Jones concocted a ruse to win back his lover. He found a heavy stone from among the many fallen stones littering the ruins' grounds, and fetched it back to the bridge over the moat. He removed his shoes and socks, his hat, his overcoat, jacket, and waistcoat and tie, and wrapped them around the stone using the arms of the overcoat to tie up the bundle. He then dropped the bundle from the bridge into the moat. I will advise in my letter that the moat be dragged near and under the bridge where I am certain the police will find the bundle.

"Mr. Jones, who was by now soaked through to the skin from the snow, then proceeded to the guards' room where he first gagged himself with the scarf and then placed his feet in both lower cuffs, dropping the pins in place to secure them. Twisting to the side he then placed his one hand into an upper cuff, closed the cuff, and dropped in the pin with his remaining free hand.

"Now, you are going to ask me, Watson, how he managed to put his free hand into the last cuff and insert the pin into the holes to secure it."

"I was not going to ask, because I knew that you were going to tell me."

"It's difficult, but I smoked a pipe over it and then attempted it myself a few days ago with a shackle from my collection. It took me nine times to succeed at it. But, no matter how many tries, it does prove that it is possible.

"Mr. Jones grasped the top of the pin between index finger and thumb and then turned his wrist into the cuff. By sliding the cuff against the wall, he was able to close it around his wrist. Once closed, he turned his wrist again to orient the holes in the cuff up and down, and the rest is co-ordination and gravity. He lined up the pin and dropped it. If it failed to find the holes, he shook open the cuff, grasped the pin, and repeated the process. As I said, it took me nine tries to succeed. Depending on his level of co-ordination, and on how badly he was shaking from the cold, it may have taken him many more attempts. But, eventually, he succeeded. And became the last prisoner to die in old de Clare's castle."

"His motive was desire?"

"You know something of the human heart do you not, Doctor?"

"Yes."

"I speak of the emotional heart of course. Yes, his motive was that he naively believed that Miss Llewellyn would not just get on the train and leave without him. He believed that she would wait for him on the platform, and, when he failed to appear, that she would run, melodramatically, through the snow to find him and save him, and thereby generate the romantic bond between them that she had up until then failed to find.

"His belief in, and his dedication to, fiction, would not allow him to conceive of the reality that Miss Llewellyn was the possessor of a reticent emotional nature, and, therefore, instead of running to the rescue, Miss Llewellyn simply got on the train and went home.

"He likely had planned on using your own criminal theory, Watson, and was going to blame his condition on a gang of robbers. Can you imagine, Miss Llewellyn, what it was like for him to hang there, waiting for you? Waiting for at least one full day and possibly into a second. Struggling at his chains until his wrists and ankles were raw. Chewing at the gag until his gums and lips bled. And then, after he had given up on waiting for you, he waited for someone else to save him – some stranger, a local out for a walk, or another visitor. But no one came. Due to the weather and the season, no one came for nearly a week. Not even the locals ventured up there because of the snow and the cold. Eventually, two boys exploring on a Saturday found him, dead from the cold."

"Death by misadventure," I said.

"Yes, the cause of his misadventure being that he had the audacity to believe that a poor actor could actually be loved by someone of your ilk, Miss Llewellyn."

I didn't even consider going to her defense this time.

"You will write the letter for me then, Mr. Holmes?" she said.

"Yes. I will send it to your solicitor's office. Leave his name and address with Mrs. Hudson on your way out."

"But will they believe it?" she asked.

192

"The police are loathe to prosecute members of the gentry. They will accept my evidence because it relieves them of the task of charging and trying you. And my evidence is the only possible explanation for the fate of your Mr. Jones."

Miss Llewellyn stood up.

I stood.

Holmes remained seated and turned away from her, towards the window.

"How may I compensate you, Mr. Holmes?" she said.

"By not consorting with actors in the future, Miss Llewellyn."

I escorted her to the door, and called for Mrs. Hudson to see her out.

When I returned to my chair, Holmes was staring at the window, seemingly oblivious to my presence.

I picked up the newspaper and read without concentrating, thinking that I should comment on how the Holmes-machine was in fine working order today. But the more he stared at nothing, and the deeper the stare went, the more I decided against it.

The Yellow Star of Cairo
by Tim Gambrell

Chapter I

I entered our rooms at 221b Baker Street to find my colleague and dearest friend, Mr. Sherlock Holmes, roaring with laughter. He was seated in his chair over against the window, an unlit pipe in his hand and that morning's *Times* draped open over the sloped thigh of his crossed legs. My closing of the door was sufficient to attract his attention, and he turned to me, barely reining in his mirth.

"My dear fellow, come. Come and witness this Grub Street balderdash. And in the columns of *The Times* of all things!" He punctuated his words with gestures and judicious handling of the newspaper in question.

I scanned down the page with my eye, looking to see what might have wrenched such mirth from my mercurial friend.

"Antiquarian murdered by Egyptian mummy?" I ventured.

"Ha!" Holmes fired off another sharp laugh like a shot from a Smith-and-Wesson. "And it's been reported as serious fact, too. Utter fantasy!"

"It says that a priceless large jewel has been stolen from the collection – "

"The Yellow Star of Cairo, yes."

I paused before continuing. "I assume that's not fantasy?"

"No indeed, my pragmatic friend." He pointed an angular digit in my direction. "And therein perhaps we'll find the truth behind this . . . farrago, which would otherwise be best off played out in the music halls."

It took some moments for the sense behind Holmes's words to sink in. Evidently, he could see the realisation track across my face. I watched him turn away with a sly grin and attend to the pipe he'd brandished unlit all this time.

I, for my part, chose to remove my topcoat and pour myself a brandy before continuing the conversation. "We have been approached, then, regarding the case?"

"The wife of the antiquarian's young assistant, yes. By the first post. An elegant hand, I'm sure you'll agree?" He held out the letter for me.

I had seen plenty like this correspondence before and would see plenty like it again. Not that it wasn't in itself without remark, of course. The lady was seeking Holmes's assistance.

"Assistance, indeed? Rarely would I agree to *assist*," ventured Holmes acerbically, guessing accurately at which point in the letter my eyes had reached. "I may lead, or I may advise."

I accused him of splitting hairs, to which he once again pointed an angular finger my way.

"Consider, if you will, Watson. In our line of work, to 'assist' is often considered a euphemism. I would not wish to be thought of thusly."

I was still convinced he was being deliberately prickly, so I left the matter and read on.

"Do you know the private collection in question?" I asked.

"Only by repute. Currently in storage. First floor of a late shipping warehouse, over against Rotherhithe Stairs."

My distaste for that area was evident. My companion continued.

"A temporary holding ground, you'll be informed, once you reach that part of the letter. Waiting for a more genteel home to become available. Yes, our petitioner has been most thorough in her scene-setting."

I didn't get any further. At that moment the doorbell rang.

"You are expecting a caller?" I asked. A lop-sided smile curled his mouth. He bounded from his chair as the anticipated knock sounded at our door.

"Enter, Mrs. Hudson," Holmes barked. The door opened slightly.

"A Mrs. Cheeke to see you, gentlemen."

"Of course, Mrs. Hudson, of course. Please, have her enter."

The door opened fully and a pretty lady of, perhaps, five-and-twenty entered. She wore a dress that was clearly a hand-me-down gift from some former role in service, along with a floral bonnet that had undoubtedly seen better – and fresher – days many summers past. I approached and saluted the lady, gesturing her to a seat. She kept her gaze to the floor. My colleague returned to his chair by the window and I sat opposite our visitor, before introducing us both and asking what we could do for her.

"Blast you, Watson," erupted Holmes. "You're a sedentary scholar at times. This is Mrs. Abigail Cheeke, the author of the letter you still hold, unread."

I was somewhat put-out at this accusation, since it was Holmes's continued interventions which had prevented me from reading much of the letter. But in the presence of a lady I swallowed the slight and asked if she required refreshment? She declined. However, she saw no objection to my partaking. While I prepared another brandy, Holmes addressed the lady.

"I presume you are seeking a response to your correspondence, Mrs. Cheeke?"

"I am indeed, Mr. Holmes. I hope you can assist me."

I flicked my gaze at my colleague, who smiled another of his lip-curlers.

"As you may have gathered," he continued, unabashed, "my good friend, Doctor Watson here, has yet to fully comprehend your predicament. Perhaps you could specify the particulars for him yourself?"

She smiled and nodded, and then commenced her story. She told us how her husband, Sebastian, was assistant to the murdered antiquarian, Rawlinson Fotherbury. He'd been dedicated to his master throughout his service, from a young age, and was lucky enough to learn from him as he worked. Abigail and her husband were poor, but prided themselves on being good, wholesome, quiet people who aimed to better themselves through hard work and application. At this I found both Holmes and myself to be nodding in accord.

It seems her Sebastian witnessed the death of his master, in the temporary warehouse accommodation at Rotherhithe Stairs. The sight of one of the mummies coming to life from within its sarcophagus, and murdering poor Fotherbury, was too much for the young man and it broke his mind. He was later found by the lady, raving and wailing. She alerted the police and a local doctor. Her poor husband had since been removed to a lunatic asylum where he now resided. However, despite the report in the press which caused Holmes so much mirth, Mrs. Cheeke was convinced the police really believed that her husband murdered his master and would place the blame on him somehow.

"So, you want us to confirm the true murderer?" I asked.

"Yes, I want you to prove without a doubt that my husband didn't kill his master," she replied.

"That's not quite the same thing," Holmes observed, caustically. "But I am intrigued enough to take you up on your offer, if only to put paid to the ridiculous notion of one of the ancient mummies animating itself and taking revenge on its current owner. And I am also intrigued by *you*, Mrs. Cheeke."

The lady caught her breath, slightly. "How so, sir?"

"I surmise you are not all you seem."

She flustered somewhat, and Holmes calmed her with a gesture and a smile.

"I simply meant that you have the manner, poise, and vocabulary of a young lady of higher status than that of which you appear."

She firmly held his gaze, this time, and complimented him on his perspicuity. He nodded to her in that way he has of indicating to the speaker that the floor is theirs. For my part, I wondered, then, if the dress had not been a gift at all, but a relic of a more affluent time. Mrs. Cheeke spoke again.

"I grew up in Surrey. My father was a businessman and we did very well for ourselves, it's true. I had a governess and was raised in abundant happiness by a caring, loving mother who doted on her only child. Alas, my father hit upon a bad business, which reduced him to a penniless drunk. It broke my mother's heart, and we left her in the village cemetery when they took the house. They left us with the clothes we had on, and a tired horse and a trap. I managed to secure some trinkets which allowed us to find accommodation here in London, under very reduced circumstances, and from thence we lived as unassuming paupers."

"I am sorry to hear that," I said, quietly, as the lady wiped her tears on a small kerchief.

"Do not be, sir," she replied. "Although I thank you from the bottom of my heart. 'Tis not all bad. I obtained work as a housemaid for Mr. Fotherbury. If it weren't for that, I would not have met my husband, and we have had many happy times together in our way. I must be grateful for the way fate has dealt our hand – although, naturally, I wish things were easier for us. Especially now."

I smiled. "Should your husband's sanity return," I ventured, "will not he inherit his master's collection?"

"I fear not, Watson," Holmes interrupted. "The newspaper states that it's been left *to those from whence it came*. So, it will be sent back to the Egyptian government, presumably."

"That's just what they wanted, too," added Mrs. Cheeke, vehemently.

"Who, my dear?"

"There's been some Egyptian-looking fellows hanging around the warehouse for weeks now. Always look like they're up to no good."

"I see," said Holmes, rising. "We'll look out for them as we head that way."

"Now?" I asked.

"Why not? We have no prior engagement, do we? And besides, we have our way in right here." He gestured to Mrs. Cheeke, who looked somewhat aghast herself. "Surely, as a member of the household, you can obtain access for us to the late Mr. Fotherbury's warehouse?"

"Of course, sir." She rose and curtsied.

Chapter II

There were no Egyptians to be seen, but a police constable had been left to guard the main street entrance to the warehouse and he willingly showed us into the building without the need for introduction. I was more than amused to note that, although Mrs. Cheeke was on staff, it was the appearance of Holmes himself and the obvious respect that the policeman held for him that gained us immediate access to the collection.

Holmes was overjoyed to find that the constable had been fully briefed. At times my friend had ventured that there was more going on in the average constable's whiskers than his head, but this fellow was able to advise that the warehouse had been fully searched, and the collection had been checked against an inventory supplied from Mr. Fotherbury's lodgings. Mrs. Cheeke smiled and curtsied at this, indicating she herself had provided the document. The constable further confirmed that only the large diamond, the Yellow Star of Cairo, was missing.

"Thank you, my man," said Holmes, before turning to me. "I remain sceptical, but we shall see. May we see the collection ourselves?" This last was to the policeman again.

The constable smiled, revealing a patchwork of teeth, and produced a keyring.

"I'll need to go first, if you don't mind, sirs? The lamps will need lighting as we go. They're not left on. Paraffin, you see. Lots of 'em."

Holmes indicated that the constable should proceed as he wished. The stench of paraffin was very much apparent even just inside the main door to the warehouse, and I'll admit to feeling a tad light-headed at first. A cigarette each from my silver case allowed Holmes and I to battle the worst of it. Mrs. Cheeke resorted to a handkerchief, I noted.

"Mr. Holmes," said the lady from behind her linen facemask. "You indicated upon entry that you were sceptical. Was that of the inventory, or of the police search, or both?"

Holmes took a long drag on his cigarette, and exhaled an equally long breath, before answering. Even then, he chose to address me rather than answer the question.

"Next time I shall remember to bring my pipe, Watson. These things of yours are abominable." He turned to the lady. "Mrs. Cheeke, you will find that I am sceptical of many things in life until I have had the opportunity to examine matters myself." And with that he continued after the constable, who was now waiting for us at the top of the stairs, by the door to the collection itself.

I'm not a squeamish man. In fact, show me a doctor who is, and I'll show you an inept practitioner. But I confess to being *uncomfortable* in the presence of such ancient body parts and artefacts. It didn't help that the collection was being stored haphazardly, not neatly displayed. The warehouse was ramshackle and the lighting poor at best. Even with the shutters open at the far end, and the breeze from the river blowing in (carrying with it the noise of the working docklands) the chamber still felt suffocating and airless. The sound of scurrying rats was a constant accompaniment to our shuffles and murmurs. I pitied Mrs. Cheeke, but it seemed she was hardened to the place through exposure and necessity.

We were having to ease ourselves through narrow gaps and gaze at an assortment of shelved items at close quarters. There is little that ancient preservatives and embalming can do over such a long period of time to totally remove the action of decomposition and the stench of degradation. Such human matter, in my view, should have been committed to the ground and allowed to take nature's course hundreds of years ago. As she did with the rats, Mrs. Cheeke appeared to take no more notice of the room's aroma than did Holmes himself.

"Constable?" Holmes called. "A lantern, if you please, for close-quarter observation. And the cross-referenced inventory if it's still here?"

The constable had waited by the door. *In case of intruders*, he'd claimed, but it was clear he had a dislike for the chamber. He fetched the requested items with alacrity, after which Holmes dismissed him back to the main street door where he'd be more comfortable. Mrs. Cheeke and I found ourselves at a loose end for quite some time while Holmes checked the inventory and busied himself about the collection. I offered to assist from time to time, but my words fell on the deaf ears of one who is entirely focussed on the task in hand to the exception of all else.

The lady and I ventured to the window for improved light and air. I apologised to Mrs. Cheeke and asked if she had other business requiring her attention. She opened her mouth to respond, but we were both surprised by an ejaculation from Holmes, instead.

"Look here, Watson!"

It took me a little time to locate him, crouched as he was at the base of some sarcophagi a small distance from the window. I thought at first that it was one whole unit, until I realised that it was four separate sarcophagi backing up against each other, rather as if they were looking out to the four corners of the globe. Mrs. Cheeke remained at the window as I joined Holmes. He lit the floor as best he could with the lantern. I could see that the wooden boards had been scuffed and scored.

"Something's been moved," I suggested. "Or could this have happened when the artefacts were originally brought in?"

Holmes kept his voice low. "It's an old warehouse – there are marks and grooves all over. But see here, the flecks of colour caught on some of the splinters?"

He was right. Tiny flecks of gold and green. These corresponded to the paint adorning the sarcophagus immediately behind it. Holmes handed me the lantern while he produced a pair of tweezers and some small stoppered glass phials from his overcoat pocket. He carefully lifted the coloured specks with the tweezers and popped them into one phial. Then he surprised me by backing up a little and plucking some fibres from another splintered floorboard. He held them up to me surreptitiously.

"And what of these, I wonder?"

"Threads from linen covers, used to protect the items from dust?" I suggested. "Or from damage during transportation?"

He held them to his nose. Then he held them to mine. There was a pungent aroma, even from such small fibres. Unmistakeable.

"Bindings?"

Holmes nodded, and I blanched.

"Upon the soul!" I leant against the rickety shelving behind me for support.

"Steady your resolve, my friend. I think it just as likely that our late antiquarian was in the habit of removing the bodies for examination." He stood and called to our companion. "Mrs. Cheeke, you say you found your husband in this chamber, after the death?"

"That is correct, Mr. Holmes."

"Did he indicate from which sarcophagus the murdering mummy emerged?"

"He did not, sir. Although the one nearest you now was, I believe, the subject of some study by Mr. Fotherbury and my Bastian."

"Internally?"

She nodded. Holmes called out to the constable, and he joined us again.

"None of these sarcophagi were opened and checked against the inventory, were they?"

"Err, no, sir," confirmed the constable, who again remained in the doorway. "The inventory doesn't specify the contents."

I was very much relieved to hear that, and my views on the sanctity of death laced my voice as I stated as much.

"Then who's to say that the inventory is correct?" Holmes countered.

I pointed to the furthest casket, facing up against the wall. There was no way that one could be opened without removing the other three first.

It was evident, under further questioning, that the poor constable was very squeamish on such matters, not to say superstitious. His pragmatic attitude on the street quickly peeled away inside to reveal someone ultimately touched by the ravings of Mr. Cheeke. If one of those mummies had come to life and strangled Rawlinson Fotherbury, the policeman didn't want to risk facing it. He insisted they'd need a priest to bless the corpses first, at least. I was very much aware that if the constable had found the binding fibres snagged on the floor as we had just done, then he might lose his wits entirely.

Holmes dismissed the constable curtly, clearly not of a mind to entertain the man's fears. Mrs. Cheeke gave a muted gasp as Holmes stepped forward and removed the lid from the sarcophagus before him. I drew my revolver as an act of caution. Holmes didn't seem concerned, though, and concentrated more on how best not to let the underside of the lid scrape along the floor. Placing the cover to one side, he took the lantern from my hand once again and held it up to better see the contents. The gruesome, emaciated face within stared back at us both. Then Holmes poked at it with a finger. I was appalled.

"Really, Holmes! Have some respect for the dead."

He glanced at me, seemingly amused to have riled me thus. "Just checking that this fellow wasn't going to try to kill us, that's all." He sank into a crouch once more. Before I could ask him what he was doing, he'd popped back up next to me and was seeking assistance to replace the lid. Then he embraced the whole sarcophagus by the elbows and lifted it with some effort. As he placed it down again, the noise echoed surprisingly in the cluttered space.

"Do be careful, Holmes," I said, raising a hand to my brow.

"Oh! Those are priceless, please don't!" moaned Mrs. Cheeke, a little way off.

"Lift one," he instructed, ignoring our censures. I did. It was narrow and surprisingly heavy. I stated as much.

"They're made of thick wood," Mrs. Cheeke advised, coming to join us now that both Holmes and I were lifting them.

"We saw," said Holmes as he strained to lift the third one.

"The bodies inside wouldn't weigh much," I observed.

"And the caskets aren't large enough to conceal a grown man." Holmes paused and stared at me, awaiting my reaction.

"Good Lord! I hadn't thought of that."

"Nor dwarf or pigmy. The adult bone structure would still be too large. An undernourished child, perhaps?"

I disliked the implication.

"My friend, it's likely such a one could easily be recruited amongst the slums."

"But my husband says he saw a mummy," pleaded Mrs. Cheeke. "It broke his mind, Mr. Holmes. Don't say he mistook a poor, ragged child?"

"And anyway," I said, "there wouldn't be sufficient air inside for them to remain for any length of time. The child would likely have suffocated."

"Feel along the tops of them, Watson. There may be a breathing hole. Or, there may be a hole large enough for the thief to have dropped the diamond inside for collection at a later date."

We did, but there was nothing. Holmes spun on his heel and moved to the open shutters, gazing out at the river and the toil of the docklands. I was about to ask what he thought we should do next when Mrs. Cheeke spoke up once again.

"I must take my leave of you, gentlemen. There are strict visiting hours at the asylum and I promised to do my duty as a wife today, if nothing else."

We thanked her for her time thus far. As we escorted her from the building my thoughts were turning to lunch, but Holmes instead begged Mrs. Cheeke's indulgence for just a little longer. She acquiesced, and, leaving the constable on guard as before, the three of us took a cab to visit poor Mr. Sebastian Cheeke. Lunch would have to wait.

Chapter III

Much has been written about London's lunatic asylums and the treatment they provide. I can't say all of it is true, but unfortunately a sufficient amount of it cannot be denied. We can but pity anyone who has to endure these establishments on top of whatever condition, medical or mental, is troubling them in the first place. The wailing, the howling, and the constant sounds of human suffering are like the torture chamber from some gruesome Renaissance drama.

As we were led through the male wing by our guide, we were positively encouraged to gaze in on each cell, like a zoological garden. And in keeping with the animals in such places, only hollow, empty souls stared back at us. The light had gone from their eyes – the life had gone from their cheeks. They were the very picture of resigned despair. These were the quiet ones. The screamers, the wailers, the howlers – they were the epitome of distress in their straitjacketed confinement. Our guide made no apology for them, or for the condition in which they were kept. Indeed, the base creature made several unseemly comments about the female wing and what could be seen or indulged in there. But his confidences were misplaced with Holmes and me, and a threat to thoroughly box the toad's ears brought him speedily back to the purpose of our visit.

Alas, visits such as ours, from gentlefolk, were something of a common occurrence and contributed much to the upkeep of the hellhole. Holmes was fascinated in the main and, I believe, recognised one or two inmates from previous investigations of his. Mrs. Cheeke, not unexpectedly, found the whole experience most distressing and I had to persist in my requests for our guide simply take us directly to Mr. Cheeke and not elaborate regarding those we passed *en route*.

202

Upon arrival, we were advised that we were fortunate. Mr. Cheeke was in one of his more contemplative moods, having previously exhausted himself with a bout of screaming.

"Terrified, poor soul," said the guide, with a grin which was not reciprocated by any of us. "Keeps yelling that it's gonna get 'im too, whatever *it* is."

"Is he always restrained thus?" I asked, observing that Mr. Cheeke wore a straitjacket.

"In calmer moments we can release 'im, but not when 'e 'as visitors."

Mrs. Cheeke was desperate to access the cell and embrace her beloved, so the door was unlocked, and this curtailed any further questioning on my part. We all entered the cell.

I found Mr. Cheeke to be an erudite man, educated and polite, but also humble – precisely what I would expect from one who had worked his way up to the role of assistant to an antiquarian of minor note. He bore the sallow, unhealthy complexion common to all the patients, and while we spoke with him, I saw little sign of the fear, nervousness, and other behaviours which had led to him being admitted. Yet I did not draw any specific conclusions from this – it is known that such patients will often appear to be perfectly normal, only to suddenly turn and go wild at the drop of an unpredictable hat. That is why it is so difficult for anyone to be released from lunatic asylums once they have been admitted.

Cheeke thanked his wife for recruiting us, although he was clearly concerned over how much the service would cost. Holmes waved this aside, advising that expenses in these endeavours were largely immaterial.

At Holmes prompting, Cheeke recounted the story of how he discovered Fotherbury's body. It was, in the main, exactly as his wife had reported it to us previously. Cheeke had returned from a visit to the Egyptian Embassy, where he'd been sent to deliver the letter offering the return and reinstatement of Fotherbury's collection. Upon entering the first-floor store at the warehouse, he found one of the sarcophagi open and a bandaged mummy strangling his employer. At this point his mind went blank until he came to himself again there in the cell, sometime later. He said he knew nothing of the missing diamond until his wife advised him of the fact. Mrs. Cheeke was careful to comfort and hold her husband during the latter part of his recollection, in case the memory caused him too much distress. Aside from a few tears and some trembling, he managed to get through his report with admirable coherence.

I glanced at Holmes, who was perched on the edge of the bed looking pensive. He nodded to me and we stood. As Holmes banged his cane on the cell door and called for our attendant, I thanked Mr. and Mrs. Cheeke for their time and indulgence today and wished them both good health. Mr. Cheeke suddenly cried out that they were going to hang him for the murder, because everyone would think that he imagined the mummy and blame him. Even though Cheek was straitjacketed, he came at me with a wild look in his eyes, spittle gathering in the corners of his mouth.

The attendant arrived at that moment. He was supposed to have been waiting right outside and I detected the scent of alcohol about him now. The attendant grabbed Cheeke and forced him back onto the bed. Mrs. Cheeke screamed and pleaded for them to be gentle with her poor Sebastian. Another attendant came running to assist. Cheeke was subdued and remained lying quietly on his bed. His wife advised us that she would remain with him for the duration allowed and urged us not to wait. We once again made our goodbyes and the new attendant showed us both back to the entrance.

"Where to, guv?" said the cabby, as we mounted.

"Scotland Yard," Holmes instructed, and we settled down for the journey. It was a pleasant day, and the sunshine helped me get over some of the traumas that we had witnessed in the asylum. I made a note to keep a close watch on the establishment in case the opportunity arose to have its practices investigated. I have not included the asylum's name in this report, but, as I indicated earlier, I fear the practices were common amongst many such asylums.

Eventually Holmes asked me what I thought. I advised him that, to the best of my knowledge in such matters, I believed Cheeke was telling the truth – at least as far as he believed it, or his mind was painting it. I did not think that Sebastian Cheeke had murdered Rawlinson Fotherbury. However, my common sense could not accept that an ancient Egyptian corpse had reanimated itself and killed the man – and certainly not doing so and then quietly returning to the sarcophagus from whence it came.

Holmes agreed that it was pure fantasy the possibility that a mummy killed the man, but not necessarily the possibility that someone made themselves up to look like a mummy to perpetrate the act.

"But why bother?" I asked.

"To create precisely the effect that it has. If the murderer was wary of being interrupted, that would make perfect sense."

"It still leaves the question of *who*. A rival collector, perhaps?"

"Interesting," Holmes agreed. "If the collection was considered to be cursed, and therefore available more cheaply – or even *gratis* – a rival collector could make considerable gains by taking it."

"Makes good sense to me," I concurred.

"Or," Holmes said, punctuating his words with a thoughtful smacking of his lips, "perhaps we should look to the original owners of the collection?"

Chapter IV

Inspector Lestrade eyed Holmes and me from across his desk.

"I don't know where that report in *The Times* came from, Mr. Holmes, but I certainly know the case in question," he said.

"So, are you looking to arrest an ancient mummified corpse for murder and theft?"

Lestrade grinned. "If you can produce one for me, Mr. Holmes, I'll put it away for life, you know that. But for the moment we're focussing on the natural, not the supernatural: An underground ring of Egyptian Nationalists. Nasty fellows in the main. They've been at large in the city for some time now. After a few scrapes and run-ins, we've been monitoring their activities pretty closely. They don't like us and, frankly, sirs, we don't like them. I'd welcome the chance to put 'em away for a bit."

I recalled what Mrs. Cheeke had said when she visited us that morning. "Have any of them been spotted around Rotherhithe Stairs at all?"

"They were keeping a watch on the premises in question, Dr. Watson," confirmed Lestrade. "We know that much."

"And the motive is there, certainly," I observed. "Their country has been rather raped of treasures and wealth."

Holmes nodded in accord. Lestrade drummed his finger tips on the desk and leaned back in his chair.

"I may be a bit cynical, Doctor Watson," the inspector said, "but my view is that the diamond would go some way to funding their ongoing operations to resist British rule."

Holmes seemed to agree. "There's certainly been trouble there ever since 1882, yes. Any thoughts on how they might have done it?"

"Sailed up the river at high tide with a ladder and climbed up and in through the window, we reckon."

"Ha!" Holmes approved. "Very simply done. And probably very likely, too."

"You don't suspect Mr. Cheeke, then?" I asked.

"The nutcase? I wish his story about mummies hadn't got out. Spooked a lot of my men, for one thing. Why, do you think he did it?"

"Oh no, no," I said. I told Lestrade that we had been to see Cheeke and that I was satisfied in his condition. "His poor wife is worried you might arrange to pin the blame on him somehow, in his fragile state, that's all."

Lestrade's pensive pause confirmed to me that this was precisely something the police had considered.

"You can tell her from me, Doctor Watson, I'd prefer to catch the real perpetrator." The inspector's magnanimity amused me.

Chapter V

After the passage of a few days, during which little of note occurred in our lives, Holmes received a telegram from Mrs. Cheeke. This appeared to be one in response to correspondence he had previously sent her, offering reassurances to the lady regarding her husband and the police, and advising that he was fully committed to the case. I rather pithily pointed out that he had done little or nothing towards the matter since we visited Lestrade. He advised me to be patient, before telling me that, according to the wife, Mr. Cheeke had now been released into her care and had immediately returned to his position to oversee the enacting of Fotherbury's will as regards the Egyptian collection.

Mrs. Cheeke further wrote that, as there did not appear to be any concern over the assistant's role in the death, she was writing to stand us down. A banker's draft for the princely sum of five shillings was enclosed, with the promise of the same again once the Estate had been settled and Mr. Cheeke had found a new position.

I was washed over with amazement, jubilant for the husband and his charming wife, but also surprised at such an expedited release. Considering the state in which we had found Mr. Cheeke only a few days ago, his recovery must have indeed been miraculous. But, more importantly – and it pains me very much to admit this of the medical profession – once one has been admitted to such an establishment, it usually requires considerable time and much effort of pleading and coercion to persuade them to release a patient.

"There is only one answer to the release," I said. "Money."

Holmes smiled and tapped his fingers along his top lip, thoughtfully. He remained silent and brooding.

Chapter VI

We'd been engaged on another investigation the following day, although our efforts turned out to be something of a wild goose chase as far as that particular case was concerned. So, it was in a somewhat disheartened, not to say sombre, mood that we returned to our rooms after dark. We found waiting for us a cold collation from Mrs. Hudson, and that morning's *Times* still to be read. I tucked into the food, grateful for a meal after such a tiring day. Holmes, on the other hand, tucked into the newspaper – presumably to satiate his own mental hunger.

"Look, Watson, see?" His sudden cry made me jump. I dashed over to him, but he rushed past me to the door, leaving me perplexed. "No time now. We must rush, or we will lose our quarry. Come, you can read it on the way – and bring your revolver!"

I grabbed my overcoat, my revolver, and a broiled chicken leg, and followed him out.

A short while later we were once again ensconced in a hansom, rushing to Rotherhithe Stairs. Holmes had grabbed one of his Irregulars out on Baker Street and slipped him a hastily-written note and half-a-crown. The poor lad's eyes bulged when he received the coin, but Holmes was at great pains to stress that Inspector Lestrade had to be handed the note personally – with all haste and at all costs. The hour was late, and if he was no longer at Scotland Yard then the boy had to track him down – hence the generosity. He could keep any change, naturally. With a nod, the young lad was off. As Holmes stepped into the road and flagged down a cab, I noticed a number of other urchins leave shaded doorways and join the boy. Holmes had quite a network or eyes and ears at his disposal, it must be said.

I did my best to read the newspaper article as quickly as I could under the rickety conditions. Holmes regularly banged on the roof with his cane, urging the driver on with maximum haste, and therefore maximum jolting for those of us inside. Cobblestones do not make for a smooth road at high speeds. Holmes remained at the lowered window, occasionally calling up to the driver, suggesting shortcuts. He was clearly very concerned. For my part, I wondered if someone had supplemented our usual copy of *The Times* for a Penny Dreadful. Something there had fired up Holmes, for sure, but for my part it was severely challenging my credulity.

I read that poor Sebastian Cheeke, lately released from his lunatic asylum, had now died in mysterious circumstances at the warehouse against Rotherhithe Stairs. His body had been found on the banks of the Thames, beneath the warehouse, at low tide the previous night. His wife had come looking for him when he didn't return home at the expected hour. She spotted his body and raised the alarm. But it was hideously aged and withered. Mrs. Cheeke confirmed the identity of the withered body for the coroner later that evening.

Further, there was now considerable panic in the area. The police constable on guard at the entrance had heard a struggle and run inside to assist, only to be faced with a walking mummy, which had sent him screaming off up the street. Residents and nearby businesses now believed an ancient curse had been released from the collection, sucking the life from those it touched. Reportedly no one knew where the mummy now was, or if indeed it had left the warehouse, but the police were refusing to return there.

Holmes was grinning at me, jubilantly, as I finished. I looked at him aghast.

"And there we have it, my friend," he said. "The final act begins."

I held up the newspaper limply. "But this is more superstitious balderdash, surely?"

"Of course, of course. And I have a strong suspicion as to the truth on that matter. But folk are credulous. No one will go near the place, now. Even the police. And that's just what the villain wants. But we men of steel are not so easily cowed, are we not?" He slapped my upper arm.

I stuttered an approximate agreement.

"I only hope we are still in time to catch the tide. This cab driver is taking an interminably long time, but with luck and a little stern resolve, I believe we can catch our thieving murderer red-handed."

The street door to the warehouse had been left wide open, but there was no indication that anyone had recently been that way. The paraffin lamps were all unlit and any traffic – including our own cab – was avoiding the whole street. (We'd been dropped off two streets along, no arguments). We lit a hooded lantern each and proceeded with caution, making as little noise as possible. As we suspected, there were no signs of any bound Egyptian cadavers haunting the abandoned warehouse.

I'd hoped that our previous visit had hardened me to the stench of paraffin and mummies, but, alas, I found myself having to pause more than once to avoid gagging – particularly as we entered the first-floor room. Someone had been busy in there. Many of the items had been boxed up or labelled for transport to Cairo. Presumably that had been the final task of Mr. Cheeke.

Holmes indicated renewed caution and vigilance, although there was a constant background of creaks and groans from the wooden beams and flooring, not to mention the scratching and scurrying of rats. Holmes crept to the shutters overlooking the river and eased them open, for which I was grateful. I joined him and gulped in several lungfuls of the less foul air. Moonlight glistened on the water. The tide was indeed high that evening. There was still much noise of activity on the water and around the dockyards, even though the hour was late. London was simply a city that never slept.

Holmes had calmed himself considerably now we were there. Holding his lantern close, he padded to the group of four sarcophagi which had interested him so much on our previous visit. Again, he scanned the floor before each one, before stepping away behind some shelving and beckoning me to join him.

"Not more ancient fibres," I muttered.

"I suspect we'll find plenty if we want them," he replied in confidential tones. "But they won't tell us anything we don't already know. What is interesting, though, is that these have changed," and he nodded to the sarcophagi.

"Changed?" I was perplexed. "How?"

"They've moved." I took my bearings quickly, but he touched my arm and shook his head. "More precisely they've *been* moved, swapped around."

I scoffed. "Surely your imagination? Blessed things all look alike."

Even in the half-light I could see that Holmes was in deadly earnest. I knew it was disrespectful to have suggested he was in error and I gave him my apologies. He continued, unabashed, indicating the nearest two sarcophagi.

"Flaking of the paint around the knuckles of the fingers on the one facing the shutters. On the casket facing us now, you will note that the left eyeball has been painted slightly off centre. Last time were here, that sarcophagus was facing the shutters. The one I opened, the one that left paint on the floor, and was facing where we are now, was the sarcophagus with the flaking knuckles. So, these two have been swapped around."

"Shipping," I hissed, with a sudden realisation. "They'll have been marked up for transportation and not been put back as they were. Simple."

"Except they haven't been marked up."

He was right. There were no shipping labels or empty packing crates at that end of the room. Holmes crept back to the sarcophagus which he'd opened last time and put his hands under its elbows. Then he released it, swiftly turned and joined me again.

"It's lighter."

"What?" I hadn't even noticed him lift it.

His eyes were gleaming with triumph. "Not by a great deal, but it's lighter."

"Was the diamond in there?"

A very slight shake of the head. "If I know my man, we shall see everything soon enough." Then he said in a loud voice, "Let us return in the morning, Watson, when the light is better." I followed him to the door, which he slammed loudly, while we remained inside. Then, with a finger to his lips, he led me silently to the far side of the room, behind more shelving and seated himself on a packing crate, in direct line of sight of the four sarcophagi. I followed, and we waited.

Chapter VII

We couldn't have been there for too long, but I must have dropped off momentarily in the dark. Holmes's grip on my knee came as some surprise – sufficient, indeed, for him to place a hand to my lips to prevent my exclamation. There were noises from downstairs, low voices and the clatter of booted feet. Judging by the snippets of conversation that reached our ears, it was a group of men trying to convince each other that the value of the spoils upstairs outweighed the threat of an ancient curse that might wither them to death.

I looked at Holmes who unhooded his lantern a fraction. I mouthed *our man* at him, but he shook his head and indicated the four sarcophagi. The moonlight filtering in provided just enough light for us to see movement. With a shuffling, scraping noise one of the sarcophagi was opening – or moving, at least. It was difficult to tell precisely. But the bound figure that emerged was unmistakeable. A walking mummy! I felt my heart leap to my throat.

"By all that's holy . . . ." I breathed.

"Steel yourself, Watson!"

The mummy plodded slowly towards the entrance, its arms held outstretched. It was met with a wash of lantern light as the fellows from below (presumably opportunist thieves) reached the top of the stairs. It emitted a lengthy moan which was then drowned out by screams from the thieves as they saw the sepulchral figure. We couldn't see much, but we heard the confused yells and dreadful clatter which followed. I assumed that this was most, if not all, of their number tumbling back down the open staircase to the ground floor. The mummy stopped in the doorway. The screams, cries, and pleas to God for forgiveness continued as the thieves clearly endeavoured to escape from the warehouse as quickly as possible with whatever injuries they'd incurred.

We took advantage of the distraction to move across the room to the group of sarcophagi once again. We found that the sarcophagus with the flaking hands, which Holmes had tested earlier and found to be lighter, had been moved completely out of the way, revealing a small shaded chamber in the middle of the group of sarcophagi, formed because they didn't all meet back to back. This was just big enough for a man to stand or sit – a small stool was there. It was from here that our "mummy" had emerged.

We remained concealed against the wall, shaded by the sarcophagi, as the mummy ceased its performance and moved in a more natural fashion over to the open shutters. It clawed at its face, separating some of the bandages and revealing the features beneath. I could only see it in profile, but it had been imprinted on my brain during our visit to the lunatic asylum a few days previously: Sebastian Cheeke.

I looked at Holmes and he nodded his recognition also, with a curling smile that indicated he had suspected Cheeke all along. A flash in my peripheral vision dragged my attention back to the open shutters. Cheeke had received a distant signal of some kind. It was repeated. A glint of light from the opposite shore. As we watched, Cheeke unhooked a hanging paraffin lamp from one of the rafters and lit it. Then he hung it in the open window. This must have been his acceptance signal.

I looked to Holmes again, but he raised a hand and indicated that we should wait further before issuing a challenge. Still unaware of our presence, the bandaged Cheeke moved to a nearby shelf of Canopic jars. He reached out and gently pushed one of the jars from the shelf, so that it might look like it had been knocked accidentally. It fell to the floor and broke into several pieces, spilling the remains it held, along with – the diamond! It glinted in the light from the paraffin lamp.

I turned to Holmes again, and again he nodded to me, raising his brows as if to confirm that this was all playing out exactly as he'd expected. Then Cheeke began removing his disguise, which seemed to have been manufactured as boots, gloves, trousers, and an over-shirt, with the head and face applied separately as one would bandage up an injury.

"Very clever, Mr. Cheeke," said Holmes, stepping out from our place of concealment and approaching the cur. Cheeke was clearly flabbergasted, not to say panicked. I moved to block his escape through the door, my revolver drawn. Cheeke's lip curled back in anger. He glanced at the open shutters again.

"Your ship has sailed, for want of a better phrase," continued Holmes. "The police have your wife and her ferryman father. That signal you received was the redoubtable Inspector Lestrade."

"I told her not to involve you, but she thought she could play you to our advantage."

"It was cunning, I'll grant her that. Now hand over the diamond and let's go and see the police outside."

"Was that your lot just now, then?"

Holmes laughed. "No, that was purely opportune. But no doubt the police will be pleased to have taken them also. I see you were taking no chances, remaining in disguise in case anyone else came looking. Must have been pretty uncomfortable, crouching in the middle of those sarcophagi for hours on end."

"It would all have been worth it in the end, for the life this little gem would have given us."

"Hardly little," I said, observing the huge diamond which Cheeke still held.

"A damn sight more than I'd have got out of old Fotherbury, I know that much. All the years I've given him, and for what? To see it all go sailing back to Egypt? Stuff that."

"And the mummy from this sarcophagus," he tapped the casket which had been moved to one side. "The mummy from here will be the body you dressed in your clothes and tossed into the lowering tide, to get caught in the riverbed for your wife to later spot."

Cheeke inclined his head in agreement.

"All very carefully planned to avoid direct suspicion and then completely remove you from consideration. But it's over now."

"That's what you think!" Cheeke turned to the open shutters, clearly with the intention of jumping. Holmes dived at him, dragging him back from the ledge and wrestling with him. In the struggle, the paraffin lamp was dislodged. Before I could do anything, it had smashed on the floor, the paraffin spreading and setting the room alight. As Holmes and Cheeke wrestled, the villain realised his bandaged boots had caught fire. He'd used ancient bindings from Fotherbury's collection and the desiccated linen went up in flames in no time at all. As he discarded Holmes and bent over to try to remove his boots, his over-shirt caught too and before we knew it the poor man was engulfed before us. There was nothing we could do. His agonised screams ripped through me.

For all that Sebastian Cheeke had done, I couldn't satisfy myself that this was a just penalty to pay, but there was no way that we could save him. Neither could we save the rest of Fotherbury's collection. In no time at all, the fire had spread through the ancient dry timbers, blocking off our own escape down the stairs.

"There's only one things for it, Holmes," I yelled, and pointed through the shutters.

"I always dreamed of being a circus performer," Holmes quipped as he dived through the flaming frame and out into the river below. I followed close behind, somewhat less elegantly, and conscious that my overcoat had caught alight as I went.

Chapter VIII

I examined the charred edges of my ruined overcoat as I sat in our sitting room the following morning. My revolver lay in pieces on the floor before the fireplace, drying out. Holmes and I were seated a little further back, our feet in a mustard bath each, while Mrs. Hudson fussed about us like an overbearing mother hen. Our clothes had already been sent for laundering – with the exception of my coat, of course, which was now good for very little.

There was a knock at the street door. We managed to persuade Mrs. Hudson that she could leave us for a few moments to answer it, although she felt the need to sternly warn us that we weren't to go, as she put it, *gallivanting off on anymore foolhardy investigations*, until we'd shaken our chills. We granted her that much, providing she answer the door before the caller walked away.

Mrs. Hudson returned with Inspector Lestrade in tow. She'd been giving him the same lecture about us and our chills as they came up the stairs. We caught the end of it as she showed him in. Much to Holmes's relief, Mrs. Hudson agreed to leave us all to our discussions, but as a parting shot she warned the inspector not to stay too long.

"You gents had an exciting time of it, then?" said Lestrade, with a smile, pouring us all a medicinal brandy from the table.

"Our compliments to your stout fellows who helped pull us from the water and bring us home," I replied as I took the drink. Lestrade inclined his head.

"I assume success?" asked Holmes, through a puff on his pipe.

"Indeed. Very fastidious, those street lads of yours, Mr. Holmes. It's a good job my wife and I weren't enjoying the theatre very much. Lawd knows how the boys got in there, mind."

Holmes grinned but said nothing.

"How did you know Mrs. Cheek's father was a ferryman?" I asked.

"From what the lady told us, Watson, it was no effort at all to discover her father's name and then to enquire as to his trade hereabouts. I always like to have as much information to hand on both sides of a case, as you should well know by now. When it came back that he was a ferryman around Rotherhithe, various aspects of the case started to make more sense and I suspected we were being played, as a form of distraction. When Cheeke's death was announced, and an obvious mummy cadaver was used to pass for his body, I was certain that things were coming to a head."

"Oh yes," I muttered, "You might want to have a word with that coroner about his professional integrity, Inspector."

"Indeed, Doctor Watson," Lestrade agreed. "He was rather taken in by the rumours of the curse, unfortunately – "

"Ha! In this day and age." Holmes interjected.

"And the lady was so very adamant that the body was her husband. She was quite detailed on a number of particulars."

"Yes," Holmes interrupted again. "I can very well believe that. The fastidious Mrs. Cheeke, *neé* Abigail Critchley of Critchley Villa, Guildford. I trust she was found where we expected?"

"Spot on, Mr. Holmes. At The Angel public house directly opposite the warehouse. Mr. Critchley's regular haunt. His ferry boat containing their luggage was moored up outside. She was a handful, and no mistake, but he was almost too drunk to stand, the old soak. Gave us the signal, though."

"It's a shame the warehouse went up like it did," I said. "I fear any insurance money is unlikely to appease the Egyptian government. You can't buy a lost heritage, after all."

"We've had them from the Embassy there already," confirmed Lestrade. "Incredibly unhappy. Devil of a job keeping them off the site. The whole place, everything inside it – incinerated. The high tide was very much in the favour of the firemen, I must say. They managed to stop it spreading to nearby properties."

"Perhaps for the best," I suggested. "The warehouse had been cursed one way or another. But what about the diamond? Surely that won't have burned?"

"No sign of it so far. We'll be able to check more closely once it's all cooled. Had to leave a squad on permanent guard at the site, in case anyone from the Embassy returns, or any further thieves fancy trying their luck."

Holmes chuckled. "Those poor fellows. Got a little more than they bargained for, didn't they?"

"Indeed they did, Mr. Holmes. And they were only too happy to be locked away for their pains, too. Seems they can assist us with a few other enquiries, as it turns out."

"You see, Watson? That's why I dislike 'assist', as I said the other day when this whole thing started."

I rubbed my brow and finished my drink. Holmes continued.

"Anyway, Inspector, I have something here that may help to appease your Embassy diplomats, if you'd care to pass it on." Holmes produced a large diamond from the pocket of his smoking jacket. By the light of the morning I could see its slightly flawed colouration, which gave it its name. Lestrade's eyes nearly popped from his head.

"Gentlemen!" Holmes cried. "The Yellow Star of Cairo!"

"You rogue, Holmes," I chided. "I thought Cheeke still held that as he burned to death."

"I wasn't going to advertise the fact that I had it, was I? I'd have been murdered at the next bend for sure."

The Adventure of the Winterhall Monster
by Tracy Revels

"I should not be here, Mr. Holmes. It is a terrible risk, but I couldn't sleep another night unless I took some action. Please, sir, assure me that I have done the right thing in seeking your help!"

The lady's words, uttered in the most heartfelt and terrified of tones, wouldn't have failed to stir the coldest of men. Holmes, as was his wont, remained calm and steely-faced, but his voice was gentle as he insisted that she take a cup of tea from his hand.

"While you are with us, you must not fear, Mrs. Pinchon. And as for your little charge, she could be in no safer hands at the moment." Indeed, the small, frail child who had been carried into Baker Street in the woman's arms was now downstairs with Mrs. Hudson, no doubt being stuffed with treats. "I understand you already know my friend, Watson."

The lady nodded. "I do, though perhaps he does not remember me? I was Miss Sullivan at the time, a novice nurse."

"Of course I remember," I said. "But you are no longer with the hospital?"

"No, for I married the year after you departed. I was happy, but then I lost both my husband and my son to consumption. I knew I would need to return to my old employment, and friends in the profession helped me find work as a private nurse. A few weeks ago, Doctor Ellingham asked me to come to his consulting room to meet a potential client. It was through this encounter that the horror began. It is like something out of a gothic novel, but every word of it is true. Will you listen?"

Holmes settled into his chair. "You have my complete attention."

Mrs. Pinchon gave me a wary glance. It was difficult for me to imagine that this little mouse of a woman, who I recalled as the most timid of all the young nurses, could have become involved in some dramatic entanglement. Still, I nodded my encouragement, and she began to speak.

"Doctor Ellingham introduced me to Mr. John Farley. He was an American, about fifty years of age, tall and slender, dressed in deepest mourning, with a great mane of iron-grey hair and pale, humorless eyes. He had come to England some five years ago and purchased Winterhall, an ancient, rather isolated estate. He was a recent widower with a young daughter, for whom he sought a nurse.

215

"'Business calls me to France,' he said, in a brusque manner, 'but Angela has been unwell since her mother's death. I have no female relations, and I am loathe to leave her with only my housekeeper as an attendant. Would you be willing to come to Winterhall for the duration of my journey? I may be away for as long as three months, and you would be in charge of all matters directly concerning Angela. You will need to make decisions about her welfare. It is essential that I not be pestered by such unimportant concerns.'

"Mr. Holmes, I was shocked by this statement. He could not tell me what ailed his daughter, beyond 'melancholy'. I did not relish the thought of rusticating in the countryside, but Mr. Farley's terms were so generous that I would finally have enough money to emigrate to Australia, where my brother resides. I agreed to come at once, and by the next morning I had arrived to take up my duties.

"Mr. Farley had said he would send his man Humbert to meet me at the station. I had expected a coach or brougham, but it was a wobbly dog-cart that arrived to transport me to Winterhall. Humbert was a dirty, uncouth American man who spat tobacco and smelled strongly of whisky. I thought that we would never reach the house, but finally it appeared, lurking in the mist – a decrepit Tudor-style manor that barely seemed fit for human habitation. It took all of my courage to climb down from the cart and walk to the door.

"A frightful woman, another American with her hair tied up in a checkered cloth and the stub of a pipe in her teeth, greeted me. She introduced herself as Mrs. Humbert and called out to Mr. Farley in a brazen tone. He came down the great stairs, dismissing her with such courtesy that she might have been our good queen instead of a common slattern. Mr. Farley's next words revealed that he had observed my apprehension.

"'You must think nothing of the Humberts. You will no doubt find them rather coarse by London standards, but Ned Humbert saved my life when I was a boy, and honor demands that I keep them on.'"

"The Humberts are the only staff?" Holmes asked.

"Yes," the lady answered. "They reside in cottage detached from the residence. Very few rooms in the house are open. The library is the only downstairs chamber that has any life about it, filled with books and comfortable chairs, though rather drafty. There is a splendid portrait of a beautiful lady above the fireplace. When I asked who she was, Mr. Farley said, quite curtly, that she was his late wife and he preferred not to discuss her. He then took me upstairs to meet my charge.

216

"'Angela is, as you have seen,' he said, 'very small for her age – she will be four years old next week. She was pale and gaunt, but she smiled broadly when her father informed her that I would be her nurse.

"'You will take care of me?' she asked.

"'Yes, I will.'

"'Just like the monster?'

"This incredible statement shocked me. I glanced back to her father, and saw that he had gone white to his lips.

"'I will take better care of you than any silly old monster does!' I answered, as lightly as I could. But before I could offer further assurance, Mr. Farley seized my elbow and roughly pulled me from the room.

"'There must be no more of such talk!" he said. "I will not have her grow up to be as nervous and foolish as her mother. If you hear her make such statements in the future, you will punish her severely. Is that understood?'"

"I nodded, even as I thought to myself that I would never follow such a cruel order.

"Mr. Farley continued my tour. We made our way to the kitchen, and through it to the lawn behind the house. Just below the shadow of the manor is a fine rose garden, with blooms of many hues, as tenderly cared for as the house is neglected. How anything so beautiful could grow in such a place is a mystery to me.

"'Do you see that tower?' Mr. Farley asked, pointing into the distance. Just beyond some apple trees, on a slight ridge, was a structure even more ancient than Winterhall. He told me that it was a watchtower built in the era of King John. My curiosity was immediately piqued.

"'Will you take me to see it?' I asked.

"'No, and you will not go to it while I am away. It is a dangerous place, and there are evil stories about it. Do not go there – and do not think to disobey me, or I will send you packing with nothing for your trouble.'"

"I promised to avoid the tower. He made me further promise to stay away from the village as well, saying I should rely on Mrs. Humbert to take care of my needs. Out of fear of losing my situation, I agreed, and before dawn the next morning Mr. Farley vanished, without even so much as a goodbye kiss for his daughter.

"I soon discovered that the only thing which ailed dear little Angela was neglect and want of sympathy. With care and gentleness, she quickly rallied and resumed interest in her playthings. She was most attached to Rex, a little Papillon dog, and the three of us soon became the best of companions, especially as I came to regard the Humberts with contempt. He was always drunk and she was often not sober. With their master away, they neglected their duties. I was forced to fill the role of housekeeper and

217

cook as well as nurse, lest my charge and I starve to death or drown in filth.

"I had been at Winterhall for two weeks when the first bizarre event occurred. Angela and I had gone down to the library and I noticed that a vase of fresh roses had been placed before the portrait. I drew this to Angela's attention.

"'See – there are beautiful flowers in honor of your mother.'

"The child shook her head. 'She is not Mama,' she said. Even as she spoke, I realized my error. Angela was as pale as her father, almost ghostly in complexion, yet the woman in the painting was olive-skinned and raven-haired, a beauty so dark she might have been Egyptian or Arabian in origin. Also, she was clad in a costume almost twenty years out of date. Later that evening, I asked Mrs. Humbert who she might be.

"'That's the *first* Mrs. Farley. Dead a long time now.'

"'She must have been a kind mistress,' I said. "I saw the flowers you placed before her picture.'

"'I've done no such thing,' she snapped, even as her husband snickered behind her back. He too denied having left the tribute. I was offended at their silly game, but later that night, as I settled into the bedroom I now shared with Angela, I wondered – if they truly did not put the flowers there, *who did*?

"The next occurrence came a few days later. Angela and I were taking some exercise in the rose garden with Rex when Humbert passed by with his great mastiff, Urian, trailing behind him. Rex began to bark and in a flash Urian leapt onto the little fellow and seized him in his teeth. I screamed and hurled my clippers at the beast. He released Rex, who fled in terror while Humbert seized the mastiff's collar and dragged him to the kennel. All our attempts to call Rex back to us failed. It distressed me to think the pup might be injured and dying. We looked everywhere on the property until there was nowhere to look except amid the grounds of the tower. I started for it, determined that the need to find Rex outweighed the order to stay away, but as I drew closer, who should lurch out from behind a tree but Mrs. Humbert. She was carrying a large basket on her arm – I saw a pair of bottles sticking out from it, and the remains of food, as if she had just come from a picnic.

"'You'll not be going there!' she snapped when I stated my intention to search for the wounded dog. 'Mr. Farley will sack you – and beat her! Be sure that I will tell him if you go one more step in that direction.'"

"Angela's misery was more than I could bear. I carried her back to the kitchen, preparing a tonic for her. Once she had quieted, I took her to her room.

"And there, Mr. Holmes, was Rex. I thought at first he was somehow cleverer than we imagined, and had found his way into the chamber. But then I wondered how this could be, for the door was firmly closed. Also, I noticed that he had a bandage tied around his leg, where the mastiff had bit him. It was neatly and carefully wrapped – I doubt a Harley Street surgeon could have better dressed the wound! Who had done this thing? I must have whispered my question, for Angela turned to me with tear-filled eyes.

"'It was the monster.'

"That evening, after Angela was abed, I demanded answers from the Humberts. At first, neither seemed inclined to speak, but finally Mrs. Humbert grunted out a few words.

"'It's a legend. Centuries ago, a Winterhall heir was born who was a beast. He was locked away in the tower, kept chained up all his life until he died. His ghost is said to wander the house. Angela's mother believed that she had seen this spirit. It made Mr. Farley angry, such talk . . . and then one morning we found Mrs. Farley at the bottom of the great staircase, her neck broken.'

"You can imagine that this story froze my blood. It was not hard for me to imagine Mr. Farley – so cold and cruel – throwing his wife down the stairs in a rage and blaming her death on some feudal superstition. But still . . . someone had tended to Rex."

"'I saved the dog,' Humbert claimed. 'There's nothing to be frightened about. I found him and brought him back inside.'

"And you bandaged him?"

"The man stared at me so blankly I knew he was lying. That night, I took a special care to lock my door, and from then on I did not move about the house unless I had a walking stick with me. I claimed it was to protect myself from Urian. In truth, I was not sure what I was guarding myself against, and that frightened me even more. Had it not been for Angela, poor child, I would have fled the place without regard to my salary. But I felt a duty to protect her against whatever lurked in the old house's shadows.

"And now I come to the final occurrence which has driven me to seek your aid. Yesterday morning, Angela begged for some apples, which had just begun to ripen. I mentioned her request to Mrs. Humbert in the kitchen, but was told that she had no time to gather them. I offered to go and pick some, but was once again threatened with expulsion should I approach the tower.

"Then cannot your husband go and fetch a few apples?"

"'No. The brat can do without!'"

Angela had slipped into the kitchen and she began to cry, pleading for the fruit. As I gathered her up, I heard something creak, and turned to see that the outer door, which had been open, was slowly swinging shut.

By bedtime, Angela seemed to have forgotten about the apples. She asked me to open the window then she said her prayers and closed her eyes. I likewise had just retired when I heard a soft thud. An apple sailed in a perfect arc through the window, followed by another, and another. Angela was giggling as this seemingly magical bounty continued to fly into our room. For a moment I was too stunned to move, then I realized my opportunity. I would see the 'monster', if such a thing existed. Angela was out of bed and gathering up the apples – it took me a minute to shoo her back beneath the covers. Then I ran to the window and leaned through it.

"Nothing was outside. I have very good eyes, and it was a bright, cloudless night, but I could see nothing unusual in the courtyard – the mastiff was sleeping, Mrs. Humphrey's laundry was limp upon a line and there was a pile of rubbish left in a corner. For an instant I believed the apples had come from the hands of angels or fairies.

"And then, Mr. Holmes, I saw it. A *thing* bolted from the far end of the rose garden, making for the cover of the trees surrounding the tower. I saw it for only a brief instant – a dark, grotesque, writhing creature that moved side to side like a crab. I was struck by the impression of a host of limbs, and two heads, something so unnatural and ungodly that – I am ashamed to say – I fainted dead on the floor. This morning, before dawn, I left a note telling Mrs. Humbert that Angela had taken ill and I was rushing her to London to consult a doctor. Now . . . tell me . . . what should I do?"

Holmes had listened to her recitation utterly spellbound. He lowered his chin onto his chest and pressed his hands together.

"You have made no contact with your employer?"

"None."

"That is for the best. I find your story fascinating, and unlike any in the annals of this agency. However, to resolve it will require you to have great courage."

Mrs. Pinchon took a deep breath. "I would prefer to run away screaming, but for Angela, I believe I can bear anything."

"Very good. You will return to Winterhall at once, and tell the Humberts that the child must be confined to her room for fear of contagion. You will also tell them that two specialists from London will be arriving tomorrow. Can you remove the couple from the house for several hours?"

"It is their usual day to go to market. They are never in a great hurry to return."

"Excellent. Perhaps one of our specialists can give you a list of necessary medications to procure at the chemist's shop, as well items for an invalid's diet, that may require a longer foray to the grocer's." Holmes shifted his gaze to me. "If he would be so kind?"

I started, having gotten so caught up in the narrative that I failed to realize I had been assigned a role. I quickly drew up a pad of paper and wrote out a list.

"Are you sure we will be safe?" Mrs. Pinchon asked.

"I am absolutely certain," Holmes said. "But stay in your room and keep the door bolted. If my Bradshaw does not lie, we will arrive at your village by eight-thirty, and be at your gate no later than ten."

The lady rose, clutching the paper I had given to her. "And the monster?"

"It obviously bears you and the child no ill will. Tomorrow, we will force it to answer to the light of day."

A short time later, we stood at the window, watching as the lady and her charge made their way down Baker Street.

"A strange story," I said.

"Indeed."

"It is the father, of course."

Holmes turned, one brow lifted. He had lit his pipe and now gave it a hard puff. "Oh?"

"Who else could it be? The servants have been eliminated. The mastiff failed to react, so no stranger approached the house. Only Mr. Farley remains – we have no proof that he is actually away from Winterhall. Clearly, he is staging this elaborate charade."

"For what purpose?" Holmes asked.

There, I confess, I was stymied. "Perhaps he fancies Mrs. Pinchon."

"If so, he has a rather ineffective way of making his passion known! It does not stand to reason, Watson. And, from the evidence of the innocent child, similar events have occurred before the lady took up residence. Remember her statement that the monster cared for her. It is also clear, from her father's actions, that he does not."

I frowned. "Very well, but then . . . what is the monster?"

Holmes clapped me on the shoulder. "We shall soon find out."

The next morning, we began our journey early. Upon arriving in the countryside, Holmes quickly procured a carriage to take us on the long ride to Winterhall. The driver was a talkative fellow who cheerfully relayed the local gossip about Mr. Farley's household to the two "medical men" from London.

"Those Humberts are a bad lot – like most Yankees! We've learned to give them a wide berth. No, Mrs. Farley wasn't an American, she was from London. Sad lady, very pale and nervous, said to be rich. Oh yes, Mrs. Farley died late last year. She fell down the stairs and broke her neck."

"Could the monster have attacked her?" I asked.

"*Monster*?" the driver exclaimed.

"The nurse told us there is a legend of a creature who lives in an old tower," Holmes explained. The man laughed heartily.

"There's no monster or ghoul that I've ever heard of, and I've lived here since I was a nipper. Maybe she's confused about the Grey Lady who walks at Stokemoor Abbey. Ah, sirs, here we are. It is a rather grim place, isn't it – perfect for a ghost, I'd say. Maybe there is one, ha! Sat empty for years before Mr. Farley bought it. Shall I come back for you at four? Thank you, sirs!"

As the carriage rattled off, the massive door of Winterhall opened. Mrs. Pinchon beckoned us inside. In her nurse's uniform, she appeared calmer and more resolute.

"There was no disturbance last evening?" Holmes said.

"None, sir. The servants left an hour ago. A telegram arrived for Humbert just after they departed. I haven't opened it."

"Indeed – that may be helpful. But let us first take a quick tour of the house."

Mrs. Pinchon obliged, leading us through a warren of wretched chambers where wallpaper hung in faded strips, paint peeled away in great patches, and dust and cobwebs reigned supreme. Clearly, one wing of the house was unused and uncared for. The section where the family resided likewise bore an aura of having seen better days. Only the nursery possessed any sense of cheer – the lady had gone to some efforts to brighten and air the room. Little Miss Angela Farley was playing with her dolls, and her pup welcomed us with a friendly yip. Holmes looked out through the window and then gestured for me to join him. Beyond the courtyard was the lawn and the rose garden, then the grove of apple trees that surrounded the tower. Of all the decay on the premises, only the tower managed the picturesque rather than the sordid.

"The outer wall is quite covered with ivy. Hello – what is this?"

Holmes reached down, plucking something from the uneven bricks and the thick foliage. He held it up to the light. Mrs. Pinchon drew back with a gasp of revulsion.

It was a long, greasy hank of black hair.

"Not, I take it, likely to have come from the head of either servant," Holmes said, in an amused manner. "Nor, I think, from the mastiff or any member of this family. Judging from the broken ivy below me, our mysterious friend must have scaled the wall."

I looked down. There were a number of torn spots in the plant life, but one thing immediately struck me. "Holmes, the damage is too wide. Even a large man could not reach so far. It would take both of us, side by side, to tear down the ivy in this pattern."

I glanced back at my friend. His eyes were gleaming.

"Watson, you are the bringer of light to dark places. Mrs. Pinchon, if you would take us to the library, and then the kitchen?"

The library had the air of a sanctuary, where an intellectual man might escape his troubles. The portrait above the fireplace was truly spectacular. The lady's ebony ringlets trailed over her shoulders, and her dark eyes and slight smile hinted at secrets eternally sealed. Her white gown bloomed around her in a style I recognized from older albums, one that our queen had favored in her youth. It emphasized the unknown lady's tiny waist and delicate shoulders.

"Magnificent, isn't she? Holmes?"

My friend had given the picture only a glance, and was now walking around the bookshelves. He stopped suddenly, his hand held out.

"It is cooler here. Much cooler."

Mrs. Pinchon eased close to me and touched my arm. "They say that a ghost can make a place very cold. I did not believe in ghosts, but . . . but now – "

Holmes turned. "There is no need to linger. Let us consult the telegram."

The kitchen was a scene of disorder. I shuddered to think what Mrs. Hudson would have said about the dishes piled in the sinks or the debris from breakfast left scattered on the counters. Holmes seized the message from its resting place on a table, ripping it open and devouring its contents.

"Ah – even better!" He thrust the paper into his coat pocket. "Mrs. Pinchon, I do not wish to be an imposition, but do you think you could add Doctor Watson to your guest list for lunch today? He is generally not a hearty eater, I am sure a sandwich or salad will do."

"Of course. But what about yourself?"

"I will need to tend to other matters. Watson, be so kind as to come with me to the garden. I'm sure Mrs. Pinchon will have her hands full without us in the way."

We exited through a rear doorway. The chained mastiff uttered a low growl, and I was grateful for the size and security of his chain. Holmes ignored him, walking blithely into the garden and pausing from time to time to savor the delectable aroma of the flowers.

"Have you ever considered, Watson, what happens when an individual is abused for many years?" he asked.

I shrugged. "I suppose that person lives only for revenge."

"Indeed. The wounded soul may become a greater fiend than his tormentor, and thus violence is perpetuated. But, on rare occasions, the sufferer becomes the exact opposite: The kindest and gentlest of creatures." He touched a red rose, stroking it velvety petals. "Not all monsters beget monsters."

"I do not understand."

"You will." He turned and we made rapid strides from the garden, across the lawn, and through the grove. There was a small clearing just before the tower door, but Holmes halted us beneath the cover of the trees.

"Now, Watson, you must do as I say without question. In a moment, I will let out a cry and start running toward the tower. You will pursue, overtake me, and, with some lively oaths, proceed to beat me senseless with your cane."

"Holmes!"

"It is a ruse, of course – though I could hardly blame you for landing a few blows in earnest! The goal is to make it look as if I am wounded and have been left for dead. You will then return to Winterhall, where you will enjoy a pleasant luncheon with the lady and her patient. I should be back in time for dessert." He put both hands on my shoulders, giving me a firm shake. "No matter what you might witness, do not return to aid me. Everything depends on you walking away. Do you understand?"

"Holmes, what is the point?"

"Are you ready?"

"Holmes, this is ridiculous. You cannot – "

With a wink, Holmes broke from the cover, shouting as if in fear for his life. There was nothing I could do but follow his lead, though I fear that my lines – "You villain! You shall pay, you blackguard!" – might have been more convincing on the stage of a melodrama. Holmes tumbled to the ground just at the door of the tower, and I pretended to pelt him with my cane. For a horrible moment I thought I had actually struck him, then I realized that he had merely slapped an overripe tomato, purloined from the kitchen, to his face. He gave a most pathetic groan and went limp at my feet. When I hesitated, and he cracked one eye open, making a face that told me if I did not continue the charade, I might find myself on the wrong end of it! I muttered a final oath and stalked away to the trees.

I was almost through the grove before I turned and saw . . . *it*. Something dark, a hideous form moving in a writhing fashion, so unnatural and ungodly, that for an instant I could not believe the thing before me was even real, but rather the product of some terrible delusion. To my horror, it hobbled close and loomed over the fallen body of my friend. I bolted toward the scene, then caught myself against a tree, recalling my promise, forcing myself to turn back toward Winterhall.

I could not look again. I had to trust that I hadn't abandoned Holmes to a monster.

"Do you think Mr. Holmes has found anything?" Mrs. Pinchon asked. We had finished our meal and were enjoying a cup of tea in the library. Miss Angela was showing us Rex's repertoire of tricks.

"I am certain he is on the trail," I said, hoping that I was speaking the truth.

"I wonder what that telegram was about," the lady whispered. "To be truthful, Doctor, I don't think I can bear another night beneath this miserable roof. Yet I love Angela dearly, and I fear that if I were to leave her in the care of the Humberts. Oh – what's got into Rex?"

The little dog had begun to bark and growl. I was pushing aside my plate to investigate when the library door swung open. Standing in the threshold was a tall, lean, silver-haired man, his face contorted with rage. Just behind him was a stout woman in a mauve travelling dress, her hair worked into a Medusa-like nest of ringlets.

"What is the meaning of this!" the man shouted. "I return home, Humbert isn't at the station to meet me, and there is a strange person lounging in my library? Mrs. Pinchon, I demand answers."

"See here," I began, stepping between them. The little girl had started to run to her father, but at his outburst she grabbed her dog and hid behind her nurse's skirts. The lady in the purple dress snorted and scowled, muttering fast words in French. Even as I drew myself up to try and manage the awkward scene, I wondered where, in the name of Heaven, was Holmes? "Mr. Farley, I believe – "

"Who the blazes are you?"

"My name is Doctor John Watson. I am a specialist in childhood diseases, and Mrs. Pinchon asked me to come from London to discuss your daughter's case."

"There's nothing wrong with Angela that a good whipping won't cure!" Mr. Farley snapped. "And you hardly look like a medical man, I doubt you have any credentials. What kind of affair is this? I thought Mrs. Pinchon was a good, decent woman, not a – "

"Chose your next word with care, sir." My friend's stern voice rang out across the room. I spun, completely astonished. It seemed that Holmes had emerged from thin air to stand before the central bookcase. "If it is an unjust word," my friend continued, "be assured that there are two of us capable of correcting you – though I would not wish to chastise even the vilest man in front of his children."

"Children?" Mr. Farley snarled. "What are . . . ."

There was a sudden rush of wind and the bookcase behind Holmes began to rotate. Something stepped out of its shadows, moving awkwardly from side to side. Mr. Farley staggered against the wall. The Frenchwoman screamed. Mrs. Pinchon clutched my arm and wavered on her feet. Only the girl and the little dog seemed unaffected by the sight. In fact, the child ran forward, arms outstretched.

"My monster!"

"Hello, Angela," the two boys said, as one. They came into the light, and suddenly I understood what I had seen. They were large, overgrown lads of maybe fifteen years, each of them clad in ragged pantaloons and a miserable, threadbare coat. Their faces were dirty and their black hair hung down to each pair of shoulders. They stood with their arms around each other, a permanent fraternal embrace necessitated by the ribbon of flesh that joined them, chest to chest, visible through large slashes in their filthy shirts. Yet nothing about them terrified the little girl, and they bent to her and caressed her head and cooed over her puppy as if they were college lads just home from Oxford.

"Their names are Edward and Edgar Farley," Holmes said. "And despite their rather unusual appearance, one could not hope to find two better boys. They saw me being attacked by a ruffian and took me into their tower abode to make sure that I hadn't been murdered."

The French woman reached out and grabbed Mr. Farley by his shirt front. She demanded to know if they were truly his children. He nodded.

"*Mon Dieu*! You would make me the mother of monsters!"

With that parting shot, she stormed out. Mr. Farley groaned loudly.

"Now you have done it. Who are you, and why must you meddle?"

"My name is Sherlock Holmes, and I 'meddle' because your boys should not be hidden away in a crumbling tower. Mrs. Pinchon, you feared an ungodly creature was stalking Winterhall. There he stands."

The miserable man made his way to a sidebar, pouring out a sniffer of brandy. "You seem to know all," he muttered.

Holmes turned and suggested to the lads that they take Miss Angela to play on the lawn. One boy lifted her easily while the other scooped up her pet. No set of siblings could have looked more natural as, laughing together, they bounded from the room.

"I know what your sons have told me," Holmes said. "I know that they are the children of your first wife, whose portrait hangs above the fireplace. She died giving birth to them, on your plantation in Missouri.

Mr. Humbert was your overseer and his lady was the midwife who delivered the children."

Mr. Farley nodded grimly, sinking into an armchair. "Deborah's death in childbed was almost more than I could bear. The boys' very existence gave the Humberts a power over me – they knew I would pay anything to keep them a secret. For ten years we lived in great seclusion, but then, somehow, word got out and the gawkers came. I felt I had to leave my country before my sons became notorious as freaks of nature. I learned of this lonely place and purchased it, but just after we arrived all my investments were wiped out in a bank panic. I needed cash, or I would be forced to sell my new home."

Mrs. Pinchon had been standing to one side, but now she stepped forward, blazing with indignation. "So you married Angela's mother for her money?"

Mr. Farley sighed over his drink. "I had no other recourse. The boys were accustomed to hiding themselves, and it was not my intention to keep them always obscured, but Margaret was a very nervous woman. Angela, however – the boys have always adored her and I suppose, in the end, one cannot keep children apart. I created the myth of a monster to explain strange happenings and dismissed Angela's growing affection for the boys as a childish fantasy. Margaret would have left me had she known the truth."

"Since you wed her for her fortune," Mrs. Pinchon said, "did you kill her for it as well?"

The wretched man shook his head. "I swear I did not kill her! She was a somnambulist, and one terrible night I forgot to secure the lock upon our bedroom door. She was sleepwalking when she fell!"

Holmes's face was dark, but he didn't challenge this explanation. Mrs. Pinchon turned to us. "I am no clearly no longer needed. I will pack my things."

"Wait! Please!" Mr. Farley reached out, seizing her hand. "Everything will be astir, and I can see that Angela is attached to you. Stay with us, just a few more days."

A new resoluteness marked Mrs. Pinchon's expression. "On one condition," she said, very firmly. "You will dismiss the Humberts immediately."

Mr. Farley sighed. "I only kept them because they knew my shame. It seems pointless now."

"Shame?" Holmes snapped. "You are the father of two intelligent, strong, and caring sons, who love you and their sister, though heaven knows you have given them no reason for such affection. You have what most men desire. I suggest you enjoy it in your remaining time on this earth. Come, Watson!"

It was not until we were on the train and halfway to London that Holmes spoke. I had been reflecting on my last vision of Winterhall, of Mrs. Pinchon on the lawn, introducing herself to the boys and shaking their hands. I turned to Holmes. His face was set like a stone, his gaze locked to the passing countryside.

"You saw it, Watson?"

"Yes – his color was dreadful. I would give him less than a year." I frowned at my friend. "You could have told me what the telegram said, so that I would have expected him!"

Holmes seemed not to have heard me. He lifted one hand, drawing a finger over the glass.

"Let us hope the disease works quickly," my friend muttered. "Mr. Farley does not deserve a long life."

Some six months after she first arrived on our doorstep in a state of terror, Mrs. Pinchon returned for a brief visit. Little Angela – now a plump, cheerful child – and Masters Edgar and Edward, smart and handsome lads in their matching suits, arrived with her. She told us she had remained at Winterhall following the dismissal of the Humberts, caring for the family as Mr. Farley succumbed to his cancer. Out of gratitude for her service, he made Mrs. Pinchon the guardian of his children. It was clear from their affectionate expressions that the youngsters regarded Mrs. Pinchon as their surrogate mother. The family was about to set sail for Australia, and we wished them *bon voyage*. Later, I noted how long Holmes stood at the window, wreathed in blue smoke from his pipe, a wistful expression on his face.

Not for the first time, I found my friend more mysterious than any of his cases.

The Grosvenor Square Furniture Van

by Hugh Ashton

Sharing rooms with Sherlock Holmes often involved my being exposed to strange, even bizarre events. In this regard, few that I can recall surpassed the case in which he saved a prominent member of the peerage from a circumstance that would have exposed him to ridicule at the very least, and possibly put an end to a promising political career.

I was opening the morning post at breakfast, prior to dividing it according to the rules laid down by Holmes. The first, and largest, pile of letters was one that he called "Fire". These were either begging letters demanding money, or requests to solve problems that he regarded as trivial, such as the tracing of missing dogs or errant husbands. Unless there was something out of the ordinary in these letters, they were consigned, unread by Holmes, to the fire burning in the grate.

The next, "Enquire", contained details of potential cases requiring further investigation before a decision could be reached as to whether or not to take on the case. This group was significantly smaller than the first.

The last group, dubbed "Hire" by Holmes, were those where he would take the case without any further ado. On most days, no letters met the exacting requirements that would justify their inclusion in this category.

On the day in question, just one fitted the bill to allow it to make its way into the "Hire" group. I placed it beside Holmes's plate and awaited his arrival at the breakfast table.

"Halloa!" he commented, as he remarked the crested envelope. "The Duke of Staffordshire requires my services? That coat of arms is familiar enough. Or rather," he added as he examined the envelope more closely, "the Duchess, if the handwriting is to be my guide in this matter."

"Indeed so," I confirmed.

I should add here that though his clientele ranged from dukes to dustmen, Holmes preferred to deal with the upper classes. Not only were they more remunerative (though he claimed to pursue his profession for its own sake, it must be confessed that he often exacted large fees for his services from the more affluent of his clients), but, he claimed, the problems that they posed were of a higher standard than those of the lower classes.

He opened the envelope and extracted the letter. "You have read this, Watson?" he enquired, having seemingly perused its contents.

"Indeed so."

"And what do you make of it?"

"If the events she describes are indeed true, then it is clear to me that she is in need of your assistance."

"I would agree. It is not in any way usual for a man such as the Duke to shut himself in his room for hours at a time, without food or drink. Moreover, he is a member of the Cabinet, though I cannot imagine that he will retain that honour for long unless his habits change in the near future. The letter also hints at other matters of a mysterious nature, which piques my curiosity."

"Does it not say that the Duchess would prefer you to visit her in Grosvenor Square, rather than her visiting us here in Baker Street?"

Holmes smiled. "She will meet us here in the first instance, or not at all. I prefer to encounter my clients in surroundings which are familiar to me but not to them. Much may be learned in the first instance from a client's adaptation to strange surroundings." He waved a hand to encompass the furnishings of the room, some of which, such as the jack-knife securing unanswered correspondence to the mantelshelf, the Persian slipper which acted as a tobacco-pouch, and the initials of our sovereign tastefully picked out in bullet pocks on the wall, might well be classified as "strange".

He picked up his pen and wrote on a page of his notebook before ringing for Billy, our page, to whom he gave the paper with instructions that it be given to the house in Grosvenor Square, with instructions that it be given to Her Grace, the Duchess of Staffordshire. Billy, suitably impressed, set off with a smile and a six-pence for his pains.

"What did you write to the Duchess?" I asked my friend.

"I merely mentioned that I was indisposed, and would welcome a chance to speak to her here."

I laughed. "May I suggest, then, that you dispose of, or at least conceal, some of those foul-smelling chemicals which have been your principal means of recreation for the past few days? I can scarcely imagine that our visitor will find them as congenial as do you."

"Very well, Watson. You remind me often of one of the principal reasons why I have never contemplated matrimony."

"That being?"

"In a marriage, it is essential that one maintains at least the semblance of affection – an attitude that it is hard to maintain when one partner continually imposes her or his wishes on the other. The same may be said of some friendships."

I could not think of a suitable rejoinder, and sat reading the newspaper's agony column out loud to Holmes as he busied himself tidying away the flasks and reagents which had polluted our air for the past few days.

"Heigh-ho," he remarked as I came to the end of my recital. "There seems to be little of interest in London these days. I trust that Her Grace will provide some respite from this *ennui* which engulfs us."

I had been observing the street as I read the newspaper to Holmes, and espied a carriage bearing the same arms as had appeared on the morning's envelope. "She has arrived," I announced.

"Excellent," he said, throwing himself into a chair and instantly assuming an air of languor, which was in complete contrast to his frenetic activity of a minute before. "Remember, Watson, that I am indisposed. A matter of a slight chill, perhaps, or a touch of influenza?" he smiled.

"Very well," I said.

In a minute, Mrs. Hudson knocked on our door to announce the arrival of the Duchess, and Holmes waved a negligent hand to indicate that she should be admitted.

I was not acquainted with the appearance of the Duchess of Staffordshire, and was not expecting the somewhat stout lady of a certain age, though dressed fashionably and well, who made her appearance. She glanced around her, using her lorgnette, and a faint smile came over her face as she remarked the singular features of our room, to which I alluded earlier in this narrative.

Her glance fell on Holmes, and her expression changed to one of what appeared to be concern.

"I am sorry to trouble you when you are unwell, Mr. Holmes." she told him. Her voice was marked by a highly pleasing musical tone, which contrasted with her almost coarse appearance.

"It is nothing," my friend informed her, in a weak voice which hardly resembled his usual ringing tones. "Watson here," indicating me, "is not only a good friend, but an excellent physician, and I am confident that with his assistance, this slight indisposition will be gone in a matter of days at the most."

"I am glad to hear it." There was a genuine warmth in her manner.

"Pray be seated and tell us what has brought you here," Holmes invited, and I helped her to the chair in which our visitors took their ease as they unfolded their mysteries to my friend.

"Why, *you* brought me here," she answered him. "I wished you to visit me at Grosvenor Square, so that you might see for yourself the impossibility of the situation, but your illness prevents this. However, if you will allow to describe the circumstances, I am hoping that you may be able to work your magic at a distance, and solve the riddle."

"There are few things in this world that one might describe as 'impossible'," Holmes replied. "Many may appear so, but on close examination, and the application of reasoning, it is almost always the case that there is a rational explanation."

"Then perhaps, Mr. Holmes, you can examine these facts, and apply your reasoning to them. My husband, the Duke, is, as I am sure you are aware, one of the foremost in the land. He holds high office in the present Government, and up to a few weeks ago, he was most conscientious in his duties in that regard." She paused and looked significantly at Holmes and me. "I am telling you all of this in confidence, you understand?"

"Naturally," Holmes murmured.

"Very well, then. Starting about two months ago, Gerald informed me that he was not going to the Cabinet meeting that morning, giving no reason."

"Perhaps it was a subject on which he felt he had nothing to contribute, or perhaps one to which he had some antipathy?" I suggested.

"I confess that I take little interest in politics, so I cannot tell you if that is correct or not. In any event, he went to his study and locked himself in for the whole of the day."

"If I might venture a guess at the reason you ascribed to his reluctance?" Holmes smiled. She nodded her assent. "You probably considered that he had taken a violent personal dislike to one or more of his Cabinet colleagues, and therefore wished to avoid meeting them."

"You are correct in your assumption of my reasoning, Mr. Holmes. However, this did not seem to be the case. Only two days after the incident I have just described, he proposed holding a dinner at Grosvenor Square, to which all members of the Cabinet were to be invited. All accepted the invitation, and I observed closely for signs of hostility or dislike between Gerald and the others. I flatter myself that I have some skill in discernment in these matters, and I can assure you that there was nothing of the sort. Some of the junior Ministers were obviously a little envious of the success of their elders, but there was nothing that I could see to indicate anything other than a body of able men, united in a common cause, and with a genuine liking and respect for each other. No, that was not the answer. Since that time, my husband has refused to attend meetings of the Cabinet several times, averaging twice a week, I would judge."

"Then we should fall back on the idea that he has some antipathy to some of the ideas expressed in the Cabinet at the meetings he does not attend," Holmes remarked. "In all honesty, Your Grace, I had expected something a little more – interesting, shall we say?"

"I have not yet begun to tell the full story," the Duchess continued. "Last Tuesday, the Duke vanished from a locked room, and then reappeared in that room." She smiled faintly as she noted the effect of her words on Holmes, who had drawn himself into a posture of alertness, fixing his eyes on her with a new intensity.

"Pray continue," he urged. "Watson, you are taking notes, I trust? Your Grace, was this disappearance and reappearance witnessed by yourself?"

She shook her head. "Allow me to explain. As I mentioned earlier, my husband locked himself in his study when he decided not to attend Cabinet meetings for the first time. This has been his practice on all such occasions since then. However, last Tuesday, the Prime Minister sent a message that the Duke should attend him at Downing Street on a matter of the utmost urgency. I therefore determined to inform him of this myself, rather than letting a servant be the bearer of the message. I knocked on the door of the study, and requested him to open it. There was no response, and I repeated my request, this time informing him that this was a matter concerning the Prime Minister. There was still no response.

"It is the custom at Grosvenor Square for a spare key to every room to be kept in the servants' hall, where it may be used in cases of emergencies, such as a fire in the building or the like.

"I judged that this was such an emergency, and availed myself of the key to the study. I knocked once more, and receiving no answer, unlocked the door, assuming that maybe Gerald had fallen asleep. You may judge my astonishment when I discovered no trace of my husband within the room. Not only had he vanished, but his clothes – that is to say, his jacket, trousers, waistcoat .and shirt – were folded neatly on a chair next to the desk. I hardly knew what to believe." She stopped as if to catch her breath. "I called Jeavons, the butler, swearing him to silence on the matter, and together we searched every possible place in the room where he might have been hiding, for whatever reason. There was nothing."

"And there is no other door leading from the room, of course?"

"None."

"And the windows?"

"The windows of that room are barred to prevent housebreakers. My husband often has occasion to bring home with him papers of the utmost confidentiality, whose loss or misappropriation might be the cause of a political crisis. A child could not make its way through those bars."

"You did not call the police?"

"Jeavons was all for following that course of action, but the resulting publicity would have been distasteful, and I forbade him to do so. We must have searched for at least thirty minutes, at the end of which time we left the room, and I relocked the door behind us. I retired to my room for about an hour, when I heard my husband's voice downstairs. I fairly ran down those stairs, Mr. Holmes, to behold Gerald, dressed in the clothes in which I had seen him dressed earlier that morning. On my enquiring of Jeavons where he had appeared, I was informed that he had come out of his study, having used his own key to unlock the door."

"And when you asked him about his disappearance from the room?"

"He simply mentioned that he had gone out, had returned, and gave me to understand that he would tolerate no further discussion on the matter. He said this last in such a tone that I felt I could question him no more."

"Curious indeed," remarked Holmes. "Has there been a recurrence of this vanishing?"

"There has been no such urgent summons that necessitated his presence, but on one occasion when the Duke had locked himself in his study, on Friday last, I took it upon myself to knock on the door on some pretext – something which I had never done before. There was no answer, but I did not enter. To tell you the truth, Mr. Holmes, I was afraid, especially after his reaction to my questions on the previous occasion."

"Understandably so," I said to her. "There is something almost of the supernatural about this, would you not agree, Holmes?" I added this last in an attempt to persuade the Duchess, using all the force of his reason and logic, that such an explanation was not to be considered. I was not disappointed, and the Duchess expressed her relief that the supernatural was not to be reckoned with in this case.

"There is one further development, which sounds so trivial that it hardly merits a mention," she added. "Yesterday was Collins', my maid's, day off. She returned to the house in the evening in a condition of some excitement. When I observed her state, I asked the cause, and she swore that she had seen the Duke coming out of a house in Holland Park at two o'clock precisely. She was sure of the time, as the clock of St. Barnabas struck the hour. At that time, I had every reason to believe that my husband was locked in his study, having retired there following luncheon."

"She was possibly mistaken in the identity of the man whom she saw?"

"I fear not. Collins is an exceptionally intelligent and observant woman, and it is unlikely that she would make such an error, especially in the case of a man whom she sees every day. In any event, the Duke suffers from a slight limp in the left leg, as the result of a bout of infantile paralysis. The man whom Collins saw had just such a limp, though he was dressed in what she describes as rough tradesman's clothes. I am satisfied that she saw my husband, but at the same time, I firmly believe that he was in a locked room in our house, from which there is no exit, and I am at a loss as to why she describes him being dressed in that way."

Holmes rubbed his hands together. "This is a most singular turn of events," he said. "When may I come to visit the scene of the disappearance? Obviously such a visit must be made in the Duke's absence."

"But you must not consider that, Mr. Holmes. You are ill, are you not?" She spoke with what seemed like genuine concern in her voice.

"I find the stimulation of such a problem to have a remarkably curative effect," he smiled.

"In that case, Gerald mentioned to me that he intended to attend a Cabinet meeting this afternoon from two o'clock. You may call at any time from then for the next two or three hours."

"Excellent. One more small matter. Did your observant Collins happen to remark the address of the building from which she claims to have seen your husband emerging?"

"She did indeed, and I have it written here." She pulled out a small slip of paper, and passed it to Holmes.

"Number 1 Holland Park Road," Holmes read out. "Thank you."

"I may expect you this afternoon, then?"

"Without a doubt," Holmes assured her, and on that note she took her leave of us.

"Well, Watson, what do you make of this?"

"If it were not for the disappearance from the room, I would suspect a vulgar intrigue being carried on at the Holland Park address. Her Grace is certainly not the most alluring example of female beauty."

"Nor was she ever," remarked Holmes. "However, as Viola Simmons, she possessed one of the most beautiful mezzo-soprano voices ever to go on the stage at Covent Garden, before the Duke married her. Her reputation was one of complete honesty and probity, unlike that of many others of that profession, and I believe the Duke was not the only contender for her hand. I believe that everything she has told us today is the truth – at least, as she sees it."

"I am puzzled about the vanishing of the Duke from a locked room, and his reappearance in another part of London."

Holmes smiled. "I am sure there will be a perfectly rational explanation. Your suggestion of an intrigue may well be the correct interpretation of the Duke's appearance in another part of London. It may well be that his change of attire is the result of his wishing to pass unremarked, which would also bolster the idea of an intrigue."

"But how," I asked, "could he leave a room, the only exit from which was locked?"

"The answer is, of course, that he did not."

"Then I am puzzled. The Duchess told us, did she not, that she had examined the room carefully, and proved that there was no other means of exit?"

"If you care to cast your mind back, that was not precisely what she told us."

I racked my brains, and consulted the notes that I had made. "I still fail to follow your reasoning, Holmes."

"Be that as it may, let us take a trip to Holland Park before we present ourselves at Grosvenor Square."

I assented. It was a fine spring morning. The night's rain had washed away much of the grime and soot, and London presented a sparkling face to the world. On our arrival at the house at which the Duke had been identified, we observed a furniture van outside the house. "Are the inhabitants moving house?" I wondered aloud.

"It is easy enough to discover," Holmes answered, striding forward to engage one of the workmen in conversation.

"Is that Miss Katherine Thornton's furniture that you are loading?" he asked. "I'd heard that she was leaving Town." I saw the glint of gold as a coin changed hands.

"No, sir. This is the gentleman who has the flat on the first floor. A Mr. Armitage, and he's not moving. These are just a few pieces which he's sold to the Dook of somewhere."

"The Duke of Staffordshire?" suggested Holmes.

"That's the one, sir. Now, if you'll excuse me, we've got to get these to him before this evening. It's a pleasure talking with you, sir," he said, displaying the half-sovereign that Holmes had slipped into his hand, "but work's work."

"Indeed it is," replied my friend, returning to join me.

"Who is Katherine Thornton?" I could not help asking.

"A dainty creature, the product of my fancy," he asked. "It is always easier to find a man ready to contradict you than to supply you with a straight answer to an open question."

"So you have discovered that Mr. Armitage who lives here is selling furniture to the Duke?"

"That is certainly what our friend there believes."

"And you do not?"

"I will reserve judgement until more facts are forthcoming. In the meantime, let us make our way to Grosvenor Square."

We were admitted by a footman who took our names and disappeared with our cards. In a minute, a man entered the hall who, from his dignified bearing, could only be Jeavons, the butler.

"Mr. Holmes. Dr. Watson. This way, if you would, gentlemen," he greeted us with a slight bow. We followed him to a drawing-room where the Duchess was reclining on a couch.

"No, pray do not disturb yourself," Holmes said to her, as she prepared to rise. "I am sure that Jeavons can conduct us to the room in question, and when I have examined that, I would like a word with Collins, if I may."

"Certainly. Jeavons, be good enough to take these men to His Grace's study. I hope that they will be able to solve the mystery that has puzzled us."

"Very good, Your Grace," he answered. He led us through the hallway to a large room at the front of the house, before making as if to leave us.

"Stay a moment," Holmes ordered him. "Tell me, what were your feelings when the door was opened and the Duke was nowhere to be seen?"

"Well, sir, I have to say that I was shocked. And then when we found his clothes, I was struck all of a heap, as they say. You'll laugh when I tell you this, but I thought he might have been taken up to Heaven by an angel or something like that. They don't need clothes up there, do they?"

Holmes laughed. "Such theological niceties are beyond me," he said. "But in any case, he came back, did he not?"

"He did, sir, and in its way that was just as shocking as him disappearing."

"I can well imagine that to be the case. It was you who searched the room with Her Grace, was it not?"

"Yes, sir, and we found nothing."

"Did you search the room together?"

"No, sir. She searched that half of the room," indicating the side with the windows facing the street, "and I searched the other part."

"And it was you who discovered the clothes?"

"It was, sir. On that chair there. Now if you will excuse me, sir, I hear the furniture van outside. His Grace has ordered some furniture, and I must supervise its delivery and unpacking. Please ring for me when you are finished here, and I will arrange for Collins to be sent to you as you requested."

"A very helpful servant," I observed as Jeavons left us in the study.

"Indeed. He told us a lot."

I was surprised at Holmes's words, since I considered we had learned very little from the butler.

"We have little enough time," Holmes told me, "so let us begin our search."

"What do you expect to find?"

"Anything that is out of the ordinary. Anything that you feel is surprising in a room such as this."

Puzzled, I moved to the window, and commenced an examination of the floor, walls, and window, together with the furnishings."

"No, not there," Holmes said. "Her Grace has already examined that side."

"But Jeavons has examined the other," I objected.

"So he tells us," Holmes said. "Come, join me."

After a few minutes' searching, Holmes let out a sharp exclamation. "Watson! Here, look!" He had rolled back the Persian rug that covered the floor behind the desk, to reveal what appeared to be a trapdoor. "Here is the solution to the mystery of the vanishing Duke!" He pulled at the ring let into the floor, to reveal a flight of wooden steps leading down to what must be the cellars of the house. "And look!" He pointed to a suit of clothes hanging on a hook let into the wall of the staircase. "Let us examine them."

The garments turned out to be a brown tweed suit of the sort worn by a tradesman who has fallen on somewhat hard times, together with a shirt and tie to match, and a brown bowler hat, to which Holmes applied his lens. Beside them was a shelf with a candlestick holding a half-burned candle. Holmes also examined this last closely, and pronounced that from the absence of dust, it had been used in the recent past.

"Where do these steps eventually lead?" I asked.

"Time enough for that later," Holmes answered. "Come, let us restore order, and talk to the maid Collins."

We replaced the candle and the clothes, and closed the trapdoor, laying the rug over it once again before ringing for Jeavons, who appeared.

"The furniture has arrived safely?" Holmes asked him by way of making conversation.

"Indeed, sir. It is now in the hall awaiting His Grace's orders as to its disposition."

"New furniture?"

There was what sounded like an audible sniff. "No, sir. Old chairs and chests and the like. Maybe hundreds of years old. If you want my personal views, sir . . . ."

"Yes?"

"I wouldn't give such things house room. Very dark and gloomy to my way of thinking. I hope you won't tell Their Graces what I have just said," he added hurriedly.

"Of course not," Holmes assured him.

"Thank you, sir. In that case, I'll just go and fetch Collins. You will talk to her in here?"

238

"If I may."

"Very good, sir."

In the few minutes while we awaited the arrival of the maid, Holmes amused himself by examining the spines of some of the books on the shelves.

"This is Collins, sir," announced Jeavons, ushering in a pleasant-faced middle-aged woman.

"Ah, Collins," Holmes greeted her. "I won't keep you from your duties for long. Thank you, Jeavons," he added, dismissing the butler. "Now, Collins, I just want to ask you about the man you saw the other day in Holland Park."

"It was His Grace, sir. I'd know his walk anywhere."

"You see, Watson?" Holmes turned to me almost triumphantly. "I have maintained for a long time that a man's gait is as distinctive as his face, and may be used to identify criminals, but those blockheads in Scotland Yard . . . ." He broke off. "I am sorry to interrupt."

"That's all right, sir," she smiled.

"What was he wearing?"

"A shabby brown suit. Not the sort of thing one of his position should be wearing in Town, if you ask me. More like a pawnbroker or something like that. And he had this brown billycock on his head which meant I couldn't see his face that clear, but I know it was him, sir. I know his boots, seeing them being cleaned often enough, and it was those boots that this man was wearing."

"Would you happen to know what size of hat His Grace wears?"

She seemed surprised at the question, but answered, "I couldn't tell you offhand, sir, but I could find out for you quickly enough."

"Please do so." She left the room on her errand.

"It seems clear to me," I said, "that this mysterious figure in Holland Park is the Duke, wearing the garments that we have just discovered."

"I agree. The hat will be the conclusive proof."

"Then you will tell the Duchess of her husband's infidelity?"

"I do not believe that to be the case here."

Before I could reply, Collins returned, bearing a silk hat. "I must give it back soon, sir. Please do whatever it is you have to do quickly."

With a word of thanks, Holmes took the hat and examined the interior minutely before handing it back.

"Thank you. That has been most helpful. You have been in this household for long?"

"I was with Her Grace before her marriage. I worked as her dress – her maid, sir. And now I must go and return the hat, if you will excuse me, sir." She bobbed a curtsey and left us.

"So she was Viola Simmons' dresser," mused Holmes. "Well, well. I believe we have discovered all we need in this place. Let us go."

We left the room and entered the hallway, where there were indeed a number of pieces of carved dark oak furniture which appeared to date from the beginning of the last century. As Jeavons had said to us, the overall impression was one of gloom. Holmes bent to examine one or two of the chairs and chests, and stood up with a look of satisfaction on his face.

Jeavons joined us. "Will you be leaving now, sir, or will you wish to see Her Grace before you go?"

"We will leave," Holmes told him. "Please thank Her Grace from me, and please inform His Grace on his return that I would very much appreciate it if he were to call on me tomorrow. He may find me at this address." He took one of his cards, and wrote a few words on it before handing it to the butler. "If he can let me know at what hour he intends to visit, I shall be much obliged."

We took our hats and sticks and walked into the street. Rather than taking the turning for Baker Street, Holmes led the way to the mews at the back of the house. "There," he exclaimed, pointing with his stick to a flaking door, seemingly little used, reached by a set of steps, which clearly led to the house's cellar. "That will be the door by which the Duke emerges in his disguise, unseen by anyone at the front of the house."

As we walked back to our rooms, Holmes was humming a tune to himself, which I recognised as "*Si vuol ballare*" from Mozart's *Figaro*. It seemed to have a certain appropriateness under the circumstances.

That evening brought a message from the Duke, informing us that he would call the next morning at nine.

At the appointed hour, the Duke made his entrance to our rooms. Although I was familiar with his features, which had been reproduced often enough in the illustrated press, I had not seen him in the flesh prior to this meeting, and was struck by his bearing, which seemed to be that more of a common man than of one of the foremost peers of the realm. Following our introductions, Holmes waved him to the chair which had been occupied by his wife the previous day and offered him a cigar, which the peer accepted.

"I have heard of you, Mr. Holmes," he said, opening the conversation. "I have heard that you are a man of discretion."

"Thank you," my friend replied. "It is one of the more flattering descriptions that has been applied to me."

"I believe you know something of Mr. Armitage of Holland Park?" was our visitor's next question.

"That is correct," answered Holmes.

"How much do you know?"

"Other that he wears a brown tweed suit with a matching bowler hat, rents a first floor flat in Holland Park, and displays a keen interest in purchasing furniture of the early eighteenth century which bears particular symbols – very little, I confess."

Our visitor's face was a picture of astonishment which appeared to be mixed with fear as Holmes recited these details. "Upon my word, I had no idea that the man was so well-known outside certain circles."

"I may also add," said Holmes, "that he is married, seemingly very happily, to a charming lady, and spends his nights and much of his days at their house in Grosvenor Square. Some of his days are spent in Westminster, or in Downing Street."

At these words, the Duke's face turned pale, and I had a momentary fear that he was about to faint. Seemingly with a great effort, he spoke in a faint voice. "You say you are a man of discretion. How much must I pay you to assure myself of that silence?"

Two spots of colour stood out on Holmes's pale cheeks. "Upon my word, sir, I you are utterly mistaken if you believe that my silence is to be purchased in the marketplace like some – some article of furniture. I have seldom been so insulted in the whole of my professional career. With all due respect, sir, I must ask you to leave immediately. My regards to your charming wife. Good day to you, sir." Sherlock Holmes was as angry as I have ever seen him.

The Cabinet minister rose to his feet. "I apologise wholeheartedly," he said in contrite tones. "I will not beg you to keep my secret, but I will no longer inconvenience you. Good day to you both."

I could see that Holmes's mood was not one in which he was willing to answer questions, and I refrained from making further enquiries about this business until sometime later, at which time he was involved with the affairs of Lord St. Simon, an account of which I have given previously in a piece entitled "The Noble Bachelor". He mentioned in passing that there was no mystery in the case of the furniture van, and that that the whole business had been obvious from the beginning. Indeed, he added, that there had been so little work for him to perform that he had not charged the Duchess for his services. Instead, he had sent her a note, reassuring her that the mysterious absences of her husband were by no means due to the agency of some supernatural force, and had nothing of the sinister or criminal about them, but for reasons of professional etiquette, he found himself unable to provide her with the precise cause, and recommending her to seek the details from her husband..

I, however, was still in the dark regarding the solution. Accordingly, when we found ourselves in a train to Dorking to investigate a case of suspected forgery of a will, I took the opportunity to ask Holmes of his conclusions regarding the Grosvenor Square case.

He drew thoughtfully on his pipe. "Quite frankly, Watson, I am surprised that you have not worked out the details yourself."

"You made it clear that the Duke of Staffordshire and this mysterious Mr. Armitage were one and the same person. We could deduce that from the description given by the maid, and the clothing we discovered in the passage under the trapdoor in the study."

"Correct. Proceed."

"But what I do not understand is why the Duke as Armitage was selling this old furniture to himself."

"He was not," Holmes answered shortly.

"But why the deception?"

Holmes sighed. "A strange mixture of vanity and reticence. The values of the Duke have always been somewhat at variance with those of his class – witness his marriage to a woman who was neither a beauty in the conventional sense, nor the possessor of great wealth. He is, however, proud of his descent from those noblemen who supported the Old Pretender in the Jacobite Rebellion of 1715. In his study in Grosvenor Square, I noted several shelves of books devoted to that particular episode in history.

"At that time, several of the great families of England, particularly in the Midlands and in the North, resented the imposition, as they saw it, of the Hanoverians on the country. Much of this resentment was also in connection with religion – the Stuarts, as you know, being inclined towards Catholicism, and the Hanoverians being staunchly Protestant. The Duke's family have been Catholics since time immemorial. It was common for such families to display their allegiances, both religious and political, in physical form, albeit discreetly."

"Such as carvings and decorations on furniture?" I hazarded.

"Precisely so. When I examined the chairs and chests in the hallway at Grosvenor Square, I discovered several crowned thistles – one of the Stuarts' badges, along with symbols associated with the Church of Rome. It is not without the bounds of possibility that many of these pieces originally belonged to the Duke's family, prior to its near-bankruptcy at the hands of a later ancestor's profligacy towards the end of last century."

"So far, I follow you," I said. "But what of the assumption of the person of Armitage?"

"Ah, there I wander a little into the realm of supposition, though I have little doubt that my theories match the facts. Firstly, the Duke would not want to draw attention to his purchases. As you know, there has been a great deal of discussion in political circles regarding undue influence by

Rome in our political affairs. It has been suggested by some that English Roman Catholics must make their choice between loyalty to Rome and loyalty to the Crown. For the Duke, a Minister of the Crown, to be seen as an active collector of items of the type that we saw would make his allegiance suspect, and it would be most injudicious at this juncture of our political life."

"And there is another, more practical, and almost farcical, possibility that strikes me. Most of these items that he acquired would be purchased through professional dealers, rather than through private dealings. I am sure that such merchants would double the price on their items should they suspect that their future owner was a duke. As Mr. Armitage, however, His Grace doubtless derived a great deal of amusement from dealing with these people on their own terms. The flat that he rented in Holland Park was, of course, the address to which the items were to be delivered."

"One thing still puzzles me, however," I said. "Why did you insist on searching that half of the study which had not been searched by the Duchess?"

"Oh, it was clear that Jeavons was fully cognisant of the whole business. I made a few casual enquiries, and discovered that he had been in service with the Duke from an early age, and no doubt his master's sympathies had transferred themselves to him. It would be he, after all, who acquired the garments for the disguise, and who maintained them, and provided the candles and so on to allow the Duke to present himself secretly to the world as Armitage."

"It all seems so simple now that you have explained it," I commented.

"It was childishly simple," he replied. "I am sorry that the Duke misjudged my motives in the way that he did. I find myself admiring his sense of humour and his ingenuity."

"Maybe an opportunity will present itself to set matters straight," I told him.

As it turned out, it was a matter of a little over a year when such an event occurred, and the Duke, clearly willing to let bygones be bygones, called on us with a problem in his Ministry to which he required Holmes to provide a solution. Though I am not as yet at liberty to provide full details of this case, let it be known that on this occasion His Grace and Holmes worked together in harmony to solve the problem, and at the conclusion of it each regarded the other with trust, and even affection.

The Voyage of
Albion's Thistle
by Sean M. Wright

At half-past eight in the morning, my snug, tidy sitting room in Pall Mall was already oppressively hot. I had ordered a late breakfast and was just finishing a third poached egg when my housekeeper, Mrs. Crosse, as thoughtful a landlady as any in the realm, brought me an odd beverage. Into a tumbler, she had poured rich coffee from the pot over bits of ice held in a strainer. It was a cool and soothing drink for what boded to be a miserably scorching day.

Despite a week-long vacation from my duties at the Foreign Office, I remained nearly drained of energy. Still at liberty on a Saturday forenoon during a mid-July heat wave in 1887, I gazed out the large front window at the traffic. I longed for the glens of Suffolk or the millponds of the West where, as a lad, I had spent many pleasant summers.

Draining the coffee, I decided myself on taking a leisurely stroll amidst wooded islets and lime trees – refreshing alternatives to the sunbaked brick and Portland stone of the city. As a concession to the informality of my ramble, I donned lavender spats in place of the usual grey. Sauntering down Pall Mall, I stopped at the tobacconist's for a pouch of black Cavendish. I was then off for Marlborough Road and St. James's Park with its canal and pond, the loveliest of all London's parks. Upon entering this little jewel-box of repose, a cooling breeze washed over me. The rustling branches of a beech tree and the sight of the greensward before me lifted my spirits. The Westminster chimes struck nine. I could look forward to a band concert beginning at ten. Newly invigorated, I stepped to the side of the path, tipping my hat to a nursemaid behind a pram as she passed. I removed a pipe from the depths of an inner pocket of my frock coat, charged it with tobacco, tested the draw, and lit it.

Gazing beyond the former royal enclosure, I took in the Mall's broad walkway, planted with elms, limes, and plane trees. Charles II had daily taken the air in this, once his own private enclosure, perhaps because, a short distance away in Pall Mall, close by my present dwelling, lived the saucy orange-seller, Nell Gwynne, darling of the groundlings.

The many homes in Carlton House Terrace now facing Pall Mall replaced the ill-famed palace where The Beau once held sway over both fashion and the Prince Regent. By way of contrast, the former residence of Lord Chancellor Jeffries, a somber brick-fronted house north of

Storey's Gate, remained a solemn guard. By special license of the King, Jeffries, the hanging judge and bane of regicides, had been allowed his own entry to the park.

To the east, now ornamenting the Horse Guards Parade, where the guards would soon be trooping the colors, sat the long Turkish cannon captured in Alexandria during the Crimean War. Next to the cannon sat the immense mortar cast at Seville by order of Napoleon, last employed by Marshall Soult at Cadiz. Abandoned during the French army's retreat from Salamanca, a grateful Spain had presented the weapon to the Regent after the Battle of Waterloo.

My good friend, General Sir Rodney Fairndails, formerly an officer in the Royal Engineers, once assured me that the heaviest shell carried by that mortar weighed one-hundred-and-eight pounds and had a range of six-thousand-two-hundred yards. Regarding the weapon's precise accuracy, he repeated a story given him by a colonel of the Horse Guards, one of Wellington's nephews. He assured Sir Rodney that he had seen a shell from this piece of ordnance shot into the Plaza de San Antonio in Cadiz when the whole of that splendid square was crowded with the rank and fashion of the city and had fallen into the very center of the square without injuring a single individual.

Betaking myself to Constitution Hill, I saw where Sir Robert Peel had been fatally injured by a fall from his horse in 1860, and where, on three occasions, the Queen-Empress had been confronted by ill-directed pistols of home rule-seeking Irish wretches whose passion to gain a wicked notoriety had degraded them into imbecilic thugs.

Beneath a dainty parasol, a demure young lady dressed in floating chiffon of canary yellow edged with white lace promenaded in my direction. She was accompanied by an enthusiastic young swain decked out in a seersucker jacket and white trousers. He very nearly crashed into me, caught himself in time, tipped his boater, and continued on, adroitly avoiding a flower-bed full of bright scarlet poppies and yellow daffodils.

Having seen gardens along the Seine, the Rhone, and the Danube, where vegetation is forced into narrow, arbitrary and artificial spaces, it cheered me to delight in the profusion of colorful flowers adding to the park's tranquil ambiance. I smiled. The English alone understand how to let Nature remain natural. True, we throw great bridges over water and construct magnificent buildings of renown, but we English design gardens, refreshing and cheerful. They can excite the imagination yet remain meditative domains of quiet and repose. I marveled that, in the very heart of the great metropolis that is London, St. James's Park lay islanded between the cobblestoned deserts of Westminster and Pimlico, an oasis of beauty blended into the majesty and greatness of England.

Ahead of me lay the lake with its little off-center island. A line of ducks waddled across the gravel walk while rare aquatic birds, all belonging to the Ornithological Society, noisily disported themselves in the water. Those of my readers who have seen these birds know them to be quite tame, happily allowing children to pet and feed them bits of bread and biscuit crumbs.

The children love this park more than any other in London, I believe. Without having to dodge landaus or hansom cabs, vendors' carts with their broad, wooden-wheels or iron-tyred lorries, lads and lasses can run and jump, roll hoops, and toss balls. Today, a few were flying kites under their parents' unobtrusive supervision – save for one father showing his little son how to play out line with a steady hand. At one point, the kite, having a mind of its own, dipped swiftly earthward. Then, suddenly, catching a sharp updraft, the line very nearly knocked the man's pipe from his mouth and the kite shot into the cloudless, cerulean vault. More sensible parents occupied themselves with laying out picnic lunches and let the children play.

Taking in all these gentle activities it came to me that, so enwrapt had I become with the responsibilities of government, I had forgotten how to enjoy a measure of rejuvenating leisure. An unexpected melancholy threatened as I realized how divorced I had become from all the merriment surrounding me, a hermit in the midst of eight millions. Watching the lively antics of the children, however, with their loud yelps, huzzahs, and laughter, provided a welcome tonic.

Finding myself on the grassy slope approaching the lake, I leant on my sturdy blackthorn. A competition of paper sailboats was to commence. The sight took me back to my youth. My brother and I had spent several summers at the home of an uncle and aunt in Devonshire where we had made boats from newsprint and sailed them across the millpond, much as a number of boys were about to do now.

They knelt at water's edge preparing paper sailboats, several ingeniously made with cunning folds – twigs served for masts, their sails cut to order with penknives. Several lads had folded peaked hats from newsprint, in imitation of the fore-and-afts of Her Majesty's naval officers. The air filled with anticipation as these young Nelsons made their final adjustments. I strode down the slope to watch more closely.

Presently, a firecracker exploded and the race was on. The boys cheered as they pushed their paper armada as far as they might. A fickle breeze caught the sail of one, blowing it a ways, then left it becalmed. When it again picked up, the breeze filled the paper sails of other boats. A few remained on tack while others, to the dismay of their creators, jibbed into each other, their progress stopped or blown off-course.

All the boats save one were pond-worthy craft. That one had skimmed the surface but a few feet before becoming waterlogged. The owner was clearly the dark-haired boy whose worried eyes reflected his dismay. Neither breeze nor cheering could save his sinking sloop. The other lads, pointing to the casualty, laughed its owner to scorn. Then they ran and skipped round to the opposite side, merrily following the paper regatta sailing hither and thither across the pond, leaving the boy whose boat had sunk quite alone.

One of his tormenters, the one who had laughed the loudest and most cruelly, was running toward the shore opposite when he looked back to hurl more insults. As fate would have it, he never saw a single laceless, left-handed, leather boot left lying on the bank. Stepping on it crookedly, he lost his balance, falling headlong into the shallow water. This event provoked more hilarity from his fellows. Stung by the laughter, the young scamp rose up in a fury – moss, mud, and duckweed clinging to his hair and clothing. Pointing to the little boy left behind he yelled, "You're the cause of this! Just wait till I get hold of you!" He made to run back, no doubt thinking to thrash the lad, but he never had the chance. I'd caught him by the scruff of the neck.

"Here, now, you rapscallion!" I exclaimed. "Leave off!" None too gently I swung him round to face me. The boy, stopped in his tracks, eyeing me warily.

"Be off with you before you feel my stick across the seat of your trousers."

The rascal looked all the way up my bulk, saw my stern expression, and thought better to offer me an impertinence. Sullenly, he trudged away to retrieve his craft.

Ambling over to the little boy, the source of his ship-building misfortune was made obvious. Not having the same paper as the others, he had found an old copy of *Tit-bits,* the penny-print published by George Newnes. Sold by every newsvendor in the city, the banner was unmistakable. Sparing every farthing in its production, Newnes had *Tit-bits* printed on newsprint of the very cheapest quality. [1] It was a feat that the lad's boat sailed as far as it had.

He was seven or eight years of age, a street Arab. His shabby clothing – a thin, formerly white shirt three sizes too large blousing over the top of a pair of patched and tattered trousers – proclaimed that he was not part of the better-dressed group. Over the shirt, he wore what had once been an elegant four-pocket waistcoat. His feet, innocent of stockings, were stuck into a pair of down-at-the-heel shoes. Holding back tears, he glanced contemptuously at the rest of the copy of *Tit-bits*, realizing how useless it would be to construct another boat from the rest of its pages.

I was struck by the boy's plight, so at odds with the gladness suffusing the park.

"Excuse me, young man."

The boy turned immediately defensive, gazing up at me with an almost ferocious stare. He brushed back a dark, lank forelock from out of his misting blue eyes.

With a friendly nod, I continued, "I see you had some trouble with your sailboat."

"Yes, sir," he said in a guarded manner. "Them others have better paper but wouldn't share it. Then I found this," he added, giving the newsprint on the ground a contemptuous little kick, "but the paper's no good."

"So I see. If you remain here until I return, I believe I can supply you with a boat that will put the others to shame."

A small spark kindled in back of his eyes. "For sure, sir?"

"You wait and see."

The hint of a lopsided smile played on his lips. "Very well, guv'nor. Let's see what 'appens."

Back in Marlborough Road, I paused momentarily before the door of a chemist's shop, just off the mews. The gilt letters on the glass I knew from my boyhood still proclaimed "*Josiah Scott, Prop. Chemist & Apothecary*".

My brother and I had frequented this shop when our parents brought us on their annual trip from our home in North Riding, to stay a number of weeks with another aunt who lived in Pall Mall. Our first visit to this shop occurred during our second visit. Mother caught the croup and had me, with Sherlock in tow, pick up a nostrum. Mr. Scott treated us with benevolence, offering us both a peppermint stick. After that, we would often stop in for a visit and let Mr. Scott show us how chemicals were mixed and reacted to each other.

It had been years since I had turned that knob, but the same old bell on the curling spring above rang out as the door opened. Two young assistants equipped with mortars and pestles grinding powders were seated at a small deal-topped table behind the counter. One of them looked up momentarily to regard the new customer, then returned to his task. Wistful recollections nudged my memory as my eyes adjusted to the shop's cool, dim quiet. Familiar aromas of licorice and almond, clove and peppermint, Sulphur and asafetida drifted in the air. How long had it been since last I had visited this wondrous shop? To an imaginative boy of fifteen, it combined the overflowing plunder of the cave of the Forty Thieves with jarsful of eye of newt and toe of lizard littering an alchemist's laboratory.

248

The walls of the shop behind the counter remained lined with shelves from floor to ceiling, containing hundreds of containers. Pasteboard packets, squared and circular, were stacked against larger cardboard cartons. Thin glass vials vied for space with long or squat glass tubes all filled with grey, white, and mustard-yellow powders. Amber, brown, blue, icy white, and coral crystals sat chockablock with innumerable sealed cylindrical and squared glass bottles brimming with colourful liquids.

When I first made the acquaintance of Mr. Josiah Scott, standing tall and thin in his long, white coat, a fringe of lengthy straight, slate-grey hair circling his bald head, I envisioned Brother Roger Bacon, the good friar and experimental scientist. I thought of him dusting the results of an experiment from off his Franciscan habit while beating out stray sparks before his robes went up in flame. After that original visit, my brother and I regularly called on the friendly apothecary. Kindliness itself, after we expressed an interest in chemical pharmacology, Mr. Scott took the Holmes boys under his wing, generously sharing his expertise.

With infinite care and precision, Mr. Scott showed us how to prepare various chemicals. Many's the day, amid test tubes, retorts, and alcohol lamps, my brother and I dabbled in experiments as Mr. Scott demonstrated the various properties of chemicals and medicinal compounds. Every so often he would look into our eager young faces and sigh deeply, saying, "You lads are more interested in the apothecary than some of my young assistants!" And he employed many over the years. These visits were, to be sure, of more than a little value to my brother in his later career.

The long, sturdy, oaken table still filled the center of what I had once thought a cavernous work area behind the counter. It still groaned under a plethora of familiar items, including the large bell jar in which ingots of pure potassium soaked in mineral oil. Mr. Scott had once terrified us, showing what happened when potassium was handled. Then, again, every so often, as a lark, the chemist would unroll a few inches of a strip of magnesium foil kept on a coil, and have one or the other of us put a lucifer to it. The result always dazzled us as it went up in an incandescent flash and thick white plume of smoke.

Mr. Scott was in the rear of the shop halfway up the tall ladder which had so fascinated me as it rolled along a trestle atop the immense cabinet bolted to the far wall, each of the shelves within filled with compounds, elixirs, and salves necessary to fill prescriptions. The old gentleman still wore the same thick, square, rimless spectacles attacked to a steel lever projecting from the thick leather band circling his brow.

Turning round at last, holding onto the ladder with one hand and shielding his eyes with the other, the chemist squinted across the room. He looked not a year older than when last I we met.

"Eh! What's this?" Mr. Scott called out in a friendly manner. "Is it Mr. Mycroft Holmes come to pay us a visit, then?"

"The same," I replied, gratified to know I was remembered.

"With you in two shakes," Mr. Scott declared in his high, raspy voice. As he clambered down the ladder I found a scrap of paper lying on the counter and dashed off the ingredients I desired. He approached, brushing powder, ashes, and soot from the sleeves of the familiar long, white-linen duster. Smiling broadly he took my hand and shook it enthusiastically.

"How good it is ter see yer again, my lad. Too many years a'gone by since last you stopped in for a visit."

"I regret that my duties have kept me away, Mr. Scott."

"Tut, tut," he said still smiling broadly. "I know your work at the Foreign Office keeps yer busy as yer keep the ship of state stay afloat, what?"

"I do what I can," I replied with rueful modesty, handing him the paper. "Your allusion has a certain aptitude regarding my calling upon you today."

"Ah, yes?" He focused on the note: "$NaHCO_3$ and $C_6H_8O_7$?" he read aloud, peering at the formula through the thick spectacles extending from the band. "Well, that's simple enough. Yer want it ter be anhydrous, then, and not monohydrate, is that it?"

"Yes. I believe it will work better that way."

He nodded. "Do yer want these ingredients mixed and combined in capsules?" the chemist asked, pulling at his long, smooth chin.

"Well, if it can be done without difficulty."

"Oh my, there's no difficulty," he chuckled, "none at all. We can combine 'em right enough, but I'd not want ter be the one ter have ter swaller 'em. Are you sure you don't want me to add some oil of clove to ease 'em down the gullet?"

"Thank you, no," I chuckled. "I assure you, no one will be swallowing them. They'll be having too much fun with them at the pond."

Old Mr. Scott's watery blue eyes widened with mirth as I told him of my morning's adventure. "Ah, now I see what yer've a mind to. Very well, my friend, but it will take some time."

"How many can you make in, say, the next forty minutes?"

"Oh, well, now," his brows knitted as he rubbed his chin, "that depends,"

"Would you be able to make up, say, one-hundred in that time?" I ventured.

He stared hard a few moments at the several orders transfixed by the spindle on the ancient receipt holder on the counter. "I have a few orders to fill ahead of yer." Then his brow relaxed as he winked, "But I can defer 'em a bit fer a friend."

I placed a sovereign on the counter.

"Good Lord, Mr. Mycroft!" Mr. Scott exclaimed. "If yer want ter spend that much, I can make yer up a couple o'thousand or so. The machinery ter roll 'em out's all shiny and clean and ready ter go."

"Thank you kindly," I replied, "I'm sure one-hundred will be more than enough at present." I pointed to the coin. "And I insist you keep it. I dare say another hundred more capsules will be wanted within the week, and throughout the summer."

Mr. Scott looked at me with a conspiratorial wink. "Just as yer say, Mr. Mycroft," he cackled genially. "Just as yer say."

"Now," I asked, "do you have a three-eighths-inch awl?"

The chemist looked up, surprised. "But of course."

"Excellent. May I trouble you for its use until I return?"

"No trouble at all." He turned to the assistants. "Ned, my lad, bring me the three-eighths-inch awl for Mr. Holmes, if yer would, please. It's in the tool chest on the workbench in the back room."

Ned departed and returned in short order, awl in hand. I took it, thanked Mr. Scott, and turned to leave.

"Oh, Mr. Mycroft, just one question."

I looked over my shoulder at the friendly chemist.

"You didn't say how much of each ingredient you want in those capsules."

"Why, enough to make capsules three-eighths of an inch in diameter, of course," I replied. "Eight-and-one-half grams of each ingredient should serve, I believe."

"Very good, Mr. Mycroft," Josiah Scott smiled creakily. "Just as you wish."

In forty minutes' time, I returned to the chemist's shop, a parcel tucked under my arm, exchanging the awl for a chip box full of capsules. In short order, I was again in St. James's Park. The little boy had kept faith with me, sitting on the slope of Constitution Hill, patiently awaiting my return. The other boys had continued playing sailor, their boats still plying the ripples on the lake.

Catching sight of me, the youngster scampered over and we walked down to the pond before I unwrapped the parcel. The butcher paper fell away and the boy's mouth fell open. He gazed at a three-masted wooden galleon. The ship was fourteen inches long and eighteen inches high, outfitted with canvas sails and festooned with thin twine for rigging, a crow's nest crowning the mainmast. After some twenty years lying in a trunk, it was still a bonny sight.

"Her name is *Albion's Thistle*," I told the boy who regarded the ship, its rigging and sails, its tiny ladders and gunports, with his eyes all agog.

"I made this ship when I was a boy." Reaching into my breast pocket I brought out a small envelope. "Here is a photograph I came across. I thought you might want to see it."

The tintype showed a round-faced boy in a frock coat, cocking an eye at the camera in order to appear more adult. "This is how I looked when I was twelve, the year my father helped me make this ship."

The boy regarded the photograph for a few moments. "Blimey, sir, look a'that. Yer've always been a toff, eh?" He gave me a sidelong glance. "'Ere now, gov'ner" he said cautiously. "You're pulling me leg, hain't cha? You don't really want me ter 'ave this 'ere boat, do ya?"

"It is a ship," I replied in gentle correction, "and it is all yours to enjoy." I spread my arms to frame my bulk. "As you can see, I'm much too big for it now."

He laughed delightedly at that all-too-obvious fact and I presented him with *Albion's Thistle*. He handed back the photograph asking, "Whatcher name, sir?"

"I am Mister Mycroft Holmes," I replied. "May I ask your name, young man?"

He looked up, smiling. "Bert. 'Erbert, actually, sir. Some's call me Wheeler, since it's me surname."

"I see. And which do you prefer?"

He thought a moment. "Bert," he replied at last.

"How do you do, Bert," I said, extending my hand.

"A lot better now, Mr. Holmes," his smile growing broader. He took my hand and gave it a friendly shake.

"Well then, Bert," I pointed out the half-inch-long hole I had dug out of the stern below the waterline with the chemist's awl. "Into this hole, you are to place one of the capsules you will find in here." I held up the chip box. "Having done so, you will be able to sail this ship on the pond any time you wish, even without a breeze to push it along."

The boy scratched behind his ear. "Ow'm I gonna do that, Mr. Holmes?"

"Through an elementary application of a principle of chemistry. Now open that box."

In my absence, the orchestra had taken the stage. The chimes in Westminster rang the hour and died away. The concert began with Von Suppe's "Light Cavalry Overture".

Bert, my new friend, remained mystified, but removed a capsule from the box and inserted it into the hole. He then placed the ship in the water.

The other boys had caught sight of *Albion's Thistle* and gathered round to see what the ship could do.

It did nothing.

The bullying lad, still damp from his wetting, began hooting that nothing was going to happen. In mid-insult, the coarse lad fell silent, as foam began to appear on the surface from the galleon's stern and, slowly at first, the ship began to move, picked up speed, leisurely voyaging across the surface of the lake.

My young friend cheered. His enthusiasm was picked up by the others, none of whom had ever seen such a thing. Walking along the water's edge we kept pace with the ship. The ducks swam out of her way as *Albion's Thistle* split the water's surface in her majestic passage. We approached the shore opposite in time to see the ship's prow strike against the bank.

Bert reached down, gingerly removing the ship from the water. He looked at it as Galahad might have beheld the Grail.

"Blimey, sir, 'ow does it work?"

The other boys crowding round picked up the question and wanted to know more about the voyage of *Albion's Thistle.*

Ignoring them Bert asked softly. "Is it magic?"

"In a way," I answered, "but the magic lies in a knowledge of chemistry. Certain reactions occur when different types of chemical compounds are brought into contact with each other. The ship was propelled by such a reaction."

The boys, although interested, were hardly comprehending me.

"Some chemicals are classified as bases, others are classified as acids. A base reacting with an acid causes small explosions of carbon dioxide gas which escapes into the air. In this case, I took sodium bicarbonate, which some people call 'aerated salt'. I wager your mother calls it 'baking soda'. It's used a great deal in cookery. When I treated the sodium bisulphate with citric acid, and placed it into the pond, the chemical reaction set in."

I looked at the pensive boys. The chemicals had reacted but they did not.

"Perhaps your mothers have made muffins or scones for your families. Sodium bicarbonate, when mixed with flour and a liquid, causes dough to rise quickly." They mulled over the notion.

"Have you ever seen your mothers make pancakes on a griddle?" I tried again, "After she spoons batter onto the griddle, have you noticed bubbles appear on the surface?"

Dawned the light.

"Sure, I've seen bubbles in the pancakes!" a red-haired boy exclaimed. The others joined in.

"Very good," I continued. "The ingredients of the pancake batter react to the hot surface of the griddle. Those bubbles are carbon dioxide gas being released into the air.

"But how's it work when there's no fire or griddle?" another boy called out.

"Good question," I replied. "There is another way to release the carbon dioxide contained in what is called an alkaline base. That is, to combine it with an acid. In this case, I used a powdered form of citric acid, made from the juices of fruits like oranges and lemons."

"I know, sir," another boy interrupted and his voice rang out, "'*Oranges and lemons sing the bells of Saint Clements*'!"

The rest of the boys laughed but were all attention as I held up one of the capsules. Breaking it open with my thumb and forefinger, white powder spilled into my lavender glove.

"But nothin's happening," my young friend said.

"And nothing will happen until water is added. The water is called a solvent. The casing of the capsule is made of gelatin. Water dissolves the gelatin, then the water saturates the powdered citric acid and the sodium bicarbonate. The two ingredients react with each other, releasing the gas called carbon dioxide."

I pointed to the hole in the ship's stern. "This gas expands and fills this hole, but the hole is too small to hold all the gas, so it escapes into the water. The explosion of those bubbles in the water force the ship to move and the continued explosions propel the ship forward."

Bert stared dubiously at the white powder in my palm.

"Have you ever seen a balloon," I asked, brushing the powder from my hands, "when the air is let out of it?"

"Oh, yes sir," Bert replied eagerly. "I seen that just last week when I watched a toy vendor blowin' up balloons. One got away from him and flew all over the street until the air was all gone out of it."

"Well," I replied, "that is much the same as what happens with the ship. The air has only one way out of the balloon, through the hole in the neck. Like the balloon, the ship goes forward, the air pushing it forward across the water until the air – the carbon dioxide gas – is gone."

"I understand, Mr. Holmes." In a softer voice Bert confided to me, "But if you ask me, it's still magic."

"It *is* magic," I smiled. "The only *real* magic. The magic of *knowledge*. The great scientist, Sir Isaac Newton, expressed it well when he said that, for every action, there is an equal and opposite reaction. The gas, trying to get out of the balloon or out of the hole in the stern of the ship, pushes the balloon into the air or the ship forward across the water."

A light began to dawn in Bert's eyes.

One of the boys held his paper boat aloft. "And we thought these were special." As he did so, something about the boat caught my eye and I asked to look at it.

"You have more of this paper?"

"A whole roll of it, sir," he replied. Then, catching himself, his attitude became more guarded. The other boys fell silent. "We, ah, found it."

"Another glass of port, Mr. Holmes?"

"Thank you, yes," The liveried attendant standing at my elbow immediately refilled my glass. "And allow me to again compliment you on this evening's superb rack of lamb, Mr. Birch. Your chef is a true artist."

Pleasant chuckles and sentiments of appreciation wafted across the table from members of the board of directors as we sat in postprandial splendor in the sumptuous private dining room of The Bank of England, J. W. Birch, Governor of the Bank, presiding. Sipping his port, he smiled broadly at me sitting in the place of honor at his right hand.

"I hope the Corona Corona is to your liking, Mr. Holmes?" he asked.

"It is one of the finest cigars I have had the pleasure of smoking, Mr. Birch. But, then, I'm partial to long-filler tobacco"

"Ah, then you must allow me to present you with a box. They come from Santo Domingo, you know. My own private stock."

"You're very kind, Mr. Birch," I replied.

"Nonsense, Mr. Holmes, nonsense. The Bank of England is very much in your debt."

Sitting to my right, the Deputy of the Mint, Charles Fremantle, leaned toward me. "You'll pardon me, Mr. Holmes if I say, having heard your story about this boy, this Bert Wheeler, I'm just a little confused as to how you solved the crime."

I sipped my port.

"In truth, sir, it was a simple matter. As the boy held up his boat, I could not help but think about the poet, Shelley."

"Good Lord!" Mr. Freemantle exclaimed. "Whatever brought him to mind?"

I smiled. "Shelly had a fondness for making paper boats in his bath, Mr. Freemantle. One day, having run out of ordinary paper, he proceeded to make a boat from a fifty-pound note. I noticed the paper from which the boy's little ship had been crafted. A quick scan of the other boats showed that the same paper had been used for all, as young Master Wheeler had earlier mentioned. The fine linen and silk threads were unmistakable. Those boats were made from that most specialized of papers, that used solely for the printing of banknotes.

"Having confirmed the type of paper, and knowing the boys could not possibly have made off with it from the Bank, I offered them each a florin if they could take me to where they had found the paper. The location was close by, a seemingly deserted house in Palmer Street, just below Petty France. A rusted-through window-latch had given the boys access.

"Peering through the window, despite their being covered by a tarpaulin, I could make out a number of large rolls of banknote paper sitting in a dark corner of the room. Smudges of black printers' ink on the tarpaulin made plain what was going on. Giving the boys their florins, I thanked and dismissed them. I then sent a wire to Scotland Yard."

"And that was all, Mr. Holmes?"

"Not entirely, Mr. Freemantle. The ruffian left on guard is presently in the Bow Street gaol nursing a bruised jaw and reflecting on the rashness of raising a sap against a member of the London constabulary. The printing press in the cellar, along with several discarded five- and ten-pound notes of inferior quality, were found by Mr. Athelney Jones, a very capable inspector at the Yard. These were taken in evidence, proof that a counterfeiting ring was headquartered in the deserted house. The premises were placed under surveillance and, after two days, five more members of the ring were taken into custody. Two culprits remain at large."

"A month ago, so as not to alarm the populace, Scotland Yard advised us not to release any news of the theft of the banknote paper," said Mr. Birch. "It was quite fortuitous, Mr. Holmes, that you came upon the cache before much of the bogus currency had passed into circulation."

"Have you had further word about the boy, Bert Wheeler?" asked Sir Thomas Farrer, one of the directors. "I believe the Bank should like to present him with a token of our appreciation."

"I am happy to say that young Master Wheeler, after a bath and a change of attire, now has a home in the loft at the chemist's shop in Marlborough Road where my friend, Mr. Josiah Scott, insisted on employing him to deliver prescriptions to his customers. You may call on him there with your expression of appreciation. When Master Wheeler enthusiastically explained to Mr. Scott just how my capsules propelled *Albion's Thistle*, and expressed a keen interest in learning more about pharmacology and chemistry, my friend insisted on taking him in."

I did not think it necessary to inform the governor and the board of the Bank of England that my brother, too, had found employment for young Bert Wheeler, as a member of his Baker Street division of the detective police force. Indeed, Sherlock put him to work within the precincts of the Old Lady of Threadneedle Street as one of his Baker Street Irregulars.

That, however, is another story.

NOTE

1. In 1891, *Tit-bits* would cease publication to become a department of Newnes's more enduring publication, *Strand Magazine*, the periodical that would famously become the home of Dr. Watson's chronicles about Mycroft's brother.

Bootless in Chippenham
by Marino C. Alvarez

I have been privy to many cases which Holmes investigated over the years. None, however, involved an actual historical relic whose storied history is recorded and on display at the Bodleian Library at Oxford University. It began on a cold November evening as rain-hardened drops pelted down against our window, with the proverbial heavy yellow fog limiting our view of the overcast sky. Holmes was reading *The Times* and seemed somewhat perplexed as he turned away, lighting his cherry-wood pipe. Several minutes passed. "Yes, Watson, it is a curious advertisement."

"Curious, Holmes? What do you mean?"

"This entry in the agony column of *The Times* that reads: "*Boot and Pole. Plough tonight. Mendoza.*" To himself, he murmured, "Something about this entry brings to mind a past remembrance." Just then, we heard the bell, followed by Mrs. Hudson ushering Inspector Lestrade up the stairs and into our room.

"Ah, Lestrade, have a glass of brandy to warm you from the night's dampness."

Lestrade took the libation that I gave him. "Thank you, Doctor. Mr. Holmes, there is a puzzling situation that may be of interest. I've just returned from Northfield Street in Ealing. We found the body of a Mr. Sidney Selden, a middle-age man, wearing a mac and lying face up in the gutter outside a pub. Seems to be a natural death. But he is known to us as a fencer of stolen goods with a criminal history. His watch, fob, and money pouch were missing. Additionally, these two papers without words, only pictures – one that seems to be a crude drawing showing a shield with three objects upon it – were on his person. You may see them for yourself." Holmes took the pieces of paper, each just a few inches across, and carefully examined both the elaborate pictorial display and the curious drawing before passing them across to me.

"Hmm. The sketch of the shield and boots is on common paper, while the other is much older. Where did you find them?"

"They were sheltered from the elements in an inside pocket, away from the water in which he was lying."

"Surely you noticed that the primitive pictorial representations in the more elaborate drawing are not European in nature?"

"Well, Mr. Holmes, I just glanced at the papers and, knowing Selden's reputation and your interest in such matters, brought them straight to you."

"Yes, of course, Lestrade. I'll keep them for further study. And now, let us go to Ealing and see what else we can learn."

I wasn't anxious to venture out into the cold night air, but with umbrella in hand I joined Holmes and Lestrade as we hailed a cab and made our way to Northfield Street. I was stunned to notice that our destination was The Plough, a pub known for its food and questionable musical performances. Recalling the agony column entry that we had recently discussed, I said, "Holmes . . . ." He noticed my gaze toward the pub and nodded, but narrowed his eyes and shook his head, as if he didn't want the connection to be revealed so soon.

A constable was on the scene when we arrived and had kept bystanders at a reasonable distance from where the body had been found. Although it had already been taken to the morgue, Holmes still made his own painstaking study of the scene. This examination was quite trying, as the area was being continually assaulted with the falling rain. Holmes, however, was not deterred. He used his lens to view closely the markings of the depressions that still remained in the nearby muddied area. When he had finished, he paused and said to Lestrade, "We are finished here. Other than it would be wise to look for a fellow with both boots having cobbled heels, one smooth rubber-soled right boot and the left with a traditional work boot design worn slightly on the instep, there is little more that can be determined. I have a fair idea of the identity of the man we seek, and I'll examine the body in the morning." With that, we said goodnight to a most surprised inspector and hailed a cab, making our way back to Baker Street.

Upon our return, Holmes went directly to the bookshelf and sorted through his scrapbooks, removing three volumes containing the letters *C*, *S*, and *W*. He paged through the entries and stopped to read two items. Carefully he made a few notations, and then sat back in his chair. It wasn't difficult to observe that he was in a brown study, frequently examining the papers removed from the body that had been found lying in the rain-soaked mire. He was still doing so when I went to bed.

The next morning found us eating a breakfast of fresh rashers and eggs, prepared by Mrs. Hudson. I assumed from observing his lens resting on the pictorial representations and the additional notes made from his scrapbooks, lying open on the desk, that Holmes had remained awake through much of the night.

"We have our starting points, Watson."

"What's that?"

"Why, the pictogram of the three boots and shield, and the boot marks in the mud last night. What remains is our examination of the body."

"Pictogram of three boots?" I asked, puzzled. However, Holmes didn't reply and, without another word, we finished our repast and then made our way to the morgue, where we were met by Doctor Whitcomb, the Medical Examiner. He told us that Selden died from an ordinary coronary heart attack. Holmes, always thorough, was given permission to examine the body. After several minutes, he announced that he concurred and thanked the Medical Examiner, and we left the premises to return to our lodgings. After again scrutinizing both papers, he told me that he would be back in time for supper and left with them in hand.

Holmes returned in the early evening and we enjoyed a meal prepared by Mrs. Hudson. Retiring into his chair and lighting his pipe, he told me what had transpired. "Watson, this afternoon was most enlightening."

"Where did you go?"

"First to the British Museum, followed by the British Library. Then I returned to The Plough before making a quick turnaround to Oxford. While at the Museum, I confirmed an interesting bit of heraldry." He held up the sketch of the shield and, as he had informed me that morning, boots. "Did you know that boots were symbolic of mounted riders and used to represent charges – often displayed as riding boots, sometimes with spurs? But of more importance is the elaborate primitive drawing." He handed it to me for further examination. "Upon visiting the Library, I was directed to read specifically about the *Codex Mendoza*, an Aztec document created to give to Charles V, the King of Spain."

"Aztecs!" I examined it in greater detail than I had the previous night. "I say! It does have pictorial designs of an eagle and other artifacts."

"Yes, Watson, it has immense antiquarian value. In Oxford, I visited the Bodleian Library, where I was given permission to examine the actual document, as the head librarian had used my services in the past. They were quite intrigued and concerned to see that ancient slip in your hands – a detail copied from the original – as until this afternoon it was believed to still be stored within the library's collections. At some point in the past it had been stolen.

"The *Codex* itself is a document, hundreds of years old, that contains Spanish explanations and commentaries regarding the tribute paid by the conquered Aztec, as well as a description of their daily life, as represented in pictograms. I learned that the *Codex* was named after the man who likely commissioned it, Don Antonio de Mendoza, a viceroy of New Spain. It was being sent on a ship of the Spanish fleet when it was taken by French privateers. It ended up in the French Court, and it was later sold to Richard Hakluyt – you may know the name. He was the same English writer Hakluyt whose work was used by Shakespeare as the source for writing *The Tempest*. But these Shakespearean associations are of no consequence to the problem at hand. The *Codex* later passed through a number of owners. The entire thing was given to the Bodleian Library in 1659 – five years after the death of one of the past owners – John Selden, an English jurist who originally possessed it at one point."

"Was he related to Sidney Selden from last night?"

"Apparently not, but he was a leading member of the Antiquarian Society for historical research during the seventeenth century. He had written his motto, '*Above all freedom*', on the top right of his copy of the *Codex Mendoza*, adding historical relevance. The document became prominent again in 1831 when Viscount Kingsborough became aware of its existence and brought it to the attention of scholars. That document is certainly a valued piece of Aztec history.

"The historical significance of the *Codex* and its influence cannot be underestimated, and one has to wonder why a known fence was showing an interest in it. Remember this point, Watson: While the detail of the *Codex* was taken and ended up in Selden's possession, the actual document is still safe, and it remains locked in a display case in the Bodleian."

The next day, Lestrade dropped around to our quarters at Holmes's invitation. When he arrived, he informed us that the unusual pieces of

261

paper taken from the body of Sidney Selden were of less interest than first imagined, as there was no evidence of foul play – which we already knew. What he had felt might be a curious fact was irrelevant, as the man had died of natural consequences, and it was of no account that his meagre possessions had been stolen after death.

Holmes chuckled and told Lestrade that there was more to this inquiry than mere stolen items. He then related the details of his travels, explaining the background of the more elaborate drawing in the *Codex Mendoza*. "And we mustn't forget the sketch of the shield and the boots," he added, repeating the heraldic connections for Lestrade's benefit.

After listening to Holmes's narrative, the inspector was puzzled. "What does heraldry and the *Codex Mendoza* have to do with our man Sidney Selden?"

"They have everything to do with what I just recounted."

"But – ?"

"Rest assured, Lestrade, the boots will soon become evident." Holmes then rose suddenly and asked us to join him in catching a train to Chippenham in Wiltshire. Lestrade appeared bewildered at this sudden decision to travel to the West Country, but he and I had learned that following Holmes's lead was the easiest way toward understanding. Without delay, we left the premises and hailed a cab to Paddington Station.

Throughout the journey, Holmes refused to be drawn into making any explanations. Instead, he ranged forth on a variety of topics, and while Lestrade was obviously wondering about the reason for our journey, he seemed to enjoy himself and a chance to leave London for the day.

In Chippenham, we left the platform and began our walk into the town. Prompted by Holmes's earlier discussion and description of the heraldry of boots and spurs, I was suddenly struck by the same symbols shown all around, including upon the Coat of Arms in front of the Council Building. With a start, I realized that the crude sketch that had been identified to me as a heraldic representation of three boots was somewhat duplicated on the colorful plaque. As Holmes and Lestrade continued up the street – Lestrade apparently oblivious of the connection – a local passerby, taking notice of my attention without my asking said, "The Coat of Arms represents two influential local families who lived here in the thirteenth and fourteenth centuries. On the sinister side, looking toward the shield on the right, are the arms of the Hussey family. They were Lords of the Manor from 1290 to 1392. Do you notice the boots?" I replied that I did, although without having had them previously identified as such, I would have likely called them something else.

He continued, "In old French, the name *Hussey* means '*booted*', and the Coat of Arms is a play on their name, showing three boots with spurs. In heraldic terminology, it is described as '*argent three boots sable*'."

The fact that Chippenham made use of a drawing of three boots in in a shield as part of its coat of arms gave me some vague indication of the reason that Holmes had brought us here. Hastily, I thanked the gentleman and hurried up the street in order to catch up with my companions.

Soon after, Holmes was able to summon a wagon and the three of us climbed aboard. Holmes gave the driver a few whispered instructions, and he took us into the countryside. Holmes was silent for much of our journey through the beautiful countryside, until we were approaching a lonely inn. It was then that Holmes turned to the inspector and me and told us the purpose of our quest. "Lestrade, please recall when, at the scene where Selden's body was found, I made a careful examination of the area. The boot prints that I described, along with an entry in that morning's Agony Column stating '*Boot and Pole. Plough tonight. Mendoza*', suggested a specific individual's involvement in the matter. I verified what I recalled about this man, Gideon Walsey –"

"Walsey!" cried Lestrade. "That thief?" He nodded. "The boot marks . . . ." he said with understanding, although I was still in the dark.

Holmes looked my way and smiled. "As I was saying, I verified what information that I had about him in my scrapbooks – you'll recall, Watson, that I examined '*S*' for *Selden*, '*W*' for *Walsey*, and '*C*' for *Chippenham* – and learned that the man in question was serving time in Dartmoor Prison – or so I thought. A wire quickly determined that he was released a month ago. But I learned something much more interesting: His cell mate was also named Selden – the Notting Hill Murderer."

"Another Selden!" I cried.

"Exactly," said Holmes, "a man whom I verified happens to have relational ties with the dead man. In fact, they are cousins.

"So," he continued, "we have Sidney Selden, a noted London fence, lying dead outside a pub that was mentioned in a newspaper entry from that very morning. He undisputedly died from natural causes, and yet there are boot prints in the mud beside where he fell that belong to a man who has recently been released from prison, where he shared a cell with the dead man's cousin. Additionally, in the dead man's coat pocket is a curious sketch of a shield and boots – indicating a connection to Chippenham, where Walsey is from – and also a detail of a rare and valuable document. And anytime that both a thief and a fence have ties to something like that is an indicator of a situation much more complex."

Lestrade questioned the connection to Chippenham, and I was able to provide an explanation of the shield and boots. Holmes raised his eyebrows at my sudden knowledge, but I related how the local man had pointed it out soon after we left the train.

"There is another connection," added Holmes. "The word *Mendoza* in the advertisement has a double meaning – a reference to the *Codex*, and something else, as you will soon see." The inspector nodded knowingly, while I remained confused.

"And now, Lestrade, we have arrived at this inn, where I have it on good authority that we will find our man. Inside, you are going to apprehend Mr. Gideon Walsey."

Lestrade and I looked at one another, both of still in a state of some bewilderment, but Holmes had clearly said all that he intended. As the horse drew to a stop, we heard a strange type of music coming from inside. We climbed down from the wagon and approached the low building. Upon entering, I was astounded to see a man standing on the far side of the room wearing one boot, with the other foot clad only in his stocking. He was playing some odd musical instrument, apparently consisting of a thick pole inserted and affixed into his other boot, resting upon the wooden floor. A series of metal bits and pieces were fastened to the pole. When shaken, they clanged together. The sound was akin to a tambourine, an effect that was enhanced as the man played the instrument by holding and applying a notched stick that combined to produce both a clicking and rattling sound.

"What is this that makes these cacophonic sounds?" I cried.

Holmes simply smiled and said to both of us, "That is Mr. Gideon Walsey, whom I mentioned outside, playing a traditional English percussion instrument – a *Mendoza*."

As we approached the man, he stopped playing and quickly gave a sigh, dropping his head on his chest. "Mr. Holmes. We meet again."

"Still playing the Mendoza, I see. I know how much this instrument means to you."

"Just like your violin does to you, Mr. Holmes."

"And . . . what's this?" he asked, reaching forward and plucking something from the man's waistcoat. "A nice watch."

Walsey swallowed. "An inheritance from my uncle when I was a lad."

"Interesting," said Holmes. He examined the pocket watch carefully with his lens. First on the outside, and then opening the back to view the inner workings. "And the initials – *S.S.*?"

"His name was, um, Samuel Stuart," replied Walsey cautiously.

"I see," said Holmes. "And you say that you were a young boy upon receiving this watch?"

"Yes."

"Did your uncle visit America?"

"I don't know," replied Walsey.

"No matter. I have made a study of pocket watches, as they are often significant in many of my cases. This particular watch was manufactured in the United States by the American Watch Company. Observe the thick glass bezel with a brass chain fob at the top. Notice when I turn the cover." We watched as Holmes unscrewed it as if he were taking a lid off a jar. "As you can see, this watch doesn't have a flip-open clasp and hinge lid."

He again took his lens and examined the inside of the watch. "Just as I thought. The case is engraved . . . " He turned it so that we could see "*SILVEROID A.W.C. Co.*" etched across the metal. ". . . and a serial number. Understanding the serial number provides a precise year when and where this watch was assembled. This particular watch was manufactured in the United States around 1884 and became the official standard for railroad watches to be used by conductors and time-keepers. Notice the winding stem at the twelve o'clock position, the black Arabic numerals on a white dial, a steel escape wheel, the open face, and . . . ."

He paused. "There are other distinguishing features, but these suffice. This watch couldn't possibly have been given to you as a youngster, since it has been recently developed to incorporate the features and the purpose I mentioned. Had you been given a watch dating from your youth, in all likelihood, it would have required a key for winding. The absence of a key on your watch fob indicated to me that this watch is a recent acquisition."

Walsey listened but didn't protest Holmes's explanation. He shrugged his shoulders and withered dejectedly into a nearby seat, waiting for what was to follow. Lestrade looked questioningly at Holmes, who held up the watch. "Selden's," mouthed Holmes silently. Without further explanation, Lestrade took hold of Walsey's arm, putting him under arrest for stealing the dead man's possessions. "Your boot prints were found beside the body," he said smugly. Then he allowed Walsey to put on his other boot and gather his Mendoza before escorting him out of the pub and into our wagon for the ride back to Chippenham, where we soon departed on the train to London.

The only time that Walsey exhibited any reaction during our journey was soon after our departure, when his facial features and his eyebrows rose in response to Lestrade telling him that he was being arrested for being in possession of a watch belonging to Sidney Selden, who had been found dead outside The Plough Pub in London two nights before. Walsey seemed surprised upon hearing that name, but he quickly regained his composure and simply turned his head to look out of the window.

As we settled in for the long journey back, Lestrade demanded further explanation. Holmes nodded, and began to take the pieces of the puzzle and arrange them into a whole. "When I first examined the mud near Mr. Selden's body, I noticed two distinct boot markings belonging to the same person. You know that when I find a matter out of place, it arouses my suspicions. Although both boots had the same heel cobbling, the right boot made a smoother impression in the mud while the left boot showed deeper tread, along with slight wear on the instep. I had already recalled the entry from *The Times'* agony column earlier in the day regarding The Plough as soon as we arrived at the pub."

I repeated the entry: "*Boot and Pole. Plough tonight. Mendoza.*" Walsey turned his head curiously.

Holmes nodded and continued. "When I noticed the odd boot marks in the mud, I recalled such characteristics have an association with certain boot-related entertainments. My thoughts turned in passing to that curious fellow, Little Tich – "

"The little chap known for the Big Boot Dance with very long soles?" I interjected.

"Indeed. The fact that the death occurred at The Plough, as mentioned in the advertisement, and additionally remembering the associated words "*Mendoza*", and "*Boot and Pole*", led me quickly to that curious musical instrument, and subsequently our friend here – a seasoned burglar whose past exploits were well-known to the police, and with whom I once had an encounter years ago when he was stealing some counterfeit plates. Clearly the message implied that Selden was to meet Walsey at The Plough, where he would be identified as the man playing the Mendoza. This fact led to other questions, which were twofold: 'What was the significance of the two papers found on the body?' and 'Why was Gideon Walsey in the proximity of a dead man known to facilitate the exchange of stolen goods?'

"As I explained, my research revealed Mr. Walsey's recent background, as well as his cell-mate, Selden. What were the odds that two Seldens could be involved in this matter without there being some connection – one found dead in the street in Ealing and other a convict in Dartmoor?

"This was a case of unexpected doubles. Two Seldens – not counting the historical John Selden. Two Mendozas – the unusual musical instrument first suggested by the bootmarks in the mud, and then the *Codex Mendoza*, as revealed by the drawing found in the dead man's pocket. The hand-drawn sheet along with it, showing heraldic boots, implied a Chippenham connection – where I learned that the man who played the Mendoza lives.

"Although I doubt that Mr. Walsey will confirm it, I theorize that what must have happened is this: Mr. Sidney Shelden conceived a desire to steal the *Codex Mendoza* – possibly after receiving the smaller related detail by someone in his capacity as a fence. As I mentioned, the Bodleian was unaware that it had been taken. Later, while on a visit to the prison in order to see his cousin the murderer, it was mentioned that Walsey is a high-profile burglar. Perhaps, thought Sidney Selden, Walsey could be commissioned to steal the *Codex* from the Bodleian. Selden the convict then approached his cellmate, who agreed. Walsey was to be released within the month. He agreed to become part of the plot and then give the stolen *Codex* to Sidney, who would then fence the document to the highest bidder. Sidney would take two-thirds of the revenue, to share with his cousin, and Walsey would take his share." He glanced at Walsey. "Perhaps the arrangement was somewhat different, but I expect that I understand the general plan." There was no reaction from the prisoner.

"But Holmes," I asked. "How would the convict who will be in prison for life make use of his share of the money?"

"That question, Watson, is one that I am not prepared to answer. Perhaps he has relatives somewhere who might benefit from his acquirement. With the finish of this scheme, I doubt that we shall ever hear of him again. In any case, a few weeks later Walsey was released.

"Walsey and Sidney Selden never actually met, as it was imperative that they not be seen together in order to avoid arousing any suspicions from the police – Walsey a paroled convict, and Sidney Selden known to the police as having a criminal background of receiving stolen artifacts.

Both communicated only by curt statements appearing in the agony column of *The Times*. But at some point a meeting must take place, so that Sidney Selden could describe what was to be stolen – and more importantly, for each man to take the measure of the other.

"On that fatal night, Walsey alerted Selden in *The Times* to meet at The Plough, and look for a man playing a Mendoza – an interesting and amusing coincidence. I was able to confirm with The Plough's owner that Walsey was performing there that night. He also indicated that Walsey was returning to his home in Chippenham the next day – yesterday.

"Unbeknownst to Walsey, Mr. Selden suffered a mortal heart attack seconds after arriving at The Plough. Somewhat ironic is that within minutes of leaving the pub after his performance, Walsey, upon seeing a strange man lying dead in the street, instinctively grabbed the man's watch and the money pouch and quickly left the premises. That man was Sidney Selden, his faceless co-conspirator, whom he had never previously met. If he hadn't taken time to steal the man's personal possessions, then Lestrade, who had no other suspicions because the man had died of natural causes, would have never involved me in the matter.

"Walsey, believing that Selden simply hadn't shown up, was none the wiser that the plan had gone awry due to the man's unexpected death. He continued on to Chippenham to entertain and wait for developments. Certainly he would have learned that Selden had died, if he hasn't already, and that the plan to fence the *Codex* would need to be revised or abandoned. As it stands now, he is guilty only of robbing the dead man's money pouch and watch – a minor offense, but more serious as the man is on parole.

"I'm sure that confirmation of my explanation, including any planned association with the theft of the *Codex Mendoza*, will be denied. Am I correct, Mr. Walsey?" He glanced at the prisoner, who had no reaction.

"I am curious, however," continued Holmes. "With every other fact serving to reinforce the others, there is one that I cannot reconcile – How did Sidney Selden come to have the sketch of the boots and shield of Chippenham, your home, in his pocket?"

Walsey was silent for a moment, and then he stirred and spoke, while continuing to stare from the window at the passing countryside. "Perhaps, Mr. Holmes, you'll find that – in addition to being simply a fence of stolen goods – he possibly also had other interests, such as heraldry and history. Possibly through his correspondence, he developed a friendship with someone of like interest – and made the sketch for use in a discussion when he was able to finally meet this friend in person.

Holmes looked at the man speculatively for a moment and then said, "I suppose that will have to do. It's as good an explanation as any."

NOTES

Places, names, and events in the story pertaining to the *Codex Mendoza* are factual:

https://publicdomainreview.org/collections/codex-mendoza-1542/)

So too, are the Mendoza, an English percussion instrument played with a boot anchor:

https://en.wikipedia.org/wiki/Monkey_stick

The town of Chippenham's coat of arms can be seen here:

http://www.chippenham.gov.uk/

Harry Ralph (Little Tich) was a prominent comedian and Big Boot dancer in the 1880's and 1900's:

https://publicdomainreview.org/collections/little-tich-and-his-big-boot-dance-1900/

The Clerkenwell Shadow
by Paul Hiscock

I have many memories of the time I spent living at Baker Street with Mr. Sherlock Holmes. Yet, among all the fascinating cases and exciting adventures, those I remember most fondly are the moments when crime in the city seemed to pause and we were able to spend a few quiet hours enjoying the comforts of bachelor life. Naturally, they never lasted long, as either a new case would arrive or Holmes would become restless. However, they were pleasant while they lasted and I was always sad when they concluded, as one such interlude did with the arrival of Miss Iris Shaw in March 1888.

It was late in the evening and, having no pressing matters to concern us, Holmes and I were sat by the fire. We were each enjoying a pipe and a glass of brandy when we heard someone knocking at the door downstairs.

"Watson, would you go see who is calling at this late hour? Mrs. Hudson has retired for the night and I am certain she will not be best pleased if she is compelled to rise and answer the door."

I complied swiftly, having no desire to antagonise our landlady, and soon returned in the company of a young woman.

"Holmes, this is Miss Iris Shaw. She has come to ask for your help at the suggestion of her employer, who we apparently aided at some point in the past."

"Miss Shaw, please take a seat and tell us the nature of your difficulty and we will try our utmost to assist you."

"Thank you," said Miss Shaw. "I am sorry to visit at such a late hour. I almost didn't come but, after it happened again, I realised that I couldn't bear another sleepless night worrying about that man."

As she spoke, she crossed the room towards Holmes. However, to my surprise, she passed the chair and picked up a plain wooden box from a shelf. She stared at it thoughtfully for a moment, before setting it down and walking back to the chair.

"It is clear that your tribulations have shaken you greatly," said Holmes. "Why else would a young lady, still new to the city, venture out so late in the evening and travel all the way across town from Clerkenwell?"

"Mr. Holmes, they said you were clever, but not that you could read minds. How did you know that I had come from Clerkenwell? Did my employers contact you?"

"I have not had any correspondence with that estimable company since I assisted them a couple of years ago. However, you told me everything that I needed to know. That you are new to London is clear from your Fenland accent. It is still strong and you are clearly self-conscious about it. If you had lived here longer, it would have faded and you would certainly be less worried about the impression it created. The traces of sawdust on your skirt and the piece of wood-shaving caught in the hem suggested to me that you are employed in an environment where wooden items are manufactured, yet it is clear from your attire and the smoothness of your hands that you do not undertake this work yourself. Therefore, I assume that you have some administrative or sales role."

"Sales," the girl stammered, obviously taken aback by Holmes's deductions.

"After that it was a simple process of elimination. You have clearly come straight from work, meaning that your employer is based in London, and I can think of only one past client of mine in the city that it could be. However, even if there had been more possibilities, only an employee of a certain games company in Hatton Garden would have been so drawn to that box, since it is an example of their exemplary craftsmanship. Watson, I assume you remember the case."

I nodded. If the croquet mallet had been swung just a little harder it would have been a case of murder as well as robbery. The box contained a very fine chess set, which had been given in gratitude for Holmes's swift and discreet handling of the matter. He had never used it. In fact, I had never seen him play chess, although I was certain he could have beaten any grandmaster at the game if he had so chosen.

Miss Shaw smiled for the first time since she had arrived. "Mr. Holmes, that's wonderful. You really are as clever as I was told. I feel safer already."

"Tell us then the full story of what brought you here," said Holmes. "Start at the beginning and leave out no detail, however insignificant it might seem."

"As you concluded, Mr. Holmes, I am from the Fenlands. I came to London from Christchurch around three months ago. My aunt and uncle found me my position and invited me to live with them, as they have no children of their own and have always cared greatly for me. I think they were lonely, as they are both quite frail and rarely leave the house. The only other person who lives there is a lodger who takes the room in the attic, but he spends most of his time in his room or out of the house. He is an elderly man with a long white beard and always wears a big black hat. You must think me terribly naive, but I did not realise this showed he was Jewish and I am afraid I wished him a happy Christmas when we first met. My uncle was so embarrassed, but Mr. Stein didn't seem offended. We don't speak often, but he is always friendly when our paths cross. It turns out there are lots of Jews living in London. I see them every day on my way to and from work."

She hesitated at this point and seemed to become more anxious again.

"It is something about your daily journey that troubles you then," said Holmes.

"That's right. How clever you are. You seem to know everything before I have a chance to say it. I'm quite sure I'm being followed. It started at the beginning of last week – well, at least I think it did. I have thought back but that is the first time that I remember noticing him. I was walking home from work, as I do every day. The first part of my journey is very busy as there are lots of shops and businesses in that part of London and most close at around the same time. However, after a while the crowds begin to thin out, and by the time I am halfway home it is much quieter. I was not far from home when I spotted him for the first time. There was hardly anyone else around, and in that instant I just knew that he was following me."

"Even on the quietest street in London one will almost always spot someone walking in the same direction," said Holmes. "This is not the countryside where one might walk for hours without seeing another soul. What made you so suspicious?"

"It wasn't anything obvious, just a feeling that I had."

"That feeling came from somewhere. Just as I deduced facts about you from your appearance when you arrived, your mind unconsciously processed the details of that scene and warned you that you were in danger. Think back. Recall those details for me so that I can see what you saw."

"I'm not sure how much there is I can tell you. It was dark. It's always dark when I leave work, although at least it is getting warmer. The first few weeks that I was here it was bitterly cold, but lately I have been able to leave the house without my scarf. Yet . . . ." she paused for a moment, "the man was still wearing a scarf. In fact he has been every time I have seen him, and not just loose around his neck but wrapped tight around his head so that you can't even see his mouth. I remember wondering how he managed to breathe under all that wool."

"He was deliberately hiding his face," I said.

"Clearly. What else did you notice about him, Miss Shaw?"

"Very little I'm afraid, Mr. Holmes. As I said, it was dark and whenever I looked at him he would seem to step into a shadow or turn away."

"Typical tricks of the inexperienced stalker," said Holmes. "He thinks he is making himself invisible when in fact he is simply drawing attention to himself. I can see why you became suspicious."

"I think you are right, Mr. Holmes, but I never thought about it like that. I just started walking faster, trying to get home as quickly as possible. Yet every time I looked back he was still there. I was starting to panic when I spotted someone ahead of me. From his big black hat I knew that he was one of the Jewish gentlemen but, when I drew closer, I realised that it was Mr. Stein himself. Once I had caught up with him I felt much safer and he walked me the rest of the way home. I offered to carry his bag for him, by way of doing something to thank him, but he refused. I wish he had let me as it was clearly very heavy. He sighed with relief when he put it down on the doorstep to find his keys."

"Did the man keep following you after you met Mr. Stein?" asked Holmes.

"Yes, he was still right behind us. He followed us all the way home, although he didn't stop when we did. As I went inside, I glanced back and saw that he had passed the house on the other side of the street."

"What did Mr. Stein say about it?" I asked. "Or your uncle when you told him?"

"I didn't tell either of them anything that night. Once I was safe inside it seemed foolish. Why would anyone want to follow me? I decided that I must have been mistaken."

"Why would anyone follow you indeed?" said Holmes quietly. Then he asked, "When did you see the man next?"

"It was the next evening. I thought I spotted him through the crowds not long after I left work, but it wasn't until it was quiet again that I became certain. This time I didn't stop to look back. I rushed towards home until once more I caught up with Mr. Stein. I was out of breath when I reached him and he was concerned for my wellbeing. It left me with little choice but to explain why I had been chasing him. However, when he looked, there was no sign of the man in the scarf behind us anymore."

"Did he not believe you then?" I asked.

"I'm not sure. He was very sympathetic, as were my aunt and uncle. I think they thought it was the strain of adapting to city life affecting me. However, since it was clear that we were both walking to the same part of London each day at around the same time, Mr. Stein offered to accompany me on my journeys, at least until I regained my confidence."

"That was kind," I said.

"Yet it did not stop your stalker," said Holmes.

"No, Mr. Holmes, I am sorry to say it did not. Every day I would still see him at some point on my journey home. Sometimes it was just a face in the crowd. Others times I was sure that I noticed someone lurking in the shadows opposite the house while Mr. Stein was searching for his key."

At this point Miss Shaw paused and yawned loudly.

"I am so sorry, gentlemen. I haven't slept well in days, because I have been having nightmares about the man following me and what he might do. This morning I was called in to the office and reprimanded for my lack of care and attention to detail. I had to tell them what was wrong and expected to be dismissed as hysterical. Yet they actually believed me and that was when someone mentioned you and how helpful you had been. I should have listened and come here right away, but I thought it would be a waste of time for a great detective such as yourself."

"What changed your mind?" I asked.

"On the journey home this evening I saw him again – and not just fleeting glances, but definitely following close behind Mr. Stein and me all the way home. Once inside, we discussed the matter with my uncle and he agreed that we needed help. Mr. Stein went out to find a hansom cab, which in turn brought me here to you. Please, Mr. Holmes, Dr. Watson, do you think you can help me?"

Holmes sat in silence for a moment, as is his custom while arranging the facts of a case in his mind. I didn't interrupt and likewise encouraged Miss Shaw to be patient.

"Your predicament is clear," Holmes said eventually, "but stopping this man may prove more problematic. After all, we cannot simply have him arrested for walking down the same street as a young woman."

Miss Shaw looked distraught. "Does that mean you cannot help me?"

"Surely we can do something, Holmes?" I said. "This man is obviously a menace who needs to be dealt with."

"We need to be patient. I have a suspicion about the truth behind this man's obsession and how we might bring this affair to a conclusion. Miss Shaw, I must ask you to be brave and return to your normal routine. Do not deviate from it in any way. It is vital that this man must not suspect any moves being made against him."

"Are you sure I will be safe? He seemed so much more brazen in his pursuit today."

"I am certain you have nothing to fear, and within a few days I hope to have resolved this matter permanently."

Miss Shaw seemed reassured and, while I did not see how Holmes could make such a sweeping promise, I trusted that he would keep his word. I escorted Miss Shaw out and found her a cab home.

"What should we do?" I asked upon my return to the sitting room.

"We should do nothing," replied Holmes. "Tonight we should sleep and tomorrow the true facts of the case will reveal themselves."

I protested again, but he would not be drawn into any further discussion. Eventually I admitted defeat and turned in for the night.

When I awoke the next morning, I was surprised to find that Holmes had already left Baker Street, having left no word for me regarding his movements. Consequently, I spent the day handling my own business and, I am ashamed to admit, I almost forgot about Miss Iris Shaw.

It was late in the evening when Holmes returned home. I had just finished a hearty supper cooked by Mrs. Hudson when he burst through the door. He tore off the black coat that he was wearing and quickly put on a smoking jacket instead. Then he rubbed his cheeks vigorously before settling himself in his chair by the fireplace as though he had been there all evening.

After years spent living with my friend, I had become somewhat inured to such antics, and so I remained calm and feigned indifference.

"Would you like me to ask Mrs. Hudson to bring you some supper?"

"Supper? We don't have time for supper. We have a client to see."

At that moment there was a knock on the door.

"Send her in please, Mrs. Hudson," shouted Holmes. Then the door opened and Miss Shaw stepped inside.

"What a pleasant surprise," I said. "Holmes, did you ask Miss Shaw to visit this evening? Does this mean you have news?"

"He did not ask me here and it is I that have news," said Miss Shaw. She was obviously angry and seemed quite transformed from the scared young woman that we had met the previous evening.

"Whatever is wrong?" I asked. "Please sit down and tell us what has happened."

"I did as he told me," she said, pointing accusingly at Holmes, "and I was almost killed."

"Nonsense," said Holmes. "You were never in any danger today."

"You are obviously safe and that is the main thing," I said. "Why don't we all sit down and discuss this calmly?"

Miss Shaw agreed to sit down and, as she did, a little of the fire seemed to leave her.

"That is better," I said. "Now tell us what happened."

"The day started so well," she said. "I slept better than I have in days once I got home last night, and was able to concentrate on my work. By the end of the day, I had almost convinced myself that the whole affair had

275

been a bad dream. However, I had only just left work and met up with Mr. Stein when I spotted the man in the crowds. As we set off he followed us, closer than ever before. It suddenly occurred to me that while Mr. Stein might be an excellent reassurance in the face of imagined threats, he was far too old to effectively protect me if I was attacked. I couldn't bear to think that this nice man might be hurt because of me, and so I decided that I must act myself."

"Against my instructions," said Holmes. "I told you to stick to your regular routine so that you did not arouse suspicion."

"I know it was probably unwise, but I couldn't bear the idea of being afraid any longer."

"So what did you do?" I asked.

"I turned around on the spot and walked right up to him. He was just a few feet behind me and I was able to reach him before he could react. 'Why are you following me?' I asked, and then I reached up and pulled down his scarf so I could see his whole face. He had blue eyes, Mr. Holmes. Blue eyes and a chubby face. I am certain that I would recognise him if I saw him again."

"I hope that will not be necessary," Holmes said. Miss Shaw looked a little concerned at his disinterest, but he asked her to continue her story.

"He panicked as soon as I removed the scarf. For a moment I thought he was going to attack me, but then he just pushed me to the ground and ran away. I think a few people in the crowd tried to hold him, but he got away. A man helped me up, one of Mr. Stein's friends, then they took charge of everything. They put me in a cab straight here, while Mr. Stein went home to tell my uncle and aunt what had happened."

"You were very brave," I said.

"And foolhardy," added Holmes. "There was no need to take such a risk. I promised that I would deal with the matter. However, now he has seen your face and you are in real danger."

"What can we do?" Most of her anger had now gone, and Miss Shaw looked more scared than ever before.

"You must not go to work tomorrow. You must not be where he expects you to be, or he might try to harm you. Better that he thinks you were injured during his flight this evening and unable to leave the house."

"I cannot hide in my uncle's house forever. If I cannot return to work, I will have to return home to my parents, and there are no prospects for me there."

"Do not fear," said Holmes. "After tomorrow, I am certain that this will all be resolved and you will be able to return to your life safely."

"Please listen to Mr. Holmes," I said. "He is only trying to keep you safe."

For a moment it looked as if Miss Shaw might protest again, but then the last of the fight drained away and she agreed. Once more, she allowed me to call her a cab and send her home.

"Where have you been all day?" I demanded once Miss Shaw had left. "You obviously knew she was coming here this evening."

Holmes smiled. "Is it not obvious, Watson? Surely you recognise my methods by now. The quick costume change? The traces of spirit gum on my face?"

"You were there, in Hatton Garden, in disguise?"

"Bravo, Watson, I knew you could figure it out. Quite obviously, I was the man who helped her up and put her in the cab to come here. The driver was quite happy to accept a small bonus in exchange for taking a longer route, giving me time to hail another hansom and get here first."

"But why the deception? I am sure the man wouldn't have recognised you."

"However, Miss Shaw would have done. I needed her to maintain her usual routine so that I, in turn, could observe her follower's routine."

"But then she scared him off and ruined everything," I said with a groan.

"I admit it was not what I had planned, but I observed enough before he fled. I'm confident that my hypothesis is correct and that by this time tomorrow night our quarry will be languishing in a jail cell."

"Will this man even appear if Miss Shaw is not present?"

"I am confident that he will be there. Tomorrow morning I need you to go to Scotland Yard and ask Lestrade for the services of a strong police constable to assist us in the evening."

"For what will they be arresting him?"

"It will be obvious when the time comes," Holmes replied cryptically.

As I expected, Inspector Lestrade complained about Holmes's request. "Anyone would think we work for him," he grumbled, but he still tasked Constable Stevens to assist us. He was well aware that a lead provided by Holmes was always worth pursuing.

Holmes's instruction was that the constable should conceal himself where he could keep a close watch on Miss Shaw's house, while we headed to Hatton Garden.

"Is Miss Shaw in danger?" I had asked.

"No, it is simply that a police constable is far too conspicuous to stalk our prey," Holmes replied. "Besides, I'm certain we will not require him until we reach the end of our journey."

Lestrade suggested sending some plain clothes officers to assist us, but Holmes had anticipated this and told me to decline the offer. "Plain clothes or not, they will still look like policemen," he said. "If they are recognised, this entire endeavour will be for naught."

If anything, Hatton Garden was even busier than I had expected. As Miss Shaw had said, there were a large number of Orthodox Jews there, far more than I had seen together anywhere else in London. It seemed as if a lot of their business was conducted in the streets. Occasionally one would hear a group of men cry out "Mazel!", which apparently meant a deal had been concluded, although I couldn't see what they were trading. However, amongst all this activity, there was no sign of a man wearing a scarf across his face.

After half-an-hour I asked, "Do you think Miss Shaw scared him away permanently when she confronted him last night? Maybe she dealt with him without our help after all?"

"No, Watson. Look over there."

Sure enough, a man with a thick burgundy scarf covering his face was walking up the road. He took up a position not far from us, leaning against the wall, and started to watch the crowd in much the same way that we had been.

"I don't see how this is going to work," I said. "He could stand there all night, but we know he is never going to spot Miss Shaw."

"Patience, Watson. He will move, I'm certain of it."

I didn't see what triggered the man's movement, but it was clear that he had seen something as he headed purposefully up the road.

"What can he have seen? Do you think he is stalking some other poor girl now? Where do you think he is going?"

"There is no great mystery about it. He is doing exactly the same as he has done every day for the last two weeks."

I still didn't understand, but there was no point in pressing the issue, as Holmes was clearly not planning to reveal the truth until the end of our pursuit. We set off after him, letting the flow of the crowd carry us along. It was easy to hide amongst so many people and I was certain we hadn't been spotted.

However, when we reached the end of Hatton Garden, the crowd started to disperse as everyone headed towards their own homes. It was still relatively busy, but I could see that as we ventured further into Clerkenwell we would soon be left exposed.

Holmes realised this too and when, a short distance further up the road, a group broke away to go in a different direction, he followed them rather than the man in the scarf, catching me by surprise.

278

"Where are you going?" I said when I caught up with Holmes, who was now running. "We are going to lose our man."

"We will lose him if we make the same mistakes he made. You heard Miss Shaw – soon the roads will become quieter and there will be nowhere for us to hide."

"But how can we follow him if we cannot see him?"

"We don't need to see him. We know where he is going and, following this road," he said as he suddenly turned around another corner, "we will be able to travel parallel to his route. If I have judged his pace correctly, then we should catch a glance of him . . . there." Holmes pointed to the left and I caught a glimpse of our quarry down a side street between the buildings.

"That's amazing, Holmes. He'll never suspect we are here."

We passed four more turnings, and each time I saw the man we were following carrying on, completely unaware. As we passed the last one, Holmes started to run again.

"We are nearing our destination," Holmes said as we ran. "Now we need to get ahead of him so that we can join the constable at the house before he arrives."

He led me through a maze of side streets. I could never have navigated them without a map, but Holmes seemed to know every twist and turn and it wasn't long until we emerged mere feet from where Constable Stevens waited.

"Mr. Holmes, Dr. Watson, I wondered when you would arrive. I was starting to think this might be some kind of practical joke. Inspector Lestrade won't be happy if I've stood here in the cold all night for nothing."

"Rest assured this is no joke, Constable. You should see the man you are going to arrest coming up the road there any minute now."

Sure enough, I saw a figure approaching us, but it wasn't the man in the scarf.

"Should I arrest him now?" asked Constable Stevens.

"No," I replied, "that isn't Miss Shaw's follower. It's Mr. Stein. What is he doing here?"

"Why, he is walking home," said Holmes, "the same as he does every day, and there is the man who has been following him." He pointed up the road and we could see the man in the scarf coming around the bend.

"Quickly, we must hide ourselves," said Holmes and pushed us back out of sight.

Constable Stevens seemed confused. "Why can't I just arrest him now?"

"What crime has he committed?" said Holmes. "I haven't witnessed anything. Have you? We need to wait just a little bit longer. You'll know when it is your moment."

By this point Mr. Stein had arrived at the house. He set down his bag on the front step and started fumbling with his keys.

"This is the moment," said Holmes, a note of triumph in his voice.

I looked down the road and saw that the man in the scarf was no longer keeping his distance, but running towards the house as fast as he could. The sound of running feet slapping against the pavement made Mr. Stein look up. As soon as he saw the man rushing towards him, Stein bent to retrieve his bag, but he was already too late. The man in the scarf grabbed it from the step as he ran past, barely slowing as he did so.

"Now, Constable! Arrest that man!" Holmes shouted. "Watson, assist the constable – we mustn't let the thief escape."

Holmes had chosen our place of concealment with great care in anticipation of this moment. We were a little further down the road and the man in the scarf still had to run past us.

Despite all Holmes's warnings, Constable Stevens seemed surprised by this sudden turn of events and didn't seem to know how to react. However, I did not hesitate and burst from our hiding place with a shout of, "Stop thief!" As soon as I was close enough, I dove at the man's legs in a flying rugby tackle that would have made my old games master proud. The thief hit his head on the ground as we landed and was knocked senseless. When he awoke, he would have a large bruise on his temple. I know as a doctor I am sworn to do no harm, but I must admit to feeling satisfied at having personally delivered a small punishment for all the anguish he had caused Miss Shaw.

Constable Stevens finally moved and came over to put his cuffs on the thief, who was just regaining consciousness. The constable hauled the prisoner to his feet roughly.

"Do you need anything else, or can I take him away?"

"I don't think he has anything useful to tell me," said Holmes, "except, just out of curiosity, what is your name sir?"

"It's Bell," the man replied sullenly.

"Very well. Constable, you may deliver Mr. Bell to Lestrade with my compliments."

While we had talked, Mr. Stein had come over to retrieve his bag, which the thief had released when I tackled him.

"Thank you so much for stopping that man," he said. "I would have been ruined if he had got away. But how did you come to be here at such a fortuitous moment?"

"I will explain everything," said Holmes, "but let us go inside first. Our client deserves to know that the man has been arrested."

We returned to the house to find Miss Shaw already waiting anxiously in the doorway.

"We heard the commotion," she said. "What happened? Has anyone been hurt?"

She went over to Mr. Stein who was clutching his bag tightly to his chest and was clearly still in a state of shock.

"The only one injured is that ruffian who was following you," I said, "but as you can see, he will not trouble you any further."

Her look of concern transformed into one of relief as she saw the man being led away by Constable Stevens, and she gladly invited us inside.

"Thank you once again, Mr. Holmes," said Mr. Stein, once we were all gathered in the parlour with a steaming pot of tea.

"It is really Miss Shaw that you should be thanking," said Holmes. "Without her unwitting intervention, Bell would certainly have struck days ago."

"I don't understand," said Miss Shaw. "What does that man have to do with Mr. Stein?"

"Have you ever wondered what kind of business Mr. Stein conducts in Hatton Garden every day?"

"I can't say that I have. As I said, we never conversed much before this affair began, and even once we started walking together regularly, I was too distracted to ask such questions."

"Were you to have asked the question, you would have learnt what I already knew. Hatton Garden is famous, not for the games and pastimes manufactured in your place of work, but for being the centre of the jewellery trade in London. Since it is a trade primarily conducted by the Orthodox Jewish community, it seemed logical to suppose that this was Mr. Stein's line of work."

"You are quite correct, Mr. Holmes. I was apprenticed to a jeweller when I was still a young boy and have worked there ever since."

"An attractive young woman might attract unwanted attention from an admirer," Holmes continued, "but how much more attractive is a man with daily access to so many precious items to members of the criminal classes."

"But Holmes," I said, "rumours are that the jewels of Hatton Garden are stored in vaults below the streets. How could a petty bag-snatcher hope to gain access to them?"

"You are correct, Watson. The vaults of Hatton Garden are nearly impregnable – and yet Mr. Stein here does not trust them, do you?"

281

Mr. Stein flushed red. "It is true, I am ashamed to say. I just cannot bear to leave my most precious pieces of work in that place. I need to keep them close to me at all times."

"Are saying that your bag is full of jewels, Mr. Stein?" I said.

"Yes. Would you care to see them?"

Before I could answer, Mr. Stein tipped up his bag and its contents slid out on to the table. There were rubies and emeralds fit to grace the fingers and throats of any monarch in Europe, and more diamonds than I had ever seen in one place. Everyone stared at them in astonishment, apart from Mr. Stein and Holmes.

Holmes gave us all a moment to enjoy the display before he continued. "Miss Shaw, I suspected the truth of the matter as soon as you described that first journey home with Mr. Stein. It was obvious that his bag was of particular importance to him. I guessed then that you had accidentally come between a thief and the treasure he coveted. Mr. Bell tried to be careful and avoid being seen by a potential witness, but in doing so he drew attention to himself in a most unfortunate fashion. Suddenly he found that his target had gained a regular walking companion and that the doorstep grab he had patiently planned had become far more risky."

"So I was never in any danger?" said Miss Shaw.

"No none at all. It seems that Mr. Bell was a patient man and was willing to wait for his opportunity. You would have been perfectly safe had you just followed my instructions. I would have stopped you approaching him in Hatton Garden yesterday, if I could only have reached you in time. Sadly, I was too late and you caught a glimpse of Bell's face. I think he might have hurt you then if I hadn't chased him off."

"That was you!" exclaimed Mr. Stein. "I thought I recognised you when we met today, but I never thought you might be the man who assisted us yesterday."

"I apologise for the deception," Holmes replied, "but I hope you will agree it was for the best possible reasons, as was my decision not to warn you that Mr. Bell would try to steal your bag today."

"There is nothing to forgive. You were protecting my young friend and myself, and I thank you for your swift intervention on both occasions."

"Likewise I forgive you, Mr. Holmes," said Miss Shaw. "Although I feel you could have let me in on the secret when I visited you yesterday evening."

If Holmes noticed the hint of a rebuke in her comment he chose to ignore it.

"Then there is nothing left to tell. I would recommend that you gather up your jewels, Mr. Stein, and consider placing them in the safety of the vault tomorrow morning. Once you have done that, you will both be able to enjoy your walks without fear. Such riches are too great a target for the thieves of London, and you will be better off without them."

The Adventure of the
Worried Banker
by Arthur Hall

"Do finish your tea, my dear Lestrade, and then, having dispensed with trivialities, you can explain to Watson and myself the reason for this sudden and most unexpected visit this afternoon."

Sherlock Holmes leaned his thin body back in the armchair and waited. I put down my own cup, curious as to what the inspector had to tell us.

"Well, gentlemen," the little detective began, "the fact is that one of our own men has disappeared. It's been a week now, and he hasn't been back to The Yard, nor has anyone heard from him."

"An inspector?" asked Holmes.

"Indeed."

"His name, pray?"

"Northbridge. One of the most recent additions to the Detective Division."

My friend nodded slowly. "I know him by sight."

"We have of course made exhaustive efforts to discover his whereabouts, and some of us have continued in our own time, but our superiors have called us off officially because of the mounting pile of cases that await our attention. 1888 has been an exceptionally busy year for us, and we are only at the beginning of summer."

"I understand your predicament, Inspector. I am aware that the demands on you and your colleagues has been especially heavy of late. Fortunately I have no current case, and so may be able to offer some assistance."

Lestrade, who did indeed appear as a man very hard-pressed, was visibly relieved.

"It would be helpful, perhaps," I ventured to suggest, "to know the nature of Inspector Northbridge's work at the time of his disappearance,"

"Excellent, Watson," said Holmes. "That is what I was about to ask. It would seem to be a good starting point."

The inspector hesitated, as was natural at the prospect of divulging Scotland Yard's business or intentions to outsiders, before informing us, "Northbridge was conducting an investigation into two particularly vicious murders, both committed within the last six weeks and thought to be connected, since the method of dispatch was identical. I doubt if he got far with his enquiries, since he had been on the case only five days when we last heard from him."

"What was the method of dispatch?"

"Strangulation of the most brutal kind. The heads were half-severed from the bodies, and the marks from the chain, or whatever it was, were distinctive."

Holmes stared thoughtfully at our sitting room ceiling. Suddenly, he got to his feet, strode over to the window, and looked down on Baker Street with a pensive air.

"I think it best if we now accompany you to Scotland Yard, Lestrade," said he. "If you would be so good as to allow me to see the file on your colleague, and any other information that you may have there. Watson, if you would inform Mrs. Hudson that we will not be in for lunch, I'll retrieve our coats from the hat-stand."

Reluctantly, I passed the message to our landlady. Five minutes later we were seated in a hansom that passed our door conveniently as we emerged into the street.

When we were settled in Lestrade's cramped office, a constable was sent to fetch Inspector Northbridge's file. He was back in minutes, and I saw at once that something was amiss. He placed the file upon the desk and addressed Lestrade.

"Inspector . . . ."

"What is it, Faring?"

The young man's expression deepened. "Sir, news has just reached us. The constable who has been checking Inspector Northbridge's house every day found the front door open and a body inside."

We all looked up, and it was Lestrade who spoke first. "Northbridge?"

"His mother, sir."

"Murdered?"

"Strangled, it appears. She had been dead for some hours."

The inspector gave a despairing shake of his head. "All right. You can go, Faring."

We could still hear the young constable's retreating footsteps growing fainter along the corridor, as Lestrade spoke again. "I must go there at once."

"One moment, Lestrade. Am I to understand that Inspector Northbridge was a bachelor, living alone but for his mother?"

"That is correct, Mr. Holmes. His father died some years ago."

"Very well. If you have no objection, Watson and I will accompany you."

285

We arrived at the Finsbury house a short time later. The two constables on guard recognised Lestrade at once and stepped aside for us to enter. The inspector examined the elderly lady's body with a single comment – "The same as the others" – but appeared to glean little else from the scene. Finally, he stood aside thoughtfully, gesturing that my friend could now apply his methods.

Holmes spent twenty minutes conducting his inspection, entering a room across the corridor briefly. Afterwards, he looked around once more before coming to stand beside us near the door.

"Well, Mr. Holmes, do you agree that the murderer has left little that can be of help?"

"Certainly his approach is that of a professional. However, we can be sure that he entered by the same door as ourselves, since there is the faint impression upon the mat of a fresh boot-mark pointing inwards. Also, as you yourself observed, the marks on the neck of the deceased and the severity of the wound agree with those of the two previous victims. He was evidently admitted willingly, since there are no signs of a struggle. There are any number of deceptions he could have used to achieve this."

Lestrade nodded. "Undoubtedly. Have you reached any other conclusions?"

"As you may have noticed, I left to make a quick examination of Northbridge's bedroom. All is in order there, his clothes tidily arranged in a wardrobe, and the floor clean." Holmes handed Lestrade an engraved visiting card. "This may be of some significance. I retrieved it from where it had fallen, behind a bedside table in a corner."

"'*Mr. Godfrey Redstrap, Assistant Governor of The Agricultural and Landowners Bank*'." The inspector read aloud.

"Indeed. With your permission, we will accompany you again, since you will undoubtedly wish to interview Mr. Redstrap this afternoon. I fear that Watson and myself would experience considerable difficulty were we to undertake this alone, since we are not attached to the official force."

Holmes said little over luncheon. I devoured Mrs. Hudson's chicken pie with relish, while he ate little.

"Clearly, you have thought more of this," I observed from his expression. "Would you care to share your conclusions?"

Holmes put down his fork. "I am asking myself why a professional killer would take the life of the elderly mother of a missing police officer. There is no profit in it for him, and so it can only be to ensure her silence. As to what she knew that was perceived as threatening, that most likely was something told to her by her son, Inspector Northbridge. Possibly he has been murdered or kept prisoner for coming into possession of the same knowledge. Perhaps our interview with Mr. Godfrey Redstrap will throw some light on this. We'll meet Lestrade at the bank, which is a short distance from the mother of all banks in Threadneedle Street, in half-an-hour, so finish your lunch, Watson, and we will see what we can learn."

Soon after, we encountered the Scotland Yard detective on the steps of The Agricultural and Landowners Bank.

"I made the appointment with some difficulty," Lestrade said. "The importance of Mr. Redstrap's position was impressed upon me, as was the fact that he is always extremely busy. Be that as it may, I will not let it stand in the way of my investigation into a murder, nor of discovering the whereabouts of a missing officer."

We were shown into a spacious chamber dominated by a huge, well-polished desk. Around the walls hung pictures of stern-looking men who I presumed were past holders of positions of high standing in the bank. Behind the desk, thick curtains hung around a single, tall window.

The man who rose to meet us was of impressive girth, florid-faced, and who quickly demonstrated an off-hand manner. He ignored Holmes and myself, and addressed Lestrade directly.

"You are an inspector from Scotland Yard, I am told," he said when we were seated.

"That is correct, sir."

"And what is it that brings you to me?"

"I understand that you were recently visited by my colleague, Inspector Northbridge."

"I cannot recall such an occasion."

Lestrade produced the card from his pocket. "This was found at his house. I assume that they are not given out indiscriminately."

Mr. Redstrap's contemptuous look vanished, and his manner changed abruptly. He withdrew a large handkerchief from his waistcoat pocket and mopped his moist face.

'Ah, yes," he said haltingly, "it comes back to me now. It was about nine days ago. I was busy at the time, but I spared him a few minutes."

"Perhaps you could tell us of the nature of the interview?" Holmes asked.

Mr. Redstrap glared at my friend for a long moment. "And who are you, sir?"

"My name is Sherlock Holmes."

Some of the banker's previous manner returned. "Indeed? I have heard of you. The consultant detective, are you not? You have no official authority, and no right to be here. I will summon a clerk to show you and your companion from the premises."

"Mr. Holmes's presence is essential to my investigation," Lestrade broke in, "and I would very much appreciate your answer to his question."

The handkerchief was retrieved from where Mr. Redstrap had dropped it on his desk. He wiped his perspiring face thoroughly once again, appearing increasingly nervous.

"The discussion was of a private nature."

Holmes fixed him with a cold glance. "The outcome may well have cost Inspector Northbridge his life."

"How can that be?"

"Northbridge has been missing for the last week," Lestrade explained. "We feel that it is possible that whatever he learned here caused him to pursue a course of action that resulted in his death."

"No, that cannot be so." Mr. Redstrap's face grew noticeably paler. "As I remember, he asked about aspects of the Bank's security which, of course, are highly confidential. He mentioned that his enquiries had led him to believe that we are in some way at risk, but I was able to reassure him."

"So there was no truth in his suspicions?"

"None whatsoever."

"And nothing else was discussed?"

"Nothing."

Lestrade looked across at Holmes. "Is there anything that you or Doctor Watson would like to add?"

"Nothing comes to mind," said I, breaking my silence.

"I think that we have learned all that is necessary," Holmes said.

We rose and left Mr. Redstrap standing by his desk, evidently much relieved. No word was spoken until we reached the street.

"That man is definitely keeping something from us," Lestrade said when we had walked a short distance.

"Without a doubt." My friend paused. "Would it suit you, Lestrade, for us to continue this investigation into Inspector Northbridge's disappearance as you requested, while you return to The Yard to deal with his mother's murder and your accumulated cases? I promise to let you know if anything significant comes to light." Before a reply could be forthcoming, my friend raised his hand to attract a passing four-wheeler. As we boarded, he turned to the Scotland Yard man with some parting words. "Despite Mr. Redstrap's assurances, it would be as well, I think, to have some sort of watch kept on the bank. His lack of sincerity was obvious. Goodbye, Lestrade."

The coach bore us away swiftly, leaving the inspector standing on the pavement.

"Your expression tells me that you have questions, Watson," my friend said as the horses slowed their pace to round a corner.

"Doubtlessly, you have learned something that I missed."

"You cannot have failed to observe Mr. Redstrap's anxiety, and his constant glances at the photographic portrait on his desk?"

"It was of a young girl of about fourteen years of age, inscribed 'Martha', and was taken at St. Alvias Convent School."

"Precisely. Judging by her age and the resemblance, it would be difficult not to conclude that she is his daughter."

I nodded. "That was my conclusion, also."

"Then why do you think he repeatedly looked so fearfully at her portrait?"

"Perhaps because she is ill."

"I think not."

"But how can you tell?"

"There are many kinds of dread, Watson, that settle upon a man's countenance for various reasons. I am accustomed to some of them."

"Could it be, then, that she is in danger of some sort?"

"Bravo, Watson! From Mr. Redstrap's secretive manner, I believe that she has been kidnapped and held hostage."

"That would certainly explain his behaviour."

"And his reluctance to speak, if he has been threatened."

"This seems likely, Holmes, but what has it to do with the disappearance of Inspector Northbridge?"

"That is what we must now endeavour to discover."

We arrived at our lodgings soon after, having stopped once at a Post Office. To my surprise, Holmes waited in the street while I went up to our rooms. He offered no explanation, but by looking from our window I quickly realised his intention.

"Did you find someone to take a message to the Irregulars?" I asked as he came in and took off his coat.

"I did indeed," he replied, smiling because I had correctly deduced his reason for accosting a young urchin. "That young fellow is a chimney sweep, but I have seen him before in the company of Wiggins."

"What service then, do you require from Wiggins and his friends?"

"The whereabouts of Hendon Warrilow's lodgings will do, for now."

"Who is Warrilow?" I asked.

"A well-known London criminal. Strangling is one of his specialities."

"You suspect that this man is involved in the murder of Inspector Northbridge's mother?"

"I consider it a distinct possibility. The marks on the lady's neck are indeed similar, and not only to the previous victims of whom Lestrade spoke. I recall that they featured in a case of some three years ago, when Warrilow was suspected but released because the evidence against him was insufficient. I was not concerned in that affair, but it is noted in my index."

I nodded. "We wait then, to hear from the Irregulars?"

"For now. It is almost time for dinner, as you no doubt have observed. Afterwards, it should not be long before a reply to my telegram is forthcoming."

In fact, it was after we had eaten, as we settled ourselves with the first pipe of the evening, when the telegram boy rang the doorbell. Holmes was on his feet in a flash and downstairs before Mrs. Hudson could emerge from the kitchen. He resumed his seat in a rush, tearing open the yellow envelope with his briar gripped between his teeth.

"As I suspected." He nodded as he discarded the form. "Miss Martha Redstrap has not attended St. Alvias Convent School for two weeks. The reason given was a mild attack of influenza. I cannot imagine this causing her father the anxiety that he was clearly suffering today. My theory, I think, is vindicated."

Before I could reply, the doorbell rang again. My friend ceased knocking out the ash from his pipe at once, reaching the top of the stairs and raising a hand to once more preclude our landlady's appearance. He was back in moments, with the air of a huntsman about him.

"Wiggins has not disappointed us!" he cried. "Our quarry resides at 85 Hyacinth Lane, which, as I recall, is just off the Tottenham Court Road. Come, Watson, we have a night's work ahead of us."

Holmes directed the driver to stop near a cluster of ancient oaks on the Tottenham Court Road. He surrendered the fare and we waited until the hansom was out of sight.

"Hyacinth Lane is about a hundred yards ahead," he said, "just past that newly-painted fence."

I could barely see the fence as we had walked some distance from the nearest street lamp, and few of the houses showed any illumination. I took out my pocket watch and held it near my face. It was after eleven.

"In here, Watson." We stepped into the lane and moved cautiously in the deepening darkness. After about five minutes, we passed several buildings lying back from the edge of the lane. The only sounds were from the shifting of the horses in the nearby stables, and the cry of a disturbed night-bird somewhere in the trees.

"I would not have expected a man such as Warrilow to live here," I whispered. "These houses seem far too grand."

Holmes said nothing, but pointed in the darkness. Because of the whiteness of his shirt-cuff, I was able to see which direction he indicated. The black shapes of two or three more houses, older and dilapidated I saw as we drew nearer, loomed ahead of us. As with the others, no rooms were illuminated. The furthest proved to be Number 85, where we peered through the windows and listened at the door to no avail.

"That narrow passage will lead us to the back of the house," Holmes said quietly and led the way, making no sound.

"The occupiers are probably in their beds by now," I remarked unnecessarily.

"But I would expect Warrilow to be at his trade at any time of day or night. For him, this would not be an unreasonable hour."

The end of the passage held nothing new for us. The rear of the house, too, had the look of a place abandoned. Holmes inspected the door as he had the front entrance, bending to get a closer view of something stuck to the stone step.

"Warrilow, or someone else, has been here quite recently," he murmured. "This lump of earth from the sole of a boot is quite moist, having had insufficient time to dry. We will return to Baker Street now, I think, and be back here a little earlier tomorrow."

We were fortunate in returning to Tottenham Court Road as a hansom delivered a fare to one of the well-spaced houses along the thoroughfare. The weary driver took us to our lodgings quickly, talking encouragingly to his horse. Once inside our rooms, Holmes bade me goodnight and retired immediately. I smoked a lonely pipe before doing the same.

The next day proved largely uneventful. I attended what seemed to be an increasing number of patients. On my return in the afternoon, I noticed a pad of telegram forms, discarded carelessly on the dining-table. Holmes lounged lazily in his armchair.

'I see that you are wondering as to my actions in your absence," he said in a tired voice. "Lestrade had informed me that the names of the previous two victims of Warrilow – if indeed it was he who murdered them – are Frederick Purcell and Stephen Mortimer. He neglected to mention their professions, and it occurred to me that they may be significant. I think we can expect his answer, soon after dinner."

But for once my friend was in error. No telegram had arrived by nine o'clock when we again set out for Warrilow's house.

Again we directed the driver of the hansom to stop on the Tottenham Court Road. The fellow was slow in complying, and so we were about to alight at a place nearer to the junction with Hyacinth Lane.

"Wait!" Holmes exclaimed suddenly.

I stopped, with one foot on the pavement, and turned to him in surprise. A cart, pulled by a coal-black horse, had emerged at a gallop from Hyacinth Lane and was speeding away in the direction from which we had come.

"Driver!" My friend called up through the little trap-door. "An extra sovereign to your fare if you turn and follow that cart at a distance. On no account must you be seen to be in pursuit."

The man's muffled response came as he turned the hansom and set the horse to a trot.

"Was that Warrilow?" I asked.

"I am quite sure of it," Holmes confirmed, "despite the darkness. He passed beneath a street-lamp and a glimpse sufficed for me to recognise him."

"Would it not have been better to enter his house while he is away, in order to see if anything that could be helpful to our investigation is there, rather than follow him without knowing his destination?"

In the poor light, I fancied that I saw Holmes smile. "Wherever Warrilow is bound, you can be sure that he is up to no good. It may be that he is meeting other members of a gang to which he is connected, or that he is on his way to claim another victim for reasons we do not yet know. In any event, I intend to choose my moment to confront and question him."

We said nothing for a while, as the horse plodded on before us, keeping the cart in sight. Now and then other hansoms and an occasional landau or four-wheeler appeared, to turn off again within a mile or two. One of these remained on the road, between us and the cart we pursued. For much of the journey, it helped to conceal us.

"We are entering Hammersmith," said I presently, breaking the silence.

Holmes lifted his head from his chest. "Indeed. Where, I wonder, is Warrilow taking us?"

We were soon to find out, for the cart took two turns to the left then three to the right, finally coming to rest before one of a group of villas that stood behind well-kept lawns. The street lamps here were bright enough for us to see Warrilow alight and tether his horse to a lamp-post as we passed.

The road curved, and the driver halted the hansom as soon as we were out of sight of the house. Holmes told him to wait, and we walked back without speaking. We arrived as Warrilow was admitted by an elderly butler. Holmes held a finger to his lips to indicate that I should remain silent, and we turned onto the path that led to the front door. I think that my friend's intention was to gain entrance at the back of the house, but he came to a sudden halt as light flared in the front room. The glow increased and he motioned me to follow as he crawled silently beneath the big bay window, where a fanlight had been opened to let in the warm night air.

We settled ourselves, I cannot say comfortably, and strained our ears.

"You cannot do this!" said a voice that I recognised. "You scoundrel, sir! How dare you keep her from me!"

"It is in your own hands," another voice replied, and Holmes mouthed the word "Warrilow" by way of identification.

"I would be betraying years of trust. It would ruin me!" The first voice, that of Mr. Redstrap, the bank official, complained despairingly.

"It is either that, or your daughter's life. The choice is yours. We have said these things before now. Let us not waste time doing so again."

There was a long silence then, and a murmuring of words that we were unable to hear.

Finally, Mr. Redstrap exploded in a burst of anger. "Take it then, and may you go to hell! When will I see my daughter?"

"This very night. I will send her to you in a hansom."

The thud of heavy footsteps reached us as Warrilow left the house and we took shelter behind a bush as he walked quickly down the path to the road. From within the house I heard the sound of someone crying softly.

When the cart disappeared from our sight we ran back to the hansom. The driver had apparently anticipated our needs and turned his vehicle around.

"Pray continue to follow that cart," Holmes instructed him, and the horse surged forward.

He said no more, but watched the road before us constantly. After a while the cart turned into a maze of dark side-streets and our driver had to proceed more slowly, lest our pursuit be discovered. We entered a long road with terraced houses along one side, while the other boasted buildings that appeared to be warehouses. Warrilow had disappeared, but this caused Holmes no great concern, since we now faced a brick wall.

"A dead-end, Watson. He cannot be far away." To the driver, he said. "You have done well. If you would care to wait for us again, you will enhance your fare even further. I do not anticipate that we will be long."

The man assented and we left the hansom quietly, walking back past several pairs of iron gates. I could see no way of telling which of these the cart had entered, but Holmes seemed absorbed in studying the locks and would, I am sure, have somehow found our way, had not the stamping of an impatient or hungry horse alerted us. We remained still and listened, until the dull impacts of iron shoes upon the stones were repeated. Holmes said nothing, but opened one of the gates slowly when it proved to be unlocked.

Once inside, we listened again and heard nothing. We crept slowly between two buildings, into a small courtyard. There the cart stood, with the horse tied to a broken pipe projecting from a crumbling wall. A wide door, used no doubt for deliveries, stood half-open before us.

"Are you armed, Watson?" Holmes whispered.

"My hand is on my service revolver."

"Excellent. I see that there is a light within."

We entered slowly, making no noise, and stood in the shadows near the door. The room was dimly lit by two oil lamps mounted on overturned storage crates, and smelled disgusting. Holmes indicated that we should do nothing for the moment, until we understood the scene before us, but the need for action was apparent.

The man I assumed to be Warrilow stood with his back to us, facing two people who were each manacled by one arm to the wall. The girl, who was clearly Martha Redstrap, was in a pitiable state. She leaned against her chains with her clothes torn and filthy. A few feet away, an unshaven man stood defiantly but in obvious distress, and in a similar condition. In full view of the prisoners but, I estimated, just out of their reach, stood an upturned box laden with a bottle of water and a loaf of mouldy bread.

"You are an obstinate man, Northbridge," Warrilow said. "You will get no more water or bread until you tell me how much Scotland Yard knows of our plans. Much has been risked for what is to come, and we cannot tolerate interference." He turned to the girl, and I felt Holmes grow tense beside me. "Perhaps some attention to Miss Redstrap, whose father has been most co-operative, will loosen your tongue."

He tore the girl's dress half from her body, with a quick sweep of his arm.

"Leave her!" Northbridge shouted. "She cannot harm your plans!"

"That is true," Warrilow agreed. "In fact, she has served her purpose well. Her father has surrendered the plans of the bank vaults, and I have promised to return her to him. As a gentleman, it grieves me not to keep that promise."

He said it with a mocking lack of sincerity, and it brought a mixture of anger and despair to Northbridge's face. "So that has become your intention?"

"That was *always* my intention."

"Then that is another reason why I shall tell you nothing."

Warrilow laughed. "You think that is how it will be? I tell you that long before you depart this life, you will be glad to pour out your soul to me."

Holmes stepped forward and new hope flared in Northbridge's eyes. Warrilow saw it at once and turned to face us. Surprise came and faded from his face quickly.

"Well, Mr. Sherlock Holmes. Such a surprise to see you here."

"We are here to escort you to Scotland Yard, Warrilow. There can be no escape this time."

Warrilow glanced calmly about him, as if searching for a weapon or a means of escape. With a shrug he walked slowly towards us, his wrists held out to invite Holmes to place handcuffs upon them. I had remained in deep shadow, and he was not yet aware of my presence. My friend stood very still as Warrilow approached, and I had an impression of a heavily moustached face with cruel eyes, advancing in the semi-darkness.

Then, with the quickness of a fairground conjuror, one of the offered hands disappeared inside the pea jacket he wore. It came out raised to strike, ready to plunge a long knife into the chest of Sherlock Holmes.

My friend had already evaded the thrust as I fired. The sound seemed as loud as a cannon in the enclosed space, and Warrilow was hurled backwards and toppled to the floor. The girl screamed as he fell near her, and I put away my revolver and stood over him. I saw at once that there was nothing that could be done to save him. His filthy shirt was moist with blood, and more dribbled from his mouth as he coughed.

"He will get you," he gasped painfully. "You will see."

His eyes went blank and he expired with a deep sigh.

"Thank you, Watson, though your action was a little premature."

"He would have killed you, Holmes!"

"So it must have appeared to you, but I had already avoided the blade. Unfortunately, we can learn nothing from him now."

Feeling rather hurt by my friend's attitude, I retrieved a bunch of keys from Warrilow's pockets and handed them to him. Both prisoners were quickly released, and I fetched fresh water from a tap in an adjoining room for them. Martha Redstrap covered herself with a tattered blanket that I discovered in an otherwise empty crate, while Northbridge sat down to regain his strength.

Holmes drew something from his pocket. "Watson, here is a police whistle. Pray be good enough to walk to both ends of the street and blow it until a constable appears. That should not take long, since the beats hereabouts are designed to intersect every fifteen minutes. Meanwhile, I will attend to our charges as best I can."

I was back with two constables within twenty minutes. Holmes explained the situation, mentioning that Inspector Lestrade's enquiries were connected also. One officer left to summon a sergeant, while the other remained. It was understood that Inspector Northbridge and Miss Martha Redstrap would be escorted to hospital for observation, that her father would be notified of her safe recovery, and that the body of Warrilow would be conveyed to the nearest mortuary.

Our driver received a generous payment on returning us to Baker Street, and seemed well pleased. It was past five o'clock as we regained our sitting room. Strangely, neither Holmes nor myself felt undue weariness as we sat either side of an unlit fire watching the new day grow lighter.

"A good night's work I think, Holmes." I remarked as I put down my empty glass.

"Indeed. Watson, I must thank you again for attempting to save my life. You must have thought me most ungrateful at the time."

"Not at all, old fellow. I understand that I unwittingly deprived us of information."

"You realise then, that this affair is not over?"

I nodded. "Warrilow referred to someone whom he expected to take revenge on us. Also, there remain unanswered questions regarding Inspector Northbridge."

"Your deductive powers improve by leaps and bounds," he said, and I felt warm satisfaction at his praise. "While you summoned the constables I talked at length to Northbridge, having first discharged the distressing task of informing him of his mother's death. His enquiries had revealed the connection between Warrilow, whom he was certain to be responsible for the previous two murders, and Mr. Redstrap of The Agricultural and Landowners Bank. I did in fact confirm Warrilow's guilt, by examining the thin chain that he kept about his waist. The shape of the links was identical to the impressions on the victims' throats."

"But Mr. Redstrap was afraid for his daughter's life and so concealed the situation, as he attempted to with us."

"Precisely. Warrilow somehow became aware of the pursuit – probably Mr. Redstrap volunteered it accidentally. He subsequently captured Northbridge, and murdered Northbridge's mother for fear of what might have been disclosed to her. He kept the inspector alive in order to learn how much Scotland Yard knew about the forthcoming crimes. I found two draughtsman's drawings in that warehouse, and one of them is clearly of Mr. Redstrap's bank."

"And the other?" I asked.

Holmes plucked two thick documents from the table, and discarded one of them. The other he unfolded, glanced at it and held it so that I could see the diagram drawn upon it.

"A building meant to contain a large number of people, I think," he observed.

"There is no writing upon it."

"And there lies the difficulty."

I looked more closely. "A hotel, perhaps?"

He frowned, but then his face lit up. "No, Watson, but you have given me the clue. Consider the design, the corridors leading to a central point and the small, regularly-spaced rooms. Can you now throw light upon it?"

For a moment more, I stared. "Of course! It is a map of the inside of a prison!"

"It is, indeed. But I see that it is almost fully light out there, and high time that we slept. We will discuss this further over a very late breakfast, but for now I bid you goodnight, or good morning, if you prefer."

He turned as I rose from my chair, picking up the documents and vanishing into his room abruptly.

The tiredness that I had kept at bay until now suddenly descended upon me. I said goodnight to my friend as I passed his door, yawning as I made my way up to my bed.

As it happened, neither Holmes nor myself slept for long. I think I had passed beyond weariness, while he would doubtlessly have remained awake to ponder the remaining problems facing us. My pocket-watch showed almost ten o'clock as we sat down to a delayed breakfast of bacon and eggs.

Strangely, and contrary to his stated intention of the early morning, my friend said nothing about the case or our discoveries. He ate automatically, maintaining an expression of deep preoccupation except for a few words of greeting.

Mrs. Hudson had no sooner cleared away our plates and coffee cups when the doorbell rang. We made ourselves comfortable in our usual armchairs as that good lady showed in Inspector Lestrade and withdrew.

"Lestrade!" Holmes called out in a surprisingly jovial manner. "Come and sit with us. Watson, pray be good enough to call down to Mrs. Hudson for another pot of coffee."

"Not for me, if you don't mind, Mr. Holmes", the inspector responded. "For once, I've managed to have breakfast before beginning my duty."

I therefore remained seated, and Lestrade settled himself in the empty chair.

"I came to discuss this Warrilow business, of course," he said. "I read the constable's report about the events of last night."

"How are Inspector Northbridge and Miss Martha Redstrap?" I enquired, despite Holmes's obvious annoyance at my interruption.

"They are recovering well, as far as I know. Miss Redstrap has been returned to her parents."

"Excellent," said Holmes, by way of dismissing the subject. "I have recovered a plan of the bank, from Warrilow. Is there any reason why a robbery should have been planned at this particular time, Lestrade?"

"The Yard has been informed that an excessive amount of bullion is on hand, to repay a number of international loans."

"That would certainly account for it. There was also another document, which Watson and I have identified as a map of the interior of a prison. Is it, by any chance, familiar to you?"

Lestrade scowled as my friend handed him the document, and I knew this was because we had removed articles from the scene, unofficially. He leaned forward to spread it out before him and gave us a sharp glance. "I have seen this before now. It is indeed a map of Pentonville Prison. You say it was recovered from Warrilow?"

Holmes had become very still, and appeared to be deep in thought. He did not answer the inspector's question, but said suddenly, "The telegram I sent to you yesterday evening, Lestrade. Did you receive it?"

"I was away from The Yard until late. I must have missed it when I called in briefly, this morning. What did it contain?"

"An enquiry about the professions of Warrilow's two previous victims."

"The first, Stephen Mortimer, was an ex-clerk from the very same bank, until he was dismissed for suspected dishonesty. No doubt Warrilow learned much from him, about the bank and the Redstrap family, before the murder. I imagine he surrendered the information after a promise of payment."

"Undoubtedly. But the second victim?"

I saw Lestrade's face go pale as he realised the implication of what he was about to say.

"Frederick Purcell was a guard at Pentonville Prison. Warrilow must have used him similarly, to obtain this plan and possibly information also."

"And Warrilow's last words were to the effect that an accomplice of his would take revenge on us."

"So there is more yet to this business," Lestrade realised. "The intentions were to rob the bank, and then break into the prison?"

Holmes declined to answer, but asked. "Is anyone of particular notoriety held there at present?"

298

"There is indeed. The Fallon gang, four men of a black-hearted family who had eluded us until now, are to be brought to trial for a number of murders and armed robberies. You believe there is some connection, Mr. Holmes?"

"I suspect that the entire sequence of events is connected," my friend replied. "The bank robbery is a distraction device, intended to engage the attention of Scotland Yard while the real crime, the releasing from prison of the Fallon Gang, is to be perpetrated. I think the two events, with Warrilow as the common factor, could not be otherwise. From this we see at once that not only must we do our utmost to discover when these acts are to be carried out, but that it is imperative that the true account of Warrilow's death be concealed. The fact that this gang, whomever they may be, are prepared to take so much trouble to extract these men from custody suggests that a much more elaborate crime awaits their participation in the near future. Something to watch for, Lestrade."

"We will, never fear. But why should the cause of Warrilow's death be hidden?"

"Because, if it were known that Watson and myself, or indeed any member of the official force, were involved, the gang would be warned that we know of their intentions and probably change them. I suggest that the newspapers are told that Northbridge and Miss Redstrap escaped, without having learned anything of value to Scotland Yard, and that Warrilow was killed as he tried to prevent this. Both sets of plans will have to be replaced where they were found of course, if it is not too late."

"No information about the incident has yet been released," the Scotland Yard man confirmed thoughtfully.

"Then we can proceed. For now, it will be a waiting game."

Nothing was heard for a week. When I commented on this, Holmes explained that this did not necessarily mean that the gang had changed its plans, since they would have to choose a replacement to take Warrilow's part in the assault on the bank and to finalise and co-ordinate the two operations. I asked if there was a possibility of an error in the construction of his theory, and my friend looked up from his newspaper with an icy glare.

"Warrilow had both sets of plans – therefore the two crimes are connected. Even if I believed in coincidence, Watson, that would be too much. Besides, this case has other features of which I will tell you after its conclusion."

For the remainder of that day, and almost all of the next, Holmes languished in that dark mood that always came upon him at times of inactivity. But in the early evening a telegram from Lestrade arrived, bearing the words: *Tomorrow. Eight o'clock.* This was in accordance with our arrangement, and meant that Scotland Yard had received information that the gang's plans were about to be set in motion.

The inspector was waiting, with fifteen constables armed with truncheons, outside the gates of Pentonville Prison when we arrived at six in the morning. Already it was fully light, and we repaired to the governor's office which overlooked the yard and main gates.

"Mr. Redstrap sent a private messenger to the Yard," Lestrade explained to us, "whose instructions were to deliver the documents he carried into my hands, which he did. They contained a message received by the bank, a reminder to the effect that a new customer, The Credit Bank of Paris, was to deliver a shipment of gold bullion at eight o'clock this morning, before the bank opens. Both the account and the delivery were arranged some weeks ago, before Northbridge disappeared and this affair began, and so no significance was placed upon it, at first. However, in the light of our current suspicions, a telegram was dispatched to Paris for confirmation. This quickly attracted a reply, telling us that they knew of no such account or delivery, and we then established that the London address that The Agricultural and Landowners Bank had dealt with was a barber's shop where the owner was in the habit of acting as a *poste restante* for a fee. That was when I arranged for these constables to be in attendance here, and notified you gentlemen as promised."

"Anticipating the second stage of the gang's plan," my friend said with approval. "But what action has been taken to protect the bank?"

"Inspectors Gregson and Bradstreet, accompanied by a dozen armed constables, are ready and waiting."

"Excellent, Lestrade," Holmes replied, and at that moment a tall stern-faced man entered and was introduced to us.

"Mr. George Wittall, Governor of Pentonville."

He shook hands with us, and his frown deepened. "This is a terrible business, gentlemen. I suppose some violence is inevitable."

"We are prepared," said Lestrade. "Myself, Mr. Holmes, and Doctor Watson, as well as five constables, are armed with revolvers, and all constables carry truncheons. Our intention is to keep the disturbance to a minimum, if that proves to be possible."

"Thank you for your consideration. Will you require assistance from the prison staff?"

"Only to bring the Fallon gang into plain view. I understand that you received notification from The Commissioner's Office at Scotland Yard that these prisoners are required for questioning?"

The governor nodded. "That is quite usual in such circumstances, where a prisoner's involvement to a further, unsolved, crime is suspected."

"And the message appeared to be no different to any other occasion?"

"Not at all."

"Then the gang has an informer at the Yard," Holmes pointed out. "Neither the wording or the presentation of these official messages are known to the general public. One of your colleagues, Lestrade, has been paid or threatened." He paused, and then added, "Such a man could also serve to intercept any request for confirmation from the prison, and to send a reply."

"Could not the information have been forced from Inspector Northbridge?" I ventured.

Lestrade shook his head. "Northbridge's duties could not have entailed anything connected with this. I will certainly look into it when I return to my office."

"As recently instructed," the governor finished, "I immediately sought confirmation."

Lestrade then dismissed the man, and our vigil began.

Holmes, Lestrade, and I looked down into the prison yard. Before long, ten convicts appeared in prison uniform, under the watchful eyes of two armed prison guards. Both of my companions nodded their approval, and I realised then that the party were actually disguised constables. They positioned themselves as if waiting to begin a daily exercise drill, and stood in silence. When two more armed guards emerged from the main building in the company of four heavily-manacled men whom I presumed these to be the Fallon gang, Lestrade consulted his pocket watch.

"It is almost time. The remaining three of my men are out of sight, and we must take up our positions. The intruders must suspect nothing until the gates are securely fastened after they enter."

A few minutes after Holmes and I had concealed ourselves in a deep doorway, and Lestrade had found cover behind the projecting brickwork of a chimney, a coach drew up outside the gates. I withdrew my watch from my waistcoat pocket sufficiently to see that the time was exactly eight o'clock.

One of the "guards" supervising the drill squad approached the gates and peered through the tiny observation port. A short conversation followed, before he shouted that the expected Scotland Yard officers had arrived. I hadn't seen the governor appear, but he stood near the entrance to the cell block and raised an arm to signal that the gate could be opened. When this was done, a long four-wheeler with police markings entered the yard slowly. The drill squad began its routine.

"This has been exceptionally well-organised," Holmes whispered. "Only a close examination would reveal that not to be an official vehicle."

We watched as the coach came to rest, the driver remaining as he was while two well-dressed men alighted. One, tall and bearded, introduced himself to the governor as "Inspector Hawkins", while his shorter companion was "Inspector Turnbull".

I noticed that the drill squad and their "guards", were already advancing slowly towards the coach.

"You will have received notification of this prisoner transfer," Hawkins began when the governor approached. "Here is further authority."

Mr. Wittall took the offered documents and spent a few minutes examining their contents. "They appear to be in order," he said.

Hawkins peered past him, at the waiting Fallon gang. "Brutal-looking lot. Still, you've got the derbies and leg-irons on them, so they shouldn't give us any trouble."

Before the governor could reply, one of the Fallon gang, a giant of a man with a scar across his forehead, shouted loudly.

"*You are trapped! All is discovered!*"

Immediately, chaos burst upon the scene.

Hawkins struck Mr. Wittall, producing a revolver from under his long coat as the governor fell. He fired twice at the guards in charge of the prisoners, and one man toppled. The other "Inspector", Turnbull, leaned into the coach and suddenly there was a shotgun in his hands, and the driver rose from his seat similarly armed. The drill squad had by this time drawn close, and Turnbull fired into their midst. The horses reared in panic, their cries alarmingly loud in the enclosed yard, spoiling the driver's aim and his balance so that he leaped to the ground. He turned in our direction, having apparently sensed our presence, but Lestrade shot him before he could bring his weapon to bear.

Dimly among the noise and the blood, I was aware of the remaining guard using his truncheon on those of the Fallon gang who resisted his efforts to return them to their cells. Holmes, meanwhile, had shot twice at Hawkins but missed as the man took shelter behind the coach. Fearing fire from the drill squad, he altered his position, and my friend brought him down with a third shot.

For an awful moment there was silence, then Turnbull ran madly towards us. He held his shotgun in his left hand and a revolver in the other aiming indiscriminately at anyone within his sight. A few inches from my head the wall exploded, splattering my face with brick dust. I fired once and he was hurled backwards. He managed to struggle to his knees as the remnants of the drill squad approached, and two disguised constables discharged their weapons until he was still. Then the danger was past and relief swept over us, as one of Lestrade's men calmed the horses, holding their heads.

The smoke from the gun-fire was already dispersing, as I avoided the patches of blood to tend the wounded, obeying the calling of my profession.

I asked Mrs. Hudson to serve a late lunch, because Holmes had accompanied Lestrade to Scotland Yard.

"How did it go, old fellow?" I asked as he entered our rooms and took off his coat.

"A constable was killed during the bank robbery, Gregson was slightly wounded. All the robbers, save one who is badly hurt and under police supervision in hospital, were killed by police gunfire."

"And from Pentonville, finally?"

He shook his head sadly. "Three constables dead, two seriously injured. One guard dead, and one with minor wounds."

"After a battle of that sort, it could have been much worse, Holmes. How is Mr. Wittall?"

"He was unaffected by the shooting. Cuts and bruises from the blow he sustained, nothing more."

"Our three adversaries were dead, I know. My examination needed to be only superficial."

"That is a pity. Much could have been learned from them."

"I thought this business was at an end. Have you discovered something more?"

"I have discovered nothing new," he said thoughtfully, "that I did not suspect from the beginning." I was about to ask for an explanation, when he suddenly smiled as the door opened. "But here is Mrs. Hudson with our lunch. Poached salmon with new potatoes, I see. We will eat first, Watson, and then retire to our chairs to smoke a pipe, after which I will answer your questions as best I can."

For once, Holmes proved himself my equal in the consumption of our lunch. He set about his food with unusual enthusiasm, and the meal ended with both our appetites satisfied. When our landlady had cleared away the remains, we took to our armchairs and smoked contentedly.

"I see that your curiosity about this case has not abated over lunch," he remarked as he knocked out his cherry-wood pipe. "Often, Watson, your expression speaks volumes."

"Only to you, I think."

"Perhaps, but let me answer your question about what remains of this affair, with a question of my own: Do you believe that Warrilow had the guile or the intelligence to plan this two-pronged assault on the resources

303

of Scotland Yard? Remember that there have been an unusual amount of minor crimes committed over the past few weeks, stretching the manpower of the official force considerably."

"Do you suspect that this was a gradual wearing down of the Yard's resources, culminating in these two major crimes?"

"I am quite convinced of it. The intention was that the robbery at The Agricultural and Landowners Bank should not only divert attention from the Pentonville break-out of the Fallon gang, but also that both crimes should take place when the Yard was least able to cope with them."

"I agree, Holmes, that I would not have thought Warrilow capable of such organisation."

"Nor I, and when we assume as much, other aspects of this affair become more credible." He replaced his pipe in the rack and sat back in his chair, his eyes half-closed. "For example, Inspector Northbridge was kept alive, and not immediately disposed of, as a threat to the forthcoming criminal operations. Inside information was obtained by one device or another, from both the bank and Scotland Yard. Then we have to consider the falsification of credentials from The Credit Bank of Paris, and of those from the Yard. There are many others, Watson, but I think those are sufficient to illustrate the point."

I considered his words, and could not deny the apparent truth in them. "Again, I cannot help but agree. But if Warrilow was a mere instrument in all this as you suggest, then who is truly behind it? Have we been battling with a shadow?"

"That is a more apt description than you realise, old fellow. You may recall that I have remarked to you on several occasions, once in the presence of Inspector MacDonald, that there is an evil influence in London that controls most of the criminal activity that we see around us. I sensed the closeness of his activities to my own some time ago, and have investigated his background. His intelligence is equal to my own, and so he is a formidable enemy. I have no doubts that we shall encounter him in the future."

The Recovery of the Ashes
by Kevin P. Thornton

In Affectionate Remembrance
OF

ENGLISH CRICKET,
WHICH DIED AT THE OVAL
ON
29th AUGUST, 1882,
Deeply lamented by a large circle of sorrowing
friends and acquaintances.

R. I. P.

N.B.—*The body will be cremated and the
ashes taken to Australia.*

Memorial in The Sporting Times, *30th August 1882,
after Australia defeated England by seven runs*

My friend, Sherlock Holmes, has been of service to some of the most famous people of our time. Royalty, industrialists, philanthropists, philosophers, and the gentry have entered our world, as well as some from the artistic and sporting worlds. People from nearly every walk of life have consulted him when troubled and he has rarely judged them, looking only to the mystery that is presented. With all my experience as his friend, fellow adventurer, and chronicler, one might think that I had become used to the nature and quality of the great man's supplicants. Yet here we were, sitting outside a committee room waiting to talk to his latest client, and I could scarce contain my excitement.

It was June. Summer was supposed to be on the doorstep, but the meteorological office noted that it was rather cold for the time of year due to the prevalence of north-easterly winds along the east coast. This cold affected everyone, and none more so than the members of the

305

organization we were visiting, as weather played a key part in their annual plans. We were seated outside the Long Room at Lords Cricket Ground, a venerable and indeed venerated place. I could scarce take in all the sights. Lords was the home of cricket, a sport that in many ways defined the Empire, and the walls and halls were bedecked with the memorials of the greats of yore. Wherever our nation had triumphed in the world we had left our mark, and cricket had spread throughout the Empire, taking with it those most English values of fighting hard and playing fair.

I said naught of my thoughts to Holmes. He had a differing world view when it came to colonisation and may very well have scoffed at my Jingoism. He seemed singularly unimpressed at his surrounds, and I wondered if I had been brought along as a translator as well as companion, for Holmes's knowledge was directed and focused, and I could easily believe he knew nothing about cricket.

The door opened and the man coming through seemed to hesitate, as if trying to get away from the conversation. The other side was muffled, but in reply the man said, "I don't know what to make of it, but I tell you the weather has gone mad. It is the middle of summer and we are still freezing. On the other side of the Atlantic they had a blizzard recently where up to four feet of snow fell in Boston. If the climate keeps changing like this you mark my words, this will be the year remembered for the decline and fall of cricket due to the continued frosting of the world's climate."

The other voice was clearer now. "Don't you mean the decline and fall of civilization, Doctor?"

The man at the door growled back. "Cricket and civilization are one and the same. If the one goes, the other will surely follow. Now if you'll excuse me gentlemen, I am late for an appointment."

He presented himself through the door, pulling it shut behind him. "Mister Holmes?" He said, looking at me.

"I am he," said Holmes. "Doctor Grace, I assume? I haven't seen you for some years. Please allow me to introduce my friend, Doctor John Watson." As he looked at me, he must have seen the stunned amazement on my face. "Have you two met?"

"I don't believe so", said Grace.

Meanwhile I was jabbering. "Doctor Grace Doctor Grace it is such an honour to meet you do you know I saw you play here in 1870 the Gentlemen versus the Players fixture where you scored a double ton magnificent innings Sir absolutely fabulous . . . ."

I was stopped in my tracks as Holmes stepped in front of me and said gently, "Watson, there will be time for that later. Work beckons."

"But this is Doctor W.G. Grace," I said, as if that explained everything.

"I know," said Holmes. "And he needs our help."

We followed him down to another room with club chairs and tables around a fireplace. There were no servants at hand and Grace himself poured us drinks.

"I dismissed the staff," he said by way of explanation. "What I have to tell you is most secret and crucial to the reputation of Queen and Empire. We have lost the Ashes."

Holmes looked puzzled as did I. As he asked the more obvious "What Ashes?" I delved further with "But you haven't even started playing for them?"

There was a pause, and then Grace said, "Doctor Watson. Your knowledge of the great game is obvious. Mister Holmes, you seem to know . . . er . . . *less*."

"I am not one for pastimes, Doctor Grace. If I need information about cricket that is pertinent to my investigation, Watson will be able to fill the gaps in my knowledge."

"But your bowling?" said Grace. "Yes, I remember you now. I assumed you were an aficionado, and I have looked forward to trying to best you at least once after the last time. No? Well, at least let me tell you briefly such history of the sport as will help you in your investigation. The first international cricket match between two countries was between the U.S.A and Canada in 1844. I say *international* lightly, as it was barely a first class match. Some of the players would have embarrassed a village cricket team. It wasn't until Australia and England played each other in 1877 that the first true test of the best players in the world came about. We, England, were victorious, and have since then had many battles royal against our antipodean enemy, so much so that the competitions are now referred to as 'test matches', as they are a test of the best. So far, they are the only two countries considered good enough to play in test matches, and it was long assumed that England's superiority would reign supreme for many years."

Holmes's patience, never one of his virtues, was wearing thin. "Please, Doctor, if you could get to the point."

Doctor Grace was unused to interruption and *harrumph*-ed his surprise. He was a big man with a beard of impressive length and girth, almost covering the size of his chest. Next to Her Majesty, he was easily the most recognizable personage in the land, loved for his skills on the cricket pitch as well as the overwhelming image of Englishness he wore so well. As such a man, on such a pedestal, he was used to being kowtowed to, and Holmes had not done so. Nevertheless he continued, but he seemed not to get to his point any sooner than he would have before.

"The cunning Australians managed to beat us here at home, and it was written about as the death of English cricket, with the Ashes being taken back to Australia to signify our momentous loss. This was all done in a jocular manner, but when my dear friend Ivo Bligh took the England cricket team to Australia, he vowed to bring back the Ashes by defeating the Australians. And he did so."

Doctor Grace paused so dramatically in his tale it was as if he was building up steam for his finish. Holmes depressurized him thus.

"The Ashes have gone missing, and you want me to find them. Doctor Grace, you have wasted my time. Good day." He stood, gathering his coat and hat, and made as if to leave, only to find that his way to the door was blocked by a new arrival. Although not as tall, and with a beard better trimmed, he looked as if he could be the doctor's older brother. Holmes did not even attempt to pass him for the door. "Your Royal Highness," he said to the Prince of Wales and Heir to the Throne. "It is indeed an honour."

"Grace thought you might need some persuading," he said, "which is why he arranged to meet you while I was here on other business. Holmes, this may seem silly to you. It is after all only a container filled with ashes. But Bligh promised to have the urn available for the duration of the test matches, and he will be discountenanced if he is unable to produce it. He has a promising future in Government and is a good friend of mine, which is why I asked Grace to intercede and ask for your help. If you won't do it for our greatest-ever cricketer, consider it as a personal favour for me. If that is not enough, do it for England."

"I will find the urn for you," said Holmes, "and have it at Lords before the competition begins."

The Honourable Ivo Bligh's father, Lord Darnley, had a house in Kent. This was where the family lived and where the urn was last seen. Holmes and I travelled there on the London and South Western Railway service from Waterloo the next day. It is a pretty journey, so I'm told. I saw nothing of it as Holmes engaged me from the moment we sat down.

"For once, Watson, your understanding of the more frivolous side of human behaviour should prove to have some value. How much of this cricket game, its rules and mores, do I need to know to solve His Royal Highness's infernal mess?" He showed me an article in *The Times*. "*Prince of Wales and Governor to attend the Test Series.*' There's the real reason I am involved. I'm told that Lord Carrington and the Prince dislike each other intensely. There is rumour of a large wager between them."

"What of it?" I asked. "It is no secret that His Royal Highness likes to gamble."

"According to my sources, the wager involves ownership of the Ashes urn, something the Prince of Wales cannot give as it is not his to wager."

"And if the urn is *not* available, Lord Carrington will take great delight in further harming the reputation of the heir to the crown."

"If that were at all possible," muttered Holmes. "So we are on a fool's errand. Never mind. Let us take this opportunity for you to explain this sorry game to me."

"Did you never play cricket at all, Holmes? Not even at school? Doctor Grace seems to think you have a talent for it?"

"I know the awe that you hold for Doctor Grace. If I promise to tell you later how I bowled him out, five out of six times, will you help me with the relevant details now? Why do people play sport, and specifically cricket?"

"I can't tell you that Holmes, because you would not understand. Idle pastimes are beyond your ken. Suffice it for you to know that cricket is a game involving batters trying to hit balls to score against the opponent, and it is made more complicated by the way it has been taken to by both the ruling classes and workers alike."

"So it is like rounders?" said Holmes. "I remember that from when we were very young, playing it in the garden."

"Yes and no," I said. "Rounders, or baseball as it is now often known, has some of the same principles, but differs in other ways. Cricket has a flat bat and a different way to convey the ball to the batter, bowling it instead of pitching. It has distinct clothing, types of running, ways of fielding, means of scoring, game length, culture, history, societal standards, and even spectator behaviour."

"Other than that, they are very similar," said Holmes. "As usual, Watson, you have entertained without enlightening. It is best perhaps to wait for the evidence. I'm sure the rules of this arcane and mysterious sport will not have any effect on the recovery of the Ashes. What of them?"

"Australia is a much better cricket team than Doctor Grace would admit to. When they beat us six years back, here on English soil, it was unexpected and even quite a shock. When Ivo Bligh, the captain of the next team to go to Australia, vowed to bring the Ashes back, it caught the public's imagination"

"And they did?" said Holmes.

'Indeed. While they were there, they were presented with an urn filled with ashes to be brought back to England. And now it is missing."

"And I am looking for it to make sure the Prince of Wales is not embarrassed. How far we have fallen, Watson. We need a good murder to whet our appetites."

"Maybe we'll be lucky and find one when we get there," I said, with a touch of asperity in my tone.

Holmes, if he even noticed, chose to say nothing, and remained within his own thoughts for the rest of the journey.

It was a short ride to the house. Cobham Hall had been in the Bligh family for at least two centuries. Previously it had been owned by the Dukes of Richmond, and before that by the Cobham Baronets. It consisted of two wings of some fifty rooms each, with a central block of similar size joining them, as well as other parts too numerous to enumerate.

"This is a house, just as Windsor Castle is a cottage," I said as we drove up to the south wing. We had passed a set of cricket nets on the lawn, practice facilities that looked well-used, as indeed they would be, for the Blighs were one of the most important cricketing families in the land. The Honourable Ivo's father, Lord Darnley, had played for the Gentlemen of Kent, and was a past president both of Kent Cricket Club and the M.C.C.. In addition, his brothers H. and E.V. Bligh, uncle J. D. Bligh, great-uncle E. Bligh, and numerous cousins had all played first-class cricket.

All this was related by the Honourable Ivo as he met us at the door and walked us through the baronial halls to the family area of the wing. He was a pleasant man, well-groomed and of the highest order of gentleman. A steadfast man, one could easily imagine him leading the charge at Waterloo or Balaclava in the same way he would face the attack of the Australian fast bowlers, Spofforth and Palmer.

"I am terribly grateful to you for coming to my aid over what you must think is such a trivial matter," he said as he led us into the end room of the wing, a large library that he had to unlock to let us enter. As he opened the door, the sound of the lock seemed to draw the most amazing creature from behind a tapestry. It was about two feet tall, with an oversized tail and tiny front paws. It nudged past Bligh and hopped through the door. Bligh saw the astonishment on my face and said, "Oh don't worry about Jerry. He was one of my presents from Australia. You will doubtless see more of the menagerie through the day. I also have a meerkat from Cape Town, a monkey, and assorted domestic animals."

310

We followed him into the room. Jerry was sitting by the fire grooming himself, for all the world like a large cat created by a mad scientist.

"He's a miniature kangaroo," said Bligh.

"A type of rock-wallaby," said Holmes. "Nocturnal, mischievous, and difficult to housetrain."

"As the touring captain, one is given all sorts of gifts. I was offered this chap or a Jeroboam of champagne, and much to my team's dismay, I chose him and named him after the bottle." He blinked suddenly and said, "I say, Holmes, I had heard of this party trick of yours, deducing things facts where no other can. How on earth did you know all that about Jerry, the jolly jumper?"

"It was not deduction but preparation, save the last point. I went back and read the accounts of your tour in *The Times* so that I could acquaint myself of all the facts. There was a small story about your pet and a description of its mannerisms which I applied to the here and now. As to the lack of housetraining, the evidence is over by the fireplace, by the door to the garden, and no doubt in several other places. As it is a smell with which I am unfamiliar, and a format I have never seen, I deduced that it came from your Australian pet. That you have had it for five years and it is still relieving itself inside the house led me to my final conclusion."

"But your conclusion was erroneous," said Bligh. "That mess, which I admit is from Jerry, could have been from another pet."

"No," said Holmes. "I am familiar with the dietary and digesting patterns of over four-dozen monkeys and apes, as well as all typical types of meerkat scat. By subtraction then, what was left came from your rock-wallaby. Is this where the urn went missing?"

"It is. I can narrow it down to a specific time period as well." He gestured towards the grand table in the centre of the room which was covered in files, dispatch, boxes, and leather-bound journals. "As you can see, I am rather involved in some tedious affairs of state, preparing for a position that may be offered to me overseas. Consequently I have set up my headquarters here, and am in the habit of locking the room whenever I leave. Two days ago, my father came to talk to me. He had been down to London on business and heard that the Ashes would be displayed for the duration of the tests. This concerned him."

"How so?" said Holmes.

"He was worried that the frivolity of the Ashes urn would take away from the *gravitas* of the series. I'm afraid we became quite heated and he insisted on seeing the urn to make his point. Because of this, I know it was here when I locked the room. It stood on the mantelpiece above the main fireplace, and it was the last thing I saw when I left. An hour later when I returned, I unlocked the door and noticed it was missing."

"What did you do next," I asked.

"I made some enquiries of my family and guests – my father in particular. I wasn't too worried at the time, although it did puzzle me. There is only one key to the room so I couldn't see how it disappeared."

Holmes was circling the room as we spoke, looking for other means of access.

"If you were not too worried," said Holmes, "what then changed your mind? This happened less than two days ago, and it has gone from a mysteriously missing trinket to a matter of national importance."

"Doctor Grace was here at the time, and he was the one who saw how serious this could become. It was he who persuaded me to reach into my connections in Whitehall and ask for assistance."

"You did not involve the local police?"

"He is a simple village constable, past retirement age. I did not see how he could help."

"And your father, Lord Darnley? What was his reaction?"

"He thought it an execrable little foible. I am sure he isn't unhappy it is missing."

"And you told him it had to be on display at Lords, as it was the feature of a bet between the Prince of Wales and Lord Carrington, the Governor of Australia."

"That's correct Holmes. It was a heated discussion. My father is not one of the Prince's supporters and was all for embarrassing him by refusing to put the Ashes on display."

"That is not quite true," said a voice behind us. "I have known Bertie, the Prince of Wales, since I was an aide-de-camp to his father. He was a spoilt little whinger back then, and nothing I've seen since has changed my mind. What I actually said was he has always been a sad bad gambler at Cowes week every year, as well as the Derby, and he is, as far as I can tell, banned from every card game in the city. Only then did I say that it would serve him right if we discomfited him in the sight of his enemy, Carrington." He held out his hand. "Darnley. You must be Holmes, and you Watson. Thank you for coming down on such a pedestrian task. I am somewhat distressed that your first time here is because of that damn pot.

"I see," said Holmes. "What is the value of the . . . pot?"

"Virtually nothing," said Bligh. "It is an old perfume jar re-labelled and filled with the ashes of a burnt cricket ball from one of the matches of our tour. Its real value is in what it represents. When the story gets out that it is the focus of the series and that there is a large amount of money on the outcome, people will demand to see it. There is talk of it being put

312

on display and charging a fee, the proceeds to go to a charity." Bligh stopped and sighed. He was still a young man of less than thirty summers, but his countenance wore wearier years than his chronology.

"What will you do when we find it?" said Holmes.

"I will honour the royal wishes," he said. "It will be on display, and if we lose, Lord Carrington will be allowed to take it away."

It was entirely possible that the *harrumph* emitted by Lord Darnley was a sailor's invective, but I presumed to give him the benefit of the doubt.

"If you don't find it," said Darnley, "Bertie will threaten to tell all that we let him down, and we'll probably end up paying his wager for him, as he never has enough money and he thinks we have too much. Still, it might be worth it if Carrington gets to lord it over him. Carrington's a good egg though, and probably wouldn't. So you have to find it Holmes. You have to find it."

Lord Darnley and Bligh left us alone while they went to attend to some business. Holmes examined the windows which were open to catch the breeze, but securely covered in metal mesh.

"What do you make of this Holmes?" I said. "All the ground floor windows seem to be covered in this stuff. Have they had other burglaries that they need to protect the windows?

"Ah, my dear Watson, as usual you have jumped as far towards the wrong conclusion as possible. The mesh, I believe we will find, is not to keep thieves out. It is there to keep a pet wallaby in. They are known to have prodigious jumping abilities." He bent down to look at the mess left by the animal next to the fireplace. "Watson, would you ring for service please. I need to talk to the head cleaning maid."

"What have you discovered, Holmes?"

"An anomaly, Watson." But he would say no more.

We waited some moments for the maid. Holmes had been pacing the room which, being both library and sitting room in its normal usage, had plenty of potential hiding places. As he paced, there was a shadowy movement at the bottom of the door and Holmes lunged forward, pulling it open.

There was a young man standing on the other side. "Mister Holmes," he said. "I am A.J. Raffles."

"I know who you are. Have you come to confess?"

"Confess?" I said. "Holmes, what do you mean? Raffles is a cricketer of note. Why I have seen him play for the Gentlemen in the annual fixture at Lords."

"He may have played for the Gentlemen," said Holmes, "but I doubt he is one."

Raffles seemed unperturbed at this accusation. "When I heard you were here, I thought I would save us both some time by coming to you directly. I was invited to Cobham Hall to take part in practice for the cricket season. You may take my word that I do not trouble my hosts with my business, and I am not interested in worthless baubles."

"You know of the Ashes urn then," said Holmes.

"Everyone who has been a guest here for longer than a couple of days has seen the urn, heard the story of the Ashes, and learned how the Honourable Ivo Bligh won them back."

Raffles stopped, as if to gather his thoughts. "I apologize if I sound mean. Bligh is a wonderful host but he is no longer a good cricketer. I was invited here along with Doctor Grace to help him practice, but his efforts are so desultory that I am wasting many practice hours that I could be using to get my own game in shape. Getting picked for England is important for me, as it will set me up for the season. There is good money to be made as an England player in the big gambling matches that will take place later in the year, and unlike Bligh, I need to make a living"

"Or else you will have to go back to your other trade," said Holmes. Raffles nodded.

"What were you doing outside there," I asked him.

"He was making sure that I saw the hinged pet door. It is remarkable work by the joiner. Unless you knew it was there, you might miss it entirely." Holmes shut the door and touched the panel at the bottom, setting it swinging. As if in answer to his action, the wallaby rose from the carpet and loped to the door where it bent down and squeezed through.

"I knew you would find it, Holmes. Your reputation precedes you, and sooner or later one of his menagerie was going to pop through and point it out." He turned to leave. "Good luck. Be assured I had nothing to do with this. I will be here until the weekend, when I return to London for trials. If you need to consult with me, Bligh will know where I am."

He left and questions flooded my tongue. Holmes stayed me. "Watson, let me answer your questions before you ask them. It will be quicker. I know Raffles professionally because I keep an eye on all villains in my city. Raffles may be one of the better cricketers in the country, but he is by far the best amateur cracksman not yet behind bars. Wherever he is invited, robberies always seem to occur, and it is only a matter of time before I will be forced to catch him."

I managed to interrupt. "But he's a gentleman," I said, as if that exonerated him.

"Gentlemen are not always gentlemen," said Holmes. "But in this instance, I think I believe him. He is a thief and a rogue, but he does have a code of sorts. He never steals from his host, and he never steals from those who can't afford it."

"That doesn't apply," I said. 'The urn is valueless."

"The urn holds the key to Bligh's next job. If it is missing and the Prince of Wales is publicly humiliated again, Bligh will take the blame, a cost to his name from which he will never recover."

The senior maid, Miss Brown, presented herself at the door. She was a tiny woman of middle age, ruddy-faced, with a keen intelligence about her. Holmes was gentle and brief in his questioning.

"I can see that you are very house-proud," he said. "If I could trouble you to look at this animal matter by the fireplace, you would do me a great service."

She drew herself up to her full height and walked with solemn dignity to where he indicated.

"I apologize for the mess," she said. "The staff and I are not always allowed into this room at the moment, as the Master is busy with his affairs. We have not been able to clean in here for at least four days, and as you can see, the animals have had the run of the place. The kangaroo and the monkey are the worst for making messes, but the little meerkat is also not correctly trained."

"Can all of these animals use the little access hatch in the main door."

"I believe so," she said. "They are all terribly fond of the Master and Mistress, and will often go into rooms they have left to see if there is any food left out. The dogs are the worst – two beagles who continually sniff for scraps – but the cats also use the hatch, and I have seen the monkey and the meerkat go through it as well."

They bent down to look at the wallaby mess underneath the mantelpiece. "Does it seem similar to other messes?" said Holmes.

If she was startled by such a question she gave no sign.

"There is one oddity. Typically Jerry leaves a line of little round black balls. But that one in the middle is flat."

I leaned over to look. "By Jove, Holmes, the thief must have stepped in it while removing the urn." I looked closer. "But how did he step only on that one when the others are so close by. Does that mean the wallaby was the thief?"

"Or the monkey, or the meerkat. The one has opposable thumbs and can grasp objects quite easily," said Holmes, "while the other often

315

carries its young in its mouth. When is the chimney in this room due to be swept?"

"Bless my soul," she said. "You haven't been here but an hour and you know of our cleaning schedule. It will be cleaned when the Master gives us permission. How did you know?"

In answer, he pointed out the window to the other wing of the house. Two small boys were walking along the parapet with their brushes attached to their waists. "They have been here a while, haven't they?"

"Nigh on four days already," she said.

"And they are very athletic, and small enough to go almost anywhere," I said.

"Indeed," said Holmes. "We are awash with suspects. Now Miss Brown, is there anything else you can tell us. Your confidentiality is guaranteed here. All I care about is finding the urn."

She paused, as if to be tactful. "It is not my place to comment on the Mistress and Master's habits in regard to their pets, but for all that they are a lovely family to work for, it is hard to keep a good house when the animals have no respect for the home. The wallaby is untrainable and smelly. The meerkat is shy, which means it always seems to make a mess in the unlikeliest of places. And as for the monkey – it will hide anywhere and jump out screeching as if it has a human sense of humour. Nearly scared me half-to-death a dozen times, Mister Holmes. Still, it could have been worse. There was a time the Master tried to tame some ravens, but that didn't last too long. Too smart for their own good they were, and they messed the walls as well as the books, so they had to go. We still have to send one of the gardeners up into their nest every now and again when something shiny is missing, just in case."

With Holmes's permission, she begged her leave and I jumped into the conversation. "Well, Holmes? Is it the ravens? Or maybe one of the other in this messy menagerie?"

Holmes did not seem as excited by this news as I. "Don't get your hopes up, Watson. Naturally we shall ask the staff to check, but a six-inch urn would be a tall task for a bird to fly with. In any event, when you come to writes your fanciful fiction, as I'm sure you will, you may end up describing this one as the locked room mystery in the room that was not locked."

I ignored his contention about my writings. I believed he did not mind them as much as he made out, and the one that I had published hadn't done his work any harm, save to make him a more obvious target for cases such as these, which he alone deemed frivolous.

It would be impossible to explain to Holmes how much cricket meant to the national identity of the country. When Bligh had returned from Australia, having vanquished the impudent colonials, he was a national hero. Even more so, he brought with him a blushing bride, Florence Morphy, whom he had met the very night the Ashes urn was presented to him. It was a story of the Age of Victoria – England rampant, the hero gets the girl and the prize, and everyone lives happily ever after. Such romantic concepts were foreign to Holmes, and I was worried that, absent his understanding of the value of the Ashes to the country, he would dismiss a likely suspect. Accordingly, I tried to steer his thoughts.

"Raffles is a very slender young man," I ventured. "Do you think he could get through the hatch?"

"I believe he could. It would require some effort, but he is fit, slim, and occasionally desperate. But why would he steal the urn? There is no value to this trinket for him. Besides, if he were trying to get inside, I have no doubt he could pick the lock – yet there is no evidence of the scratches and marks left by such tools on this door's mechanism."

"But if he had the urn, he could sell it to those who didn't wish to be embarrassed," I said.

Holmes smiled. "But he is a gentleman and a cricketer, is he not? By your own standards then, how could he also be a blackguard?"

I hesitated. Holmes was calling into judgement much of what I held dear and true about decency and sportsmanship. How could a thief like Raffles play our national game to the same moral standard of Bligh or Grace?

Holmes must have read my face so clearly. "One of the reasons you are so dear to me Watson is that you believe in such outdated concepts as 'honour' and 'rectitude', as if they were tangible parts of the nation, and you assume that others of like mind have similar views. I regret to tell you that your favourite sport is one that encourages much gambling, and to know that is to presuppose the sport is not always honest. Did you know that many of the so-called 'amateur gentlemen' of the game are paid large fees to play, and are given a cut of the gambling winnings?"

"That cannot be so," I said. "If they receive money, they cannot be amateurs, and if they are not amateurs . . . ."

"Then they are not, by societal definition, gentlemen either. Even your hero, Doctor Grace, bends the rules, Watson, and if it were to come out he would be disgraced. He is a medical doctor who has no practice and he spends his life playing cricket. How else do you think he makes a living?" Holmes looked almost sad for me, as if he had taken my apple in the schoolyard and was now pondering my starvation. "It will do no one any good if the display of the Ashes urn focuses the story of the game on the gambling instead of the state of play on the field. If illegal wagering, such as the bet between the Prince of Wales and Lord

317

Carrington, becomes public knowledge, people like Grace stand to lose much of their livelihood."

"Surely you don't think Grace had something to do with it."

"It would be a foolish man who called in Sherlock Holmes to investigate a crime he committed, but the hubris of the famous is not to be ignored. We raise them onto pedestals that change the focus of the world for them, and some start to believe all they hear about themselves. I hope your hero, the Good Doctor, is not one of them. There is much of the game that is good, Watson. But there is much that is not. We are here because of an illegal bet between the Heir to the Throne and one of his barons. Let us not forget that."

"So you do believe there is an as yet obscured motive behind this crime?"

"My dear Watson. I'm not yet sure that a crime exists. We have a plethora of motives and suspects, yet little in the way of facts."

Bligh rejoined us and said that his wife was available if we so desired. We did, and we left he locked the room behind us. We didn't have far to walk as a door burst open and a young girl ran out, giggling, chased by an athletic-looking woman. She picked up the little girl and swung her around before putting her back on the ground.

"Go back to your doll house, Izzy. I'll come and join you once I've talked to Uncle Ivo's friends."

Izzy wasn't happy and stamped her feet. "But you said you would take me into the garden and help me pick flowers to put in my dolly home."

"And I will later. In the meantime, go with Nanny." She turned to talk to us, only to find Holmes crouching down to get to the little girl's eye level.

"My name's Sherlock," he said. "Do you have a favourite doll?"

"My best doll is called Florence," she said. "I named it after Auntie Flo. It's in the doll house. Would you like to come and see her?"

"Maybe later," said Holmes.

"You are good with children," said the Honourable Mistress Bligh.

"I don't know that I am," said Holmes.

"Well, you don't talk down to them, which is most important." She watched Izzy disappear back into the room. "She's such a delight, but she bores easily. If you do visit her, Mister Holmes, it will mean so much to her, and to me as well."

"I shall not let either of you down," said Holmes. "Can you tell me how the urn came about? I haven't seen it. Was it crafted in Australia for the events of the series?"

"Oh, dear heavens, no. Ivo was a guest of my employer in Melbourne, Sir William Clarke. Once the cricket was won, we thought it would be fun to present him with the Ashes that everyone had been going on about, so we found an empty perfume jar, filled it, stoppered it, and gave it to him. It has been a lucky jar for us. We talked all that evening and came to know each other better. Not long after that he proposed, and here we are."

"Have you had any luck yet," said Bligh. "Any suspects?" He said the last with a slight wince, as if the thought that any of his guests would do such a thing made him dyspeptic. "The fact is, that's not all that's gone missing. Doctor Grace has just arrived from London and he told me his diamond tiepin and cufflinks, which he left here in his room, have vanished. They were given to him by the Maharaja Jam Saheb, Jashwantsinhji Vibhaji II. Apparently the Prince's son is a prodigious talent and Grace coached him last year. Anyway, they are worth a princely sum and Grace is most displeased. The servants are tearing apart his room as we speak."

"Ah," said Holmes. "I believe I have a solution to that as well. If you will indulge me for thirty minutes, let us meet then in your library where all will be revealed."

As always at such moments, he said no more and retreated down the main hall at an impressive pace.

Left to my own devices, I went to the smoking room and made myself a drink. Holmes seemed to think he had the case solved, but for the life of me I couldn't see it.

I was just about to leave the room when Holmes came in, clutching something inside a large white cloth. "Quick, Watson. Take this and fill it. Then affix the stopper, dust it off, and put it inside your right jacket pocket before you join us in the library. I must go there immediately. You come along as soon as you can." He dashed off and I opened the cloth and saw what had to be done.

Two minutes later I edged into the library, hoping to be inconspicuous. Holmes seemed to wish the opposite as he walked over to me in an importunate manner, looking as if he wished to berate me. As he came closer he grabbed me by the arm and said "Watson, this is most ill-timed of you. We have been waiting."

Even though I was expecting his sleight of hand, I couldn't be sure that he had been near my pocket. Yet as he moved back to the centre of the room, I felt inside and found it to be empty. I looked around. None of the assembled *dramatis personae* – Lord Darnley, Doctor Grace, Raffles, Ivo Bligh, and his wife – seemed to have noticed.

Holmes began thus. "Right from the start there were two questions to answer. If the Ashes were stolen, why? And if they were *not* stolen, where were they? In quest of the first, I asked who would profit from this theft. Was it someone who disliked the Prince of Wales?" He looked at Lord Darnley, who met his gaze evenly. "Someone who did not wish the underbelly of cricket gambling exposed?" This time Holmes looked at the doctor, who had the grace to lower his eyes. "Or was it someone with an entirely different agenda?"

As he looked at Raffles, the young man piped up. "I say, that reminds me. One of the servants was cleaning my cufflinks and he must have left these in my room. Does anyone know who they belong to?" He placed a small box on the table. Inside was a diamond pin with matching cufflinks.

"Those are mine," growled Grace. He looked suspiciously at Raffles, who somehow managed to maintain an air of insouciant charm. "Thank you," he said. "Indeed, thank you Raffles. That is most decent of you."

Holmes continued. "I concluded it was none of those. Stealing the urn to achieve any of these aims was too complicated, and could have been done in a far easier manner than attempting to breach a locked room."

"But it is not exactly a locked room," I said.

"Thank you, Watson. Although the room is secured, with the door to the garden always locked and the windows safe from entry due to the zoological nature of the house, the animal hatch could have been accessed in any number of ways. We had information that a famous burglar was in the area, but crawling through the hole in the door may have proved too much for him, as talented as he indubitably is."

"I'll say," murmured Raffles and then had the temerity to smile a little at the very thought.

"There were also the chimney sweeps, save they had not done this room due to Bligh's work laid out on the table. Also, sweeps are almost always messy, and again – what would be the motive?

"But what if the theft was not human in design. There seemed to be almost too many types of creatures who could have accidentally caused this event to unfold. The dogs have access to the room and beagles are notorious for their curiosity. Cats in turn are renowned for knocking things over and batting them around. There are ravens outside still familiar with the house from the time you tried to domesticate them, and while they would struggle to fly holding an object six inches long, it was certainly a possibility. Then there is a meerkat somewhere, strong enough to carry its young in its mouth. The prowling monkey with opposable thumbs and mischievous intent, and the wallaby which comes with its own pouch and obviously a means by which it could place objects therein."

"So you are saying that one of the animals did it."

"I am saying that I don't know, nor do I care. I was hired to find the urn, and that I will do." He began to walk up and down the bookcases, stopping and staring intently before moving on. At one point he rounded a corner so fast that we were unable to keep up. To a sharp "A-ha!" we caught up with him just as he was seen reaching behind a binding of an ancient book. His hand appeared, and it was holding the urn.

Even I, expecting the trick, was impressed by the presentation. As for the others, it was if they had seen a man walk on water. Even Lord Darnley was impressed

"Jolly good show, Holmes! Capital job, capital. You'll stay the night then. Plenty to celebrate."

"Thank you, but no. I have one more appointment with Mister Raffles at your cricket nets, and then I think we will still make the last train back to Waterloo."

Bligh looked delighted, his wife relieved, Doctor W.G. Grace looked confused, and A.J. Raffles like a man who had escaped the hangman's noose. As we made our way down the hall, I asked him, "How did you find it?"

"I listened to everyone and I deduced. Question; Why would a little girl want to be taken out to cut flowers? Answer: Because she had a new vase, which she had been directed to go and purloin from the library when the door was locked. Little Isabel crawled through the hatch, went to the mantelpiece, reached up and grabbed the urn, and returned with it to her co-conspirator. She only made one mistake. She stepped in the mess left by the animal, and it was done in such a way that only a tiny foot could have fit the clue."

"Where was it?" I said.

"I would have ended up at little Izzy's doll house eventually – it was the obvious hiding place. I didn't realize it is a mansion of enormous size, fully ten-feet-by-five-by-six high. It has a room all to itself. It was quite easy for the two of them to hide the urn inside, and it took a lot of searching to find, which was why I was nearly late. I take it you found some ash to put back in the urn then? The original contents were upended somewhere when it became a doll's plaything. Thank you, Watson. I always know I can count on you in a crisis."

"Yet we have lost the ashes of Bligh's cricket ball."

Holmes snorted. "We have done no such thing. This prize was created on a whim by a gaggle of society ladies. Do you think they stood outside reducing a cricket ball to carbon on a fire, or did they do what

321

you just did – filling it with household ash from a cold grate? Regardless, the urn is as genuine as it ever was."

"Wait, wait Holmes. Who was the co-conspirator?"

"The Honourable Mistress Bligh. She made it quite clear that I needed to look in the doll house."

I had listened to everything Holmes heard in that conversation yet missed that part. "But why? Why did the mistress of the house steal from her husband?"

"I suspect it is some romantic claptrap leading back to when he received it from her and her friends. Maybe it was all her idea, the Ashes, and the urn came to mean more to her than it did to anyone else. When it seemed possible she would lose the urn to the Prince of Wales' bet, she resolved to do something about it, and didn't realize how big the incident would become. She became entrapped in the theft, and now we have rescued her. I think we will leave everyone guessing at the truth. I suspect Lord Darnley has his suspicions. Bligh too, and Raffles, rogue that he is, will have worked it out. Perhaps you can suggest that Conan Doyle to craft a suitable story as to a woman's motivation. Did you not you say he was dabbling in romances now?"

I ignored his jibe. My relationship with anyone who was involved in my storytelling was always contentious, and Arthur and Holmes were never the best of friends.

"And Doctor Grace?"

"He has no clue, save that the Ashes are back and he can continue playing his game. The medical world was saved a lot of anxiety when Grace decided cricket was the life for him. He is easily befuddled, as I proved all those years ago, and a cricket bat is a much safer tool in his hands than a scalpel."

"You promised that story to me, Holmes, how you bowled him out five times."

"I did. If we hurry to the cricket nets, I will tell you as we go. I was auditing classes at Bristol Medical School. This would have been the summer of my sixteenth year. Grace was attempting to study medicine, but in reality was the catalyst for the first season of Gloucestershire cricket, a new club at the time. Consequently, he spent as much time practicing in the special nets they set up for him as he did in class. I was interested in physics as it applied to objects flying through the air, and a cricket ball seemed the perfect study. I asked him if I could try to bowl at him, and by manipulating my fingers round the seam of the ball, shining one side of the leather and scuffing the other, I was able to bamboozle him by making the ball appear to go one way when it actually went the other."

"And that's the only six balls you have ever bowled in your life? Holmes, you are truly amazing."

"Thank you. Now, I must try to see if I can remember how to do it again. I promised Raffles a lesson in how to bowl the ball that Grace can't play."

"What a good idea!" I said. "Maybe if he has more success at cricket, he'll give up his career as an amateur cracksman."

"Ah, Watson. You are as always the last ray of hope and decency in a world of despair and decay. What would I do without you?"

The Golden Star of India
by Stephen Seitz

At last!

Baker Street hadn't been a happy home for much of the summer, for my friend Sherlock Holmes had been extremely bored. He indexed his documents, tidied his laboratory, and even cleaned the ashtrays for the first time in what seems like years. Having done as much as he could in that rare spell of domesticity, Holmes whiled his days away in his mouse-coloured dressing gown, smoking and scanning the newspapers for any problem which might break his funk.

Then a great weight lifted from my heart when I heard a light tread on the steps which led to our sitting room. Holmes's head snapped toward the door. "Someone has sent a servant," Holmes said.

I answered the door after three gentle knocks. Before me stood a slender and delicate gem of a young woman, in age around four-and-twenty, her lush auburn hair styled in a French twist which allowed the full appreciation of her high cheekbones, sapphire eyes, and thin lips. She dressed simply, as might a maid or governess.

Holmes rose and greeted her warmly.

"It is good to see meet you, Miss Cusack," he said. "To what do we owe the pleasure of your company?"

"Holmes, would you please – "

"Of course. Where are my manners? Miss Catherine Cusack, this is my friend and colleague, Dr. John Watson. Upon what errand has the Countess sent you? I can tell from your demeanor that it is a pressing one."

"Countess?" I asked.

"The Countess of Morcar, Watson. Don't you remember the business of the blue carbuncle back in December? Miss Cusack is the Countess's waiting maid." He raised an eyebrow. "I'm surprised that you've still retained your position, however, after the events related to the loss and recovery of the jewel."

The girl looked at him curiously, trying to see just how much he might know regarding her connection with the jewel's theft. However, Holmes, who had promised not to reveal what he had learned about the true thief's identity, apparently chose not to educate her on his conclusions – and neither did he ask what she might know. When, after a moment, she made no comment, he said, "Have a seat, Miss Cusack. Some tea?"

She nodded and, knowing that Mrs. Hudson was away, I put a tea kettle on Holmes's Bunsen burner.

"Mr. Holmes," said the girl, "do you know the Golden Star of India?"

Holmes indicated one of the bookshelves with a nod of his head, and said, "Watson, would you mind?"

I found the relevant volume and flipped through it. "It is a rare yellow diamond from the mines at Golconda in the south of India," I read. "It was fashioned by a sultan's craftsmen to seemingly absorb all light around it, magnify it, and radiate golden rays from its many exquisite facets. It weighs about one-hundred-and-forty carats. For years, the sultan wore it on special state occasions, and it disappeared after his death. The jewel surfaced again some two-hundred years later, having somehow become the possession of one our less-noble nobles. Its value is said to be beyond measure. It cannot be insured." I closed the book, returned it to the shelf, and finished preparing the tea. After we had been served, I returned to my own chair before the fireplace.

"Are we to understand that it is currently owned by the Countess?" Holmes asked the girl.

"It is."

"And where is the jewel now?" asked Holmes.

"We don't know," said Catherine Cusack. "That's why I'm here."

"Why did the Countess send you, instead of seeking an appointment herself – either here, or by summoning us to her presence?"

"She was notified of the theft this morning, when the police and a bank manager arrived at the Hotel Cosmopolitan, where we are staying while in London. She was assured that the police have the matter in hand, but privately she isn't satisfied. She doesn't want to excite any attention by inviting you to travel to her, and of course she . . . she wouldn't visit here." She had the good grace to appear embarrassed at this statement.

Holmes, his legs crossed at the ankles, pressed his fingertips together, and said, "Pray tell me what happened, and do not omit any details."

"As you know," said Miss Cusack, setting aside her teacup, "the Countess is a connoisseur of jewelry. Her most valuable possessions are held in the vaults of the Cox and Company Bank. Sometime during the night, someone has robbed the bank and taken the contents of the Countess's safety deposit box. And now, sir, you know as much as I do."

"Did the thieves disturb more than one box?"

"I do not know."

"And you say that the police visited you this morning?"

"Inspector Lestrade is the gentleman on the case, I believe."

"That should ease everyone's mind," said Holmes, an amused twinkle in his eye. "I'm surprised that we haven't heard from the good inspector by now."

No sooner had Holmes uttered those words than we heard the doorbell. Within moments I had admitted Lestrade.

"I see that Miss Cusack has told you of my errand," said he upon entering the sitting room.

"But I haven't heard the details from your perspective, Lestrade. What do you know so far?"

"Precious little, I'm afraid. Last night, someone somehow got past a time lock, and then a massive vault door, using the combination, which no single bank officer has in its entirety. It takes two to open the vault, and once inside, the safety deposit boxes are kept in a chamber behind locked bars."

"Besides the Countess's jewels, was anything else taken?" I asked, somewhat concerned. The Countess had chosen the very bank that I also use. I had a slight fear that my own valuables, in the form of highly sensitive manuscripts and evidence related to a number of Holmes's cases, and stored in a tin dispatch box from my army days, might have been violated.

"Yes," replied the inspector. "The thieves pried open several of the boxes. They took cash and jewelry."

"I take it you've been talking to jewelers and known fences."

"Thus far," Lestrade said, "no one has noticed anything unusual. But it may be too soon for anything to show up."

"Well, Watson," said Holmes, abruptly standing. "Do you fancy a visit to Cox and Company?"

I nodded. Outside, we sent Miss Cusack on her way back to the Countess to inform her that Holmes had taken the case. Then, along with Lestrade, Holmes and I hired a growler and were soon on our way to Charing Cross.

The bank manager, a slight and nervous man by the name of David McTavish, greeted us. From a distance, he looked more like an adolescent boy than a grown man, except for his moustache. He couldn't stop himself from wringing his hands. He wore a suit as black as his hair, and a somber gray tie held in place by a stickpin. But for his manner, I should have thought he was an undertaker.

"I'll be ruined over this," he said after we exchanged introductions. "This is the first such incident in our history, and it had to happen under my stewardship. I'll never work again."

"Come now, Mr. McTavish," said Holmes. "This can hardly be your fault. You didn't leave the vault unlocked, did you?"

"Of course not!" he barked. "We use a time lock. No one can get in between the hours of six p.m. and seven a.m. And once inside, opening the vault door requires both myself and my assistant manager, Cornell Huston, to provide our unique halves of the combination. Mr. Huston has one half and I the other. Neither one of us knows the other's combination."

"Who discovered the crime?"

"I did, when Mr. Huston and I opened the vault this morning."

"Did either of you notice anything unusual?"

"Immediately. We saw that the safety deposit room had been breached. We ran right in."

"Like curious buffalo, no doubt. I'll do what I can. Have you a key to the safety deposit room, Mr. McTavish?"

The manager did, and handed it him. Then he led us down and into the vaults, whereupon Holmes set to work. He went to the chamber, unlocked the door, and examined the lock carefully. Beyond the bars, we could see that the thieves had apparently used crude tools to get into the boxes, five or six of them, which lay bent and scattered on the floor. Holmes pored over every inch of the vault, muttering and measuring. I noticed a slight aroma of cigar hanging in the air, as if the thieves had felt that they had all the time in the world. Holmes examined the dust and dirt, pausing to scrape some into a small envelope. The moved along the drawers which held the safety deposit boxes and ran his sensitive fingers along the walls. He then gave the time lock mechanism at the entrance to the vault particularly close scrutiny. Finally, after thirty minutes' time, he emerged.

"Well?" both Lestrade and McTavish ejaculated.

"Does anyone in your employ smoke Cuban cigars?" Holmes asked. "There is a quantity of said ash near the section where the boxes were opened. If nothing else, our culprit has expensive tastes."

"That's all you have?" McTavish cried.

"We are looking for a single thief," Holmes said. "In height, I should say no taller than yourself, Lestrade. He has dark brown hair, recently cut. He carried his booty in a large carpet bag. He most certainly knows this particular bank extremely well. Tell me, Mr. McTavish, have you encountered anyone who has suddenly come into a lot of money?"

McTavish shook his head.

"Do you trust your guards?"

"They are trusted men, yes. But we don't staff the bank overnight."

"You might want to ponder that. You'll be relieved to know, Watson, that the thief did not deem your dispatch box worthy. He apparently limited himself to items which can't be traced easily." Holmes then turned said, "Might I ask all of you to wait here for five minutes? There is something which I want to test."

Without waiting for a response, he turned and left the vaults. We waited, with McTavish becoming more impatient as the time passed. However, as promised, Holmes was back in five minutes, a gleam in his eyes.

"Have you a theory, Mr. Holmes?" asked Lestrade.

"I have several, all of which fit our meagre facts. In your shoes, I would visit the bank's wealthiest customers, especially those who have jewelry collections. It is entirely possible that whoever did this was hired by such an individual."

"Could you provide a list?" Lestrade asked McTavish.

"I'll set Huston to it."

"Where is he?" Holmes asked.

"He is at a meeting in the City concerning bank business. He won't be back before two o'clock."

"Then I'll return about that time," said Lestrade. "Time to knock on some doors. I assure you, Mr. Holmes, good old-fashioned policing will make short work of this. Those jewels will surface somewhere. What about you?" he asked. "What is the next step?"

"Lunch. I feel a mite peckish." And with that, he and I made our way outside and to a nearby corner pub, where we ordered sandwiches and beer.

"What do you make of it, Watson?" asked Holmes as were nearly finished with our meal..

"You know all the cracksmen. Might one of them have done it?"

"I shall be enquiring along those lines, of course."

"I should say that a bank employee is a strong possibility."

"You're doing very well, Watson. What did you glean from McTavish?"

"He struck me as being more at home in a funeral parlor than a bank. Typical functionary."

"Did you observe anything about his clothing?"

"Nothing in particular stood out."

"Watson, have I taught you nothing? In spite of the expense of his clothing, the condition shows that his wife has ceased to love him." He took a sip of beer, and then said, "I don't suppose you paid any attention to the deposit room door?"

"That's hardly my purview."

"There wasn't a mark on it. Someone used a key – another indicator that someone in the bank participated."

Seeing that we were both finished, I made as if to rise and go, but Holmes did not move.

"I'll see you in Baker Street, Watson. I have an errand to run, and a theory to test."

I returned to our rooms and spent the next several hours reading a new collection of stories by Rudyard Kipling. When Holmes returned, I said, "You're rather later than I expected."

"I've had a busy day, but an extremely productive one."

"Did you talk to Mr. Huston?"

"Ah, you suspected that was part of my plan. I did speak with him. He is an ambitious young man."

"What did he say?"

"He pays particular attention to his appearance. He is current in men's fashions, and is undoubtedly a favorite among the ladies, to judge from the lingering perfume on him. He also takes great care to maintain his physique, and he doesn't drink or smoke. Hmm," he said, dropping into his chair. "The scent of perfume keeps ringing a bell. I know I've smelled it somewhere. It is somehow a vital clue, but I can't quite put my finger on it. Now I wish you had been with me, Watson. You might have been able to enlighten me."

He lapsed into silence and, despite my entreaties for more, Holmes kept his thoughts and theories to himself. "When I am certain, my dear Watson – when I am certain!"

The next day, I ran out of cigars, and as I returned and was approaching our front door, a grinning Lestrade joined me.

"He won't get the best of me this time!" Lestrade said with a cackle. "I have one of the men involved!"

Without asking for particulars, I let Lestrade in and we went upstairs to share his news. "Capital, Lestrade," said Holmes. "Who is our burglar?"

"Someone we know very well," Lestrade said. "Roy Slade. He traffics in jewels, and sure enough, he had some of the booty in his possession. It won't be long before we have the full story from him and recover the rest."

"Well done, Inspector! Shall we share our happy news with the men of Cox and Company?"

With that, Holmes donned his frock coat and top hat and off we went with Lestrade in high spirits as he regaled us with the story of his prowess – his interview with Slade had tripped the man up. Holmes took this in good humor. Sooner or later, Lestrade was bound to crack a difficult case on his own, but I disliked the relish he was taking in his feat. One would have thought he'd never made an arrest before. In that moment, I realized just how jealous he sometimes was of my friend's spectacular abilities.

Lestrade's glee continued in McTavish's office, where he told the manager and his assistant, Cornell Huston, how he had found some of the jewels in the possession of the known fence. McTavish exhaled a sigh of relief. "Are you certain, Inspector?" he asked, clearly pleased. "You have the man?"

Lestrade nodded and said, "He is in the nick even as we speak. Sooner or later, he will talk, and we'll find the rest of the loot – and who stole it as well!"

At that moment, Holmes reached into his pocket and produced an exquisitely cut yellow stone. "Did you think to ask him about this, Inspector?"

Lestrade's jaw fell to the floor, and Huston blushed a rich hue of scarlet. "That's imposs – " the inspector blurted.

McTavish looked at Holmes and asked, "The Golden Star of India! Where – ? How did you recover it?"

"There is your mastermind, Lestrade." He nodded toward the younger man, who was moving toward the door. "Cornell Huston."

The assistant froze, not knowing whether to stay or flee. Then he stammered, trying to deny the accusation, but he was so flustered that he quickly confessed. "Mr. McTavish!" he cried, turning to the bank manager. "I am so sorry!"

"But wait, Huston," said Holmes. "You mustn't simply confess to *this* crime. Why don't you also tell us about your partner? And also the other person who led you to this mess . . . ."

"Mr. Holmes!" sobbed the young man. "I can't do that."

"But it would be better coming from your lips."

Huston stepped to a sideboard and poured himself a glass of water. Then, casting a guilty glance toward his superior with defeat in his voice, he said, "It's . . . Adelaide."

"My wife?" barked McTavish. "I knew it! I just didn't know who!"

Holmes gave a slight smile as Lestrade studied the floor. He had the air of a small child who has had his candy taken directly from his hand.

Then Holmes said, his expression becoming more serious. "I'm sorry to tell you this, Mr. McTavish, but your wife, who I've interviewed and has confessed all, was plotting with this young man to run off to America. They decided that your bank's depositors should finance the trip. Do yourself a favor, Huston – give us your side of the details."

"We're in love!" Huston declared. "Adelaide is so miserable and unhappy. She came here looking for Mr. McTavish one afternoon, and she started crying. She felt trapped in a loveless and childless marriage, but you all know the laws of England. To obtain a divorce here would be almost impossible. So we . . . we thought of a plan where we could have money and freedom."

Holmes picked up the narrative.

"Mr. McTavish keeps his copy of the vault's complete combination in his desk, in case of emergency. While you waited downstairs in the vault yesterday, I came up and searched. It took me only moments to locate it. Mrs. McTavish knew it was here, and she made that information available to her lover." Turning to Huston, he said, "Would you care to name the third conspirator?"

"My brother," said Huston. "He's a locksmith."

"I hope he got more out of it than a Cuban cigar," Holmes said. Huston looked puzzled, and Holmes added, "He left traces in the vault."

"They needed more than just my combination," McTavish interjected. "There is the time lock? How did they defeat that?"

"Huston's brother was given access at an earlier date, at some time when you were otherwise occupied. He changed the timing mechanism to open last night. While Huston didn't assist in the actually robbery, he gave his brother his own vault key and identified which boxes to take – those having valuable jewels. Sadly for them, neither thought to put the empty boxes back, so that they wouldn't be noticed the next morning."

"But the Golden Star of India!" McTavish bellowed. "How did you get it back?"

Holmes turned to Lestrade and handed him the jewel.

"Lestrade, I present you with the Golden Topaz of Scotland Yard."

Lestrade took the stone, held it to the light, and then slammed the jewel to the floor, where it shattered into dust. Then he handcuffed Huston and left without a further word.

Holmes chortled for a few seconds, and then said, "I must ask your forgiveness, Mr. McTavish. I cannot resist a touch of the dramatic. I had a copy of the stone made to spark a reaction."

"How then did you discover Huston's secret?" I asked.

"When I realized where I had first encountered the perfume that I smelled on Huston while interviewing him. I had smelled it just that morning." He turned to the disheartened bank manager. "Mr. McTavish, does your wife wear jasmine?"

"She does."

"I detected it on you when we first met," Holmes said, lighting a cigarette, "and then realized later that it was on Mr. Huston as well. Everything fell into place once I realized that. She was wearing it when I interviewed her. You wouldn't notice the scent yourself, of course, and therefore didn't notice it on your assistant."

"Do you know where the jewels are?"

"I'm afraid that we'll have to obtain that information from Mr. Huston. The Countess will be disappointed that the Golden Star is still unrecovered, but I believe that we'll track it down quickly. In fact, Huston may have even brought the rest of the jewels back here, you know, after selling a few of them to Roy Slade. See if anyone, perhaps matching the description of Mr. Huston's brother, has opened a new safety deposit account lately."

"I can't thank you enough!"

"You're perfectly welcome, Mr. McTavish, though you may not be so grateful when you receive my bill. Come, Watson. Some most excellent beer is waiting for us at the corner pub."

The Mystery of the
Patient Fisherman
by Jim French

T*his script has never been published in text form, and was initially performed as a radio drama on October 27, 2002. The broadcast was Episode No. 32 of* The Further Adventures of Sherlock Holmes, *one of the recurring series featured on the nationally syndicated* Imagination Theatre. *Founded by Jim French, the company produced over one-thousand multi-series episodes, including one-hundred-twenty-eight Sherlock Holmes pastiches – along with later "bonus" episodes. In addition, Imagination Theatre also recorded the entire Holmes Canon, featured as* The Classic Adventures of Sherlock Holmes, *the only version with all episodes to have been written by the same writer, Matthew J. Elliott, and with the same two actors, John Patrick Lowrie and Lawrence Albert, portraying Holmes and Watson, respectively. Mr. French passed away at the age of eighty-nine on December 20th, 2017.*

This script is protected by copyright.

CHARACTERS

- SHERLOCK HOLMES
- DR. JOHN H. WATSON
- MRS. HUDSON
- HENRY MONCRIEF
- MRS. AMHURST
- HASWELL
- MAN IN THE STREET
- OLD WOMAN IN THE STREET
- THE FISHERMAN

SOUND EFFECT: OPENING – BIG BEN

ANNOUNCER: *The Further Adventures of Sherlock Holmes*

MUSIC: *DANSE MACABRE* UP AND UNDER

WATSON: My name is Doctor John H. Watson, the associate and close confidante of that most illustrious detective of the nineteenth century,

333

Mr. Sherlock Holmes. You will be aware through my descriptions of his procedures, that Holmes – though he possessed no more than the usual five senses given to us all – had learnt to so attune himself to the use of those senses, that he seemed to possess a sixth sense – which, to the consternation of the regular police, gave him powers of deduction that seemed to border on the supernatural. (Holmes, of course, heatedly denied that.) But sometimes, he knew what was going to happen before it happened . . . .

MUSIC: SEGUE TO HOLMES VIOLIN, SOFTLY IN BACKGROUND

SOUND EFFECT: A LOW FIRE SNAPS OCCASIONALLY. HORSE TRAFFIC ON WET STREET IN BACKGROUND

WATSON: I had returned to my old quarters in Baker Street following the death of my dear wife Constance. I'd given up my medical practice, although it would have been beneficial for me, as well as those in need of my services, if I had busied myself treating patients instead of grieving alone. But as it happened, Sherlock Holmes came to my rescue by asking for my assistance in several cases, one of which was the mystery I'm about to relate. Holmes had been playing his Stradivarius by the window as he watched the rain stream down one dark afternoon, when the pensive mood was interrupted by the doorbell . . . .

SOUND EFFECT: DOORBELL RINGS. VIOLIN STOPS

WATSON: Ah, what a pity.

HOLMES: Hmm. Here, take the Strad and the bow, will you Watson, and put them on my bed.

WATSON: Certainly.

SOUND EFFECT: HUSHED STEPS (UNDER)

HOLMES: (OFF) And while you're in there, bring me my waterproof, will you?

WATSON: (UP) Are you going out?

HOLMES: (OFF) Very likely.

334

WATSON: Hmm. Well then, I'll get mine too.

SOUND EFFECT: WATSON OPENS CLOSET, REMOVES WATERPROOF, CLOSES CLOSET DOOR. HE WALKS BACK INTO SITTING ROOM AND PUTS THE WATERPROOFS DOWN ON A CHAIR

WATSON: (NARRATING DURING ABOVE) I laid the priceless violin on his un-made bed and fetched his rain slicker and my own, while Holmes went round the sitting room turning up the gas lamps.

HOLMES: (OFF, MOVING ON) Now we should be ready to have a good look at our caller, who is obviously here on some urgent mission, by all appearances.

SOUND EFFECT: A MAN'S TAP ON THE DOOR

WATSON: I'll get it.

SOUND EFFECT: DOOR OPENS

WATSON: Yes, Mrs. Hudson?

MRS. HUDSON: A gentleman to see Mr. Holmes. He says his name is Moncrief. He says it's urgent.

HOLMES: (OFF) Show him in, Mrs. Hudson.

MRS. HUDSON: Go right in, sir.

MONCRIEF: (SLIGHTLY OUT OF BREATH) Thank you so much.

SOUND EFFECT: TWO STEPS ON RUG

MRS. HUDSON: Will you be wanting anything, Mr. Holmes? Doctor?

WATSON: No, I think not.

MRS. HUDSON: Very good, gentlemen.

SOUND EFFECT: DOOR CLOSES

MONCRIEF: Then I am addressing Mr. Sherlock Holmes?

HOLMES: At your service. And this is my friend Doctor Watson.

MONCRIEF: How do you do. My name is Henry Moncrief. I apologize if this is an inconvenient time. I'd have waited till morning, but I've decided I can't live another hour without your help!

HOLMES: Which would explain why you had your driver racing up Marylebone High Street and cutting west to get here.

MONCRIEF: How would you know that?

HOLMES: Oh, by the simplest observation. Your hired coach is a Culligan brougham – the style used only by Marble Arch Livery. You've only just rented it because it isn't yet splashed with much soil from the street. And the fastest route from Marble Arch to our address would of course be by way of the High Street – the only street where a gallop would be possible at this busy hour – thereby saving several minutes by avoiding the Baker Street shopping district. And the poor horse that pulled you here was clearly not accustomed to being driven that hard. But now, why the haste?

MONCRIEF: Mr. Holmes, you take my breath away! You're as clever as they say you are! Let me explain why I sought you out.

HOLMES: Please.

MONCRIEF: But you must promise that you won't dismiss me as a raving lunatic!

HOLMES: I won't dismiss you at all. Please go on.

MONCRIEF: Well I'm being tormented. Followed. Night and day.

HOLMES: Threatened?

MONCRIEF: Not in words, he never speaks. Do you hold with . . . spiritualism?

HOLMES: With spiritualism?

336

MONCRIEF: Appearances of the dead.

HOLMES: Since none of the dead has ever appeared to me, I've had no experience along those lines.

MONCRIEF: Well, neither had I. But in the strictest of confidence, I must tell you . . . Either I am being tricked, or I am being haunted. Now, I am not a type of man given over to his emotions, but in the last month I have come to believe that a man who is dead and buried is pursuing me!

HOLMES: Who would that be?

MONCRIEF: His name is Joseph Amhurst.

HOLMES: Your former business partner?

MONCRIEF: Ah! Then you read the report in the papers at the time?

HOLMES: That's how I recognized your name. He jumped from Waterloo Bridge, I believe, something over a month ago?

MONCRIEF: Yes, the fifth of September. I saw him do it. So I know he's dead. But. . . blast it all! He comes back!

HOLMES: What sort of business are you in?

MONCRIEF: My firm holds various properties to let.

HOLMES: You are a rental agent?

MONCRIEF: That's right. Moncrief and Amhurst.

HOLMES: Were you and Amhurst on good terms at the time of his death?

MONCRIEF: Actually, no. I caught him stealing from me. When I confronted him, he promised he'd pay me back, but we both knew that would be impossible – the amount he'd taken was too great. But he begged me to give him twenty-four hours before turning him in, saying he'd come up with a solution.

HOLMES: So what did you do?

MONCRIEF: I gave him his twenty-four hours. He asked me to meet him on Waterloo Bridge at midnight where he would "make everything right", as he put it.

HOLMES: And so . . . ?

MONCRIEF: I met him on the bridge. We spoke for just a minute or so. He begged my forgiveness, and then he suddenly vaulted over the rail.

HOLMES: I see.

WATSON: Uh, May I, Holmes?

HOLMES: Of course.

WATSON: Well, the drop from the bridge to the water wouldn't necessarily be fatal, and last month the Thames wasn't all that cold. We'd had quite a warm spell, if you remember, so a man could survive in the water for some little time. He could have clung to one of the piers that support the bridge, perhaps hailed a passing boat and made it to shore.

MONCRIEF: No, no, no, Doctor. When he jumped he didn't hit the water, he landed on one of those brick piers and dashed his brains out. The water police fished his body out at Blackfriars Bridge and I had the lovely job of identifying it. No, it was him.

HOLMES: And where have you been seeing this, ah . . . ghost?

MONCRIEF: Everywhere! Not an hour ago I saw him on Waterloo Bridge. That's why I finally decided to come to you.

MUSIC: UNDERCURRENT

WATSON: Sherlock Holmes is the least superstitious individual I ever knew. He dismissed the notion that Moncrief was seeing a ghost, and of course I agreed with him. But Moncrief implored us to follow him down to Waterloo Bridge to take a close look at the scene of his partner's death.

MUSIC: OUT

SOUND EFFECT: (FADE IN) CARRIAGE IN MOTION

WATSON: Holmes.

HOLMES: Yes?

WATSON: How did you know we'd have to go out? You asked for your raincoat before we even me Moncrief! Remember?

HOLMES: (WEARILY) Watson, must you make a mystery of everything I do? You'll recall that from our window I saw him dash out of his brougham and run to our door. His horse had been driven at high speed, indicating that whatever he wanted of me, time was of the essence. That being the case, I asked you for my waterproof to save a few moments if I needed to leave at once.

WATSON: (GLUM) Well. Once again you humble me with the speed of your brain.

HOLMES: Not speed alone, Watson. I was thinking ahead. If you were called to see a patient in serious distress, you'd make arrangements in advance for an ambulance to take him to hospital if it were needed, wouldn't you? It's the same thing.

WATSON: (PAUSE) What do you expect to find at Waterloo Bridge?

HOLMES: Nothing.

WATSON: Then, why –

HOLMES: Why go out in this filthy weather? I assure you we are not searching for a ghost. You would do well to bring all your knowledge of the human condition to bear on Mr. Moncrief . . . . (UP) Pull up here, driver, behind that brougham stopping at the end of the bridge, then wait for us here. We won't be long.

MUSIC: SOMBER STING

SOUND EFFECT: HEAVY CARRIAGE TRAFFIC IN THE RAIN

MONCRIEF: Here. It was just here that we had our final interview.

HOLMES: Who chose this spot on the bridge?

MONCRIEF: Amhurst. We arrived in separate cabs. As you know, they can't stop on the bridge, so we had them leave us off here and drive on, and we stood here by the rail, talking. And then all of a sudden he sprang up and plunged over the rail.

HOLMES: And how did he jump? Head first? Feet first?

MONCRIEF: I . . . I . . . I really don't remember.

HOLMES: What did you do?

MONCRIEF: I was stunned. I looked over the rail and saw his body strike the pier and bounce off into the river.

HOLMES: How could you have seen that, at midnight?

MONCRIEF: Well, we were right under this double street lamp, and there were lights along Victoria Embankment and in Somerset House there on the shore.

HOLMES: Did anyone else see it happen?

MONCRIEF: Well, I did see a fisherman down on the Embankment. He was the only other living soul who could have seen it. Then a hansom came by a minute later and I flagged it down and told the driver to find a policeman, and he must have done, because one showed up shortly afterwards.

WATSON: And this is where you think you saw Amhurst's ghost today?

MONCRIEF: Yes! He was perched on the rail, right here where we're standing, hanging onto this double lamppost . . . waiting for me to come by!

HOLMES: Were you alone?

MONCRIEF: No, I was riding in a cab with a business acquaintance.

HOLMES: And did he see the ghost as well?

MONCRIEF: I suppose not.

HOLMES: The other times. Tell me about them.

MONCRIEF: He shows up anywhere . . . everywhere. Just a glimpse of him. Haymarket. Foley Street Mews. . . just anywhere. I catch sight of him and then he's gone.

HOLMES: Have you attempted to speak to him?

MONCRIEF: (PAUSE) No. (PAUSE) You think it's all in my mind, don't you?

HOLMES: I have made no conclusion. There is much more to learn, but I prefer to learn it somewhere other than in the middle of a bridge in a driving rain. Suppose we retire to your offices.

SOUND EFFECT: RAIN SEGUE TO

MUSIC: UNDERCURRENT

WATSON: Moncrief and Amhurst did business out of a modest three-room suite on Sabine Road in Lavender Hill.

MUSIC: FADE OUT

MONCRIEF: Can I offer you some tea? Or something stronger? I'm going to have a drink.

HOLMES: Nothing for me.

WATSON: I'm a bit chilled. Perhaps a spot of tea?

MONCRIEF: I'll put the pot on. Miss Railton usually takes care of the tea but she leaves at five. I'll only be a second.

SOUND EFFECT: (BACKGROUND) POURING WATER INTO TEAKETTLE. PUT KETTLE ON A HARD SURFACE

HOLMES: (OVER SOUND EFFECT) This photograph on the wall. Two men shaking hands in front of this building. I take it the other fellow is Amhurst?

MONCRIEF: (OFF) Oh that, yes. We had that made when we went into business together.

HOLMES: He looks a bit older than you.

MONCRIEF: He was.

HOLMES: Just how did you find out that Amhurst was stealing from the company?

MONCRIEF: (OFF) Well, every night I tally the receipts against the cash on hand. Some of our tenants began to fall behind in their rents, or so Amhurst said. He told me not to worry, that he'd take stern measures to get what was owed to us. But the shortages continued for weeks and months and got worse! Finally, I went to some of our delinquent tenants myself, and that's when I found that they'd been paying Amhurst but Amhurst had been pocketing the money. (MOVING ON) Well, at first Amhurst denied it, but I persisted and finally he broke down and admitted he'd stolen the money. Over a thousand pounds in all. Said he'd had debts he had to pay. Begged me not to turn him in. But I told him we were quits. Bloody awful scene. He did have a wife to support. I suppose I could have given him another chance, but who wants to be in partnership with a crook? Anyway, that's when he asked me to give him twenty-four hours. I thought perhaps he'd return some of what he'd taken from the business. . . . Excuse me, you sure you wouldn't like a drink, gentlemen?

MUSIC: UNDERCURRENT

WATSON: It was all too clear that Henry Moncrief felt responsible for Amhurst's suicide. That would account for his seeing what he took to be the ghost. After we left Lavender Hill, Holmes and I had supper at the Holborn Restaurant, and he outlined a simple plan.

MUSIC: SEGUE TO

SOUND EFFECT: GENTEEL RESTAURANT (BACKGROUND)

HOLMES: What Moncrief wants is for me to rid him of his guilt over his partner's demise, but no one can do that for him.

WATSON: I quite agree.

HOLMES: So I'd like you to be at his side wherever he goes tomorrow, and if Moncrief sees someone he thinks is his dead partner, you'll follow him and learn his true identity. Then, when Moncrief finally admits that his mind has been playing tricks on him, it would seem to me that our job is done. What do you think?

WATSON: It seems that would be all we can do.

HOLMES: And see if you can locate Amhurst's widow, and get what you can from her. In the meantime, will make a few inquiries of my own, and then tomorrow night we'll compare notes.

MUSIC: UNDERCURRENT

WATSON: So before Moncrief opened his office the next day, I called on Mrs. Joseph Amhurst. She lived in a comfortable house in Upper Norwood.

MUSIC: OUT

MRS. AMHURST: You work with Sherlock Holmes? Is he looking into the death of my husband?

WATSON: It's not that, exactly.

MRS. AMHURST: Then what is it?

WATSON: I wonder if I might ask you to tell me everything your husband told you about the last few days of his work with Mr. Moncrief?

MRS. AMHURST: That's what the police asked. I can only tell you what I told them. He was upset about something, he wouldn't say what. I gathered it had to do with something personal between the two of them.

WATSON: But he never said what that was.

MRS. AMHURST: Joseph always protected me from his business worries. That's the kind of husband he was to me.

WATSON: Very considerate. What was his age at the time of his . . . .

MRS. AMHURST: Fifty.

WATSON: Now, forgive me, this is a very delicate thing to ask you and I hope it won't seem rude of me, but I should like to know if you and Mr. Amhurst were happy in your marriage.

MRS. AMHURST: Very happy.

WATSON: And he wasn't in any kind of financial difficulty that you know of?

MRS. AMHURST: No, Doctor Watson, he left me quite well off. Perhaps you should talk to our solicitor, Mr. Haswell in Regent Street, if you have any more questions.

SOUND EFFECT: STORMY CITY PERSPECTIVE THROUGH WINDOW

HASWELL: And the purpose of your inquiry is?

WATSON: Sherlock Holmes is looking into the Amhurst matter, Mr. Haswell.

HASWELL: Good! Maybe we'll get to the bottom of it then!

WATSON: Sir?

HASWELL: I happen to know that Scotland Yard hasn't closed the book on Joseph Amhurst's death. How did Holmes get into it?

WATSON: Well, he's . . . acting for a client. That's really all I can say.

HASWELL: Mrs. Amhurst?

WATSON: I, uh, really can't say. Mr. Holmes has established a rule that he never discloses the name of his clients.

HASWELL: Who does he think he is, a solicitor? Well, never mind. I'll tell you this much, Doctor Watson. The facts don't fit. Amhurst wasn't the suicidal type. And he certainly wasn't a thief.

WATSON: But the police haven't made any charges.

HASWELL: No. They need evidence. Let us hope your Mr. Holmes sheds some new light on this tragedy.

SOUND EFFECT: CARRIAGE IN STREET, (INTERIOR)

MONCRIEF: Keep a sharp lookout, Doctor. He could be on the sidewalk, or crossing the street . . . He could be anywhere!

WATSON: You seem to be most afraid of seeing the ghost on Waterloo Bridge, Mr. Moncrief.

MONCRIEF I suppose that's because that's the last place I saw him alive.

WATSON: Well, we're only two blocks from the bridge.

MONCRIEF: I know.

WATSON: What sort of clothes would this ghost be wearing?

MONCRIEF: Oh, he wore what any gentleman wears in business. Black coat and trousers. A black hat . . . something like this one I'm wearing.

WATSON: Amhurst seemed a bit taller than you, in that photograph.

MONCRIEF: He was. And he wore a beard and moustache. Look, you watch the street and I'll watch the sidewalk on the left.

WATSON: Right. And if either one of us spots someone you think looks like Amhurst, I'll take out after him. Although I'm not as fast as I once was. When I was in the army, I –

MONCRIEF: Look! There! I think that's him! The tall man! Standing in the crowd!

WATSON: I see him! Driver, stop the cab!

WATSON: Stay there!

SOUND EFFECT: WATSON TROTS ON STREET

WATSON: (OUT OF BREATH, TO HIMSELF) Wait! Where is he? Where'd he go?

SOUND EFFECT: STEPS STOP

WATSON: I don't see him! (UP) Excuse me . . . did you see a tall man in black? He was just here on the curb . . . .

MAN: I didn't see no one.

WATSON: Madam! Pardon me! Did you see where that tall man went? He was standing right here

OLD WOMAN: What are you talking about? I didn't see anyone.

WATSON: I see. Thank you. Sorry.

SOUND EFFECT: WATSON WALKS BACK TO THE CAB, GETS IN

WATSON: (EXERTION AS HE GETS IN AND SITS DOWN) I'm sorry. I lost him.

MONCRIEF: He disappeared, didn't he? Just like he always does! But now at least you've seen him! You know he's real! (UP) All right, driver.

SOUND EFFECT: CAB STARTS UP AGAIN

WATSON: He could have gone into one of those doors.

MONCRIEF: How does he know where I'll be? That's what I want to know! If it's a living person, how does he know how to find me? But if it's a ghost. . . I'll never be rid of him!

346

WATSON: Mr. Moncrief, I will stake my career in medicine and my years investigating crime on one thing: There is no such thing as a ghost! Your mind is playing tricks on you.

MONCRIEF: You think I'm crazy, don't you? . . . Well, maybe I am. He's driven me to it! I don't know how much longer I can go on.

WATSON: Are you married, Mr. Moncrief?

MONCRIEF: No! I was. She left me. It's been years. No woman will have me! It's all right. I'm happier by myself.

WATSON: Whom do you talk to? Whom have you told about seeing your ghost?

MONCRIEF: No one! Not one living soul! Not one – living – soul.

WATSON: We're onto Waterloo Bridge now.

MONCRIEF: I'm not going to look! I'm going to shut my eyes!

WATSON: Please, Mr. Moncrief –

MONCRIEF: Yes! I should have done this before! I won't open my eyes until we're off the bridge! Tell me when we're off the bridge, Doctor Watson!

WATSON: Really. Now, I'm going to write a prescription for some medicine I want you to take that will ease your anxiety. When we're through collecting rents today, I want you to stop by a chemist's and have him –

MONCRIEF: (PAUSE) Yes? What? What is it? Did you see something?

WATSON: (SHAKEN) Uh, it's nothing. Just, uh . . . keep your eyes closed, Mr. Moncrief. We'll be off the bridge in a minute.

MUSIC: UNDERTONE

WATSON: I didn't tell Moncrief, but just as we were passing the center of Waterloo Bridge, I saw a figure dressed in black, squatting on the

347

rail, hanging onto the double lamp post . . . in the same spot where Amhurst had jumped to his death! I rode with him to three addresses where he picked up his rent money, and then he dropped me off at 221b Baker Street. To my surprise, although it wasn't yet four o'clock, Holmes was there.

MUSIC: OUT

HOLMES: Ah, Watson. Did you meet the widow Amhurst?

WATSON: Yes, I did.

HOLMES: And did you chaperone Henry Moncrief on his rounds?

WATSON: Yes, I've just come back.

HOLMES: Well . . . ?

WATSON: Mrs. Amhurst says her marriage was a happy one, and her husband left her well off. She did say he seemed to have had something on his mind prior to the night of his death but he wouldn't say what it was. She referred me to her solicitor, a Mr. Haswell.

HOLMES: And did you see him?

WATSON: Yes. He doubts that Amhurst committed suicide, and he said Scotland Yard is still investigating, which I didn't know.

HOLMES: Interesting. And what else? You're saving the best for last, aren't you?

WATSON: What do you mean?

HOLMES: You have more to tell. Oh, come, Watson. I can read you like a book.

WATSON: Well, I may have seen him myself.

HOLMES: Who?

WATSON: I saw someone who vaguely fit Amhurst's description and I gave chase, but he vanished. And then, as we crossed Waterloo

348

Bridge, I saw – well, I saw someone again who fit the description. Perched on the bridge rail, right where Amhurst jumped.

HOLMES: And how did Moncrief react to that?

WATSON: He didn't see him. He had his eyes shut.

HOLMES: Too bad. Well, are you now converted to a belief in ghosts? Shall we book a séance or two?

WATSON: Don't make light of it, Holmes. I don't know what I saw, but I did see someone . . . and I know that Moncrief isn't having delusions!

HOLMES: And I agree.

WATSON: You do?

HOLMES: I've spent an informative day myself. The result of which I expect will bring this case to a conclusion tonight . . . with your help.

MUSIC: UNDERCURRENT

WATSON: Holmes then busied himself with writing materials and a concoction of foul-smelling chemicals for the next hour. Then he made up a small parcel and gave it to a delivery boy he often hired, along with a generous tip.

HOLMES: And now, what say we see if Mrs. Hudson has any of that mutton left over. I'm ravenous, and we have work to do at midnight!

WATSON: By ten o'clock we had finished our supper, chatting about inconsequential things. Finally he suggested I get into my warmest clothes and some wading boots . . . and bring my gun.

MUSIC: OUT

HOLMES: By no later than eleven, Watson, you are to take up a position just east of the north end of Waterloo Bridge, down on the Victoria Embankment in front of Somerset House. Conceal yourself and keep watch.

349

WATSON: Keep watch? For what?

HOLMES: A solitary fisherman.

WATSON: At that hour?

HOLMES: You don't know what he's fishing for.

MUSIC: MYSTERIOUS UNDERCURRENT

WATSON: And so, at twenty-minutes-to-eleven, I left Holmes and took a cab down through Bloomsbury to Waterloo Bridge. Fog was rolling down the Thames, forming haloes of light round the streetlamps. I found a nesting place beneath the stonework at the end of the bridge, and settled in to wait for – I didn't know what. Fifteen minutes later, a fisherman lumbered down to the Embankment. He carried a wicker creel and a jointed fishing pole, which he patiently assembled. Then he dropped his line in the water and sat on the edge of the seawall. He was an older man, wearing a hood over his head. In a few minutes, another man walked down from the road toward the fisherman, approaching from the back. I crept out of my hiding place and followed him. The fog was wafting up from the river. Then, the newcomer spoke.

SOUND EFFECT: RIVERBANK SOUNDS

MONCRIEF: Well, a boy delivered your putrid note and I'm here.

FISHERMAN: I see you are, Henry. My apologies for the smell. Everything I touch smells that way . . . now.

MONCRIEF: I've hired Sherlock Holmes. If you're real, he'll get you.

FISHERMAN: Even Sherlock Holmes can't help you now.

MONCRIEF: You . . . your voice doesn't sound the same.

FISHERMAN: Being dead changes one, Henry. You'll find that out.

MONCRIEF: I don't believe you! Let me see your face!

FISHERMAN: You don't want to see my face, Henry. There's not much left of it after what you did.

MONCRIEF: You left me no choice! You were going to report me!

FISHERMAN: So you went from thievery . . . to murder.

MONCRIEF: What do you want?

FISHERMAN: I want to hear your confession. It may help save your soul – if you have one.

MONCRIEF: And then you'll let me alone? Say you'll let me alone!

FISHERMAN: You won't ever see me again.

MONCRIEF: All right! I stole from the company! I stole your half of the earnings! And then . . . when you found me out . . . .

FISHERMAN: Yes?

MONCRIEF: . . . . I lured you out here to the bridge and . . . and I smashed your head with a hammer and pushed you into the river! There! I've confessed! Now let me go!

HOLMES: (NATURAL VOICE) I think not. (CALLING OUT) Watson! Train your gun on him!

MONCRIEF: Sherlock Holmes! You! You tricked me!

HOLMES: Along with six Scotland Yard policemen made up to look like your victim. Ah. And here they come now.

SOUND EFFECT: SCOTLAND YARD MEN ENTER

HOLMES: You see, Watson, I learned that Scotland Yard had been laying their own trap for Moncrief, stationing men along his usual routes through London, dressed as Amhurst had dressed.

WATSON: And your plan to force Moncrief to admit his guilt was the final touch.

HOLMES: Yes, but you and I will no doubt be called as witnesses for the Crown, and Moncrief s defense will surely be the insanity plea.

WATSON: But if he *was* insane, it was his own crime that had driven him mad.

HOLMES: Yes, Watson. But either way, a grim lesson to those who would commit murder: The evil that men do lives on – after the deed.

MUSIC: *DANSE MACABRE* UP AND UNDER

WATSON: And this is Doctor John H. Watson. I'll have another Sherlock Holmes adventure to tell you . . . *when next we meet!*

MUSIC: UP AND OUT

Sherlock Holmes in Bedlam
by David Friend

I had never visited Bedlam before that windswept night and, as I made my way unsurely through the tall iron gates, I hoped I would never have to do so again. The clouds which covered me were grim and gun-smoked, the sputtering rain had sluiced my skin, despite my Norfolk jacket, and I was eager for shelter – though not, I dearly add, whatever else the wretched place had in store for me.

Tales had been told of the infamous mental hospital which I did not care to recall. Stories of starving, naked men chained to walls, tortured beyond endurance. And of Bryan Crowther, butcher and chief surgeon, who inhabited the morgue and dissected the brains of dead patients in an effort to discover the secrets of insanity.

I flatter myself to think that after a short but shameless military career in Afghanistan and, not least, the many remarkable adventures alongside my famous friend which had so often jangled the nerves and thrilled the soul, I had been left with a constitution which was not easily influenced. Nonetheless, a building of such legend lent me considerable pause.

The iron door of Bethlem Royal Hospital was tall and imposing and seemed to have been closed forever. I noticed a flickering of a lantern above, its thin sharp shadows stretching out as though trying to reach the palisade circumvallating the yard and escape. With a grim purpose, I balled my hand into a fist and thumped a couple of hollow beats against the door.

At first, nothing happened.

I had decided no answer was forthcoming, and I might as well leave, when a rectangular peephole slid across and a pair of wide, curious eyes peered without.

I was momentarily discomforted – they were those sort of eyes – but tried to summon a calm and composed demeanour not ordinarily associated with a man splattered with mud and rainwater.

"I'm Dr. John Watson," I said.

The peephole snapped closed and, for a moment, I considered myself rebuffed. Then a small door whined open and I stepped cautiously inside.

A short, plump man with sideburns and a mess of ginger hair watched me keenly. There was bare ground beneath my feet and a wide yard ahead of me. Two doors were on either side – leading, I supposed, to opposite

353

wings of the hospital. The place was somehow colder than it had been outside and I couldn't help but shiver.

"You scared?" said the guard, without smiling.

I shook my head, but didn't even manage to convince myself. "Just cold."

It seemed he had not heard me. "Lots of people get scared here," he said teasingly.

"I am here to see a patient," I said with dignity.

He fished a piece of paper from his pocket and studied it suspiciously. "What's his name?" he asked. He seemed to be testing me.

"Sherlock Holmes."

The guard nodded. "You'll find Mr. Grout around, I shouldn't wonder."

I frowned. "You mean *Doctor*, surely?"

The guard smiled. It wasn't pleasant, though this had nothing to do with the few yellowed, crooked teeth. "There ain't many doctors here," he said. "Not . . . proper ones."

He pointed to the door, through which I found a cavernous, dimly lit corridor with rising damp crawling up the walls. It was difficult to properly recognize the smell, but it reached the back of the throat and wouldn't leave. Most rooms, I quickly found, were unfurnished, and what little wallpaper there was had long since begun to peel. I glimpsed a couple of vermin scurrying past and winced. It reminded me of a castle in an Ann Radcliffe novel.

I walked cautiously through the darkness, my footsteps echoing into the gloom. There was another sound too. Dimly, in the distance. Someone, somewhere, was moaning. As I moved nearer, it become clearer and turned into a throaty wail of distress. In the army, I had observed strange episodes of hysteria which had seemed quite natural in the devil's playground of dirt and death. But here, in the stillness of the night, where even whispers were forbidden, it was alien and unsettling.

Moving swiftly and without sound, I passed around the corner and into the first room that I reached. I still do not know if this was fortunate or not, but I found myself in a place of near total darkness. The air within was close and had the putrid smell of rotten cabbages. By virtue of what little light there was behind me, my eyes gradually adjusted, strange blurs thickened into three dimensions, and I could finally see something.

The reader may recall, in my chronicle of the Neville St Clair case, the night in which I ventured into an opium den to retrieve the husband of my wife's friend. This was not an altogether dissimilar experience. With no little lament, I can only describe the people I now saw as human wreckage. They were all men, chained to the walls, with sallow faces, ragged clothes, and no energy. With such darkness, it was as though they had been smuggled through a backdoor into Hell itself. Despite the singular appearance of these men, I knew it was I who stood apart, for I was the intruder. They may even have feared me. I certainly feared them. Then, in the corner, there was someone of far greater significance. A cadaverous figure, stretched out on a pile of dirty rags, his head tipped back towards the ceiling as though he had left this world and was staring sombrely into the next.

"Holmes," I said, kneeling down beside him. "It seems so foolish to ask how you are."

His face creased with cynical amusement. "And yet you will do so anyway," he said. "How was your trip?"

The enquiry surprised me. I did not wish to waste time in speaking of my stay in Powys with an army friend, or how I had been offered a temporary post as a *locum* at a local cottage hospital. Such thoughts, which had sat so heavily during my journey home, were of no consequence now.

"Uneventful," I conceded, "though I understand the same cannot be said of yours."

My friend nodded wearily, his pale face greased with sweat. "You must hear of this, Watson. We have no time! Despite what you have been told, and how you presently behold me, I am quite sane. So, I believe, are a couple of other patients here." He gripped my forearm intently. "Something is not right!"

"Careful, Holmes," I said, gripping his shoulders and leaning him back into the rags. "You mustn't get excited. If only I had stayed in London, I could have helped you."

I watched his face recover from the first transports of earnest desperation and steely purpose. "Hear me, Watson," he begged, "for we may be interrupted. Soon after you left for Wales, I was visited by a man named Herbert Wainwright. A short, restless individual with wide and anxious eyes, he said he was a member of the Diogenes Club and had heard of me through Mycroft. It was clear at once that he was superstitious. From the window, I observed his approach and the way he would avoid cracks in the pavement. He admitted as much himself, and spoke of other ways in which he endeavoured to bring himself good fortune.

"Indeed, it was this which was troubling him. His wife had recently purchased a diamond necklace of which, he had heard, was cursed. It had been owned by a Mrs. Sybil Cuthbertson, who was said to have gone mad. It was inherited by her husband, Victor, a quiet soul and not in the least excitable. However, one afternoon at home, he took up his gun and began firing it at his housekeeper. And that is not all. A couple of days after he visited me, Wainwright himself was seated in the Diogenes when he suddenly leapt to his feet and shouted that he was on fire. Both men are now detained at this very hospital, Watson, by the same man who placed me here – Dr. Norbeck. During my investigation – "

Suddenly the door creaked open behind me and there came the rustle of movement. Our time, I knew instinctively, was over. My muscles tensed coldly and I turned to face the new arrival.

It was a short woman of late middle age with a round, pale face, a surly mouth, and a bun of grey hair. "There should be no visitors at this hour," she said in a thin and husky voice.

"I'm a doctor," I said with calm authority.

"This is your patient?" she asked, her head jutting keenly forward like a pigeon.

Already, however, I had been defeated. I may have lied to the guard outside, but I was unlikely to get so far again. "A friend," I corrected. "He was recently committed by a Harley Street man named Norbeck."

A look of grim satisfaction settled over her face. "In that case, Doctor, I shall kindly ask you to leave."

"And who might you be?" I enquired, for I was not so obsequious as to leave immediately.

"Miss Cropper. I am in charge of this hospital."

"Mr. Holmes," I said archly, "will not be here long. I trust that he will not want for anything."

From my pocket, I pulled out the latest issue of *Knowledge* and handed it to him silently. He nodded, but didn't speak.

"Good night, Doctor," she said primly, and I nodded in reply.

I felt utterly wretched for leaving my friend in such a place. With every step, I was even more the traitor. I feared that Holmes's illness might be genuine, and that he was fooling himself into believing that there was a conspiracy in order to make sense of his situation.

Back home, I clambered out of my cab and walked wearily inside. Mrs. Hudson, despite the late hour, appeared anxiously in the hallway. It was she who had told me of Holmes's incarceration and I had headed immediately without. Now, exhausted, remorseful, and not a little shocked, I recounted all that Holmes had told me. Speaking of such queer senselessness – of guilt and paranoia and night-time terror – felt all the stranger in the firelight of a comfortable sitting room. Our landlady already seemed familiar with much of what I said, however, and nodded in sorrowful confirmation.

"I should have remained here," I said ruefully. "If only I hadn't left London."

She took hold of the teapot and poured another cup. I was too distracted to drink my own. "You were not to know, Doctor," she said consolingly.

"I wish, then, that I had left him with some case or other. Was there nothing to keep him occupied while I was away? No clients to speak of at all?"

Mrs. Hudson considered. "Well, a lady named Mrs. Blundell waited upstairs until he came back, but she wanted him to find her cat and he dismissed her immediately."

"In which case, I cannot blame him," I said, remembering my friend's intolerance for trifles. "It takes more than a missing cat to hold his interest." I leant forward, over my steaming cup. "Were you alarmed, yourself, when you heard that he had made a fool of himself?"

Mrs. Hudson inclined her head to one side reflectively. "I hadn't seen him for days, at that point, but I thought he had a case at last." She poured herself more tea. "What will you do?" she asked with worry. The dear lady seemed to think I would end up going mad myself. It certainly seemed possible.

I thought obscurely of Llanwrtyd Wells and the offer that my old comrade Joseph Barrington had made. It had been an enticing one, I will admit that, with the possibility of turning into a permanent position. A small part of me resented my friend for spoiling such plans. Indeed, in view of his possible illness, I wasn't sure whether I was equipped to handle Holmes anymore, even if I did remain in London. His symptoms, whatever the reason, were always of the most extreme. Added to which, he was intolerably stubborn and, if the mood took him, was even known to decline medicine. Most often, he ignored any ailment altogether and focussed instead on the latest investigation which had so ensnared his attention.

"It is better if you sleep now, Doctor," said our landlady concernedly. "You must be most uncomfortably tired."

"Very well, Mrs. Hudson," I said and drained my tea-cup. The day, with its travels and traumas, had indeed been an exhausting one, however, and it was with relief that I retired to bed.

Sleep, it so proved, was irritatingly elusive. I could not help but think of Holmes and how he was trapped in that house of madness. I thought of the nocturnal excursion which had precipitated his removal – how he had run fearfully through the darkness of London's midnight streets from, perhaps, Grimesby Roylott and his slinking serpents or maybe even Miss Irene Adler. This did nothing for my own constitution and I had to shake off such nightmares myself.

The next day, after reading the news reports of Holmes's attack, I set off for Harley Street and the offices where Dr. Ruben Norbeck had rooms.

I had visited the building before on a different matter, and was familiar with its wide spaces, parquet floors, blue-grey walls, and Louis IV furniture. I felt rather awkward, consulting another doctor about a patient who was not my own. We do not take kindly to such interference. Dr. Norbeck, however, proved to be most reasonable – at first. He was a tall, barrel-chested man with a smooth, pale face, bright blonde hair and a neat moustache, and I was surprised to recall that we had met a few months earlier at a social event.

"I wish to speak with you in a matter concerning my friend, Mr. Sherlock Holmes."

The physician winced apologetically, but there was something slightly slow and unnatural about it, as though the gesture had been rehearsed. "I am afraid, Dr. Watson, that I am unable to oblige," he said in a brittle Swedish accent. "I have a full morning ahead of me and, as you are not a patient yourself, I must instead return to those who are."

"This will only take a moment," I said, a little too keenly. Holmes, for his flaws, was able to invoke a certain authority. "As you may be aware, Mr. Holmes and I shared rooms together until his sudden removal last week. I wonder, if he were to be discharged, whether such an arrangement would be permitted to continue – with my careful ministration, of course."

The question hung, unanswered, for a few moments and I wondered earnestly whether he would afford it one at all. Then Norbeck said, "Unfortunately not, Doctor."

This did not ring true. Most physicians – though by no means all – are rather good at conveying bad news, but there was no such effort from the Swede. "I have little doubt, upon meeting Mr. Holmes and then witnessing the episode when he departed here, that he requires some considerable specialist treatment. You are, naturally, entitled to visit him on particular days, but I cannot allow for anything else."

I could not accept this. "Holmes believes that he is sane," I said curtly, "and I concur."

"Your loyalty is commendable, Doctor."

I wanted to mention that he was Holmes's physician only by chance – that my friend's attack had occurred just after leaving Norbeck's office, leading to his committal by this same doctor. Instead, I said, "I also believe that two other patients there are sane as well. Mr. Victor Cuthbertson and Mr. Herbert Wainwright."

"That is unfortunate," said the doctor, "because both men, I can assure you, are mentally unfit. It is all quite tragic." And, with an air of finality, he lifted a hand for me to shake. I did so mechanically. "Excuse

358

me," he nodded. Briskly, he turned into his consulting room and left me stranded, stunned, in the corridor.

Perhaps it was arrogance on my part, but I did not expect such a request to be denied, nor for our meeting to end so abruptly. Norbeck, it was obvious, believed that he was right in sectioning Holmes. I knew, however, that I could not return to my friend without news of some kind. Until this point, I had only been interested in Holmes's health, but my mind now turned to his current preoccupation. With a swift glance to check that no one else was around, I decided to indulge my friend and investigate.

The notion of handling a case on my own was, admittedly, a most attractive one. I flatter myself to think that, over the years of our association, I have been of some use to Holmes, not only in offering myself as a listening post, but also as an agent he could dispatch to uncover information. I had acted alone for much of the spectral hound case – and, I believe, conducted myself rather well – though I occasionally came up short.

During my time accompanying Holmes on his investigations, there have been occasions in which he hasn't adhered to conventional laws as meticulously as I would have liked. He broke into another man's property three times, and once I even refused, though I later acquiesced. I understand that he only ever did this as he believed that in doing so he could prevent something far worse from occurring. For this same reason, I took it upon myself to make a search without any due consent. I knew from experience that medical records are usually kept in filing cabinets, and these tend to be shunted off into a backroom somewhere and out of the way. It was, then, with a quickening pulse that I tripped down the hallway and followed a line of doors to the end.

Sneaking inside, I found the cabinets stocked with such records and began rummaging through them assiduously. It felt dangerous, deceitful, and wickedly uncouth, and I was so distracted with the clandestine nature of my investigation that I struggled to concentrate on the task at hand. Within moments, however, I had located the papers pertaining to Mr. Herbert Wainwright and read the notes that Norbeck had made. Apparently, Wainwright's malady had first manifested itself at the Diogenes. At first, there was little more information, other than the crisp diagnosis that he was suffering from a psychosis of some sort. There was nothing about Holmes in the records whatsoever, and it Victor Cuthbertson's file simply had a list of his appointments and the routine prescriptions that had been provided to him, befitting a man of his age.

An hour later, I found myself at Cuthbertson's villa in Richmond. It rested on fifteen acres, with patterned bricks, bargeboards, and sliding sash windows. The interiors were just as striking, with oak herringbone parquet floors and kimono wallpaper, while a portrait from Cézanne's dark period stood above an imitation Adam fireplace. Suitably impressed, I folded into an armchair and accepted a cup of tea from the housekeeper. Mrs. Cornford was short and elderly, with an elfish face and an apparent eagerness to oblige most any whim.

"What sort of person, in your view, is Mr. Cuthbertson?" I asked her, deciding to focus on the man himself.

Mrs. Cornford considered. "A gentle man. Very quiet. Owned a brewery, till he retired. Mainly, however, he was preoccupied with birds. A member of the British Ornithologists' Union, don't you know."

"I didn't. And have you worked for him long?"

"Nearly seventeen years," she said reminiscently, "and never in that time had he seemed odd in any way. He seldom ever spoke." Her eyes glittered. "But then, of course, came the evening that changed everything."

"Indeed?" I said, replacing my cup carefully upon the saucer. "I must confess, Mrs. Cornford, that I am quite ignorant of what actually transpired."

The old lady swallowed. She did not want to dwell, it seemed, on such a troubling incident again. I tended towards tact, but I knew that Holmes would have remained. My friend possesses a kind and polite nature but, nonetheless, will not be deterred from obtaining the relevant facts in any unsettling matter.

"Mr. Cuthbertson was relaxing with a book," she recounted, "as he so regularly did. Henry G. Vennor's *Our Birds of Prey*, I seem to recall. As I was walking upstairs, on my way to deliver to him his afternoon tea, I heard a cry."

I tried to feign a certain civilised detachment, of which Holmes, I am sure, would have been most proud. "What was the matter with him?"

"I could not say," said Mrs. Cornford. "I called up to him to enquire, but he began shouting warnings. 'Keep back!' he said. 'Don't come near!' It was alarming, to say the least."

"I can imagine," I said. The old lady was wincing uncomfortably at the memory, and I was sympathetic.

"Of even more concern," she continued, having gathered her composure, "was what happened next. I was higher on the stair, about to walk further on, when two loud cracks cut savagely through the air."

I felt myself tense. "He had a gun?" I said.

"Oh yes, and he was firing it wildly and without reason." She shook her head, her brow folded in confusion, still unable to comprehend her employer's sudden and quite dangerous behaviour. "I was scared witless," she recalled, and there was a hardness in her voice which bespoke of an unexpected anger.

360

"I would imagine you were," I said, not unkindly.

"The bullets went straight through the wall. It was a most awful noise. Deafening, in fact. Like a war was going on in the house."

"What did you do?"

"Well, what could I do, Doctor?" she said rather harshly. Sometimes, I regret asking certain questions. Holmes is much more at ease with such enquiries. "I threw my hands up in the air – though it was more out of panic than rage – and clattered down the stairs again." Mrs. Cornford pressed a hand against her chest as though the fear and panic was coming back to her. "I fled to our neighbour, Mrs. Hibbert, whose husband went and fetched a constable."

"I see," I said, and started to reach out a hand to comfort her, but decided against it. Mrs. Cornford, I could see, was a formidable lady who would not take kindly to such gestures.

"And I did not return to the house for days," she added bitterly, her eyes now closed. "For weeks thereafter, I would dream of such noises and scare myself awake again."

"Has this changed your opinion of Mr. Cuthbertson?" I asked gently.

Even this question, however, was met with fierce intolerance. "I am angry with him, if that is what you mean."

"Did you consider his mental state, perhaps, ironic? Considering, I mean, what happened to his wife."

The housekeeper's face hardened. "Mrs. Cuthbertson's condition was unfortunate," she said, "and most incurable."

"She owned a necklace, I understand. A diamond necklace."

"Indeed," Mrs. Cornford nodded. She seemed ready to say something else, but then came the sound of the door. Her brow darkened. "That will be Miss Bennett. Mr. Cuthbertson's only cousin, who is staying here since Mr. Cuthbertson's been in hospital."

I rose from my chair as another lady entered the room.

Eleanor Bennett was a tall woman of early middle age, dressed in a large bustle, with a thin, oblong face of a darkened cast, wavy brown hair, and wide, questioning eyes which leant her appearance a somewhat cynical, sophisticated beauty.

"Good morning," I said. "My name is Dr. Watson. I'm an associate of Mr. Sherlock Holmes." I enunciated these last three words so theatrically it was as though I were demonstrating their pronunciation. Mentioning my friend was, I realise now, a somewhat curious thing to do. I wanted to undertake an investigation myself, after all, without involving Holmes. Yet, apparently I had no qualms about invoking his name if it expedited my progress.

The lady's face was without animation. "Good morning," she said flatly.

"I wonder if I could speak to you concerning your cousin. Your only one, I understand. His internment must have come as quite a shock to you."

Miss Bennett's shoulders relaxed and she considered the remark with a cool detachment. "I don't know him well, Doctor. I've only recently returned from America, where I have been living for years, and only met him briefly out of curiosity. Please, sit down."

I did so. "You . . . got on well?" I asked as Mrs. Cornford removed herself.

"Indeed," said Eleanor Bennett. "He was quite a sweet man. He spoke mostly of birds, something of which I know very little."

"Yes, I understand that is rather a hobby of his. I also hear that you have taken possession of this house."

"Only temporarily," she said, without surprise. "I'm told that my cousin won't be returning, and it wouldn't feel right, living here myself, so it will be sold soon after repairs are made. That is, frankly, costlier than I expected, so I am selling some of Mr. Cuthbertson's antiques in order to pay for them."

"I see. You seem most organized, Miss Bennett."

"As a spinster, Doctor, without any considerable means, one has to be."

"I gather your cousin owned a necklace, formerly belonging to his wife. Is that something you have sold?"

"Indeed it is."

"Quite so," I said. "In that case, maybe I can ask who bought the necklace."

The lady paused in calm remembrance. "Mrs. Henrietta Wainwright of Hillingdon," she said at last, almost reluctantly.

Having confirmed the information that I sought, I made my excuses and left, but knew just where I was bound.

The Diogenes Club was guarded from without by a lanky, sharp-featured man, the better of six foot, with an assertive jaw and the kind of dark, leathery skin which had seen much sun. He knew of my connection to one of its oldest members and let me within. Holmes and I had visited the club some months earlier, during the case of the prisoner and the linguist, and I passed the same old, slumbering men as I had on that unexpectedly stimulating occasion. I went in search of the Stranger's Room and awaited my friend's brother.

Mycroft Holmes presently appeared, his not inconsiderable stoutness pressing against the doorframe as he shuffled awkwardly through it. His eyes, as ever, were deep-set and watery grey and seemed to stare into other men's souls, while a thin, firm mouth refused to speak of what they saw there. My friend was always both frustrated and impressed with his brother. He believed Mycroft was the more intelligent, yet deplored his brother's laziness and reluctance to implement any practical effort into the problems which he so effortlessly solved.

"You have visited Sherlock," Mycroft stated.

"He doesn't consider himself ill," I countered. "Why do you suppose that is?"

As Holmes's sibling, Mycroft's view was the nearest thing to a self-diagnosis. He raised his broad shoulders in a disconsolate shrug. "Pride, perhaps. He is not the most humble of men."

"He is convinced, also," I said, "that a couple of his fellow patients are similarly sane. Do you credit that?"

The elder Holmes paused, his brows knitted together contemplatively. "Not particularly," he confessed. "Sherlock is, it would seem, for the moment, rather delusional. It grieves me to pronounce such things, of course."

"Quite so," I agreed. "Out of loyalty, I am looking into the matter myself. Holmes gave me two names of the patients whom he believes are wrongfully incarcerated: Mr. Victor Cuthbertson and Mr. Herbert Wainwright. I know the latter suffered an episode of some sort here at the club."

Mycroft nodded without surprise. "Indeed he did, Doctor. Wainwright is a boisterously jovial man, restless in both movement and intellect. He reads omnivorously on all manner of arcane subjects and paces up and down as he does so, book aloft, as though he is unable to stop moving. Thin, also. You would not think he paused even to eat."

"Not the sort of person you usually have here," said I, remembering the voluminous supply of food on offer at the club.

"Indeed. Our other members are unsociable – it's very nearly a rule – and are fairly confounded by his energy. They are powerless against him, however, as the chap doesn't speak when he's here. As you know, silence is our standard. Iron-clad. Men have even tried to wheedle him into speech, just so he can be expelled. Hasn't worked, of course, though he is too damned cheerful to even notice the trap. In fact, the silly fool wouldn't think ill of anyone. Modest, too, despite his varied achievements."

"Oh really? And what are they?" I asked with interest.

"Well," said Mycroft, and his eyes dulled wearily with boredom, "he's an explorer, ethnologist, cartographer, translator, and Orientalist to boot. Far too much time on his hands," he added disagreeably. "Just thinking of it all makes me exhausted. And then there's the madness itself."

"Perhaps you could describe the incident," I pursued, though I could see he would have continued anyway. Mycroft, I now know, was just as intolerant as his brother.

"Well," said Mycroft dreamily, "he was sitting in his armchair – for once, quite still and staring around himself, lost in thought, as it were. But then, to everyone's surprise, he sprang to his feet and declared – with a roar which these walls have never heard – that he was on fire."

"On fire?" I said, interested.

"Indeed. Awfully embarrassing, I must say. Others tried to calm him but, but to no effect, until someone tossed a glass of port in his face. He was well again after that, but it manifested itself later, apparently, in other ways."

"How strange," I reflected. "Maybe he really is mad, and your brother is wrong."

Mycroft seemed quite taken with this idea and nodded agreeably. "This could indeed be the case," he said, and paused. "What have you done?"

"Well," I considered, and then explained by visit with Cuthbertson's cousin, Eleanor Bennett.

Mycroft's broad face stretched into a smile. "I may be able to help you," he said with some pleasure. "The lady of whom you speak has had quite an interesting life."

"Indeed?" I said, surprised.

"I remember reading of her in *The Daily News* a few months ago. Not the sort of thing one would forget. She was living in Fair Haven, Vermont, and pretending to be the Duchess of Argyll, when she was found out and deported."

Such words fell over me like a wave. "She was a fraudster?" I said with the sort of slow bemusement which often followed one of Holmes's extravagant deductions.

"More to the point," said Mycroft, "she may still be one. Are you certain that she *is* Cuthbertson's cousin? She could be playing fraudulent again."

As I made my way back out, Mycroft gestured limply towards an armchair and I supposed this was where Wainwright had been sitting when he suffered his unfortunate episode. I paused contemplatively, looking about the room. Finally, I decided to sit in the chair myself and did so for a few moments, bathed in silence, as Mycroft watched me with a bland, indulgent smile. I wondered if he expected me to give up the case, without Holmes on hand to solve it, and I wanted to prove him wrong. Therewith, I made directly for Scotland Yard and asked Inspector Gregson to make inquiries into Eleanor Bennett's identity.

I also wanted to discover more about Cuthbertson himself and, remembering that Mrs. Cornford had told me about her employer's keenness for bird-watching, I decided to visit the British Ornithologists' Union. The man to whom I wished to speak, it so followed, had more letters after his name than any I have otherwise met. Indeed, I expected to find him in a dusty old library somewhere. As it was, however, I managed to locate him in a wood towards Greyhound Hill in Hendon.

There I walked beneath a bare blue sky and a sun of stabbing brightness. At once, I came upon a man of long and narrow proportions standing by a tree, his thin and rather waxen face hidden almost fearfully behind a pair of heavy binoculars. He was, it seemed, preternaturally still and could easily have made for a perfectly fine tree himself. I sauntered over, twigs snapping underfoot, and noticed him bristle unpleasantly.

"Do you mind?" he asked, half-turning, in an agitated whisper. "We are trying to inspect a European goldfinch!"

I paused, surprised. "I beg your pardon?"

"There!" he said, and reached out a bony finger towards the edge of the woods. "We have been looking for him all afternoon."

I was not to be gainsaid. "Well, I have been looking for someone myself. Mr. Silas Goodman."

Face tensed with irritation, the young man pointed ahead, beyond the wood, and to a mound of old earth. Reaching it, I found a portly figure in tweed lying sprawled across it, his binoculars pressed patiently against a head of grey curls.

"Mr. Goodman?" I asked tentatively, and knelt down beside him. "I would like to speak to you," I said, "regarding Mr. Victor Cuthbertson of Richmond. Would that be possible?"

The old man didn't relax his attention for a moment. "What is it you want to know?" he asked, his voice hoarse and authoritative.

This, I concluded, was the best I could expect. "Firstly," I tried, "do know Mr. Cuthbertson well?"

"Oh, yes," the secretary growled in response, his jaw hanging loose in concentrated effort. "He played an important part in the Union's activities for many years and was the sort of expert that even his peers could admire."

"And what is your opinion of Mr. Cuthbertson's instability? I take it you've heard."

The man lifted his shoulders to shrug, but became distracted by a swooping starling and followed it with his binoculars. "He seemed most sensible," he managed to mutter. "Like most people, I was tremendously shocked by what happened."

"Did you know that he owned a gun?"

For once, the secretary put down his binoculars and looked at me seriously. His face was tanned, as though he migrated abroad as often as the birds which so fixated him. "Yes," he said, though he spoke with a certain reservation. "I don't think it was used much, however. In my belief, Cuthbertson did not approve of shooting – particularly birds. In fact, now I think of it . . . ." His brow creased with remembrance, his birdwatching forgotten for the moment. "Ah, I know it now."

"You do?" I said hopefully.

"One day, at his house, I noticed the gun. A Beaumont–Adams revolver, and I asked Cuthbertson about it. He said a soldier had given it him during the Great Rebellion, at which time Cuthbertson was working for the East India Company." He shook his head sorrowfully. "The carnage had quite an effect on his constitution, it seemed, as not only did Cuthbertson insist on carrying a gun which he barely understood how to use, but he also took early retirement soon after, due to nervous exhaustion." The ornithologist frowned with quizzical concern. "Are you all right, Doctor?"

I recovered, smiling politely. "Yes, Mr. Goodman. I apologise. I just remembered something, that is all. Thank you for your time."

Returning to Baker Street, I stopped and sent several telegrams. Then, ensconced in our sitting room, I sat in my armchair, and thought. *The Daily News* was draped across my lap, but I had no intention of doing anything but thinking. I wished that Holmes was investigating the matter himself. It was the sort of case that would stimulate him and keep his mind febrile and away from the needle. I thought of the diamond necklace and the fear that it had inspired within Herbert Wainwright. I thought of Victor Cuthbertson and the gunshots that had chased his housekeeper away. And I thought, stirringly, of how I would save my friend.

Over the course of the afternoon, I received a number of replies to my wires, and elaborated upon the information received by locating entries in Holmes's scrapbooks. Finally I felt that I understood.

I took a hansom to the Yard and met Inspector Gregson. From there we proceeded to a certain house in the East End, where an interview confirmed what I had already theorized. Then on to Richmond, where we continued to gain understanding of the conspiracy. By that point, I knew virtually everything that I needed to know. All that was required was more men, for I was ready for something which was, I confess, frighteningly familiar. I was ready for battle. And I knew where it was to be held.

I had visited Bedlam once before, on that windswept night when I found Holmes held as more prisoner than patient, and as I made my way determinedly through the tall iron gates, I hoped I would never have to go there again.

After a firm knock, a peephole slid back and two eyes glimmered suspiciously back.

"Scotland Yard," barked Inspector Gregson.

The door opened and the inspector's men charged inside.

We found what we sought in the operating theatre. It was dimly lit, with a surgical table in the center, in front of a wide curtain hanging from the ceiling. Miss Cropper was there by the table, facing in our direction, and I eyed the physician standing just beyond her. Lying on the table before him was an elderly man covered by a sheet. I couldn't tell if he was alive or dead.

"It is too late, Norbeck," I said quietly.

"Perhaps you should explain yourself, Dr. Watson!" said the doctor angrily.

I took a breath, patient but purposeful. What I was about to relate was partly fact and partly unverified theory, and yet I was certain that I was right. "I have learned that Eleanor Bennett is a criminal who was deported from America some months ago. She returned here, virtually penniless, and decided to ask her only living relative, Victor Cuthbertson, for a loan. He was a wealthy man, after all, who had founded a successful brewery and owned a beautiful villa in Richmond. The moment Miss Bennett saw the place, however, she resolved to take that instead. If she could inherit such a property, her money woes would be over. Unfortunately for her, Cuthbertson was in fine health and would likely live for many more years. She knew this for certain, having contrived a meeting with his physician – *you*, Dr. Ruben Norbeck."

The doctor glowered. "This is all conjecture," he complained. "You know nothing."

I did not agree and set about proving it. "You, too, Doctor, are a devious schemer," I said, and turned back to the inspector. "He knew Cuthbertson need not die for Miss Bennett to inherit the house. Instead, the old man could become, in some way, incapacitated, like Cuthbertson's wife, and maybe even be incarcerated. As his doctor, he would see to that himself."

"You may possess a certain authority, Dr. Norbeck" Gregson added, "but you cannot simply remove someone from society at will."

"You made it look properly authentic, Doctor," I added. "Earlier today, I asked some of Sherlock Holmes's associates to research your background. They quickly learned that you have been in league with Harry Stokes, the drug peddler, who – in addition to his other connections – purchases narcotics from you and sells them on the black market, with the proceeds then split between you. Mr. Stoker is now in custody, and has happily cooperated, relating to us various aspects of your plot. It wasn't wise to share so much with him, Doctor. He revealed that he was able to obtain, at your request, a hallucinogen named *uigilans somniauit* – Latin for 'waking dream' – and he passed this on to you, and so on to Miss Bennett, who has also been under arrest for several hours. She confirmed her part of the plot. After an early morning bird-watching in the local park, Cuthbertson fell asleep, as he often did, and Miss Bennett contaminated his whisky flask with the hallucinogen. This caused him to suffer, later that day, some sort of vivid hallucination, leading to his breakdown."

"And then there was Wainwright," added Gregson. "By then, you weren't content to stop with Mr. Cuthbertson."

"In order to pay you, Doctor," I continued, "Miss Bennett needed to sell something belonging to her cousin. She chose the diamond necklace that had once been worn by his wife. She sold it to Henrietta Wainwright and then handed the money that she received to you as payment. But you realized that Wainwright was also your patient, and conceived the idea of being paid twice. You slipped some of the 'waking dream' into his medications. After he was institutionalized – at your recommendation as his doctor – you then planned to steal the necklace back in the confusion.

"I've examined your patient records and determined that you wrote a prescription for him just a day before his hallucination at the Diogenes Club."

"And then," said Inspector Gregson ominously, "you went after Mr. Holmes."

"Herbert Wainwright was superstitious," I said. "He had heard of Cuthbertson's supposed madness and believed that the necklace was cursed. He asked Holmes to investigate his theory, which seemed to prove itself true when Wainwright also went mad. Somehow you were able to poison him with the same drug you'd used on Wainwright and Cuthbertson."

"Not quite," said a voice from behind the curtain. Gregson and I, as well as the constables around us, gaped in surprise as Sherlock Holmes stepped around the edge and into the light. "I visited Dr. Norbeck to question him about the fact that two of his patients had suffered mental breakdowns. He seemed most anxious that I take advantage of his offer of tea, and his relief when I appeared to drink it was almost ludicrous in its obviousness. Soon after, I appeared to evince the same symptoms as the other men. Dr. Norbeck was happy to step in, and I quickly ended up in here with them – where I needed to be in order to understand the rest of the doctor's plot."

Norbeck had initially been shocked when the gaunt figure of Holmes stepped into the light. He took a step closer to the table where the old man lay, a knife poised over the man's throat. "I'll kill him!" he growled. "I swear it!"

Holmes continued to move slowly toward him, his eyes boring into those of the doctor. Mrs. Cropper hissed and backed away.

"So far you haven't committed a capital offense," said Holmes. "If you kill Mr. Cuthbertson, as his cousin no doubt insisted, you will most surely hang."

The doctor's hand twitched, the scalpel that he held poised just inches from the old man's throat. Holmes, now only a few feet away, suddenly lunged with a speed I would have found impossible, landing a blow which caused Norbeck to stagger backwards into the nearby curtain, tugging it for support, and causing it to fall on top of him, revealing all that was hidden behind it.

It was the patients, standing and staring and blocking what little light dribbled in from the door behind them. Their faces were grim, their fingers curled into fists. They were far from the pitiful ravages that they had been before.

I felt my insides twist into a knot. I was fitter and healthier than they – surely – but the way in which they held themselves, so firm and tall, made me doubt it. There was something eerie too about their blank stares, as though they were not quite living things anymore at all. It wouldn't have surprised me to learn that they were in possession of a sort of hive mind which caused them to act together and move with a unified consciousness. All I had were my wits and strength. I hoped that Holmes had his.

My friend swept a glance over this horde of walking corpses and I noticed a flash of amusement in his eyes. He was taut and alert and I could sense his energy. I also had the vague feeling that he was just as pleased with this turn of events as I was horrified. He stretched out a leg and stepped forward. It was the slowest movement I had ever seen and I was glad of it. I didn't want these men to think we would attack. For that matter, I didn't want to think we would either.

"I freed these men in case I needed and army," said Holmes. "I may have made an error."

The patients who had been standing at the back took a few steps forward and joined those further in front. A few of them were holding onto their chains and clinking it in their hands.

"When I give the word," said Holmes to Gregson, me and the other policemen, so quiet that it was almost under his breath, "we will run for the other door. All right?"

For the only time that I could remember, he sounded like one of the sergeant-majors barking us into battle.

Then, before I could react, there was a tinkle of chains from close behind me. I made to turn, when I suddenly felt a length of cold, hard rings loop about my neck and press against the skin.

I stopped breathing.

Holmes pivoted, revealing from his rags a Webley No. 5 Express Revolver. He pointed its four-inch barrel at the patient behind me in a silent threat. The chain tightened purposefully, the hard metal digging into my neck. I began making choking noises, eyes wide in fear and fright. A thick beard brushed the back of my neck and I could feel the man's hot sour rasps against my ear. He was panting with all the breath I no longer had.

"Let him go or I shall shoot," said my friend calmly, but his words were not obeyed.

Holmes continued to stare, his mouth lipless, the revolver fixed in his firm grasp. Gregson was saying something, and the other patients surrounding us were becoming restive. I felt the chains tightening further, squeezing my larynx. I couldn't cry out, but my lungs were certainly trying. They were burning raw against my chest. I felt the heat rising uncomfortably to my face and was dimly aware that my hyoid could crack at any moment.

Holmes's eyes fixed themselves on mine. "Watson," he said, "if I fire this gun, it will be a call to arms. The place will erupt and you will need to recover quickly. The other patients are almost upon me. I can hear their steps as they slowly advance. They can see me, but I can't them, which means that I am at a disadvantage. I have the gun, so they will attack me first. I will be floored in seconds, with the gun snatched from me and most likely fired upon me too. These will be the moments in which you shall have to escape. There will be no other chance for you. Take it."

I stared stiffly back. The chain had loosened ever so slightly and I was able to rasp a reply. "I won't leave you here," I said. As a soldier, I understood the need to follow orders. As a friend, I refused.

"You must," he said. His voice was still calm, emotionless even.

The gun was cocked and he was ready. It was aimed directly at my captor.

I felt my face crease in distress. "This is madness!" I managed.

Holmes's finger tickled the trigger. "You forget," he said, and smiled weakly, "according to Dr. Norbeck, so am I."

The gun snarled, the chains round my neck suddenly slackened, and a roar went up. The men were charging. In one fluid movement, Holmes wheeled around, fired another shot, and rocked back on his heels, toppling gracefully onto the floor and out of their grasp. He fired out another round and a couple of the closest men, brutal and broad, jerked back as bullets ripped into their shoulders.

He was saving my life for the second time in as many moments.

A weight, I realised, had pushed against my back. I moved aside and the tall, hairy-faced man who had wanted to kill me seconds earlier now fell lifelessly away. I looked about me, tense and ready to recoil.

I watched as Dr. Norbeck and Miss Cropper were overwhelmed by a sea of madmen. They were bellowing with fury, their voices drowning out their own echoes. They charged forward like a battalion, nearly surrounding us. "Get away!" I yelled.

Just seconds earlier, these men had been languid and pathetic and looked as though they had not moved a muscle in months. Now, the promise of violence and excitement had them electrified.

"Police!" yelled Gregson, rallying the constables, and in spite of Holmes's instructions to run, they charged forward, truncheons flying. In moments the chaos had abruptly ceased.

In the aftermath, I examined Cuthbertson on the table, and found that he would recover. Later, I found Wainwright in a cold and dank cell. He would not be so lucky.

As I stood with a sigh, Holmes was suddenly beside me. "Thank you, Watson," he said. "I think that we should leave here now."

"I quite agree," I said, and we made our way out of that hellish chamber.

The Adventure of the
Ambulatory Cadaver
by Shane Simmons

It had been a long and miserable night by the time I came knocking on the front door of 221b, looking for answers I expected only Sherlock Holmes would be able to provide. The first hint of sun was coming up on a day so grey, it was hardly any brighter than it had been during my last few hours of confused wandering. It was a match for my mood.

Mrs. Hudson weren't so pleased to greet one of The Irregulars that early, but Mr. Holmes was up. Had been all night by the looks of his stubble and the state of his chemical experiments that had burnt a fresh hole in the carpet.

"I'm sorry to call on you so late – or early – Mr. Holmes, but I don't know who else to turn to!"

"Ah, Wiggins," he said, like he was pleased to see me. He was the only one who ever was. "Have you located the whereabouts of the organ grinder with the one-eyed monkey? I am most anxious to discuss the matter of Lady Vandermir's missing correspondence with him."

"You sure that old organ-grinding geezer knows something?" I asked, reminded of the task I was supposed to be working on.

"No, I expect him to be quite ignorant of the matter," said Mr. Holmes. "But I look forward to interrogating his monkey."

"He hasn't turned up yet," I informed the detective. "I was out asking after him last night, but I got distracted."

"How so?"

Mr. Holmes was probably concerned about the shilling investment he'd already made in my inquiries.

"Something came up," I said. "A mystery. A different one. I practically tripped right over it in the street."

I'd more than practically tripped over it. I'd literally tripped over it in the wee hours, and had landed face-first in the gutter. I didn't want to share that embarrassing detail with Mr. Holmes, but I expect he'd already deduced what I'd landed in by the smell of me.

"There's foul play about. That much I'm sure of," I continued. "How foul it is, I don't know, but I feel as though someone is playing a game with me, sure enough!"

372

Dr. Watson arrived in the room at that moment, wearing his night shirt and a face that looked only half awake.

"Ah, Watson," said Mr. Holmes. "You're the only one who had any sleep last night, and you look like you've had the least rest of any of us."

The doctor had been seeing more patients lately. Probably trying to earn enough money to pay for his upcoming wedding I didn't expect to be invited to. I understand wives and weddings can get fiercely expensive and are best avoided. Mr. Holmes would agree, and since he's the smartest person I've ever met, that settles that as far as I'm concerned.

"Wiggins was just about to tell me of some intrigue he stumbled upon in the night. Given his state of agitation, and in light of his experience dealing with such matters, I suspect we are in for quite a tale. You may wish to take notes."

Dr. Watson yawned wide and made no move to collect his pad of paper as he sat down heavily in an arm chair. I expected the story I had to tell would get him up and about in no time. Certainly Mr. Holmes was giving me his full attention.

"A body, Mr. Holmes!" I began. "Dead in the street, lying on his back like he was having hisself a rest, but stone cold dead to be sure. I double-checked myself, though he looked quite alive and well – other than the fact he weren't breathing and didn't have a beating heart."

"A man dropping dead in the streets of London, or any widely populated city, is not so uncommon an occurrence as to rattle a seasoned street urchin, surely. Why bring this to me? Why not point the poor wretch out to the police and be done with the matter?"

"I been to the police already," I said. "Repeatedly. The last bobby I tried to drag along to have a look threatened to stick me in a cell for the night if I didn't quit having them on. Word has spread along the beat, and now they all think I'm pulling a prank. Or worse, that I've gone mad."

"Why would they think that?"

"Because this dead bloke don't stay put. I brought the first bobby around to the exact spot where I found him, only he weren't there no more."

"Gone you say?"

I nodded. "No sooner did the bobby scold me and leave did I find the same body again, a block away from the first spot."

"You're quite sure you weren't mistaken about the original location?" asked Dr. Watson, suddenly more interested in my tale than he was in stealing another few minutes of sleep in his chair.

It was a fair question, but I still had to make an effort to not get offended. I know my way around, sure enough.

"That's just what the next bobby I found had to say. Right until I brought him to that second spot, and there weren't no corpse there neither. He thought I was having him on as well."

"When did you next encounter this wayward cadaver?" asked Mr. Holmes, anticipating where my misadventure was going.

"Three blocks away this time. I was only trying to forget about the whole business and get back to my job at hand. I weren't looking for the blighter, but it's like he found me on his own. Still lying there on his back like he'd never budged an inch."

"What did you do then?" asked the doctor.

"This time I got smart. I figured I'd drag him to a bobby myself, just in case he got the idea in his dead head to wander off again. That way there'd be no denying what I'd found – no accusing me of making some foolish joke."

"A suitable notion," agreed Mr. Holmes. "But it did not work as planned."

"Not a bit of it," I admitted. "Like I said, the bloke looked perfectly healthy, other than being dead. And he was well fed. Too well fed. He was a great big fatty, and too heavy for me to move more than a few doors down before I had to give up. I don't expect I need to tell you what happened next."

"So after the third bobby in a row failed to find the corpse where you said it would be, what then?"

"I'd had quite enough of him, as you might expect, so I took off, trying to put as much distance as I could between him and where I'd last seen him. Four blocks later, there he bloody well was again! By then I'd wasted half the night and I was done wasting any more of it. I came here figuring you to be the last man in London who might still believe me."

"I would never doubt your word," Mr. Holmes assured me. "Something peculiar is afoot, to be sure. Tell me, Wiggins, where was the final location you witnessed this body?"

"He won't be there no more," I said, not wanting to waste Mr. Holmes's time looking for it. "Sure enough, he'll have moved on by the time we get to the spot."

"I'm certain you're right, Wiggins. Nevertheless, I shall have that location."

"It was on Bethnal Green, near the corner of Chance Street."

"Where before that?"

"Navarre Street."

"And before that?"

"Redchurch."

"And the first place you saw it?"

374

"Along the Old Nichol."

You could practically see the whole city playing out across that great forehead of his, in the lines of his thoughtful brow. Nobody knew the streets of London like Mr. Holmes. Not even me, nor the best cabbie you could ever hope to wave down. While Dr. Watson was busy looking for a map to better remind hisself how one street related to the other, Mr. Holmes already had a picture, clear in his head.

"The sightings of this phantom corpse occur at opposing points, growing more distant with each incident," Mr. Holmes concluded in mere moments.

"He does seem to get around," I agreed.

"Surely the man was only a drunk," suggested Dr. Watson, "slipping in and out of consciousness, and wandering about when he was awake."

"I don't need no man of medicine to tell me who's living and who's dead as a doornail!" I argued. "I'm telling you, this fellow was stone cold, down for the count, ready to start pushing up daisies!"

"You said yourself he didn't even look dead," Dr. Watson reminded me.

"Dressed well, was he?" Mr. Holmes asked, ignoring his companion's comments.

"A suit," I said. "Cheap but nice enough. And clean."

"Tell me, Wiggins, when you had occasion to view the fellow up close, did you notice the state of his shoes?"

I was worried then that Mr. Holmes's line of thinking was taking the same path as the doctor.

"You think he's been wearing his shoe leather down, traipsing about town? Mr. Holmes, I don't know so much as you, but I know a dead bloke when I seen one. This one was dead and done, and the dead don't go for a walk."

"Have I suggested we're dealing with some unusually energetic decedent, Wiggins? No, I asked after the state of his shoes."

I tried to answer Mr. Holmes as best I could so as not to try his patience.

"Well, erm," I contemplated, trying to remember them. "There were two. And they was on his feet."

I could tell Mr. Holmes was after something more specific.

"No matter," he said with a wave of his hand. "I can well anticipate their state of wear and tear."

Mr. Holmes had his coat and hat in hand not a moment later.

"The pattern we see here is not of a corpse that won't stay still, but rather that of an as-yet unresolved argument."

"You think this man got hisself into a fight about something and was killed for it?" I wondered.

"No, Wiggins, I do not expect he ever expressed an opinion in the matter. Never committed to a side. And therein lies the heart of the matter!"

"Do you know where he's likely to show up next?" I asked.

"Not in the least," said Mr. Holmes, much to my disappointment. "As the points of discovery widen, so too do the possibilities of a final destination. No, our best chance of discovering where your late fat man will get to next is to determine where he started this circuitous journey. For that, we must search the central-most point of the various sightings. That is where lies his origin."

Mr. Holmes threw the door open and asked, over his shoulder, "Coming, Watson?"

But Dr. Watson made no move to follow. He was back in his chair, having nodded off, with his gaping mouth sucking deep breaths.

"Ah, let the poor fellow sleep," decided Mr. Holmes. "He's had a long day of it, and another awaits him in in short order. Besides, I doubt very much he would care to chronicle this particular inquiry of mine. I expect to have the matter resolved within the hour."

"Is it so simple a puzzle, then?" I asked, feeling disappointed in myself for bothering the detective with it.

"It is a minor diversion," he said. "But a diversion nevertheless after so fruitless a night of chemical experiments. The scorched rug will thank me to try my luck elsewhere, at any rate!"

Boundary Street, which touched upon most of the thoroughfares that had briefly been host to London's most well-travelled corpse, was our destination. Once the cab let us off, Mr. Holmes began his search – not of the curbs and gutters of the road, mind you. His eyes were cast up, not down, as he looked at the various bits of signage that hung over shop doors and other places of business.

"This one looks promising," he announced, pointing us at one display across the street.

"That's where dead bodies ought to end up," I noted. "It's not a place likely to make much coin setting them free."

"The proprietor will likely agree once he discovers he's short one client."

The funeral parlour still had a card in the window saying it was closed at that early hour, but the undertaker was up and about and fussing with something inside. He finally answered after Mr. Holmes persistently knocked for a third time.

"Sir, I do apologise, but we are not yet open to customers. And I am afraid our display room is in disarray and shall need tidying."

"A quick look is all I ask," said Mr. Holmes. "We shall be careful where we step so as not to suffer any cuts or splinters."

"Why . . . how did you?" began the man in the doorway before growing suspicious. "I say, you didn't have anything to do with this break-in, did you?"

"I am investigating the matter as we speak."

"You are with the police then?" we were asked.

"Scotland Yard and I have an arrangement of mutual cooperation," said Mr. Holmes vaguely.

"But I haven't even had a chance to summon them."

"And I wouldn't expect them to respond for hours yet. Which is why you are better off letting me have my look. I am, after all, the one who already stands here, before you."

The mortician stepped aside and allowed us entry, showing us through the double doors that led to the principal display room.

"As you can see," he said, "they made quite a mess of things."

Several loose planks of wood littered the floor, some of them snapped in two, with shards scattered across the carpeting. The box they had once helped compose was still largely intact, but had been smashed on the floor and mangled to such a degree that it wasn't immediately recognizable for what it was – an upended coffin of a non-standard size. So giant it was, it looked more like something that should be packed on a ship, carrying freight.

"I take it nothing else is missing, other than the former occupant of that box," commented Mr. Holmes, as his eyes searched the room.

"The late Herbert Garamond, poor fellow. A big man with a big heart that gave out too soon. Dropped dead at his local, not far from here, and was delivered directly."

"Quite a burden to remove him from these premises," said Mr. Holmes, observing the twin furrows in the carpet where the body had been dragged.

"Twenty-two stone, by my reckoning," said the mortician. "The coffin was a custom job. Nothing in stock would have fit him."

"Unfinished pine," Mr. Holmes noted. "A modest funeral."

The mortician nodded. "He died almost penniless. This funeral accounted for the last of his savings, and now he shall not even have that much. A terrible shame after I put my best efforts into his presentation."

"That accounts for his lifelike appearance, Wiggins," Mr. Holmes told me. "A funeral director's makeup. Some blush and powder to bring back a hint of colour to the grey flesh of a man recently deceased."

"It is," the mortician declared, "an art form."

But Mr. Holmes wasn't interested in hearing the man talk about his paints or his morbid canvass. Something had captured his interest. There was a liquid stain on the intact side of the coffin.

"What is it?" I asked, not so sure I wanted to know. "Corpse bile?"

"Nothing of the sort!" exclaimed the mortician, quick to defend the honour of his business. "I run a clean parlour. Nor is it embalming fluid, I assure you. Sutton Undertakings guarantees leak-free funereal services, regardless of the weight or volume of a client."

"It is castor oil," Mr. Holmes announced after a single sniff at the fluid.

"We use no such oils," said the mortician.

"Of course not," replied Mr. Holmes. "The source comes from outside."

At this suggestion, the mortician looked up at the ceiling, like he might spot a leak from the roof that was letting in a drizzle of oil rather than rain. Mr. Holmes, who was never much for explaining himself, was already on to the next subject that interested him.

"Tell me, is there a Mrs. Garamond that I might speak to?"

"Ah yes," the mortician recalled. "Such a slight woman compared to her husband. I believe she said she lives on Sclater Street. Allow me to check our copy of the invoice."

The mortician wasn't long looking through his papers. The bill for his next scheduled funeral was up near the top of the stack.

"No, no, it appears I am mistaken," he said, reading it over. "Mr. Garamond's residence is on Hocker Street, just off the Arnold Circus."

"Did you interact with the widow Garamond often?" Mr. Holmes asked.

"Only twice," was the reply. "Both times the dear lady was inconsolable. I could barely understand her between her sniffles and tears, and I dare say she hardly understood what I was saying back to her. We had to go over the details of the funeral in full both times we met. And she was so out of sorts, she even attempted to pay me my fee a second time. I, of course, refused her. Some less ethical funeral directors are known to take advantage of grieving families at times of tragedy, but we hold ourselves to a higher standard here at Sutton."

"You say she was a frail woman?"

"I wouldn't go so far as to say frail, but she was quite thin. They say black mourning attire is slimming, but she was slight by any measure."

"So she wore a mourning dress?" Mr. Holmes asked.

"Both times we met. I expect she'll remain in mourning for a good long time, given her obvious grief."

378

"Complete with hat and veil?"

"Oh yes. All very proper."

"Well then," said Mr. Holmes, clapping his hands together in satisfaction, "we mustn't disappoint the widow. A funeral for her husband has been paid for, and that won't happen without his body. I shall have Mr. Garamond's remains delivered back here in short order."

"Do you know where he's got to?" I asked.

"No, Wiggins, but I know where he shall be."

We were back on the street and walking briskly to a new destination no more than two minutes later.

"I don't want to ask if you're sure about this, Mr. Holmes, sir," I said, running to keep up with the pace of his long legs, "but are you sure you're sure?"

"A simple enough mental calculation, Wiggins. Given the last known whereabouts of Mr. Garamond, the amount of time that has passed since then, the pattern of his relocations, and now a probable destination, I can safely surmise we are most likely to catch up with him somewhere in or about Calvert Avenue."

"If you say so, Mr. Holmes," I said, because what he said always seemed to turn out to be right.

"Now," he said, as we turned the corner into Calvert, "let us see if we can catch our man in transit this time."

That early, there was hardly a soul to be found on the road. As such, it was easy enough to spot someone walking only a couple of blocks away – or more accurately, waddling. It took me a moment to realise this person was only walking so funny because they was walking backwards. Once they started to turn the corner, I saw why: Dragging a body they were, one that was big and bulky.

"There, Mr. Holmes! There's my dead fatty and the thief what stole him!"

We raced down the avenue, quick to catch up, and the body-burglar must have heard us because by the time we'd rounded the corner, the thief gone from sight. But old Herbert Garamond was there, lying peacefully, just as I kept finding him. It was like he was having hisself another rest between legs of his journey.

"Reunited at last, Wiggins. Here is your wandering cadaver – though not wandering by his own will, nor under his own power it would seem. Observe the state of the heels of his shoes and you shall see just how far he's been dragged over the course of the last few hours."

"But why one way and then back the other? It makes no sense! And who's been doing it?"

"Do you not yet see, Wiggins?"

I gave it a few moments of good hard thinking.

"Of course! Mrs. Garamond!" I cried. "It has to be."

"Not strong enough to move her heavy husband more than a block or so at any one try, but she is certainly persistent."

"But why would she do it? And never in the same direction?"

"Does the oil slathered on Mr. Garamond's left hand not tell you her motives?"

"No," I admitted. "But I'll be sure to ask her when I catch her. There she is!"

I pointed at a figure who was watching us from behind the garden hedges of Arnold Circus, a road that ran in a circle and touched upon many intersections. She was dressed head to toe in black, with gloves and a veil covering so much of her pale skin, it was hard to spot her in the dim light, creeping through the foliage as she was.

My feet acted on instinct long before my head could catch up, and I was across the street and after her at a full run a moment later.

"Wiggins, stop! Stay with the body!" I heard Mr. Holmes shout behind me.

The widow bolted away, through the garden. By the time I arrived at the central gazebo, I couldn't tell which direction she'd gone, or what branching street she'd chosen to escape me. Mr. Holmes caught up a moment later and urged me to give up the pursuit.

"Let her go," he said. "I am quite certain we have not seen the last of Mr. Garamond's widow just yet."

"Why would she come back now that she's been discovered?"

"Because she hasn't yet acquired what she is after – what she has been in stubborn competition for all night long."

This he told me on our walk back to the body, which was only a short distance away. Even so, the widow Garamond, who I'd last seen running far away from her dead husband, had somehow beat us back to his latest resting place.

"How'd she get to him so fast?" I wondered, seeing the skinny black-clad woman hunched over her man on the sidewalk like she was praying for his soul.

Mr. Holmes held a finger to his lips, cautioning me to be quiet as we both snuck up on the lady. Once we were only a few paces off, Mr. Holmes announced himself.

"Had you resorted to that option earlier, this conflict might have long been resolved."

The woman sprung to her feet in an instant and turned on us with an angry hiss. Mr. Holmes had known to keep his distance, and even put a hand out to stop me from advancing any further towards the danger he anticipated. Somehow he'd known she'd be armed. It was a nasty great bread knife she pointed at us, the serrated blade coated with blood. In her other hand was a dripping stump – one of her husband's chubby fingers, freshly severed.

"Back, you cutpurses, or I'll be the one cutting you!" she growled at us.

"There will be no call for that," Mr. Holmes told her. And then, quick as a snake strike, he grabbed her by the wrist before she could do any more damage. With a minimum of pressure, he got her to drop the knife. The finger, though – that she was much more interested in keeping a grip on, holding it tight in her fist.

"Drop it at once, Mrs. Garamond!" Mr. Holmes demanded, and she finally did, letting the digit fall to the road, where it did its best to roll away from the woman who'd cut it off.

"And you, as well, Mrs. Garamond!" Mr. Holmes added, turning to address the second woman who had darted out from behind a corner to try to snatch up the finger for herself. She, too, was dressed all in black mourning, and was of a slight build similar to the first woman. Once Mr. Holmes caught her in the act, she threw back her veil and yelled at him.

"Don't you stick your nose in my personal family business!"

"That wedding band is mine by rights!" hollered the first woman as Mr. Holmes released her.

"You'll only pawn it the moment you get your greedy mitts on it!" countered the second one in the street.

The first widow tore off her own hat and veil as the argument heated up.

"And what would you do with it, eh? Keep it forever in a shrine? Bollocks!"

With their head covers off, I could see the twin widows weren't so alike after all. The size and shape of them was a match, but their faces were completely different – except in as much as they were all twisted up in anger and hatred for each other.

"I was the first he married!" snarled one.

"And I he married once he knew you weren't such a fine catch!" the other snarled right back.

"He spent more time with me! Four days a week!"

"You can have your four days! It was most nights he spent with me!"

It looked like it might come to blows at any moment. Mr. Holmes ignored the fracas as he explained the finer points of the mystery to me.

"One might think a bigamist would seek variety, but as you can see, the late Mr. Garamond was consistent in his taste in women. Once his untimely death led to them discovering each other's existence, the race to obtain his one remaining possession of value before it went to the grave with him began. I expect they both made an attempt to remove that wedding band from his finger as he lay in state, only to find it immoveable, thanks to Garamond's weight gain since his last nuptial."

"That's when one of them broke into the funeral home and tried to get it off with the oil!" I said.

"Quite right, Wiggins," said Mr. Holmes, as the two widows wrestled and tore at each other's dresses. "When that failed, the coffin was indelicately pulled from its platform and an attempt was made to steal the body and bring it home where further attempts at the gold band could be made at leisure. Unfortunately, both ladies had the same notion. As one grew tired and retreated to seek a tool that might ease the burden or assist in a more timely ring-removal, the other would take up the cause to procure the body and drag it to their own safe harbour. And so the argument went, with each woman redoubling her efforts, until a final desperate impromptu amputation was decided upon before the streets could fill with potential witnesses."

"You had it all figured out the moment my story spilled out of my mouth, didn't you?" I said.

"I may have surmised a good deal of it, but how the specific details revealed themselves was worth the small effort it took to look into the matter," said Mr. Holmes.

"So what do we do about them?" I said of the two widows, who were so busy fighting they'd forgotten the ringed finger at their feet.

"Ladies!" announced Mr. Holmes, clearing his throat. It was enough to get them to interrupt their scuffle for a moment and listen.

"By my reckoning, your claims to the inheritance hold equal merit," he continued. "As neither of you seems willing to share the proceeds with the other, I can only suggest a decision made by pure impartiality."

Mr. Holmes reached into his pocket and produced a single shilling coin. They knew at once what he had in mind, even before he flipped it into the air.

"Heads!" shouted the first Mrs. Garamond before the other could think to choose. And when the coin hit the cobblestones and revealed Her Royal Majesty's profile – a third woman in mourning appropriately enough – she howled at her victory.

Without any further fuss, the woman snatched up her prize and yanked it off the stump end of the oily finger, tossing away the bit of gristle and tucking the ring where her bitter enemy couldn't get at it.

"Then that tossed shilling is mine!" said the empty-handed one, reaching for it.

Mr. Holmes stepped on the coin before she could snatch it away.

"The shilling goes to young Wiggins here, for bringing this early morning diversion to my attention," said Mr. Holmes, before consulting his pocket watch. "Alas, there was less than an hour of distraction to be had. Not even enough time to see the sun fully risen. But at least it has not kept me from my breakfast."

The detective tipped his hat to the two ladies who weren't so lady-like.

"Allow me to offer you my sincerest condolences."

He then went about his next set of instructions.

"Wiggins," he said, "round up some more of The Irregulars. Half-a-dozen should suffice. And see to it that you help the second Mrs. Garamond convey her late husband back to the undertaker. I expect she's quite strained her back enough for one night."

With the case closed and the dispute resolved – at least to one party's satisfaction – Mr. Holmes turned and strode away with no further comment.

"Who the bloody hell was that, then?" said one of the Garamond widows.

I didn't put myself to the bother of explaining to them that they had just been the subjects of an investigation by the great Sherlock Holmes. Neither of them struck me as a big reader of books or newspapers.

With a final sneer at her competition, the winner of the ring turned and headed off – either to her home, or the first pawnbroker who was likely to open shop that morning. The remaining widow spat after her departing rival. Well practised, she got good distance, but her shot fell just short of the hem of the other woman's mourning dress.

Alone with the losing Mrs. Garamond, I thought it only polite I should express my regrets for her misfortune.

"I'm sorry you lost the ring, but I suppose, when it comes to a coin-flip chance, somebody's got to lose."

"Never you mind, young lad," she said. "I expect I'll still come out ahead."

She knelt down next to the body of the unfaithful Herbert Garamond and pulled back his cold lips. I could spy a few glints of yellow metal above his gum line.

"My husband did like his sweets, as you might be able to tell from the size of him. All them candies and bon-bons and such he ate went and ate him right back. They put all sorts of holes in his teeth, they did. Over our years together, he spent all his money keeping not just two wives, but one dentist as well. A dozen fillings or more he must have, each of them gold. And there's my end of the inheritance. All for me and none for her.

383

She'd know about that fortune in fillings if only she made him smile more often, like I did."

"You really did care for him, didn't you ma'am?" I commented, catching the hint of genuine grief in her voice.

"Indeed I did. The love of my life, he was," she said, choking back a tear. Then it was back to business. "Now pass me that brick, boy."

I did as I was told, reaching for a loose bit of masonry that was left over from a repair job to the wall of the building nearest us. She took it in hand and drew her arm back, taking careful aim. I needn't describe what happened next for fear of putting off more delicate readers. I've been warned against indulging in that sort of grisly sensationalism when describing these tales of logic and deductive reasoning. Best to keep to the facts and the relevant data, or so I've been told. Suffice to say, a man who'd spent his life lying through his teeth went to his grave without a tooth in his head, and leave it at that.

The Dutch Impostors
by Peter Coe Verbica

Chapter I – A Silver Coin

Crossing York Street on a brisk morning walk to Holmes's Baker Street flat, my breath issued puffs as if I were a locomotive. I was glad to have a hat pulled down close to my ears and woolen scarf wrapped around my neck. I climbed the steps, found the door unlocked, and stepped into the sitting room of 221b. The familiar ambience of a Persian rug, the buttoned upholstered chairs, and an orange glow behind the fireplace screen provided a welcome contrast to the chill outside. A beam of light streamed through the windows – had I not braved the cold, it would have given a perception of warmth outside despite the inclement weather.

Mrs. Hudson acknowledged me with a brief smile and handed me a steaming cup of tea, leaving a blue and white china teapot upon its tray. She left and I steadied the cup in its saucer, waiting for the liquid to cool. Holmes was seated, wearing a dark smoking jacket and facing a small table strewn with eclectic scientific apparatuses. I stepped forward to get a better view of his side and observed his long, thin fingers forming a steeple at the base of his chin. He appeared deep in thought. An old and oily black clay pipe rested in a dish filled with ashes next to him. A blue horizon of smoke hung mid-air, evidence that he had been ruminating over some mystery for hours.

"I say, Watson," Holmes began without turning around, and pointed offhandedly to a copy of *The London Times* on the floor. "Have you read about the untimely death of Sir John Newbarth? The gentleman dropped while tending his rose garden and never recovered."

"The Regal Academy of Arts director?" I replied, my hands rising involuntarily in surprise. "He was as spry as they come – a force of nature. He single-handedly helped raise the funds for the Academy. My wife was the governess for one of his benefactors before we married. It's hard to picture him dead," I said, raising my eyebrows.

"One and the same. His fine character helped him negotiate a very favorable long-term lease with the Royal Family for the Academy's premises. He proceeded to build an impressive museum collection of van Rijn, Hals, Hobbema, ter Brugghen, and Vermeer at a breakneck pace. The *Times'* writer speculates that Sir John was struck dead by an adder."

"An adder? Aren't adders normally found in more forested areas? You would think that he would spot it easily in the open terrain of a rose garden," I ventured.

"Excellent observation! My thoughts exactly. Unfortunately, he had all of the symptoms of being poisoned by a viper. And, our ever-vigilant, but often unimaginative, Inspector Lestrade, found a decapitated snake about a foot-and-a-half in front of Sir John's feet. Its head had been chopped off by a garden hoe and was found on the opposite side of its victim."

Holmes stood up and walked to the door. "Speaking of the devil, Watson," he said before he opened it. "Inspector, to what do we owe this pleasure?" Holmes said, looking benignly down upon the man.

Lestrade ignored the question and walked to the middle of the room, blinking his ferret-like eyes as they adjusted to the dim interior light. He picked up a curio from Holmes's table and inspected it.

"That scarab is from an ancient Egyptian tomb, Inspector, and its base is somewhat delicate. Certain collectors believe the relic to be more valuable than a country manor."

Lestrade looked at Holmes in disbelief and set the item down carefully.

"You're an odd duck, Mr. Holmes."

"I've been called worse, Inspector. May I take your hat?"

"No, that won't be necessary. I won't be long. I'm here at the behest of Sir John's stubborn widow."

"Lestrade, if your men haven't disturbed the site of Sir John's demise, I would be happy to review the scene and share with you any clues."

"Clues, Mr. Holmes!" the inspector replied, his voice beginning to break and his face looking more pinched than usual. "The man died of a snakebite to his forearm. What clues are needed? He was holding the very hoe in which he attempted to protect himself. The gardeners, out of respect for the deceased's family, have neatly raked the area to prepare for the upcoming wake."

"Of course." Holmes raised an eyebrow at me and turned back to Lestrade. "But something seems to be troubling you."

"Not troubling me, Mr. Holmes. But you have a fascination for peculiar things. His widow found this in his pocket," Lestrade said, handing Holmes a silver dollar.

Holmes turned the coin over in his fingers. "Go on, Lestrade."

"Well, she seems to think it's important, though I'm disinclined to agree. She said that in their thirty-five years of marriage, the man never had loose change in his pockets. She said that he always kept it in a coin purse."

"A U.S. trade dollar," Holmes said, letting me inspect the currency. "Ninety-percent silver. Ten-percent copper. The thirteen stars represent the original thirteen colonies."

"Trade dollar?" I repeated, peering at the obverse.

"Issued, as you well-know, Watson, by a variety of countries," he explained. "Our country, France, the United States, and even Japan use these for trading abroad. This one, featuring Lady Liberty, was designed by William Barber and minted in San Francisco. She faces the left, in homage to Pacific commerce, and sits on items for sale. In her hand is an olive branch, signifying her peaceful intentions."

"There's a small mark on it, I notice," I said. "It looks like a small stick figure of a man – or even, with a bit of imagination, a tangled spider."

"Obviously, the work of someone bored and thoroughly untalented," Lestrade interjected gruffly.

"Perhaps a schoolboy," Holmes chuckled, "not reprimanded on the consequences of defacing money?"

"I wouldn't have noticed it, but for the widow's insistence," Lestrade offered, a slight scowl upon his face.

"That doesn't surprise me, Inspector," Holmes said neutrally. "May I keep this for a while?"

"It's of no use to me," Lestrade answered abruptly. He turned on his heels.

Holmes replied, "We'll let you know if we can make heads or tails of it . . . ."

Chapter II – Men Surrounding a Book

My small medical practice required my attention and kept me away from Holmes's latest mystery. I came to visit him after the span of a week. My work included a particularly gruelling surgery on a charity patient, paid for by The Church of England's "Widows and Orphans Fund". A visit to my friend was a welcome reprieve.

I discovered his diverse sitting room in more than its usual bachelor's disarray. The divan, tables, and other furniture had been pushed against the walls and into the four corners. The lean private detective hovered over a large, unframed oil painting propped in the room's center. The dark piece, at least five feet across, featured a group of men surrounding a large open book. Holmes was peering at the canvas through a magnifying glass.

I announced myself (as if it were necessary), and Holmes took a studied look in my direction. His glance found me rubbing my temple lobe with one of my thumbs. There was a long pause and then he returned his attention to the painting. "Grab something stronger than tea, Watson. I can tell from the faint smell of carbolic acid, the measure of your gait, the shadows beneath your eyes, and your headache that you had a difficult surgery this week. You have the telling marks of adrenal fatigue."

I opened the beak of a hinged silver stopper on a decanter crafted into an eagle's head and poured a medicinal portion. Sipping from an etched crystal glass, I slowly returned to normality. "True, Holmes. Your power to diagnose is keener than most physicians."

Holmes set down the magnifier and clapped his hands with a sharp report. He rubbed his palms together. "Most see rather than observe. Watson, if I may distract you with a less somber topic . . . let us discuss an ubiquitous fraud which surrounds Her Majesty's subjects, of which most are blissfully unaware."

He pointed to the painting and raised an eyebrow. "What do you know of forgeries?"

"Rather little, Holmes. I can tell you how to properly clean and oil a service revolver, but I can barely tell the difference between a Rembrandt and a Rossetti."

"I suspect you're being a bit modest, Watson. But, if you'll bear with me, I'll give you a quick primer on how far more than thirty-percent of art is misattributed." He set his magnifying glass down upon the mantelpiece. "Help me negotiate this alleged Dutch masterpiece against the wall and return the furniture to its proper orientation."

After we re-arranged the room, rather than stand like Holmes, I placed myself squarely in my chair. I could feel the remnants of a Jezail bullet causing my shoulder to throb slightly.

My initial malaise was contrasted by Holmes's boundless energy when on the scent of a trail. He dug his pipe into a Persian slipper and filled it with shag tobacco. He pushed its contents down with his thumb but was too animated by the topic to light the pipe. Instead, he used it like a conductor's baton and began explaining the basics of detecting art forgeries.

"Art has been copied for as nearly as long as men began taking up chisels and brushes. The Romans imitated the Greeks, and of course, dutiful apprentices slavishly copied their masters in various 'schools' of art. Scientific detection still needs to make great progress. I am seeking to perfect better ways of determining paint composition and the age of a canvas, for example. But we can still search for an abundance of helpful *indicia* to determine whether a piece is forged or genuine."

I leaned forward, picked up Holmes's decanter, and splashed two fingers of the amber-hued tonic into my tumbler. I rarely had a second glass, especially given my brother's excessive enthusiasm for liquor, but in this instance I took an exception. I rotated the glass unconsciously and noticed an embedded symbol of a square and compass. (It was a simple, distracting reminder to me that for Holmes, many mysteries – even the sacred geometries of nature, art and music – hide in plain sight.)

"I imagine that one has to be careful not to damage the painting while determining if it is genuine," I offered, regaining my focus.

Holmes suspended the well-used briar pipe upside down over a flickering gas lamp and then deftly rotated it upright, puffing until he had sufficiently enshrouded himself in a blue cloud.

"Of course," he said, waving his hand dismissively. "Now, you can look for the obvious, such as anachronistic inclusions in a piece, or marks when a canvas is reframed. I have seen pieces soaked in tea and others smeared in India ink to appear older. Even Michelangelo reportedly forged a cupid which he interred in acidic dirt to give it the appearance of an antiquity. The more skilled and resourceful forgers learn the techniques of earlier masters, including how to manufacture their own paints and even construct brushes out of period-appropriate materials, such as badger hair. Clever forgers will also search for old canvases and frames to repurpose for their schemes."

Holmes cleared his throat. "The Dutch forgery you helped me prop against the wall is particularly well done. Even the cracks of the paint are superbly imitated, probably by heating the canvas itself. The forger washed the piece with ink to make it appear older, but not all of it was absorbed in between the flakes of paint."

I looked toward the painting. It emanated a sense of antiquity and painstaking details, including folds in a tablecloth and light behind the figures which gave each a saintly radiance.

"I've unveiled dubious pieces in Florence, Vienna, Fontainebleau, and Buckingham Palace. But, enough of my sounding my own trumpet, Watson. Rest up. Tomorrow afternoon, we are set to attend a salon where art will be discussed."

I grimaced. "As I say, Holmes, I know little about art and would be at my best simply to keep quiet and listen in on the banter."

"Do just that, Watson, and assuredly you will be the most popular attendant at the party. Rare, indeed, is a man who listens more than he talks."

Chapter III – The Salon

"Do you come to please or educate, Mr. Holmes?" asked Lady Emily, the hostess, upon our arrival at the salon. Holmes took the lady's hand and kissed it reverently. She had flowing locks of brown hair, a delicate but determined oval face, large, searching brown eyes, and lips which formed a subtle smile. She was dressed in finery which revealed her attributes almost to the edge of acceptability.

Holmes had primed me on her noteworthy transformation. Though titled, her family was landless. Over the span of several years, she had changed from an autodidact employed by W.H. Smith and Sons Lending Library to a life of apparent ease and privilege. When pressed by the impudent, she dismissed such inquiries, explaining her good fortune was due to a distant relative who died *sans* spouse or children. She demurred in a society section article that she was simply "the last leaf on her family's tree".

A prim, overly dressed man wearing a Frenchman's beret – despite being indoors – stood next to her and introduced himself. "I am Henri, the painting instructor," the gentleman said with an accent. He extended his hand as if it were an *object d' art*. He wore a poet's shirt and his clothes were impeccably tailored. The ends of his lips turned down in disdain, and he surveyed us with cold eyes.

"We come bearing gifts," Holmes answered, ignoring the man. He produced a large rectangular present from behind his back and bestowed it upon the hostess. It was wrapped with crème-colored paper and tied with scarlet ribbon. The mistress of ceremonies took the package and handed it to a servant, who was dressed in a formal black *changshan* robe and wearing white gloves. "Thank you, Wu," she said to him.

She guided Holmes by the elbow as we strolled into the main room of the well-appointed residence. The early afternoon's light cascaded through the tall windows, bringing life to large porcelain vases, gilded mirrors, rows of books, oil paintings, and – to my amusement – a collection of neatly arranged Meerschaum pipes and ivory carvings of bearded men. Holmes paused to admire one of the carved pieces and picked it up, flashing me a glimpse of hieroglyph on its base which read:

"Mr. Holmes, please," the hostess entreated to regain his attention. "You may be a brilliant man, but like a bright child, you are easily distracted!"

"Forgive me," he responded. "I'm cursed with an insatiable curiosity."

We walked past a female musician tucked in the adjacent hallway, playing a large concert harp, her feet working the pedals for sharps and flats. She wore a shimmering dark blue dress which gave her the appearance of an exotic bird.

"Lady Emily, you are like the scent of pine which enchants a forest," Holmes continued. "May I introduce Dr. Watson – one of London's most respected physicians?"

I bowed awkwardly, taken by Holmes's new-found gentility. The *salonnière* placed her hand to the exposed top of her bosom and looked at me inquisitively.

"Dr. Watson," she began in her pleasing voice. "I have read with fascination studies which show that cholera outbreaks are waterborne. Is it true that upstream water is safer than downstream water?"

"Yes, my Lady. Because of the number of sewers," I answered before thinking.

"Because of the sewers," she repeated loudly to an audience of well-dressed gentlemen and ladies which had gathered about us. "Here is a man who calls it as he sees it! Mr. Holmes, you came not just to flatter with words and gifts, I see, but, thanks to Dr. Watson, to educate as well." A short, balding man with lamb chop sideburns guffawed with delight.

I could feel my face reddening.

"Let's get ourselves an *hors d'oeuvre*, Watson, now that you've made the proper impression upon our hostess," Holmes said, pointing to a long table. "What would the world be without goose-liver or fish eggs, eh?" He winked discreetly.

I surveyed the room and, though I did not know different artistic periods, I was captivated by the difference in styles of the still life paintings and portraits. Some were dark. Some were light. Some detailed and others seemed to be sketches in paint in a style which I didn't completely recognize.

Holmes whispered to me, "Watson, play along. I haven't finished embarrassing you for the afternoon, I'm afraid." He began hitting a small fork against a toasting flute and the murmur of the room quickly quieted.

"Ladies and gentlemen, indulge me if you would! For those of you who don't know it, today is my good friend, Dr. Watson's birthday. I would first like to propose a toast to the man. Happy birthday to the Good Doctor!" Holmes said loudly raising his glass.

After a chorus of agreement and tippling, Holmes, to my chagrin as it wasn't actually my birthday, continued. "I am sad to say that though it is my good friend's birthday, I have nothing to present to him." He shrugged his shoulders sheepishly and the audience responded with gentle scolding.

"And, so," Holmes continued, "I am enlisting your help. Since we are a gathering of those who relish art, I would like to request that our esteemed hostess open her gift box which I brought and share its contents with us."

Lady Emily obliged, untying the ribbon and unwrapping the box. After unfolding the flaps, she pulled out neat bundles of charcoal pencils, erasers, and artist's paper.

"My request of you all is that we remedy my shortcoming and ask Dr. Watson to sit for a portrait. There is abundant paper and pencils for all attendees. Let us take half-an-hour out of our afternoon and sketch the features of this sturdy gentleman. What say all of you? Are we going to let this man leave empty-handed on his birthday? Help me gather chairs in a semicircle, and let's have Dr. Watson sit where the light accents his features! When you're finished, be sure to sign your piece for posterity."

"Holmes, Holmes!" I whispered. "This is insufferable."

He ignored my pleadings and at the end of the drawing session, collected each piece and thanked the participants effusively. "Mademoiselle," Holmes said to Lady Emily, "your composition is compelling."

"You're a poor liar, Mr. Holmes. We both know that my drawing wouldn't buy you a potato!"

Chapter IV – A Thread through the Labyrinth

A few days later, I visited Holmes in his upstairs lair. I was still smarting from having been propped up like a store mannequin when he posed a question.

"Watson, how many people were in the room at the salon?"

"I would wager about two-dozen."

"Very close, Watson. There were twenty-six, including the Oriental server, the harpist, ourselves, and the hostess."

"Why do you ask?"

"How many of the drawings of you do you suppose that I possess, Watson?"

"Well, if you exclude me, the musician, and the manservant, there should be twenty-three."

"Watson, I'm both pleased and saddened to report that I am in possession of that number of drawings."

"Why saddened, Holmes?" I inquired.

"It connects with my theory that Newbarth didn't die by happenstance. And, if not, then who would benefit the most from his untimely demise?"

"Not his spouse, I would suppose, unless he was planning to divorce her, which would appear at odds with his steadfast character."

"Agreed, Watson. What other connections do you see?"

"Was the couple a policy-holder where Sir John's widow would gain from a life insurance settlement?"

"Excellent question! I do have access to the records of the Society for Equitable Assurances on Lives and Survivorship, due to previous, very private work I completed for their Court of Directors. The answer is 'Yes', but the Newbarths own a multitude of property holdings and mercantile interests. His wife will receive an annual insurance stipend as the result of his passing, but, in the context of their wealth, it is quite inconsequential."

"If no pecuniary motive, Holmes, then a scorned lover?"

"Watson, you are ratcheting through the alternatives – commendable, but for your lack of evidence. Given Sir John Newbarth's age, I would say that an amorous sub-plot would be unlikely, but I did interview the housekeeper, winning her over with a glass of fortified wine and idle chit-chat. She confessed that Lady Newbarth did weary over certain of her husband's eccentricities, such as sequestering himself in an outbuilding next to the main estate at wee hours. But, by and large, their wedlock was as tranquil as a Thames backwater in June."

"I am confounded, Holmes. It seems to be a dead end at every twist and turn."

"Remember Socrates, who admonishes, 'Η μόνη αληθινή σοφία είναι να γνωρίζετε ότι δεν γνωρίζετε τίποτα,' which translates to, 'The only true wisdom is knowing you know nothing.' Do not despair, Good Doctor, for as we eliminate odds, we find ourselves closer to the truth. In part, this was why I had the salon guests and Lady Emily create your 'birthday' drawings. It was a simple way to determine whether any among the attendees had the artistic talent to create the masterful forgeries I've been quietly identifying recently among some our island's rarest collections. While I seemed indifferent, I also ascertained whether any among our group tried to sketch using their non-dominant hand as a means to foil my research. The exercise proved most fruitful, leading me closer to the truth, but not in the way I had anticipated."

"The art teacher with the French accent?" I asked, leaning forward in my chair.

"This is the frustrating dilemma, Watson. Not a single submission showed the level of innate genius required to produce what I've been seeing.

"But, I have a theory which bears testing later this evening. It will take us to a treacherous alley or two in the Limehouse area of the East of London. I would be grateful to have the company of you and your trusted Webley revolver."

Chapter V – Retribution

The night sky was moonless as we stepped from a hansom cab a short distance from a crowd of gloomy buildings. Holmes led the way toward a foreboding three-story structure. It had high, jagged gables and a turret capped with a black witch's hat. My determined friend walked with a stout shillelagh, its brass ferrule muted by a rubber tip. Looking ahead, I noticed a dim light emanating from an upper window.

"Holmes," I hissed through clenched teeth. "You're not taking me to a God-forsaken opium den, are you?"

"Courage, Watson," he whispered back. "As our famed countryman, Lord Tennyson, said in 'The Lotus Eaters': '*This mounting wave will roll us shoreward soon*!' I've had my irregulars – that singularly resourceful network of overlooked street urchins – surreptitiously monitoring these premises for the past two weeks. Be at the ready, for if I am correct, we may encounter a brute of unbridled malevolence."

The balustrade-lined stairway creaked under our feet and I tightened my grip on my revolver's grip in my coat pocket. We quietly made our way through a curtained front door, and down a narrow, high-ceilinged hallway. Upon turning the corner, I observed a large, haze-filled room, strewn with cots, slumped bodies, and long pipes. I shivered at the distinct floral and earthy smell of opium, which was countered by the stench of stale food, body odor, and dung. Throughout the room, I spied what appeared to be bell jars upon dishes. An attendant wearing a Manchurian hat and a long, braided queue held a tray in his hands. He eyed us morosely.

We stepped past the listless figures and passed through another door, and down a cramped set of servant's stairs. We could hear muffled cries and the unpleasant thumps of someone being beaten. I withdrew my revolver, my finger out of the trigger guard, and kept the weapon pointed away from Holmes's shoulder. Holmes quietly opened a door and we stepped into a brick-walled basement. I quickly stepped to one side for a clear field of fire.

A large coal furnace occupied the corner. A small man with a slumped head was tied to a chair while a bearded hulk overshadowed him, wielding a cudgel. A single kerosene lamp painted the dim room with dark silhouettes.

"I told you not to come down here unless I called for something!" the man barked at us.

"I can see that you've been up to no good, Treviss," Holmes answered flatly.

The victim in the chair murmured incomprehensibly and rocked his head.

"What ho! Who in the dickens are you rogues and how did you know my name!" the cudgel-wielding man raged, stepping forward.

Holmes's shillelagh had the advantage of length, and despite the close quarters, my friend struck the would-be assailant three times with astounding speed and viciousness. The ogre dropped to the dirt floor and lay still.

I moved to the man in the chair, and despite the sheet of blood that covered his face, I recognized him as Wu, the domestic in the employ of Lady Emily. His hands and forearms were tied to the chair's arms. I extracted a pocket knife and severed the bonds. His fingers and hand bones were irreparably broken and beginning to balloon with swelling. I helped the man stand and, putting one of his arms over my shoulders, aided him as he wobbled to the stairs.

I turned to Holmes, whose face was drawn tight. "I apologize, Watson, especially given your sworn duty to heal, but this sadist must suffer retribution. It is my unfortunate obligation to mete it out." He set his shillelagh down and picked up the man's stout cudgel. He knelt next to the unconscious man and began to methodically strike the man's hands. I turned to make my way up the stairs with my charge who was still weak on his feet.

Holmes greeted me outside with a stoic countenance. Cabbies who didn't want to be robbed by unsavory riders skirted the area, but a hansom pulled up in front of us, evidence of Holmes forethought. "Whitechapel Road to the London Hospital!" Holmes shouted to the driver. He helped me load the wounded manservant into the cab and waved us along.

"I'm going to walk for a bit, Watson," he said.

I heard the crack of the cabbie's whip and the hansom's start jostled me. Looking back, I watched as Holmes's dark figure disappeared into the darker night.

Chapter VI – A Meeting with Mycroft

Three days had passed since my bizarre trip with Holmes to Limehouse, but it seemed like a fortnight. An ill-dressed ruffian appeared at the door of my small medical practice in the Paddington district and rang the bell. I went to greet the street urchin – due to malnourishment, he was undoubtedly older than his size implied. He wore the flat cap of a chimney sweep.

"A note for you, sir, from Mr. 'Olmes."

I traded him a small coin in exchange for the note. The boy's dirty fingermarks liberally marked the sealed envelope. I was thankful that Holmes hadn't resorted to his periodic habit of a riddle. The message was mercifully blunt, and read:

W –

Meet me at the Diogenes Club at 4:45 pm today.

– SH

Though terse, his style was immediately recognizable. Holmes's fascination with graphology provided encouragement for me to mull over the private detective's style of handwriting as well. His lines were school-boyishly neat and deliberate. Though not overly cramped, the letters were written with economy, in contrast to the generous space between each of the rows: His *t*'s were crossed with short, careful strokes – he habitually left the loops of his *p*'s unclosed, his capital letters invariably showed a more liberal use of ink, the first leg of his capital *H* had the telltale foot, jutting as if ready to kick a ball. His *g*'s, *j*'s, and *y*'s were never finished with any flourish, but rather ended with a straight, downward stroke. With time, perhaps I might be able to discern how his cursive reveals his intense psyche, his placing reason on a plane far above that of emotion, of observing even the minutest of details and culling relevant facts from common chaff.

I headed directly towards the Diogenes. My preoccupation with Holmes's handwriting whisked away the time and, drifting from my private reverie on Pall Mall, I found myself stretching my memory to locate the discreet entrance to the club of Holmes's older brother. Holmes had summarized it as the queerest club in London, of which his brother was the queerest of members. I envisioned Mycroft and Sherlock vying with each other while observing the near imperceptible traits of some oblivious gentleman, to determine which brother was the better deducer. Holmes stood in front of the building, as if prescient of my inevitable disorientation. His face bore no signs of the horrors we had both witnessed as he pointed to his watch.

"Watson, I commend you on your punctuality. Remember to remain silent until we reach the Stranger's Room."

I sat in the room facing Pall Mall until Holmes returned with his brother. Mycroft's weight far exceeded his brother's, but I could see in their faces a similarity, an alertness which each took to problems like stealthy lions ready to pounce. Mycroft exhaled as he lowered himself heavily into a leather club chair. He placed his hands upon the table-top and formed a triangle with his outstretched fingers. He cleared his throat. Only the three of us were present.

A wiry club waiter dressed in black tie entered, his posture was ramrod straight, to a nearly comical extent. He carried tumblers, Scotch, a burled cigar box, a crystal dish, and a Seltzer bottle on a silver tray. He mixed the drinks efficiently, served us, and passed coasters as if he were dealing from a deck of cards. With care, he placed the cigar box and ashtray side-by-side in the table's center. After a short bow, he closed the door so quietly that one didn't hear even the clicking of the latch.

"Gentlemen," Mycroft said, "what I am about to discuss with you must stay within the confines of this room. It is an intrigue which involves certain illustrious individuals who wish these issues to remain confidential."

"That won't be necessary, Mycroft," Sherlock replied. "I've already tied together each separate strand of this mystery."

"I would expect no less, Sherlock. Then, you're aware that you've blunted one of the more effective tools of our government?"

The large host produced a cigar from out of the box, along with a silver cutter and box of matches. He snipped the cigar's end, set it down on the ashtray, placed the cutter on the table top, and struck a match. Then he rotated the end of the cigar over the flame without puffing on it. When he was finished with the ritual, he extinguished the match and began puffing on the cigar.

"Treviss? I have no regrets," Holmes responded. "I humbly suggest that new implements be chosen."

"May I interject, gentlemen, and politely ask for a more detailed explanation? I am in the dark here."

Mycroft gestured with a glance and upward nod towards his brother.

"Of course, Watson. Like a set of dominos carefully stacked by a child – when the lead is toppled, the rest predictably fall. Sir John's death was caused by an adder's venom. Even with the elimination of evidence by Lestrade, I realized that because of the position of the hoe, Sir John had to have killed the viper *before* he was struck. This left two possibilities: Another snake was present, or a more remote probability. Imagine, Watson: Sir John despairing under this cloud of looming disgrace – pieces of his collected works of art might be exposed as forgeries. He seeks solace in his garden tasks. There, as fate would have it, he encounters an adder and kills it. His mind loosened, he seizes upon the chance to escape infamy and perhaps preserve the family name. Given the facts, it becomes clear that Sir John injected himself with the venom after the snake's head had been severed. If the adder had attacked first, Sir John should have been bitten in his calf, rather than his forearm."

"Why would the man kill himself?" I asked, perplexed.

"My initial question, Watson. I surmised it must relate to the museum, and I began to survey carefully the Academy's inventory. Sir John elevated its worldwide reputation with a striking, but rapidly assembled, collection of Dutch Masters. Despite supposedly unassailable provenances according to the curators, I began to wonder if some of the collection could be counterfeit. My suspicions fell upon the patroness Lady Emily – which inspired our visit to her salon."

"Thus, the drawing episode over my purported birthday!" I offered.

"Imaginative, Sherlock, but sophomoric," Mycroft chided.

"I realized that none of the invitees who participated had the innate skill to forge at the level which would be necessary to dupe a well-trained art collector or museum curator. Watson, do you remember my compliment toward Lady Emily?"

"Even for you, Holmes, I thought it a bit odd. Something about pine trees."

Mycroft exhibited a slight and uncharacteristic smile: "A reference to turpentine."

"Turpentine?" I asked.

"Made from distilled pine gum, Watson. I discerned it on her fingers when I kissed her hand. As you know, it's a staple solvent used in oil painting. After reviewing the sketches, I noticed that Lady Emily's was the most allegorical, in terms of composition, but lacked technical skill. I surmised that though she had insufficient skill to perform the finish work, she could easily have rendered the underpainting and guided a more accomplished counterfeiter – an accomplice. As you may recall, Watson, she had a collection of detailed meerschaum pipes and intricate ivory carvings on display, as well as a notable array of paintings. It was evident to me that she had the eye, but who had the skill to execute? One immediate clue was the character which I showed you on the base of the ivory carving."

"I didn't know how to read it," I admitted.

"Understood, Watson. Most Englishmen are woefully ignorant in terms of deciphering characters from the Orient. It translates to the name of the carver, a name which is one of the ten most common and shared by millions of people. It's simplified version looks like a man waving, similar to the mark found on Sir Newbarth's coin. When translated to the King's

English it means, 'affairs', or 'business'. It also can be associated with 'military' or 'courage'."

"A strong coincidence implicating one of the unassuming players in this drama," Mycroft said, "one that might confirm one's suspicions – if joined with other evidence."

Holmes continued, "When I realized that none of the guests had the prerequisite skills of a counterfeiter, my attention turned to those who didn't participate."

"The harpsichordist and the Chinese server," I exclaimed.

"Indeed, Watson. My suspicions were immediately on Wu, the server, because his hands were covered by white gloves. Lady Emily would know of my powers of discernment. If the server's hands were exposed, I could easily deduce whether he was an avid painter with a simple shake of the man's hand."

"Thus Treviss' smashing the man's hands!" I blurted.

"A brutal payback for Lady Emily's blackmail of Sir John Newbarth, don't you think, Mycroft?" Sherlock asked his brother.

"There are some at the highest echelons of our government who wanted to send a message. The Academy's reputation is one and the same as Her Majesty's. The man is lucky to be alive," Mycroft replied.

Holmes leaned forward and resumed his summary.

"My educated guess is that Lady Emily overstepped her leverage with Sir John. She threatened to reveal cracks in the foundation of the Academy's collection. He, on the other hand, must have been concerned about the pace upon which the collection was being built, and how the provenance of too many 'discovered' pieces could be explained. Lady Emily's favorite buyer and benefactor had turned off the spigot. The trade dollar which Inspector Lestrade provided me was helpful for a number of reasons. It's very minting was designed to facilitate trade to the Orient, so it directed my attention to the East. The crude marking you observed on the coin's obverse is a "chop mark", made by a Chinese trader to verify the coin's weight and silver content, a common practice given the risk of counterfeit money. Can you guess the name which the chop mark translates to, Watson? It is a simpler version of the character on the ivory object's base which I showed you in the salon."

"Wu!"

"Bravo, Watson! The West doesn't have a monopoly of counterfeiting goods. The Chinese have long had a history of copying ancient art and artifacts. I've read one scholar who argues that the culture of Confucius, which is based on memorizing and reciting, inculcates the value of copying well. These counterfeits at present are a minor menace.

With industry, willpower, and improved techniques, I prophesy in the future they will become an epidemic."

"As the proverb states, '*Imitation is the highest form of flattery*'," Mycroft interjected.

"More to the point," Sherlock continued, "because of my contacts in Hong Kong, I learned that Wu was a master forger, an orphan taken from the streets and trained by a vast Chinese criminal enterprise. His skill is such that his works hangs in the Vatican, the Tsar's court, the Louvre, and in the some of the most revered museums across the Continent. But he double-crossed the Tong syndicate on a deal in hopes to purchase his own freedom with the proceeds. Instead, he was discovered and had to flee to escape its wrath."

Sherlock Holmes took a sip of his beverage, recommencing. "Lady Emily, being both well-read and resourceful, discovered Wu's aptitude and harnessed it for her own gain. If the forgeries in the museum were revealed, it would undermine tremendous goodwill – not just at a personal or regional level, but at an international one as well. Sir John had gained the trust of society's most renowned patrons, including the Queen, and could not bear the thought of their condemnation. There is no greater or more effective reprimand than being shunned by your peers. This dark cloud enshrouded any hope the man had. He became devastated to the point of taking his own life."

"My advice to you, Sherlock, is that you quietly extricate yourself from this matter. You've stepped on some well-clad toes in the process. My confidants are satisfied with my solemn guarantee that both of you will keep your discoveries secret."

"The counterfeits stay hung proudly upon the walls for the public to admire, I take it," Holmes stated, rather than asked.

"Match your powers of perception with a dollop of politics, Sherlock."

Holmes stood suddenly and dusted off his coat. "Watson, let us take leave of my brother, so that he may enjoy a quiet meal. His counsel has left me positively dyspeptic!"

Chapter VII – A "Thank You" Gift

Despite Holmes's complaint, when we returned to 221b we enjoyed a simple but hearty repast of stew, courtesy of Mrs. Hudson. When the dishes were cleared, Holmes sat with his legs crossed comfortably on a footstool. His pronounced forehead was unworried and his grey eyes were directed toward the ceiling of the familiar sitting room. His aquiline features were accented by the gaslight behind him.

My attention was drawn to a knock at the door, but Holmes remained at ease. I walked over and opened it. To my surprise, it was Lady Emily, unattended. She wore a sable coat and black hat which covered a majority of her face. She held a wooden box and extended it to me, exposing her pale arms. I accepted the item, which weighed more than anticipated.

"I've come to say thank you for what you gentlemen did the other evening. Wu appreciates your rescuing him as well. He insisted that I bring you this as a token of his gratitude. Mr. Holmes, I also want you to keep the Old Masters painting of '*Scholars Surrounding an Open Book*' which I asked you to inspect on my behalf."

Holmes stood. "We are honored, Lady Emily. May we offer you a beverage?"

"It's late and I need to get back to helping Wu recuperate. I hope you understand." She curtsied politely.

"Indeed, we do. Please tell Wu that he's one of the most talented artists I've ever encountered, living or dead."

"He'll appreciate the compliment, Mr. Holmes. As you know, his talents have been largely unacknowledged."

"For his sake and yours, they should remain so. Watson, would you be so kind as to ensure Lady Emily gets a cab safely?"

"Of course," I replied.

"He'll probably never be able to paint again," the beautiful woman lamented. "And to think, I saved him from a merciless Tong gang only to encounter similar brutality here."

"Your recent misfortunes are sufficient sentences for you both, I presume," Holmes said quietly.

"Silence is a true friend who never betrays," she answered.

"Confucius has rubbed off on you, I see," Holmes replied, as I escorted her to the door.

Making my way back up the flight of stairs, I found Holmes setting out ivory carvings which appeared yellowed with age.

"The eight immortals, revered by Taoists and important mythological characters in Chinese culture, Watson. Each has its own attribute and power."

"Where do you plan to hang the counterfeit painting, Holmes?"

Holmes looked towards where the substantial painting still resided, propped against the wall. I detected the hint of a smile on his normally reserved face.

"Why, Watson, given the recent turn of events, I think it should hang high in a gilded frame with its cousins. I can think of no better beneficiary than the Academy."

The Adventure of the
Missing Adam Tiler
by Mark Wardecker

I recall my friend Mr. Sherlock Holmes once remarking upon the extraordinary occurrences that sometimes befall "when you have four million human beings all jostling each other within the space of a few square miles." In that case, it was after Commissionaire Peterson had introduced him to the first link in a chain of unusual events involving the theft of the Countess of Morcar's blue carbuncle, but time and again, we have witnessed what would seem the wildest of coincidences come together to form, with the aid of Holmes's uncanny insight and imagination, a picture as clear and coherent as crystal. Another such adventure began with a visit from one of the unlikeliest clients to have ever been received at 221b Baker Street. It was a Friday evening, and since my wife Mary was going to be away for several days visiting a friend, I decided to call upon Holmes after completing my rounds. I was greeted at the door by a beaming Mrs. Hudson who was eager for news of my life, and I must admit, I enjoyed commiserating briefly with my former landlady over the undiminishing eccentricities of her most notorious tenant.

"Last week, a courier tried to deliver several pounds of cormorant guano to him! It was for one of those experiments of his. You'd hardly credit it. 'Not in the house!' I told him. You should see who's up there with him now. A wrong 'un if ever I saw, and up to no good, Dr. Watson."

"Well, then I had best be on hand just in case," I said as I eagerly turned and ascended the seventeen steps to the rooms I used to share with Holmes. As I was about to knock, I heard Holmes call out from within.

"Please come in, Watson, I have someone here I would like you to meet."

I entered to find the sitting room unchanged, with both Holmes and a blazing fire there to welcome me. It was satisfying to see the Persian slipper containing Holmes's tobacco still hung from the mantel, and his correspondence was impaled upon it as always with a jackknife. As I greeted Holmes and took off my coat, a short and roughly dressed man rose from the basket chair by the table. He had a long, hooked nose and broad, toothy grin. I took his proffered hand as Holmes declared, "This is Mr. Vinto Jones. I'd watch his hands, Watson, for you are in the presence of possibly the most talented pickpocket in the entire city."

"Well, bless you for a gentleman, Mr. Holmes, and a pleasure to meet you, Dr. Watson. There are precious few outside the trade as can appreciate the craft of it as Mr. Holmes here."

"Please, both of you have a seat. I trust you do not mind if Dr. Watson joins us, Mr. Jones."

"Not at all Mr. Holmes, I'd be honoured. And if he can help me track down my old Adam Tiler, then the more the merrier."

Holmes and I took our accustomed places in the two easy chairs by the fire, and I pulled a small notebook and pencil from my coat pocket. "So this is about a missing person? This Mr. Tyler?" I asked.

At this, they both started chuckling.

"Ah, bless my soul! But, of course, he wouldn't, would he, Mr. Holmes?"

"No, my friend Watson is an honest man and, much to his credit, has almost certainly never heard of an 'Adam'. You see, Watson, 'Adam Tiler', with an 'i', is thieves' cant for a particular sort of henchman."

"He holds the bread, you see. The routine is that I secretly hand my pickings to the Adam, quick as you please, before returning to my business. That way, should anyone, especially the Old Bill, suspect and try to search me, there's nothing to be found."

"It is a very common arrangement that goes back long enough that it has given birth to its own slang," said Holmes as he leaned back in his chair and closed his eyes. "Why don't you tell the story again from the beginning, Mr. Jones, so that Watson can also be put into the picture."

"As you please, Mr. Holmes. Last Wednesday, my mate and I were down in Ravey Street near Mark Square. It was a fine day, and business was brisk. Late in the afternoon, I made my last dive, handed the proceeds to my Adam, and we went our separate ways to reconvene in an alley by the butcher's shop around the corner on Blackall Street. Other people tend to avoid the spot, since it pongs a bit on account of the shop's offal. That made it a convenient spot to split the loot and for the Adam to change his clothes. You see, he always played posh, to make himself look less suspicious. To be honest, I think it probably came honestly to him. Anyway, when I arrived at our meeting place, he was nowhere to be found. I waited around for an hour, but he never did turn up. I've asked around after him at all our usual haunts, but no one's seen hide nor hair of him. It's not so much the bread and honey, Mr. Holmes – I can make that up in a day. It's just that I'm worried about the lad. He's the first apprentice I've ever had and all. I can pay if you're willing to help me find him."

Holmes opened his eyes and gazed at Jones over his tented fingertips.

"No offense, Mr. Jones, but I am not sure I can readily accept payment from you, given your line of work. But let us not get into that just now. What was your associate's name or alias, and how did you come to meet him?"

"He went by Vernon Jule, so you tell me. I have no idea what his real name is. He sort of saved my life. I was diving over in Liverpool Street, and one of the marks noticed his wallet was missing. He started raising an unholy racket and then pointed me out. Without thinking twice, I turned to drop the dosh into the pocket of someone beside me, but as I was finishing, I looked up to see the lad staring right down at me. I was sure I was done for, but before I could turn away, he smiled at me and winked. Then, he wandered off, while I, with utmost indignation, turned out all of my pockets for the angry gentleman and a bobby whose undesirable attention he'd attracted. After I had satisfied their curiosity and expressed my dissatisfaction at such shoddy treatment at the hands of all involved, I made my way to the Fancy Griffin pub. To my surprise, the lad fell in beside me along the way, introduced himself, and joined me for a few pints. He wouldn't go into detail, but he said he had fallen out with his old man and done a runner with some of the family's finest. That was a little over a month ago, and we've worked together ever since."

"Do you know where Jule was living?" asked Holmes.

"I've no idea. We started off at midday every day by meeting at that alley. If he's anything like me, his digs aren't really appointed for company."

"What did he look like?

"He was tall, almost as tall as you, Mr. Holmes. About twenty-five years old, clean shaven, and ginger. That curly red mane would stand out, no matter the titfer. He could be dressed as a thief or a gentleman and carry himself as such. That's what made him so indispensable."

"Did he have any enemies? Could anyone be after either of you? Did you see anything unusual?"

"Perish the thought, Mr. Holmes. Like I said, he was new to all this. As you know, I'm not and am always careful about not working on anyone else's patch. As for the rest, I saw a few of the regulars, beggars and shopkeepers, but no one unusual."

"Is there anything else you can tell me that might help me to locate this mysterious young man?"

"I'm sorry, Mr. Holmes. I know it's not much to go on. There is one thing, though," he said as he produced a silver locket and chain from his waistcoat pocket.

"This was lying in the back of the alley where we were to divvy up the haul. It may be meaningless, but I'm positive this wasn't something I lifted. I also think I see a bit of a resemblance to him here."

Holmes took the opened locket from him and said, "It's a photograph of a mother with a small child, Watson. Do you mind if I hang on to this, Jones? Very well, I shall try to find your Adam Tiler. If I can lay hands on the man, despite having so little with which to begin, it would be a feather in my cap. Where can I reach you?"

"God bless you, Mr. Holmes. I'm staying above the The Gilded Shoe Tavern in Shoreditch. Any message you leave with the landlord will get to me." And with that, Vinto Jones donned his cap and bid us farewell.

After he had departed, I asked Holmes, "This could be an ugly business. Should you even be assisting a pickpocket, Holmes?"

"Yes. A young man from a wealthy family who has fallen in with criminals is more than a little vulnerable. As for Jones' status, arresting common divers is the business of the police. You and I have more important matters to pursue."

"How on earth do you intend to find this young man? You do not even have a name with which to proceed."

"I must admit, I am used to having a mystery at one end of a case, but to have one at both ends does create a challenge. But even if I am not up to it. I've been at his game long enough to know at least one person who may be able to assist me in the matter. Can your wife and practice spare you for a few days?"

"Yes, that is what I came here to tell you. She is away for a few days, and I have already arranged to take a few days' holiday."

"Excellent. Then we shall begin tomorrow. Tonight, we shall see what Mrs. Hudson has prepared for us."

I stayed in my old room upstairs at Baker Street that night after one of Mrs. Hudson's wonderful roast beef dinners. After I had dressed and had breakfast, with Holmes having opted for a less conventional repast of coffee and cigarettes, we set out into the chilly autumn morning. Holmes had adopted his usual reticence, and I knew better than to intrude upon him while he was concentrating on the case in hand. There was a crisp breeze indicating that, despite the colorful leaves on the trees that were visible from our hansom as it passed St. James's Park, an impatient winter was fast approaching. Soon we were deposited before a club on St. James's Street that I immediately recognized as housing the notorious Langdale Pike. This society gossip monger was a columnist for several of the garbage papers, and Holmes could always rely on him to navigate the swirls and eddies of scandal within London's social scene.

A porter in livery led us to an oak-panelled reading room scantily populated by older gentleman reading newspapers in sumptuous leather wingback chairs, but it was not in these chairs that Pike was to be found. The journalist was seated in one of the bow windows at the farthest end of

405

the room, languidly smoking a cigarette with a long holder and watching the people bustling about below, like a velvet-jacketed bird of prey. He turned to us drowsily as we approached and said, "Ah, Sherlock Holmes and Doctor Watson. It is good to see you both. Better still if you have a story for me."

"Hello, Pike. I am afraid that it is I who am in need of your services today, but if you can help me, rest assured I will repay the debt."

With this, Holmes fed Pike, eagerly playing with the ends of his elaborate moustache, many of the details Jones provided the night before.

"You know, Holmes, if I had a penny for every well-to-do young ne'er-do-well who has been turned out his house by his father . . . ."

"You would have?"

"Precisely two shillings and thruppence . . . if we count only this month, and it is still early days. In any case, it *is* your lucky day. The red hair is a dead giveaway – you are looking for Gavin Brayslow, son and heir to Lord Simeon Brayslow. The lad has always been work-shy, and the pater turned him out last month. The mother died years ago, and Gavin is the epitome of an only child. Rumor has it the boy helped himself to some of the family's silver on his way out. You will find Lord Brayslow at his home in Camden. Do promise to let me know how it all turns out, Holmes?"

Holmes assured him he would return after he had found young Brayslow, and we took our leave.

"Well, things are a little more straightforward now that we at least have a name to go with our description."

"Indeed, Watson. Pike has once again proven his worth. Let's telegraph Lord Brayslow now to see if we can arrange an appointment for this afternoon."

After we had posted the missive and emerged from the post office, Holmes hailed another cab and asked to be taken to Mark Square.

"I doubt there is much to be learned there, especially after the passing of several days, but I feel it would be remiss of us not to look over Brayslow's last known whereabouts."

We alighted into a square that was no less busy for being relatively small. People in heavy coats milled about, their frozen breath hanging in the air as they spoke. The traffic thinned out somewhat as we turned onto Ravey Street and then Blackall Street. There we found several small establishments lining the sidewalks, including, in addition to the butcher's shop by the alley, a tea room, a cigar shop, and several clothiers, all of which were quite busy. In front of the cigar shop, a stout man with a flat cap and wooden leg was selling *The Morning Post*. Holmes approached him and purchased one.

"By any chance, were you here last Wednesday evening."

"Yes, sir," he said smiling. "I'm here every day, rain or shine."

"I am looking for someone," said Holmes as he fished a guinea from his coat and handed it to the man. "A young man, about my height with red hair."

"You must be joking. Look at all these people here. Sorry, but even if he had a paper off me, I wouldn't remember him."

Holmes nodded, and we strolled over to a blind beggar huddled on the ground beside his hat.

"Holmes, what could he possibly tell you?"

"Oh, Watson, you would be surprised," he said as he dropped another guinea into the hat.

"Were you here last Wednesday?" he asked the beggar.

"Aye, I'm here every day."

"I am looking for a young man who may have been here last Wednesday," he said as he nodded to me. I dropped a few more shillings into the hat, and he resumed, "About my height with curly red hair."

"Sorry, I don't recall anyone by that description. Perhaps, if he had been more generous, I might have noticed him."

"Well, this has been about as productive as I had anticipated. It looks like there is only one more possible regular to ask. I have saved the best for last," said Holmes as he looked toward a millenarian preacher, shouting fire, brimstone, and the end times from the opposite corner. My heart sank as I reconciled myself to approaching this lunatic with his bulging eyes and spittle flying from his lips as he ranted. His clothes were nice enough but ill-fitting, possibly donated. An opera hat that was slightly too small was pulled tightly down over his long white hair. He noticed our approach and focused his wild black eyes upon us.

"You, sirs. Would you hear the word of the Lord and learn about The Following? For the end is upon us, and there is little time in which to save your souls from everlasting damnation and the torments of Hell!"

"Actually, Reverend, I am engaged in trying to save the soul of another. A young man of about my height with red hair. He may have been here last Wednesday."

"Only The Following can show you all the true way! I saw no such man last Wednesday, but when you find him, get you all to our church and learn The Truth. Here, take a pamphlet, and God willing, I will see you both at our new church tomorrow."

Holmes left it to me to take the pamphlet and extricate us from the man. Then we made our way to the small alley by the butcher's shop that Jones had said was their rendezvous point. Despite Jones being quite accurate about the smell, Holmes dropped to the ground and began a

407

minute investigation, but I could tell by his lack of zeal that he held out little hope. After twenty minutes, he sprang back to his feet, dusted off his knees, and announced, "At least we can say we have done our due diligence here. The good news is that there are no signs of violence or a struggle, but that is only because there are really no signs of anything that might interest us. I suggest we return to Baker Street for lunch and to see if we have had a reply from Lord Brayslow."

As we were finishing our sandwiches and coffee, a messenger arrived with a telegraph from the young man's father: "*If you must come, then do so at two p.m..*"

"I know it is an impersonal medium, Holmes, but I would have expected him to sound a little more concerned."

"Still, we have received less courteous responses to our inquiries. I think there is just time for another pipe and a quick check of the papers before we go."

The newspapers yielded nothing, and I could tell that Holmes was becoming concerned about the dearth of clues as we made our way to Lord Brayslow's home in Camden. I confirmed this by attempting to sound him out in the cab.

"A name, a description, and a locket. Eh, Holmes?"

"Indeed. It is a meager foundation upon which to build, is it not?"

"And the locket might not even be his."

"It may very well not. With some luck, maybe Lord Brayslow will shed a little light on the proceedings."

But Lord Brayslow was clearly not interested in discussing the business at all. At the neat, white stucco house, we were led to the library by a kindly and somewhat apologetic butler who insisted under his breath that the Lord really was concerned about his son. Lord Brayslow's behavior, however, seemed to contradict this sentiment. A squinting, clean-shaven, old man, he did not rise from his desk upon our entrance and seemed to be more interested in the papers on it, from which he barely glanced up. As we approached, I caught Holmes's nod toward a framed picture on a shelf behind the desk. It was, without a doubt, the woman from the locket. Introductions were short and we were not invited to sit down.

"So what manner of trouble has the juvenile delinquent got himself into now? And do not think for a moment that I am going to spend a single farthing to rescue him. I gave him opportunities enough."

"As of yet, Lord Brayslow, we are uncertain as to your son's whereabouts. A concerned friend of his consulted me yesterday and says he has not seen him since Wednesday. I was hoping you might have some idea as to where he might be."

"I have not seen him in over a month, not since he made off with half the silver, the little toe rag. Must take after my wife's felonious brother. He was smart enough not to leave a forwarding address, though. If you do find him, please do tell him to remain out of touch. Good day."

"Thank you, Lord Brayslow, but there is just one more thing," said Holmes as he fished the locket from his waistcoat. "Do you recognize this?"

"What do you have there?" he said with a wince. "That is an old photograph of my wife and the boy."

"His acquaintance found it after your son had presumably left it behind. It does belong to your son?"

"It could, but I have to admit that I have not seen it before," he said as he returned it to Holmes, having visibly softened. "Look . . . Mr. Holmes. If you do manage to find the boy, please let me know."

With that, we took our leave.

"Where to now?" I asked.

"Any suggestions would be welcome. There is simply no data."

And with that, Holmes sank into one of his moods, and I could get nothing further out of him. He spent the remainder of the day sitting cross-legged and immobile in his chair by the fire, smoking plug after plug of noxious tobacco in his greasy clay pipe. When I awakened in my room and rolled over in the small hours, I could hear the mournful sound of his violin from below. In the morning, I breakfasted as he, again, drank coffee and smoked a succession of cigarettes. It was as I was reading one the papers he had cast aside in frustration that I was finally able to intrude upon his thoughts.

"Is it not always the way of things? You remember Filcote Hardiman, of course?"

"The notorious gang leader and extortionist," he brusquely replied. "He is serving his sentence at Dartmoor."

"Yes, and there has a emerged a movement, led by the prison chaplin, the free him early. Apparently, he has become quite religious and has even been ministering to the other prisoners. It is funny how so many only turn to religion after they have been nicked."

As I finished speaking, I raised my eyes from the paper and saw Holmes regarding me with a disturbing intensity.

"Watson, you may have just supplied the clue we need to find the missing young Brayslow."

"But Holmes, I fail to see how Filcote Hardiman can have anything to with it."

"Not Hardiman, Watson. Hardiman's *behaviour*. As you said, it is a pattern we see time and again."

"But what does that have to do with our young man's disappearance."

"The locket, Watson. What if it does not belong to young Brayslow?"

"But it contains a picture of him and found at his last known whereabouts. I fail to understand this train of thought."

"And yet I can imagine it all quite vividly," he muttered as he lunged from his chair.

"Do you still have the pamphlet the old man gave you yesterday?"

"Yes," I said as I got up to retrieve it from my coat and hand it to Holmes, who had already begun putting on his hat and overcoat.

"I need to go out, Watson. Please wait here in case anything turns up."

Disappointed, I sank back into my chair and tried to resume reading the papers. On the other hand, it was nice to be once again ensconced in Baker Street, enjoying the nostalgia of the surroundings and Mrs. Hudson's cooking while waiting on news from Holmes. Nothing did, in fact, turn up, though, and I retired for the evening with still no word from my friend. It would be late afternoon the following day before he finally put in an appearance, strolling into the flat and hanging up his hat and coat as nonchalantly as if he had only gone out for a walk around the block.

"Holmes, where have you been all this time?"

"I am sorry, Watson. I would have taken you with me but, as I was at that point only operating on a conjecture, I was unsure as to whether I would need you to be on hand here in Baker Street."

"You need not worry on that score."

"Ah, well, if it is any consolation, I have located young Brayslow," he announced as he turned from warming his hands by the fireplace and leaned against the mantel.

"But how? Before you left, you were uttering some gibberish about Filcote Hardiman finding God and whether or not Brayslow was the owner of a locket that contained a picture of himself and his mother."

"Yes, Watson, but it was far from gibberish, for once again, you have proven yourself a great conductor of light. It was when you began trying to draw me into conversation with your account and observations on Hardiman that I caught the merest glimpse of a possibility. You will recall that, while we were questioning Lord Brayslow, he mentioned his son being like his 'wife's felonious brother'. It was when you mentioned the tendency of criminals to strongly embrace religion that I saw a thread on which to pull. I needed to begin gathering more data. My first stop was the church of The Following. I got the address from your pamphlet. I was in time for the second service, and what a production it was. The acoustics suited our reverend acquaintance from Blackall Street, and I could almost smell the brimstone in the air. I was seated behind one of the six attendees whom I gathered were also members of the cult, and at the end of the sermon, praised his performance to her and asked the reverend's name. It was Sidney Horrocks.

"I managed to slip out before Horrocks emerged to speak with his congregation and headed back to Lord Brayslow, who confirmed that our reverend is indeed his wife's brother and had, in fact, discovered religion while still in prison for embezzling from the law firm at which he had worked. Watson, your flash of brilliance identified our man.

"So the locket belonged to the uncle, who was the lunatic preaching in the street? Incredible."

"There were other indicators. For instance, you will remember Vinto Jones stating that he saw 'no one unusual' in the square and 'a few of the regulars'. Surely, he would have recognized Horrocks as a regular and described him as something other than 'usual'. His being absent last Wednesday was irregular.

"My next errand was to make some arrangements with Vinto Jones. I headed to the Gilded Shoe and, upon his return, arranged to meet him in Blackall Street this afternoon. During the evening, I staked out the church of The Following in Hampstead. In addition to the church itself, an old gray stone structure dating back to the last century, there was a large residence that housed Horrocks and his fellow cult members and a few small outbuildings. Last night, after dark, Horrocks emerged from the house with a tray of food and a carafe, and entered one of these. It, too, was made of stone, windowless, and looked like a small shed. He left an hour later, alone with the empty tray. Neither he nor anyone else visited the shed that night, but he did repeat the ritual this morning.

"This afternoon, I returned to Blackall Street – or rather, an alley around the corner from it. At the appointed time, Vinto Jones came to meet me with the good reverend's keys, which he had lately borrowed while the man was terrifying passersby with great gusto, just as we witnessed the other day. I made some quick wax impressions, and gave the keys back to Jones to, hopefully, return to Horrocks before he was the wiser. He is going to meet us here in few hours to assist us with liberating young Brayslow."

"This is all utterly remarkable. But why has Horrocks abducted his nephew?"

"That we shall have to discover this evening. Now, I believe that is Mrs. Hudson coming up the stairs, and unless I am mistaken, I can smell curry. I recommend supper and a brief nap before Jones arrives. We are going to have a crowded evening."

At eleven o'clock, Jones arrived and the three of us hired a growler to take us to Hampstead. The closer we got to the church, the more the

411

traffic of the city began to thin, and by the time we arrived at our destination, there were very few people about. After we alighted from the cab about a block away, we began to walk slowly toward the church, which took up the entirety of the next block.

"If last night's routine holds, Horrocks and the other zealots should be tucked up in the house by now. But be on the lookout nonetheless."

It was very cold and quiet, and the full moon painted the scene with a dim glow. There was a low, stone wall bordering the churchyard, and we followed Holmes as he shimmied over it and silently made his way across the frosty ground through the old, stunted headstones. There were three small outbuildings behind the church and the house, and Holmes began making his way toward the nearest of them. When we reached the shed, Holmes motioned for us to stand behind him as he examined the door's lock and produced some keys from his coat. He selected what he thought was the appropriate one and took a step towards the door to unlock it. At that exact moment, however, the door's knob began to turn and the door swing outward. Instinctively, Jones hid behind it as it opened while Holmes and I braced for what was to come next. It was Horrocks who emerged, and before the old man could utter a sound, Holmes had maneuvered behind him, covered his mouth with his hand, and tackled him to the ground with one of the man's arms pinned behind him. I quickly removed my scarf and gagged the cult leader while Holmes produced some handcuffs. The three of us then entered the shed with our captive, and after Holmes gave a last look outside to make sure no one had seen, he noiselessly closed the heavy door behind us.

The stone building was musty with age and had a damp dirt floor. Within, illuminated by a single lamp hanging from a beam beneath the roof, sitting on the edge of a cot in his shirt sleeves with a blanket thrown over him and a chain leading from his wrist to the wall, was a tall, thin young man with curly red hair.

"Jones!" he cried. "Am I glad to see you! I hope you are as good as picking locks as you are at picking pockets. This lunatic has had me locked up in here for days. Who is that with you?"

"Master Jule – Or should I say Brayslow? If you aren't a sight for sore eyes! I was so worried about you I went and hired Sherlock Holmes and Doctor Watson to find you."

Holmes produced another key from his pocket. "And a good thing he did, but in the future I would strongly suggest you be a bit more selective about the company you keep, young man."

"You do not intend to involve the police, do you Mr. Holmes?"

"Please do not be apprehensive on that score, Brayslow. Dr. Watson and I are concerned with more weighty matters than apprehending pickpockets. If I were to truly administer justice in this case, it would be this reprobate I would hand over to the police. Please check his gag again, Watson, since we are going to be here for a few more minutes," he said as he turned again to young Brayslow and freed him from his chain.

"With the help of Watson, I was able to discover that it was your uncle who had abducted you and where he was keeping you, but I would very much appreciate it if you could fill in the details for me."

"I confess, I had no idea who he was when I passed him on the way to the alley, but he certainly recognized me. He followed and cornered me in the alley while I was waiting for you, Jones – crying out my name and yelling about what a horrible sinner I was. Then he showed me a picture of my mother and said that if I didn't let him help me to redeem myself, he would call the police. That he had heard all about my gambling and carousing. I was afraid he would give our whole game away, Jones. I decided it would be better to humour him, at least until we got to the church, but as soon as we got there, he coshed me. The next thing I knew, I was lying here with him looming over me, ranting about all sorts of angels and demons and the various circles of Hell. I kept telling him I had repented, but he wouldn't credit it. He told me that when I was ready to stay with The Following forever, then he would set me free. I've been here for days! And what's worse, Jones, he took our dosh."

"It was the locket that helped lead us to you," said Holmes. "He must have dropped it there. Well, you are free now, and I must ask you . . . What do you intend to do now that you are free? I should point out that your father provided me with information that helped me to trace you, and would like to know that you are safe. I cannot say for certain, but returning to him seems to be your best course. No offense meant, Jones."

"None taken, Mr. Holmes. Though I would hate to lose touch, I think he has point. The son of a Lord should have an easier time of it than a pickpocket," said Jones sheepishly.

"You may have no worries on that score, gentleman. I think I have had more than enough of youthful adventures."

"Very good. Then it is time we took our leave. But," added Holmes, "if I or the Brayslow family hears from you again, Sidney Horrocks, rest assured you will be the worse for it."

"What exactly are we going to do with him?"

"That is simple enough, Watson," he said as he advanced toward the reverend and started patting his pockets. He pulled out a key exactly like the one he was going to use to open the door and then produced the key to the handcuffs from his coat. He then blew out the lamp, and I heard a tinkle of metal as he tossed both keys into the darkness. With that we filed out, and he locked the door behind us with the key he had made, leaving Horrocks behind to find his own way outside.

After we had returned to Baker Street, having dropped off young Brayslow in Camden and having seen Jones off to Shoreditch, Holmes and I poured ourselves some brandy and sat down by the fire.

"I must say," I observed, "that this visit to Baker Street certainly did not disappoint."

"Yes, I always enjoy our time together. As I have said, I am lost without my Boswell."

"Well, Mary is not due to return for another few days. Perhaps you will be visited by another worthy client before I go. Do you think young Brayslow really intends to reform?"

"Who is to say, Watson? He had not gone terribly far down the path toward the dock, and after all, there are worse criminals to fall in with than Vinto Jones. Judging by what he told us:

> "*Consideration like an angel came*
> "*And whipt th' offending Adam out of him.*'"

Showing admirable restraint, Langdale Pike never did publish the story and contented himself with some of Holmes's latest sidelights on the affair of the politician, the lighthouse, and the trained cormorant that he had managed to gather, despite Mrs. Hudson's protestations over his recent unsavoury deliveries.

About the Contributors

The following contributions appear in this volume:
The MX Book of New Sherlock Holmes Stories
Part XIII – 2019 Annual (1881-1890)

Marino C. Alvarez, Ed.D., BSI, is professor *emeritus* at Tennessee State University. His book, *A Professor Reflects on Sherlock Holmes*, and other Sherlockian articles appear in the *Baker Street Journal*, *Canadian Holmes*, and *Saturday Review of Literature*, among others.

Hugh Ashton was born in the U.K., and moved to Japan in 1988, where he remained until 2016, living with his wife Yoshiko in the historic city of Kamakura, a little to the south of Yokohama. He and Yoshiko have now moved to Lichfield, a small cathedral city in the Midlands of the U.K., the birthplace of Samuel Johnson, and one-time home of Erasmus Darwin. In the past, he has worked in the technology and financial services industries, which have provided him with material for some of his books set in the 21st century. He currently works as a writer: Novelist, freelance editor, and copywriter, (his work for large Japanese corporations has appeared in international business journals), and journalist, as well as producing industry reports on various aspects of the financial services industry. Recently, however, his lifelong interest in Sherlock Holmes has developed into an acclaimed series of adventures featuring the world's most famous detective, written in the style of the originals. In addition to these, he has also published historical and alternate historical novels, short stories, and thrillers. Together with artist Andy Boerger, he has produced the *Sherlock Ferret* series of stories for children, featuring the world's cutest detective.

Brian Belanger is a publisher and editor, but is best known for his freelance illustration and cover design work. His distinctive style can be seen on several MX Publishing covers, including *Silent Meridian* by Elizabeth Crowen, *Sherlock Holmes and the Menacing Melbournian* by Allan Mitchell, *Sherlock Holmes and A Quantity of Debt* by David Marcum, *Welcome to Undershaw* by Luke Benjamen Kuhns, and many more. Brian is the co-founder of Belanger Books LLC, where he illustrates the popular *MacDougall Twins with Sherlock Holmes* young reader series (#1 bestsellers on Amazon.com UK). A prolific creator, he also designs t-shirts, mugs, stickers, and other merchandise on his personal art site: *www.redbubble.com/people/zhahadun*.

Derrick Belanger is an educator and also the author of the #1 bestselling book in its category, *Sherlock Holmes: The Adventure of the Peculiar Provenance*, which was in the top 200 bestselling books on Amazon. He also is the author of *The MacDougall Twins with Sherlock Holmes* books, and he edited the Sir Arthur Conan Doyle horror anthology *A Study in Terror: Sir Arthur Conan Doyle's Revolutionary Stories of Fear and the Supernatural*. Mr. Belanger co-owns the publishing company Belanger Books, which released the Sherlock Holmes anthologies *Beyond Watson, Holmes Away From Home: Adventures from the Great Hiatus* Volumes 1 and 2, *Sherlock Holmes: Before Baker Street*, and *Sherlock Holmes: Adventures in the Realms of H.G. Wells* Volumes I and 2. Derrick resides in Colorado and continues compiling unpublished works by Dr. John H. Watson.

417

S.F. Bennett was born and raised in London, studying History at Queen Mary and Westfield College, and Journalism at City University at the Postgraduate level, before moving to Devon in 2013. The author lectures on Conan Doyle, Sherlock Holmes, and 19th century detective fiction, and has had articles on various aspects from The Canon published in *The Journal of the Sherlock Holmes Society of London* and *The Torr*, the journal of *The Poor Folk Upon The Moors*, the Sherlock Holmes Society of the South West of England. Her first published novel is *The Secret Diary of Mycroft Holmes: The Thoughts and Reminiscences of Sherlock Holmes's Elder Brother, 1880-1888* (2017).

Andrew Bryant was born in Bridgend, Wales, and now lives in Burlington, Ontario. His previous publications include *Prism International*, *On Spec*, *The Dalhousie Review*, and second place in the 2015 *Toronto Star* short story contest. "The Shackled Man" is his first Sherlock Holmes story, written after visiting 221b Baker Street.

Sir Arthur Conan Doyle (1859-1930) *Holmes Chronicler Emeritus*. If not for him, this anthology would not exist. Author, physician, patriot, sportsman, spiritualist, husband and father, and advocate for the oppressed. He is remembered and honored for the purposes of this collection by being the man who introduced Sherlock Holmes to the world. Through fifty-six Holmes short stories, four novels, and additional Apocryphal entries, Doyle revolutionized mystery stories and also greatly influenced and improved police forensic methods and techniques for the betterment of all. *Steel True Blade Straight.*

Steve Emecz's main field is technology, in which he has been working for about twenty years. Following multiple senior roles at Xerox, where he grew their European eCommerce from $6m to $200m, Steve joined platform provider Venda, and moved across to Powa in 2010. Today, Steve is Chief Revenue Officer at CloudTrade, a company that digitises large companies' accounts payables. Steve is a regular trade show speaker on the subject of eCommerce, and his tech career has taken him to more than fifty countries – so he's no stranger to planes and airports. He wrote two novels (one a bestseller) in the 1990's, and a screenplay in 2001. Shortly after, he set up MX Publishing, specialising in NLP books. In 2008, MX published its first Sherlock Holmes book, and MX has gone on to become the largest specialist Holmes publisher in the world. MX is a social enterprise and supports three main causes. The first is Happy Life, a children's rescue project in Nairobi, Kenya, where he and his wife, Sharon, spend every Christmas at the rescue centre in Kasarani. In 2014, they wrote a short book about the project, *The Happy Life Story*. The second is the Stepping Stones School, of which Steve is a patron. Stepping Stones is located at Undershaw, Sir Arthur Conan Doyle's former home. Steve has been a mentor for the World Food Programme for the last two years, supporting their innovation bootcamps and giving 1-2-1 mentoring to several projects.

Edwin A. Enstrom is a budding pasticheurs and an Army veteran who spent one year in Vietnam. Now retired, he worked for forty-plus years for one company in various capacities, mostly within Information Technology. He is an avid reader, especially of fair-play detective mysteries. He is a puzzle lover, especially cryptic crosswords. Additionally, he's an internet junkie, spending several hours daily surfing the web, but with no smart phone, no television, and no Facebook or social media.

James R. "Jim" French became a morning Disc Jockey on KIRO (AM) in Seattle in 1959. He later founded *Imagination Theatre*, a syndicated program that broadcast to over one-hundred-and-twenty stations in the U.S. and Canada, and also on the XM Satellite Radio system all over North America. Actors in French's dramas included John Patrick Lowrie,

Larry Albert, Patty Duke, Russell Johnson, Tom Smothers, Keenan Wynn, Roddy MacDowall, Ruta Lee, John Astin, Cynthia Lauren Tewes, and Richard Sanders. Mr. French stated, "To me, the characters of Sherlock Holmes and Doctor Watson always seemed to be figures Doyle created as a challenge to lesser writers. He gave us two interesting characters – different from each other in their histories, talents, and experience, but complimentary as a team – who have been applied to a variety of situations and plots far beyond the times and places in The Canon. In the hands of different writers, Holmes and Watson have lent their identities to different times, ages, and even genders. But I wanted to break no new ground. I feel Sir Arthur provided us with enough references to locations, landmarks, and the social conditions of his time, to give a pretty large canvas on which to paint our own images and actions to animate Holmes and Watson." Mr. French passed away at the age of eighty-nine on December 20th, 2017.

David Friend lives in Wales, Great Britain, where he divides his time between watching old detective films and thinking about old detective films. Now thirty, he's been scribbling out stories for twenty years and hopes, some day, to write something half-decent. Most of what he pens is set in an old-timey world of non-stop adventure with debonair sleuths, kick-ass damsels, criminal masterminds, and narrow escapes, and he wishes he could live there.

Tim Gambrell lives in Exeter, Devon with his wife, two young sons, two cats, and seven chickens. He has had short stories published in *Lethbridge-Stewart: The HAVOC Files 3* and *The Lethbridge-Stewart Quiz Book* (both Candy Jar books, 2017), *Bernice Summerfield: True Stories* (Big Finish, 2017) and *Relics . . . An Anthology* (Red Ted Books, 2018). Tim has written a novella, *The Way of The Bry'hunee*, for the Erimem Range from Thebes Publishing (due 2019), and his first full novel, *Lucy Wilson and The Bledoe Cadets*, will be published by Candy Jar Books in 2019 as part of the *Lethbridge-Stewart: The Laughing Gnome* series. Tim has contributed to a number of charity publications, including *A Time Lord For Change* (2016) and *Whoblique Strategies* (2017) from Chinbeard Books, and *You and 42 & Blake's Legacy: 40 Years of Rebellion* from Who Dares Publishing (both 2018).

Mark A. Gagen BSI is co-founder of Wessex Press, sponsor of the popular *From Gillette to Brett* conferences, and publisher of *The Sherlock Holmes Reference Library* and many other fine Sherlockian titles. A life-long Holmes enthusiast, he is a member of *The Baker Street Irregulars* and *The Illustrious Clients of Indianapolis*. A graphic artist by profession, his work is often seen on the covers of *The Baker Street Journal* and various BSI books.

Melissa Grigsby Executive Head Teacher of Stepping Stones School, is driven by a passion to open the doors to learners with complex and layered special needs that just make society feel two steps too far away. Based on the Surrey/Hampshire border in England, her time is spent between relocating a great school into the prestigious home of Conan Doyle, and her two children, dogs, and horses, so there never a dull moment.

John Atkinson Grimshaw (1836-1893) was born in Leeds, England. His amazing paintings, usually featuring twilight or night scenes illuminated by gas-lamps or moonlight, are easily recognizable, and are often used on the covers of books about The Great Detective to set the mood, as shadowy figures move in the distance through misty mysterious settings and over rain-slicked streets.

419

Arthur Hall was born in Aston, Birmingham, UK, in 1944. He discovered his interest in writing during his schooldays, along with a love of fictional adventure and suspense. His first novel, *Sole Contact,* was an espionage story about an ultra-secret government department known as "Sector Three", and was followed, to date, by three sequels. Other works include five Sherlock Holmes novels, *The Demon of the Dusk*, *The One Hundred Percent Society*, *The Secret Assassin*, *The Phantom Killer*, and *In Pursuit of the Dead*, as well as a collection of short stories, and a modern detective novel. He lives in the West Midlands, United Kingdom.

Paul Hiscock is an author of crime, fantasy, and science fiction tales. His short stories have appeared in several anthologies and include a seventeenth century whodunnit, a science fiction western, and a steampunk Sherlock Holmes story. Paul lives with his family in Kent, England, and spends his days chasing a toddler with more energy than the Duracell Bunny. He mainly does his writing in coffee shops with members of the local NaNoWriMo group, or in the middle of the night when his family has gone to sleep. Consequently, his stories tend to be fuelled by large amounts of black coffee. You can find out more about his writing at *www.detectivesanddragons.uk.*

Roger Johnson BSI, ASH is a retired librarian, now working as a volunteer assistant at the Essex Police Museum. In his spare time, he is commissioning editor of *The Sherlock Holmes Journal*, an occasional lecturer, and a frequent contributor to The Writings About the Writings. His sole work of Holmesian pastiche was published in 1997 in Mike Ashley's anthology *The Mammoth Book of New Sherlock Holmes Adventures*, and he has the greatest respect for the many authors who have contributed new tales to the present mighty trilogy. Like his wife, Jean Upton, he is a member of both *The Baker Street Irregulars* and *The Adventuresses of Sherlock Holmes.*

David Marcum plays *The Game* with deadly seriousness. He first discovered Sherlock Holmes in 1975, at the age of ten, when he received an abridged version of *The Adventures* during a trade. Since that time, David has collected literally thousands of traditional Holmes pastiches in the form of novels, short stories, radio and television episodes, movies and scripts, comics, fan-fiction, and unpublished manuscripts. He is the author of *The Papers of Sherlock Holmes Vol.'s I* and *II* (2011, 2013), *Sherlock Holmes and A Quantity of Debt* (2013), *Sherlock Holmes – Tangled Skeins* (2015), and *The Papers of Solar Pons* (2017). He is the editor of *Sherlock Holmes in Montague Street* (2014) *Holmes Away From Home* (2016), *Sherlock Holmes: Before Baker Street* (2017), *Imagination Theatre's Sherlock Holmes* (2017), *Sherlock Holmes: Adventures Beyond the Canon*, (2018) and *The New Adventures of Solar Pons* (2018). He edited the authorized reissues of the *Solar Pons* stories, and is currently editing *The Complete Dr. Thorndyke*. Additionally, he is the creator and editor of the ongoing collection, *The MX Book of New Sherlock Holmes Stories* (2015-Present), now at fifteen volumes, with more in preparation as of this writing. He has contributed stories, essays, and scripts to a variety of Sherlockian anthologies, *The Baker Street Journal*, *The Strand Magazine, The Watsonian, Beyond Watson, Sherlock Holmes Mystery Magazine, About Sixty, About Being a Sherlockian, Sherlock Holmes is Like, The Solar Pons Gazette, Imagination Theater, The Art of Sherlock Holmes, The Proceedings of the Pondicherry Lodge*, and *The Gazette*, the journal of the Nero Wolfe *Wolfe Pack*. He began his adult work life as a Federal Investigator for an obscure U.S. Government agency. When the organization was eliminated, he returned to school for a second degree and is now a licensed Civil Engineer, living in Tennessee with his wife and son. He is a member of *The Sherlock Holmes Society of London, The Nashville Scholars of the Three Pipe Problem* ("The Engineer's Thumb"), *The Occupants of the Full House, The Diogenes Club* *of Washington, D.C.*, *The Tankerville Club* (all Scions of *The Baker Street Irregulars*), *The Sherlock Holmes Society of India* (as a Patron), *The John H. Watson Society* ("Marker"), *The Praed Street Irregulars* ("The Obrisset Snuff Box"), *The Solar Pons Society of London*, and *The Diogenes Club West (East Tennessee Annex)*, a curious and unofficial Scion of one. Since the age of nineteen, he has worn a deerstalker as his regular-and-only hat. In 2013, he and his deerstalker were finally able make his first trip-of-a-lifetime Holmes Pilgrimage to England, with return Pilgrimages in 2015 and 2016, where you may have spotted him. If you ever run into him and his deerstalker out and about, feel free to say hello!

Jacquelynn Morris, ASH, BSI, JHWS, is a member of several Sherlock Holmes societies in the Mid-Atlantic area of the U.S.A., but her home group is Watson's Tin Box in Maryland. She is the founder of *A Scintillation of Scions*, an annual Sherlock Holmes symposium. She has been published in the BSI Manuscript Series, *The Wrong Passage*, as well as in *About Sixty* and *About Being a Sherlockian* (Wildside Press). Jacquelynn was the U.S. liaison for the Undershaw Preservation Trust for several years, until Undershaw was purchased to become part of Stepping Stones School.

Mark Mower is a member of the *Crime Writers' Association*, *The Sherlock Holmes Society of London*, and *The Solar Pons Society of London*. He writes true crime stories and fictional mysteries. His first two volumes of Holmes pastiches were entitled *A Farewell to Baker Street* and *Sherlock Holmes: The Baker Street Case-Files* (both with MX Publishing) and, to date, he has contributed chapters to six parts of the ongoing *The MX Book of New Sherlock Holmes Stories*. He has also had stories in two anthologies by Belanger Books: *Holmes Away From Home: Adventures from the Great Hiatus – Volume II – 1893-1894* (2016) and *Sherlock Holmes: Before Baker Street* (2017). More are bound to follow. Mark's non-fiction works include *Bloody British History: Norwich* (The History Press, 2014), *Suffolk Murders* (The History Press, 2011) and *Zeppelin Over Suffolk* (Pen & Sword Books, 2008).

Sidney Paget (1860-1908), a few of whose illustrations are used within this anthology, was born in London, and like his two older brothers, became a famed illustrator and painter. He completed over three-hundred-and-fifty drawings for the Sherlock Holmes stories that were first published in *The Strand* magazine, defining Holmes's image forever after in the public mind.

Tracy J. Revels, a Sherlockian from the age of eleven, is a professor of history at Wofford College in Spartanburg, South Carolina. She is a member of *The Survivors of the Gloria Scott* and *The Studious Scarlets Society*, and is a past recipient of the Beacon Society Award. Almost every semester, she teaches a class that covers The Canon, either to college students or to senior citizens. She is also the author of three supernatural Sherlockian pastiches with MX (*Shadowfall*, *Shadowblood*, and *Shadowwraith*), and a regular contributor to her scion's newsletter. She also has some notoriety as an author of very silly skits: For proof, see "The Adventure of the Adversarial Adventuress" and "Occupy Baker Street" on YouTube. When not studying Sherlock, she can be found researching the history of her native state, and has written books on Florida in the Civil War and on the development of Florida's tourism industry.

Brenda Seabrooke's stories have been published in sixteen reviews, journals, and anthologies. She has received grants from the National Endowment for the Arts and Emerson College's Robbie Macauley Award. She is the author of twenty-three books for young readers including *Scones and Bones on Baker Street: Sherlock's (maybe!) Dog and the Dirt Dilemma*, and *The Rascal in the Castle: Sherlock's (possible!) Dog and the Queen's Revenge*. Brenda states: "It was fun to write from Dr. Watson's point of view and not have to worry about fleas, smelly pits, ralphing, or scratching at inopportune times."

Stephen Seitz has reported for newspapers as politically diverse as the *Brattleboro Reformer* and the *New Hampshire Union Leader*. He has covered everything from natural disasters to presidential campaigns, and has interviewed an original cast member from every *Star Trek* television series. Other notables include James Earl Jones, Jodi Picoult, Jerry Lewis, James Whitmore, Senator George McGovern, and many others. He is also the host of cable TV's *Book Talk*. Sherlock Holmes has been a part of Steve's life since the age of twelve, when, while putting homework off, he discovered *The Hound of the Baskervilles* in the stacks at Brooks Memorial Library in Brattleboro, Vt. More than forty years later, he is still an avid Sherlockian and speaks to scion societies on occasion. Naturally, more of his Sherlock Holmes stories are on the way.

Matthew Simmonds hails from Bedford, in the South East of England, and has been a confirmed devotee of Sir Arthur Conan Doyle's most famous creation since first watching Jeremy Brett's incomparable portrayal of the world's first consulting detective, on a Tuesday evening in April, 1984, while curled up on the sofa with his father. He has written numerous short stories, and his first novel, *Sherlock Holmes: The Adventure of The Pigtail Twist*, was published in 2018. A sequel is nearly complete, which he hopes to publish in the near future. Matthew currently co-owns Harrison & Simmonds, the fifth-generation family business, a renowned County tobacconist, pipe, and gift shop on Bedford High Street.

Shane Simmons is a multi-award-winning screenwriter and graphic novelist whose work has appeared in international film festivals, museums, and lectures about design and structure. His best-known piece of fiction, *The Long and Unlearned Life of Roland Gethers*, has been discussed in multiple books and academic journals about sequential art, and his short stories have been printed in critically praised anthologies of history, crime, and horror. He lives in Montreal with his wife and too many cats. Follow him at *eyestrainproductions.com* and *@Shane_Eyestrain*

Robert V. Stapleton was born and brought up in Leeds, Yorkshire, England, and studied at Durham University. After working in various parts of the country as an Anglican parish priest, he is now retired and lives with his wife in North Yorkshire. As a member of his local writing group, he now has time to develop his other life as a writer of adventure stories. He has recently had a number of short stories published, and he is hoping to have a couple of completed novels published at some time in the future.

Will Thomas is the author of ten books in the Barker and Llewelyn Victorian mystery series, including *Some Danger Involved*, *Fatal Enquiry*, and most recently *Blood is Blood*. He was nominated for a *Barry* and a *Shamus*. He lives in Oklahoma, where he studies Victorian martial arts and models British railways.

Kevin P. Thornton has experienced a Taliban rocket attack in Kabul and a terrorist bombing in Johannesburg. He lives in Fort McMurray, Alberta, the town that burnt down in 2016. He has been shortlisted for the *Crime Writers of Canada* Unhanged writing award six times. He's never won. He was also a finalist for best short story in 2014 – the year Margaret Atwood entered. We're not saying he has luck issues, but don't bet on his stock tips. Born in Kenya, Kevin was a child in New Zealand, a student and soldier in Africa, a military contractor in Afghanistan, a forklift driver in Ontario, and an oilfield worker in North Western Canada. He writes poems that start out just fine, but turn ruder and cruder over time. From limerick to doggerel, they earn less than bugger-all, even though they all manage to rhyme. He also likes writing about Sherlock Holmes and dislikes writing about himself in the third person.

Peter Coe Verbica grew up on a commercial cattle ranch in Northern California, where he learned the value of a strong work ethic. He works for the Wealth Management Group of a global investment bank, and is an Adjunct Professor in the Economics Department at SJSU. He is the author of numerous books, including *Left at the Gate and Other Poems*, *Hard-Won Cowboy Wisdom (Not Necessarily in Order of Importance)*, *A Key to the Grove and Other Poems*, and *The Missing Tales of Sherlock Holmes (as Compiled by Peter Coe Verbica, JD)*. Mr. Verbica obtained a JD from Santa Clara University School of Law, an MS from Massachusetts Institute of Technology, and a BA in English from Santa Clara University. He is the co-inventor on a number of patents, has served as a Managing Member of three venture capital firms, and the CFO of one of the portfolio companies. He is an unabashed advocate of cowboy culture and enjoys creative writing, hiking, and tennis. He is married with four daughters. For more information, or to contact the author, please go to *www.hardwoncowboywisdom.com*.

Mark Wardecker is an instructional technologist at Colby College. He is the editor and annotator of *The Dragnet Solar Pons et al.* (Battered Silicon Dispatch Box, 2011) and has contributed Sherlockian pastiches to *Sherlock Holmes Mystery Magazine*, Solar Pons pastiches to *The New Adventures of Solar Pons*, and an article to *The Baker Street Journal*, as well as having published other fiction and nonfiction.

Sean Wright BSI makes his home in Santa Clarita, a charming city at the entrance of the high desert in Southern California. For sixteen years, features and articles under his byline appeared in *The Tidings* – now *The Angelus News* – publications of the Roman Catholic Archdiocese of Los Angeles. Continuing his education in 2007, Mr. Wright graduated *summa cum laude* from Grand Canyon University, attaining a Bachelor of Arts degree in Christian Studies. He then attained a Master of Arts degree, also in Christian Studies. Once active in the entertainment industry, in an abortive attempt to revive dramatic radio in 1976 with his beloved mentor the late Daws Butler directing, Mr. Wright co-produced and wrote the syndicated *New Radio Adventures of Sherlock Holmes* starring the late Edward Mulhare as the Great Detective. Mr. Wright has written for several television quiz shows and remains proud of his work for *The Quiz Kid's Challenge* and the popular TV quiz show *Jeopardy!* for which The Academy of Television Arts and Sciences honored him in 1985 with an Emmy nomination in the field of writing. Honored with membership in *The Baker Street Irregulars* as "The Manor House Case" after founding *The Non-Canonical Calabashes, The Sherlock Holmes Society of Los Angeles* in 1970, Mr. Wright has written for *The Baker Street Journal* and *Mystery Magazine*. Since 1971, he has conducted lectures on Sherlock Holmes's influence on literature and cinema for libraries, colleges, and private organizations, including MENSA. Mr. Wright's whimsical *Sherlock Holmes Cookbook* (Drake) created with John Farrell BSI, was published in 1976 and a mystery novel, *Enter the Lion: a Posthumous Memoir of Mycroft Holmes* (Hawthorne), "edited" with Michael Hodel BSI, followed in 1979. As director general of The Plot Thickens Mystery Company, Mr. Wright originated hosting "mystery parties" in homes, restaurants, and offices, as well as producing and directing the very first "Mystery Train" tours on Amtrak beginning in 1982.

Part XIV – 2019 Annual (1891-1897)
and
Part XV– 2019 Annual (1898-1918)

Maurice Barkley lives with his wife Marie in a suburb of Rochester, New York. Retired from a career as a commercial artist and builder of tree houses, he is writing and busy reinforcing the stereotype of a pesky househusband. His other Sherlock Holmes stories can be found on Amazon. *https://www.amazon.com/author/mauricebarkleys*

Matthew Booth is the author of *Sherlock Holmes and the Giant's Hand*, published by Breese Books and the co-author of *The Further Exploits of Sherlock Holmes*, a collection of new stories, commissioned by Sparkling Books in 2016. He contributed two original Holmes stories to *The Game is Afoot*, a collection of Sherlock Holmes short stories published in 2008 by Wordsworth Editions and contributed a story to Wordsworth Editions' collection of original crime tales, *Crime Scenes*. He is the creator of Anthony Rathe, a disgraced former barrister seeking redemption by solving those crimes which come his way. The character first appeared in a series of radio plays produced and syndicated by *Imagination Theatre* in America. Rathe now appears in Matthew's latest book, *When Anthony Rathe Investigates* published by Sparkling Books. A lifelong devotee of crime and supernatural fiction, Matthew has provided a number of academic talks on such subjects as Sherlock Holmes, the works of Agatha Christie, crime fiction, Count Dracula, and the facts and theories concerning the crimes of Jack the Ripper. He is also a member of the *Crime Writers Association* and a contributor to their monthly newsletter, *Red Herrings*.

Thomas A. Burns, Jr. is the author of the *Natalie McMasters Mysteries*. He was born and grew up in New Jersey, attended Xavier High School in Manhattan, earned B.S degrees in Zoology and Microbiology at Michigan State University, and a M.S. in Microbiology at North Carolina State University. He currently resides in Wendell, North Carolina. As a kid, Tom started reading mysteries with The Hardy Boys, Ken Holt and Rick Brant, and graduated to the classic stories by authors such as A. Conan Doyle, Dorothy Sayers, John Dickson Carr, Erle Stanley Gardner, and Rex Stout, to name a few. Tom has written fiction as a hobby all of his life, starting with The Man from U.N.C.L.E. stories in marble-backed copybooks in grade school. He built a career as technical, science, and medical writer and editor for nearly thirty years in industry and government. Now that he's truly on his own as a novelist, he's excited to publish his own mystery series, as well as to contribute stories about his second-most-favorite detective, Sherlock Holmes, to *The MX anthology of New Sherlock Holmes Stories*.

Nick Cardillo has been a devotee of Sherlock Holmes since the age of six. His first published short story, "The Adventure of the Traveling Corpse" appeared in *The MX Book of New Sherlock Holmes Stories – Part VI: 2017 Annual*, and he has written subsequent stories for both MX Publishing and Belanger Books. In 2018, Nick completed his first anthology of new Sherlock Holmes adventures entitled *The Feats of Sherlock Holmes*. Nick is a fan of The Golden Age of Detective Fiction, Hammer Horror, and Doctor Who. He writes film reviews and analyses at *Sacred-Celluloid.blogspot.com*. He is a student at Susquehanna University in Selinsgrove, PA.

Leslie Charteris was born in Singapore on May 12th, 1907. With his mother and brother, he moved to England in 1919 and attended Rossall School in Lancashire before moving on to Cambridge University to study law. His studies there came to a halt when a publisher accepted his first novel. His third one, entitled *Meet the Tiger*, was written when he was twenty years old and published in September 1928. It introduced the world to Simon Templar, *aka* The Saint. He continued to write about The Saint until 1983 when the last book, *Salvage for The Saint*, was published. The books, which have been translated into over thirty languages, number nearly a hundred and have sold over forty-million copies around the world. They've inspired, to date, fifteen feature films, three television series, ten radio series, and a comic strip that was written by Charteris and syndicated around the world for over a decade. He enjoyed travelling, but settled for long periods in Hollywood, Florida, and finally in Surrey, England. He was awarded the Cartier Diamond Dagger by the *Crime Writers' Association* in 1992, in recognition of a lifetime of achievement. He died the following year.

Harry DeMaio is a *nom de plume* of Harry B. DeMaio, successful author of several books on Information Security and Business Networks, as well as the ten-volume *Casebooks of Octavius Bear – Alternative Universe Mysteries for Adult Animal Lovers.* Octavius Bear is loosely based on Sherlock Holmes and Nero Wolfe in a world in which *homo sapiens* died out long ago in a global disaster, but most animals have advanced to a twenty-first century anthropomorphic state. "It's Time" is Harry's first offering treating Holmes and Watson in their original human condition. A retired business executive, consultant, information security specialist, former pilot, and graduate school adjunct professor, he whiles away his time traveling and writing preposterous articles and stories. He has appeared on many radio and TV shows and is an accomplished, frequent public speaker. Former New York City natives, he and his extremely patient and helpful wife, Virginia, and their Bichon Frisé, Woof, live in Cincinnati (and several other parallel universes.) They have two sons living in Scottsdale, Arizona and Cortlandt Manor, New York, both of whom are quite successful and quite normal – thus putting the lie to the theory that insanity is hereditary.

Ian Dickerson was just nine years old when he discovered The Saint. Shortly after that, he discovered Sherlock Holmes. The Saint won, for a while anyway. He struck up a friendship with The Saint's creator, Leslie Charteris, and his family. With their permission, he spent six weeks studying the Leslie Charteris collection at Boston University and went on to write, direct, and produce documentaries on the making of *The Saint* and *Return of The Saint,* which have been released on DVD. He oversaw the recent reprints of almost fifty of the original Saint books in both the US and UK, and was a co-producer on the 2017 TV movie of *The Saint.* When he discovered that Charteris had written Sherlock Holmes stories as well – well, there was the excuse he needed to revisit The Canon. He's consequently written and edited three books on Holmes' radio adventures. For the sake of what little sanity he has, Ian has also written about a wide range of subjects, none of which come with a halo, including talking mashed potatoes, Lord Grade, and satellite links. Ian lives in Hampshire with his wife and two children. And an awful lot of books by Leslie Charteris. Not quite so many by Conan Doyle, though.

C.H. Dye first discovered Sherlock Holmes when she was eleven, in a collection that ended at the Reichenbach Falls. It was another six months before she discovered *The Hound of the Baskervilles*, and two weeks after that before a librarian handed her *The Return.* She has loved the stories ever since. She has written fan-fiction, and her first published pastiche, "The Tale of the Forty Thieves", was included in *The MX Book of New Sherlock Holmes Stories – Part I: 1881-1889.* Her story "A Christmas Goose" was in *The MX Book of New*

Sherlock Holmes Stories – Part V: Christmas Adventures, and "The Mysterious Mourner" in *The MX Book of New Sherlock Holmes Stories – Part VIII – Eliminate the Impossible: 1892-1905*

Anna Elliott is an author of historical fiction and fantasy. Her first series, *The Twilight of Avalon* trilogy, is a retelling of the Trystan and Isolde legend. She wrote her second series, *The Pride and Prejudice Chronicles*, chiefly to satisfy her own curiosity about what might have happened to Elizabeth Bennet, Mr. Darcy, and all the other wonderful cast of characters after the official end of Jane Austen's classic work. She enjoys stories about strong women, and loves exploring the multitude of ways women can find their unique strengths. She was delighted to lend a hand with the "Sherlock and Lucy" series, and this story, firstly because she loves Sherlock Holmes as much as her father, co-author Charles Veley, does, and second because it almost never happens that someone with a dilemma shouts, "Quick, we need an author of historical fiction!" Anna lives in the Washington, D.C .area with her husband and three children.

Edwin A. Enstrom – *In addition to a story in this volume, Ed also has stories in Parts XIV and XV*

Thomas Fortenberry is an American author, editor, and reviewer. Founder of Mind Fire Press and a Pushcart Prize-nominated writer, he has also judged many literary contests, including the Georgia Author of the Year Awards and the Robert Penn Warren Prize for Fiction. His Sherlock Holmes stories have appeared in such works as *An Improbable Truth* and various volmes of *The MX Book of New Sherlock Holmes Stories.*

Jayantika Ganguly BSI is the General Secretary and Editor of the *Sherlock Holmes Society of India*, a member of the *Sherlock Holmes Society of London*, and the *Czech Sherlock Holmes Society*. She is the author of *The Holmes Sutra* (MX 2014). She is a corporate lawyer working with one of the Big Six law firms.

Dick Gillman is an English writer and acrylic artist living in Brittany, France with his wife Alex, Truffle, their Black Labrador, and Jean-Claude, their Breton cat. During his retirement from teaching, he has written over twenty Sherlock Holmes short stories which are published as both e-books and paperbacks. His contribution to the superb MX Sherlock Holmes collection, published in October 2015, was entitled "The Man on Westminster Bridge" and had the privilege of being chosen as the anchor story in *The MX Book of New Sherlock Holmes Stories – Part II (1890-1895).*

Denis Green was born in London, England in April 1905. He grew up mostly in London's Savoy Theatre where his father, Richard Green, was a principal in many Gilbert and Sullivan productions. A Flying Officer with RAF until 1924, he then spent four years managing a tea estate in North India before making his stage debut in *Hamlet* with Leslie Howard in 1928. He made his first visit to America in 1931 and established a respectable stage career before appearing in films – including minor roles in the first two Rathbone and Bruce Holmes films – and developing a career in front of and behind the microphone during the Golden Age of radio. Green and Leslie Charteris met in 1938 and struck up a lifelong friendship. Always busy, be it on stage, radio, film or television, Green passed away at the age of fifty in New York.

Jack Grochot is a retired investigative newspaper journalist and a former federal law enforcement agent specializing in mail fraud cases. He has written three books of Sherlock

Holmes pastiches and a fourth nonfiction book, *Saga of a Latter-Day Saddle Tramp*, a memoir of his five-year horseback journey across twelve states. Grochot lives on a small farm in southwestern Pennsylvania, where he writes and oversees a horse-boarding stable.

Liz Hedgecock grew up in London, England, did an English degree, and then took forever to start writing. Now Liz travels between the nineteenth and twenty-first centuries, murdering people. To be fair, she does usually clean up after herself. Liz's reimaginings of Sherlock Holmes, her Pippa Parker cozy mystery series, and the Caster & Fleet mystery series (written with Paula Harmon) are available in ebook and paperback. Liz lives in Cheshire with her husband and two sons, and when she's not writing or child-wrangling, you can usually find her reading, messing about on Twitter, or cooing over stuff in museums and art galleries. That's her story, anyway, and she's sticking to it.

Arthur Hall – *In addition to a story in this volume, Arthur also has a stories in Parts XIV and XV*

Carl L. Heifetz Over thirty years of inquiry as a research microbiologist have prepared Carl Heifetz to explore new horizons in science. As an author, he has published numerous articles and short stories for fan magazines and other publications. In 2013, he published a book entitled *Voyage of the Blue Carbuncle* that is based on the works of Sir Arthur Conan Doyle and Gene Roddenberry. *Voyage of the Blue Carbuncle* is a fun and exciting spoof, sure to please science fiction fans as well as those who love the stories of Sherlock Holmes and *Star Trek*. Carl and his wife have two grown children and live in Trinity, Florida.

Stephen Herczeg is an IT Geek, writer, actor, and film-maker based in Canberra Australia. He has been writing for over twenty years and has completed a couple of dodgy novels, sixteen feature-length screenplays, and numerous short stories and scripts. Stephen was very successful in 2017's International Horror Hotel screenplay competition, with his scripts *TITAN* winning the Sci-Fi category and *Dark are the Woods* placing second in the horror category. His work has featured in *Sproutlings – A Compendium of Little Fictions* from Hunter Anthologies, the *Hells Bells* Christmas horror anthology published by the Australasian Horror Writers Association, and the *Below the Stairs*, *Trickster's Treats*, *Shades of Santa*, *Behind the Mask*, and *Beyond the Infinite* anthologies from *OzHorror.Con*, *The Body Horror Book*, *Anemone Enemy*, and *Petrified Punks* from Oscillate Wildly Press, and *Sherlock Holmes In the Realms of H.G. Wells* and *Sherlock Holmes: Adventures Beyond the Canon* from Belanger Books.

Mike Hogan writes mostly historical novels and short stories, many set in Victorian London and featuring Sherlock Holmes and Doctor Watson. He read the Conan Doyle stories at school with great enjoyment, but hadn't thought much about Sherlock Holmes until, having missed the Granada/Jeremy Brett TV series when it was originally shown in the eighties, he came across a box set of videos in a street market and was hooked on Holmes again. He started writing Sherlock Holmes pastiches several years ago, having great fun re-imagining situations for the Conan Doyle characters to act in. The relationship between Holmes and Watson fascinates him as one of the great literary friendships. (He's also a huge admirer of Patrick O'Brian's Aubrey-Maturin novels). Like Captain Aubrey and Doctor Maturin, Holmes and Watson are an odd couple, differing in almost every facet of their characters, but sharing a common sense of decency and a common humanity. Living with Sherlock Holmes can't have been easy, and Mike enjoys adding a stronger vein of "pawky humour" into the Conan Doyle mix, even letting Watson have the second-to-last word on occasions. His books include *Sherlock Holmes and the Scottish Question*,

427

the forthcoming *The Gory Season – Sherlock Holmes, Jack the Ripper and the Thames Torso Murders*, and the Sherlock Holmes & Young Winston 1887 Trilogy (*The Deadwood Stage*, *The Jubilee Plot*, and *The Giant Moles*), He has also written the following short story collections: *Sherlock Holmes: Murder at the Savoy and Other Stories*, *Sherlock Holmes: The Skull of Kohada Koheiji and Other Stories*, and *Sherlock Holmes: Murder on the Brighton Line and Other Stories*. www.mikehoganbooks.com

Christopher James was born in 1975 in Paisley, Scotland. Educated at Newcastle and UEA, he was a winner of the UK's National Poetry Competition in 2008. He has written two full length Sherlock Holmes novels, *The Adventure of the Ruby Elephant* and *The Jeweller of Florence*, both published by MX, and is working on a third.

Kelvin I. Jones is the author of six books about Sherlock Holmes and the definitive biography of Conan Doyle as a spiritualist, *Conan Doyle and The Spirits*. A member of *The Sherlock Holmes Society of London*, he has published numerous short occult and ghost stories in British anthologies over the last thirty years. His work has appeared on BBC Radio, and in 1984 he won the Mason Hall Literary Award for his poem cycle about the survivors of Hiroshima and Nagasaki, recently reprinted as "Omega". (Oakmagic Publications) A one-time teacher of creative writing at the University of East Anglia, he is also the author of four crime novels featuring his ex-Met sleuth John Bottrell, who first appeared in *Stone Dead*. He has over fifty titles on Kindle, and is also the author of several novellas and short story collections featuring a Norwich-based detective, DCI Ketch, an intrepid sleuth who investigates East Anglian murder cases. He also published a series of short stories about an Edwardian psychic detective, Dr. John Carter (*Carter's Occult Casebook*). Ramsey Campbell, the British horror writer, and Francis King, the renowned novelist, have both compared his supernatural stories to those of M. R. James. He has also published children's fiction, namely *Odin's Eye*, and, in collaboration with his wife Debbie, *The Dark Entry*. Since 1995, he has been the proprietor of Oakmagic Publications, publishers of British folklore and of his fiction titles. He lives in Norfolk. (See *www.oakmagicpublications.co.uk*)

David Marcum *– In addition to a story in this volume, David also has stories in Parts XIV and XV*

Jacquelynn Morris *– In addition to a poem in this volume, Jacquelynn also has a poem in Part XIV of this set.*

Mark Mower *– In addition to a story in this volume, Mark also has a story in Part XV*

Will Murray is the author of over seventy novels, including forty *Destroyer* novels and seven posthumous *Doc Savage* collaborations with Lester Dent, under the name Kenneth Robeson, for Bantam Books in the 1990's. Since 2011, he has written a number of additional Doc Savage adventures for Altus Press, two of which co-starred The Shadow, as well as a solo Pat Savage novel. His 2015 Tarzan novel, *Return to Pal-Ul-Don*, was followed by *King Kong vs. Tarzan* in 2016. Murray has written short stories featuring such classic characters as Batman, Superman, Wonder Woman, Spider-Man, Ant-Man, the Hulk, Honey West, the Spider, the Avenger, the Green Hornet, the Phantom, and Cthulhu. A previous Murray Sherlock Holmes story appeared in Moonstone's *Sherlock Holmes*: *The Crossovers Casebook*, and another is forthcoming in *Sherlock Holmes and Doctor Was Not*, involving H. P. Lovecraft's Dr. Herbert West. Additionally, his Sherlock Holmes stories have appeared in *The MX Book of New Sherlock Holmes Stories*.

Robert Perret is a writer, librarian, and devout Sherlockian living on the Palouse. His Sherlockian publications include "The Canaries of Clee Hills Mine" in *An Improbable Truth: The Paranormal Adventures of Sherlock Holmes*, "For King and Country" in *The Science of Deduction*, and "How Hope Learned the Trick" in *NonBinary Review*. He considers himself to be a pan-Sherlockian and a one-man Scion out on the lonely moors of Idaho. Robert has recently authored a yet-unpublished scholarly article tentatively entitled "A Study in Scholarship: The Case of the *Baker Street Journal*". More information is available at *www.robertperret.com*

Gayle Lange Puhl has been a Sherlockian since Christmas of 1965. She has had articles published in *The Devon County Chronicle*, *The Baker Street Journal*, and *The Serpentine Muse*, plus her local newspaper. She has created Sherlockian jewelry, a 2006 calendar entitled "If Watson Wrote For TV", and has painted a limited series of Holmes-related nesting dolls. She co-founded the scion *Friends of the Great Grimpen Mire* and the Janesville, Wisconsin-based *The Original Tree Worshipers*. In January 2016, she was awarded the "Outstanding Creative Writer" award by the Janesville Art Alliance for her first book *Sherlock Holmes and the Folk Tale Mysteries*. She is semi-retired and lives in Evansville, Wisconsin. Ms. Puhl has one daughter, Gayla, and four grandchildren.

Tracy J. Revels – *In addition to a story in this volume, Tracy also has stories in Parts XIV and XV of this set*

Roger Riccard of Los Angeles, California, U.S.A., is a descendant of the Roses of Kilravock in Highland Scotland. He is the author of two previous Sherlock Holmes novels, *The Case of the Poisoned Lilly* and *The Case of the Twain Papers*, a series of short stories in two volumes, *Sherlock Holmes: Adventures for the Twelve Days of Christmas* and *Further Adventures for the Twelve Days of Christmas*, and the new series *A Sherlock Holmes Alphabet of Cases,* all of which are published by Baker Street Studios. He has another novel and a non-fiction Holmes reference work in various stages of completion. He became a Sherlock Holmes enthusiast as a teenager (many, many years ago), and, like all fans of The Great Detective, yearned for more stories after reading The Canon over and over. It was the Granada Television performances of Jeremy Brett and Edward Hardwicke, and the encouragement of his wife, Rosilyn, that at last inspired him to write his own Holmes adventures, using the Granada actor portrayals as his guide. He has been called "The best pastiche writer since Val Andrews" by the *Sherlockian E-Times.*

GC Rosenquist was born in Chicago, Illinois and has been writing since he was ten years old. His interests are very eclectic. His eleven previously published books include literary fiction, horror, poetry, a comedic memoir, and lots of science fiction. His latest published work for MX Books is *Sherlock Holmes: The Pearl of Death and Other Stories* (April 2015). He has had his work published in *Sherlock Holmes Mystery Magazine*. He works professionally as a graphic artist. He has studied writing and poetry at the College of Lake County in Grayslake, Illinois, and currently resides in Lindenhurst, Illinois. For more information on GC Rosenquist, you can go to his website at *www.gcrosenquist.com*

Geri Schear is a novelist and short story writer. Her work has been published in literary journals in the U.S. and Ireland. Her first novel, *A Biased Judgement: The Diaries of Sherlock Holmes 1897* was released to critical acclaim in 2014. The sequel, *Sherlock Holmes and the Other Woman* was published in 2015, and *Return to Reichenbach* in 2016. She lives in Kells, Ireland.

Mark Sohn was born in Brighton, England in 1967. After a hectic life and many dubious and varied careers, he settled down in Sussex with his wife, Angie. His first novel, *Sherlock Holmes and the Whitechapel Murders* was published in 2017. His second, *The Absentee Detective* is out now. Both are available from Amazon.com.
https://sherlockholmesof221b.blogspot.co.uk/
https://volcanocat.blogspot.co.uk/

Robert V. Stapleton – *In addition to a story in this volume, Robert also has a story in Part XV of this set.*

S. Subramanian is a retired professor of Economics from Chennai, India. Apart from a small book titled *Economic Offences: A Compendium of Crimes in Prose and Verse* (Oxford University Press Delhi, 2012), his Holmes pastiches are the only serious things he has written. His other work runs largely to whimsical stuff on fuzzy logic and social measurement, on which he writes with much precision and little understanding, being an economist. He is otherwise mainly harmless, as his wife and daughter might concede with a little persuasion.

Tim Symonds was born in London. He grew up in Somerset, Dorset, and Guernsey. After several years in East and Central Africa, he settled in California and graduated Phi Beta Kappa in Political Science from UCLA. He is a Fellow of the *Royal Geographical Society*. He writes his novels in the woods and hidden valleys surrounding his home in the High Weald of East Sussex. Dr. Watson knew the untamed region well. In "The Adventure of Black Peter", Watson wrote, *"the Weald was once part of that great forest which for so long held the Saxon invaders at bay."* Tim's novels are published by MX Publishing. His latest is titled *Sherlock Holmes and the Nine Dragon Sigil.* Previous novels include *Sherlock Holmes and The Sword of Osman, Sherlock Holmes and the Mystery of Einstein's Daughter, Sherlock Holmes and the Dead Boer at Scotney Castle*, and *Sherlock Holmes and the Case of The Bulgarian Codex.*

William Todd has been a Holmes fan his entire life, and credits *The Hound of the Baskervilles* as the impetus for his love of both reading and writing. He began to delve into fan fiction a few years ago when he decided to take a break from writing his usual Victorian/Gothic horror stories. He was surprised how well-received they were, and has tried to put out a couple of Holmes stories a year since then. When not writing, Mr. Todd is a pathology supervisor at a local hospital in Northwestern Pennsylvania. He is the husband of a terrific lady and father to two great kids, one with special needs, so the benefactor of these anthologies is close to his heart.

Charles Veley has loved Sherlock Holmes since boyhood. As a father, he read the entire Canon to his then-ten-year-old daughter at evening story time. Now, this very same daughter, grown up to become acclaimed historical novelist Anna Elliott, has worked with him to develop new adventures in the *Sherlock Holmes and Lucy James Mystery Series.* Charles is also a fan of Gilbert & Sullivan, and wrote *The Pirates of Finance*, a new musical in the G&S tradition that won an award at the New York Musical Theatre Festival in 2013. Other than the Sherlock and Lucy series, all of the books on his Amazon Author Page were written when he was a full-time author during the late Seventies and early Eighties. He currently works for United Technologies Corporation, where his main focus is on creating sustainability and value for the company's large real estate development projects.

Peter Coe Verbica – *In addition to a story in this volume, Peter also has a story in Part XV of this set.*

I.A. Watson is a novelist and jobbing writer from Yorkshire who cut his teeth on writing Sherlock Holmes stories and has even won an award for one. His works include *Holmes and Houdini*, *Labours of Hercules*, *St. George and the Dragon* Volumes 1 and 2, and *Women of Myth*, and the non-fiction essay book *Where Stories Dwell*. He pens short detective stories as a means of avoiding writing things that pay better. A full list of his sixty-plus published works appears at:
http://www.chillwater.org.uk/writing/iawatsonhome.htm

Darryl Webber is a journalist and author who lives in Essex, England. As well as penning stories under the banner of *The Secret Adventures of Sherlock Holmes* with fellow writer Duncan Wood, he also works for a number of newspapers and runs a film blog called *Chillidog Movies*. Darryl was born in Romford, Essex in 1968 and studied art and design at college before becoming a compositor at his local newspaper. After taking a career break to do a psychology degree at the University of East London, he retrained as a journalist and has held various senior editorial positions in newspapers in the southeast of England, specialising in culture and the arts, as well as working on the sports section of *The Sunday Times*. In 2016, Darryl co-authored a book called *The Man Who Fell To Earth* about the Nicolas Roeg film of the same name starring David Bowie. In this year, he became a part of the team that runs the Chelmsford Film Festival. Darryl's favourite stories from the Conan Doyle Canon are "The Bruce Partington Plans", "Silver Blaze", and "The Blue Carbuncle", and he firmly believes that the game is always afoot.

Marcia Wilson is a freelance researcher and illustrator who likes to work in a style compatible for the color blind and visually impaired. She is Canon-centric, and her first MX offering, *You Buy Bones*, uses the point-of-view of Scotland Yard to show the unique talents of Dr. Watson. This continued with the publication of *Test of the Professionals: The Adventure of the Flying Blue Pidgeon* and *The Peaceful Night Poisonings.* She can be contacted at: *gravelgirty.deviantart.com*

The MX Book of New Sherlock Holmes Stories

"This is the finest volume of Sherlockian fiction I have ever read, and I have read, literally, thousands." – Philip K. Jones

"Beyond Impressive . . . This is a splendid venture for a great cause! – Roger Johnson, Editor, *The Sherlock Holmes Journal,* The Sherlock Holmes Society of London

Part I: 1881-1889
Part II: 1890-1895
Part III: 1896-1929
Part IV: 2016 Annual
Part V: Christmas Adventures
Part VI: 2017 Annual
Part VII: Eliminate the Impossible (1880-1891)
Part VIII – Eliminate the Impossible (1892-1905)
Part IX – 2018 Annual (1879-1895)
Part X – 2018 Annual (1896-1916)
Part XI – Some Untold Cases (1880-1891)
Part XII – Some Untold Cases (1894-1902)
Part XIII – 2019 Annual (1881-1890)
Part XIV – 2019 Annual (1891-1897)
Part XV – 2019 Annual (1898-1917)

In Preparation

Part XVI – Whatever Remains . . . Must be the Truth
Part XVII – 2020 Annual

. . . and more to come!

Publishers Weekly says:
Part VI: *The traditional pastiche is alive and well . . . .*

Part VII: *Sherlockians eager for faithful-to-the-canon plots and characters will be delighted.*

Part VIII: *The imagination of the contributors in coming up with variations on the volume's theme is matched by their ingenious resolutions.*

Part IX: *The 18 stories . . . will satisfy fans of Conan Doyle's originals. Sherlockians will rejoice that more volumes are on the way.*

Part X: *. . . new Sherlock Holmes adventures of consistently high quality.*

Part XI: *. . . an essential volume for Sherlock Holmes fans.*

Part XII: *. . . continues to amaze with the number of high-quality pastiches . . .*

434

The MX Book of New Sherlock Holmes Stories
Edited by David Marcum
(MX Publishing, 2015-   )

MX Publishing

MX Publishing is the world's largest specialist Sherlock Holmes publisher, with several hundred titles and over a hundred authors creating the latest in Sherlock Holmes fiction and non-fiction.

From traditional short stories and novels to travel guides and quiz books, MX Publishing caters to all Holmes fans.

The collection includes leading titles such as *Benedict Cumberbatch In Transition* and *The Norwood Author*, which won the 2011 *Tony Howlett Award* (Sherlock Holmes Book of the Year).

MX Publishing also has one of the largest communities of Holmes fans on *Facebook*, with regular contributions from dozens of authors.

www.mxpublishing.co.uk (UK) and *www.mxpublishing.com* (USA)